A Theoretical and Practical Grammar of the French Language

SALZWASSER VERLAG

M. de Levizac

A Theoretical and Practical Grammar of the French Language

Reprint of the original.

1st Edition 2023 | ISBN: 978-3-37514-410-4

Verlag (Publisher): Salzwasser Verlag GmbH, Zeilweg 44, 60439 Frankfurt, Deutschland
Vertretungsberechtigt (Authorized to represent): E. Roepke, Zeilweg 44, 60439 Frankfurt, Deutschland
Druck (Print): Books on Demand GmbH, In de Tarpen 42, 22848 Norderstedt, Deutschland

A

THEORETICAL AND PRACTICAL GRAMMAR OF THE FRENCH LANGUAGE.

BY

M. DE LEVIZAC.

TWENTY-NINTH EDITION,

REVISED, CORRECTED, AND IMPROVED,

BY J. C. TARVER,

LATE FRENCH MASTER OF ETON SCHOOL.

LONDON:
DULAU AND CO., 37, SOHO SQUARE.
1858.

PREFACE.

The distinguished success, which (as it has been justly affirmed in former editions) has attended the Grammar of M de Levizac, adopted in the most celebrated schools in England, cannot be a matter of surprise to those who are acquainted with the high reputation of its learned author in this country. Nor indeed is that reputation confined to England alone; for M. de Levizac has been ranked in France among her ablest grammarians, and his works, considered as standard, are frequently quoted when a good authority is required.* Under such circumstances, the rules, definitions and explanations which he has given in the elementary part of the present work, as well as on the most difficult points of French grammar and construction, could not be any thing but correct and good; whilst the judicious choice of the French sentences of which he has given the translation for the subject of his exercises, is all that one could wish for the application of the rules laid down. It must also be added that those sentences (being selected from pure and unexceptionable writers) must necessarily leave moral impressions of a beneficial nature on the mind of the young learner, improve his taste, and enlighten his mind.

* See La Grammaire des Grammaires, etc.

These are the real advantages to be derived from M. de Levizac's Grammar, such as he left it to us. His views, his arrangement of the exercises, his constant assistance in the course of the latter, by pointing out the order in which the words are to stand, have been scrupulously adhered to in the present edition, with which great pains have been taken to restore that which in the last, had been considerably altered and disfigured. Some transpositions have, however, been thought advisable, and it is necessary here to explain the reason. M. de Levizac had divided the Syntax into two parts under the denominations of "*Syntax of the Article, the Adjective, the Pronoun, etc. etc.*" And "*Particular rules of the Substantive, of the Article, of the Adjective, etc. etc.*" It is reasonable to suppose that in adopting this division, the Author had in view to introduce the Learner to the difficulties of the Language by degrees. This notion no doubt was also entertained by those to whom the revising of his work has been intrusted since his death, as they have made no alterations in this respect; for, on examining the rules in both parts, one is certainly surprised to find some in the latter, which, from the great simplicity or familiarity of their subject, unquestionably belong to the former, and *vice versâ;* as well as with the unnecessary repetition of the same rules in each part. These considerations have appeared a sufficient inducement to give up that division, and throw the two parts into one, which has accordingly been done. *

But whilst M. de Levizac's Grammar was every thing one could wish, as far as regards the laying down of the rules, and giving appropriate exercises for their application, still in another point of view, the grammar was incomplete, in-

* This will account for the difference in the setting of the Exercises, observable in pages 290, 292.

asmuch as it was confined to definitions of *what the French Language is, without any reference to the English Language*, through which French is learned, and in which people must necessarily (in the beginning, and for a long time at least) conceive their thoughts, and from which they must translate them into French. M. de Levizac has given proofs of his knowledge of the English Language in his excellent English and French Pocket Dictionary, and yet, strange to say, he has almost entirely lost sight of that Language in his Grammar, and forgotten that the English who attempt to speak in French must unavoidably be led by the force of habit to give the construction and idiom of their own language to the foreign one. He consequently neglected a very important thing in his practical grammar of a language so much spoken as French; he did not foresee those innumerable cases in which the learner would fall into error. In not comparing the two languages wherever they happen to differ, and pointing out the difference, he lost the opportunity which would thus have been afforded, of checking habit and preventing mistakes attendant on literal translation. Whenever the two languages clash in their construction, as, for instance, in the subjunctive mood and government of verbs, the difference has been noticed, and wherever the case has suggested some English idioms of a particular construction, directions have been given on the manner of rendering it into French. To say, however, that the present edition gives everything that can be wished for in this respect, would be an absurd and foolish assertion; but that a great effort has been made to supply the deficiency just noticed is sufficiently proved from the fact that this Grammar, which in former editions contained 422 pages,* now contains 508.

* M. Pasquier's.

The same considerations have rendered some alterations, or rather additions necessary in the Exercises, in which some English sentences of a more conversational and idiomatical nature have been thrown.

The French Academy has lately fixed the disputed orthography with regard to the *ais,* instead of *ois,* in those words in which the latter combination is to be sounded *ès*, especially in verbs; and with regard also to the plural of words ending in *ant, ent,* to which they add an *s* without dropping the *t*, this has appeared sufficient authority to deviate from the orthography adopted by M. de Levizac in those cases. Besides that it seemed reasonable to abide by the decision of the learned Academy, there was another motive equally important, namely, to facilitate pronunciation by adopting that spelling, which represents the two distinct and different sounds *ois, ais,* in *Anglais, Danois, paraître, croître,* and others formerly spelled alike.

This also appeared an excellent opportunity to render references easier. For this purpose, the rules have been numbered, one series running from the beginning to the end of the book. Occasional references to various parts of the book, by means of these numbers, will enable the learner to find those rules which are connected with that which is under consideration. With the same view, the *Table of Contents* has been altered and enlarged. The number of the rules as well as of the page, wherein they are to be found, have both been given. A learner cannot be too well acquainted with the elementary book placed in his hands; it is of great moment that he should not only know what the book contains, but where it is to be found. The new table of contents, may, therefore, be considered as a *Résumé détaillé* of the whole matter.

Eton, May 6th, 1836

CONTENTS.

N.B.—*The Figures on the left show the number of the Rule, or of the Subject; the Figures on the right show the number of the Page.*

CHAPTER V.

VERB.

CHAPTER VI.

CHAPTER VII.

CHAPTER VIII.

CHAPTER IX.

PART II.

CHAPTER I.

SUBSTANTIVE.

CHAPTER II.

CHAPTER III.

ADJECTIVE.

CHAPTER IV.

PRONOUNS.

CHAPTER V.

THE VERB.

EXPLANATION

OF THE

ABBREVIATIONS USED IN THE EXERCISES.

---

m.	stands for	masculine.
f.	———	feminine.
pl.	———	plural.
s. *or* sing.	———	singular.
h m.	———	*h* mute.
h asp.	———	*h* aspirated.
pr. *	———	preposition.
art. *	———	article.
pr-art.	———	article and preposition contracted.
pron.	———	pronoun.
inf-1	———	present of the infinitive.
inf-2	———	the past of the infinitive.
p. pr.	———	participle present.
p. p-4	———	participle past.
ind-1	———	present of the indicative, *je parle.*
ind-2	———	imperfect. *Je parlais.*
ind-3	———	preterit definite. *Je parlai.*
ind-4	———	preterit indefinite. *J'ai parlé.*
ind-5	———	preterit anterior. *J'eus parlé.*
ind-6	———	pluperfect. *J'avais parlé.*
ind-7	———	future absolute. *Je parlerai.*
ind-8	———	future anterior. *J'aurai parlé.*
cond-1.	———	present of the conditional. *Je parlerais.*
cond-2.	———	first conditional past. *J'aurais parlé.*
cond-3	———	second conditional past. *J'aurais eu parlé.*
imp.	———	imperative. *Aie.*
subj-1	———	present of the subjunctive. *Que je parle.*
subj-2	———	imperfect. *Que je parlasse.*
subj-3	———	preterit. *Que j'aie parlé.*
subj-4	———	pluperfect. *Que j'eusse parlé.*

* In the Exercises, denotes that the word under which it is placed, is not expressed in French.

— Denotes that the English word is spelt alike in French, or at least the part under which this sign is placed.

* Art. in the Exercises, before a word, shows that the definite article is used.

† Prep. shows the preposition is to be used.

= Denotes that the French word differs from the English only by its termination. See 27.

In filling the Exercises, the order of the figures placed sometimes in the phrases after the French words, is to be observed.

In the exercises, when several English words are included between a parenthesis, they must be translated by the only words placed under.

FRENCH GRAMMAR

1. Grammar, in general, is the art of *speaking* and *writing* correctly.

To Speak—is to convey our thoughts by means of articulated sounds.

To Write—is to render those thoughts permanently visible by means of certain signs or characters, called *Letters*, and the latter, disposed in proper order, constitute what is called the Alphabet.

2. OF THE FRENCH ALPHABET.

Roman Letters.		Italic Letters.		Old Appellation.	New Appellation.
A	a	*A*	*a*	*ah—*	*ah*
B	b	*B*	*b*	*bay**	*bay**
C	c	*C*	*c*	*say*	*ke*
D	d	*D*	*d*	*day*	*de*
E	e	*E*	*e*	*a—*	*a*
F	f	*F*	*f*	*eff*	*f*
G	g	*G*	*g*	*jay*†	*ghe*
H	h	*H*	*h*	*ash*	*he*
I	i	*I*	*i*	*e—*	*e*
J	j	*J*	*j*	*jee*†	*je*†
K	k	*K*	*k*	*kah*	*ke*
L	l	*L*	*l*	*ell*	*le*
M	m	*M*	*m*	*emm*	*me*
N	n	*N*	*n*	*enn*	*ne*
O	o	*O*	*o*	*o—*	*o*
P	p	*P*	*p*	*pay*	*pe*
Q	q	*Q*	*q*	*ku*‡	*ke*
R	r	*R*	*r*	*heir*	*re*
S	s	*S*	*s*	*ess*	*se*
T	t	*T*	*t*	*tay*	*te*
U	u	*U*	*u*	*u*‡	*u*‡
V	v	*V*	*v*	*vay*	*ve*
X	x	*X*	*x*	*eeks*	*kse*
Y	y	*Y*	*y*	*e greo*	*e greo*
Z	z	*Z*	*z*	*zed*	*ze*

* Here both the old pronunciation and the new are expressed by sounds, and, in the new, the letter *e* after each consonant is sounded as in the English word *battery*.

† When *g* is soft, it is sounded like *s* in *pleasure*, or *z* in *azure*. Such is also the sound of *j*, which is always soft.

‡ See the second note, page 5.

PRONUNCIATION,

OR SOUNDS OF THE FRENCH TONGUE.

3. OF LETTERS IN GENERAL,

The French ALPHABET contains, it is seen, *twenty-five letters*, which are divided into *Vowels* and *Consonants*.

A *vowel* is the simple emission of the *voice* forming an articulate sound by itself.

A *consonant*, on the contrary, cannot be articulated without the assistance of a *vowel*.

The *vowels* are *a*, *e*, *i*, *o*, *u*, and *y*, which sometimes has the sound of *one i*, and sometimes of *two*.

The nineteen remaining letters, *b*, *c*, *d*, *f*, *g*, *h*, *j* *k*, *l*, *m*, *n*, *p*, *q*, *r*, *s*, *t*, *v*, *x*, *z*, are consonants.

4. OF ACCENTUATION.

In reading and writing, great attention must be paid to the accents; for they not only change the sound of the vowels, but also the meaning of words. Ex. *péche*, a peach; *péché*, a sin; *la*, the; *là*, there; *ou*, or; *où*, where.

Three accents are used on the vowels; they are the *acute* (´) placed on *e* alone, as in *bonté*.* The *grave* (`) used solely on the letter *e*, as in *procès*, *prèt*, and on the three following words, *à*, to; *là*, there; *où*, where. The *circumflex* (^) used on every

* The acute accent is used on the final *e* of the part. past of the first conjugation, *aimé*, *estimé*, and of all nouns derived from those Latin words of the third declension, ending in *as*, *vérité*, veritas; *cité*, civitas; *cécité*, cecitas: *générosité*, generositas, etc. etc.

one of the five vowels, which it makes long, *plâtre, rêve, épître, apôtre, vous fûtes**.

The *cedilla*,(ç) *cédille*, placed under *c*, gives it the sound of *s* before *a, o, u*, as in *façade, façon, reçu.*

The *diæresis* or *tréma* (¨) is placed over the vowels *e, i, u*, whenever they form one distinct syllable, as *haïr, naïf, Esaü, ciguë, Raphaël*, which are pronounced *ha-ïr, na-ïf, E-sa-ü, ci-gu-ë, Ra-pha-ël.*

The *hyphen* or *tiret*, (-) is used in connecting compound words, as in *Belles-lettres, tout-puissant, arc-en-ciel*, &c.

5. OF THE SOUNDS OF THE VOWELS,

AND OF THEIR COMBINATIONS.

Independently of the radical sounds of the five vowels, *a, e, i, o, u,* there are others which are formed by means of the accents which are placed upon them, according as the case requires, so that the number of *simple sounds* is altogether ten, *a, â, e, é, è, ê, i, o, ô, u.*

The sound of *i*, and of *u* is not affected by the apposition of the circumflex accent.

There are besides *three* other *simple sounds*, each represented by the following combinations of vowels, *eu, eû, ou.*

There are also *four nasal simple sounds*,† which, for want of more appropriate signs, are represented

* The ^ accent takes the place of the *s* or of the double vowel which were used in old orthography, *aage, fluste*, now *âge, flûte;* it is also used in words derived from the Latin language, especially verbs, from which a syllable is cut off, *âme*, anima; *vous aimâtes*, amavistis.

† Seventeen simple sounds. *See* TABLE I.

1*

by the combinations of *m* or *n* with each of the vowels, *an, em, an, en—im, in—om, on—um, un.*

All vowels are long which have the ^ accent upon them, as *pâte;* others may be long by position, as *rose.*

Besides the *simple,* there are also the *compound* sounds, in which two vowels are distinctly heard by a single emission of the voice; these are the *diphthongs.*—*See* Table III.

The sound of one or more letters, pronounced with a single emission of the voice, is called a syllable; one or more syllables make a word.

TABLE I.

6. THE SEVENTEEN SIMPLE SOUNDS OF THE FRENCH TONGUE.

Sounds.	*Examples.*	*Sounded as*
1. a *short*	ami, *friend*	a in *amateur*
2. â *long*	pâte, *paste*	a — *bark*
3. e	tenir, *to hold*	e — *battery*
4. é	*été, summer*	a — *paper*
5. è	modèle, *model*	e — *met*
6. ê (*)	tête, *head*	e — *there*
7. i.	imiter, *to imitate*	i — *timid*
8. o. *short*	école, *school*	o — *scholar*
9. ô *long*	côte, *rib*	o — *note*
10. u	vertu, *virtue*	(†)
11. eu *short*	jeune, *young*	u — *shun*
12. eû *long*	jeûne, *fast*	(†)
13. ou	soupe, *soup*	ou — *soup*
14. an (†)	*ange, angel*	en — *encore*
15. in (†)	lin, *flax*	en — *length*
16. on (†)	long, *long*	on — *long*
17. un (†)	brun, *brown*	un — ——

* Besides these four sorts of *e*, there is one entirely mute at the end of many words, as in the above *modèle, tête, école, côte;* and sometimes in the beginning and middle, as in *cependant, javeline, Roquefort, Souquenille, l'empereur,* &c.

† The sound of the French *u*, to which there is no similar, nor even approximate, sound in English, must be heard from the master; and it may be well to add, that, although we have attempted to give an idea of the French sounds by means of English ones, yet they can be correctly learnt only by hearing them from the lips of a native. The nasal sounds cannot be conveyed by any combination of English letters, but a correct notion of the way in which they are pronounced may be had by observation and comparison. In uttering *attention,* as it is pronounced in both languages, it will be seen that the lips do not move when spoken in French, whereas they do, when spoken in English. To stop the moving of the lips, is, therefore the only way of arriving at the right utterance of French nasals.

TABLE II.

7. COMBINATIONS OF LETTERS REPRESENTING SEVERAL OF THE SEVENTEEN SIMPLE SOUNDS.

The Figures refer to Table I.

1	a	ea	il gagea	*he betted*
2	â	acs, as, eât, ats*	appats	*charms*
4	é	ai	aigu	*sharp*
		eai	geai	*jay*
		ée	année	*year*
		œ	œsophage	*œsophagus*
5	è	ai	aide	*aide*
		aie	baie	*bay*
		ei	baleine	*whale*
		eoi, eai	je nageois, geais.	*I did swim*
		oi, ai	foible, faible	*weak*
		oie, aie	monnoie, naie	*money*
6	ê	ai	aîné	*eldest*
		oi	boire	*to drink*
			paroître, raître	*to appear*
7	î	ie	folie	*folly*
8	o	au	aurore	*dawn*
		eo	flageolet	*flageolet*
9	ô	au	auteur	*author*
		eau	marteau	*hammer*
		eo	geole	*goal*
10	u	eu	gageure	*wager*
		eue	eue f.	*had*
		ue	laitue	*lettuce*
11	eu	œu	sœur	*sister*
12	eû	œu	nœud	*knot*
		eue	queue	*tail*
13	ou	oue	il joue	*he plays*
		aoû	Août	*August*
14	an	an	jambe	*leg*
		ean	affligeant	*afflicting*
		em	membre	*member*
		en	entendre	*to hear*
15	in	aim	essaim	*swarm*
		ain	crainte	*fear*
		ein	peinture	*picture*
		im	impoli	*impolite*
		ym	symbole	*symbol*
		yn	syntaxe	*syntax*
16	on	eon	pigeon	*pigeon*
		om	ombre	*shade*
17	un	eun	à jeun	*fasting*
		um	Parfum	*perfume*

TABLE III.

DIPHTHONGS.

8. *Compound Sounds represented by Examples.*

7*	*i*	ia	fi*a*cre	*hackney-coach*
1 or 2	*a*		galimat*ias*	*nonsense*
7	*i*	iai	je déf*iai*	*I challenged*
4	*é*	ié	amit*ié*	*friendship*
7		iez	vous r*iez*	*you laugh*
		iai	b*iais*	*bias*
	i	iè	b*iè*re	*beer*
5	*è*	ie	c*ie*l	*heaven*
		ioi, iai	je purif*iois*, f*iais*	*I purified*
7	*i*	io	v*io*lon	*violin*
8 or 9	*o*	iau	m*iau*ler	*to mew*
7	*i*	iu	rel*iu*re	*binding*
10	*u*			
7	*i*	ieu	rel*ieu*r	*bookbinder*
11 or 12	*eu*		m*ieu*x	*better*
7	*i*	iou	ch*iou*rme	*crew of a galley*
13	*ou*			
7	*i*	ian	v*ian*de	*meat*
14	*an*	ien	aud*ien*ce	*audience*
7	*i*	ien	chrét*ien*	*christian*
15	*in*			
7	*i*	ion	pass*ion*	*passion*
16	*on*			
		oi	b*oi*s	*wood*
8	*o*	oî	b*oî*te	*box*
2	*â*	oie	f*oie*	*liver*
		oe	m*oe*lle	*marrow*
8	*o*	oi	v*oi*sin	*neighbour*
6	*ê*	eoi	nag*eoi*re	*fin*
8	*o*	oin	bes*oin*	*want*
15	*in*			
10	*u*	ua	n*ua*ge	*cloud*
1	*a*			
		uai	je rem*uai*	*I moved*
10	*u*	ue	étern*ue*r	*to sneeze*
4	*é*	ué	dén*ué*	*stript*
		uée	n*uée*	*cloud*

* These figures refer to the numbers of the sounds in the preceding page.

TABLE III.

DIPHTHONGS CONTINUED.

Compound Sounds represented by Examples.

10	*u*	ue	men*u*et	*minuet*
5	*è*	uoi, uai	il s*uoit*, *uait*	*he perspired*
10	*u*	ui	b*ui*sson	*bush*
7	*i*	uie	parapl*uie*	*umbrella*
10	*u*	uo	imp*é*t*uo*sité	*impetuosity*
8	*o*			
10	*u*	ueu	l*ueu*r	*glimmering*
11	*eu*			
10	*u*	ueu	majest*ueu*x	*majestic*
12	*eû*			
10	*u*	uan	n*uan*ce	*shade*
14	*an*	uen	infl*uen*ce	*influence*
10	*u*	uin	*Juin*	*June*
15	*in*			
10	*u*	uon	t*uon*s	*let us kill*
16	*on*			
13	*ou*	oua	r*oua*ge	*wheel-work*
1	*a*			
		oue	dén*oue*r	*to untie*
13	*ou*	oué	déj*oué*	*frustrated*
4	*é*	ouée	fille enj*ouée*	*cheerful girl*
		ouai	je j*ouai*	*I played*
13	*ou*	oue	f*oue*tter	*to whip*
5	*è*	ouoi, ouai	je dén*ouois*, *ouais*	*I untied*
13	*ou*	oui	camb*oui*s	*cart grease*
7	*i*	ouie	l'*ouie*	*hearing*
13	*ou*	oueu	b*oueu*r	*scavenger*
11	*eu*			
13	*ou*	oueu	n*oueu*x	*knotty*
12	*eû*			
13	*ou*	ouan	l*ouan*ge	*praise*
14	*an*	ouen	R*ouen*	*Rouen, a city*
13	*ou*	ouin	bab*ouin*	*baboon*
15	*in*			
13	*ou*	ouon	j*ouon*s	*let us play*
16	*on*			

9. OBSERVATIONS

UPON THE TWO FIRST TABLES (SEE ALSO LETTERS M.N.)

Am, an, do not take the nasal sound when *m* or *n* are doubled, as in *constamment, année.* *Am* is not nasal at the end of some foreign names, as *Abraham, Roboam, Rotterdam, Potsdam, Cham,* &c.; except *Adam.*

Em and *en* are articulated as in the English words *hem* and *men:*

1. In words from Latin, as *abdomen, amen, solen. hymen, item, décemvirat, décemvirs,* and proper names *Jérusalem, Sem;* except *examen, memento, agenda, mentor,* in which *en* has the sound of *in.*

2. *E* before double *nn,* is sounded like *è,* as *étrennes, ennemi, moyennant;* also in some persons and tenses of the verbs, *tenir, venir, prendre,* and their compounds, as *que je vienne, que tu soutiennes, qu'il comprenne,* &c. in the pronouns feminine, *la mienne, la tienne, les siennes,* in many other words, as *antienne, magicienne, Vienne en Autriche,* &c. See letter N.

Also in many nouns and persons of verbs ending in *ène, ème,* as in *arène, ébène,* je me *promène,* il *égrène,* il *sème,* where, however, the *e* is somewhat more open.

Aen has the sound of the French nasal *an* in *Caen,* a town of Normandy. *Aon* is sounded *an* in *Laon,* another town of France, in *faon,* a fawn, and in *paon,* a peacock; but these letters have the sound of *on* in *taon,* an ox-fly.

N, in the monosyllable *en,* both when a preposition and when a pronoun, in *on, mon, ton, son* pronouns, and in *bon, bien, rien,* ceases to be nasal when these words are immediately followed by a vowel or an *h* mute, as *en Italie, on en aura, mon ami, c'est un bon homme, on a bien essayé, je suis bien aise qu'il n'ait rien oublié.* But *en* and *on* remain nasal, when they are placed after the verbs; as *donnez-en à votre sœur. A-t-on essayé? Va-t'-en au logis.*

1. *Im, in,* are not nasal, 1. in the word *intérim,* and in proper names taken from foreign languages, as *Sélim, Ephraïm, Ibrahim.* However the nasal sound is preserved in *Benjamin, Joachim.*

2. In the beginning and middle of words, when *m* or *n* is followed by a vowel or an *h* mute, as *inanimé, inimaginable, unanimité,* &c.

3. Whenever *m* or *n* is doubled, as *immoler, immersion, innover, inné, innocent,* though in this latter word only one *n* is sounded.

Un has the sound of *u* close, as in *une, unième, unanime,* when followed by a word beginning with a vowel or an *h* mute, as *un homme, un esprit, aucun ami, commun accord.*

Um is pronounced *omm* in some words adopted from the Latin, as *centumvirs, album, quinquennium, ladanum, laudanum, géranium,* except *pensum, factotum.*

U after the consonants *q* and *g* is generally silent, as in *quatre, guerre,* &c. See those letters.

10. OF THE *Y.*

This letter has the sound of *i,* in all words derived from Greek; *lyre, physique,* and in *y* adverb. In *pays, paysan, paysage,* it is sounded like two *i,* as if these words were spelled *pai-is, pai-i-san, pai-i-sage.* *Y,* placed between two vowels, is also pronounced as two *i,* one of which alters the sound of the first vowel, and the other making a diphthong with the second, thus, *payer*, is pronounced as if it were spelled *pai-ier*, *monnoyer* or *monnayer*, as if *mo-nai-ier*.*

EXAMPLES.

ab-ba-ye	*Abbey*	nous é-ga-yons	*we enliven*
a-bo-yer	*to bark*	es-su-yer	*to wipe*
ap-pu-yer	*to support*	mo-yen	*means*
ba-la-yer	*to sweep*	net-to-yer	*to clean*
bé-ga-yer	*to stammer*	je pa-yais	*I was paying*
cra-yon	*pencil*	je ra-ye-rais	*I would stripe*
cro-ya-ble	*credible*	ro-yau-me	*kingdom*
é-cu-yer	*esquire*	vo-ya-ge	*voyage*
il ef-fra-ye	*he frightens*	vo-ya-geur	*traveller*

11. OF CONSONANTS.

B, *b*, at the beginning of a word or of a syllable, is sounded as in English.

Bal	*ball*	bo-bi-ne	*bobbin*
Ba-bel	*Babel*	bar-ba-ris-me	*barbarism*
ba-bil	*prating*	bi-bli-o-thè-que	*library*
ba-bouin	*baboon*	bur-les-que	*burlesque*

B is sounded in the middle of words, as *ab-di-quer*, *sub-ve-nir*, *ob-vi-er*: and at the end of proper names, as *Job*, *Caleb*, *Moab*; also in the words, *ra-doub*, the refitting of a ship, *rumb*, point of the compass; but it is not sounded in *plomb*, lead.

Double *bb* is not sounded, *abbé*, abbot; *rabbin*, rabbin; *sabbat*, sabbath; which pronounce *a-bé*, *ra-bin*, *sa-bat*, but it is heard in *Abbatial*, *Abbeville*.

C, c, is { *Hard*, as in English, before *a*, *o*, *u*, *l*, *n*, *r*.
Soft, before *e*, *i*, *y*, and also before *a*, *o*, *u*, when it has the cedilla *ç*,

* *Baïonnette*, *biscaïen*, *païen*, are sometimes spelt *bayonnette*, *biscayen*, *payen*, but the *y* must be sounded as one *i*.

HARD.		SOFT.	
Cal-cul	*calculation*	ce-ci	*this*
ca-co-pho-nie	*cacophony*	cé-ci-té	*blindness*
clérical	*clerical*	cé-ta-cée	*cetaceous*
Cra-co-vie	*Cracow*	cer-ceau	*hoop*
co-que-li-cot	*wild poppy*	Cir-cé	*Circe*
cro-co-di-le	*crocodile*	ci-li-ce	*hair-cloth*
cris-tal	*crystal*	cy-ni-que	*cynic*
cu-cur-bi-te	*cucurbite*	cy-près	*cypress*
A-rach-né	*Arachne*	le-çon	*lesson*

Double *cc* and *cq*, in the middle of words, are sounded as one *c* before *a, o, u, la, le, li, lo, lu, ro, re, ri ;* thus *a-cabler*, &c. except, *pec-cable, pec-cant, pec-cadille, pec-cavi, sac-cholactique,* in which the sound of the double *c* is distinctly heard. But before *é, i,* the two *cc* are heard distinctly; *succès, accident, vaccine,* are, therefore, pronounced, *suc-cès, ac-cident, vac-cine,* &c.

C is sounded as *g* hard in *second* and its derivatives, and by many in *Claude,* and *Reine Claude,* and even by some, but improperly, in *secret.*

C, at the end of words, is usually sounded harsh, as in *cognac, lac,* (a lake), *avec, bec, pic, syndic, roc, froc, estoc, duc, aqueduc, agaric, arc, zinc,* &c. and in the singular of *échec :* but it is not sounded in *croc, accroc, arc-boutant, banc, broc, clerc, marc d'argent, cric, estomac, flanc, jonc, lacs* (toils,) *tabac, tronc, échecs,* nor in *donc* before a consonant; but

It is always sounded in *croc-en-jambe, franc étourdi, du blanc au noir,* and in both syllables of *mic-mac, tric-trac, ric-à-ric,* and *porc-épic.*

In words ending in *ct,* both consonants are generally sounded; as in *tact, contact, intact, exact, inexact, abject, correct, direct, infect, strict, succinct ; c* alone is heard in *respect ; ct* are silent in *amict, instinct, respects ;* both letters are always heard in *suspecte, circonspecte, respecte, distincte,* as well as in the middle of other words, such as *recteur*, *vecteur*, *séducteur*, *rédacteur*, *humecter*, *injecter*, *dactyle*, *ductile*, *tactique*, &c.

Ch has two sounds { one, which is most general like *sh*, in *she*, *shake*; the other, which very rarely occurs, is that of *k* in *chimera*. }

EXAMPLES OF *sh*.

Chat	*cat*	ché-ru-bin	*cherubim*
che-val	*horse*	ca-té-chis-me	*catechism*
cher-cher	*to seek*	chou-et-te	*screech-owl*
chi-che	*stingy*	chu-te	*fall*
ar-chi-tec-te	*architect*	chu-cho-ter	*to whisper*
ar-chi-tra-ve	*architrave*	chy-le, &c. &c.	*chyle*

It has also sound in *Achille*, *Zachée*, &c.

EXAMPLES OF *ch* AS *k*.*

A-chab	Cham	Ma-chi-a-vel	Cal-chas
A-ché-lo-us	Cha-na-an	Mi-chel-ange	Bac-chus
An-ti-o-chus	Chi-o	Pul-cné-rie	Cha-ron
A-cha-ïe	Cho-rè-be	Ti-cho-Bra-hé	Zurich
A-nar-char-sis	Cho-ro-ès	Dyr-ra-chi-um	é-cho
a-na-cho-rète	Chal-da-ï-que	chi-ro-man-cie	scho-li-e
ar-chan-ge	Chal-dée	chœur	cha-li-bé
ar-chan-gel	cha-os	cho-ris-te	chon-dril-le
ar-ché-type	ché-li-doi-ne	or-ches-tre	chi-ra-gre
ar-chon-tes	cher-so-nè-se	i-cho-reux	ar-cha-ïs-me
ar-chi-é-pis-co-pal	chi-li-ar-que	cho-rè-ge	
chal-cé-doi-ne	chal-co-gra-phie	Na-bu-cho-do-no-sor	
eu-cha-ris-tie	ca-té-chu-mè-ne		
	Za-cha-rie		

EXAMPLES OF *cht* AS *k*.

Yacht, U-trecht, Maes-tricht } are pronounced { Yak, Utrek, Mastrik } without sounding the *t*.

Ch has the hard sound of *g* in *drachme*, but is silent in *almanach*. On account of their Italian ori-

* The harsh sound of *ch* is heard in words of Greek or oriental etymology, which have not yet become popular and are not entirely Frenchified.

gin, *vermicelle* and *violoncelle* are, by some, pronounced *violonchelle, vermichel.*

Ch has uniformly the sound of *k*, in all words where it is followed by a consonant, as *Christ, chrétien, chloris, chronique, isochrone, chronomètre. Arachné, ichneumon, technique*, &c.

D, d, is sounded as in English.

Dé-da-le	*labyrinth*	Dry-ade	*Dryad*
do-du	*plump*	dro-ma-dai-re	*dromedary*
din-don	*turkey*	dé-di-ca-toi-re	*dedicatory*

D is always sounded in the middle of words, as *adjectif, adverbe, admirable.*

It is likewise heard at the end of proper names, as in *David, Obed, Gad, Alfred*, &c. and in some other words, as *Cid, Sud, Sund, Talmud, éphod, lamed. D* final, before a word beginning with a vowel, is sounded as *t*, as *quand il viendra ; un grand homme ; vend-il ?* which are pronounced *quan-til-viendra*, &c. The *d* final of the following words is always silent in *bond, gond, fond, nid, nœud, muid*, and *pied ;* except in *de fond en comble, de pied en cap, tenir pied-à-boule, avoir un pied-à-terre*, where it is sounded as *t*.

Double *d* is heard in some few words derived from the Latin, as in *ad-dition, ad-ducteur, red-dition.*

F, f, is sounded like the same letter in English.

EXAMPLE.

Far-fa-det	*hobgoblin*	fé-bri-fuge	*febrifuge*
fau-fi-ler	*to baste (in sewing*	fruc-ti-fi-er	*to fructify*
fet-fa	*edict of the Mufti*	fi-fre	*fifer*
fan-fa-ron	*boaster*	for-fait	*crime*

Final *f* is sounded in all nouns and adjectives ending in *af, ef, if, of*, as *bref, brief, chef, fief, nef, nerf, grief, serf, relief, méchef, Azof, lof, tof, tuf, ouf, pouf, œuf, veuf, bœuf*, and *neuf* (new); *f* is silent in *clef, éteuf, chef-d'œuvre, œuf frais*, and in these plurals *nerfs, œufs, bœufs, neufs* (new). In *neuf* (nine) when alone, or when it terminates the sentence, *f* is distinctly sounded, but it takes the sound of *v* before a vowel, and is silent before a consonant.

Double *f* is generally sounded as one *f* alone; however, in some few words, as *effusion, affadir, effraction*, it seems more proper to sound both.

G, g, has { before *a, o, u*, the hard sound of *g* in the English word *go*, and before *e, i, y*, the soft sound of *s* in *pleasure*. }

EXAMPLES OF *g* HARD.

Gan-grè-ne	*gangrene*	gut-tu-ral	*guttural*
Gro-nin-gue	*Groningen*	gom-me	*gum*
gai	*cheerful*	gla-ce	*looking-glass*
go-gue-nard	*joker*	Gor-go-ne	*Gorgon*

EXAMPLES OF *g* SOFT.

Geai	*jay*	gé-né-ral	*general*
gé-or-gi-ques	*georgics*	gens	*people*
gen-re	*gender*	gin-gem-bre	*ginger*
gé-mir	*to groan*	gym-ni-que	*gymnastic*

G final is hard in *joug*, and in proper names, as *Agag, Doeg*. When *rang, sang, long*, precede a word beginning with a vowel, *g* final is sounded as *k*. It is silent in *faubourg, Luxembourg, bourg, Bourg-l'abbé, Bourg-la-Reine*, &c.; and likewise in *sang-sue, de sang froid, sang-de-dragon*, in *rang, sang, long* before a consonant, and always in *doigt, legs, poing, vieux-oing, hareng, étang, seing*, and *vingt*.

Bourg-mestre is pronounced *bourgue-mestre*, and by some persons it is now, and not improperly, written in this latter manner.

Gu forms a distinct syllable in *ar-gu-er, aiguë, suraiguë, ciguë, ambiguë, contiguë, exiguë*, and *bésaiguë*. *Gui* is sounded as a diphthong, that is, the two vowels are heard in *aiguille, aiguillade, aiguillon*, and in the proper names, *d'Aiguillon, de Guise, le Guide*. But the *u*, in the inflections of more than forty verbs ending in *guer*, and in many other words, where it stands before *e* and *i*, as intended only to give to *g* the hard sound, is entirely silent, as in *anguille, aiguière, aiguade, bague, bègue, figue, dogue, fougue, fugue, onguent, langue, longue, nargue, vergue, morgue, distingue, gué, gui, guérir, guinder, guise, languir, guinguette*, &c.

Gua takes the mixed sound of the diphthong *goua* in some few words, as *lingual, paraguante, Guadeloupe, Guadalquivir, Guatimala, Guastalla*.

Double *g* is only sounded before *e* and *i*, then the first *g* retains the *hard*, and the second adopts the *soft* sound, as in *suggérer, suggillation*.

G before *h*, and before several consonants, in the middle of words, retains its hard sound, as in *Berghen, Enghien, église, énigme, segment, amygdales*. Before *l* there are two exceptions, in the words *imbroglio* and *de Broglio*, where it is sounded liquid, as in *seraglio*, and these words are generally pronounced as if written *imbroille, de Broille*.

Gn has two sounds: one *hard* as in the English word *ignorant*, and the other liquid, as in the last syllable of *onion*.

EXAMPLES OF THE HARD SOUND.

Gni-de	gna-pha-li-um	ag-na-ti-que	rég-ni-cole
Gno-me	gnos-ti-que	cog-na-ti-que	mag-né-sie
gno-mi-de	ag-nat	ag-nus	stag-nant
gno-mi-que	ag-na-ti-on	ig-nee	stag-na-ti-on
gno-mon	cog-nat	ig-ni-cole	di-ag-nos-ti-que
gno-mo-ni-que	cog-na-ti-on	ig-ni-ti-on	mag-nats

EXAMPLES OF LIQUID SOUNDS.

di-gni-té	*dignity*	ré-gner	*to reign*
i-gno-rant	*ignorant*	cham-pa-gne	*Champaign*
com-pa-gnie	*company*	Bou-lo-gne	*Boulogne*
si-gner	*to sign*		
ré-pu-gner	*to feel a repugnance*		

G is silent in *signet* and *Regnard*, which are pronounced *sinet*, *Renard*.

H is sometimes aspirate, sometimes mute, as in English; thus, *l'homme*, *le héros;* but there is this difference that the breathing is much softer in French than in English.

h IS ASPIRATED IN		*h* IS MUTE IN	
'Habler	*to romance*	ha-bit	*coat*
'ha-che	*axe*	her-be	*grass*
'ha-ïr	*to hate*	heu-re	*hour*
'har-pe	*harp*	heu-reux	*happy*
'haut	*high*	hé-ro-ïne *	*heroine*
'hé-ros *	*hero*	hé-ro-ïque *	*heroic*
'hé-ris-son	*hedge-hog*	hé-ro-ïs-me *	*heroism*
'hideux	*hideous*	his-toi-re	*history*
'hon-te	*shame*	hi-ver	*winter*
'hur-ler	*to howl*	hor-reur	*horror*

The aspirate *h* is generally marked in dictionaries, as no general rule can be given on the subject.

H is never aspirated in the middle of a word, except when that word is the compound of another, beginning with an *h* aspirated, as in *s'aheurter*, *déhaler*, *déhanché*, *déharnacher*, *enharnacher*, *s'enhardir*, *dehors*.

N.B.—Though there is no aspirated *h* before *onze*, *onzième*, and *oui*, it is customary to pronounce and write *le onze*, *le onzième*, and not *l'onze*, *l'onzième;* we say likewise *le oui et le non* without elision.

* Observe that *h* is aspirated in *héros*, but not in its derivatives

S final in *mes, tes, ses, nos, vos, leurs, ces,* and *les,* is never sounded when placed before the words *oui, onze,* as *tous vos oui et vos non; sur les onze heures,* nor even before *une* in *sur les une heure.*

For what concerns *h,* placed after *c* or *g,* see the remarks on those letters.

H, after *r* or *t,* is always silent, as *rhéteur, Rhône, rhubarbe, thé, Thomas, thym.*

J, j, has constantly the sound of *z* in *azure,* or of *s* in *pleasure.*

EXAMPLE.

jus	*gravy*	jou-jou	*toy*
ja-mais	*never*	ju-ju-be	*jujube*
jo-vi-al	*jovial*	jeu-nes-se	*youth*

K, k has always a hard sound, as in the English word *king.*

This letter can hardly be considered as belonging to the French alphabet, as it is found only in some few words borrowed from foreign languages, as

Kan-ga-rou	*kangaroo*	ki-os-que	*Turkish pavilion*
ker-mès	*cochineal*	ky-ri-elle	*tedious enumeration.*

L, l has two sounds, the { first, is precisely the same as *l* in the English words *lily, law,* &c.
second, resembles that of *ll* in *brilliant,* in which case *l* is called *l mouillée* (liquid.)

EXAMPLE OF THE FIRST

La-té-ral	*lateral*	li-las	*lilac*
lé-gis-la-teur	*legislator*	lo-cal	*local*
li-bel-le	*libel*	lu-ni-so-lai-re	*lunisolar*

SECOND SOUND.

It is impossible to define exactly the peculiar liquid sound which *l* has in French, in combinations of letters such as these, *ail, eil, œil, euil, ouil, aill, eill, euill, ouill,* &c.; it must be heard from the mouth of a native. It may not be useless, however, to make the following observation, that that liquid sound does not in the least affect that of the vowel or combination of vowels which precede or follow *il, ill.* Thus, in *tailleur,* the sound of *ta* and *eur* must be pure and distinct; nearly as if the word were thus spelt, *ta-ieur;* the liquid sound of *ill,* forming a sort of diphthong with the last syllable. In *bouillon, bou* must be pure and distinct, thus, *bou-ion;* in *treillage, trè* is also pure—thus, *trè-iage.* In *bail, travail, sommeil,* the liquid sound is final, and is sounded something between *ie* and *lie,* but rapidly and as it were whispered, *ba-ie, tra-va-ie, so-mè-ie:* when followed by a word beginning with a vowel, this final liquid sound blends itself with it thus, *travail utile, tra-va-iu-tile; sommeil agréable, so-mmè-ia-gré-able.*

EXAMPLES.

écureuil	é-cu-reu-ie	*a squirrel*
merveilleux	mer-vè-ieux	*wonderful*
gazouillage	ga-zou-iage	*warbling*
orgueil	or-gueu ie	*pride*
orgueilleux	or-gueu-ieux	*proud*
œillade	eu-ia-de	*glance*
oreille	o-rè-ie	*ear*
périlleux	pé-ri-ieux	*dangerous*
treillage	trèi-age	*lattice work*
bouillon	bou-ion	*broth*

Il final is liquid in *babil, avril, Brésil, cil, mil, péril,* but the *l* is silent in *baril, chenil, coutil, fenil, fusil, outil, gril, nombril sourcil persil* In *fils,* a son, the *l* is silent, but it is sounded, though not liquidly, in *fil*, thread; *fils*, threads; *poil*, hair.

Observe that *Milhaut*, *Pardalhac*, and *Sully*, proper names, are pronounced *liquid*, contrary to the established rule, and that the two latter are nearly the only known instances of an *l* or *ll* sounded *liquid*, without being immediately preceded by the vowel *i*.

Ill, is not liquid in *illégal*, *illuminer*, *distiller*, *instiller*, *osciller*, *scintiller*, *titiller*, *vaciller*, *fritillaire*, *imbécille*, *mille*, *tranquille*, *ville*, *Achille*, *campanille*, *codicille*, *fibrille*, *Gill*, *maxillaire*, *pupille*, *la Sibylle*, and *sille*. But it is liquid in *famille*, *fille*, *charmille*, *souquenille*, *carillon*, *piller*, *pillage*, &c.

Double *l* is sounded in the following words, *allégorie*, *allusion*, *appellatif*, *appellation*, *belligérant*, *belliqueux*, *collation de bénéfices*, *follicule*, *malléole*, *velléité*, *collusion*, *constellation*, *constellé*, *ébullition*, *Gallican*, *Gallicisme*, *intellect*, &c. *malléable*, *médullaire*, *palliatif*, *pellicule*, *équipoller*, *hellénisme*, and in proper names, as *Apollon*, *Bellone*, *Dolabella*, *Pallas*, *Sylla*, &c.

M, *m*, corresponds in sound with the same letter in English.

EXAMPLES.

Mar-me-la-de	*marmalade*	mo-mie	*mummy*
mar-mot-te	*marmot*	mo-ment	*moment*
mé-mo-ra-ble	*memorable*	Mu-sul-man	*Mussulman*
mir-mi-don	*myrmidon*	mur-mu-re	*murmur*
mi-mi-que	*mimic*	mys-tè-re	*mystery*

M final is nasal and not sounded in *faim*, *daim*, *nom*, *renom*, *parfum*; it is not nasal, and is sounded in *Amsterdam*, *Rotterdam*, *Sem*, *Cham*, *item*, *Jérusalem*, *Sédim*, *Ibrahim*, and most proper names, except *Joachim*.

M, *n*, are both articulated in *amnistie*, *calomnie*, *hymne*, *insomnie*, *indemnité*, (pr. *indamnite*), *somnam-*

bule, *automnal*, but are sounded as one *n* alone in *automne*, *damner*, and derivatives.

Double *m* is sounded as one *m*, except in words beginning with *imm*, such as *immortel*, *immensité*. In compound words such as *emmancher*, *emmener*, the preposition is heard distinctly *en-man-cher* ; *Emmanuel* is pronounced *Emanuel*. In *femme*, *différemment*, *ardemment*, the *e* preceding *mm* is sounded *a*, *fa-me* ; but in *lemme*, *e* is sounded è. See Observations,

N, *n*, is sounded as in English.

EXAMPLES.

Né-nu-far	*Nenuphar*	non-ne	*nun*
na-ti-o-nal	*national*	Ni-ni-ve	*Nineveh*
no-mi-nal	*nominal*	noc-tur-ne	*nocturnal*
no-na-gé-nai-re	*a măn of ninety*	nym-phe	*nymph*

N nasal, see Tables I and II and observations following.

Gn have two sounds, which see at letter *g*.

The termination *ent* of the third person of verbs is sounded *e*, *ils parlent*, *ils aimeraient*, pr. *ils par-le*, *ils ai-me-raie*.

Double *n* is not sounded except in *an-nexe*, *annal*, *an-nuel*, *an-notation*, *annuler*, *in-né*, *in-nové*, *innovation*, and a few other cases.

En final, and in all the persons of *venir*, *tenir*, and their compounds, is sounded like *in*, *ancien*, *mien*, *chien*, *citoyen*, *il vient*, *il tiendra*

En is sounded nasally at the beginning of the following compound words, *enivrer*, *enamourer*, *enorgueillir*, *ennuyer*, *enhardir*, *enharmonique*.

P, *p* is sounded as in English.

EXAMPLES.

Pa-pil-lon	*butterfly*	pou-pée	*doll*
pe-pin	*pippin*	po-pu-lai-re	*popular*
pied-plat	*mean fellow*	pour-pre	*purple*
prin-ci-pe	*principle*	pur-pu-rin	*purplish*
pro-pos	*discourse*	py-ra-mi-de	*pyramid*

Ph is sounded as *f*, *philosophe*, *phosphore*, *physique*.

P is sounded distinctly in *adapter*, *adopter*, *capter*, *captieux*, *baptismal*, *aptitude*, *exception*, *exemption*, *inept*, *contempteur*, *gypse*, *Septembre*, *Septuagésime*, *corruption*, *rupture*, *apsides*, *rapsodies*, *symptome*, *rédemption*, *rédempteur*; but is silent, in *baptême*, *baptiser*, *baptistère*, *Baptiste*, *exempt*, *exempter*, *sculpter*, *sculpteur*, *sculpture*, *je romps*, *il corrompt*, *sept*, *septième*, *temps*, *printemps*, *prompt*, and derivatives.

Final *p* is always sounded in *Alep*, *cap*, *Gap*, *jalap* and *julep*, it is also heard in *trop*, *beaucoup*, and *coup*, when before a vowel, but never in *champ*, *camp*, *drap*, *loup*, *sirop*, and *galop*.

In *aps*, *relaps*, and *rapt*, both the final consonants are pronounced, but both are silent in *ceps de vigne*.

Double *p* is sounded as one only.

Q, has generally the sound of *k* in *king*.

Qu has three sounds,
- *ke*, by far the most general before any vowel.
- *kou*, before *a* in some particular words.
- *ku* before *e*, or *i* in some others.

EXAMPLES OF *k*.

Quai	*wharf*	ques-tion	*question*
qua-li-té	*quality*	sé-ques-tre	*sequestration*
quel-que	*some*	queue	*tail*
qui-con-que	*whosoever*	a-queux	*watery*
qui-pro-quo	*blunder*	a-que-duc	*aqueduct*
quo-li-bet	*pun*	é-qui-vo-que	*ambiguity*
quin-qui-na	*Peruvian bark*	se re-quin-quer	*to trick oneself out*
que-nouil-le	*distaff*		

&c. &c. &c.

EXAMPLE OF *kou*.

A-qua-ti-que	*aquatic*	qua-ter-ne	*quaternion*
é-qua-teur	*equator*	qua-dra-gé-naire	*a man of forty*
é-qua-ti-on	*equation*	qua-dra-gé-si-mal	*quadragesimal*
qua-cre	*quaker*	a-qua-ti-le	*aquatile*
qua-dra-ture	*quadrature*	a-quar-el-le	*water colour*
qua-dri-ge	*ancient chariot, with four horses*	li-qua-tion	*liquation*
qua-dru-pè-de	*quadruped*	in quar-to	*quarto size*
qua-dru-ple	*quadruple*	lo-qua-ci-té	*loquacity*

EXAMPLE OF *ku*.

E-ques-tre	*equestrian*	é-qui-mul-ti-ple	*equi-multiple*
li-qué-fac-tion	*liquefaction*	é-qui-ta-tion	*horsemanship*
ques-teur	*questor*	quin-tu-ple	*quintuple*
ques-tu-re	*questura*	quin-tile	*quintile*
quin-quen-nium	*quenquennium*	quin-quen-nal	*quinquennial*
équi-la-tè-re	*of equal dimensions*	quin-dé-cem-vir	*squindecemviri*
é-qui-la-té-ral	*equilateral*	quin-qué-rème	*ancient galley*
é-qui-an-gle	*equiangular*	quin-quer-ce	*a term of the ancient gymnasium*
é-qui-dis-tant	*equi-distant*		

In *quinquagénaire*, a man of fifty, and *quinquagésime*, quinquagesima, the first syllable corresponds with the sound of *qu* in *équestre*, and the second corresponds with the sound of *qu* in *aquatique*. *Q* final is sounded in *coq*, *cinq*, except when *cinq* precedes a word beginning with a consonant, *cinq livres*.

R, is sounded as in English.

EXAMPLES.

Ra-re-té	*scarcity*	rhyth-me	*rhythm*
ra-ssu-rer	*to hearten*	sour-dre	*to spring*
ra-bou-gri	*stunted*	cour-roux	*wrath*
re-brou-sser	*to recoil*	il cour-ra	*he will run*
ri-gou-reux	*rigorous*	cor-ro-de-ra	*it will corrode*
rom-pre	*to break*	cor-ro-bo-re-ra	*it will corroborate*
rou-vrir	*to open again*	ir-ra-dia-ti-on	*irradiation*
ru-gir	*to roar*	ir-ro-ra-ti-on	*irrigation*
ru-ral	*rural*	tor-ré-fac-ti-on	*torrefaction*
rus-tre	*a boor*		

R is always sounded at the end of words after the vowels *a, i, o, u*, except in *Monsieur*, in which it is silent.

Er, ier, the terminations of the infinitive of verbs of the first conjugation, and of many adjectives and nouns, are pronounced *é* and *ie*. *Parler, marcher, jouger, premier, singulier, cordonnier, boulanger.*

But in the following words the termination *er* is pronounced *air*.

EXAMPLES.

Cher	*dear*	ou-tre-mer	*ultramarine*
fer	*iron*	bel-vé-der	*belvidere*
ver	*worm*	Lu-ci-fer	*Lucifer*
mer	*sea*	Pa-ter	*the Lord's prayer*
fier	*haughty*		
gas-ter	*stomach*	fra-ter	*hair-dresser*
hi-er	*yesterday*	ma-gis-ter	*village school-master*
hi-ver	*winter*		
a-mer	*bitter*	Stat-hou-der	*Stadtholder*
can-cer	*cancer*	Ju-pi-ter	*Jupiter*
en-fer	*hell*	Al-ger	*Algiers*
é-ther	*ether*	Gess-ner	*Gessner*
a-vant-hier	*the day before yesterday*	Ni-ger	*Niger, a river*
		cuiller	*a spoon*

In terminations like *ers, ert, erd, art, ard, arts, ort, ord, ords, orts, r* alone is sounded *canard, morts, pervers.*

When the following adjectives and a few others precede a substantive beginning with a vowel, the *r* is sounded, that is, there is what is called a *liaison.*

R sounded	Le premier acte	*the first act*
	son dernier ouvrage	*his last work*
	un singulier évènement	*a singular event*
	un entier abandon	*an entire cession*
	un léger obstacle	*a slight obstacle*
R not sounded	Il est le *premier* à vous promettre et le *dernier* à vous tenir parole.—*He is the first to promise, and the last to keep his word.*	

R not sounded { C'est un homme *léger* et inconstant, *entier* en tout ce qu'il veut, et *singulier* en tout ce qu'il fait.—*He is a light versatile character, positive in all he undertakes, and singular in all he does.*

Final *r* in the present of the infinitive of all the verbs, of the first conjugation, may be sounded when preceding a word beginning with a vowel; in conversation, this distinction is, however, seldom observed.

Rh. See *h*.

Double *r* is not sounded, except, 1st, in *aberration*, *abhorrer*, *horreur*, *errer*, *torréfier*, and their derivatives: 2dly, in words beginning with *irr*, as *irrévocable*, *irrégulier*, *irruption*, &c.; 3rdly, in the future and conditional of the verbs *acquérir*, *courir*, *mourir*, and their derivatives—*j'acquerrai*, *je mourrais*, *nous cour-rions*, &c.

S, *s* has two sounds, { *hard*, as in the English word *sister*. *soft*, as in *rose* and *please*.

S has the hard or hissing sound at the beginning of words, and the soft sound, in the middle, between vowels.

EXAMPLES.

Sai-son	*season*	sour-noi-se	*a sullen woman*
sai-sie	*seizure*	sup-po-sez	*suppose*
sé-sa-me	*se-samum*	sé-dui-sant	*alluring*
si-se	*situate*	Su-se	*Susa*
sou-bi-se	*soubise*	Sy-ra-cu-se	*Syracuse*
sot-ti-se	*silly action*	Syn-thè-se	*Synthesis*
sous-en-ten-te	*mental reservation*		

In *Sbire*, *Svelte*, *Sganarelle* and *Sdili* for *Delos*, it has the *soft* sound; and, in familiar conversation, *aller à Sedan*, *il est le second de sa classe*, are pronounced as if these words were written *azdan*, *le zgon*. Before *ch*, *s* is mute, as in *Schall*, *Schaffhouse* *Schelling*, *Schiste* *Schorl.*

Sh in *shérif*, a sheriff, is sounded as in English.

Sce, sci, scy, are pronounced as *se, si, sci*, at the beginning of words, and as double *s*, in the middle, as *Scène, science, Scythie*, &c. *efferves-cence, effores-cence, turges-cence, incandes-cence, reminis-cence, re-sipis-cence, mis-cible, res-cinder, sus-ception, sus-citer, sus-citation, vis-cère, vis-céral, trans-cendance*, and a few others. But *sc* before *a, o, u*, and *l, r*, have the hard sound of *sk*, as *scapulaire, scolie, sclérotique, scribe, esclave, scrupule*, &c.

S has the *hard* sound, in the middle of a word, when preceded or followed by a consonant, as in *transe, transir, Transylvanie, convulsion, valse, espace, ustensile, statistique, jasmin, dispos, aspirant, prisme, digestion, austérité, obstacle*, &c. &c. &c. However, it takes the *soft* sound, or that of *z*, in *Alsace, Arsace, Asdrubal, asbeste, balsamine, balsamique, bisbille, Israël, Israélite, Esdras, Thisbé, presbitère, transaction, transiger, transitoire, intransitif, transalpin, Lesbos, Isboseth, Brisgaw, Ryswick, Louisbourg, Augsbourg, Presbourg, Philipsbourg*, and some few others.

S takes the *soft* sound when between two vowels, as in *base, Thèse, bise, rose, ruse*, &c. Except compound words, in which it has the *hard* sound of the *initial s* of the radical word, as in *désuétude, entresol, monosyllable, polysyllable, parasol, tournesol, préséance, présupposer, resaisir, resaluer, vraisemblable*, and some derivatives.

Final *s* is heard in *as, atlas, argus, bibus, blocus, bolus, agnus, fœtus, sinus, Phébus, les, us, virus, aloes, bis, jadis, iris, gratis, lapis, les lis, la Lys*, (a river), *maïs, métis, vis, tournevis, Amadis, Adonis, Paris* (the shepherd), *pathos, Athos, Lesbos, Minos, Délos, Paros, Brutus, Vénus, Régulus, Protésilas, Blas, Gil Blas, Las Casas, Rheims, Sens, Mars, Rubens, Cérès, Damoclès*, finally in all Latin words not in common use, and in proper names, Greek, Latin and foreign, &c. But it is always silent as the mark of the plural, *les hommes, les chats, les livres, les canifs, les chefs,* &c. in all persons of verbs, *tu parlas, tu mangeais, nous rions,* &c. in all words in common use, *repas, des bas, cas, appas, trépas, tapis, souris, propos, clos, depuis, toujours,* &c. and in *Jésus-Christ, fleur-de-lis.*

The *s* final of an adjective, pronoun and adverb, is joined to the initial vowel of the next word, and has the soft sound, *vous avez,* pron : *vou zavez.*

Though there is no *s* in *quatre,* yet, before *yeux,* it is, in conversation, pronounced as if there were one, *quatre zieux.*

Finally, double *s* is commonly sounded as one, as in *je ressassasse, assassinasse, Mississipi, etc.* There are some words, however, in which the double *s* is heard, as *assation, assonance, dissonance, accessible, inaccessible, admissible, inadmissable, missive, scissile, scission, scissure, fissure, fissipède, assentiment, asservir.* Thus there is a difference in pronunciation between these phrases: *C'est un homme à* SENTIMENS, *il aime à* SERVIR *ses amis,* and *il faut son* ASSENTIMENT, *cet ambitieux voudrait* ASSERVIR *l'univers,* and again between *l'alun de plume est* SCISSILE, and LA SICILE *est une île triangulaire,* &c.

T is sounded as in English.

EXAMPLES.

Tac-ti-que	*tactics*	a-mi-tié	*friendship*
tes-ta teur	*testator*	sou-tien	*support*
thé-â-tre	*theatre*	nous par-tions	*we were going*
to-ta-li-té	*totality*	ti-are	*tiara*
tour-te-rel-le	*turtle*	bas-ti-on	*bastion*
ti-tu-lai-re	*titulary*	bi-jou-tier	*jeweller*
ti-thy-ma-le	*tithymal*	Ma-thi-as	*Mathias*
chré-tien	*christian*	Pon-thieu	*Ponthieu*
le tien	*thine*	tu sou-tiens	*thou supportest*
pitié	*pity*	&c. &c. &c.	

3*

Ti is sounded *ci* in words derived from the Greek or the Latin languages, in all words ending in *tion*, *attention*, *portion*, &c. except *question*, *gestion*, *digestion*, *combustion*, *mixtion*. In all words ending in *tie*, *démocratie*, *inertie*, *ineptie*, &c. except *partie*, *modestie*, *dynastie*, *Eucharistie*, *hostie*, *repartie*.

Tieux, *tial*, *tient*, are also sounded *cieux*, *cial*, *cient*, *ambitieux*, *captieux*, *patient*, *patienter*.

Tien final is sounded *cien*, in names of nations and proper names, *Doclétien*, *Egyptien*, *Bœotien*.

EXAMPLES.

Par-tial	*partial*	pa-tient	*patient*
par-tia-li-té	*partiality*	pa-tien-ter	*to bear patiently*
par-tiel	*partial*	Ga-la-tie	*Galatia*
pa-tien-ce	*patience*	Bé-o-tie	*Beotia*
im-pa-tien-ce	*impatience*	ac-tion	*action*
quo-tient	*quotient*	bal-bu-tier	*to stammer*
cap-tieux	*captious*	i-ni-tier	*to initiate*
ar-gu-tie	*cavil*	bal-bu-tia	*he stuttered*
cau-tio-nne-ment	*bail*	bal-bu-tie-ment	*stammering*
am-bi-tion	*ambition*	i-ner-tie	*inertness*
am-bi-tio-nner	*to wish*	Vé-ni-tien	*Venetian*

Th is sounded as a single *t*, *théologie*, *théâtre*, *thé*. In the combinations *st*, the *s* and *t* are heard distinctly. *T* final is not heard; *goût*, *rat*, *défaut*, *statut*, &c. except in the following words: *apt*, *rapt*, *fat*, *malt*, *mat*, *pat*, *opiat*, *exeat*, *transeat*, *vivat*, *spalt*, *spath*, *Goliath*, *net*, *fret*, *tacet*, *Thibet*, *aconit*, *déficit*, *granit*, *introït*, *prétérit*, *transit*, *subit*, *dot*, *Astaroth*, *azimut*, *brut*, *comput*, *chut*, *bismuth*, *indult*, *lut*, *occiput*, *sinciput*, both *s* and *t* are articulated in *Le Christ*, *l'est* (east) *l'ouest*, *Brest*, *lest*, *test*, *Pest*, *toast*, and *entre le zist et le zest*; but neither of these letters is heard in *Jésus-Christ*, which is pronounced *Jésus-Cri*.

The final *t* of *sept*, *huit*, is heard at the end of a

sentence, and before a vowel, but not before a consonant, *j'en ai huit, huit livres, sept ans.*

In words ending in *art, est, ort, ourt,* the *t* final is silent. *T* is always silent in the conjunction *et,* which is pronounced *é.*

Double *tt* is not heard except in *atticisme, attique, Atticus, guttural,* and *pittoresque.*

V, v, has the same sound in French as in English.

EXAMPLES.

Val-ve	*valve*	vi-vo-ter	*to live poorly*
val-vu-le	*valvule*	vi-re-vol-te	*quick irregular walk.*
vau-de-vil-le	*ballad*	vi-re-veau	*windlass*
ver-ve	*poetic fire*	veu-ve	*widow*
vi-va-ce	*vivacious*	veu-va-ge	*widowhood*
vis-à-vis	*opposite*		
vi-vre	*to live*		

W is generally pronounced as single *v* in *Wolfram, Warwick, Windsor, Walcourt, Wallon, Warsovie, Westphalia, Wirtemberg, Wolga, Weser, Wendover, Ryswick,* &c. except in *wist* and *wiski,* where it has the English sound; but, in *Newton,* the first syllable *new* is pronounced as *neu,* in *neutralité.*

X, x, has the four different sounds of
- *ks,* in *axe, expense*
- *gz,* in *exhibit, exhale*
- *ss,* in *bliss, mossy*
- *z,* in *Xenophon*

EXAMPLES OF THE FIRST SOUND, *ks.*

axe	*axis*	Xan-tip-pe	*Xantippe*
sexe	*sex*	o-xy-gè-ne	*oxygen*
ri-xe	*altercation*	pa-ra-do-xe	*paradox*
bo-xer	*to box*	flu-xi-on	*defluxion*
lu-xe	*luxury*	ex-sic-ca-ti-on	*exsiccation*
ex-cé-der	*to exceed*	ex-suc-cion	*exsuction*
ex-cel-ler	*to excel*	ex-su-da-ti-on	*exsudation*
ex-cès	*excess*	ex-su-der	*exude*
ex-cep-ter	*to except*	ex-ci-per	*to plead an exception*
ex-ci-se	*excise*		
A-lex-an-dre	*Alexandre*		

EXAMPLES OF THE SECOND SOUND, *gz*.

Xa-vi-er	*Xaverius*	ex-au-cer	*to hear favorably*
Xé-no-phon	*Xenophon*	ex-haus-ser	*to raise*
ex-il	*exile*	ex-hi-ber	*to produce*
ex-or-de	*exordium*	ex-hu-mer	*to disinter*
ex-ubé-ran-ce	*exuberance*		
ex-a-men	*examination*		

EXAMPLES OF THE THIRD SOUND, *ss*.

Aix	*Aix*	Soixante	*Sixty*
Aix-la-Chapelle	*Aix-la-Chapelle*	Bruxelles	*Brussels*
Auxerre	*Auxerre*	Luxeu-il	*Luxeuil*
Auxonne	*Auxonne*		

EXAMPLES OF THE FOURTH SOUND, *z*.

Deuxième	*second*	dix écus	*ten crowns*
sixième	*sixth*	dix hommes	*ten men*
dizième	*tenth*	deux aunes	*two ells*
dix-huit	*eighteen*	beaux yeux	*fine eyes*
dix-neuf	*nineteen*	&c. &c.	

The first sound of this letter, (*ks*,) is by far the most general, and is found in words beginning with *exce*, *exci* and *exs*.

The second sound (*gz*) takes place in all words beginning with *x* or *ex*, followed by a vowel, or the letter *h*, as *le Xanthe*, *Xénocrates*, *Ximenès*, *exorable*, and several others with those already mentioned in the second examples.

The third sound *ss* is only found in the above examples, and in *six* and *dix*, when unaccompanied by substantives, as in *de seize ôtez six*, *reste dix*, where *six* and *dix* are pronounced with the hissing sound of *ss* in the English word *bliss*.

The final *x* of adjectives, *doux*, *heureux*, and such like, is silent before a consonant, and has the fourth sound when before a vowel, *doux accent*, *heureux père*.

The *x* final of ***six***, ***dix***, is sounded like ***ss*** at the end of a sentence, ***il en a dix***; like ***z***, before a vowel, ***il a dix ans***, and is silent before a consonant, ***six livres***.

X final is silent, *je veux*, *prix*, *perdrix*, *feux*, *flux*, &c. except *Ajax*, *Astianax*, *borax*, *storax*, *Halifax*, *Hipponax*, *Dax*, *climax*, *thorax*, *Pertinax*, *Syphax*, *index*, *perplex*, *Béatrix*, *Erix*, *Félix*, *préfix*, *phénix*, *Fox*, *Palafox*, *Coysevox*, *lynx*, *sphinx*, *larynx*, *syrinx*, *onyx*, *Styx*, and *Pollux*.

N.B.—*X* takes the sound of *sh* only in *Don Quixote*, generally pronounced *Don Kishot*, or rather *Don Ghishot*.

Z, *z*, is generally pronounced as *z* in *zone*, or *s* in *rose*.

EXAMPLES.

Zi-za-nie	*tare*	zig-zag	*zigzag*
zé-nith	*zenith*	zin-zo-lin	*reddish purple*
zo-ne	*zone*	Zuy-der-zée	*Zuyder-see*

In *assez*, *chez*, *nez*, and in the second person of verbs, *vous avez*, *vous parlez*, the termination *ez* is pronounced *és*.

In proper names, especially Spanish names, the same termination *ez* is sounded *èce*, *Alvarez*, *Senez*, and also in *Metz*.

ZZ in Italian words is either sounded as one *z* or according to Italian pronunciation, by those to whom it is familiar.

12. PRACTICAL EXERCISES

ON THE PRONUNCIATION OF MONOSYLLABLES.

Gras	*fat*
ma	*my*
ta	*thy*
sa	*his, her, it*
la	*the, her, it*
las	*tired*
pas	*step*
un plat	*a dish*
bac	*ferry-boat*
sac	*sack, bag*
arc	*arch, bow*
parc	*park*
bal	*ball*
cap	*cape*
car	*for*
par	*by, through*
part	*share*
art	*art*
cha	*chariot*
dard	*dart*
lard	*bacon*
tard	*late*
quand	*when*
rang	*rank*
blanc	*white*
sans	*without*
dans	*in*
gland	*acorn*
pan	*skirt of a coat*
cran	*notch*
plant	*plantation*
plan	*plan*
flanc	*flank*
grand	*great*
en	*in*
il fend	*he splits*
gens	*people*
lent	*slow*
main	*hand*
il ment	*he lies*
il pend	*he hangs*
il prend	*he takes*
ceint	*girt*
cinq	*five*
sain	*wholesome*
sein	*bosom*
saint	*holy*
seing	*signature*
il rend	*he returns*
il sent	*he smells, feels*
je vends	*I sell*
je	*I*
me	*me*
ne	*not*
te	*thee*
ce	*this, that*
se	*himself, etc.*
le	*the, him, it*
de	*of*
lé	*breadth*
né	*born*
mais	*but*
mes	*my*, pl.
tes	*thy*, pl.
ses	*his, her, its*, pl.
les	*the, them*
pré	*meadow*
près	*near*
prêt	*ready*
ver	*worm*
vers	*towards*
vert	*green*
il perd	*he loses*
il sert	*he serves*
peur	*fear*
il meurt	*he dies*
pleurs	*tears*
leur	*their, them*
sel	*salt*
tel	*such*
quel	*which*
sec	*dry*

bec	*beak*	roc	*rock*
chef	*chief*	bloc	*block*
bref	*short*	troc	*exchange*
neuf	*new*	dot (pr. dote)	*dowry*
Est	*East*	on	*one, people, they*
vingt	*twenty*	bon	*good*
crin	*horse-hair*	bond	*bound*
lin	*flax*	ton	*thy*
brin	*sprig*	son	*his, her, its*
pain	*bread*	ils sont	*they are*
pin	*pine*	mon	*my*
vin	*wine*	don	*gift*
fi	*fy*	dont	*of which, etc.*
fils	*son*	donc	*therefore*
frit	*fried*	front	*forehead*
lis	*lily*	rond	*round*
pris	*taken*	blond	*light (hair)*
prix	*price*	pont	*bridge*
ris	*laugh*	long	*long*
riz	*rice*	fond	*bottom*
ni	*neither, nor*	ils font	*they do*
nid	*nest*	jonc	*rush*
si	*if*	non	*no*
il fit	*he did*	gond	*hinge*
mis	*put*	nom	*name*
plis	*folds*	plomb	*lead*
fil	*thread*	nu	*naked*
vil	*vile*	du	*of the*, sing. m.
vif	*lively*	il dut	*he owed*
sot	*fool*	bru	*daughter-in-law*
tôt	*soon*	brut	*rough*
clos	*shut up*	il but	*he drank*
nos	*our*	cru	*raw*
vos	*your*	il crut	*he believed*
gros	*big*	je fus	*I was*
trop	*too much*	jus	*juice*
trot	*trot*	lu	*read*
croc	*hook*	il lut	*he read*
or	*gold*	plus	*more*
bord	*edge*	tu	*thou*
fort	*strong*	vu	*seen*
tort	*wrong*	flux	*flux*
je sors	*I go out*	glu	*bird-lime*
sort	*fate*	duc	*duke*
port	*port*	suc	*juice*
il mord	*he bites*	sur	*upon*
vol	*theft*	mur	*wall*
choc	*shock*	nul	*no, none*

bout	*end*	mou	*soft*
joug	*yoke*	tout	*all*
nous	*we, us*	toux	*cough*
vous	*you*	pou	*louse*
clou	*nail*	cour	*yard*
cou	*neck*	il pleut	*it rains*
coup	*blow, stroke*	peu	*little, few*
trou	*hole*	il veut	*he is willing*

13. ON DISSYLLABLES.

OR WORDS OF TWO SYLLABLES.

A-bus	*abuse*	bri-gand	*robber*
a-chat	*purchase*	brus-que	*abrupt*
ac-teur	*actor*	bru-te	*brute*
â-ge	*age*	bu-ffet	*cupboard*
ai-greur	*acidity*	bu-reau	*office*
â-me	*soul*	bus-te	*bust*
a-nneau	*ring*	ca-deau	*present*
ar-deur	*ardour*	ca-fé	*coffee*
ar-gent	*money*	ca-hot	*jolt*
as-tre	*star*	ca-non	*cannon*
au-cun	*none*	ca-ve	*cellar*
a-veu	*confession*	cau-se	*cause*
a-vis	*advice*	cer-cle	*circle*
au-tre	*other*	ci-seau	*chisel*
bal-con	*balcony*	clé-ment	*clement*
ban-que	*bank*	cli-mat	*climate*
bar-que	*a bark*	cloi-son	*partition*
ba-teau	*boat*	co-hue	*mob*
bâ-ton	*stick*	co-mmun	*common*
beau-té	*beauty*	com-pas	*compasses*
bè-gue	*stammerer*	com-te	*earl*
bê-te	*beast*	con-gé	*holiday*
beur-re	*butter*	con-te	*tale*
bi-ble	*bible*	co-quin	*rogue*
blâ-me	*blame*	cor-deau	*line*
bon-heur, *pr.* bo-nheur	*happiness*	côté	*side*
		cou-ple	*couple*
bonté	*goodness*	cou-reur	*runner*
bos-quet	*grove*	cou-ssin	*cushion*
bou-quet	*nosegay*	cou-vent	*convent*
bour-geon	*bud*	crê-me	*cream*
bour-ru	*surly*	cri-me	*crime*
bra-sseur	*brewer*	crot-te	*dirt*

croû-te	*crust*
da-me	*lady*
dan-seur	*dancer*
dé-bit	*sale*
de-bout	*standing upright*
de-mi	*half*
dé-pôt	*deposit*
dé-sert	*wildernes*
dessert	*dessert*
dis-cours	*speech*
dou-leur	*pain*
é-cu	*crown*
en-clin	*inclined*
en-fant	*child*
é-poux	*spouse*
es-poir	*hope*
é-tain	*pewter*
ex-cès	*excess*
fes-tin	*feast*
fê-te	*festival*
fi-lou	*pickpocket*
fla-con	*decanter*
flam-beau	*flambeau*
flû-te	*flute*
fo-rêt	*forest*
fou-dre	*thunderbolt*
four-mi	*ant*
fri-pon	*knave*
fu-reur	*fury*
gaie-té	*cheerfulness*
gar-çon	*boy*
gâ-teau	*cake*
ga-zon	*turf*
gen-dre	*son-in-law*
gen-re	*gender*
gi-got	*leg of mutton*
gla-çon	*piece of ice*
goû-té	*luncheon*
gout-te	*drop*
grâ-ce	*favour*
gron-deur	*grumbler*
gru-au	*gruel*
guè-re	*little*
guer-re	*war*
gueu-le	*mouth (of a beast)*
gui-de	*guide*

hai-ne	*hatred*
‘ hal-le	*market-hall*
‘ har-pe	*harp*
‘ hâ-te	*haste*
‘ hau-teur	*height*
‘ ha-sard	*chance*
‘ hê-tre	*beech*
hom-me, *pr.* ho-mme	*man*
hon-neur, *pr.* ho-nneur	*honour*
‘ hon-te	*shame*
hor-reur	*horror*
hô-te	*landlord*
hu-main	*human*
im-pie	*impious*
ju-ge	*judge*
jour-née	*day*
lai-teux	*milky*
la-quais	*footman*
lar-cin	*theft*
lar-geur	*breadth*
li-queur	*liquor*
lo-gis	*dwelling*
lon-gueur	*length*
mar-bre	*marble*
mar-chand	*tradesman*
ma-ri	*husband*
mè-re	*mother*
meu-ble	*furniture*
mon-de	*world*
mons-tre	*monster*
mou-le	*mould*
mou-lin	*mill*
ni-gaud	*silly fellow*
nou-veau	*new*
œu-vre	*work*
on-guent	*ointment*
or-dre	*order*
ou-bli	*oblivion*
pa-rent	*relation*
par-rain, *pr.* pa-rrain	*godfather*
pâ-te	*dough*
pâ-té	*pie*
pat-te	*paw*
pê-che	*fishing*
pé-ché	*sin*

pê-cheur *fisherman*
pé-cheur *sinner*
pei-ne *trouble*
pein-tre *painter*
pè-re *father*
peu-ple *people*
peu-reux *fearful*
pin-te *pint*
plu-me *feather*
por-trait *picture*
pour-pre *purple*
prin-ce *prince*
pru-neau *prune*
ra-goût *ragout*
rè-gle *rule*
rè-gne *reign*
rei-ne *queen*
ren-te *annuity*
rê-ve *dream*
ri-re *laughing*
rou-te *road*
ru-se *trick*
sa-bre *sabre*
sa-lut *salute*
sa-tin *satin*
sau-ce *sauce*
sau-teur *tumbler*
sé-jour *residence*
si-gnal *signal*
si-gne *sign*
som-bre *dark*
sou-hait *wish*
sou-pe *soup*
sou-ris *smile*
su-cre *sugar*
sus-pec *suspicious*
ta-che *spot*
tâ-che *task*
tam-bour *drum*
tom-beau *grave*
to-me *volume*
tou-pie *top*
tour-neur *turner*
traî-neau *sledge*
trô-ne *throne*
trou-peau *flock*
veu-ve *widow*
vi-gne *vine*
zè-le *zeal*
zé-lé *zealous*

14. WORDS OF THREE SYLLABLES.

A-bî-me *abyss*
a-bré-gé *abridgment*
a-bri-cot *apricot*
ab-so-lu *absolute*
ab-sur-de *absurd*
ac-tri-ce *actress*
a-ffai-re *business*
am-pou-le *blister*
a-ppé-tit *appetite*
â-pre-té *asperity*
a-rai-gnée *spider*
ar-moi-re *cabinet*
ar-tis-te *artist*
as-si-du *assiduous*
a-tro-ce *atrocious*
au-ber-ge *inn*
a-voi-ne *oats*
aus-tè-re *austere*
ba-bio-le *bauble*
bas-ses-se *baseness*
bâ-ti-ment *building*
bê-le-ment *bleating*
ber-gè-re *shepherdess*
bê-ti-se *stupidity*
bien-fai-sant *benevolent*
bien-sé-ant *becoming*
bien-ve-nu *welcome*
blan-châ-tre *whitish*
bles-su-re *wound*
boi-se-rie *wainscot*
bor-du-re *edging*
bou-lan-ger *baker*
bou-ta-de *whim*
bou-ti-que *shop*
bras-se-rie *brewhouse*
bra-vou-re *valour*

breu-va-ge	*drink*
bro-de-rie	*embroidery*
brou-et-te	*wheelbarrow*
brû-lu-re	*burning*
brus-que-ment	*bluntly*
ca-de-nas	*padlock*
cam-pa-gne	*country*
ca-rê-me	*lent*
car-ross-e	*coach*
cein-tu-re	*girdle*
ce-pen-dant	*however*
cham-pi-gnon	*mushroom*
cha-pe-lier	*hatter*
cha-pel-le	*chapel*
cha-pi-tre	*chapter*
char-la-tan	*quack*
char-ret-te	*cart*
châ-ti-ment	*chastisement*
chau-de-ment	*warmly*
chau-diè-re	*copper*
chau-ffa-ge	*fuel*
chau-ssu-re	*shoes, stockings*
ci-viè-re	*hand-barrow*
cla-ve-cin	*harpsichord*
clo-a-que	*sewer*
co-li-que	*colic*
co-llé-ge	*college*
co-lli-ne	*hill*
co-lo-nne	*column*
co-lo-ris	*colouring*
co-mé-die	*comedy*
co-mé-dien	*comedian*
co-mmer-çant	*merchant*
com-pa-gnie	*company*
com-pa-gnon	*companion*
con-dui-te	*behaviour*
con-qué-rant	*conqueror*
con-quê-te	*conquest*
cons-tam-ment	*constantly*
con-ti-gu	*contiguous*
cor-do-nnier	*shoemaker*
co-ri-a-ce	*tough*
cor-ni-chon	*girkin*
cou-chet-te	*couch*
cou-ro-nne	*crown*
cou-te-las	*hanger*
cou-te-lier	*cutler*
cou-tu-re	*seam*

cra-moi-si	*crimson*
cré-du-le	*credulous*
cri-ti-que	*critic*
cru-au-té	*cruelty*
cui-si-ne	*kitchen*
cul-bu-te	*tumble*
cu-re-dent	*tooth-pick*
dé-com-bres	*rubbish*
dé-goû-tant	*disgusting*
dé-jeû-ner	*breakfast*
de-meu-re	*abode*
dés-ho-nneur	*dishonour*
des-po-te	*despot*
dis-ci-ple	*pupil*
dis-grâ-ce	*disgrace*
dro-guis-te	*druggist*
droi-tu-re	*uprightness*
é-cha-fand	*scaffold*
é-chel-le	*ladder*
é-che-veau	*skein*
é-cu-me	*froth*
em-pe-reur	*emperor*
em-plâ-tre	*plaster*
em-plet-te	*purchase*
en-clu-me	*anvil*
en-ga-geant	*engaging*
en-ne-mi	*enemy*
en-sei-gne	*sign*
é-pa-gneul	*spaniel*
é-pi-ce	*spice*
é-pi-cier	*grocer*
é-pou-se	*wife*
es-ca-lier	*stair-case*
es-pa-ce	*space*
es-pè-ce	*kind*
es-quis-se	*sketch*
es-tra-gon	*stragon*
é-tei-gnoir	*extinguisher*
é-tour-di	*thoughtless*
é-vê-ché	*bishoprick*
é-veil-lé	*awake*
ex-ces-sif	*immoderate*
ex-em-ple	*example*
fa-bu-leux	*fabulous*
fa-ça-de	*front*
fai-en-ce	*delft ware*
fa-ri-neux	*mealy*
fa-rou-che	*fierce*

fi-las-se	*flax*
fleu-ris-te	*florist*
fai-bles-se	*weakness*
fo-lâ-tre	*playful*
fou-droy-ant	*thundering*
four-bi-sseur	*sword-cutler*
four-ru-re	*fur*
fram-boi-se	*raspberry*
fri-su-re	*curling*
froi-ssu-re	*bruising*
gi-ro-fle	*cloves*
go-be-let	*goblet*
gou-lû-ment	*speedily*
gué-ri-son	*cure*
gui-mau-ve	*marsh-mallow*
ha-lei-ne	*breath*
‘ har-di-ment	*boldly*
‘ ha-ri-cot	*French bean*
hor-lo-ge	*clock*
hor-ri-ble	*horrid*
hô-tes-se	*landlady*
i-gno-rant	*ignorant*
im-men-se	*immense*
im-pu-ni	*unpunished*
in-cen-die	*conflagration*
in-con-nu	*unknown*
in-gé-nu	*ingenuous*
i-nhu-main	*inhuman*
in-sec-te	*insect*
ins-truc-tif	*instructive*
i-voi-re	*ivory*
i-vro-gne	*drunkard*
ja-quet-te	*jacket*
jour-na-lier	*journeyman*
lai-tiè-re	*milk woman*
lan-gou-reux	*languishing*
len-til-le	*lentil*
li-ma-çon	*snail*
ma-ga-sin	*warehouse*
mal-a-droit	*awkward*
ma-nœu-vre	*labourer*
mar-mi-ton	*scullion*
mas-cu-lin	*masculine*
mé-con-tent	*discontented*
mé-moi-re	*memory*
mé-na-ger	*thrifty*
men-son-ge	*falsehood*
mé-pris-e	*mistake*
mé-tho-de	*method*
mo-des-tie	*modesty*
mon-ta-gnard	*highlander*
mou-tar-de	*mustard*
mur-mu-re	*murmur*
na-tu-rel	*natural*
nau-fra-ge	*shipwreck*
né-an-moins	*nevertheless*
no-bles-se	*nobility*
noi-râ-tre	*blackish*
o-bli-geant	*obliging*
om-bra-ge	*shade*
o-ppro-bre	*disgrace*
o-ra-geux	*stormy*
or-fè-vre	*goldsmith*
or-phe-lin	*orphan*
pa-moi-son	*fainting fit*
pan-tou-fle	*slipper*
pa-pe-tier	*stationer*
pa-ra-sol	*umbrella*
pa-ren-te	*kinswoman*
pa-rois-se	*parish*
pa-ssa-ble	*tolerable*
poi-ssar-de	*fishwoman*
poi-tri-ne	*breast*
por-tiè-re	*coach door*
pos-tu-re	*posture*
po-ta-ge	*porridge*
pou-ssiè-re	*dust*
pré-tex-te	*pretence*
prin-ces-se	*princess*
pro-mes-se	*promise*
pro-tec-teur	*protector*
pu-é-ril	*childish*
pui-ssan-ce	*power*
que-rel-le	*quarrel*
ra-piè-re	*rapier*
ra-tiè-re	*rat-trap*
ré-col-te	*crop*
ré-ser-vé	*reserved*
re-ssour-ce	*resource*
re-trai-te	*retirement*
rê-ve-rie	*meditation*
rou-geâ-tre	*reddish*
rus-ti-que	*rural*
scan-da-leux	*scandalous*
scru-pu-leux	*scrupulous*
sé-an-ce	*sitting*

[illegible]u-re	*lock*
si-ffle-ment	*whistling*
sim-ple-ment	*plainly*
so-bri-quet	*nick name*
so-le-nnel, pronounced *la*	*solemn*
so-nnet-te	*little bell*
so-no-re	*sonorous*
sou-cou-pe	*saucer*
soup-ço-nneux	*suspicious*
spec-ta-cle	*sight*
splen-di-de	*splendid*
suc-ce-sseur	*successor*
su-prê-me	*supreme*
symp-tô-me	*symptom*
tein-tu-re	*dyeing*
ten-dres-se	*tenderness*
té-né-breux	*darkness*
thé-â-tre	*theatre*
thé-iè-re	*tea-pot*
toi-let-te	*toilet*
tour-ne-vis	*screw-driver*
tou-te-fois	*nevertheless*
tri-che-rie	*cheat*
tri-om-phe	*triumph*
trom-pet-te	*trumpet*
tu-mul-te	*tumult*
va-can-ces	*holidays*
ver-get-te	*brush*
ver-mi sseau	*small worm*
vic-toi-re	*victory*
vi-gou-reux	*vigorous*
vi-lla-geois	*countryman*
voi-tu-re	*carriage*
zé-phir	*zephyrus*

15. OF GENDER.

There are but two genders in French, the masculine and feminine.

The masculine gender expresses the male kind, as *un homme*, a man; *un lion*, a lion.

The feminine gender denotes the female kind, as *une femme*, a woman; *une lionne*, a lioness.

The French language has no neuter; consequently, inanimate objects are either masculine or feminine. Foreigners experience great difficulty in that respect, for, as the article, pronoun and adjective which refer to a noun, must agree with it *in gender*, as well as *in number*, much attention must be paid to ascertain the former. To enable them to do this, no general rules can efficiently be given, on account of the numberless exceptions which occur. We think that *ear* and *practice* are the safest and most correct guides which can be followed, and, in fact, they are the only ones which the French themselves have,

4*

who hardly ever make a mistake, if we except the uneducated; we, therefore, strongly recommend them to the English learners. Unwilling, however, to withhold from them any part of the assistance they may look for in a grammar like this, we will give some general rules with their exceptions.

16. GENERAL RULES,

TO ASCERTAIN THE GENDER OF NOUNS SUBSTANTIVES IN FRENCH, WITH THEIR EXCEPTIONS.

1. God, his angels, cherubim and seraphim, are of the masculine gender.

2. All *diminutives of animals*, when there is but one common denomination for both sexes, are of the masculine gender, whatever may be the gender of the root from which they are derived, as *un lionceau, un souriceau, un perdreau, un cornillas, un carpillon, un couleuvreau, un vipereau, un bécasseau*, &c. except *une bécassine;* but these two latter, although derived from the word *bécasse*, and belonging to the *genus*, are not of the same *species*. In other cases, the diminutives follow the gender their sex indicates, as *un poulain, une pouliche, un cochet, une poulette*.

3. Diminutives of inanimate objects generally follow the gender of their roots, as *batelet, maisonnette, globule*, from *bateau, maison, globe*, &c.; but *un corbillon, un soliveau, un cruchon, une savonnette, un trousseau*, from *la corbeille, la solive, la cruche, le savon*, and *la trousse*, and many others do not.

4. All the names of the days, months, and seasons of the year, are of the *masculine gender*, except *automne*, which is of both genders; when, however,

the diminutive *mi* (half) is prefixed to the name of a month, the compound word then takes the feminine gender, as *la mi-mai, la mi-août, la mi-carême; mi* standing for *demi*, f.; *la St. Jean, la St. Michel*, and other saints' days are feminine; *fête de* being understood, as *la* FÊTE DE *St. Jean.*

5. NAMES — ARE MASCULINE.
- of *trees*, except *yeuse*, a sort of oak.
- of *shrubs*, with some exceptions,
- of *metals*, without excepting *platine*, formerly feminine,
- of *minerals*, a few excepted,
- of *colours*, without excepting *l'Isabelle, le Feuille-morte*, &c. though they have a feminine termination.

6. NAMES — ARE MASCULINE.
- of *mountains*, except when the words *Montagne côte*, are understood; *les Cordillières, les Alpes.*
- of *winds*, except *la bise, la tramontane, la brise*, and *les moussons.*
- of *towns*, except those which necessarily take the article *la* before them, as *la Rochelle, la Ferté-sur-Aube*, &c. and others.

7. Ordinal, distributive, and proportional numbers, adjectives, and infinitives of verbs, prepositions and adverbs, all these, when used substantively, are masculine, as *le tiers, le quart, un cinquième, le quadruple, le beau, le sublime, le boire, le manger, le mieux, le pour, le contre, un parallèle*, (a comparison,) &c. except *la moitié*, and the elliptical forms of speech, *une courbe, une tangente, une perpendiculaire, une parallèle, une antique*, used for *une ligne courbe, une ligne tangente*, &c. *Antique* is feminine, for the same reason; the word *médaille*, or *statue* appearing to be understood.

8. Names of *virtues* are of the feminine gender, except *courage, mérite.*

17. GENDERS OF NOUNS,

TO BE KNOWN FROM THEIR TERMINATION.

9. The termination in an *e* mute, is called a feminine termination; any other is called masculine. This distinction arises probably from the circumstance that most nouns of the feminine gender end with an *e* mute, thus *la table, la rivière, la rue, la plante, la tête, la fenêtre;* but to this general rule there are innumerable exceptions, which we will notice as we speak of other terminations.

10. *Names of states, empires, kingdoms and provinces* are of the gender which their terminations indicate; except *le Bengale, le Mexique, le Péloponèse. le Maine, le Perche, Rouergue, le Bigorre, le Vallage, la Franche-comté,* and perhaps a few more.

1.. The names of fruits, grain, plants, and flowers, follow pretty generally the gender of their terminations, but there are too many exceptions to be introduced here.

18. TABLE,

SHOWING THE GENDER OF ALL WORDS WHICH DO NOT END IN *e* MUTE.

	MASCULINE.		FEMININE.	
0	0	-tié	amitié, inimitié, moitié. pitié	4
11	Aparté, arrêté, bénédicité, comté, côté, été, pâté, traité, lé, thé, Léthé	-tié	absurdité, beauté, charité, cité, dignité, fidélité, générosité, etc. etc. .	500
40	alibi, biribi, lundi, gui, grand merci, etc.	-i	Fourmi, merci, gagui, après-midi . .	4
15	convoi, effroi, etc.	-oi	foi, loi, paroi	3
30	ergo, vertigo, indigo, etc	-o	albugo, virago	2
10	fichu, cru, écu, tissu, etc.	-u	bru, glu, tribu, vertu.	4
200	aloyau, anneau, etc. etc	-au	eau, peau, surpeau, sans-peau.	4
6	bref, chalef, chef, fief, grief, relief.	-ef	clef, nef, soif.	3
3	daim, essaim, abatfaim	-aim	faim, male-faim	2
100	an, ban, cran, écran, pan, etc	-an	maman	1
200	bain, baise-main, avant-main, garde-main, tourne-main, essuie-main, gain, frein, basin, etc . .	-in	fin, main, nonnain. . .	5
4	scion, bastion, bestion, Ixion	-cion -sion -tion -gion -nion -xion	succion, cession, friction, gestion, région, opinion, réflexion, fluxion, etc. etc. etc.	1100
30	gabion, taudion, million, lion, ardélion, fourmilion, trémion, capion, turion, camion, lampion, septentrion, brimborion, gavion, etc.	-bion -dion -lion -mion -pion -rion -vion	rébellion, dent-delion, alluvion	3

	MASCULINE.		FEMININE.	
8	alcyon, clayon, crayon, rayon, sayon, trayon, lamproyon, Amphictryon. . . .	-yon	. . . .	0
1	brise-raison.	-aison	cargaison, etc. etc . . .	30
11	peson, bison, grison, groison, horizon, sison, tison, oison, poison, contre-poison, buson	-eson -ison -uson	garnison, guérison, prison, trahison, cloison, foison, moison, pamoison, toison, camuson. .	11
15	basson, caisson, cavesson, taisson, poisson, cosson, buisson, frisson, hérisson, maudisson, nourrisson, palisson, polisson, unisson, saucisson, courson	-sson	paisson. boisson, moisson, cuisson, salisson mousson . .	6
4	arcanson, échanson, tenson, pinson. . .	-nson	chanson.	1
20	charançon, caveçon, courçon, pinçon, suçon, etc..	-çon	façon, contrefaçon, malfaçon, leçon, rançon	5
30	bridon, guéridon, etc. .	-don	dondon.	1
150	tendron, jeune tendrop, baron, etc . .	-lon -ron	laideron, souiilon, tatillon	3
70	abattis, appentis, iris, tourne-vis, etc. . .	-is	brebis, souris, chauve-souris, vis iris.	5
15	bois, mois, carquois, harnois, etc.	-ois	fois	1
12	adent, chiendent, liondent, claquedent, cure-dent, occident, trident, etc	-dent -gent	dent, surdent, gent. . .	3
700	acharnement, assortiment, etc	-ment	jument	1
250	ballet, billet, bosquet, minuit, conduit, réduit, etc. billot. brulot, complot, etc. bout, goût, ragoût, etc	-et -uit -ot -out	forêt, nuit, dot, glout .	4
15	paix, choix, crucifix, prix, etc. taux, houx, courroux, époux, etc.	-ix -aux -oux	paix, croix, noix, poix, voix, perdrix, chaux, faux, toux.	9

20	art, départ, champart, rempart, effort, port, sort, tort, etc.	-art -ort	hart, part, mort, malemort	4
40	fer, ver, hiver, etc. air, éclair. etc. tour, contour, four, etc.	-er -air -our	cuiller, mer, chair, cour, tour	5
900	bonheur, malheur, labeur, honnéur, déshonneur, cœur, anticœur, crève-cœur, chœur, chou-fleur, pleurs, équateur, secteur, etc. etc.	-eur	aigreur, ampleur, ardeur, blancheur, candeur, chaleur, chandeleur, clameur, couleur, douceur, douleur, épaisseur, erreur, fadeur, défaveur, ferveur, fleur,	76

passe-fleur, sans-fleur, fraîcheur, frayeur, froideur, fureur grandeur, grosseur, hauteur, horreur, humeur, laideur, langueur, largeur, lenteur, liqueur, longueur, lourdeur, lueur, maigreur, moiteur, noirceur, odeur, pâleur, pesanteur, peur, primeur, profondeur, puanteur, pudeur, impudeur, rigueur, raideur, rondeur, rougeur, rousseur, rumeur, saveur, senteur, sœur, souleur, splendeur, sueur, teneur, terreur, tiédeur, torpeur, touffeur, tumeur, valeur, non-valeur, vapeur, verdeur, vigueur, and mœurs; *besides* basseur, rancœur, trémeur, *three words now obsolete, making in the whole the number of seventy-six*

There are a great many proper names of females, which, though they may not have the feminine termination, are of that gender, as the learner, from their nature, will easily comprehend; such are, among the heathens, *Pallas, Cérès, Thétis, Vénus, Junon, Didon, etc.* Among christian names, *Sara, Deborah, Elizabeth, Agnès*, etc. and many of these are contractions, as *Fanchon* for *Fanny, Lison, Louison, Marion, Manon, Nanon, Jeanneton, Madelon, Tonton, Cataut, Margot, Goton, Babet, Babeau, Isabeau.*

As this list of exceptions will be found pretty accurate, all other nouns, that belong to this termination, must be strictly considered as being of the masculine gender, since they are not enumerated in this Table.

19. A TABLE OF SUBSTANTIVES.

THAT ARE MASCULINE IN ONE SIGNIFICATION AND FEMININE IN ANOTHER.

MASCULINE.		FEMININE.
Assistant, helper	Aide	*Aid, help, support*
eagle, a great genius	aigle	*a standard*
an angel	ange	*a kind of thornback*
an alder tree	aune	*an ell, a sort of measure*
barb, a Barbary horse	barbe	*beard*
Bard, a poet	barde	*a slice of bacon, horse-armour*
red-breast	berce	*cow-parsnip*
a sort of privateer	câpre	*caper (a fruit)*
a scroll or ornament in painting	cartouche	*cartouch, cartridge*
a caravan, a boy	coche	*a notch, a sow*
cornet, a standard bearer	cornette	*a woman's head-dress*
a couple, a man and wife	couple	*a brace, a pair, two of a sort*
Croat, a Croatian soldier	cravate	*a cravat, neckcloth*
a crape	crêpe	*a pancake*
an echo	écho	*Echo, a nymph*
ensign, an officer	enseigne	*a sign post*
example, model, instance	exemple	*a copy for writing*
a gimlet, a piercer	forêt	*a wood, a forest*
a large vat	foudre	*lightning, thunderbolt*
keeper, warden	garde	*watch, hilt, nurse*
hoar frost	givre	*a snake (in heraldry)*
the rolls, a register	greffe	*a graft*
gules in heraldry	gueule	*the mouth of beasts*
guide, director	guide	*reins in driving*
heliotrope, sunflower	héliotrope	*heliotrope, jasper*
iris, the rainbow, iris of the eye	iris	*sprig-crystal, a proper name*
lacker, a kind of varnish	laque	*lacca, gum-lac*
a book	livre	*a pound*
a hat of otter's hair	loutre	*an otter*

N.B. Of this table it is to be remarked, that the French word stands in the middle column and its signification on the right hand and on the left. When it has the meaning which stands on the left, it is masculine; when that which stands on the right it is feminine.

MASCULINE.		FEMININE.
handle of a tool	manche	*a sleeve, English channel*
a labourer	manœuvre	*the working of a ship*
memoir, a bill	mémoire	*memory*
thanks	merci	*pity, mercy*
mood, mode	mode	*fashion*
a pier, or mound	môle	*mole, moon-calf*
mould, cast, form	moule	*muscle, a shell-fish*
a ship-boy	mousse	*moss, a plant*
the philosopher's stone	œuvre	*action, an author's work*
office, prayers	office	*pantry, larder, buttery*
ombre, a game at cards	ombre	*shade, shadow*
singular is mas.	orgue	*plural is feminine*
page of a prince, etc.	page	*page in a book*
a merry andrew	paillasse	*a straw bed*
a hand's breadth	palme	*the branch of a palm tree, victory*
pantomime	pantomime	*a dumb show*
Easter, Easter-day	pâque	*the passover*
a comparison	parallèle	*a parallel*
pendulum	pendule	*a clock*
le Perche, in France	perche	*pole, perch, a fish*
summit, highest pitch	période	*period, epocha*
anybody, nobody (a pronoun)	personne	*a person, (a noun)*
spade, at cards	pique	*a pike*
gnatsnapper, a bird	pivoine	*peony, a flower*
a plane-tree	plane	*plane, an instrument*
a stove, a canopy	poèle	*a frying-pan*
post, a military station	poste	*the post for letters*
punto at cards	ponte	*the laying of eggs*
purple colour, purples, (a disease)	pourpre	*purple fish, purple dye*
a pretence	prétexte	*pretext*
quadril at cards	quadrille	*party of horse in a tournament*
the calling back a hawk	réclame	*a catch-word (in printing)*
rest, relaxation	relâche	*harbour*
a glass coach	remise	*a coach-house, a remittance*
a sort of pear-tree	sans-peau	*a sort of pear*
Satyr, a sylvan god	satyre	*a satire, a lampoon*
serpentarius	serpentaire	*snake-root, dragon's wort*
nap, slumber	somme	*sum, load, name of a river*
a smile	souris	*a mouse*
a porter	suisse	*Switzerland*
holder, a book-keeper	teneur	*tenor, purport, content*
a tour, turn, trick	tour	*tower, rook at chess*
triumph	triomphe	*a trump*

trumpeter	trompette	*trumpet*
space	vague	*a wave, surge*
a vase, vessel	vase	*the slime in ponds, lakes, etc.*
a hat of vigonia wool	vigogne	*a vigon, or llama*
a veil	voile	*a sail*

---

20. A VOCABULARY,

FRENCH AND ENGLISH.

IN TWENTY-THREE CHAPTERS.

*** In the following Vocabulary, the Gender has been affixed only to those Nouns that are not included in the preceding Rules.

OF THE UNIVERSE IN GENERAL.

Dieu	*God*	nature	*nature*
créateur	*creator*	univers	*universe*
Jésus-Christ	*Jesus Christ*	monde *m.*	*world*
Trinité	*Trinity*	élément	*element*
Saint-Esprit	*Holy Ghost*	terre	*earth*
ange	*angel*	eau	*water*
archange	*archangel*	feu	*fire*
prophète	*prophet*	air	*air*
Messie	*Messiah*	firmament	*sky*
sauveur	*saviour*	étoile	*star*
rédempteur	*redeemer*	planète	*planet*
Vierge Marie	*Virgin Mary*	comète	*comet*
apôtre	*apostle*	constellation	*constellation*
évangéliste	*evangelist*	soleil	*sun*
martyr	*martyr*	rayon du soleil	*sun-beam*
saint	*saint*	lune	*moon*
paradis	*paradise*	éclipse	*eclipse*
ciel	*heaven*	orage *m.*	*storm*
enfer	*hell*	tonnerre *m.*	*thunder*
diable	*devil*	éclair	*lightning*

brouillard	*fog*
pluie	*rain*
arc-en-ciel	*rainbow*
ondée	*shower*
neige	*snow*
grêle	*hail*
glace	*ice*
gelée	*frost*
dégel	*thaw*
rosée	*dew*
créature	*creature*
globe *m.*	*globe*
sphère	*sphere*
hémisphère *m.*	*hemisphere*
horizon	*horizon*
degré	*degree*
longitude	*longitude*
latitude	*latitude*
points cardinaux *pl.*	*cardinal points*
orient, *ou* est	*east*
occident, *ou* ouest	*west*
septentrion, *ou* nord	*north*
midi, *ou* sud	*south*
climat	*climate*
région	*region*
continent	*continent*
Europe	*Europe*
Asie	*Asia*
Afrique	*Africa*
Amérique	*America*
empire *m.*	*empire*
royaume *m*	*kingdom*
république	*republic*
pays	*country*
colonie	*colony*
principauté	*principality*
électorat	*electorate*
province	*province*
comté	*shire* or *county*
île	*island*
presqu'île / péninsule	*peninsula*
Chersonèse	*Chersonesus*
cap	*cape*
promontoire *m.*	*promontory*
isthme *m.*	*isthmus*
montagne	*mountain*
mont	*mount*
colline	*hill*
sommet	*summit*
pente, *ou* penchant	*declivity*
hauteur	*eminence*
vallée	*valley*
vallon	*dale*
abîme *m.*	*abyss*
désert	*desert*
plaine	*plain*
marais	*marsh or fen*
rive	*bank (of a river)*
rivage *m.*	*shore*
côte	*coast*
rocher*	*rock*
roche*	*rock*
roc*	*rock*
écueil*	*shoal*
banc*	*sand bank*
récif*	*reef of rocks*
brisans*	*breakers, surf*
cime	*top*
pierre	*stone*
pont	*bridge*
chaussée	*causeway, road*
gué	*ford*
quai	*wharf or quay*
route	*road*
sentier	*path*
fossé	*ditch*
gravier	*gravel*
sable *m.*	*sand*
sablon	*small sand*
poussière	*dust*
océan	*ocean*
mer	*sea*
golfe *m*	*gulf*
baie	*bay*

* These seven words do not convey in French the same idea; the four latter relate to the sea.

rade	*road (for ships)*	charbon de terre	*pit coal*
anse	*creek*	charbon de bois	*charcoal*
canal	*channel*	braise	*small coal*
détroit	*strait*	tourbe	*turf*
courant	*current*		*peat*
marée	*tide*	bois	*wood*
flux	*flowing*	bûche	*log of wood*
reflux	*ebbing*	fagot	*faggot*
vague	*wave*	coupeaux *pl.*	*chips*
flots *pl.*	*billows, waves*	cendre	*ashes*
ondes *m.*	*waters*	suie	*soot*
hâvre *m.*	*haven*	feu	*fire*
port	*harbour*	atmosphère	*atmosphere*
lac	*lake*	vent	*wind*
rivière	*river*	zéphyr	*zephyr*
fleuve *m.*	*great river*	vapeur	*vapour*
embouchure	*mouth of a river*	lumière	*light*
ruisseau	*brook*	ténèbres *pl.*	*darkness*
débordement	*overflow*	chaleur	*heat*
déluge *m.*	*deluge*	froid	*cold*
inondation	*inundation*	nue, nuée	*cloud*
écluse	*flood-gate, sluice*	nuage *m.*	*cloud*
digue	*dyke*	nielle	*blight*
étang	*pond*	humidité	*dampness*
vivier	*fish-pond*	serein	*mildew*
réservoir	*bason*	tourbillon	*whirlwind*
abreuvoir	*horse-pond*	orage *m.*	*storm*
bain	*bath*	tempête	*tempest*
citerne	*cistern*	ondée	*shower*
fontaine	*fountain*	calme *m.*	*calm*
source	*source*	éternité	*eternity*
puits	*well*	temps	*time*
pompe	*pump*	siècle *m.*	*age or century*
bateau	*boat*	époque	*epoch*
barque	*bark*	période *m.*	*period*
bac	*ferry-boat*	date	*date*
coche d'eau *m.*	*barge*	an, année	*year*
gabare	*lighter*	mois	*month*
navire *m.*	*ship*	janvier	*january*
vaisseau	*vessel*	février	*february*
paquebot	*packet-boat*	mars	*march*
flamme	*blaze*	avril	*april*
étincelle	*spark*	mai	*may*
chaleur	*heat*	juin	*june*
fumée	*smoke*	juillet	*july*
incendie *m.*	*conflagration*	août	*august*
chauffage *m.*	*fuel*	septembre	*september*
charbon	*coals*	octobre	*october*

novembre	*november*
décembre	*december*
semaine	*week*
jour	*day*
journée	*day*
aujourd'hui	*to-day*
demain	*to-morrow*
hier	*yesterday*
lundi	*monday*
mardi	*tuesday*
mercredi	*wednesday*
jeudi	*thursday*
vendredi	*friday*
samedi	*saturday*
dimanche	*sunday*
heure	*hour*
demi-heure	*half an hour*
quart-d'heure	*quarter of an hour*
aurore	*aurora*
aube	*dawn*
matin	*morning*
matinée	*forenoon*
midi	*noon*
l'après-midi, l'après-dinée	*the afternoon*
soir, soirée	*evening*
crépuscule *m.*	*twilight*
nuit	*night*
minuit	*midnight*
minute	*minute*
seconde	*second*
moment	*moment*
instant	*instant*
saison	*season*
printemps	*spring*
été	*summer*
automne	*autumn*
hiver	*winter*
carnaval	*carnival*
carême *m.*	*lent*
mi-carême	*midlent*
pâque	*easter*
pentecôte	*whit-sunday*
la Saint Jean	*midsummer*
l'avent	*advent*
noël	*christmas*
fête	*festival*
équinoxe *m.*	*equinox*
solstice *m.*	*the solstice*
canicule	*the dog-days*
fenaison	*hay-harvest*
moisson	*harvest*
vendange	*vintage*
tonte	*shearing-time*
semailles *pl.*	*sowing-time*
congé	*holiday*

II. OF MAN.

genre humain	*mankind*
homme	*man*
femme	*woman*
sexe	*sex*
enfant	*child*
garçon	*boy, youth, lad*
fille	*girl*
vierge	*virgin*
virginité	*virginity*
enfance	*infancy*
jeunesse	*youth*
adolescence	*adolescence*
virilité	*manhood*
vieillesse	*old age*
décrépitude	*decrepitude*
jeune homme	*young man*
jeune fille	*young girl*
vieillard	*old man*
géant	*giant*
nain	*dwarf*
pigmée *m.*	*pigmy*
mari	*husband*
femme	*wife*
veuf	*widower*

veuve	*widow*
orphelin	*orphan (boy)*
orpheline	*orphan (girl)*
héritier	*heir*
héritière	*heiress*
maître	*master*
maîtresse	*mistress*
hôte	*landlord*
hôtesse	*landlady*
domestique	*man servant*
servante	*maid servant*
voisin *m.*	*neighbour*
voisine *f.*	
compagnon *m*	*companion*
compagne *f.*	
corps	*body*
membre *m.*	*member*
tronc	*trunk*
tête	*head*
crâne *m.*	*skull*
front	*forehead*
visage *m.*	*face*
traits *pl.*	*features*
œil	*eye*
yeux *pl.*	*eyes*
sourcils *pl.*	*eye-brows*
paupière	*eye-lid*
nez	*nose*
narines *pl.*	*nostrils*
bouche	*mouth*
lèvres *pl.*	*lips*
dent	*tooth*
gencives *pl.*	*gums*
mâchoire	*jaw-bone*
langue	*tongue*
palais	*palate*
joues *pl.*	*cheeks*
fossette	*dimple*
menton	*chin*
barbe	*beard*
tempes *pl.*	*temples*
oreille	*ear*
cheveux *pl.*	*hair*
cou	*neck*
gosier	*throat*
sein	*bosom*
poitrine	*chest*
ventre *m*	*belly*

ceinture	*waist*
côté	*side*
hanche	*hip*
reins *pl.*	*loins*
genou	*knee*
jarret	*ham*
rotule	*knee-pan*
jambe	*leg*
mollet	*calf of the leg*
pied	*foot*
talon	*heel*
orteil	*toe*
bras	*arm*
coude *m.*	*elbow*
aisselle	*the arm-pit*
épaule	*shoulder*
main	*hand*
poing	*fist*
poignet	*wrist*
doigt	*finger*
pouce	*thumb*
ongle *m.*	*nail*
côte	*rib*
cerveau	*brain*
cervelle	
squelette *m.*	*skeleton*
cœur	*heart*
poumon	*lungs*
foie *m.*	*liver*
rate	*spleen*
estomac	*stomach*
entrailles *pl.*	*entrails*
sang	*blood*
humeurs *pl.*	*humour*
glande	*gland*
poil	*hair*
chair	*flesh*
peau	*skin*
pores *m. pl.*	*pores*
nerf	*nerve*
artère	*artery*
veine	*vein*
os	*bone*
moelle	*marrow*
ride	*wrinkle*
bouton	*pimple*
santé	*health*
tempérament	*constitution*

embonpoint	*plumpness*
maigreur	*leanness*
teint	*complexion*
rougeur	*redness*
pâleur	*paleness*
port	*carriage*
démarche	*gait*
geste *m.*	*gesture*
vivacité	*liveliness*
enjouement	*sprightliness*
gaieté	*gaiety*
beauté	*beauty*
charmes *m.*	*charms*
attraits *pl.*	*attractions*
appas *pl.*	*beauties*
agrément	*pleasantness*
laideur	*deformity*
taille	*figure, size*
voix	*voice*
parole	*speech*
silence *m.*	*silence*
action	*action*
mouvement	*motion*
repos	*rest*
grimace	*grimace*
ris, rire *m.*	*laughter*
souris, sourire *m.*	*smile*
humeur	*temper*
soupir	*sigh*
gémissement	*groan*
assoupissement	*drowsiness*
sommeil	*sleep*
songe *m.*	*dream*
rève *m.*	*dream*
souffle *m.*	*breath*
haleine	*breath*
respiration	*respiration*
éternuement	*sneezing*
vue	*sight*
ouie	*hearing*
odorat	*smell*
goût	*taste*
toucher	*touch*
sentiment	*sense*
obscurité	*darkness*
ombre	*shade*
son	*sound*
bruit	*noise*
odeur	*smell*
puanteur	*stench*
saveur	*flavour*
sensations *pl.*	*sensations*
chatouillement	*tickling*
plaisir	*pleasure*
joie	*joy*
douleur	*pain*
faim	*hunger*
soif	*thirst*
dégoût	*distaste*
maladie	*disease*
mal	*complaint*
incommodité	*illness*
infirmité	*infirmity*
indisposition	*illness*
mal de dents	*tooth-ache*
mal de tête	*head-ache*
mal aux yeux	*bad, sore eyes*
migraine	*megrim*
vertige *m.*	*dizziness*
évanouissement	*swoon*
défaillance	*fainting, sinking*
faiblesse	*swoon*
démangeaison	*itching*
pesanteur	*heaviness*
engourdissement	*numbness*
insomnie	*sleeplessness*
coup	*blow*
contre-coup	*counter-blow*
égratignure	*scratch*
écorchure	*excoriation*
entorse	*sprain*
foulure	*strain*
enflure	*swelling*
tumeur	*tumour*
meurtrissure	*bruise*
contusion	*contusion*
blessure	*wound*
cicatrice	*scar*
ulcère *m.*	*ulcer*
gangrène	*mortification*
coupure	*cut*
brûlure	*burn*
cor	*corn*
durillon	*callosity*

enrouement	*hoarseness*	sage-femme	*midwife*
rhume *m.*	*cold*	consultation	*consultation*
toux	*cough*	ordonnance	*prescription*
coqueluche	*hooping-cough*	remède *m.*	*remedy*
surdité	*deafness*	drogues *pl.*	*drugs*
frénésie	*frenzy*	poudres *pl.*	*powders*
folie	*lunacy*	pillules *pl.*	*pills*
rage	*madness*	saignée	*bleeding*
goutte	*gout*	lancette	*lancet*
convulsions *pl.*	*convulsions*	gouttes *pl.*	*drops*
vapeurs *pl.*	*vapours*	bain	*bath*
fièvre	*fever*	régime *m.*	*diet*
frisson	*shivering*	sirop	*syrup*
accès	*fit*	agonie	*agony*
délire *m.*	*delirium*	mort	*death*
crise	*crisis*	cadavre *m.*	*corpse*
médecine	*physic*	vie	*life*
médecin	*physician*	guérison	*recovery*
chirurgien	*surgeon*	rechute	*relapse*
apothicaire *m.*	*apothecary*	symptôme *m.*	*symptom*
accoucheur	*man-midwife*	convalescence	*convalescence*

III. OF THE MIND AND ITS FACULTIES.

âme	*soul*	apparence	*appearance*
esprit	*mind, talent, wit*	méprise	*mistake*
génie *m.*	*genius*	bévue	*oversight*
raison	*reason, sense*	science	*science*
entendement	*understanding*	connaissance	*knowledge*
jugement	*judgment*	pénétration	*penetration*
sens	*sense*	sagacité	*sagacity*
pensée	*thought*	disposition	*disposition*
idée	*idea*	inclination	*inclination*
imagination	*imagination*	capacité	*capacity*
fantaisie	*fancy*	mémoire	*memory*
caprice *m.*	*caprice*	souvenir	*remembrance*
volonté	*will*	oubli	*forgetfulness*
liberté	*liberty*	stupidité	*stupidity*
bel esprit	*wit*	passions *pl.*	*passions*
opinion	*opinion*	affections *pl.*	*affections*
sentiment	*sentiment*	amour	*love*
vérité	*truth*	amours *pl.*	*amours*
erreur	*error*	haine	*hatred*
vraisemblance	*likelihood*	désir	*desire*

probabilité	*probability*	crainte, peur	*fear*
appréhension	*apprehension*	patience	*patience*
espérance	*hope*	prudence	*prudence*
confiance	*confidence*	économie	*economy*
honte	*shame*	habileté	*skill*
timidité	*bashfulness*	industrie	*industry*
hardiesse	*boldness*	soin	*care*
assurance	*confidence*	diligence	*diligence*
colère	*anger*	exactitude	*exactness*
courroux	*wrath*	honneur	*honour*
fureur	*fury*	probité	*probity*
rage	*rage*	désintéressement	*disinterestedness*
ressentiment	*resentment*		
vengeance	*revenge*	sagesse	*wisdom*
dépit	*spite*	constance	*constancy*
déplaisir	*displeasure*	bienveillance	*benevolence*
tristesse	*sadness*	émulation	*emulation*
chagrin	*grief*	faveur	*favour*
peine	*sorrow*	valeur	*valour*
désespoir	*despair*	bravoure	*stoutness*
doute *m.*	*doubt*	courage *m.*	*courage*
soupçon	*suspicion*	finesse, ruse	*cunning*
envie	*envy*	adresse	*skill*
jalousie	*jealousy*	chasteté	*chastity*
pitié	*pity*	innocence	*innocence*
miséricorde	*mercy*	libéralité	*liberality*
compassion	*compassion*	générosité	*generosity*
terreur	*terror*	reconnaissance	*gratitude*
épouvante	*fright*	frugalité	*frugality*
indignation	*indignation*	prospérité	*prosperity*
vertu	*virtue*	adversité	*adversity*
charité	*charity*	mœurs *pl.*	*manners*
justice	*justice*	bonheur	*happiness*
tempérance	*temperance*	récompense	*reward*
sobriété	*sobriety*	prix	*prize*
force	*fortitude*	présent	*present*
modestie	*modesty*	don	*gift*
civilité	*civility*	prêt	*loan*
pudeur	*bashfulness*	grâce	*grace*
politesse	*politeness*	réputation	*fame*
honnêteté	*honesty*	vice *m.*	*vice*
complaisance	*complaisance*	défaut	*defect*
douceur	*sweetness*	imperfection	*imperfection*
bonté	*goodness*	avarice	*avarice*
amitié	*friendship*	avidité	*greediness*
union	*union*	orgueil	*pride*
concorde	*concord*	paresse	*idleness*

fainéantise	*slothfulness*
tranquillité	*tranquillity*
paix	*peace*
luxe *m.*	*luxury, pomp*
mollesse	*effeminacy*
impureté	*lewdness*
débauche	*revel*
dissolution	*dissoluteness*
libertinage *m.*	*libertinism*
désordre *m.*	*disorderly life*
dérèglement	*licentiousness*
mépris	*contempt*
raillerie	*jest*
moquerie	*mockery*
médisance	*detraction*
calomnie	*calumny*
crime *m.*	*crime*
malice	*malice*
méchanceté	*wickedness*
tromperie	*deceit*
parjure *m.*	*perjury*
friponnerie	*knavery*
fourberie	*roguery*
enchantement	*witchcraft*
injustice	*injustice*
tort	*wrong*
usure	*usury*
achat	*purchase*
vente	*sale*
troc	*barter*
gage *m.*	*pledge*
dépôt	*trust*
contrat	*contract*
marché	*bargain*
bassesse	*meanness*
impudence	*impudence*
effronterie	*effrontery*
audace	*audaciousness*
témérité	*temerity*
poltronnerie	*cowardice*
opiniâtreté	*stubborness*
obstination	*obstinacy*
cruauté	*cruelty*
dispute	*dispute*
querelle	*quarrel*
brouillerie	*broil*
babil	*babbling*
caquet	*prating*
nonchalance	*carelessness*
lâcheté	*sluggishness*
prodigalité	*prodigality*
gourmandise	*gluttony*
impolitesse	*rudeness*
incivilité	*incivility*
dissension	*dissension*
impatience	*impatience*
imprudence	*imprudence*
négligence	*negligence*
malhonnêteté	*rudeness*
déshonneur	*disgrace*
exil	*exile*
bannissement	*banishment*
pusillanimité	*pusillanimity*
trahison	*treachery*
perfidie	*perfidiousness*
punition	*punishment*
châtiment	*chastisement*
légèreté	*levity*
coquetterie	*coquetry*
badinage *m.*	*sport*
larcin	*robbery*
vol	*theft*
friponnerie	*roguery, cheating*
tromperie	*deceit*
ivrognerie	*drunkenness*
ivresse	*ebriety*
assassinat	*murder*
meurtre *m.*	*manslaughter*
mensonge *m.*	*lie*
fausseté	*falsehood*
conte *m.*	*tale*
serment	*oath*
malheur	*misfortune*
folie	*folly*
extravagance	*madness*
coutume	*custom*
usage *m.*	*use*
pratique	*practice, custom*
habitude	*habit*
licence	*licentiousness*
excès	*excess*
tour	*trick*
bagatelles *pl.*	*trifles*
faute	*fault*

faiblesse	*weakness*	faible *m.*	*foible*
inconstance	*inconstancy*	affront	*affront*
ingratitude	*ungratefulness*	outrage *m.*	*outrage*
ambition	*ambition*	insulte	*insult*

IV. OF MEATS AND DRINKS.

nourriture	*nourishment*	jambon	*ham*
alimens *pl.*	*food*	lard	*bacon*
vivres *pl.*	*victuals*	moutarde	*mustard*
provision	*provisions*	soupe	*soup*
repas	*meal*	potage *m.*	*pottage*
déjeûner	*breakfast*	bouillon	*broth*
dîner	*dinner*	consommé	*gravy soup*
goûter, collation	*formerly a light meal between dinner and supper*	ragoût	*ragout*
		fricassée	*fricassee*
		jus	*gravy*
		sauce	*sauce*
souper	*supper*	poisson	*fish*
festin	*feast*	salade	*sallad*
régal	*treat*	sel	*salt*
pain	*bread*	huile	*oil*
croûte	*crust*	vinaigre *m.*	*vinegar*
mie	*crumb*	verjus	*verjuice*
farine	*flour*	anchois	*anchovies*
son	*bran*	épices *pl.*	*spices*
pâte	*dough*	poivre *m.*	*pepper*
levain	*leaven*	gingembre *m.*	*ginger*
morceau	*bit, morsel*	muscade	*nutmeg*
tranche	*slice*	mâcis	*mace*
bouchée	*mouthful*	girofle *m.* (clous de)	*cloves*
viande	*meat*		
bouilli	*fresh boiled beef*	canelle	*cinnamon*
rôt, rôti	*roast meat*	oublies *pl.*	*wafers*
bœuf	*beef*	sucre *m.*	*sugar*
mouton	*mutton*	cassonade	*moist sugar*
agneau	*lamb*	dessert	*dessert*
veau	*veal*	fruit	*fruit*
porc	*pork*	pâté	*pie*
venaison	*venison*	gâteau	*cake*
volaille	*fowls*	tourte, tarte	*tart*
gibier	*game*	biscuit	*biscuit*
gigot	*a leg of mutton*	macaron	*macaroon*
andouille	*chitterlings*	crêpes	*pancakes*
saucisse	*sausage*	confitures *pl.*	*sweetmeats*

gelée	*jelly*	thé	*tea*
marmelade	*marmalade*	café	*coffee*
conserve	*preserves*	chocolat	*chocolate*
tablettes *pl.*	*lozenges, cakes*	limonade	*lemonade*
dragées *pl.*	*sugar-plums*	ponche *m.*	*punch*
pralines *pl.*	*burnt almonds*	vin	*wine*
fromage *m.*	*cheese*	bière	*beer*
beurre *m.*	*butter*	eau-de-vie	*brandy*
lait	*milk*	nectar	*nectar*
crême	*cream*	ambroisie	*ambrosia*
œuf	*egg*	cidre *m.*	*cider*
coque	*shell*	poiré	*perry*
blanc	*white*	hydromel	*mead*
jaune *m.*	*yolk*	sirop	*syrup*
boisson	*drink*	lie	*dregs*
liqueur	*liquor*		

V. OF THE DRESSING APPAREL, ETC.

habillement	*dress*	redingote	*great coat*
hardes	*clothes*	linge *m.*	*linen*
habit	*coat*	toile	*linen*
habit complet	*a suit*	batiste	*cambric*
veste	*jacket, round jacket*	mousseline	*muslin*
		linon	*lawn*
gilet	*waistcoat*	chemise	*shirt*
gilet de laine	*flannel waistcoat*	jabot	*frill*
gilet de peau	*under waistcoat*	cravate	*cravat*
manches *pl.*	*sleeves*	bas *pl.*	*stockings*
poches *pl.*	*pockets*	jarretières *pl.*	*garters*
bouton	*button*	laine	*wool*
doublure	*lining*	fil	*thread*
couture	*seam*	coton	*cotton*
culotte	*breeches*	maille	*stitch*
pantalon	*pantaloon*	trou	*hole*
gousset	*fob*	chaussons *pl.*	*socks*
drap	*cloth*	guêtres *pl.*	*gaiters*
soie	*silk*	souliers	*shoes*
velours	*velvet*	escarpins *pl.*	*pumps*
serge	*serge*	semelle	*sole*
basin	*dimity*	bottes *pl.*	*boots*
flanelle	*flannel*	boucles *pl*	*buckles*
étoffe	*stuff*	cuir	*leather*
manteau	*cloak*	chapeau	*hat*
surtout	*surtout*	perruque	*wig*

jupe	*petticoat*
jupon	*under-petticoat*
satin	*satin*
taffetas	*taffety*
gaze	*gauze*
coiffure	*head-dress*
coiffe	*cap*
collier	*necklace*
boucles d'oreilles *pl.*	*ear-rings*
gants *pl.*	*gloves*
mitaines *pl.*	*mittens*
tablier	*apron*
mules *pl.* / pantoufles *pl.*	*slippers*
bague	*ring*
bijou	*jewel*
bracelet	*bracelet*
dentelle	*lace*
blonde	*blond lace*
éventail	*fan*
manchon	*muff*
agrafe	*clasp*
épingle	*pin*
aiguille	*needle*
étui	*case*
dé	*thimble*
masque *m.*	*mask*
voile *m.*	*veil*
tabatière	*snuff-box*
tabac (en poudre)	*snuff*
tabac (à fumer)	*tobacco*
bourse	*purse*
argent	*money*
porte-feuille *m.*	*pocket-book*
ciseaux *pl.*	*scissars*
crayon	*pencil*
mouchoir	*handkerchief*
lunettes *pl.*	*spectacles*
lorgnette	*opera-glass*
conserves *pl.*	*spectacles*
bouquet	*nosegay*
canne	*cane*
cordon	*string*
épée	*sword*
montre	*watch*
boite	*box or case*
chaîne	*chain*

VI. OF A HOUSE AND FURNITURE.

maison	*house*
hôtel	*mansion*
——	*hotel, lodging house*
hôtellerie	*inn*
château	*castle, country seat*
palais	*palace*
couronne	*crown*
trône *m.*	*throne*
sceptre *m.*	*sceptre*
aile	*wing*
pavillon	*pavillion*
fondements *pl.*	*foundation*
mur, muraille	*wall*
bâtiment	*building*
matériaux *pl.*	*materials*
pierre	*stone*
brique	*brick*
mortier	*mortar*
chaux	*lime*
plâtre *m.*	*plaster*
ciment	*cement*
tuile	*tile*
ardoise	*slate*
charpente	*timber work*
poutre	*beam*
solive	*joist*
échelle	*ladder*
cave	*vault*
cellier	*cellar*
tonneau	*cask*
futaille	*vessel*
boutique	*shop*
atelier	*work-shop*
magasin	*warehouse*

vestibule *m.*	*hall*
salle, salon	*parlour or sitting room*
escalier	*stairs*
office	*pantry, butler's room*
cuisine	*kitchen*
garde-manger *m.*	*larder*
boulangerie	*bakehouse*
brasserie	*brewhouse*
lingerie	*laundry*
écurie	*stable*
remise	*coach-hous*
puits	*well*
étage *m.*	*story*
appartement	*apartment*
chambre	*room*
antichambre	*anti-chamber*
salle à manger	*dining-room*
salon de compagnie	*drawing-room*
cabinet de toilette	*dressing-room*
chambre à coucher	*bed-room*
galerie	*gallery*
cabinet	*closet*
boudoir	*lady's sitting room*
garderobe	*wardrobe*
porte	*door*
porte-cochère	*gate*
seuil	*threshold*
jalousie	*lattice*
gond	*hinge*
marteau	*knocker*
serrure	*lock*
clé, *or* clef	*key*
verrou	*bolt*
venêtre	*window*
vitre	*glass*
volet	*shutter*
balcon	*balcony*
store *m.*	*blind*
grenier	*garret*
toit	*roof*
gouttière	*gutter*
ulle	*trunk*
boite	*box*
caisse	*chest*
cassette	*casket*
coffre *m.*	*coffer*
logement	*lodging*
ameublement	*furniture*
cheminée	*chimney*
âtre *m.* foyer	*hearth*
soufflet	*pair of bellows*
pelle	*shovel*
pincettes *pl.*	*tongs*
fourgon	*poker*
garde-feu *m.*	*fender*
bouilloire	*boiler*
couvercle *m.*	*lid*
poêle	*frying-pan*
poêlon	*skillett*
casserole	*saucepan*
fourneau	*stove*
allumette	*match*
pierre à fusil	*flint*
briquet	*steel*
four	*oven*
clou	*nail*
essuie-main	*towel*
bassinoire	*warming-pan*
panier, corbeille	*basket*
faïence	*delft ware*
poterie	*earthenware*
pot	*pot*
cruche	*pitcher*
lampe	*lamp*
lanterne	*lantern*
savon	*soap*
amidon	*starch*
balai	*broom*
banc	*seat, form*
escabeau	*stool*
plancher	*floor*
parquet	*(drawing-room) floor*
plafond	*ceiling*
lambris	*wainscot*
cloison	*partition*
tapisserie	*hangings, tapestry*
tapis	*carpet, cloth*

lit	*bed*
alcove	*alcove*
châlit	*bedstead*
chevet	*bolster*
oreiller	*pillow*
paillasse	*straw mattrass*
matelas	*mattrass*
draps *pl.*	*sheets*
couvertures *pl.*	*bed-clothes*
courte-pointe	*counterpane*
rideau	*curtain*
tringle	*curtain-rod*
anneau	*ring*
sofa	*sofa*
fauteuil	*arm-chair*
siége *m.*	*seat*
chaise	*chair*
coussin	*cushion*
armoire	*press*
commode	*chest of drawers*
trumeau	*pier-glass*
toilette	*toilet*
miroir	*looking-glass*
peigne *m.*	*comb*
pomade	*pomatum*
poudre	*powder*
houppe	*puff*
parfum	*perfume*
tableau	*picture*
dessin	*drawing*
coloris	*colouring*
portrait	*portrait*
paysage *m.*	*landscape*
miniature	*miniature*
chandelier	*candlestick*
bobèche	*socket*
chandelle	*candle*
bougie	*wax-light*
cire	*wax*
mouchettes *pl.*	*snuffers*
porte-mouchettes *m.*	*snuffer-stand*
éteignoir	*extinguisher*
vergettes *pl*	*brush*
buffet	*cupboard*
cabaret	*stand*
tasse	*cup*
soucoupe	*saucer*
théière	*tea-pot*
cafetière	*coffee-pot*
chocolatière	*chocolate-pot*
sucrier	*sugar-bason*
jatte	*bowl*
table	*table*
nappe	*cloth*
serviette	*napkin*
assiette	*plate*
plat	*dish*
couteau	*knife*
cuiller, *ou* cuillère	*spoon*
salière	*salt-cellar*
huilier	*oil cruet*
moutardier	*mustard pot*
aiguière	*ewer*
coupe, tasse	*cup*
gobelet	*goblet*
verre *m.*	*glass*
bouteille	*bottle*
bouchon	*cork*
tire-bouchon *m.*	*corkscrew*
carafe	*flagon, decanter*
bibliothèque	*library*
bureau	*bureau*
tiroir	*drawer*
cachet	*seal*
lettre	*letter*
enveloppe	*cover*
adresse	*direction*
signature	*signature*
sonnette	*bell*
estampe	*print*
médaille	*medal*

VII. OF THE CITY.

ville	*town, city*
village *m.*	*village*
bourg	*borough*
rue	*street*
carrefour	*cross-way*
passage *m.*	*passage*
place	*square*
cul-de-sac	*blind alley*
pyramide	*pyramid*
obélisque *m.*	*obelisk*
pavé	*pavement*
ruisseau	*kennel*
marché	*market*
denrées *pl.*	*provisions*
boucherie	*meat market*
poissonnerie	*fish market*
friperie	*rag fair*
édifice *m.*	*edifice*
façade	*front*
frontispiece	*frontispiece*
colonne	*column*
pilastre *m.*	*pilaster*
base	*base*
piédestal	*pedestal*
statue	*statue*
arcade	*arcade*
portique *m.*	*portico*
aqueduc	*aqueduct*
dôme *m.*	*dome*
paroisse	*parish*
salle de comédie	*play-house*
théâtre *m.*	*theatre*
coulisses *pl.*	*scenes*
décorations	*decorations*
toile	*curtain*
foyer	*green-room*
orchestre *m.*	*orchestra*
parterre *m.*	*pit*
loge	*box*
amphithéâtre	*first gallery*
paradis	*upper gallery*
billet	*ticket*
couvent	*convent*
monastère *m.*	*monastery*
cellule	*cell*
hermitage *m.*	*hermitage*
solitude	*solitude*
retraite	*retirement*
université	*university*
collége *m.*	*college*
école	*school*
pension	*boarding-scho.*
parlement	*parliament*
chambre des pairs	*house of lords*
chambre des communes	*house of commons*
prison	*prison*
cachot	*dungeon*
hôpital	*hospital*
infirmerie	*infirmary*
taverne	*tavern*
cabaret	*public-house*
auberge	*inn*
café	*coffee-house*
enseigne	*sign*
affiche	*bill*
pont	*bridge*
arche	*arch*
pilier	*pillar*
bateau	*boat*
quai	*quay*
bourse	*exchange*
banque	*bank*
agiotage *m.*	*stock-jobbing*
douane	*custom-house*
poste	*general post*
petite poste	*twopenny post*
trésorerie	*treasury*
amirauté	*admiralty*
arsenal	*arsenal*
faubourg	*suburbs*
boulevards *pl*	*bulwarks*
remparts *pl*	*ramparts*

barrière	*turnpike*
guinguette	*tea-garden*
forge	*forge*
verrerie	*glass-house*
fonderie	*foundry*
carrosse *m.*	*coach*
impériale	*roof*
portière	*door of a coach*
glaces *pl.*	*windows*
timon	*coach-pole*
roue	*wheel*
essieu	*axle-tree*
équipage *m.*	*equipage*
harnois *pl.*	*harness*
rênes *pl.*	*reins*
bride	*bridle*
licou	*halter*
selle	*saddle*
bât	*pack-saddle*
arçon	*saddle-bow*
sangle	*girth*
étriers *pl.*	*stirrup*
éperons *pl.*	*spurs*
berline	*berlin*
cabrioles	*curricle*
chaise	*chaise*
fiacre *m.*	*hackney-coach*
charrette	*cart*
fourgon	*waggon*
remise	*coach-house*
rasoir	*razor*
cuir	*strap*
moule	*mould*
machine	*machine*
moulin	*mill*

VIII. OF TRADES, ARTS, PROFESSIONS, ETC.

boulanger	*baker*
barbier	*barber*
forgeron	*blacksmith*
relieur	*book-binder*
libraire *m.*	*bookseller*
chaudronnier	*brazier*
brasseur	*brewer*
boucher	*butcher*
ébéniste	*cabinet-maker*
charpentier	*carpenter*
charron	*wheelwright*
sculpteur	*sculptor*
chimiste	*chymist*
horloger	*clock-maker*
confiseur	*confectioner*
carrossier	*coach-maker*
tonnelier	*cooper*
corroyeur	*currier*
coutelier	*cutler*
fourbisseur	*sword-cutler*
teinturier	*dyer*
distillateur	*distiller*
droguiste	*druggist*
graveur	*engraver*
maréchal	*farrier*
poissonnier	*fishmonger*
fondeur	*founder*
fruitier	*fruiterer*
fourreur	*furrier*
jardinier	*gardener*
doreur	*gilder*
verrier	*glass-maker*
vitrier	*glazier*
gantier	*glover*
orfèvre	*goldsmith*
épicier	*grocer*
armurier	*gun-smith*
chapelier	*hatter*
aubergiste	*innkeeper*
joaillier	*jeweller*
menuisier	*joiner*
serrurier	*locksmith*
maçon	*bricklayer*
couturière	*mantua-maker*
maître d'hôtel	*steward*
mercier	*mercer*
meûnier	*miller*
peintre	*painter*

pâtissier	*pastry-cook*
paveur	*pavior*
colporteur	*pedlar*
parfumeur	*perfumer*
médecin	*physician*
plâtrier	*plasterer*
plombier	*plumber*
potier	*potter*
imprimeur	*printer*
sellier	*sadler*
singère	*sempstress*
cordonnier	*shoe-maker*
pelletier	*skinner*
forgeron	*smith*
chirurgien	*surgeon*
apothicaire	*apothecary*
arpenteur	*surveyor*
tailleur	*tailor*
tanneur	*tanner*
bijoutier	*jeweller*
tourneur	*turner*
entrepreneur	*undertaker*
tapissier	*upholsterer*
horloger	*watch-maker*
tisserand	*weaver*
perruquier	*hair-dresser*
ouvrage	*work*
ouvrier	*workman*
ouvrière	*workwoman*
manœuvre	*labourer*

IX. OF THE COUNTRY, HUSBANDRY, FLOWERS, TREES, ETC.

campagne	*country*
chemin	*way*
sentier	*foot-path*
boue	*mud*
fange	*mire*
poussière	*dust*
bourbier	*slough*
ornière	*cart-rut*
hameau	*hamlet*
enclos	*close*
château	*castle*
terre	*estate*
cour	*yard*
basse-cour	*poultry yard*
colombier	*pigeon-house*
laiterie	*dairy*
écurie	*stable*
fruiterie	*fruit-loft*
jardin	*garden*
jardinage m.	*gardening*

X. FLOWERS.

fleuriste	*florist*
parterre	*parterre*
fleur	*flower*
iris	*flags*
primevere	*cowslip*
narcisse m.	*narcissus*
jacinthe	*hyacinth*
tulipe	*tulip*
violette	*violet*
pensée	*heartsease*
églantier	*sweet-briar*
marguerite	*daisy*
impériale	*turk's cap*
martagon	*mountain lily*
lis	*lily*
muguet	*may-lily*
oreille d'ours	*auricula*
anémone	*anemone*
renoncule	*ranunculus*
jonquille	*jonquil*
giroflée	*stock-gilliflower*
œillet	*carnation*

campanule gantelée	} *bell flower*	tournesol	*sun flower*
rose	*rose*	camomille	*camomile*
jasmin	*jasmine*	belle-de-nuit	*great nightshade*
tubéreuse	*tuberose*	éternelle immortelle	} *cassidony*
réséda	*mignionette*	balsamine	*balsam*
chèvre-feuille *m.*	*honey-suckle*	ancolie	*columbine*
seringat	*seringa*	passe-rose	*hollyhock*
lilas	*lilac*	hépatique	*hepatica*
souci	*marigold*	pied d'alouette	*lark-spur*
amaranthe	*amaranth*	pivoine	*piony*
pavot	*poppy*	scabieuse	*scabious*
coquelicot ponceau	} *wild-poppy*	julienne	*rocket*
bluet, barbeau	*blue-bell*	planche	*bed*
		plate bande	*flower-border*

XI. FRUITS.

amande	*almond*	melon	*melon*
pomme	*apple*	mûre	*mulberry*
abricot	*apricot*	brugnon	*nectarine*
cerise	*cherry*	noisette	*hazel-nut*
guigne	{ *black heart cherry*	orange	*orange*
châtaigne	*chesnut*	pêche	*peach*
marron	*large chesnut*	poire	*pear*
groseilles *pl.*	*currants*	citrouille	*pumpion*
groseille	*gooseberry*	coin	*quince*
figue	*fig*	framboise	*raspberry*
aveline	*filbert*	fraise	*strawberry*
raisin	*grapes*	noix	*walnut*
prune	*plum*	épine-vinette	*barberries*
reine-claude	*green-gage*	grenade	*pomegranate*
citron	*lemon*	olive	*olive*
ananas	*pine apple*	cerneaux	{ *fresh or unripe walnuts*
nèfle	*medlar*		

XII. OF HERBS AND PLANTS.

aloès	*aloe*	moutarde	*mustard*
angélique	*angelica*	capucine	*nasturtium*
artichaut	*artichoke*	ortie	*nettle*
asperge	*asparagus*	ognon	*onion*
citron	*plant*	persil	*parsley*
basilic	*basil*	panais	*parsnip*
fève	*bean*	pois	*peas*
haricot	*French bean*	pariétaire	*pellitory*
poirée	*beet*	plante	*plant*
betterave	*beet-root*	plantain	*plantain*
bourrache	*borage*	pavot	*poppy*
bardane	*burdock*	pomme de terre	*potatoe*
primprenelle	*burnet*	courge	*pumpkin*
chou	*cabbage*	pourpier	*purslain*
carotte	*carrot*	rave	*radish*
céleri	*celery*	radis	*Spanish radish*
cerfeuil	*chervil*	roseau	*reed*
choux-fleurs *pl.*	*cauliflowers*	rue	*rue*
mâches *pl.*	*corn-salad*	jonc	*rush*
cresson	*cresses*	rhubarbe	*rhubarb*
concombre *m.*	*cucumber*	safran	*saffron*
dent-de-lion	*dandelion*	sauge	*sage*
patience	*dock*	sariette	*savery*
chicorée	*endive*	ciboule	*scullion*
fenouil	*fennel*	échalotte	*shallot*
fougère	*fern*	oseille	*sorrel*
ail	*garlick*	véronique	*speedwell*
calebasse	*gourd*	épinards *pl.*	*spinage*
ciguë	*hemlock*	tanaisie	*tansy*
herbe	*herb*	ivraie	*tare*
raifort	*horse-radish*	estragon	*stragon*
joubarbe	*house-leek*	chardon	*thistle*
lierre *m.*	*ivy*	thym	*thyme*
poireau	*leek*	serpolet	*wild thyme*
laitue	*lettuce*	trèfle *m.*	*clover*
réglisse	*licorice*	navet	*turnip*
mauve	*mallows*	valériane	*valerian*
guimauve	*marsh-mallows*	végétaux *pl.*	*vegetables*
marjolaine	*marjoram*	légumes *m. pl*	*vegetables, greens*
réséda	*mignionette*		
menthe	*mint*	verveine	*vervain*
gui	*misletoe*	absynthe	*wormwood*
mousse	*moss*	mille-feuille	*yarrow*

XIII. OF TREES AND SHRUBS.

arbre *m.*	*tree*	hêtre	*beech-tree*
arbrisseau	*shrub*	bouleau	*birch-tree*
écorce	*bark*	buis	*box*
branche	*branch*	genêt	*broom*
feuille	*leaf*	sureau	*elder-tree*
graine	*seed*	orme	*elm*
rejeton	*sucker*	sapin	*fir-tree*
abricotier	*apricot-tree*	coudrier	*hazel-tree*
cerisier	*cherry-tree*	houx	*holly*
châtaignier	*chesnut-tree*	lilas	*lilac*
citronnier	*lemon-tree*	tilleul	*lime-tree*
coignassier	*quince-tree*	myrte	*myrtle-tree*
figuier	*fig-tree*	chêne	*oak*
noyer	*walnut-tree*	osier	*osier*
oranger	*orange-tree*	romarin	*rosemary*
pêcher	*peach-tree*	églantier	*sweet briar*
pommier	*apple-tree*	épine	*thorn*
poirier	*pear-tree*	buisson	*thorn bush*
prunier	*plumb-tree*	aubépine	*white-thorn*
arbousier	*arbutus*	vigne	*vine*
frêne	*ash-tree*	saule	*willow tree*
tremble	*aspen*	if	*yew-tree*

XIV. PROMISCUOUS WORDS.

grange	*barn*	haie	*hedge*
hutte	*hut*	bruyère	*heath*
chaumière	*thatched-house*	dunes	*downs*
seigneurie	*manor*	lande	*waste land*
dîme	*tithe*	commune	*common*
métairie	*farm*	plaine	*plain*
sillon	*furrow*	garenne	*warren*
pré, prairie	*meadow*	fondrière	*bog*
arpent	*acre*	marais	*marsh*
fossé	*ditch*	platebande	*border*
champ	*field*	serre	*green-house*
pâturage *m.*	*pasture-ground*	serre chaude	*hot-house*
terroir	*soil*	boulingrin	*bowling-green*
parc	*park*	berceau	*bower*

bosquet	*grove*	orge	*barley*
grotte	*grotto*	avoine	*oats*
vignoble *m.*	*vineyard*	riz	*rice*
pépinière	*nursery*	seigle *m.*	*rye*
taillis	*coppice*	millet	*millet*
hallier	*thicket*	lin	*flax*
paysage *m.*	*landscape*	chanvre *m.*	*hemp*
perspective	*prospect*	chènevis	*hemp-seed*
vue	*view*	épi	*ear (of corn)*
cascade	*cascade*	gerbe	*sheaf (of corn)*
canal	*canal*	tige	*stalk*
agriculture	*agriculture*	tuyau	*blade*
labourage *m.*	*tillage*	paille	*straw*
bétail	*cattle*	chaume *m.*	*stubble*
fumier	*dung*	foin	*hay*
terreau	*mould*	fourrage *m.*	*fodder*
récolte	*crop*	fermier	*farmer*
moisson	*harvest*	paysan	*peasant*
vendange	*vintage*	laboureur	*ploughman*
houblon	*hops*	moissonneur	*reaper*
grain	*corn*	faucheur	*mower*
blé	*wheat*	berger	*shepherd*

XV. OF QUADRUPEDS.

bête	*beast*	buffle *m.*	*buffalo*
animal	*animal*	taureau	*bull*
animal domestique	*domestic animal*	vache	*cow*
		génisse	*heifer*
bête de somme	*beast of burden*	veau	*calf*
monture	*saddle horse*	bouvillon	*bullock*
cheval	*horse*	renne *m.*	*rein-deer*
cavalle	*mare*	brebis	*ewe*
jument	*mare*	mouton	*wether*
étalon	*stallion*	bélier	*ram*
poulain	*colt*	agneau	*lamb*
pouliche	*filly*	chèvre	*she-goat*
bidet	*pony*	bouc	*he-goat*
âne	*ass*	chevreau	*kid*
ânesse	*she-ass*	cochon	*hog*
ânon	*young ass*	porc	*pig*
mulet	*mule*	pourceau	*pig*
mule	*she-mule*	truie	*sow*
bête à cornes	*horned beast*	cochon de lait	*sucking pig*
bœuf	*ox*	cochon d'inde	*guinea pig*

verrat	*boar*
sanglier	*wild boar*
laie	*wild sow*
marcassin	*young wild boar*
bête fauve	*deer*
cerf	*stag*
biche	*hind*
faon	*fawn*
daim	*fallow-deer*
daim mâle	*buck*
daim femelle	*doe*
chevreuil	*roe-buck*
chevrette	*roe*
lion	*lion*
lionne	*lioness*
lionceau	*lion's whelp*
tigre	*tiger*
tigresse	*tigress*
ours	*bear*
ourson	*bear's cub*
zèbre *m.*	*zebra*
giraffe	*camel-leopard*
léopard	*leopard*
cameléopard	*camel-leopard*
rhinocéros	*rhinoceros*
hippopotame, *m.*	*river-horse*
éléphant	*elephant*
chameau	*camel*
dromadaire *m.*	*dromedary*
lama	*lama*
buffle *m.*	*buffalo*
hiène	*hyena*
panthère	*panther*
once	*ounce*
licorne	*unicorn*
élan	*elk*
loup	*wolf*
louve	*she-wolf*
louveteau	*wolf's cub*
lynx	*lynx*
renard	*fox*
taisson	*brock*
blaireau	*badger*
castor	*beaver*
hermine	*ermine*
marte, zibeline	*marten, sable*
écureuil	*squirrel*
'hérisson	*hedge-hog*
porc-épic	*porcupine*
loutre	*otter*
raton	*racoon*
fure	*ferret*
lièvre	*hare*
'has	*doe-hart*
levraut	*leveret*
lapin	*rabbit*
chien	*dog*
chienne	*bitch*
lévrier	*greyhound*
levrette	*greyhound bitch*
dogue	*bull dog*
mâtin	*mastiff*
limier	*blood-hound*
bichon	*lap-dog*
épagneul	*spaniel*
basset	*terrier*
barbet	*shagged-dog*
chien d'arrêt	*pointer*
meute de chiens	*pack of hounds*
chat, matou	*cat, tom-cat*
chatte	*cat, puss*
chaton	*kitten*
minon	*puss*
minet, minette	*young kitten*
singe *m.*	*monkey*
guenon	*ape*
magot, babouin	*baboon*
gazelle	*antelope*
belette	*weasel*
putois	*pole-cat*
fouine	*pole-cat*
loir	*dormouse*
marmotte	*marmot*
taupe	*mole*
rat	*rat*
souris	*mouse*
tortue	*tortoise*
bétail, bestiaux	*cattle*
troupeau	*flock, herd*
pâtre, berger	*shepherd*
bergère	*shepherdess*
vacher, bouvier	*cow-herd*
porcher	*swine-herd*
chasse	*hunting*
chasseur	*hunter*
braconnier	*poacher*

gibier, venaison	*game*
fusil	*gun*
gibecière	*pouch*
tiré	*shooting*
tireur	*shooter*
garde-chasse	*gamekeeper*

XVI OF BIRDS.

oisean	*bird*
oiselet, oisillon	*little bird*
volaille	*fowl*
coq	*cock*
poule	*hen*
poulet	*chicken*
poussin	*young chicken*
cochet	*cockerel*
poularde	*pullet*
chapon	*capon*
coq-d'Inde, dindon	*turkey-cock*
dinde	*turkey-hen*
dindonneau	*young turkey*
oie	*goose*
jar	*gander*
oison	*gosling*
canard	*drake*
cane	*duck*
caneton, canette	*duckling*
pigeon	*pigeon*
colombe	*dove*
serin, canari	*canary bird*
perroquet	*parrot*
perruche	*parroquet*
moineau, passereau	*sparrow*
hirondelle	*swallow*
martinet	*marten*
rossignoi	*nightingale*
chardonneret	*goldfinch*
pinson	*chaffinch*
verdier	*greenfinch*
bouvreuil	*bullfinch*
linot, linotte	*linnet*
rougegorge *m.*	*redbreast, robin*
merle *m.*	*blackbird*
grive	*thrush*
geai	*jay*
pie	*magpie*
alouette	*lark*
bergeronnette	*wagtail*
alcyon, ou martin-pêcheur	*king's-fisher*
pivert	*wood-pecker*
mésange	*tit*
pluvier	*plover*
roitelet	*wren*
vanneau	*lapwing*
butor	*bittern*
becfigue *m.*	*beccafico*
étourneau	*starling*
sansonnet	*starling*
bruant	*yellow-hammer*
coucou	*cuckoo*
freux, grolle	*rook*
corbeau	*raven*
corneille	*crow*
hibou	*owl*
chouette	*screech-owl*
buse	*buzzard*
choucas	*chough*
aigle	*eagle*
aiglon	*eaglet*
épervier	*sparrow-hawk*
émouchet	*musket-hawk*
milan	*kite*
faucon	*falcon*
cormoran	*cormorant*
plongeon	*didapper*
héron	*heron*
cicogne	*stork*
outarde	*bustard*
pélican	*pelican*
autour	*goshawk*
vautour	*vulture*
griffon	*griffin*
huppe	*lapwing*

mouette	*gull*	poule d'eau	*moor-hen*
perdrix	*partridge*	paon	*peacock*
bartavelle	*large red partridge*	paonne	*peahen*
perdreau	*young partridge*	paonneau	*young peacock*
caille	*quail*	cygne *m.*	*swan*
cailleteau	*young quail*	autruche	*ostrich*
faisan	*pheasant*	pintade	*pintado*
faisandeau	*young pheasant*	fou-de-bassan	*gannet*
bécasse	*woodcock*	pingoin	*razor-bil.*
bécassine	*snipe*	chauve-souris	*bat*
ortolan	*ortolan*	chasse aux oiseaux	*fowling*
tourterelle	*turtle-dove*	appeau	*bird-call*
gélinotte	*godwit*	gluaux	*lime twigs*
francolin	*francoline*	trébuchet	*bird-trap*
ramier	*wood-pigeon*	filets	*nets*
marceuse	*sea-duck*	oiseleur	*bird-catcher*
sarcelle	*teal*	oiselier	*bird-seller*
grue	*crane*	volière	*aviary*
courlis	*curlew*		
foulque	*coot, moorcock, or hen*		

XVII. OF FISHES.

poisson	*fish*	sardine	*sprat*
esturgeon	*sturgeon*	thon	*tunny*
turbot	*turbot*	plie	*plaice*
saumon	*salmon*	congre *m.*	*conger*
rouget	*roach*	merlan	*whiting*
brochet	*pike*	merluche	*haddock*
carpe	*carp*	hareng	*herring*
truite	*trout*	sèche	*cuttle fish*
perche	*perch*	limande	*burt, bret-fish*
cabillaud	*haddock*	lamproie	*lamprey*
morue	*stock fish*	homard, langouste, écrevisse de mer	*lobster*
raie	*skate*		
tanche	*tench*		
éperlan	*smelt*		
maquereau	*mackerel*	écrevisse	*crawfish*
surmulet	*mullet*	crabe *m.*	*crab*
carrelet	*flounder*	salicoque	*prawn*
barbeau	*barbel*	chevrette	*shrimp*
alose	*shad*	anguille	*eel*
sole	*sole*	anchois	*anchovy*

goujon	*gudgeon*
véron	*minnow*
lotte, barbotte	*eel-pout*
loche	*loach, groundling*
morue salée	*salt-fish*
barbue	*brill*
marsoin	*sea-hog, porpoise*
espadon	*saw-fish*
porcelaine	*sea-snail*
tortue	*tortoise*
huître	*oyster*
pétoncle	*cockle*
moule	*muscle*
baleine	*whale*
cachalot	*cachalot*
requin	*shark*
dauphin	*dolphin*
chien marin	*sea-dog*
loup marin	*sea-wolf*
hérisson de mer	*sea-urchin*
frai	*fry*
fretin	*young fish*
laite	*soft roe*
œufs	*spawn, hard roe*
museau	*snout*
oules	*gills*
nageoires	*fins*
écailles, coquilles	*scales*
arrêtes	*bones*
pinces	*claws*
appât, amorce	*bait*
pêcheur	*fisherman*
pêche	*fishery*
pêche à la ligne	*angling*

XVIII. OF REPTILES AND INSECTS.

grenouille	*frog*
serpent	*serpent*
couleuvre	*adder*
vipère	*viper*
scorpion	*scorpion*
aspic	*aspick*
basilic	*basilisk*
dragon	*dragon*
tarentule	*tarantula*
crapeau	*toad*
lézard	*lizard*
sangsue	*leech*
limace	*slug*
ver	*worm*
ver-luisant	*glow-worm*
ver-coquin	*vine-grub*
ver-à-soie	*silk-worm*
escargot	*snail*
escarbot	*beetle*
grillon	*cricket*
perce-oreille *m.*	*ear-wig*
teigne	*moth*
ciron	*hand worm*
fourmi	*ant*
charançon	*weevil*
cloporte *m.*	*wood-louse*
tique	*tick*
pou	*louse*
lente	*nit*
puce	*flea*
punaise	*bug*
chenille	*caterpillar*
papillon	*butterfly*
mouche	*fly*
abeille	*bee*
frelon	*hornet*
bourdon	*drone*
guêpe	*wasp*
taon	*oxfly*
cousin	*gnat*
cantharide	*Spanish-fly*
hanneton	*cockchafer*
sauterelle	*grasshopper*
cigale	*balm-cricket*
araignée	*spider*
toile d'araignee	*cobweb*

essaim d'abeilles	*swarm of bees*	rayon de miel	*honeycomb*
miel	*honey*	ruche	*hive*
cire	*wax*	fourmilière	*ant-hill*

XIX. OF METALS &c.

or	*gold*	mercure	*mercury*
argent	*silver*	vif-argent	*quicksilver*
platine	*platina*	soufre	*sulphur*
vermeil	*silver-gilt*	nitre	*nitre*
cuivre	*copper*	salpêtre	*saltpetre*
airain	*brass*	bitume	*bitumen*
laiton	*latten*	antimoine	*antimony*
bronze	*bronze*	arsenic	*arsenic*
similor	*pinchbeck*	alun	*alum*
fer	*iron*	couperose *f.*	*copperas*
fil d'archal	*wire*	vitriol	*vitriol*
acier	*steel*	carmin	*carmine*
fer-blanc	*iron-tinned*	pastel	*pastel*
étain	*pewter*	ocre *f.*	*ochre*
plomb	*lead*	vermillon	*red lead*

XX. OF COLOURS.

blanc	*white*	rouge	*red*
noir	*black*	jaune	*yellow*
bleu	*blue*	brun	*brown*
vert	*green*	pourpre	*purple*
gris	*grey*	écarlate	*scarlet*
orangé	*orange colour*	indigo	*indigo*

XXI. OF PRECIOUS STONES.

diamant	*diamond*	améthyste	*amethyst*
topaze	*topaz*	cornaline	*cornelian*
émeraude	*emerald*	onix	*onyx*
saphir	*sapphire*	agathe	*agate*
escarboucle	*carbuncle*	corail	*coral*
rubis	*ruby*	perle	*pearl*

XII. OF THE PRINCIPAL COUNTRIES.

France	*France*	Malabar	*Malabar*
Italie	*Italy*	le Japon	*Japan*
Espagne	*Spain*	Barbarie	*Barbary*
Portugal	*Portugal*	Egypte	*Egypt*
Turquie	*Turkey*	Biledulgerid	*Biledulgerid*
Allemagne	*Germany*	Zaara	*Zaara*
Suisse	*Switzerland*	Nigritie	*Nigritia*
Prusse	*Prussia*	Guinée	*Guinea*
Pologne	*Poland*	Ethiopie	*Ethiopia*
Bohême	*Bohemia*	Zanguebar	*Zanguebar*
Hongrie	*Hungary*	Monomotapa	*Monomotapa*
Hollande	*Holland*	Monoémugi	*Monoemugi*
les Pays-Bas	*the Netherlands*	Caffrerie	*Caffraria*
Angleterre	*England*	Abyssinie	*Abyssinia*
Ecosse	*Scotland*	Canada	*Canada*
Irlande	*Ireland*	Pensylvanie	*Pennsylvania*
Russie	*Russia*	le Maryland	*Maryland*
Danemarc	*Denmark*	la Virginie	*Virginia*
Suède	*Sweden*	la Caroline	*Carolina*
Norvège	*Norway*	la Géorgie	*Georgia*
Tartarie	*Tartary*	le Pérou	*Peru*
Arabie	*Arabia*	le Paraguay	*Paraguay*
Perse	*Persia*	le Chili	*Chili*
Inde	*India*	le Brésil	*Brazil*
Chine	*China*	la Guiane	*Guiana*
Mogol	*Mogul*	St. Dominigue	*St. Domingo*
Bengale	*Bengal*	la Jamaïque	*Jamaica*

XXIII. COMMON NATIONAL NAMES.

Français, *e*	*French*	Flamand, *e*	*Flemish*
Italien, *ne*	*Italian*	Anglais, *e*	*English*
Espagnol, *e*	*Spanish*	Ecossais, *e*	*Scotch*
Portugais, *e*	*Portuguese*	Irlandais, *e*	*Irish*
Turc, *que*	*Turkish, Turk*	Russe	*Russian*
Allemand, *e*	*German*	Danois, *e*	*Dane*
Prussien, *ne*	*Prussian*	Suédois, *e*	*Swede*
Suisse, *esse*	*Swiss*	Norvégien, *ne*	*Norwegian*
Polonais, *e*	*Pole*	Persan, *e*	*Persian*
Bohémien, *ne*	*Bohemian*	Chinois, *e*	*Chinese*
Hongrois, *e*	*Hungarian*	Américain, *e*	*American*
Hollandais, *e*	*Dutch*	Japon, *e*	*Japanese*
Autrichien, *ne*	*Austrian*	Lapon	*Laplander*

INTRODUCTION

TO THE

EXERCISES.

22. OF THE PREPOSITIONS *of, from, to,* AND OF THE ARTICLE *the, a.*

The English definite article *the,* is rendered by

le before a noun masculine } in the singular.
la before a noun feminine }

and *les* before nouns of either gender, in the plural.

The indefinite *a* or *an* is rendered by *un* before a noun masculine, and by *une* in the feminine.

EXAMPLES.

Le livre	*the book*	*un* homme	*a man*
la rue	*the street*	*une femme*	*a woman*
les plantes	*the plants*	*un* héros	*a hero*

EXERCISES.

The wood; *the* forest; *the* houses; *the* men; *the* court;
bois m. *forêt* f. *maisons* pl. *hommes* pl. *cour* f.

the foot; *the* arms; *the* room; *the* garden; *the* windows
pied m. *bras* pl. *chambre* f. *jardin* m. *fenêtres* pl.

a history; *a* novel; *a* foreigner; *a* walk; *a* day;
histoire f. *roman* m. *étranger* m. *promenade* f. *jour* m.

a night; *the* sun; *the* moon; *the* stars; *a* body: *a* card:
nuit f. *soleil* m. *lune* f. *étoiles* pl. *corps* m. *carte* f.

a crown.
écu m.

23. The prepositions *of* and *from* are rendered literally by *de,* and *to* by *à.*

When followed by the definite article, they are rendered in this manner:

of the and *from the*, by	*du** before a noun masculine singular beginning with *a consonant* or *h* aspirated *de la* before a noun feminine singular *de l'* before any noun beginning with *a vowel* or *h* mute *des* before any noun in the plural.
to the by,	*au* before a noun masculine singular beginning with *a consonant* or *h* aspirated *à la* before a noun feminine singular *à l'* before any noun beginning with *a vowel* or *h* mute *aux* before any noun in the plural.

And when these prepositions are followed by *a* or *an*, thus :

of a or *from a* by	*d'un* before a noun masculine *d'une* before a noun feminine
to a by	*à un* before a noun masculine *à une* before a noun feminine.

EXAMPLES.

Du parc	*of the park*	à l'esprit	*to the mind*
de la rivière	*of the river*	aux carrosses	*to the coaches*
de l'esprit	*of the mind*	d'un jour	*of a day*
des carrosses	*of the coaches*	d'une nuit	*of a night*
au parc	*to the park*	à un jour	*to a day*
à la rivière	*to the river*	à une nuit	*to a night*

EXERCISES.

The palace *of the* king; *of the* queen; *of the* man; *of the*
palais m. *roi* m. *reine* f. *homme h* m.

men; *to the* king; *to the* queen; *to the* man; *to the* men;
hommes pl.

from a balcony; *from a* window: *of a* prince; *to a* princess;
balcon m. *fenêtre* f. — m. *princesse* f.

of the gardens; *of the* evening; *to the* courtiers; *of a* table; *to*
jardins pl. *soir* m. *courtisans* pl. ——— f.

the master; *to a* lady; *of the* soul; *of the* horse; *to a* cat;
maître m. *dame* f. *âme* f. *cheval* m. *chat* m.

of the houses; *of a* carpet.
maisons pl. *tapis* m.

24. These same prepositions, when followed by

* Observe that you must not say *de le*, *à le*, *de les*, *à les*, but that the article and preposition are contracted into one word, *du*, *au*, *des* *aux*.

the possessive pronouns, *my*, *thy*, *his*, *her*, *its*, *our*, *your*, and *their*, will be both rendered thus:

			singular. m.	singular. f.	plural. m. *and* f.
of or *from*	*my*	by *de*	*mon*	*ma*	*mes*
	thy		*ton*	*ta*	*tes*
	his, her, or *its*		*son*	*sa*	*ses*
	our		*notre*	*notre*	*nos*
	your		*votre*	*votre*	*vos*
	their		*leur*	*leur*	*leurs*
of	*my*	by *à*	*mon*	*ma*	*mes*
	thy		*ton*	*ta*	*tes*
	his, her, its		*son*	*sa*	*ses*
	our		*notre*	*notre*	*nos*
	your		*votre*	*votre*	*vos*
	their		*leur*	*leur*	*leurs*

And likewise, when followed by the demonstrative *this* or *that*, *these* or *those*:

of or *from this* or *that*, by *de* *to this or that, by à*	*ce*	before a noun masculine beginning with a consonant or *h* aspirated
	cet	before a noun masculine beginning with a vowel or *h* mute
	cette	before a noun feminine

of or *from these* or *those*, by *de ces* *to these* or *those*, by *à ces*	before nouns plural of either gender.

EXAMPLES.

de mon père	*of my father*	à leur travail	*to their work*
à ta mère	*to thy mother*	de cette terrasse	*from this terrace*
de son frère	*of his brother*	de ce lieu	*of that place*
de notre ville	*of our town*	de cet homme	*of this man*
à votre maison	*to your house*	de ces arbres	*of these trees*

EXERCISES.

Of my clothes; *of thy* handkerchief; *of his* pocket; *from your*
habits pl. *mouchoir* m. *poche* f.

letters; *of our* treasure; *to their* house; *of this* steeple; *of that*
lettres pl. *trésor* m. *maison* f. *clocher* m.

hero; *of this* tower; *of these* models; *from my* sister; to
héros m. *h* asp. *tour* f. *modèles* pl. *sœur* f.

7**

your relations; the top *of the* mountain; *to my* friend
parens pl. *sommet* m. *montagne* f. *ami* m

from these pleasures; *of our* duties; *to their* connexions; *of*
plaisirs pl. *devoirs* pl *liaisons* pl.

his acquaintances; *to my* neighbours.
connaissances pl. *voisins* pl.

25. OF ELISIONS.

The *apostrophe* (') marks the suppression of a *vowel* before a word beginning with a *vowel* or *h* mute, as in *l'église*, for *la église*, etc. This suppression is called *elision: a, e,* are the only two vowels which are thus cut off; *i* is cut off in *si*, before *il* and *ils*, *s'il*, *s'ils*, *o* and *u* are never cut off.

The *a* is suppressed only in *la* feminine, both when an article and a personal pronoun.

But the *elision* of *e* occurs, not only in the definite article and personal pronoun *le*, but also in many monosyllables, such as *je, me, te, se, de, ce, ne, que*, and in the compound of *que*, such as, *parceque, quoique, puisque, jusque, vû que*, etc.

EXAMPLES OF ELISIONS.

of	*la*	in l'amitié	for	*la* amitié	*the friendship*
	la	..l'herbe		*la* herbe	*the grass*
	le	..l'oiseau		*le* oiseau	*the bird*
	le	..l'honneur		*le* honneur	*the honour*
	je	..j'ai		*je* ai	*I have*
	me	..il m'oublie		il *me* oublie	*he forgets me*
	te	..je t'aime		je *te* aime	*I love thee*
	se	..il s'habille		il *se* habille	*he dresses himself*
	le	..vous l'aidez		vous *le* aidez	*you help him*
	la	..vous l'obligez		vous *la* obligez	*you oblige her*
	ce	..c'est vrai		*ce* est vrai	*it is true*
	de	..un coup-d'œil		un coup *de* œil	*a glance*
	ne	..n'oubliez pas		*ne* oubliez pas	*do not forget*
	que	..qu' attendez-vous		*que* attendez vous	*what do you expect?*

of	*si*	in s'il arrivait	for	si il arrivait *if it happened*
	il	.. s'ils pouvaient		si ils pouvaient *if they could*
	parceque	.. parcequ'il faut		parceque il faut *because it is requisite*
	quoique	.. quoiqu'il fasse		quoique il fasse *whatever he may do*
	puisque	.. puisqu'on vous dit		puisque on vous dit *since they tell you*
	jusque	.. jusqu' à demain		jusque à demain *till to-morrow*
	vu que	.. vû qu'il obtiendra		vu que il obtiendra *since he will obtain*
	dès que	.. dèsqu'on saura		dès que on saura *as soon as it is known*
	quelque	.. quelqu'un vient		quelque un vient *somebody comes*

The *e* of the preposition *entre* is not cut off generally before *eux*, *elles*, *autres*, good writers prefer leaving it, thus, *entre eux*, *entre elles*, *entre autres*; but in the following compound words there must be an elision :

Entr'acte	*an interlude*	for	entre-acte
s'entr'aider	*to help another*		se entre-aider
entr'ouïr	*to hear imperfectly*		entre-ouïr
entr'ouvrir	*to half open*		entre-ouvrir

EXERCISE.

The soul; *the* heroine; *the* mind; he loves *him*; she
âme f. *héroïne* f. *esprit* m. *il aime* 2 *le* 1; *elle*

loves *her; I* love this man; you understand *me;* he es-
2 *la* 1; *je aime* *homme* m. *vous entendez* 2 *me* 1; *il es-*

teems *thee;* he goes away; *it* was *the* golden age; do not go
time 2 *te* 1; *se en-va ce était de or* 2 *âge* 1; * *ne aller*

there; *if* he comes; *if* they please; *what* has he said? *till*
pas là; si vient: ils veulent; que a-t-il dit? jusque

night; *though* he says; *since* he knows; *when* he saw;
au soir m. *quoique dise; puisque sait; lorsque vit;*

between them; somebody is come.
entre eux; quelque un est venu.

26. OF NEGATIONS.

The negation *not*, is rendered by *ne-pas*, cf which *ne* is placed *before* the verb, and the *pas after*.

Never is rendered by *ne-jamais; nobody* by *ne-personne; nothing*, by *ne-rien*, which are placed in the same order as *ne-pas*.

EXAMPLES OF NEGATIVE PHRASES.

N.B. The ^ shows the place of the verb.

Not	ne ^ pas / ne ^ point	as	je ne *suis* pas, etc. / nous *n'avons* point	*I am not*, etc. / *we have not*
never	ne ^ jamais		il ne *joue* jamais	*he never plays*
nothing	ne ^ rien		vous ne *dites* rien	*you say nothing*
nobody	ne ^ personne		je ne *vois* personne	*I see nobody*
not a jot	ne ^ goutte		je ne *vois* goutte	*I do not see, or I see not in the least*
no where	ne ^ nulle part		je ne *vais* nulle part	*I go no where*

In compound tenses, the negations are always placed before and after the auxiliary verb; as nous n'*avons* point parlé, *we have not spoken*; on n'*aurait* jamais cru, *one could never have believed.*

EXERCISE.

I do *not* say; I have *not* said; I have *never* seen; I *never* (tell a
* *dis* *ai* *dit* *ai* *vu* *mens*

falsehood); I do *nothing*; I have done *nothing*; is he *not* ar-
fais *ai* *fait* *est-il* *ar-*

rived? does *not* he come? I see *nothing*; has he *never* seen? he
rivé * 2 *vient* 1 *vois* *a-t-* *vu*

never loses his time; that (is worth) *nothing*; I met *nobody*.
perd *temps* m. *cela* *vaut* *rencontrai*

27. OF WORDS WHICH ARE ALIKE IN BOTH LANGUAGES.

There are many words which are alike in both languages, and others which differ only in their termination.

The expressions, which are perfectly alike, are particularly those that have the following terminations:

-al	as	animal, cardinal, fatal, général, local, moral, natal, original, principal, etc.
-ble	..	capable, fable, etc. bible, éligible, etc. noble, double, soluble, insoluble, etc.
-ace	..	face, grimace, grace, place, préface, race, surface, trace, etc.
-ance	..	chance, complaisance, extravagance, ignorance, lance, tempérance, etc.
-ence	..	abstinence, conférence, continence, diligence, éloquence, patience, etc.
-ice	..	artifice, auspices, édifice, justice, injustice, office, orifice, précipice, solstice, etc.
-acle	..	miracle, oracle, obstacle, réceptacle, tabernacle, spectacle, etc.
-ade	..	ambuscade, cavalcade, brigade, esplanade, sérénade, rétrograde, etc.
-age	..	Âge, adage, bandage, cage, cordage, image, page, plumage, rage, etc.
-ege	..	collége, privilége, sacrilége, siége, etc.
-ge	..	vestige, doge, barge, charge, orange, forge, rouge, refuge, déluge, etc.
-ule	..	globule, ridicule, animalcule, corpuscule, formule, module, mule, pustule, valvule, etc.
-ile	..	bile, débile, agile, docile, ductile, facile, fragile, nubile, reptile, versatile, etc.
-ine	..	carabine, fascine, doctrine, héroïne, machine, marine, famine, mine, rapine, etc.
-ion	..	action, fraction, légion, nation, opinion, passion, question, religion, etc.
-ant	..	arrogant, constant, élégant, éléphant, pétulant, piquant, poignant, vigilant, etc.
-ent	..	absent, accident, compliment, augment, content, élément, fréquent, serpent, etc.

28. Many other English words require only the change of termination, in the following manner:

-ary	into	-aire	as	*military*	militaire
-ory	....	-oire	..	*glory*	gloire
-cy	....	-ce	..	*clemency*	clémence
-ty	....	-té	..	*beauty*	beauté
-ous	....	-eux	..	*dangerous*	dangereux
-our	....	-eur	..	*favour*	faveur

-or	into	-eur	as	*error*	erreur
-ine	....	-in	..	*clandestine*	clandestin
-ive	....	-if	..	*expressive*	expressif
-ry	....	-rie	..	*fury*	furie
-cracy	....	-cratie	..	*aristocracy*	aristocratie

N.B. Adjectives in { -eux, -if, -in } make their feminine in { -euse, -ive, -ine }

EXERCISE.

The beauty of that fable ; the horror of vice ; the utility of
f. *cette* f. f. *h.* m. art. m. f. art

science ; the atrocity of this action ; the violence of his passions ,
f. f. *cette* f. f. *ses* pl.

the simplicity of that machine ; an audacious conspirator ; the
f. *cette* f. 2 m. 1

absurdity of that opinion ; the military evolutions ; an industrious
f. *cette* f. pl. 2 pl. 1 2

nation ; an important victory ; an alimentary pension ; a dangerous
f. 1 2 f. 1 2 f. 1 2

animal ; a figurative expression ; a famous general ; his constant
m. 1 2 f. 1 m. *sa* 2

generosity ; he is incapable of attention ; his impudence is visible ;
f. 1 *il est* *son*

his fidelity is indubitable ; she is very attentive ; your clemency is
sa f. *elle est très-* f. *votre* f.

admirable ; the dèstruction of his fortune was the consequence of
f. *sa* f. *fut* f.

his temerity ; she is very scrupulous ; his condition is horrible ; his
sa f. *très-* f. *sa* f. *ses*

parents are very miserable ; this history is incontestable ; your
pl. *sont très-* pl. *cette* f. *votre*

facility is prodigious ; his perfidy is odious ; it was a horrible
f. *sa* f. f. *ce étoit*

famine ; the sublimity of his sentiments is still preferable to the
f. f. *ses* m. *encore*

energy of his expressions ; it was a decisive action ; the carnage
ses f. *c'était* f. 2 f. 1 m.

was terrible ; that obstacle is invincible ; this instrument is not
cet *cet* m.

harmonious ; the prosperity of the wicked is not durable ; your
f. *méchans* pl. *vos*

insidious presents are not acceptable ; his memory is truly extra-
2 pl. 1 *sont* pl. f. *vraiment*

ordinary ; that is his principal occupation ; a central position ; his
ce est son f. 2 f. 1 f. 2 f. 1 *son*

extravagance is visible ; these arguments are insoluble.
f. *ces* m. pl.

PART I.

OF WORDS CONSIDERED IN THEIR NATURE AND INFLECTIONS.

There are in French nine sorts of words, or parts of speech, namely :

1. Substantive, or Noun,
2. Article,
3. Adjective,
4. Pronoun,
5. Verb.
6. Adverb
7. Preposition,
8. Conjunction,
9. Interjection.

CHAPTER I.

29. OF THE SUBSTANTIVE, OR NOUN.

The substantive is a word which serves to name a person, or thing, as *Pierre*, Peter ; *livre*, book, etc.

There are two sorts of substantives, the *substantive proper*, or *proper name*, and the *substantive common*, also called *appellative*.

The *proper name* is that which is applied to a particular person, or thing, as *César*. Cesar ; *la Tamise*, the *Thames*.

The *substantive common* is that which belongs to a whole class of objects. The word *homme*, man, is a substantive common, as it is applicable to any individual, that is to *Pierre*, or *Paul*, or *Jean*.

Of these nouns some are *collective*, and others *abstract*.

Collectives express either a whole mass, as *une armée*, an army; *une forêt*, a forest; or a partial assemblage, as *une quantité de*, etc. a certain quantity of; *la plupart*, most part, etc.

Abstract nouns are the names of qualities abstracted from their subjects: as, *surface*, *rondeur*, *science*, *sagesse*; surface, roundness, knowledge, wisdom, etc.

In substantives are to be considered *Gender* and *Number*.

30. OF GENDERS.

There are *only* two genders, the *masculine* and *feminine*.

The masculine belongs to the male kind, as *un homme*, a man; *un lion*, a lion, etc.

The feminine belongs to the female kind, as *une femme*, a woman; *une lionne*, a lioness, etc.

This distinction applies also, in French, to inanimate objects, which are either masculine or feminine, as, *un livre*, a book, is masculine; *une table*, a table, is feminine, etc.

31. OF NUMBER.

There are two numbers; the *singular* and the *plural*.

The *singular* expresses *one single* object, as *un homme*, *un livre*.

The *plural* announces *more* objects than *one*. as *des hommes*, *des livres*

Some nouns have no plural, such as names of passions, senses, metals : *l'ivrognerie,* drunkenness; *l'ouïe,* hearing; *le courage,* courage; *l'or,* gold; *l'argent,* silver.

Some have no singular : *les annales,* annals ; *les ancêtres,* ancestors ; *les mouchettes,* snuffers ; *les épinards,* spinach.

Proper names have no plural, as *Londres, Paris, Milton,* etc.

32. OF THE FORMATION OF THE PLURAL OF SIMPLE SUBSTANTIVES.

GENERAL RULE.

The plural is formed in French, as in English, by the addition of an *s* to the singular.

EXAMPLES.

Singular.		Plural.	
le roi	the king	*les rois*	the kings
la reine	the queen	*les reines*	the queens

EXCEPTIONS TO THE GENERAL RULE.

1. Words ending in *s, x, z,* in the singular, remain the same in the plural.

EXAMPLES.

Singular.		Plural.	
le fils	*the son*	les fils	*the sons*
la voix	*the voice*	les voix	*the voices*
le nez	*the nose*	les nez	*the noses*

2. Words ending in *au, eu, ou* form their plural by adding an *x*.

EXAMPLES.

Singular.		Plural.	
bateau	*boat*	bateaux	*boats*
feu	*fire*	feux	*fires*
bijou*	*jewel*	bijoux	*jewels*
vœu	*vow*	vœux	*vows*

3. Words ending in *al, ail,* change their terminations into *aux* to form the plural.

EXAMPLES.

Singular.		Plural.	
cheval†	*horse*	chevaux	*horses*
travail‡	*work*	travaux	*works*

4. Polysyllables ending in *ant, ent* form their plural by the addition of an *s*, thus : *enfant, enfants, moment, moments, commençant, commençants.*

M. Levizac's rule on this subject was to drop the *t* and put an *s*, *enfant, enfans,* and it has long been optional to adopt the one or the other way ; but the French Academy having, in the new edition of their dictionary, adopted the first orthography, it has been thought right to follow their example.

Monosyllables ending in *ent, ant* form their plural by the addition of an *s* : as *gant, gants, chant, chants, dent, dents.*

5. The following six words are quite irregular as to the formation of the plural :

Singular.		Plural.	
ail	*garlic*	aulx	*heads of garlic*
bétail	*cattle*	bestiaux	*cattle*
aïeul	*grandfather*	aïeux	*ancestors*
ciel	*heaven*	cieux	*heavens*
œil	*eye*	yeux	*eyes*
bercail	*sheepfold*	*has no plural*	

* Those in *-ou*, that take *x* in the plural, are *chou, caillou, bijou, genou, hibou, joujou, pou ;* the others now follow the general rule and take *s*, as *clou, clous ; verrou, verrous,* &c.

† Several nouns in *-al*, as *bal, cal, pal, régal, carnaval, local,* &c. follow however the general rule, simply taking *s*.

‡ Those in *-ail*, making their plural in *aux*, are particularly *bail, sous-bail, corail, émail, soupirail, travail, vantail, ventail ;* the rest, as *attirail, détail, éventail, gouvernail, portail, serail,* &c. follow the general rule.

33. OF THE FORMATION OF THE PLURAL OF COMPOUND SUBSTANTIVES.

1. When the word is composed of an adjective and un, both take the mark of the plural.

un *chef-lieu*	county town	*des chefs-lieux*
un *petit-maître*	a dandy	*des petits-maîtres*
un *loup-garou*	a hobgoblin	*des loups-garous*
un *franc-alleu*	a free-hold	*des francs-alleus*
un *arc-boutant*	a buttress	*des arcs-boutants*

To this rule there are exceptions : in some words compounded of a noun and an adjective, one of them takes the *s*, and the other does not ; in some both remain in the singular, as :

un *rouge-gorge*	a robin red-breast	*des rouge-gorge*
un *hôtel-Dieu*	a hospital	*des hôtels-Dieu*
un *arc-en-ciel*	a rainbow	*des arcs-en-ciel*

These differences and apparent contradictions arise from the following considerations :

Rouge gorge is an elliptical form of which the full sense is *oiseau à rouge gorge ; des rouge gorge*, consequently, means *des oiseaux à rouge gorge*, and cannot assume the sign of the plural. *Hôtel Dieu* is also elliptical, and its full sense is *hôtel de Dieu ;* there may be more hotels than one, but there is but one *Dieu*. The same may be said of *arcs* and *ciel*, in *des arcs-en-ciel.*

From what precedes may be established into a precise rule, viz. : that the *s* cannot be affixed to those words to which an idea of plurality cannot be attached.

2. One of the components of a compound substantive, or even each of them, may be a verb, an adverb,

a preposition, all undeclined parts of speech to which the *s* cannot be attached.

un essuie-mains	a towel	*des essuie-mains*
un essuie-main	———	*des essuie-main*
un passe-partout	a master key	*des passe-partout*
un avant-coureur	a fore runner	*des avant-coureurs*
un vice-amiral	a vice admiral	*des vice-amiraux*

3. When the component words are taken from the Latin or from any foreign language, no *s* is added to the plural.

des te-deum	des post-scriptum
des mezzo-termine	des vade-mecum
des auto-da-fè	

4. In all words compounded of *porte* and a noun substantive, no *s* is to be added to the latter.

un porte-étendard	standard bearer	*des porte-étendard*
un porte-épée	sword bearer	*des porte-épée*
un porte-mouchettes	snuffers stand	*des porte-mouchettes*

EXERCISE.

The flowers of the gardens; the niceties of the languages; the
fleur jardin délicatesse langue

palaces of the kings; the woods of those countries; the wallnuts of
palais roi bois ces pays noix

their orchards; the pictures of those painters; the feathers of these
leurs verger tableau ces peintre plume ces

birds; the melody of their voices; the gods of the pagans; the
oiseau =f. s. *leurs voix dieu païen*

jewels of my sisters; the cabbages of our gardens; these charming
bijou mes sœur chou nos jardin ces charmant

places; the horses of my stables; the fans of these ladies; the
2 *lieu* 1 *cheval mes écurie éventail ces dame*

(front gates) of those churches; the actions of my ancestors; the
portail ces église — *mes aïeul*

evils of this life; the victories of those generals; the works of
mal cette vie — *ces* — *travail*

those architects; the corals of those seas; the (learned men) of
ces ——*tecte corail ces mer savant*

those times; the presents of my parents; the teeth of your combs;
ces temps-là — *mes* — *dent* *votre peigne*
the playthings of our children; the heads of these nails.
joujou *nos enfant* *tête* *ces clou.*

CHAPTER II.

OF THE ARTICLE.

34. The *Article* is a small word prefixed to substantives, to determine the extent of their signification.

The French article is { *le* before a masculine substantive / *la* before a feminine substantive } the plural is *les* for both genders.

EXAMPLE.

Singular.		Plural.	
le jour	*the day*	*les* jours	*the days*
la nuit	*the night*	*les* nuits	*the nights*

EXERCISE.

The sun, the moon, and *the* stars are *the* glory of nature.
soleil m. *lune* f. *étoile* f.pl.*sont* = f. art—f.

The king, *the* queen, and *the* princes are well pleased. *The* rose,
roi m. *reine* f. —m.pl. *très-satisfaits* — f.

the violet, *the* tulip, *the* narcissus, *the* hyacinth, *the* gilliflower,
violette f. *tulip* f. *narcisse* m. *jacinthe* f. *giroflée* f.

the jasmine, *the* lily, *the* honeysuckle, *the* ranunculus are *the*
jasmin m. *lis* m. *chèvre-feuille* m. *renoncule* f.

delight of *the* sight. Poetry, painting and music are
délices f. pl. *vue* f. art. *poésie* f. art. *peinture* f. art. *musique*

(sister arts). *The* day and *the* night are equally necessary.
sœur f. pl. *jour* m. *nuit* f. *également nécessaire.*

OF THE ELISION OF THE ARTICLE *le, la.*

35. The articles *le, la* form but one word with the noun following, if the latter begins with a vowel or an *h* not aspirate. This suppression of a letter is called *Elision.*

EXAMPLE.

l'argent	instead of	le argent	*the money*
l'histoire		la histoire	*the history*

36. The same elision takes place also with regard to the preposition *de*, when it precedes a word beginning with a vowel, or an *h* not aspirate.

EXAMPLE.

gage d'amitié	token of friendship.
parole d'honneur	word of honour.

EXERCISE.

The soul of man without cultivation is like a diamond
âme f. art.*homme h.* m *sans* *culture* f. *est comme diamant* m.

(in the rough) The history of Spain is sometimes very interesting.
brut *h.* m. *Espagne quelquefois très intéressante.*

(Look at) *the* amaranthe and *the* anemone ; what beauty ! Self-
Considérez *amaranthe* f. ——f. *quelle* —f. art.*amour-*

love and pride are always the offspring of a weak mind.
propre art.*orgueil toujours* *partage* m. *faible* 2*esprit* m.1.

Honesty, innocence, honour, and *the* love of
art.*Honnêteté h.* m.art.—— art. *honneur*.h.m. *amour* art.

virtue are (very much) esteemed. Summer, autumn, and
vertu f. *très-* *estimés* art. *été* art. *automne* art.

winter are very changeable. France is separated from Italy
*hiver h.*m. *variables* art. — *séparée* *de* *Italie*

by the Alpes, and from Spain by the Pyrenees (An act) of
par *Alpes* pl. art. — — pl. *acte*

ambition. She was struck with horror. He is full of vanity.
—— *Elle était frappée de* — *Il est rempli* *orgueil*

In a fit of humour.
dans un accès ——

CONTRACTION OF THE ARTICLES *le, la, les,* AND PREPOSITION *de, à.*

37. It has been observed page 37 that the articles *le, la, les* are contracted into one word with the prepositions *de, à,* when they are used in connexion before a word beginning with a consonant or an *h* aspirate.

EXAMPLES.

Du roi	is instead of	*de le* roi	*of the king*
du héros	———	*de le* héros	*of the hero*
au roi	———	*à le* roi	*to the king*
au héros	———	*à le* héros	*to the hero*
des rois	———	*de les* rois	*of the kings*
des reines	———	*de les* reines	*of the queens*
ux rois	———	*à les* rois	*to the kings*
aux reines	———	*à les* reines	*to the queens*

EXERCISE.

. The top *of the* mountains and the bottom *of the* vallies are
sommet m. *montagne* *fond* m. *vallée*

equally agreeable. Silk is soft to the touch. The happiness
également agréables.art. *Soie* f. *douce* *toucher* m. *bonheur* m.

of a feeling man is to relieve *the* wants *of the* poor. A man
sensible 2 1 *de subvenir à* *besoin* *pauvre* m.s.

given *to* pleasure was never a great man. He obeyed *the* orders
livré art. *plaisir* m. *ne fut* *grand* *Il obéit à* *ordres*

of the king. The warbling *of* birds, the murmuring of
gazouillement m. art. *oiseau* ——*re* m. art.

streams, the enamel *of* meadows, the coolness of woods,
ruisseau *émail* m. art. *prairie* *fraîcheur* f. art. *bois*

the fragrance *of* flowers, and the sweet smell *of* plants,
parfum m. art. *fleur* *douce odeur* f. art. *plante*

contribute greatly *to the* pleasure of the mind and tc the health *of*
contribuent beaucoup *esprit* *santé* f.

the body.
corps m.

De and *à* are never contracted with *la*.

EXAMPLES.

De la reine	of the queen	*à la reine*	to the queen

Nor are *de* and *à* contracted with *le*, before a masculine substantive singular, beginning with a vowel or *h* mute.

EXAMPLES.

De l'esprit	of the mind	*de l'homme*	of man
A l'esprit	to the mind	*à l'homme*	to man

Contraction does not take place either when the adjective *tout*, all, every, intervenes between *de* or *à*, and the article.

EXAMPLES.

de tout le monde	of every body
de tous les hommes	of all men
à tout le monde	to every body
à tous les hommes	to all men
de toutes les vertus	of all virtues
à toutes les maisons	to all houses

The hope *of* success strengthened the cause of virtue
espérance f. art. *réussite* f. *fortifia* —f. art. *vertu* f.

and weakened the audaciousness *of* rebellion. Fire *of*
affaiblit *audace* f. art. —f. art. *Feu* m. art.

imagination, strength *of* mind, and firmness *of* soul,
———f. art. *force* f. art. *esprit* art. *fermeté* f. art. *âme*

are gifts of nature. We saw with horror that man
des dons m.pl. art. —f. *Nous vîmes avec* =

given up *to* avarice and to voluptuousness. Good cultivation
livré * art. — *à* art. *volupté* f. art. *Bonne culture* f.

is that which contributes most *to the* fertility of the soil. More
est ce qui contribue le plus = *terre* f. *Plus*

or less pain is the lot *of* every body. The history
ou moins de peine *partage* m. *tout* art. *monde* m. =

f man under all the circumstances *of* life, is the study of the
art. *sous toutes* art. *circonstance* f. art. *vie* f. *étude*

wise Playfulness does not become all ages, nor
sage m. art. *Enjouement* m. * *ne sied ni à tout* art.—m.pl. *ni à*

all dispositions
art. *caractère* m.pl.

OF THE ARTICLE.

38. In French, the article always agrees in gender and number with the substantive to which it relates.

EXAMPLES.

le *livre que je cherche*	the book which I am looking for
la *femme que je vois*	the woman whom I see
les *hommes qui étudient*	the men that study.

EXERCISE.

The father and the mother, the brothers and the sisters, the
père m. *mère* m. *frère* m.pl. *sœurs* f.pl.art.

uncles and the aunts, and several other relations were
oncles m.pl. art. *tante* f.pl. *plusieurs autres parent* m.pl. *étaient*

present. What we value is health, frugality, liberty,
présens. Ce que nous estimons c'est art. *santé* f. art. =f. art. =f.

vigour of mind and body; it is the love of virtue,
art. *vigueur* f. art. art. *corps* m. *ce* *amour* m. art. f.

the fear of the gods, fidelity to all mankind,
crainte f. *de* *dieu* m.pl. art. =f. *envers* art. *monde* m. art.

moderation in prosperity, fortitude in adversity,
——f. *dans* art. =f. art. *force* f. art. =f. art.

courage, good morals, and the abhorrence of flattery.
—m. art. *bonnes mœurs* f.pl. *horreur* f.*h*.m. art. =f.

OF THE PARTITIVE ARTICLE.

39. *Some*, signifying a little of, a small portion or quantity of, a few, is rendered by *du*, *de la*, *des*, *de l'* before a vowel and *h* not aspirate; but *some* is hardly ever used in English, whereas *du*, *de la*, *des* must always be expressed in French.

EXAMPLES.

Je mange du *pain*	I eat bread
Il prend de la *peine*	He takes pains
Nous mangeons du *hachis*	We eat some hash
Elle conçoit de la *haine*	She conceives a hatred
Vous avez de l'*amitié*	You have friendship
Vous prenez de l'*humeur*	You get into an ill humour
Nous cueillons des *pommes*	We gather apples
Ils vendent des oranges	They sell oranges

EXERCISE.

Give me *some* bread and butter. Offer him *some*
donnez-moi *pain* m. pr. part. *beurre* m. *Offrez-lui*

meat. Take *some* salt. (There is) mustard. We
viande f. *Prenez* *sel* m. *Voilà* pr. art. *moutarde* f. *Nous*

have *some* girkins. Shall I offer you *some* fowl? Shall I
avons *cornichons* pl. *Vous* *offrirai-je* *poulet* m. *Vous*

help you to *some* fruit? I will take (with pleasure) *some*
servirai-je * — m. *Je prendrai* *volontiers*

broth. Bring me *some* bread. Pour me out *some* beer.
bouillon m. *Apportez-moi* *Versez-moi* * *bière* f.

Drink *some* wine. Take *some* tea. Put (in it) *some* sugar
Buvez *vin* m. *Prenez* *thé* m. *Mettez-y* *sucre* m.

and milk. I hear *some* noise. It hails. She
pr. art. *lait* m. *J'entends* *bruit* m. *Il tombe* *grêle* f. s. *Elle*

has pride. Have you any ink and pens?
a pr. art. *orgueil* m. *Avez-vous* pr. art. *encre* f. pr. art. *plumes* pl.

Put *some* oil and vinegar in the sallad.
Mettez *huile*, *h*. m. pr. art. *vinaigre* m. *dans* *salade* f.

Eat *some* lobster. He has received *some* gold and
Mangez pr. art. *homard* m. *h*. asp. *Il* *a* *reçu* *or* m.

silver.
pr. art. *argent* m.

40. *Du, de la, des, de l'* are not used generally after a negation, nor before a noun preceded by an adjective. In those cases, *de* alone is used without any distinction of gender or number.

EXAMPLES.

Je ne mange pas de pain,	*I do not eat bread.*
Il ne prend jamais de peine	*he takes no pains.*
Ils vendent de bonnes oranges	*they sell good oranges.*

EXERCISE.

Do not give me any bread. We have good girkins. I will not
Ne me donnez pas *avons* *bons* *Je ne prendrai pas*

take broth. We drink excellent wine. She has no pride.
bouillon *nous* *buvons* ——— *vin* *Elle n'a pas*

Have you no ink? Do you not take salt? We never drink wine
Ne prenez-vous pas *jamais*

Do you never eat fruit?
mangez-vous jamais

CHAPTER III.

OF THE ADJECTIVE.

41. The adjective is a word, which is added to a substantive to express its quality, as,

bon père	*good father*	bonne mère	*good mother*
beau livre	*fine book*	belle image	*fine image*

These words *bon, bonne, beau, belle,* are adjectives, because they express the qualities of *père, mère, livre, image.*

A word is known to be an adjective, when it can be properly joined with the word *personne,* or the word *chose.* Thus, *habile,* skilful, and *agréable,* agreeable, are adjectives, because we can say *personne habile,* skilful person, *chose agréable,* agreeable thing.

In French, the adjective agrees in *gender* and *number* with the substantive to which it relates. This difference of *gender* and *number* is generally marked by the termination of the adjective.

42. OF THE FORMATION OF THE FEMININE OF FRENCH ADJECTIVES.

All adjectives ending, in the singular, in *e* mute, are of *both* genders.

EXAMPLES.

Un homme aimable,	An amiable man
Une femme aimable,	An amiable woman

Adjectives ending, in the masculine, in *e*, *i*, *u*, *t*, *d*, form their feminine by the addition of an *e* mute

EXAMPLES.

m.	*f.*	
prudent	prudent*e*	*prudent*
sensé	sensé*e*	*sensible*
poli	poli*e*	*polite*
tortu	tortu*e*	*crooked*
instruit	instruit*e*	*well-informed*
grand	grand*e*	*large*

Adjectives in *-el*, *-eil*, *-ien*, *-on*, *-et*, *-as*, *-ès*, *-ais*, *-os*, *-ot*, *-ul*, *-il*, form their feminine, by doubling the final consonant, and adding *e* mute.

EXAMPLES.

m.	*f.*			
cruel	cruel*le*	*cruel*	= 50	of each termination.
pareil	pareil*le*	*like*	= 3	
ancien	ancien*ne*	*ancient*	= 80	
bon	bon*ne*	*good*	= 18	
net	ne*tte*	*clean*	= 34	

m.	*f.*		*m.*	*f.*	
bas	bas*se*	*low*	épais	épais*se*	*thick*
cas	cas*se*	*cracked*	métis	métis*se*	*mongrel*
gras	gras*se*	*fat*	gros	gros*se*	*big*
las	las*se*	*tired*	sot	sot*te*	*silly*
exprès	expres*se*	*express*	vieillot	vieillot*te*	*oldish*
profès	profes*se*	*professed* { *monk* or *nun*	nul	nul*le*	*no*
				gentil*le*	*genteel*

Adjectives ending in *f*, change this letter into *ve*.

EXAMPLES.

bre*f*	brè*ve*	*short*
acti*f*	acti*ve*	*active*
naï*f*	naï*ve*	*ingenuous*
neu*f*	neu*ve*	*new*

Adjectives ending in -*x* change -*x* into *se*.

EXAMPLES.

honteu*x*	honteu*se*	*ashamed*
vertueux	vertueu*se*	*virtuous*
jalou*x*	jalou*se*	*jealous*

Adjectives ending in *eur*, derived from verbs, and which might be more properly called substantives, were it not that they have a feminine, form that feminine in various manners; they are few in number, and change as follows :

EUR, EUSE.

complimenteur	—teuse	*fond of compliments*
connaisseur	—sseuse	*connaisseur, judge*
demandeur	—deuse	*one who asks*
flatteur	—tteuse	*flattering*
menteur	—teuse	*deceiving*
parleur	—leuse	*talker*
rêveur	—veuse	*dreamer*
moqueur	—ueuse	*sneering*
trompeur	—peuse	*deceiver*

etc., etc.

EUR, ERESSE.

bailleur	bailleresse	*donor*
demandeur	——deresse	*plaintiff*
défendeur	——deresse	*defendant*
enchanteur	——teresse	*charmer*
pêcheur	——cheresse	*sinner*
vengeur	——geresse	*avenger*

etc. etc.

EUR, RICE.

accusateur	—trice	*accuser*
acteur	—trice	*actor*

bienfaiteur	—trice	*benefactor*
admirateur	—trice	*admirer*
séducteur	—trice	*seducer*
protecteur	—trice	*protecttor*
conservateur	—trice	*preserver*
conducteur	—trice	*leader*
ambassadeur	—drice	*ambassador*

Auteur, docteur, imprimeur, professeur, have no feminine.

All *real* adjectives ending in *eur*, form their feminine by the addition of an *e*; they are about twelve in number: *antérieur, citérieur, extérieur, intérieur, inférieur, meilleur, mineur, majeur, postérieur, supérieur, ultérieur, prieur.*

EXERCISE.

She is *decent.* This house is well *situated.* This pear
Elle — *Cette maison* f. *bien situé* *poire* f.

is too ripe. She is *tall* and well *formed.* This story is
trop mûr *grand* *bien fait* *histoire* f.

very *entertaining.* This person is very *volatile.* This mountain
très-amusant *personne* f. *bien léger* *montagne* f.

is *steep.* This road is not very *safe.* The door is not
escarpé *route* f. *sûr* *porte* f.

open. This room is *dark.* This street is too *narrow.* It is
ouvert *chambre* f. *obscur* *rue* f. *étroit* *Ce*

is an *ancient* custom. She has *carnation* lips. His
coutume f. *a* *vermeil* 2 art. *lèvre* f. pl. 1. *Sa*

memory will be *immortal.* His manners are *natural.* The
= f. *sera* ——*tel* *Ses manières* f. pl. *naïf*

engagement was *warm.* (That is) an *original* thought. This
action f. *fut* *vif* *Voilà* *neuf* 2 *pensée* f. 1.

cloth is the *best* of all. These are *delusive* promises.
étoffe f. *meilleur* f. pl. *trompeur* 2 *promesse* f. pl. 1.

He seduces by his *fawning* manners. The *delightful* valley
séduit par *flatteur* 2 *manières* f. pl. 1. *délicieux* *vallée* f.

of Tempe is in Thessaly. The grass is very *thick.* The soup
Tempé *dans* art. = f. *herbe* f. *soupe* f.

is too *fat.* It is a *foolish* undertaking. This water is not *clean.*
sot *entreprise* f. *Cette eau* f. *net*

It is a very *silly* *story*. The law is *express* upon that point.
C'est *histoire* f. *loi* f. *sur* *ce* — *ro*.

The *avenging* thunder smote that *impious* wretch. He
vengeur 2 *foudre* f. 1 *frappa* *cet* *impie* *

(held out to us) a *protecting* hand.
tendit 2 *nous* 1 ——*teur* 2 *main* f. 1.

OF IRREGULAR ADJECTIVES.

43. There are some adjectives which are irregular in the formation of their feminine. They will be found nearly all contained in the following list.

m.	f.		m.	f.	
*beau †bel	bel*le*	*fine*	*fou †fol	fol*le*	*mad*
*nouveau *nouvel	nouvelle	*new*	*mou †mol	mol*le*	*soft*
*vieux †vieil	vieil*le*	*old*			

m.	f.		m.	f.	
blanc	blan*che*	*white*	fau*x*	fau*sse*	*false*
franc	fran*che*	*frank*	rou*x*	rou*sse*	*red*
frai*s*	fraî*che*	*fresh*	dou*x*	dou*ce*	*sweet*
Grec	Grec*que*	*Greek*	aigre-dou*x*	aigre-dou*ce*	*tartish, sweet*
public	publi*que*	*public*	tier*s*	tier*ce*	*third,* etc.
caduc	cadu*que*	*frail*	tor*s*	tor*se, or* tor*te*	*twisted*
Turc	Tur*que*	*Turkish*	coi	coi*te* or *coie*	*still, snug*
long	lon*gue*	*long*	favori	favori*te*	*favorite*
béni*n*	béni*gne*	*benign*	jumeau	jume*lle*	*twin*
malin	mali*gne*	*malignant*	traître	traître*sse*	*traitor*
sec	sè*che*	*dry*			

The following adjectives ending in *et*, not only form their feminine by the addition of *e* mute, but require the grave accent on the penultimate *e*.

* *Beau, nouveau, vieux, fou, mou*, before a consonant or *h* not aspirate.

† Before a vowel and *h* mute.

m.		f.
concret		concrète
discret		discrète
indiscret		indiscrète
inquiet		inquiète
complet	make	complète
incomplet		incomplète
replet		replète
suret		surète
prêt		prête

Préfix m. makes *préfixe* f. and is the only adjective in *-x*, which retains this letter and follows the SECOND RULE.

Some adjectives have no feminine, as *bisché, dispos, fat, paillet,* etc.; others have no masculine, as *blette,* etc,

SINGULARITY OF DEMI, FEU, NU.

43*. *Demi, nu,* have a peculiarity which must be noticed. When they precede the noun, they are undeclined; when they follow it, they agree with it.

une demi-livre	*half a pound*
une demi-heure	*half an hour*
un demi-cent	*half a hundred*
une livre et demie	*one pound and a half*
deux heures et demie	*half past two*
trois cents et demi	*three hundred and a half*

nu-pieds	les pieds nus	*bare feet*
nu-tête	la tête nue	*bare head*

Feu is undeclined when preceding the article and a possessive pronoun; it is declined when following them.

Feu la reine	la feue reine	*the late queen*

The adjectives *bas, bon, court,* etc. being used with a verb, become adverbs, and are not declined.

ces fleurs sentent bon	*these flowers smell nice*
elle parle bas	*she speaks low*
ils demeurèrent court	*they stood short*
elle se fait fort d'y aller	*she takes upon herself to go*

REMARKS ON TOUT, QUELQUE.

44. Tout, *all*, means also *every*, in a sort of distributive sense.

je vous souhaite toute espèce de bonheur, *I wish you every happine*

Tout is very frequently prefixed to an adjective in the sense of *quite, entirely*, and is, consequently, undeclined.

ces enfants, tout aimables qu'ils sont, me fatiguent	*amiable as these children are, they fatigue me*
ils étaient tout étourdis	*they were quite astounded*

But it has this peculiarity that, when placed before an adjective feminine, beginning with a consonant, it is declined.

c'est une tête toute vide	*it is a head quite empty*
elles étaient toutes tremblantes	*they trembled all over*

Quelque, before a noun plural, qualified or not by an adjective, takes an s.

quelques richesses que vous ayez, ne soyez pas prodigue.	*whatever be your riches do not be lavish.*
quelques bonnes actions que vous fassiez, soyez modeste.	*whatever good actions you do, be modest.*

Quelque before an adjective, means *however*, and is not declined.

quelque riches qu'ils soient, ils ne donnent rien.	*however rich they be, they give nothing.*

Quel que, quelle que, quels que, quelles que; here, *quel* is a sort of pronoun adjective which must agree in gender and number with the noun to which it refers, and which is the subject of the verb following.

quels que soient vos desseins, et quelles que soient vos vues	*whatever be your designs and your views.*
quelles que soient votre naissance et votre fortune	*whatever be your birth and fortune.*

Observe that the verb is in the subjunctive mood after *quelque, quelques, quel que.*

EXERCISE.

He drank a glass of brandy *quite pure.* My sisters were
but *verre* m. *eau de vie* f. — *étaient*

quite *put out.* Hope, *deceitful* as it is, leads us to the
déconcerté art. *espérance* *trompeur* f. *nous mène*

end of life through a pleasant path. She was quite
fin f. art. *vie* *par* *agréable* 2 *chemin* m. 1. *fut*

astonished when she saw us. *Whatever* advantages you
étonnée *vit* 2 *nous* 1. *avantages* *que vous*

have, (do not make) too sure of success. (I will not have
ayez *ne soyez pas* art. *succès* m. *Je ne veux pas*

her), however *beautiful* she may be. You must conquer your
d'elle *jolie* *qu'elle soit.* *il* *faut* *vaincre*

inclinations *whatever* they be. (Let us know) your choice
penchants m. *soient* *faites-nous savoir* *choix* m.

whatever it may be. That soup is very *good.* There is *no* truth
soupe f. *Il n'y* *a* *nul* *vérité* f.

in all that. It is in the *newest* fashion. It is a *fine* statue
dans *tout* *cela.* *à* *nouveau* *mode* f. *beau* = f.

He lives in a state of *luxurious* idleness. This wax is not
Il *vit* *dans* * * *mou* *oisiveté* f. *cire* f.

very *white.* She is as *fresh* as a rose. The paint on that
* *comme* — f. *peinture* f.

wainscot is not *dry.* His answer is a *mere* evasion. The
lambris m. *réponse* f. *franc* *défaite* f.

thing is *public.* That plant possesses a *pernicious* property.
chose f. *herbe* f. *a* *malin* 2 *qualité* f. 1.

She is of a *benevolent* disposition. This woman is *jealous* and
a * *benin* 2 *humeur* f. *femme* f. *jaloux*

deceitful. His temper is *gentle.* This colour is too red.
faux *Son* *humeur* f. *doux* *couleur* f. *trop* *roux*

These *old* clothes are *good* for nothing. He ran *bare*
hardes f. *pl.* *ne* *à* *rien* *il* *courait* *nu*

legged in the streets. Give me a guinea and a *half.*
les jambes f. *par* *Donnez-moi* *guinée* f. *

Cut *half* a yard. / *Coupez en* — *aune* f.
The late princess was *idolized.* / — *cesse* *chéri*

Do not stand in the cold air (without your hat).
Ne restez pas art. *tête* f. *nu à l'air.*

OF THE FORMATION OF THE PLURAL OF FRENCH ADJECTIVES.

45. General Rule. The formation of the plural in adjectives follows the same rules as those given for the plural of substantives. All adjectives having the feminine termination in *e* mute, or ending in *e, i, u, c, d, g, f, n, t,* form their plural by the addition of an *s*, as : *aimable, aimables ; docile, dociles ; poli, polis ; goulu, goulus ; grand, grands ; long, longs.* This rule applies to the participles past, *aimé, aimés ; reçu, reçus,* etc.

EXCEPTIONS.

1. Adjectives ending in *-s*, or *-x*, do not change their termination in the plural, as *gros, gras, hideux.*

2. Those ending in *-au*, take *x* in the plural, as *beau, beaux, nouveau, nouveaux.*

Those in *-al*, change this termination into *aux*, as *égal*, equal, *égaux ; général, généraux ;* but most of these have no plural masculine, as *amical, austral, boréal, canonial, conjugal, diamétral, fatal, filial, final, frugal, jovial, lustral, matinal, naval, pastoral, pectoral, spécial, vénal,* and some others.

Canonical, clérical, conjectural, colossal, déloyal, diaconal, ducal, électoral, équinoxial, final, fiscal, are seldom used in the plural masculine ; wherever they are, they follow the general rule.

Amical, automnal, colossal, frugal, glacial, jovial, total have no plural masculine.

Pascal makes *pascals,* but *fatals* ought to be avoided.

4. Polysyllables ending in *-nt*, according to general practice, may drop the *t* in the plural, as *excellent*, *excellens*; but the Academy keep the *t*, (see page 86). Monosyllables retain it, as *lent*, slow, *lents*; but the adjective *tout*, all, makes *tous*.

EXERCISE.

They are *envious* and *jealous*. Those fowls are large and
Ils = *jaloux* *poulet* m. pl. *gros*

fat Owls are *frightful* birds. (These are)
gras art. *Hibou* m. pl. *des* *hideux* 2 *oiseau* m. pl. 1. *Voilà*

beautiful jewels. The two *new* operas have succeeded.
de beau *bijou* m. pl. *deux nouveau* — m. pl. *ont* *réussi*

Men are only *equal* (in the) infirmities of nature. The
art. 2 *ne* 1 *que* 4 *égal* 3 *par les* = art. — f.

general officers are *assembled*. This fruit is *excellent*.
— 2 *officiers* m. pl. 1. ——*blé* *ces* — m. pl. *sont* —

His improvement is *slow*, but *solid*. *All* his friends have
Ses progrès, m. pl. *sont lent* *solide* *ses* *ami* m. pl.

been very *glad* to see him. Those ladies are *tired* with
été *bien* *aise* *de* *voir* 2 *le* 1 *ces* *dame* f. pl. *las* *de*

walking. You have powerful enemies; but their efforts
marcher *Vous avez de puissant* *ennemi* m. pl. *mais leurs* — m. pl.

will be *vain* and *useless*. The four *cardinal* points are the
seront — *inutile* *quatre* — 2 *point* pl. 1

east, west, south, and north.
orient, m. art. *occident* m. art. *midi* m. art. *nord* m.

OF THE DEGREES OF SIGNIFICATION OF THE ADJECTIVE.

46. Grammarians commonly reckon *three* degrees of comparison; the *positive*, the *comparative*, and the *superlative*.

The *positive* is the adjective expressing the quality of an object, without any increase or diminution, as *beau*, *belle*.

EXAMPLES.

A child *gentle*, *amiable*, and *docile*, is beloved by every body
enfant m. *doux* *aimable* — *aimé de tout le monde*

An *ingenuous* candour, an *amiable* simplicity and a *lively*
——*nu* 2 =f. 1. =f. *piquant* 2

artlessness are the charm of youth. The sight of an *agreeable*
naïveté f.1. *charme* m. art.*jeunesse* f. *vue* f. *agréable*

landscape is a *varied* and rapid source of *delightful* sensations.
paysage m. *varié* 2 *rapide* 3—f.1 *délicieux* 2 —f.pl.1

47. The *comparative* is so called, because it draws a comparison between two or many objects. When two things are compared, the one is either superior, inferior, or equal to the other; hence three sorts of comparison, that of *superiority*, of *inferiority*, and *equality*.

The *comparative of superiority* is formed by putting *plus*, more, before the adjective, and *than* is rendered by *que*.

EXAMPLES.

La rose est plus belle que la violette.	The rose is more beautiful than the violet.

By, in comparison before a noun of number, is rendered by *de*.

He is taller by two inches. *Il est plus grand de deux pouces*

EXERCISE.

The republic of Athens was *more illustrious* than that of
république f. *Athènes a été* *illustre* *celle*

Lacedemon. Homer was perhaps a *greater* genius than Virgil
Lacédémone *Homère était peut-être* *grand génie* m. *Virgile*

but Virgil had a *more delicate* and *more refined* taste than Homer.
mais *a eu* *fin* 2 *délicat* 3 *goût* m. 1. *h* m.

Milton appears (to me) *more sublime* than all the other epic
paraît 2 *me* 1 ——— *autre* 1 *épique* 3

poets. The river is deeper *by* four feet.
poète m.pl.2. *rivière* f. *profond*

The *comparative of inferiority* is formed by prefixing *moins*, less, to the adjective, and rendering also *than* by *que*.

EXAMPLES.

La violette est moins belle que la rose	The violet is less beautiful than the rose

EXERCISE.

Shipwreck and death are *less fatal* than the pleasures which
art. *Naufrage* m. art. *mort* f. *funestes* *plaisirs* m. *qui*

attack virtue. The violet is *less brilliant* to the eye than the
attaquent art. f. f. *brillant* *yeux*

lily, a true emblem of modesty and of pride
lis m. * *véritable* 2 *emblème* m 1. art. = f. *de* art. *orgueil* m

Autumn is *less varied* than spring, but it is richer.
art. *Automne* f. *varié* art. *printemps* m. *elle* *riche*

In the *comparative of equality* the first *as* is rendered by *aussi* in affirmative, and by *si*, in negative phrases; the second *as* is rendered by *que*.

EXAMPLE.

La tulipe est aussi belle que la rose.	the tulip is as beautiful as the rose.
La tulipe n'est pas si belle que la rose	the tulip is not so beautiful as the rose.

EXERCISE.

Pope's images are *as perfect* as his style is harmonious.
De Pope 2 art. —f.pl.1. *parfait* *son* —m =.

Delicacy of taste is a gift of nature *as scarce* as
art. *Délicatesse* f. art. *goût* m. *don* m. art. —f. *rare*

true genius. The love of our neighbour is *as necessary* in
art. *vrai génie* m. *amour du* * *prochain* = *dans*

society for the happiness of life, *as* in christianity for
art. = *pour bonheur* m. art. *vie* f. art. ——*nisme* m.

eternal salvation. It is *as easy* to do good *as* to do
art. —*nel* 2 *salut* m. 1. *aisé de faire* art. *bien* m. *de*

evil. Paris is not *so* large *as* London. James will not be
art. *mal* m. — m. *grand Londres Jacques ne sera pas*

so rich *as* his brother.
riche son frère.

Meilleur, *pire*, *moindre* are the comparatives of *bon*, *mauvais*, *petit*, which are irregular in the formation of the degrees. Thus :

bon,	good	*meilleur*,	better	*le meilleur*,	the best
mauvais,	bad	*pire*,	worse,	*le pire*,	the worst
petit,	small	*moindre*,	smaller	*le moindre*,	the smallest

48. N.B. As most beginners are apt to confound these comparative adjectives with the comparative adverbs, MIEUX, PIS, and MOINS, because they are generally rendered by the same English words *better*, *worse* and *less*, it may be advisable to subjoin here these comparative adverbs with their positives, that the difference of meaning may serve as a distinction.

ADJECTIVES.

Meilleur, better, is the comparative of *bon*, good, and is used instead of *plus bon*, which is never said.

Pire signifies *plus mauvais*, worse, or more wicked, and is used instead of this.

Moindre means *plus petit*, less, or smaller, and is used instead of these terms.

ADVERBS.

Mieux,* better, is the comparative of *bien*, well, and is used instead of *plus bien*, more well, which is said in neither language.

*Pis** is the comparative of *mal*, badly, and is used for *plus mal*, worse, which, however, may be used.

Moins is the comparative of *peu*, little, and is used for *plus peu*, which is never said.

* There are some instances of *pis* and *mieux* used adjectively, but this is not the place to mention them.

EXAMPLES.

Ce fruit-là est bon, mais celui-ci est meilleur	*That fruit is good, but that is better*
Sa condition est mauvaise, mais elle a été pire	*His condition is bad, but it has been worse.*
Ma dépense est petite, mais la vôtre est moindre	*My expense is small, but yours is smaller*
Il se conduit bien, mais elle se conduit encore mieux	*He behaves well, but she behaves still better*
Il se portait mal, mais il est pis que jamais	*He was badly, but he is worse than ever*
Je parle peu, vous parlez encore moins.	*I speak little, you speak still less*

EXERCISE.

His reasoning is not *better* than yours. Your style is a
Son raisonnement m. *le vôtre* *Votre* — m. *de*

great deal *better* than that of his brother. The thickness of this
beaucoup *celui* *son* *épaisseur* f. *ce*

wall is less than that of the next wall. This column is *less* than
mur m. *celle* *voisin* 2 1 *Cette colonne* f.

the other in height and thickness. The remedy is *worse*
autre en hauteur f. *en grosseur* f. *remède* m.

than the disease. Your horse is *worse* than mine.
mal m. *cheval* m. *le mien.*

49. The adjective is in the *superlative* degree, when it expresses the quality in a high or in its highest state: hence there are two sorts of superlatives, the *absolute* and the *relative*.

50. The *superlative absolute* is formed by putting *très*, *fort*, *bien*, very, before the adjective; it is called *absolute*, because it does not express any comparison with, or relation to, any other objects.

EXAMPLE.

Londres est une très-belle ville	*London is a very fine city.*

REMARK. The adverbs *extrêmement*, extremely, *infiniment*, infinitely, are likewise marks of the superlative absolute.

EXAMPLE.

Cet homme est extrêmement savant	*That man is extremely learned.*
Dieu est infiniment heureux	*God is infinitely blessed.*

EXERCISE.

That landscape is *very diversified, very extensive,* and *infinitely*
Ce paysage m. *varié étendu*
agreeable on every side. The Alps are *very high* and *very steep.*
agréable de toutes parts f. pl. *haut escarpé*
The style of Fénélon is *very rich,* and *very harmonious,* but it is
—m. ——— = *il*
sometimes prolix ; that of Bossuet is *extremely sublime,* but it is
quelquefois prolixe celui élevé
sometimes harsh and unpolished.
dur rude

51. The *superlative relative* is formed by prefixing the article *le, la, les,* according to the gender of the noun, to the comparative, and is called *relative* because it expresses comparison with, or relation to, another subject.

The article *le, la, les* is not used in the superlative degree when a possessive pronoun precedes the noun.

EXAMPLES.

Londres est la plus belle des villes	*London is the finest of cities*
Je préfère une maison de campagne au plus beau palais	*I prefer a country house to the finest palace*
C'est mon plus grand ennemi	*He is my greatest enemy*
Voici nos meilleurs voisins	*These are our best neighbours.*

Plus and *moins,* with the article, are repeated before every adjective.

EXERCISE.

The most beautiful comparison that there is perhaps in any
beau comparaison f. *que il y ait peut-être dans aucun*

anguage is that which Pope has drawn from the Alps, in his Essay
langue f. *celle que* *tiré* f. *de* *Alpes, dans son essai*

on Criticism. *The most able men* are not always *the most*
sur art. *critique* f. *habile gens* m. pl. *toujours*

virtuous. *The most ancient* and *most general* of all kinds of
vertueux. f.—*nne* f. art. *espèce* f. pl.

idolatry was the worship rendered to the sun. *The least excu-*
= *était* *culte* m. *rendu* *soleil* m. —

sable of all errors is that which is wilful. I will show you
art. — f. *celle qui* *volontaire. Je montrerai*2 *vous*1

my prettiest flowers. These are her richest gifts. I have not
mes joli fleur f. *précieux don* m. *Je ai*

read his best work.
lu son *ouvrage* m.

CONCORD OF THE ADJECTIVE WITH THE SUBSTANTIVE.

52. The adjective always agrees in gender and number with the substantive to which it relates.

Le bon père	*The good father*
La bonne mère	*The good mother*
De beaux jardins	*Fine gardens*
De belles promenades	*Fine walks*

Bon is masculine singular, because *père* is masculine, and in the singular; *bonne* is feminine singular, because *mère* is feminine, and in the singular; *beaux* is in the masculine plural, because *jardins* is masculine, and plural, etc.

EXERCISE.

These hills are *covered* with trees *loaded* with
ces coteau m. pl. *couvert de* *arbre* m. pl. *chargé de*

fruit, already *ripe*. A *pure* stream rolls its *limpid*
— m. pl. *déjà* *mûr.* *clair ruisseau* m. *roule son limpide* 2

water through the midst of meadows *enamelled* with
cristal m. 1 *à* *milieu* m *prairie*, f. pl. *émaillé de*

flowers. (Every thing) interests the heart in this abode
fleur f. pl. tout intéresse cœur m. ce séjour m.

which is *full* of charms. Fly, *inconsiderate* youth,
* * plein attrait m. pl. Fuyez, —déré 2 jeunesse f. 1

fly from the *enchanting* allurements of a *vain* world; its
* —teur 2 attrait 1 — 2 monde m. 1. ses

perfidious sweets are a *slow* poison, which (would destroy
—de 2 douceur f. pl. 1. lent 2 — m. 1. qui détruirait

in your soul the *noble* enthusiasm of goodness, and the
dans âme — enthousiasme m. art. bien m.

precious seeds of *sublime* virtues.
= germe m. art. — 2. vertu 1.

53. When the adjective relates to two substantives singular, of the same gender, it must be put in the plural, and agree with them in gender.

EXAMPLE.

Le roi et le berger sont égaux après la mort	*The king and the shepherd are equal after death*
Ma mère et ma sœur sont vives	*My mother and sister are quick*

EXERCISE.

Uprightness and piety are much *esteemed*, even by the
art. droiture f. art. piété f. très-estimé même de

wicked. Man, in the most elevated rank, and
méchant pl. art. dans (le plus élevé) 2 art. rang m. 1

man in the most obscure situation, are equally *precious*
art. obscur 2 art. état m. 1 également =

in the eyes of God. Pilpay and Confucius are very *celebrated*
à m. pl. célèbre

among the nations of Asia.
parmi peuples art.

54. When the two substantives, to which the adjective relates, are of different genders, the adjective is to be put in the masculine plural.

EXAMPLE.

Mon père et ma mère sont contents	*My father and mother are contented.*

EXERCISE.

His probity and disinterestedness are *known* (every where).
= f. *son désintéressement* m. *connu partout*

The love of life, and the fear of death, are
amour m. art. *vie* f. *crainte* f. art. *mort* f.

natural to man. Ignorance and self-love are
— *rel* art. art. —f. art. *amour-propre m.*

equally *presumptuous.* My sister and brother were very *atten-*
présomptueux Ma f. *mon* m. *ont été* =

tive to the instructions of their masters.
— *leur maître* m. pl.

NOUNS AND ADJECTIVES OF NUMBER.

55. Numbers are divided into five classes, viz: *cardinal, ordinal, collective, distributive, and proportional.*

CARDINAL NUMBER.	ORDINAL NUMBER.		NUMERICAL COLLECTIVE NOUNS.
1 un, une	*premier*	*first*	unité, *unit*
2 deux	deuxième, *second*	2d	couple, paire, *couple*
3 trois	troisième	3rd	trio
4 quatre	quatrième	4th	deux couples, *two couples*
5 cinq	cinquième	5th	
6 six	sixième	6th	demi-douzaine, *half a dozen*
7 sept	septième	7th	
8 huit	huitième	8th	huitaine, *week*
9 neu*f*	neuvième	9th	neuvaine, *nine days of prayer*
0 dix	dixième	10th	dizaine, *half a score*
11 onze	onzième	11th	
12 douze	douzième	12th	douzaine, *dozen*
13 treize	treizième	13th	
14 quatorze	quatorzième	14th	
15 quinze	quinzième	15th	quinzaine, *fortnight, etc.*
16 seize	seizième	16th	

CARDINAL NUMBER.	ORDINAL NUMBER.		NUMERICAL COLLECTIVE NOUNS.
17 dix-sept	dix-sept*ième*	17th	
18 dix-huit	dix-huit*ième*	18th	
19 dix-neu*f*	dix-neu*vième*	19th	
20 vingt	vingt*ième*	20th	vingtaine, *a score*
21 vingt et-un	vingt-et-un*ième*	21st	
22 vingt-deux	vingt-deux*ième*, etc.	22nd	
30 trent*e*	trent*ième*	30th	trentaine, *a score and a half*
31 trente-et un, etc.	trente-un*ième*	31st	
40 quarante	quarant*ième*	40th	quarantaine, *two score*
41 quarante-et un, etc.	quarante-un*ième*	41st	
50 cinquante	cinquant-*ième*	50th	cinquantaine, *two score and a half*
51 cinquante et-un, etc.	cinquante-un*ième*	51st	
60 soixant*e*	soixant*ième*	60th	soixantaine, *three score*
61 soixante-et-un, etc.	soixante-un*ième*	61st	
70 soixante-dix	soixante-dix*ième*	70th	
71 soixante-onze	soxiante-onz*ième*	71st	
72 soixante-douze, etc.	soixante-douz*ième*	72d	
80 quatre-vingts	quatre-vingt*ième*	80th	—— *four score*
81 quatre-vingt-un, etc.	quatre-vingt-un-*ième*	81st	
90 quatre vingt-dix	quatre-vingt-dix-*ième*	90th	
91 quatre vingt-onze, etc.	quatre-vingt-onz-*ième*	91st	
100 cent	cent*ième*	100th	1 centaine, *one hundred*
101 cent-un, etc.	cent-un-*ième*, etc.	101st	
200 deux-cents	deux-cent*ième*	200th	2 centaines, 2 *hundred*
1000 mill*e*	mill*ième*	1000th	1 millier, 1 *thousand*

CARDINAL NUMBER.		ORDINAL NUMBER.	NUMERICAL COLLECTIVE NOUNS.
2000	deux, mille, etc	deux-millième, etc. 2000th	2 milliers, 2 *thousand*
10,000	dix mille	dix-millième 10,000th	1 myriade, 1 *myriad*
1,000,000	mille fois mille	million-*ième*, millionth	1 million 1 *million*

Un milliard or *billion*, a thousand millions, *un trillion*, etc.

Cent takes an s when immediately before the noun; it does not take it when followed by another number. *trois cents hommes ; trois cent cinquante hommes.*

Mille never takes the *s* in the plural : *deux mille hommes.*

In dates, *mille* is contracted into *mil: mil huit cent trente-cinq.*

There are many other numerical expressions used in poetry, music, games, etc. : as, *distique*, *tercet*, *quatrain*, *sixain*, *huitain*, etc. *solo*, *duo*, *trio*, *quatuor*, *quinque*, *quinte*, *octave*, etc. *beset*, *sonnez*, etc.

Un millier is very often employed for one thousand *weight*, but *quintal* is never used except in the sense of one hundred weight.

The distributive numbers are those which express the different parts of a whole : as, *la moitié*, the half; *le quart*, the quarter ; *un cinquième*, a fifth, etc.

The proportional denote the progressive increase of things : as, *le double*, the double ; *le triple*, the treble; *le centuple*, a hundred fold, etc.

CHAPTER IV.

OF THE PRONOUN.

56. A *pronoun* is a word substituted in the place of a noun.

There are several kinds of pronouns, as the *personal possessive, relative, absolute, demonstrative,* and *indefinite.*

SECTION I.

OF THE PERSONAL PRONOUNS.

57. *Personal pronouns* are used in the places of persons and things, to avoid their being repeated.

58. There are three *persons:* the first who speaks, the second who is spoken to, and the third is the person or thing spoken of.

Singular.

Subject.	je			je loue Dieu	*I praise God*
Object.	me	*for* à moi I		il me donne	*he gives me, or to me*
	me	.. moi	*to me*	il me blesse	*he hurts me*
	moi	.. à moi	*me*	donnez-moi	*give me, or to me*
	moi	.. moi	*to me*	aidez-moi	*help me*
	de moi	.. ——	*of me*	il parle de moi	*he speaks of me.*

Plural.

Subject.	nous		*we*	nous louons Dieu	*we praise God*
Object.	nous	*for* à nous	*to us*	il nous donne	*he gives us*
	nous	.. nous	*us*	il nous blesse	*he hurts us*
	de nous	.. ——	*of us*	il parle de nous	*he speaks of us.*

They are both masculine and feminine; that is, of the same gender as the person or persons they represent.

59. In general, *je* and *me* are put before the verb; *moi, de moi, à moi* after it, and *nous* before or after, as the case requires.

EXERCISE.

I cast my eyes upon the objects which surrounded *me*, and
portai vue f. s. *sur objet environnaient me*

saw with pleasure that all was calm and tranquil. Do you not
je vis avec que était calme tranquille * 3 1-4

see in all the features of my father that he is satisfied with
voyez 2 *dans trait* m. pl. *que content de*

me? *We* have told the truth. What were they saying of *us*?
moi avons dit vérité f. *Que* * *on* 2 *disait* 1

If *we* desire to be happy, *we* must not deviate from the
Si désirons de ne devons pas nous écarter de

path of virtue.
sentier m. art.

60. PRONOUNS OF THE SECOND PERSON.

Singular.

Subject.	tu		*thou*	tu crains Dieu	*thou fearest God*
Object.	te	*for* à toi	*to thee*	il te parle	*he speaks to thee*
	te	.. toi	*thee*	il te voit	*he sees thee*
	toi	.. à toi	*to thee*	donne-toi la peine	*give thyself the trouble*
	toi	.. toi	*thee*	habille-toi	*dress thyself*
	de toi	.. —	*of thee*	nous parlons de toi	*we speak of thee.*

Plural.

Subject.	vous		*ye, or you*	vous louez Dieu	*you praise God*
Object.	vous	*for* à vous	*to you*	il vous parle	*he speaks to you*
	vous	.. vous	*you*	il vous respecte	*he respects you*
	de vous	.. —	*of you*	il parle de vous	*he speaks of you.*

In general, *tu* and *te* are put before the verb; *toi, de toi, à toi* are placed after; *vous* is placed either before or after, according as the case requires.

REMARK. Politeness has led to the use of the plural *vous*, instead of the singular *tu*: as, *vous êtes bien bon* you are very good, for *tu es bien bon*.

EXERCISE.

Thou art greater than I; and from *thee* I have (at once)
es *moi* *toi* *ai* *en même temps* 2
learnt humility and wisdom. I (was telling) you that
appris 1 art. = f. art. *sagesse* f. *disais* *te* *que*
dancing is to the body what taste is to the mind. *You* have
art. *danse* f. m. *ce que* art. *goût* m. *esprit* m. *avez* 2
shown us great talents; when (will *you* show) us great virtues?
montré 3 1 *de* ——m. *quand montrerez-vous* 2 1 *de* f.pl.
How amiable *you* are! How good *you* are to have thought of
Que 3 1 *êtes* 2 3 1 2 *de* vous *être occupé*
us! (It was said) of *you* the other day, that *you* intended to
On disait *autre jour* m. *vous vous proposiez de*
spend a winter in London (in order to) see every thing curious
passer m. *à* *—dres* *pour* *voir* *tout* *ce* =6
which that city presents.
que 1 *cette* 2 *ville* 3 *offre* 4 *de* 5

61. PRONOUNS OF THE THIRD PERSON.

Singular

Sub.	il *m.*	. . . . *he*		il perd son temps	*he loses his time*
	elle *f.*	. . . . *she*		elle travaille toujours	*she is always at work*
Obj.	lui *m.*	*for* à lui	*to him*	dites-lui que je *lui* parlerai	*tell him that I will speak to him*
	lui *f.*	.. à elle	*to her*	dites-lui que vous *lui* donnerez	*tell her that you will give her*
		de lui	*of him*	il parle de lui	*he speaks of him*
		.. d'elle	*of her*	il parle d'elle	*he speaks of her*
	lui *m.*	lo	*him*	je ne connais que *lui* de capable	*I know but him capable*
		..			
		.. avec lui	*with him*		
	le *m.*	*for* lui	*him*	je *le* méprise	*I despise him*
	la *f.*	.. elle	*her*	je *la* respecte	*I respect her*
	elle *f.*	elle	*her*	Il ne connaît qu'*elle*	*he know but her*
				venez avec elle	*come with her*
	le *m.*	*for* cela	*it*	je ne *le* savais pas	*I did not know it.*

Plural.

Sub.	ils *m.*	*they*		*ils* chantent	*they sing* (gentlemen
	elles *f.*	*they*		*elles* rient	*they laugh* (ladies)
Obj.	leur *m.*	*for* à eux	*to them*	payez-*leur* ce que vous *leur* devez	*pay* them *what you owe to* them, (to men)
	leur *f.*	*for* à elles	*to them*	dites-*leur* que je désire *leur* parler	*tell* them *that I wish to speak* to them (to ladies)
	les *m.*	*for* eux	*them*	vous *les* trouverez	*you will find* them (men)
	les *f.*	*for* elles	*them*	il *les* admire	*he admires* them (ladies)
	eux *m.*		*them*	je ne vois qu'*eux*	*I see but* them (gentlemen)
				allez sans eux	go without them
	elles *f.*		*them*	il ne connaît qu'*elles*	*he knows but* them (ladies)
				partez sans elles	go without them

Il, ils, le, les masculine, *elle, elles, le, les* feminine are used in speaking of things as well as of persons; but *de lui, d'elle, d'eux, d'elles, lui, leur* are not. See *Y, en.* *No.* 64, 65.

62. When the verb is interrogative, the pronoun, which is its subject, is always put after it; the interrogative *do*, used in English, has no equivalent in French, and is consequently not expressed.

Singular.

Subject	je	*I*	dois-*je* payer?	*must* I *pay?*
	tu	*thou*	as-*tu* dit?	*hast* thou *said?*
	il	*he*	chante-t-*il* bien?	*does* he sing *well?*
	elle	*she*	travaille-t-*elle*?	*does* she *work?*

Plural.

Subject	nous	*we*	irons-*nous*?	*shall we go?*
	vous	*you*	viendrez-*vous*?	*will you come?*
	ils *m.*	*they*	chantent-*ils*?	*do they sing?*
	elles *f.*	*they*	travaillent-*elles*?	*do they work?*

EXERCISE.

He loved *them* because *they* were gentle, attentive, and grateful.
aimait m. *parce que* *doux* = *reconnaissant*

He (was saying) (to *them*,) do you not know that the nature
disait * 3 1-4 *savez* 2 *que* *propre* m.

merit is to excite envy? *She* often exhorted me
art. *mérite* m. *de exciter* art. *envie* f. *souvent* 2 *exhortait* 1

the study the most useful, that of the human heart. *They* make
étude f. *utile* *celle* 2 m.1 *font*

love virtue, more by their examples than by their words,
aimer art. f. *par* *leur* *exemple* *parole* f. pl.

What has been said of *them?* Did they speak of *them?*
Que 1 *on* 3 *a-t-*2 * *dit* *eux* * *on* 2 *parlait* 1 *elle*

Do you not see *her?* With what pleasure she plays! Look at
* 4 1-5 *voyez* 3 2 *quel* *joue* *Regardez*

that magnificent building, it unites gracefulness to beauty.
ce *magnifique* *bâtiment* m. *réunit* art. *grâce* f. art. *beauté* f.

Ignorance is vain, it sees difficulties in nothing. Do not judge
art. ——f. *vain* *ne voit de* = *à* *rien* *ne jugez pas*

from appearances, they are deceitful. Take one of these
sur art. *apparences* f. *trompeur* *Prenez* *ces*

roses, they smell so sweet.
——f. *sentent* *si* *bon.*

63. REFLECTED AND RECIPROCAL PRONOUNS OF THE THIRD PERSON.

	Singular.			*Examples.*
Object.	soi	with a *preposition*	chacun tire *à soi*	*every one draws* to himself
	soi	governed by the *verb*	l'égoïsme fait qu'on ne voit que *soi*	*selfishness makes a person see none but* himself
Object.	se	for *à soi, à lui-même*	il *se* donne des louanges	*he gives* himself *praises*
	se	.. *à elle-même*	elle *se* fait illusion	*she imposes* on herself.
	se	.. *soi,* or *lui-même*	il *se* perd	*he ruins* himself
	se	.. *soi,* or *elle-même*	elle *se* flatte	*she flatters* herself

	Plural.			Examples.
Object.	se	for à eux-mêmes	ils s'attribuent la la gloire, etc.	they attribute to themselves the glory of, etc.
	se	.. à elles-mêmes	elles se prescrivent pour règle de etc.	they prescribe to themselves as rule to, etc.
	se	.. l'un à l'autre	ils s'entredonnent, ou se font des cadeaux	they exchange gifts
	se	.. eux-mêmes	ils se sont déshonorés	they have disgraced themselves
	se	.. elles-mêmes	elles se sont flattées	they have flattered themselves
	se	.. l'un l'autre	ils s'entr'aident	they help one another
	se	.. les uns les autres	les rats, dit-on, s'entre-dévorent	rats, it is said, eat one another

REMARK. *Se* is placed before a verb, and *soi* after a preposition.

EXERCISE.

In a thousand instances, we do not watch sufficiently over *ourselves*.
* *mille* *occasion* f. *on* * *veille* *assez* *sur* *soi*

The glory of the world (passes away) in an instant. He gives
=f. *monde* m. *s'évanouit* *en* ——m. *donne*

himself (a great deal) of trouble. She tires *herself*. People should
se *beaucoup* *peine* f. *lasse* *se* *On* *doit*

(very seldom) speak of *themselves*. Virtue is amiable in *itself*. We
rarement *parler* *soi* art. f. *de soi*. *On*

must take upon *ourselves* the care of our own affairs.
doit prendre sur *soi* *soin* m. *ses propre affaire* f.pl.

OF THE PERSONAL AND RELATIVE *EN*.

64. This pronoun is personal when it means *of him*, *of her*, *of them*, *of it*, *of them*, and may be called the genitive case of *je*, *nous*, *tu*, *vous*, *il*, *elle*, *ils*, *elles*. It is relative when it is used in reference to an object or

place antecedently named, and signifies *out of it*, *out of them*, *some of it*, *some of them*, and *from that place*, or *thence.*

As a personal pronoun, it may be used in speaking of persons, although its chief use is about things; but, as a relative pronoun, its use is confined to things and places.

EXAMPLES.

EN *for*	de lui *of him*	cet homme vous plaît, vous *en* parlez souvent	*that man pleases you, you speak* of him *often*
	d'elle *of her*	je ne crois pas cette femme sincère, je m'*en* méfie	*I do not believe that woman sincere, I distrust her*
	" *of it*, m.	lisez son poème, et dites-moi ce que vous *en* pensez	*read his poem, and tell me what you think of it*
	" *of it*, f.	sa conduite est mauvaise, je m'*en* plaindrai	*his conduct is bad; I will complain of it*
	" *of them* m.	quant à ces événements nous *en* parlons souvent	*as for these events, we often mention them*
	" *of them* f.	que dites-vous de ces gravures, *en* êtes-vous content?	*what do you think of these plates, are you pleased with them?*
	" *some of them*	ces fruits paraissent bons, j'*en* mangerais volontiers	*these fruits look good, I should like to eat* some of them
	" *some of them*	voilà de belles oranges, voulez-vous m'*en* donner?	*these are beautiful oranges, will you give me some?*
	de cela *of that*	on ne m'a pas trompé, j'*en* suis sûr	*I have not been imposed upon, I am sure of it*
	d'ici *hence*	il arriva à Paris, comme j'*en* partais	*he arrived at Paris as I was setting off*
	de là *thence*	vous allez à Paris, et monsieur *en* vient	*you are going to Paris, this gentleman comes* from thence

OF THE PERSONAL AND RELATIVE PRONOUN *Y.*

65. The use of *y*, as a pronoun, is strictly confined to things. It is employed in all those cases in which the objective case is marked by the preposition *à*. Speaking of persons, we say: *je pense à votre frère, je donne mes soins à votre frère*; and, when not naming the person, we say: *je pense à lui, je lui donne mes soins*; thus, speaking of things, we must say: *je pense à votre affaire, je donne mes soins à votre affaire*, and, speaking relatively, *j'y pense, j'y donne mes soins.*

Y is also used in reference to a place antecedently named, and when *here, there* are understood in English.

EXAMPLES.

for	à lui à elle	*to him* *to her*	c'est un honnête homme, fiez-vous *y* *	*he is an honest man, trust* to him *
	,,	*to it*, m.	la poussière gâtera ce tableau, si on n'y met pas un verre	*the dust will spoil this picture, if you don't put a glass to it*
	,,	*to it*, f.	si votre lettre est finie, mettez-y l'adresse	*if you have finished your letter, put the direction to it*
	,,	*to them*, f.	ce sont de belles promesses, mais je ne m'y fie pas	*these are fine promises, but I do not trust to them*
	,,	*to them* m.	donnez-moi vos ordres, et j'y obéirai ponctuellement	*give me your commands, and I will punctually obey them*
	,,	*in them*	ces arguments sont pressants, je n'*y* vois point de réplique	*these arguments are cogent, I see no reply to them*
	à *cela*	*to it*	allons, n'en parlons plus, il ne faut plus y penser	*come, say no more, we must not think about it any longer*
	ici	*here*	nous partons de Londres, quand vous *y* venez	*we set off from London, when you come* hither
	là	*there*	c'est un endroit charmant, je compte m'y fixer	*it is a fine place, I intend to settle* there

REMARK. *Y* and *en* are always put before the verb, except with the imperative affirmative second person.

EXERCISE.

They speak (a great deal) *of it*. You like French authors,
On parle beaucoup *aimez* art. *français* 2 *auteur* 1

you are always speaking *of them*. That is a delicate affair; the
* 2 *parlez* 1 *Ce* *délicat* 2 =f. 1.

success of it is doubtful. See them; I consent *to it*, but do
succès m. *douteux* *Voyez* *consens* 2 1 *

not trust *them*. That is a fine appointment: he had
1-5 *vous* 2 *fiez* 4 *y* 3 *Ce* *place* f. *

long aspired *to it*. He has done it; but he
depuis long-temps —*rait* 2 1 *a* *fait* *ne* 1

will get nothing *by it*.
gagnera 3 *rien* 4 *y* 2

§ II.

OF POSSESSIVE PRONOUNS.

66. These pronouns denote the possession of things. When we say, *mon habit*, my coat; *votre maison*, your house; *son jardin*, his, or her garden; it is the same, as saying *l'habit qui est à moi*, the coat which belongs to me; *la maison qui est à vous*, the house which belongs to you; *le jardin qui est à lui*, or *à elle*, the garden which belongs to him, or to her.

67. These pronouns are of two sorts, the *conjunctive*, which are always joined to a noun, which they precede, *mon livre*, my book; and the *relative*, which are used in reference to a noun, as *le mien*, mine.

By some, these pronouns have also been called adjectives, because they agree in gender and number with the noun. *Mon frère*, my brother; *ma sœur*, my sister.

POSSESSIVE PRONOUNS CONJUNCTIVE RELATING TO ONE PERSON.

		Singular		Plural		
for the	*1st person*	mon, *m.*	ma, *f.*	mes, *m f.*	*my*
	2nd ——	ton, *m.*	ta, *f.*	tes, *m. f.*	*thy*
	3rd ——	son, *m.*	sa, *f.*	ses, *m. f.*	*his, her, its*

POSSESSIVE PRONOUNS CONJUNCTIVE RELATING TO MANY PERSONS.

		Singular	Plural	
for the	*1st person*	notre, *m. f.*	nos, *m. f.*	*our*
	2nd ——	votre, *m. f.*	vos, *m. f.*	*your*
	3rd ——	leur, *m f.*	leurs, *m. f.*	*their*

EXAMPLES.

Mon père, ma mère et mes frères sont à la campagne, avec vos amis et leurs enfants.	*My father, mother, and brother are in the country, with your friends and their children.*
Mon cousin est allé consoler sa sœur, qui a perdu son fils.*	*My cousin is gone to visit and console his sister, who has lost her son.*

68. *Mon, ton, son,* are used before a noun feminine, when beginning with a vowel, or *h* mute, *mon âme,* my soul; *ton humeur,* thy humour; *son amitié,* his friendship, in order to avoid the meeting of the two vowels, or hyatus, *ma âme, ta humeur, sa amitié.*

EXERCISE.

My principles, *my* love, of retirement, *my* taste
——*pe* *goût* m. *pour* art. *retraite* f. *amour* m.
for (every thing) that (is connected) with learning, and
tout *ce qui* *tient* *à* art. *instruction,*
my detestation of all spirit of party, (every thing) has
haine f. *h.* asp. *pour* *esprit* *parti* *tout* *a* 2
induced me to prefer a life passed in the closet, to the
porté 3 1 *préférer* * art. *vie* f. * *de* * *cabinet*

* Observe that the pronoun does not agree with the possessor as in English, thus, *his father, her father* are both rendered by *son père*, and *his mother, her mother*, by *sa mère*, no regard being paid to *his* or *hers*, but to the gender of *father* and *mother*.

active life of the world. Do not think, *my* daughter, that *thy*
— 2 f. 1 m. * *pense* *que*

candour, *thy* ingenuousness, *thy* taste, so delicate and so
= f. *ingénuité* f. *goût*, m. *délical*

refined, and even *thy* graces, can shelter thee from
fin *même* — *puissent* *mettre à l'abri* *de*

censure. *His* wit, *his* talents, *his* honesty, and
art. — f. *esprit* m. — m. *honnêteté* f. *h.* m.

even *his* (good nature) make him beloved by every body.
même *bonhomie* f. *font* *aimer* *de* *tout* *le monde*

Our constancy and *our* efforts will (at last) surmount all
— f. — m. * *enfin* 2 *surmonteront* 1

obstacles. I see nothing that can (be censured)
art. — m. pl. *vois* 2 *ne* 1 *rien* 3 *que on puisse* *reprendre*

in *your* conduct. *Their* taste for the fantastical, the mon-
dans *conduite* f. *pour* *bizarre*, m. *mon-*

strous, and the marvellous gives to all *their* compositions
strueux, m. *merveilleux* m. *donne* —— f.

although very fine in themselves, an air of deformity, which
quoique *en elles-mêmes* — m. *difformité* f. *qui*

shocks at first sight.
choque *à* art. *coup-d'œil*, m.

69. POSSESSIVE PRONOUNS RELATIVE, REFERRING TO ONE PERSON.

	m. Sing.	*f. Sing.*	*m. Plur.*	*f. Plur.*	
1st.	Le mien,	la mienne,	Les miens,	les miennes,	*mine*
2nd.	Le tien,	la tienne,	Les tiens,	les tiennes,	*thine*
3rd.	Le sien,	la sienne,	Les siens,	les siennes,	*his, her, its*

POSSESSIVE PRONOUNS RELATIVE, REFERRING TO SEVERAL PERSONS.

	m. Sing.	*f. Sing.*	*Pl. of both Gen.*	
1st.	Le nôtre,	la nôtre,	Les nôtres,	*ours*
2nd.	Le vôtre,	la vôtre,	Les vôtres,	*yours*
3rd.	Le leur,	la leur,	Les leurs,	*theirs*

The use of these pronouns is to avoid the repetition of a noun antecedently named.

EXAMPLE.

Avez-vous toujours votre cheval? je n'ai plus le mien; *for* je n'ai plus mon cheval

Have you still your horse? I have no longer mine.

EXERCISE.

Is it your temper or *hers*, that hinders you from living well
ce *humeur* f. *qui empêche* 2 1 *de vivre*

together? If it be *yours*, it is easy for you to remedy it
ensemble *ce est* *il* 2 *aisé* 3 * 1 *d'y porter remède*

by mastering (your temper); if it be *hers*, redouble your
en prenant sur vous-même; *ce* *redoublez de* *

kindness, attention, and good behaviour; it is
complaisance de — *de* *procédé* m. pl. *il*

very seldom that this method (proves unsuccessful). If my
très-rare *ce* *moyen* *ne réussisse pas* *Si*

friends had served me with the same zeal as *yours*, it
avaient 2 *servi* 3 1 *même zèle* m. *que*

is very certain that I (should have) succeeded: but *yours* have
très *sûr* *aurais* *réussi* *ont*

been all warmth, and *mine* all ice. All the pictures which we
été *de feu* *de glace* *tableau* m. *que*

expected from Rome are arrived: there are some that are a
attendions *arrivés* *il y en a qui*

little damaged; but *yours, his,* and *mine,* are in good
peu *endommagés* *en*

condition. We know perfectly well what are your
état m. *savons* *parfaitement* * *quels*

amusements in town, and I assure you we are very
— *à* art. *ville* f. — 2 1 *que* *sommes bien*

far from envying you them; but if you knew
éloigné pl. *envier* 3 1 2 *connaissez quels*

ours in the country, it (is most likely) you
sont *à* *campagne* f. *il y a toute apparence que*

(would not be long) in giving them the preference. You
ne tarderiez pas *à* *donner* 2 *leur* 1 *préférence* f.

have opened your heart to me with that noble frankness.
avez 2 *ouvert* 3 1 — *franchise* f.

which so well becomes an honest man: this confidence well
qui si 2 3 *sied* 1 *à* *honnête* *confiance* f. 2
deserves *mine.*
mérite 1.

Remark. When through politeness *vous* is used for *tu*, then *votre, vos*, are used instead of *ton, ta, tes*, and *le vôtre, la vôtre, les vôtres*, for *le tien, la tienne, les tiens, les tiennes.*

EXAMPLES.

Que vous ressemblez peu à vos ancêtres?	*How little you resemble your ancestors.*
Quand vous aurez entendu nos raisons, nous écouterons les vôtres.	*When you have heard our reasons, we will listen to yours.*

§ III.

70. OF DEMONSTRATIVE PRONOUNS.

The demonstrative pronouns serve to designate and point out objects. They are of two sorts, the *conjunctive*, which are always placed before the noun, and the *relative*, which are used in reference to a noun antecedently named. Both agree in gender and number with the noun.

CONJUNCTIVE DEMONSTRATIVE PRONOUNS.

71. The demonstrative relative pronouns are in the singular.

Ce masc. before a consonant or an *h* aspirate.
Cet, masc. before a vowel or an *h* mute.
Cette, fem. in all cases.

MASCULINE SINGULAR.

Ce livre, *this* or *that book*	Cet homme, *this or that man*
Ce héros, *this or that hero*	Cet enfant, *this or that child*

FEMININE SINGULAR.

cette fille,	*this or that girl*
cette âme,	*this or that soul*
cette histoire,	*this or that story*
cette haine,	*that hatred*

The plural of *ce*, *cet*, *cette* is *ces*. It is common to both genders, and is used before vowels and consonants.

ces livres, *these or those books*	ces hommes, *these men*
de ces héros, *of these or those heroes*	ces enfants, *those children*
à ces filles, *to these or those girls*	ces histoires, *these stories*

Ci and *là* are often added to the noun, either to point it out more distinctly or speak of it more emphatically.

Cet homme-là, *that man.*	Ces poires-ci sont bonnes, *these pears are good.*

RELATIVE DEMONSTRATIVE PRONOUNS.

72. The relative demonstrative agree also in gender with the noun, and are

MASCULINE SINGULAR AND PLURAL.

Celui-ci, *this*	Celui-là, *that*
Ceux-ci, *these*	Ceux-là, *those*

FEMININE SINGULAR AND PLURAL.

Celle-ci, *this*	Celle-là, *that*
Celles-ci, *these*	Celles-là, *those*

Celui, *celle*, *ceux*, *celles*, are used without *ci*, *là*, before a preposition and a relative pronoun.

J'aime mieux mon jardin que celui de mon frère.	*I like my garden better than my brother's.*
On ne peut les comparer à ceux que nous avons vus à Paris.	*They are not to be compared with those we saw at Paris.*
Je le donnerai à celui qui arrivera le premier.	*I will give it to him who comes in first.*

73. *Ceci*, this; *cela*, that; are, as it were, of the neuter gender, and are used to express *this thing, that thing*, when the object is not named.

Je n'aime pas cela.	*I do not like that.*
Ceci n'est pas pour vous.	*This is not for you.*

CE QUI, CE DONT, &c. FOR WHAT.

74. *Ce* is much used in conjunction with the relative pronoun.

Ce qui me plaît	*That which (or what) pleases me.*
Ce dont je parle	*What I speak of (or that of which I speak.)*
Ce à quoi je m'applique	*What I apply to, (or that thing to which I apply.)*
Ce que je dis	*What I say (or that thing which I say)*
Ce dont je dépends	*What I depend upon (that thing upon which I depend.)*

Observe that the pronoun *what* is commonly used in English as if a contraction of *that which*, and is, accordingly, always expressed by two words in French, a demonstrative and a relative pronoun.

75. *CE* IN EXPLANATORY SENTENCES.

Ce is also much used in French, as the nominative or subject of *être*, in descriptive sentences, that is, when we name the nature, object of a thing, and even a person.

C'est une tabatière,	*It is a snuff-box.*
C'est un officier général,	*He is an officer general.*
Ce sont de bons enfants,	*They are good children.*

See *Syntax. Demonstrative Pronouns.*

EXERCISE.

Nothing is so opposite to *that* true eloquence, the office
ne 2 *rien* 1 *opposé* *véritable* — f. *fonc-*

(of which) is to ennoble (every thing), as the use of
tion f. 2 1 *de* 1 *ennoblir* 3 *tout* 2 * *que* *emploi* m.

those refined thoughts, and hunting after *those* light,
fin 2 *pensée* f. 1. art. *recherche* f. *de* *léger* 2

airy, unsolid ideas, which, like a leaf of
délié 3 *sans consistance* 4 *idée* f. 1. *qui* *comme* *feuille* f.

beaten metal, acquire brightness only by losing
battu 2 — m. 1. *ne prennent* *de* art. *éclat* m. *que* *en* *perdant*

part of their solidity. *This* man has nothing in common
* * art. = f. *h* m. *de* *commun*

with *that* hero. *This* long restrained hatred broke,
h asp. 1 *long-temps* 3 *contenu* 4 *haine*, f. 2. *éclata*

and was the unhappy source of *those* dreadful events.
fut *malheureux* — f. *terrible* *événe-*

It is a great pleasure to me. *It* was a great
ment m. pl. *Ce* *plaisir* m. * *fut*

pain to us. The pleasures of the wise resemble in
déplaisir m. * *nous.* *ressemblent* 2-3

nothing *those* of a dissipated man. *He that* suffers himself to (be
1 4 *à* *dissipé* 2 1. *se laisse* *

ruled) by his passions, must renounce happiness.
dominer *doit* *renoncer à* art. m.

This stuff (will suit) you admirably. I desire you
étoffe-ci f. *siéra* 2 1 *à merveille* *que*

to take *this*. *That* action is blameable. *This*
preniez m. *-là* *digne de blâme*

scene is calculated to interest all men, but *that* cannot
-ci *faite* *pour* *intéresser* art. *-là* *ne saurait*

succeed. (Here are) certainly two charming prospects, *this*
réussir. *Voilà* *certainement* *beau* *perspective* f. pl.

has something (in it) more cheerful, but many people
quelque chose de * *riant* *bien de* art. *personne* f. pl.

that more striking and more majes-
troment à quelque chose de imposant de majes-

tic. The body perishes, the soul is immortal: yet all
tueux. périt cependant

the cares are for *that*, while we neglect *this*. What
m. tandisque négligeons f

means *this?* *That* is true. It is not *that*. *This* is low and
veut dire Ce bas

mean, but *that* is grand and sublime.
rampant

OF THE RELATIVE PRONOUNS.

76. *Relative pronouns* are those which relate to a noun preceding, called the *antecedent*. In the phrase *l'homme qui joue*, the man who plays, *qui* relates to the substantive *homme; l'homme* is then the *antecedent* of the pronoun relative *qui*.

Relative pronouns are used as follows according as they refer to persons and things:*

qui, common to persons and things	who	Dieu *qui* voit tout	*God* who *sees every thing*
	which	les chevaux *qui* courent	*the horses* which *are running*
de qui, said of persons only; *dont*, common to persons and things, *d'où*	of whom, *or* from whom	l'homme *dont* or *de qui* vous parlez	*the man of whom you speak*
		les femmes *dont*, or *de qui* il se moque	*the women whom he laughs at*
	of which, *or* from which	le livre *dont* vous parlez	*the book of which you speak*
		les livres *dont* vous parlez	*the books of which you speak*
		la maison *d'où* (de laquelle) il est sorti	*the house out of which he came*
	whose	le marchand *dont* le magasin est brûlé	*the merchant whose warehouse is burnt*
		les enfants *dont* il a placé le père	*the children whose he placed the father*
à qui, said of persons only	to whom	l'homme *à qui* vous vous adressez	*the man to whom you apply*

*Much attention must be paid to the distinction between persons and things as the use of some of the pronouns is common, and the use of others is restricted to persons

auquel, à laquelle, auxquels, auxquelles common, but especially applied to things, *où*	to which	l'affaire *à laquelle* vous mettez tant d'intérêt	*the business in which you are so interested*
		les dépenses *auxquelles* vous êtes obligé	*the expences to which you are obliged*
		le but *où* (auquel) vous tendez	*the thing at which you aim*
que, common to persons and things	whom	l'homme *que* vous cherchez	*the man* whom *you seek*
	which	les lois *que* nous observons	*the laws* which *we observe*

RELATIVE PRONOUNS WITH PREPOSITIONS.

qui referring to persons	pour qui est cette lettre?	*for whom is this letter?*
	avec qui irez-vous à Paris?	*with whom do you go to Paris?*
lequel, laquelle, lesquels, lesquelles, common, but chiefly said of things of which the gender is known	ce sont de ces choses avec *lesquelles* il ne faut pas badiner	*these are things with which you must not trifle*
	c'est bien là la maison dans *laquelle* il est entré	*this is indeed the house which he went in*
quoi, said of things not named, of which the gender has not been expressed	*pourquoi* faites-vous cela	*what do you do that for? (for what reason?)*
	de quoi parlez-vous?	*what are you speaking of?*
	avec quoi fait-on de l'encre?	*what is ink made of?*

Qui, que, and *dont,* are of both genders and both numbers.

Lequel is a compound of *quel* and of the article *le, la, les,* with which it is joined, and forms but one word.

Singular.		*Plural.*		
lequel	laquelle	lesquels	lesquelles	*which*
duquel	de laquelle	desquels	desquelles	*of which*
auquel	à laquelle	auxquels	auxquelles	*to which*

This pronoun always agrees in gender and number with its antecedent.

Quoi is always governed by a preposition.

77. *Qui*, relative, is common to persons and things

and is of both genders and numbers; the verb which follows it, and adjective which refer to it, must be of the same number and gender as the antecedent.*

EXAMPLES:

Moi qui suis son fils	I who am his son.
Mon frère qui est si bon	My brother who is so kind.
L'enfant qui joue	The child who plays.
Les enfants qui étudient	The children who study.
Vous qui riez	You who laugh.
Les livres qui instruisent	The books which instruct.

In the first example, the verb is in the first person singular, to agree with *moi*, and, in the second, *bon* is masculine singular, to agree with *frère*.

78. *Dont*, whose, of whom, of which, from whom, from which, is common to persons and things, and *duquel*, *de laquelle*, *desquels*, *desquelles* have the same meaning, but are used only when the object is particularly pointed out, or distinguished from others of the same nature.

EXAMPLES:

La tour dont nous apercevons les créneaux doit être très-élevée.	*The tower whose battlements we perceive must be very high.*
Ce dont je vous ai parlé l'autre jour n'a pas réussi.	*What I was speaking to you of the other day did not succeed.*
C'est une démarche de laquelle tout dépend.	*It is a step on which every thing depends.*

79. *A qui*, of both genders and numbers, (to whom, to which,) is never used in reference to things, but *auquel*, *à laquelle*, *auxquels*, *auxquelles*, which agree in gender and number with the antecedent.

EXAMPLES.

L'homme à qui vous avez écrit, n'a pas repondu.	*The man to whom you wrote, did not answer.*
Sont-ce là les choses auxquelles vous pensez?	*Are those the things you think of?*

* The relative pronoun is so important a part of a sentence, its use in French so different from what it is in English, that it has been thought better to anticipate a little, and to place here at once rules which properly belong to the syntax, but which it is quite necessary the learner should understand whilst he is doing the exercises which precede that part of the grammar, which belongs to the relative pronoun according to the usual order.

EXERCISE.

I who did not suspect (so much) falsehood, cunning,
* *soupçonnais tant de fausseté* f. pr. *ruse* f.

and perfidy, in a man whom I loved blindly, followed
pr. = *j'aimais aveuglément, je suivis*

his counsels. Thou, *who* art candour and innocence itself,
conseil m. *es* art. = f. art. = f. *même*

trust not too lightly. The great empire of the Egyptians
te confie légèrement. — m. ——*tien*

which was, (as if) detached from all others, was
fut comme détaché art. *fut*

not of long duration. We *who* know the value of time
durée f. *connaissons prix* m. art.

ought to make a good use (of it), instead of wasting
nous devons * *emploi* m. *en au lieu perdre*

it in idleness and frivolity. What! is it you, my
dans art. *oisiveté* f. art. *inutilité* f. *Quoi ce*

daughter, *who* (would wish) that I (should love) you less? The
voudriez que aimasse

greatest men, *who* were the ornament and glory of Greece,
étaient ornement art. = f. art. *Grèce* f.

Homer, Pythagoras, Plato, even Lycurgus and Solon, went
Homère, ——*gore Platon, même* —*gue.* —— *allèrent*

to learn wisdom in Egypt. Is this the man whose house
* *apprendre* art. *sagesse* f. *en Egypte. Est-ce là*

was burnt down last week. I know the books of which
a été brûlée * 2 art. *semaine* f. 1 *connais*

you (are speaking). It is a project to which he has devoted
parlez —*jet* m. *a consacre*

much time. Who is the lady to whom you (paid a visit) this
bien du avez fait visite ce

morning? Come in the (drawing room) I will show you the
matin Venez salon m. *montrerai*

table on which he (was writing).
à écrivait.

80. *Que* is also common to persons and things, and is of both genders and numbers.

EXAMPLES.

c'est moi que l'on demande,	*it is I whom they ask for*
c'est toi que l'on appelle,	*it is thou whom they cal*

la femme que je vois si bien parée,	*the woman whom I see so well dressed*
c'est nous que vous offensez,	*it is we whom you offend*
c'est vous que je cherche,	*it is you I am seeking*
les dames que vous voyez	*the ladies whom you see*

EXERCISE.

I whom temptation surrounded on very side fell
art. *séduction* f. *environnait* *de* *tout part* f. pl. *je tombai*

into the snare. It is you *whom* the public voice calls to that
dans *piége* m. *Ce* 2 f. 1. *appelle*

office. A power, *which* terror and force have founded,
place f. *puissance* f. art. = f. art. —f. *fondé*, f.

cannot be of long duration. It is we *whom* they persecute with
ne peut *durée* f. *l'on* *poursuit* *avec*

unexampled rage. You *whom* every body respects,
une *sans example* 2 *fureur* f. 1. *tout* *le monde* *respecte*

hasten to (show yourself). (Every thing) in the universe
hâtez-vous *de* *paraître* *Tout* *dans* *univers* m.

alters and perishes; but the writings *which* genius has
s'altère *périt* *écrit* m. pl. art. *génie* m.

dictated, shall be immortal.
dicté m. pl. *seront* ——*tel.*

81. *D'où* is very often used for *duquel, de laquelle, desquels, desquelles*; and *où* for *auquel, à laquelle, auxquels, auxquelles.*

EXAMPLES.

Voilà le but, où (auquel) il tend	*That is the object he has in view.*
Ce sont des affaires, où (auxquelles) je suis embarrassé	*Those are affairs with which I am perplexed.*
Voilà une chose d'où (de laquelle) dépend le bonheur public	*That is an affair on which the public happiness depends.*
Tels sont les lieux par où (par lesquels) il a passé	*These are the places through which he passed.*

82. *Lequel, laquelle, lesquels, lesquelles,* are generally used after prepositions, and also in the sense of *which,* when it is necessary to distinguish between objects of the same nature.

EXAMPLES.

Sont-ce là les personnes avec lesquelles il passe son temps?	*Are those the people with whom he spends his time.*

12*

Ce sont de ces moments dans lesquels on oublie tous ses chagrins.	*These are the moments in which a man forgets all his sorrows.*
C'est une de ces dames, mais je ne sais laquelle	*It is one of these ladies, but I do not know which.*

83. *Quoi* comes after prepositions, and is used in speaking of things of which the gender is not ascertained; it is generally used to express *what, what thing, which thing.*

EXAMPLE

Dites-moi en quoi je puis vous être utile	*Tell me in what thing I can be of use to you.*
De quoi a-t-il été question ?	*What has been the matter?*
On dansa jusqu'à minuit, après quoi il y eut un souper superbe.	*They danced until twelve, after which there was a beautiful supper.*

EXERCISE.

The protection on *which* he relied has been too weak
—f. *sur* *comptait* *faible*

That after *which* a true philosopher sighs most ardently
Ce après *vrai* —*phe* m. *soupire* art. *ardemment*

is to spread that sentiment of universal benevolence which
de répandre — m. —*sel* 2 *bienveillance* f. 1

should unite and (bring together) all men. These are con-
devrait unir *rapprocher* art. *Ce sont de* art.

ditions without *which* the thing (would not have been) concluded.
sans f. *n'aurait pas été* *fait* f.

Nature, of *whose* secrets we (are ignorant) (will
art. — f. * 1 art. — m. pl. 4 2 *ignorons* 2 *sera*

always be) a source of conjecture to mankind. What does
toujours — f. 3 — f. pl. 4 *pour* 1 art. *homme* 2 *

he complain of so bitterly? The only moments, *in which* his
se plaint *amèrement* *seul* — pl.

soul is yet opened to pleasure, are those which he devotes
s'ouvre encore art. *ceux* *consacrer*

to study. The mountains *from whence* gold (is
art. f. pl. *on* 1 art. *or* 3

extracted), are not in general barren. The different countries
tire 2 * *en* — *infertile* pl. — *pays* m. pl.

through *which* he has passed have furnished his pencil with
par *a passé* *ont* *fourni* *à* *pinceau* m. *de*
romantic and picturesque scenes.
art. — *tique* 2 *pittoresque* 3 — 1.

84. OF THE PRONOUN ABSOLUTE *QUI*, AND OTHER PRONOUNS USED IN QUESTIONS.

Who and *whom* are rendered by *qui*, in questions.

EXAMPLES.

Qui vous a dit cela?	*Who told you that?*
Qui voulez-vous inviter?	*Whom do you wish to invite?*
Savez-vous qui l'a dit?	*Do you know who said so?*

What (or what thing) is rendered by *que*.

EXAMPLES.

Que voulez-vous dire?	*What do you mean?*
Que fait-il en haut?	*What is he doing up stairs?*

Quoi must be used after prepositions, and also with adjectives.

EXAMPLES.

À quoi pensez-vous?	*What are you thinking of?*
Quoi de plus beau?	*What can be finer?*

What, *which*, joined to a noun, is rendered by *quel*, *quelle*, *quels*, *quelles*.

EXAMPLES.

Quel habit mettrez-vous?	*What coat shall you put on?*
On ne sait quelle route il a pris.	*No one knows which road he has taken.*
Quel homme est-ce?	*What sort of a man is he?*

What and *which*, used relatively, are rendered by *lequel*, *laquelle*, *lesquels*, *lesquelles*.

EXAMPLES.

Voilà deux habits; lequel mettrez-vous?	*There are two coats, which will you put on?*
Avec laquelle de ces dames voulez-vous danser?	*With which of those ladies do you wish to dance?*

EXERCISES.

Who (will not agree) that life has few real pleasures and
ne conviendra pas art. f. *peu de vrai plaisir*, m.

many dreadful pains? (Some one) entered
beaucoup de affreux 2 *peine* f. pl. 1. *On entra*

secretly; guess *who* it was. *What* have you read in that book
secrètement, *devinez* * * *lu* m.

that can have excited in your soul emotion and enthu-
qui puisse avoir porté art. — f. art. *enthou-*

siasm? I know not *what* to think (of it). About *what* did you
siasme m. *ne sais penser* 2 *en* 1 *à avez-vous*

find them occupied? (There is) in that discourse I know
trouvés occupé m. pl. *Il y a discours* m. *sais* 2

not *what* which appears to me designing. *What* have you
ne 1 *sembler* * *insidieux*

remarked good, beautiful and sublime in Homer? *What*
remarqué de pr. pr.

more brilliant, and, at the same time, more false, than the
pr. *brillant en* * *même* pr.

expressions of a man, who has (a great deal) of wit; but
—— *beaucoup esprit qui*

wants judgment? *What* grace, *what* delicacy, *what* har-
manque de jugement? grâce f. *délicatesse* f.

mony, *what* colouring, *what* beautiful lines in Racine! *What*
= f. *coloris* m. *vers* m. — 1

then must have been that extraordinary man, to whom seven
donc 3 *doit* 2 *avoir été* = 2 —

cities contested the glory of having given birth? He
se sont disputé = f. *avoir donné* art. *jour* m.

(does not know) what model to follow. I have told you *what* man
ne sait pas modèle m. * *suivre ai dit*

it is. *Which* of those ladies do you think the most amiable?
ce f. *dames* f. * ? *trouvez* 1 f.

Choose *which* of those two pictures you like best.
Choisissez m. 4 5 6 *tableau* m. 7 1 *aimez* 2 art. *mieux* 3

§ VI.

OF INDEFINITE PRONOUNS.

85. *Indefinite pronouns* are those which have a vague and indefinite signification, and which have reference to persons and things in general, without particularizing.

They are of four sorts.

FIRST CLASS.

86. Those that are never joined to a substantive.

ON*	one	on aime à se flatter	one *is apt to flatter ones self*
	a man	*on* n'est pas toujours maître de soi	*a man cannot always command his own temper*
	a woman	*on* n'est pas toujours maîtresse d'aller où* *l'on* veut	*a woman cannot always go where she pleases*
	somebody	*on* frappe à la porte	somebody *knocks at the door*
	people	*on* pense et* *l'on dit* tout haut	people *think and say openly*
	they	*on* raconte diversement cette histoire	they *relate that story differently*
	we	*on* acquiert l'expérience à ses dépens	we *acquire experience at our own expense*
	you	*on* trouve partout de importuns	you *will find troublesome people every where*
	I	*on* prévient qu'on n'a point eu l'intention de, etc.	I *beg to observe, that* I *had no intention to,* etc.
	I	quand *on* vous dit que† l'*on* compte sur vous	*when* I *tell you that* I *depend upon you*
	they	si † l'*on* vous blâme et si † on le loue, *on* a tort	*if* they *blame you, and praise him,* they *are wrong.*

* *On* is an abbreviation or a contraction of *homme*, which in old French was spelt *hom*. No doubt but that formerly it was usual to say, when speaking in a vague sense, *homme dit*, *homme étudie*, from which mode of expression *on* has been derived.

† Instead of *et on*, *ou on*, *si on*, it is better for euphony, to part these words with an *l'*, thus: *et l'on*, *ou l'on*, *si l'on*, when the next word does not begin with an *l*, as seen by the examples; and instead of *les habitudes* qu'on *contracte*, *ce après quoi* on *court*, *quoiqu'*on *croie*, *un homme à qui* on *reproche*, say rather: *les habitudes que* l'on *contracte*, *ce après quoi* l'on *court*, *bien que* l'on *croie*, *un homme à qui* l'on *reproche*.

quelqu'un	*one* *somebody* *some one*	quelqu'un m'a dit, *somebody to'd me.*
quiconque	*whoever* *whosoever*	qui connaît les hommes, apprend à s'en défier, *whoever knows mankind, learns to distrust them.*
chacun	*each* *every one*	chacun s'en plaint, *every one complains of him.*
autrui	*other people* *others*	n'enviez pas le bien d'autrui, *do not covet the property of others* ne faites pas à autrui ce que vous ne voudriez pas que l'on vous fît, *do not do to others what you would not have done to you*
personne	*nobody* *no one*	la fierté ne convient à personne, *pride becomes nobody*
rien	*nothing* *not anything* *any thing*	rien ne lui plaît, *nothing pleases him.* y a-t-il rien qui puisse lui plaire? *is there any thing that can please him?*

SECOND CLASS.

87. Those which are always joined to a substantive.

quelque	*some*	si cela était vrai, quelque historien en aurait parlé, *if that were true, some historian would have mentioned it*
chaque	*each, every*	à chaque jour suffit sa peine, *sufficient for the day is the evil thereof*
quelconque	*whoever* *whatever*	il n'y a raison quelconque qui puisse l'y obliger, *no reason whatever can oblige him to it*
certain	*certain* *some*	certain homme, *a certain man* certaines nouvelles, *some news*
un	*a, an*	j'ai vu un homme, *I saw a man* prenez une orange, *take an orange*

THIRD CLASS.

88. Those which are sometimes used in conjunction with a substantive, and sometimes relatively.

nul	*no, one*	nulle raison ne peut le convaincre, *no reason can convince him* nul d'eux ne l'a rencontré, *not one of them has met him*
pas un	*no, not one*	il n'y a pas une erreur dans cet ouvrage, *there is not one error in that work* pas un ne le dit, *not one says so*
aucun	*no, none*	je ne connais aucun de vos juges, *I know none of your judges* il n'a fait aucune difficulté, *he has made no difficulty*
autre	*other*	servez-vous d'une autre expression, *make use of another expression* je vous prenais pour un autre, *I took you for another*
même	*same*	c'est le même homme que je vis hier, *he is the same man I saw yesterday* cet homme n'est plus le même, *that man is no longer the same*
tel	*such* *like*	il tint à peu près un tel discours, *he made nearly such a discourse* je ne vis jamais rien de tel, *I never saw any thing like it*
plusieurs	*several* *many*	il est arrivé plusieurs vaisseaux, *several vessels have arrived* il ne faut pas que plusieurs pâtissent pour un seul, *many must not suffer for one*
tout	*all* *every* *every thing*	tous les êtres créés, *all created beings* tout disparaît devant Dieu, *everything vanishes before God.*

FOURTH CLASS.

89. Of those which are followed by *que*.

qui que	*whoever*	qui que tu sois, *whoever thou mayest be* qui que ce soit, *whoever it may be*
quoi que	*whatever*	quoi que ce soit, *whatever it may be* quoi que vous disiez, *whatever you may say*
quelque	*whatever* *however*	quel que soit cet homme, *whoever that man may be* quel que soit votre courage, *whatever your courage may be*

telque	*such as*	cette étoffe est telle que vous la voulez, *this stuff is such as you wish for*
quelque—que	*whatever* / *however*	quelque raison que vous donniez, *whatever reason you may give* quelque puissant que vous soyez, *however powerful you may be*
tout—que	*however*	tout savant qu'il est, *however learned he may be.*

CHAPTER V.

OF THE VERB.

90. The *Verb* is a word, the chief use of which is to express action, feeling, existence; it has persons, moods, and tenses.

In the phrase *la vertu est aimable*, virtue is amiable, it is affirmed that the quality *aimable* belongs to *la vertu;* likewise in this sentence, *le vice n'est pas aimable*, vice is not aimable, it is affirmed that the quality *aimable* does not belong to *le vice;* the word *est* expresses this affirmation.

That concerning which we affirm or deny a thing is called the *subject*, and what is affirmed or denied is called its *attribute*. In the two preceding sentences, *vertu* and *vice* are subjects of the verb *est*, and *aimable* is the attribute affirmed respecting the one, and denied with respect to the other.

91. There are in verbs *two numbers*, the singular and plural, and, in each number, *three persons*.

I. The first person is that who speaks; it is designated by *je*, I, in the singular, and by *nous*, we, in the plural: as, *je pense*, I think; *nous pensons*, we think.

II. The second is the person spoken to, expressed by *tu*, thou, in the singular, and by *vous*, you, in the plural: as, *tu penses*, thou thinkest; *vous pensez*, you think.

III. The third is the person spoken of, known by *il*, he, or *elle*, she, in the singular, and by *ils* or *elles*, they, in the plural: as, *il* or *elle pense*, he *or* she thinks; *ils* or *elles pensent*, they think.

All substantives, either common or proper, are of the third person, when not addressed or spoken to: as, *les lions rugissent*, lions roar; *ces arbres sont beaux*, these trees are beautiful; *les soldats se battent*, soldiers are fighting.

Rem.—A word is known to be a *verb*, when it admits the personal pronouns: thus, *finir*, to finish, is a verb, because we can say, *je finis, tu finis, il*, or *elle finit*, etc.

92. There are *five moods*, or modes of conjugating verbs.

I. The *infinitive mood* expresses the nature of the action, feeling, without any reference to persons, numbers or time, as, *aimer*, to love; *avoir aimé*, to have loved.

II. The *indicative* simply indicates and asserts a thing in a direct manner; as, *j'aime*, I love; *il aima*, he loved.

III. The *conditional* affirms a thing with a condition, as, *j'aimerais, si*, etc. I should love, if, etc.

IV. The *imperative* is used for commanding, exhorting, requesting, or reproving; as, *aime*, love (thou); *aimons*, let us love.

V. The *subjunctive* mood expresses an action in a manner which is subordinate; it is always preceded of a verb, conjunction, or phrase implying the necessity, desire, apprehension that a thing should be, as *il faut que nous partions*, it is necessary that we should go.

93. There are three tenses, the *present*, which declares a thing now existing, or doing, as, *je lis*, I read; the *past*, denoting that the thing has been done, as, *j'ai lu*, I did read; the *future*, denoting that the thing will be done, as, *je lirai*, I shall read. In order to specify in a precise and correct manner, the moment when the action has taken, or will take place, the verb has several forms: thus, *je lisais*, I was reading; *je viens de lire*, I have just read; *je venais de lire*, I had just read, etc. Numerous examples of these latter forms are given at the end of the grammar. See No. 19, *Examples on the Difficulties*.

There are five kinds of verbs, the *active*, *passive*, *neuter*, *pronominal*, and *impersonal*.

94. The *verb active*, or *transitive*, is that which expresses an action, the object of which may be *quelqu'un*, some person, or *quelque chose*, some thing; as, *aimer Dieu*, to love God; *aimer l'étude*, to love study. The object of this action is called the *regimen*, or *government* of the verb active.

N.B. A simple question will show this *regimen* as, *qu'est-ce que j'aime?* what do I love? answer, *Dieu*, God. *Dieu* is then the regimen of the verb *j'aime*.

95. Passive verbs express that the action is suffered by the subject; they are conjugated by means of the auxiliary *être*, and the participle past of the active voice, as *je suis aimé*, I am loved. Thus, to change the verbs from active to passive in these sentences, *mon père m'aime*, my father loves me; *le milan a enlevé le serin*, the kite has carried off the canary bird, they must be turned in this way, *je suis*

aimé de mon père, I am loved by my father; *le serin a été enlevé par le milan*, the canary bird has been carried off by the kite.

96. The *verb neuter*, or *intransitive*, is that which has no direct regimen, that is, after which you cannot put a substantive, without a preposition. *Aller* to go, is a neuter verb, because one cannot say, *aller Londres*, to go London, but *aller à Londres*, to go to London. *Plaire*, to please, is likewise a verb neuter, as we cannot say in French, *plaire quelqu'un*, to please somebody, but *plaire à quelqu'un*.

The *pronominal verbs* are those in which each person is conjugated through all the tenses, with two pronouns.

as	*je me*,	I myself	*nous nous*	we ourselves
	tu te,	thou thyself	*vous vous*	you yourself, *or* ye yourselves
	il se,	he himself	*ils se*	they themselves
	elle se,	she herself	*elles se*	they themselves

There are four sorts of *pronominal verbs*:—

97. I. The *reflective*, when the action of the verb falls upon the subject, as *je me flatte*, I flatter myself; *il se loue*, he praises himself. Almost all active verbs are susceptible of being *reflective*.

II. The *pronominal verb neuter*, which indicates only a state, a disposition of the subject as, *se repentir*, to repent; *se désister*, to desist; *s'enfuir*, to run away.

III. The *reciprocal verb* expresses a reciprocity of action between two or more subjects, and consequently has no singular; such are, *s'entr'aider*, to help one another; *s'entre-donner*, to give each other.

IV. The *pronominal verb impersonal*, is only used in the third person singular. Active verbs frequently assume this form in a passive sense, for the sake of brevity and energy; as, *il se bâtit*, there is building; *il se faisait*, there was doing; *il se conclut*, there was concluded; *il s'est dit*, it has been said; *il se donnera une grande bataille*, a great battle will be fought.

98. The *impersonal verb* is only used in the third person singular, with the pronoun *il* for its subject. *Neiger*, to snow, is an impersonal verb, as it cannot be applied to any person, or thing; *il neige*, it snows, *il neigeait*, it did snow. *Neuter* verbs may be used impersonally, as *il vint un homme*, there came a man, instead of *un homme vint*, a man came.

Though the greater part of the French verbs are regular, there are, however, as in other languages, some that are *irregular*, and others that are *defective.* Regular verbs are those which are conjugated conformably to a general principle. Irregular verbs are those which deviate from that general principle in the formation of their persons and tenses; and defective verbs are those which, in certain tenses, or persons, are not used.

OF CONJUGATIONS.

99. To conjugate is to give all the persons and tenses of a verb through all its different inflections.

The French generally admit four regular conjugations, which are distinguished by the termination of the present of the infinitive.

The	FIRST	ends in	-er	as, parl*er*, aim*er*, chant*er*, donn*er*, etc.
	SECOND		-ir	as, fin*ir*, avert*ir*, pun*ir*, tern*ir*, etc.
	THIRD		-oir	as, recev*oir*, apercev*oir*, dev*oir*, etc.
	FOURTH		-re	as, rend*re*, vend*re*, mord*re*, batt*re*, etc.

100. The French, like most modern nations, not having a sufficient number of inflections in their

verbs to specify exactly the moment at which the action takes place, supply this deficiency with two auxiliary verbs, *avoir* and *être*, to have and to be.

Besides AVOIR and ÊTRE, which are the only verbs generally recognised as auxiliaries, there are four others which are as fully deserving of that name, in consequence of their being frequently used in conjunction with the infinitive, to express *times* and *circumstances*, which the simple tenses are insufficient to do. These four verbs are *aller*, *venir de*, *devoir*, *pouvoir*. (*See models of their use, No.* 19, *of the* EXAMPLES ON DIFFICULTIES.)

Those tenses, which are formed from the infinitive, are called simple tenses, as *parler*, *je parle*, *je parlais*, *je parlai*, *je parlerai*, etc. Those which are formed by the conjunction of the participle with *être* and *avoir*, or of the infinitive with *venir de*, *aller*, *devoir*, *pouvoir*, are compound tenses, as *j'ai parlé*, *je viens de parler*, etc.

101. CONJUGATION

OF THE

VERB *AVOIR*, TO HAVE.

INFINITIVE.

SIMPLE TENSES.		COMPOUND TENSES.	
PRESENT.		PAST.	
avoir	*to have.*	avoir eu	*to have had.*

PARTICIPLES.

PRESENT.		PAST.	
ayant	*having*	ayant eu	*having had*
PAST.			
eu, *m.* eue, *f.*	*had*		

INDICATIVE.

PRESENT.		PRETERIT INDEFINITE, *or compound of the present.*	
j'ai	*I have*	j'ai eu	*I have had*
tu as	*thou hast*	tu as eu	*thou hast had*
il, *or* elle a	*he* or *she has*	il a eu	*he has had*
nous avons	*we have*	nous avons eu	*we have had*
vous avez	*you have*	vous avez eu	*you have had*
ils, *or* elles ont	*they have*	ils ont eu	*they have had*

EXERCISE.

102. In the following exercises, the substantive being taken in a partitive sense, it will be necessary to use the partitive *du, de l', de la, des*, according to the gender and number. See Rule the 39th.

SIMPLE TENSES.		COMPOUND TENSES.	
IMPERFECT.		**PLUPERFECT, *or compound of the imperfect.***	
j'avais	*I had*	j'avais eu	*I had*
tu avais	*thou hadst*	tu avais eu	*thou hadst*
il avait	*he had*	il avait eu	*he had*
nous avions	*we had*	nous avions eu	*we had*
vous aviez	*you had*	vous aviez eu	*you had*
ils avaient	*they had* } *or was having*	ils avaient eu	*they had* } *had*
PRETERIT DEFINITE.		**PRETERIT ANTERIOR, *or compound of the preterit.***	
j'eus	*I had*	j'eus eu	*I had*
tu eus	*thou hadst*	tu eus eu	*thou hadst*
il eut	*he had*	il eut eu	*he had*
nous eûmes	*we had*	nous eûmes eu	*we had*
vous eûtes	*you had*	vous eûtes eu	*you had*
ils eurent	*they had*	ils eurent eu	*they had* } *had*

PRESENT.

I have books. Thou hast friends. He has honesty. She
livre — *ami* — *honnêteté* f. *h* m.

has sweetness. We have credit. You have riches. They
douceur f. — m. *richesse* pl. m.

have virtues. They have modesty.
vertu f. — f.

PRETERIT INDEFINITE.

I have had pleasure. Thou hast had gold. He has had patience
plaisir m. *or* m. — f

She has had beauty. We have had honours. You have had
— f. *honneur*

friendship. They have had sentiments. They have had feeling.
amitié f. m. — f. *sensibilité* f.

IMPERFECT.

I had ambition. Thou hadst wealth. He had sincerity. She
— f. *bien* m.

SIMPLE TENSES.		COMPOUND TENSES.	
FUTURE ABSOLUTE.		FUTURE ANTERIOR, *or compound of the future.*	
j'aurai	*I shall* or *will have*	j'aurai eu	*I shall* or *will have*
tu auras	*thou shalt* or *wilt have.*	tu auras eu	*thou wilt have*
il aura	*he will have*	il aura eu	*he will have*
nous aurons	*we shall have*	nous aurons eu	*we shall have*
vous aurez	*you will have*	vous aurez eu	*you will have*
ils auront	*they will have*	ils auront eu	*they will have*

(*had*)

had graces. We had oranges. You had pears. They had apples.
— — *poire* m. *pomme*

They had lemons.
f. *citron*

PLUPERFECT.

I had had apricots. Thou hadst had nectarines He had had
abricot *brugnon*

walnuts. She had had hazel-nuts. We had had chesnuts. You
noix *noisette* *châtaigne.*

had had figs. They had had medlars. They had had filberts.
figue m. *nèfle* f. *aveline.*

PRETERIT DEFINITE.

I had plums. Thou hadst cherries He had strawberries. She
prune *cerise* *fraise*

had pine-apples. We had almonds. You had currants. They had
ananas *amande* *groseille* m.

raspberries. They had grapes.
framboise f. *raisin* m. pl.

103. In the following exercises, the addition of an adjective, after the substantive, will make no difference as to the use of *du, de la, de l', des.*

PRETERIT ANTERIOR.

I had had very black ink. Thou hadst had honest
fort 2 *noir* 3 *encre* f. 1. *honnête* 2

CONDITIONAL.

SIMPLE TENSES.		COMPOUND TENSES.	
PRESENT.		PAST, *or compound of the conditional.*	
j'aurais	*I should* or *would have*	j'aurais eu	*I should* have had.
tu aurais	*thou shouldst have*	tu aurais eu	*thou shouldst* have had.
il aurait	*he should have*	il aurait eu	*he should* have had.
nous aurions	*we should have*	nous aurions eu	*we should* have had.
vous auriez	*you should have*	vous auriez eu	*you should* have had.
ils auraient	*they should have*	ils auraient eu	*they should* have had.

---

friends. She had had uncommon graces. We had had very ripe
amis. *rare* 2 1. 2 *mûr* 3

grapes. You had had exquisite melons. They had had ready
1. *exquis* 2 — m. 1. *comptant* 2

money.
argent m. 1.

FUTURE ABSOLUTE.

I shall have studious pupils. Thou wilt have horrid
appliqué 2 *élève* m. 1. *horrible* 2

pains. He will have ridiculous ideas. We shall have use-
peine f. 1. *ridicule* 2 *idée* f. 1. *inu-*

less cares. You will have true and real pleasures. They will
tile 2 *soin* m. 1. 2 *réel* 3 m. 1.

have poignant griefs.
cuisant 2 *chagrin* m. 1.

104. But if the adjective precedes the substantive, then *de*, or *d'*, only is to be used without any regard to the number or the gender of the noun.

FUTURE ANTERIOR.

I shall have had good paper. Thou wilt have had excellent
papier m.

fruit. She will have had charming flowers. We shall have had
m. pl *charmant fleurs* f.

good pens. You will have had large buildings. They will
plume f. *grand bâtiment* m.

have had fine clothes.
superbe habit m.

PRESENT OF THE CONDITIONAL.

I should have fine engravings. Thou shouldst have pretty play-
gravure f. *joli jou-*

things. He should have immense treasures. We should have
jou m. *trésor* m.

beautiful pictures. You would have pretty houses. They should
tableau m. f.

have long conversations.
— f.

105. *De* is also to be used alone, without any regard to the gender or number of the noun, after an adverb of quantity, such as *beaucoup*, a great deal, great many; *peu*, little, few; *plus*, more; *moins*, less; *trop*, too much, too many, etc; except *bien*, much, many, which requires *du, de la, de l'*, *des*.

CONDITIONAL PAST.

I should* have had *a great deal of* trouble. Thou wouldst have
peine f.

have had *more* pleasure. He would have had *(a vast deal)* of
de *infiniment*

knowledge. We should have had *more* opportunities of succeeding.
connaissance f.pl. *de occasion* f.pl. *réussir*

You would certainly have had *many* advantages over him.
certainement 1 *beaucoup de avantage* *sur lui*

They would have had *many* enemies.
bien ennemi

* *Would, should, could* are not always mere signs of the conditional; they are on the contrary, more frequently used as having a distinct and separate sense, expressing *will, duty,* or *power*. In such cases, they are also to be rendered in French by separate words, such as *vouloir, devoir, pouvoir*. The attention of the scholar will be called to that necessary distinction hereafter; but for the present, that is, in the course of the following introductory exercises on the conjugation of verbs, he must consider *would, could,* and *should* as being used in their first capacity only that is, as *Signs of the Conditional*.—See 386.

N.B. *J'eusse eu, tu eusses eu, il eût eu, nous eussions eu, vous eussiez eu, ils eussent eu,* I should have had, &c. is also used for the conditional past.

IMPERATIVE.

aie, or aye	*have (thou)*
qu'il ait	*let him have*
ayons	*let us have*
ayez	*have (ye)*
qu'ils aient	*let them have*

SUBJUNCTIVE.

SIMPLE TENSES.		COMPOUND TENSES.		
PRESENT.		PRESENT.		
que	*that*	que	*that*	
j'aie	*I may have*	j'aie eu	*I may*	*have had*
tu aies	*thou mayst have*	tu aies eu	*thou mayst*	*have had*
il ait	*he may have*	il ait eu	*he may*	*have had*
nous ayons	*we may have*	nous ayons eu	*we may*	*have had*
vous ayez	*you may have*	vous ayez eu	*you may*	*have had*
ils aient	*they may have*	ils aient eu	*they may*	*have had*

---

106. When the verb is followed by several substantives, the proper article and preposition must be repeated before each.

IMPERATIVE.

Have thou patience, perseverance, and courage. Let him have
——f. ——f. ——m.

modesty and more correct ideas. Let her have more decency. Let
——f. 2 *juste* 3 1 *décence*

us have courage and firmness. Have ye gravy soup, nice roast
——m. *fermeté* f. *un gras* 2 *soupe* f.1. *un bon ros-*

beef and a pudding. Let them have ale, rum, and punch. Let
bif m. *pouding* m. m. *aile* f. *rum* m. *ponche* m.

them have morals and conduct
f. *mœurs* f.pl. *conduite* f.

SUBJUNCTIVE.

PRESENT.

That I may aave many friends. That thou mayest have good
beaucoup

reasons to give him. That he may have elevated sentiments. That
donner lui *élevé* 2 ——m.1.

we may have courage and magnanimity. That you may have
bravoure f. =f.

delightful landscapes, and beautiful sea-pieces. That they may
délicieux 2 *paysage* m.pl. *marine* f.pl.

have more condescension and more prepossessing manners.
——*dance* 2 *prévenant* 3 *manière* f.pl.1.

PRETERIT.

That I may have had wine, beer, and cider. That thou mayest
vin m. *bière* f. *cidre* m.

have had a good horse, and a fine dog. That he may have had
cheval m. *chien* m.

enlightened judges. That we may have had snow, rain, and wind.
éclairé 2 *juge* m.1 *neige* f. *pluie* f. *vent* m.

That you may have had a great dining-room, and a beautiful drawing-
salle à manger f. *superbe* *salon de*

room, a pretty dressing-room, and a delightful bed-
compagnie m. *joli* *cabinet de toilette* m. *charmant chambre-*

room. That they may have had vast possessions, fine meadows,
à coucher f. *vaste* ——f. *prairie* f.

and delightful groves.
délicieux 2 *bois* m.1

SIMPLE TENSES.		COMPOUND TENSES.	
IMPERFECT.		PLUPERFECT, or *compound of the imperfect.*	
que	*that*	que	*that*
j'eusse	*I had, or might have*	j'eusse eu	*I might have had*
tu eusses	*thou might'st have*	tu eusses eu	*thou mightest have had*
il eût	*he might have*	il eût eu	*he might have had*
nous eussions	*we might have*	nous eussions eu	*we might have had*
vous eussiez	*you might have*	vous eussiez eu	*you might have had*
ils eussent	*they might have*	ils eussent eu	*they might have had*

IMPERFECT.

That I might have a sword, a musket, and pistols. That thou
épée f. *fusil* m. *pistolet* m.

might'st have a knife, a spoon, and a fork. That we might
couteau m. *cuillère* f. *fourchette* f.

have a penknife, pencils, and good copies. That he might have
canif m. *pinceau* m. *modèle* m.

a coach, a good house, and furniture, simple but elegant. That
carrosse m. f. *meuble* m.pl. —— *mais* ——

you might have health and great respect. That they might have
santé f. *un* *considération* f.

fruitful lands.
fertile 2 *terre* f.1.

PLUPERFECT.

That I might have had friendship. That thou might'st have had
amitié f.

gloves, boots, and horses. That he might have had zealous and
gant m. *botte* f. *cheval* m. *zélé* 2

faithful servants. That we might have had fine clothes, precious
fidèle 3 *domestique* m.1. =f. 2

jewels, and magnificent furniture. That you might have had warm
bijou m.1 *magnifique* 2 1 *chaud* 2

friends. That they might have had greatness of soul and pity.
1 *grandeur* f. *pitié* f.

SENTENCES ON THE SAME VERB, WITH A NEGATIVE.

107. *De, d'* is also used, without any regard to the gender or the number of the noun, after a negative phrase.

EXAMPLES :

Je n'ai pas de livres	*I have no books*
tu n'avais pas de bien	*thou hadst no wealth*
nous n'avons pas eu d'amitié	*we have had no friendship*
si vous n'aviez pas eu de puissants amis	*if you had not had powerful friends*
ils n'auront pas d'ennemis	*they will not have enemies*
il n'aurait pas de plaisir	*he would not have any pleasure.*

INDICATIVE.

PRESENT.

I have no precious medals. We have no useless things.
=2 *médaille* f.1 *inutile* 2 *chose* f.1

PRETERIT INDEFINITE.

I have had no perseverance. We have had no generosity.
—f. =f.

IMPERFECT.

Thou hadst not a beautiful park. You had no good cucumbers.
parc m. *concombre* m.

PLUPERFECT.

He had had no fine houses. They had had no money.
argent m.

PRETERIT DEFINITE.

He had no answer to his letter. They had no carpets.
réponse f. *lettre* f. *tapis* m.

PRETERIT ANTERIOR.

Thou hadst had no kindness. You had had no great talents.
complaisance f. ——m.

FUTURE ABSOLUTE.

I shall have no great difficulty. We shall not have company at dinner
grand difficultés f. *monde à dîner*

FUTURE ANTERIOR.

You will not have had quiet days.
tranquille 2 m. 1

CONDITIONAL.

PRESENT.

He would not have bad pictures. They would have no leisure.
mauvais tableau m. *loisir* m

PAST.

I should have had no griefs. We should have had no troubles
chagrin m.pl. *veine* f.

IMPERATIVE.

Have no such whims. Let him not have such absurd ideas.
caprice m. *si absurde* 2 f.pl.1

Let us not have discussions of this sort. Have no such whims.
——— *espèce* f. *tel caprice* m.

Let them not have foreign servants.
étranger domestique

SUBJUNCTIVE.

PRESENT.

That I may have no protectors. That we may have no success.
=m. *succès* m.

PRETERIT.

That he may have had no perseverance. That they may have had
———f.

no valour.
bravoure f.

IMPERFECT.

That thou might'st have no taste. That you might not have a just
goût m. *juste*

reward.
récompense f.

PLUPERFECT.

That I might not have had good advice. That we might not have
avis m.pl.

had any news.
nouvelle f.pl.

THE VERB *AVOIR*, INTERROGATIVELY AND AFFIRMATIVELY

108. In interrogations, the pronoun, which is the subject of the verb, is placed after it, and they are joined by an hyphen, *ai-je?* In compound tenses, the pronoun is placed immediately after the auxiliary *ai-je eu?* When the third person singular of the verb ends with a vowel, *-t-* is placed between the verb, and *il*, *elle*, in order to avoid the hiatus occasioned by the meeting of the two vowels: ***a-t-il?*** ***aura-t-il?*** This applies to ***on:*** ***aura-t-on?***

EXAMPLES:

ai-je des livres?	*have I books?*
avais-tu du bien?	*hadst thou wealth!*
eut-elle ce courage?	*had she that courage?*
Jean a-t-il de l'argent?	*has John any money?*
avons-nous eu de bons conseils?	*have we had good counsels?*
aviez-vous eu de la prudence?	*had you had prudence?*
aura-t-il de l'argent?	*will he have money?*
aura-t-elle eu des protecteurs?	*will she have had protectors?*

INDICATIVE.

PRESENT.

Hast thou needles? Have you coloured maps?
aiguille f. *enluminé* 2 *carte* f. 1

PRETERIT INDEFINITE.

Have I had good friends? Have we had much fortune?
bon *ami* ——— f.

IMPERFECT.

Had she time? Had they large buildings?
le temps *grand bâtiment* m.

PLUPERFECT.

Had she sufficient means? Had they extensive fields?
suffisant *moyens* m. *spacieux* 2 *champ* m. 1

PRETERIT DEFINITE.

Had he good shoes? Had they looking glasses?
soulier m. f. *miroir* m.

PRETERIT ANTERIOR.

Hadst thou had lace? Had you had odoriferous shrubs?
dentelle f. *odoriférant* 2 *arbuste* m. 1

FUTURE ABSOLUTE.

Shall I have gold and silver? Shall we have (good luck)?
m. *argent* m. *bonheur*

FUTURE ANTERIOR.

Will they have had company?
compagnie f.

CONDITIONAL.

PRESENT.

Shouldst thou have happy moments? Would you have good
heureux —— m.

wine and nice liqueurs?
vin m. *fin* 2 *liqueur* f. 1

PAST.

Would he have had uncommon patience? Would they have had
extraordinaire

rich clothes.
habit m.

THE SAME VERB INTERROGATIVELY AND NEGATIVELY.

109. This form is the same as the preceding, except that the first negative *ne* is placed before the verb, and the second, *pas* or *point*, after the pronoun: *ai-je? n'ai-je pas? ai-je eu? n'ai-je pas eu?*

EXAMPLES.

n'a-t-elle pas beaucoup d'esprit?	*has she not a great deal of wit?*
n'avons-nous pas eu de bons procédés?	*have we not had considerate regards?*
n'aviez-vous pas eu de nouvelles robes?	*had you not had new gowns?*
n'aura-t-il pas de ressources?	*will he have no resources?*

109. (*bis*). It has been said (107) that, after negations, *de* must be used before the noun substantive, without any regard to its gender or number, instead

of *du, de la, des,* used in affirmative sentences: as *je n'ai pas d'argent, elle n'a pas d'amis.* Yet, *in interrogative and negative sentences,* there are some cases when *du, de la, des,* may be used, and others when *de* must: thus,

1st.	n'ai-je pas du mépris pour lui?	*have I not contempt for him?*
	n'avez-vous pas des livres?	*have you* not *books?*
	n'avez-vous pas de l'argent?	*have you* not *money?*
2nd.	n'avez-vous pas de livres?	*have you* no *books?*
	n'avez-vous pas d'argent?	*have you* no *money?*

Although the first examples are under the interrogative form, they are intended for affirmations. By a figure, called *litote,* one form has been substituted to another, thereby to convey more meaning than the simple assertions *j'ai du mépris pour lui; vous avez des livres; vous avez de l'argent,* would be able to do. Thus, for instance, *you complain of being dull, how can that be, have you not books?* instead of saying *since you have books?*

EXAMPLES.

n'ai-je pas des livres?	*have I no books?*
n'avais-tu pas des amis?	*hadst thou no friends?*
n'auront-elles pas eu des consolations?	*will they have had no consolations?*

In the second examples, on the contrary, nothing but mere questions is intended, there is no substitution of form, no other meaning *understood,* but the one expressed. The difference is also somewhat marked in English.

INDICATIVE.

PRESENT.

Hast thou no diamonds? (*diamant* m.) Have you no indulgent parents? (—— 2 —— m. 1)

PRETERIT INDEFINITE.

Hast thou not had contempt (*mépris* m.) and even (*même*) hatred (*haine* f. *h.* asp.) for that (*pour cet*) man?

Have you not had better (*meilleur*) examples? (*exemple* m.)

IMPERFECT.

Had he not a rigid censor? Had they not inattentive children?
sévère 2 *censeur* m.1 =2 *enfant* m.1

PLUPERFECT.

Had I not had other views? Had we not had amethysts, rubies,
autre vue f.pl. *améthyste* f. *rubis* m.
and topazes?
topase f.

PRETERIT DEFINITE.

Had we not perfidious friends?
perfide 2 1

PRETERIT ANTERIOR.

Had he not had too studied expressions? Had they not had
2 *recherché* ——f.1
excellent models?
—— *modèle* m.

FUTURE ABSOLUTE.

Wilt thou not have a more regular conduct? Will you not have
plus 2 *réglé* 3 *conduite* f.1
fashionable dresses?
à la mode 2 *robe* f.1

FUTURE ANTERIOR.

Shall we have had sufficient time then?
assez de temps

CONDITIONAL.

PRESENT.

Should she not have clear and just ideas? Would they not have
clair 2 3 f. 1
more extensive knowledge?
2 *étendu* 3 *connaissances* f.pl.1

PAST.

Would she not have had any objection? Would they have had no
——
reward?
récompense f.

110. CONJUGATION

OF THE

AUXILIARY VERB *ETRE*, TO BE.

INFINITIVE.

SIMPLE TENSES.		COMPOUND TENSES.	
PRESENT.		PAST.	
être	*to be*	avoir été	*to have been*

PARTICIPLES.

PRESENT.		PAST.	
étant	*being*	ayant été	*having been*
PAST.			
été	*been*		

INDICATIVE.

PRESENT.		PRETERIT INDEFINITE.	
je suis	*I am*	j'ai été	*I have been*
tu es	*thou art*	tu as été	*thou hast been*
il, *ou* elle est	*he* or *she is*	il a été	*he has been*
nous sommes	*we are*	nous avons été	*we have been*
vous êtes	*you are*	vous avez été	*you have been*
ils / elles } sont	*they are*	ils ont été	*they have been*

111. General Rule. In those sentences in which there is an adverb, it must be placed between the verb and the adjective or participle : *il n'est jamais content ; il est toujours récompensé.*

SIMPLE TENSES.		COMPOUND TENSES.	
IMPERFECT.		**PLUPERFECT.**	
j'étais	*I was*	j'avais été	*I had been*
tu étais	*thou wast*	tu avais été	*thou hadst been*
il était	*he was*	il avait été	*he had been*
nous étions	*we were*	nous avions été	*we had been*
vous étiez	*you were*	vous aviez été	*you had been*
ils étaient	*they were*	ils avaient été	*they had been*
PRETERIT DEFINITE.		**PRETERIT ANTERIOR.***	
je fus	*I was*	j'eus été	*I had been*
tu fus	*thou wast*	tu eus été	*thou hadst been*
il fut	*he was*	il eut été	*he had been*
nous fûmes	*we were*	nous eûmes été	*we had been*
vous fûtes	*you were*	vous eûtes été	*you had been*
ils furent	*they were*	ils eurent été	*they had been*

The following exercises, on the verb *être*, are composed of four forms of sentences, affirmative, interrogative, and negative; interrogative and negative.

When, in a question, the substantive is expressed, it must always begin the sentence, and the pronoun still be put after the verb.

EXAMPLES.

Mon frère est-il venu?	*is my brother come?*
la reine n'est-elle pas arrivée?	*is not the queen arrived?*

PRESENT.

I am very glad to see you. Art not thou pleased with that book,
aise de voir *satisfait de*

Is she really amiable? We are happy. Are you not too
véritablement *heureux*

obliging? Are your friends still in London?
complaisant *encore à Londres*

* Exercises upon this tense would be as yet too complicated, as may be seen by this sentence: *à peine y eus-je été cinq ou six minutes qu'il arriva*, I had scarce been there five or six minutes when he arrived.

PRETERIT INDEFINITE.

Have not I been constant? Hast thou always been steady? She
posé

has been faithful. Have we not been firm and courageous? You
fidèle *ferme* =

have been charitable. Have those men always been good and
———

benevolent?
bienfaisant

IMPERFECT.

I was too busy to see you. Wast not thou troublesome?
occupé pour recevoir *importun*

Was this girl idle? Were we not too untractable? You were
fille paresseux *indocile*

not quiet enough. They were vain, light, and coquettish.
tranquille 2 *assez* 1 f. — *frivole* *coquette*

PLUPERFECT.

I had hitherto been very indifferent. Hadst not thou been too
jusqu'alors *insouciant*

imprudent? Had his wife been sufficiently modest and reserved?
——— *épouse* *assez* *assez réservé*

We had not yet been sufficiently attentive. Had you been envious
encore *appliqué* =

and jealous? They had not been grateful.
jaloux *reconnaissant*

PRETERIT DEFINITE.

Perhaps I was not sufficiently prudent. Wast thou discreet
peut-être que *assez* ——— *discret* 2

enough on that occasion? Was not that princess too proud? We
1 *en* ———f. ———*cesse* *fier*

were very unhappy. Were not you too hasty? They were not
prompt

much satisfied.
fort satisfait

SIMPLE TENSES.		COMPOUND TENSES.	
FUTURE ABSOLUTE.		**FUTURE ANTERIOR.**	
je serai	*I shall* or *will be*	j'aurai été	*I shall* or *will* have been
tu seras	*thou wilt be*	tu auras été	*thou wilt* have been
il sera	*he will be*	il aura été	*he will* have been
nous serons	*we shall be*	nous aurons été	*we shall* have been
vous serez	*you shall be*	vous aurez été	*you will* have been
ils seront	*they shall be*	ils auront été	*they will* have been

FUTURE ABSOLUTE.

To-morrow I shall be at home till (twelve o'clock.) Wilt thou
demain *chez moi jusqu'à* *midi*

always be restless, brutal, and sour? Will your father be
inquiet *bourru* *chagrin* *Monsieur*

at home this evening? Shall not we be more diligent? You will
chez lui *soir* m. 1

then be ever capricious, obstinate, and particular. Will not your
2 1 3 *quinteux* *opiniâtre* *pointilleux*

scholars be troublesome?
écolier *incommode*

FUTURE ANTERIOR.

Shall not I have been too severe? Thou wilt have been too

distrustful. Shall we not have been desirous enough? Will not
défiant *empressé* 2 1

you have been inconsiderate? Will not the judges have been just?
indiscret *juge*

CONDITIONAL.

SIMPLE TENSES.		COMPOUND TENSES.	
PRESENT.		PAST.	
je serais	*I should, would,* or *could be*	j'aurais été	*I should have been*
tu serais	*thou wouldst be*	tu aurais été	*thou wouldst have been*
il serait	*he would be*	il aurait été	*he would have been*
nous serions	*we should be*	nous aurions été	*we should have been*
vous seriez	*you would be*	vous auriez été	*you should have been*
ils seraient	*they would be*	ils auraient été	*they would have been*

This form ***j'eusse été, tu eusses été, il eût été, nous eussions été, vous eussiez été, ils eussent été,*** is also used instead of the conditional past, ***j'aurais été.***

CONDITIONAL.

PRESENT.

I would not be so rash. Wouldst thou be as consistent in thy
téméraire *conséquent dans*

behaviour as in thy language? Would not his son be ready in time
conduite f. *propos* m.pl. *fils* *prêt à*

Should we always be incorrigible? You would not be disinterested
*désintéressé*2

enough. Would not those ladies be always ready?
1 *dame* *prêt*

PAST.

(But for) your instructions, I should have been proud and
sans *conseil* m.pl. *dédaigneux*

haughty. Wouldst not thou have been malicious and sarcastic?
hautain *malin* *ricaneur*

Would not that man have been quite destitute? Certainly, we
entièrement dépourvu

should not have been so ridiculous. Would not you have been
si *ridicule*

more kind and indulgent? They would not have been so
doux *plus complaisant*

rude.
malhonnête

IMPERATIVE

sois	*be (thou)*
qu'il soit	*let him be*
soyons	*let us be*
soyez	*be (ye)*
qu'ils soient	*let them be*

SUBJUNCTIVE.

SIMPLE TENSES.		COMPOUND TENSES.	
PRESENT.		PRETERIT.	
que	*that*	que	*that*
je sois	*I may, can,* or *should be*	j'aie été	*I may, can,* or *should* (have been)
tu soit	*thou may'st be*	tu aies été	*thou mayest* (have been)
il soit	*he may be*	il ait été	*he may* (have been)
nous soyons	*we may be*	nous ayons été	*we may* (have been)
vous soyez	*you may be*	vous ayez été	*you may* (have been)
ils soient	*they may be*	ils aient été	*they may* (have been)

112. When the noun is expressed, its place is immediately after *que : que votre fils soit plus poli*, let your son be more polite.

Be liberal, but with discretion. Do not be so lavish. Let us be
sing. —— *avec* —— sing. *prodigue*

equitable, humane, and prudent. Let us not be greedy. Be economical
—— *humain* —— *avide* *économe*

and temperate. Do not be thoughtless. Let him be more patient,
sobre pl. *léger* ——

Let her be ready at six o'clock. Let your children be better
prêt à six heures *enfant* *mieux*

(taken care of). Let these (poor men) be admitted. Let them
soignés *malheureux* *admis*

not be so hasty in their conclusions.
prompt à porter un jugement

OF THE SUBJUNCTIVE MOOD.

113. In the preceding exercises, and in the tenses of the subjunctive mood, we have given such English

sentences as might lead the learner to suppose that the French *que je parle*, and the English *that I may speak*, are always equivalent, and that the use of the subjunctive mood corresponds in both languages; but it is indeed very far from being the case, as the following examples will show.

1. Je désire qu'il vienne	*I wish him to come*
2. Voulez-vous que je vous le dise?	*do you wish me to tell it you?*
3. Je ne crois pas qu'il vienne	*I do not think he will come*
4. Cachez cela, de peur qu'il ne le voie	*hide that, lest he sees it,* or *lest he should see it*
5. Dites-le lui, afin qu'il vienne à temps	*tell it him, in order that he may come in time*
6. Il faut que j'y sois à deux heures	*I must be there at two o'clock*

Here are six sentences in which the subjunctive mood is *necessarily* used in French, and there is but one in which it is used in English, the fifth. The use of the subjunctive mood in French depends upon the preceding or governing sentence, and is determined by rules which will be found in their proper place. (*See Syntax*) We will confine ourselves, for the present, in these exercises on the various tenses of the subjunctive, to giving full sentences; that is, we will add the introductory part after which that mood is required.

It must further be added that the conjugation *that* is often omitted in English, whereas *que* is and must always be expressed in French.

PRESENT OF THE SUBJUNCTIVE.

Is it possible that he is so credulous? We wish that thou
est-il possible ——*le* *nous désirons*

mayest be more modest. Is it true that she is so obstinate? They
——*te* *est-il vrai* *entêté*

wish you to be more assiduous. It is not expected that you should
désire ——*du* *on ne s'attend pas*

be back so early. We fear they will be deceived.
de retour de si bonne heure. *nous craignons* *trompé*

SIMPLE TENSES.		COMPOUND TENSES.	
IMPERFECT.		**PLUPERFECT.**	
que	*that*	que	*that*
je fusse	*I might* or *could be*	j'eusse été	*I might*, or *could* have been
tu fusses	*thou mightst be*	tu eusses été	*thou might'st* have been
il fût	*he might be*	il eût été	*he might* have been
nous fussions	*we might be*	nous eussions été	*we might* have been
vous fussiez	*you might be*	vous eussiez été	*you might* have been
ils fussent	*they might be*	ils enssent été	*they might* have been

PRETERIT.

It is possible that I may have been too hasty and too impatient,
'l se veut *emporté* ——

I cannot believe that he may have been so puffed with pride. It is
je ne saurais croire *bouffi d' orgueil* m. *c'est*

(a pity) that she has been so fickle. My father regrets that we have
dommage *volage* *mon père regrette*

been so headstrong. It is wrong that you should have been so
entêté *il est mal*

covetous. I cannot think that they have been so unreasonable.
avare *je ne puis croire* *déraisonnable.*

IMPERFECT.

Could you doubt my being humane and generous? We wish
avez-vous pu douter *humain* = *nous voudrions*

thou wert more careful. We told it to her in order that she might
soigneux *nous le lui avons dit afin*

not be so arrogant. Prayers were offered to the gods that we might
—— *on offrit des prières aux dieux pour*

be victorious. It would be better if you were not so stern. We
= *il vaudrait mieux que* *sévère* *nous*

used all our efforts that they might be successful.
avons fait tous nos efforts afin que *heureux*

PLUPERFECT.

That I might have been more studious. That thou mightst have
=

been more circumspect. That she might have been more attentive
circonspect =

to her duties. That we might have been less addicted to
devoir m. pl. *livré* à

pleasure. That you might have been more assiduous and more
art. m. pl. *assidu* *plu*

grateful. That they might have been less daring.
reconnaissant *hardi*

FIRST CONJUGATION.

114. GENERAL REMARKS ON THE ORTHOGRAPHY OF SOME OF THE VERBS ENDING IN *er*.

The infinitive ends in *er:* as, *aimer*, to love; *parler*, to speak.

I. In verbs ending in *-ger*, the *e* is retained in those tenses where *g* is followed by the vowels *a* or *o*, in order that the *g* may have the soft sound, in every tense and person, as in the infinitive: as, *mangeant, jugeant, je négligeai.*

II. In verbs ending in *-cer*, a cedilla is put under c, for the same reason, when followed by *a* or *o*: as, *suçant, plaçant, j'effaçai.*

III. In verbs ending in *-oyer* and *-uyer*, the *y* is changed into *i* before a mute *e*: as, *j'emploie, il essuie, j'appuierai, il nettoierait.*

IV. This practice is extended by some to verbs in *-ayer*, and *-eyer*: as, *il paie, j'essaierai, elle grassèye*, or *grassèie.*

V. In some few verbs ending in *-eler* and *-eter*, the *l* and *t* are doubled in those inflections, which receive an *e* mute, after these consonants: as, from *appeler*, *il appelle*, from *jeter*, *je jetterai*, etc.

VI. The first person singular of the present of the indicative changes *e* mute into acute *é*, in interrogative sentences; as, *négligé-je? aimé-je?* This remark is also applied to some verbs of the second conjugation ending in *-vrir*, *-frir*, and *-lir:* as *offré-je? cueillé-je?*

There are but two irregular verbs in *er:* *aller*, *envoyer*, which will be found in their proper place.

115. PARADIGM, OR MODEL.

INFINITIVE.

SIMPLE TENSES.		COMPOUND TENSES.	
PRESENT.		PAST.	
parl-*er*	*to speak*	avoir parl*é*	*to have spoken*

PARTICIPLES.

PRESENT.		PAST.	
parl-*ant*	*speaking*	ayant parl*é*	*having spoken*
PAST.			
parl-*é* m. -*ée* f.	*spoken*		

REMARKS.

All the verbs of the first conjugation follow the terminations of the verb *parler*.

EXAMPLE.

	parl-*er*	aim-*er*	expliqu-*er*	avou-*er*
	parl-*ant*	annonç-*ant*	engag-*eant*	défray-*ant*
	parl-*é*	agré-*é*	décri-*é*	dédommag-*é*
je	par-le	dans-*e*	ignor-*e*	renvoi-*e*
tu	parl-*es*	dîn-*es*	rejet-t*es*	renouvel-l*es*
il	parl-*e*	chant-*e*	bégai-*e*	grassèy-*e*
nous	parl-*ons*	berç-*ons*	choy-*ons*	chang-*eons*
vous	parl-*ez*	régn-*ez*	essuy-*ez*	épel-*ez*
ils	parl-ent	caress-*ent*	ennu-*ient*	appel-l*ent*

And so on through the whole verb.

It must be remembered, in writing the following exercises on the various conjugations,

1. That the adverb comes after the verb, in simple tenses, or between the auxiliary and the participle, in compound ones.

INDICATIVE.

SIMPLE TENSES.		COMPOUND TENSES.	
PRESENT.		PRETERIT INDEFINITE.	
je parl-*e*	*I speak, am speaking,* or *do speak*	j'ai parl-*é*	*I have* } *spoken*
tu parl-*es*	*thou speakest*	tu as parl-*é*	*thou hast*
il parl-*e*	*he speaks*	il a parl-*é*	*he has*
nous parl-*ons*	*we speak*	nous avons parl-*é*	*we have*
vous parl-*ez*	*you speak*	vous avez parl-*é*	*you have*
ils parl-*ent*	*they speak*	ils ont parl-*é*	*they have*

II. That *du, de la, de l', des,* are always placed before any noun which is not taken in the general sense, and whenever *some* may be understood.

III. That *de* alone is used, after negations, without regard to the gender or the number, and also when the noun is preceded by an adjective.

IV. That personal pronouns, in the objective case are generally placed before the verb, except the imperative affirmative 1st pers. pl. 2nd pers. sing. & pl.

V. That the signs of the interrogation *do, did,* are not rendered in French; nor are they rendered when emphatically joined to the English verb thus: as, *I do love.*

INDICATIVE PRESENT.

I readily give that plaything to your sister. Do I prefer
volontiers donner *joujou* m. f. *préférer*

pleasure to my duty? Dost not thou incense thy enemies? He
art. m. *devoir* m. *irriter* *ennemi*

does not give salutary advice to his friends. We do sincerely love
donne un =2 *avis* m.1. *sincèrement*

peace and tranquillity. We do not neglect (any thing) to please
art. *paix* f. art. =f. *négliger* *rien* *pour plaire*

SIMPLE TENSES.		COMPOUND TENSES.	
IMPERFECT.		PLUPERFECT.	
je parl-*ais*	*I did speak*, or *was speaking*	j'avais parl-*é*	*I had* } *spoken*
tu parl-*ais*	*thou didst speak*	tu avais parl-*é*	*thou hadst*
il parl-*ait*	*he did speak*	il avait parl-*é*	*he had*
nous parl-*ions*	*we did speak*	nous avions parl-*é*	*we had*
vous parl-*iez*	*you did speak*	vous aviez parl-*é*	*you had*
ils parl-*aient*	*they did speak*	ils avaient parl-*é*	*they had*

---

you. Do you not admire the beauty of that landscape? Do not
admirer =f. *paysage* m.

your parents comfort the afflicted? They (make use of) every
——— *consoler* *affligé* m.pl. *employer* *tous* art.

means to succeed.
moyen m *pour* *réussir*

PRETERIT INDEFINITE.

I have (given up) my favourite horse to my cousin. Hast thou
céder *favori* 2 *cheval* m.1 ——m.

not exchanged watches with my sister? Has the tutor given
changer de montres *précepteur* *de*

fine engravings to his pupil? We have spoken (a long while) of
gravure f. pl. *élève* *long-temps*

your adventure. Have you not insisted too much on that point
aventure f. *insister* * *sur* — m

Have your aunts prepared their ball dresses?
tante *préparer* *de bal* 2 *habit* m. pl 1.

IMPERFECT.

I unceasingly thought of my misfortunes. Didst thou dread
sans cesse *penser* *à* *malheur* m.pl. *redouter*

his presence and firmness? He exhibited in his person all the
———f. pron. *fermeté* f. *retracer* *en* f.

virtues of his ancestors. Did not that woman accuse her friend of
f. *ancêtre* *accuser* *ami* f.

levity? We did not protect that bad man. You despised a vain
légèreté f. *protéger* *méchant* *mépriser* —2.

erudition. Did the Romans disdain so weak an enemy!
———f.1 *Romain* *dédaigner* *faible* 2 m.1.

SIMPLE TENSES.		COMPOUND TENSES.	
PRETERIT DEFINITE.		PRETERIT ANTERIOR.	
je parl-*ai*	*I spoke*	j'eus parl-*é*	*I had* spoken
tu parl-*as*	*thou spokest*	tu eus parl-*é*	*thou hadst* spoken
il parl-*a*	*he spoke*	il eut parl-*é*	*he had* spoken
nous parl-*âmes*	*we spoke*	nous eûmes parl-*é*	*we had* spoken
vous parl-*âtes*	*you spoke*	vous eûtes parl-*é*	*you had* spoken
ils parl-*èrent*	*they spoke*	ils eurent parl-*é*	*they had* spoken

PLUPERFECT.

I had drained (*dessécher*) an unhealthy (*malsain* 2) marsh (*marais* m. 1). Hadst thou not married (*épouser*) a rich man, but unluckily (*malheureusement*) without (*sans*) education (—— f.)? Had his father rejected (*rejeter*) these advantageous (*avantageux* 2) offers (*offre* f. 1)? We had not long (*long-temps*) listened (*écouter*) to the (*) singing (*chant* m.) of the birds (*oiseau* m.). Had you already (*déjà*) studied (*étudier* art.) geography (== f.) and history (art. ==)? Had not his friends procured (*procurer* 2) him (*lui*) a troop (*compagnie* f.) of cavalry (*cavalerie*)?

There is a fourth preterit, called *preterit anterior indefinite*, which is used instead of the preterit anterior, when speaking of a time not entirely elapsed: as, *j'ai eu achevé mon ouvrage ce matin, cette semaine*, etc. and not *j'eus achevé*, as it is found in every conjugation. We shall insert it here: *j'ai eu parlé, tu as eu parlé, il a eu parlé, nous avons eu parlé, vous avez eu parlé, ils ont eu parlé*.

PRETERIT DEFINITE.

I gave them (*leur*) peaches (*pêche* f.pl.) and flowers (*fleurs* f.pl.) out of my garden (*de mon jardin*). Thou forgottest (*oublier*) an essential (*essentiel* 2) circumstance (*circonstance* f.). Did not your cousin relate (*raconter*)

SIMPLE TENSES.		COMPOUND TENSES.	
FUTURE ABSOLUTE.		FUTURE ANTERIOR.	
je parl-*erai*	*I shall* or *will speak*	j'aurai parl-*é*	*I shall* or *will* have spoken
tu parl-*eras*	*thou shalt speak*	tu auras parl-*é*	*thou shalt* have spoken
il parl-*era*	*he shall speak*	il aura parl-*é*	*he shall* have spoken
nous parl-*erons*	*we shall speak*	nous aurons parl-*é*	*we shall* have spoken
vous parl-*erez*	*you shall speak*	vous aurez parl-*é*	*you shall* have spoken
ils parl-*eront*	*they shall speak*	ils auront parl-*é*	*they shall* have spoken

that charming history with (a great deal) of grace? He lightly
—mant = f *avec beaucoup* *légèrement*

judged of my intentions. Did we not show courage
juger * ——— *montrer de* art. —— m. pl.

perseverance, and firmness. Did you not visit the grotto and
art. *persévérance* pr. art. *fermeté* f. *visiter* *grotte* f.

the grove? They did not generously forgive their enemies?
bois m. *généreusement pardonner à*

PRETERIT ANTERIOR.

I had soon wasted my money, and exhausted my resources.
bientôt manger argent m. *épuiser* *ressource* f.

Hadst thou very soon reinforced thy party. Had not Alexander
* *vite renforcer* *parti* m. *Alexandre*

soon surmounted all obstacles. We sat down to table as soon
surmonter tous art. = m. pl. *nous nous mîmes à* —— *aussitôt*

as we had closed the shutters and drawn the curtains. Had you not
que *fermer* *volets* *tirer* *rideau*

quickly dined. They retired to their quarters when they
promptement dîner ils rentrèrent aux casernes quand

had dispersed the mob.
disperser *populace* f.

FUTURE ABSOLUTE.

I shall relieve the poor. Wilt thou faithfully keep that secret?
soulager pauvre m. pl. *fidèlement garder* — m.

Will he consult enlightened judges? He will support you
consulter de art. *éclairé* 2 *juge* 1 *appuyer*

with all his credit. We shall not prefer pleasure to glory,
de —— m. *préférer* art. m. art. f.

CONDITIONAL.

SIMPLE TENSES.		COMPOUND TENSES.	
PRESENT.		PAST.	
je parl-*erais*	*I should, would,* or *could speak*	j'aurais parl-*é*	*I should, would,* or *could* have spoken
tu parl-*erais*	*thou shouldst speak*	tu aurais parl-*é*	*thou shouldst* have spoken
il parl-*erait*	*he should speak*	il aurait parl-*é*	*he should* have spoken
nous parl-*erions*	*we should speak*	nous aurions parl-*é*	*we should* have spoken
vous parl-*eriez*	*you should speak*	vous auriez parl-*é*	*you should* have spoken
ils parl-*eraient*	*they should speak*	ils auraient parl-*é*	*they should* have spoken

J'eusse parlé, tu eusses parlé, il eût parlé, nous eussions parlé, vous eussiez parlé, ils eussent parlé, are also used for the conditional past. This remark holds good for every verb.

---

and riches to honour. With such conduct will you not
art. pl. art. *par une telle conduite*

grieve your father and mother? Will they not astonish their
affliger pron. *étonner*

hearers?
auditeur m.pl.

FUTURE ANTERIOR.

I shall soon have finished this book. By thy submission wilt thou
achever m. *soumission* f.

not have appeased his anger? The country will be happy when
appaiser *colère* f. *ce pays* *heureux*

the king shall have triumphed over his enemies. We shall be better
triompher de *plus*

pleased with ourselves, when we shall have rewarded the merit of
content de' nous *récompenser* *mérite* m.

this good man. Will you not have flown to his assistance then?
de bien 2 1 *voler* *secours* m.

Will not our servants have (brought back) our horses then?
domestique m. *ramené* *cheval*

CONDITIONAL PRESENT.

I would not plan such vain projects. Thou wouldst not avoid so
former —— *projet* m. *éviter* 2

IMPERATIVE.

parl-*e**	*speak (thou)*
qu'il parl-*e*	*let him speak*
parl-*ons*	*let us speak*
parl-*ez*	*speak (ye)*
qu'ils parl-*ent*	*let them speak*

SUBJUNCTIVE.

SIMPLE TENSES.		COMPOUND TENSES.	
PRESENT.		PRETERIT.	
que	*that*	que	*that*
je parl-*e*	*I may* or *can speak*	j'aie parl-*é*	*I may* or *can* (have spoken)
tu parl-*es*	*thou mayest speak*	tu aies parl-*é*	*thou mayest* (have spoken)
il parl-*e*	*he may speak*	il ait parl-*é*	*he may* (have spoken)
nous parl-*ions*	*we may speak*	nous ayons parl-*é*	*we may* (have spoken)
vous parl-*iez*	*you may speak*	vous ayez parl-*é*	*you may* (have spoken)
ils parl-*ent*	*they may speak*	ils aient parl-*é*	*they may* (have spoken)

great a danger. Would not his attorney (clear up) that business?
3 1 4 *procureur débrouiller affaire* f.

We would (drive away) the importunate. Would you not discover
chasser importun m. pl. *dévoiler*

that atrocious plot? They would not unravel the clue of that
atroce 2 *complot* m. 1 *démêler fil* m.

intrigue.
——— f.

PAST.

I should have liked hunting, fishing, and the country.
aimer art. *chasse* f. art. *pêche* f. *campagne* f.

Wouldst thou not have played? Would he not have bowed to the
jouer saluer *

company? Would we gladly have praised his pride and
compagnie f. *avec plaisir* 2 *louer* 1 *orgueil* m.

incivility? You would have awakened every body. Would
pron. *malhonnêteté* f. *éveiller tout le monde*

those merchants have paid their debts?
négociant payer dette f. pl.

* The second person singular of the imperative of this conjugation, and likewise of some verbs of the second ending in *vrir, frir, lir*, take an *s* after *e*, before the word *y* and *en*, as, *portes-en à ton frère*, carry some to thy brother; *offres-en à ta sœur*, offer some to thy sister; *cueilles-en aussi pour toi*, gather some alike for thyself; *apportes-y tes livres*, bring there thy books.

IMPERATIVE.

In all thy actions, consult the light of reason. Never
dans —f.pl. *consulter* *lumière* art. f.

yield to the violence of thy passions. Let us love
te abandonner ——— f. ———

justice, peace, and virtue. Let us not cease to
art. ——— f. art. f. art. f. *cesser de*

work. Sacrifice your own interest to the public good. Do
travailler. *sacrifier* * *intérêt* m. pl. 2 *bien* 1

not omit such useful and interesting details.
négliger de si utile 2 *intéressant* 3 art. ——— m. pl. 1.

SUBJUNCTIVE.

PRESENT.

Must I ever listen to a severe censor of my defects? I wish
faut il toujours 2 *écouter* 1 * ——2 =m.1. *défaut* m.pl. *je souhaite*

that thou mayest find real friends. He must study, in order
trouver de vrai *il faut qu'il travaille afin*

that he may adorn his speeches with the graces of a pure diction.
parer *discours* *de* —2 ———f.1

We have retired in order that she may remain alone and quiet.
nous nous sommes retirés afin *rester*

Provided we do not so hastily condemn the world. It is not
pour que *légèrement condamner* *monde* m. *il n'est*

well to sulk incessantly. We pay them well that they may
pas bien *bouder* *sans cesse* *nous les payons bien afin que*

work more willingly.
travailler plus volontiers

PRETERIT.

It is not unlikely that I have spoken rashly. Do you not
il n'est pas improbable *imprudemment ne croyez-*

believe that he has carried despair into the heart of his
vous pas *porter* art. *désespoir* m. *dans* *âme*

friend? Can any one imagine that we should have blamed a conduct
pourra-t-on s'imaginer. *blâmer conduite* f.

so prudent and so wise? I easily conceive your having exasperated
——— *sage. je conçois facilement que* *exaspérer*

so petulant a disposition That they may not have (taken advantage)
———2 *caractère* m.1 *profiter*

of the circumstances.
circonstance f pl

SIMPLE TENSES.		COMPOUND TENSES.	
IMPERFECT.		PLUPERFECT.	
que	*that*	que	*that*
je parl-*asse*	*I might, could or would*	j'eusse	*I might, could or would*
tu parl-*asses*	*thou mightst*	tu eusses	*thou mightst*
il parl-*ât*	*he might*	il eût	*he might*
nous parl-*assions*	*we might*	nous eussions	*we might*
vous parl-*assiez*	*you might*	vous eussiez	*you might*
ils parl-*assent*	*they might* — *speak*	ils eussent — parl-*é*	*they might* — *have spoken*

IMPERFECT.

That I might not copy his example. That thou mightest (give up)
imiter *exemple* m. *abandonner*

perfidious friends. That he might inhabit a hut
de ——*de* 2 art. 1 *habiter* *chaumière* f.

instead of a palace. That we might fall at the feet of an
au lieu *palais* m. *tomber à* *pied* m.

illegitimate king. That you might respect the laws of your
illégitime 2 1 *respecter* *loi* f. pl.

country. That they might not speak at random.
pays m. *à tort et à travers*

PLUPERFECT.

That I might not have burnt that work. That thou mightest not
brûler m.

have contemplated the beauties of the country. That he might have
contempler = *campagne*

improved his natural abilities. That we might not have
perfectionner ——*rel* 2 *moyens* m. 1

gained the victory. That you might have delighted the public.
remporter = f. *enchanter* — m.

That they might have struck their enemies with fear.
frapper *de* *crainte*

116. SECOND CONJUGATION.

IN -*IR*.

This conjugation is divided into five branches, which are distinguished by the *participle present*, the *first person of the indicative*, and the *preterit*, thus:

1 punir	punissant	je punis	je punis
2 dormir	dormant	je dors	je dormis
3 ouvrir	ouvrant	j'ouvre	j'ouvris
4 venir	venant	je viens	je vins
5 courir	courant	je cours	je courus

The first branch contains upwards of two hundred and eighty verbs, the second contains seven radical verbs, and eleven derivatives.

As there are many verbs of the first branch, the infinitives of which end in *mir, tir, vir*, like those of the second branch, as may be seen from the following table, some confusion may arise in conjugating the one or the other, that is, the learner might be led, by analogy, to say *ralentant, je ralentais*, or *dormissant, je dormissais*. To avoid this confusion effectually, he will do well to learn the second branch by heart, especially as the few verbs of which it is composed, are very commonly used.

The third branch has four radical verbs, and five derivative.

The fourth branch has two radical verbs and twenty-three derivatives.

The fifth has one radical, and seven derivative verbs.

TABLE OF THE FIVE BRANCHES.

FIRST BRANCH.

ralent-*ir*	*to slacken*	asserv-*ir*	*to inslave*
retent-*ir*	*to resound*	sév-*ir*	*to punish*
appesant-*ir*	*to make heavy*	assouv-*ir*	*to glut*
nant-*ir*	*to pledge*	appauvr-*ir*	*to impoverish*
renform-*ir*	*to plaster*	tern-*ir*	*to tarnish*
afferm-*ir*	*to strengthen*	vern-*ir*	*to varnish*
répart-*ir*	*to distribute*	garn-*ir*	*to garnish*
avert-*ir*	*to inform*	fourn-*ir*	*to furnish*
dessert-*ir*	*to unset a stone*	bén-*ir*	*to bless*
sort-*ir*	*to obtain*	henn-*ir*, etc.	*to neigh*
assort-*ir*	*to match*		
essort-*ir*	*to be under the jurisdiction of*		

SECOND BRANCH.

Roots.		Derivatives.	
dor-*mir*, je dors	*to sleep*	redor-*mir*	*to sleep again*
		endor-*mir*	*to lull asleep*
		se rendor-*mir*	*to fall asleep again*
men-*tir*, je mens,	*to lie*	démen-*tir*	*to give the lie*
sen-*tir*, je sens,	*to feel*	consen-*tir*	*to consent*
		pressen-*tir*	*to foresee*
		ressen-*tir*	*to resent*
par-*tir* *, je pars,	*to set out*	dépar-*tir*	*to divide*
		repar-*tir*	*to set out again*
sor-*tir* *, je sors,	*to get out*	ressor-*tir*	*to go out again*
ser-*vir*, je sers,	*to serve*	desser-*vir*	*to clear the table*

se repen-*tir*, je me repens, *to repent*, has no derivative.

THIRD BRANCH.

ou-*vrir*	*to open*	rou-*vrir*	*to open again*
		entr'ou-*vrir*	*to half open*
cou-*vrir*	*to cover*	décou-*vrir*	*to discover*
		recou-*vrir*	*to cover again*
off-*rir*	*to offer*	mésof-*frir*	*to underbid*

souff-*rir* *to suffer* has no derivative.

* N.B.—*Partir*, *repartir*, *sortir*, and *ressortir*, of the second branch, take the auxiliary *être*. *Venir*, and its derivatives, are likewise conjugated with *être*, except *prevenir* and *subvenir*, which take *avoir*; *convenir* also takes *avoir*, when it means *to suit*, but it takes *être*, when it signifies *to agree*. *Avenir* is a defective and obsolete verb, only used impersonally.

FOURTH BRANCH.

Roots.	Derivatives.		Roots.	Derivatives.	
VENIR *to come*	contre-*venir*	*to contravene*	TENIR *to hold*	s'abs-*tenir*	*to abstain*
	a-*venir*	*to happen*		appar-*tenir*	*to belong*
	con-*venir**	*to agree*		con-*tenir*	*to contain*
	de-*venir*	*to become*		dé-*tenir*	*to detain*
	discon-*venir*	*to deny*		entre-*tenir*	*to keep up*
	inter-*venir*	*to intervene*		main-*tenir*	*to maintain*
	par-*venir*	*to attain*		ob-*tenir*	*to obtain*
	pré-*venir*	*to prevent*		re-*tenir*	*to retain*
	pro-venir*	*to proceed*		sou-*tenir*	*to uphold*
	re-*venir*	*to come again*			
	sur-*venir*	*to befall*			
	sub-*venir**	*to relieve*			
	se sou-*venir*	*to remember*			
	se ressou-*venir*	*to recollect*			

FIFTH BRANCH.

COURIR, COURANT, JE COURS, *to run*	accourir,	*to run to*	parcourir,	*to run over*
	concourir,	*to concur*	recourir,	*to recur*
	discourir,	*to discourse*	secourir,	*to succour*
	encourir,	*to incur*		

117. PARADIGMS OF THE SECOND CONJUGATION.

INFINITIVE.

PRESENT.

Branch 1.	Branch 2.	Branch 3.	Branch 4.	Branch 5.
to punish	*to feel*	*to open*	*to hold*	*to run*
pu-*nir* †	sen-*tir* †	ou-*vrir* †	t-*enir* †	cou-*rir* †

PARTICIPLE PRESENT.

punishing	*feeling*	*opening*	*holding*	*running*
pu-*nissant*	sen-*tant*	ou-*vrant*	te-*nant*	cou-*rant*

PARTICIPLE PAST.

punished	*felt*	*opened*	*held*	*ran*
pu-*ni*	sen-*ti*	ou-*vert*	te-*nu*	cou-*ru*

* See Note in page 182.

† The italics show the letters which are altered from the infinitive, in the formation of the different persons.

to have punished avoir pu-*ni* *having punished* ayant pu-*ni*	*felt* sen-*ti*	*opened* ou-*vert*	*held* t-*enu*	*ran* cou-*ru*

INDICATIVE.

PRESENT.

I punish	*feel*	*open*	*hold*	*run*
je pu-*nis*	sen-*s*	ou-*vre*	t-*iens*	cour*s*
tu pu-*nis*	sen-*s*	ou-*vres*	t-*iens*	cour*s*
il pu-*nit*	sen-*t*	ou *vre*	t-*ient*	cour*t*
nous pu-*nissons*	sen-*tons*	ou-*vrons*	te-*nons*	cou-*rons*
vous pu-*nissez*	sen-*tez*	ou-*vrez*	te-*nez*	cou-*rez*
ils pu-*nissent*	sen-*tent*	ou-*vrent*	t-*iennent*	cou-*rent*

PRETERIT INDEFINITE.

I have punished	*felt*	*opened*	*held*	*ran*
j'ai pu-*ni*	sen-*ti*	ouv-*ert*	t-*enu*	cou-*ru*

IMPERFECT.

I did punish	*feel*	*open*	*hold*	*ran*
je pu-*nissais* *	sen-*tais* *	ouv-*rais* *	t-*enais*	cou-*rais* *

INDICATIVE.

PRESENT.

I choose this picture. I feel all the unpleasantness of your
choisir *tableau* m. *désagrément* m.

situation. Whence comest thou? Does he thus define that word?
— *d'où* *venir* * *ainsi* *définir* *mot* m.

Does his mother (go out) so early? Do we not (set off) for the
* *sortir* *tôt.* * *partir*

country? Do you not sympathise with his sorrows? Do you
campagne f. * *compatir à* *mal.* m. pl. *

not (tell a lie)? They (are finishing) at this moment. They
mentir *finir* *dans* * art. — m.

(act contrarily) to your orders.
contrevenir *ordre.*

* The first person only of those tenses, which are invariably conjugated alike, will now be given, the scholar will easily supply the rest. Those tenses are, the imperfect. je *punissais*, the future and conditional, *je punirai*, *je punirais*

PLUPERFECT.

I had punished	*felt*	*opened*	*held*	*ran*
j'avais pu-*ni*	sen-*ti*	ouv-*ert*	t-*enu*	cou-*ru*

PRETERIT DEFINITE.

I punished	*felt*	*opened*	*held*	*ran*
je pu-*nis*	sen-*tis*	ouv-*ris*	t-*ins*	cou-*rus*
tu pu-*nis*	sen-*tis*	ouv-*ris*	t-*ins*	cou-*rus*
il pun-*it*	sen-*tit*	ouv-*rit*	t-*int*	cou-*rut*
nous pu-*nîmes*	sen-*tîmes*	ouv-*rîmes*	t-*înmes*	cou-*rûmes*
vous pu-*nîtes*	sen-*tîtes*	ouv-*rîtes*	t-*întes*	cou-*rûtes*
ils pu-*nirent*	sen-*tirent*	ouv-*rirent*	t-*inrent*	cou-*rurent*

PRETERIT ANTERIOR.

I had punished	*felt*	*opened*	*held*	*ran*
j'eus pu-*ni*	sen-*ti*	ou-*vert*	te-*nu*	cou-*ru*

FUTURE ABSOLUTE.

I shall punish	*feel*	*open*	*hold*	*run*
je pu-*nirai*	sen-*tirai*	ou-*vrirai*	t-*iendrai*	cour-*rai*

FUTURE ANTERIOR.

I shall have punished	*felt*	*opened*	*held*	*ran*
j'aurai pu-*ni*	sen-*ti*	ouv-*ert*	te-*nu*	cou-*ru*

IMPERFECT.

I fortified his soul against the dangers of seduction. I served
prémunir *contre* — art. — f. *servir*

my friends warmly. Didst not thou amuse him with fair
avec chaleur * *entretenir* *de beau*

promises? He generally complied with the wishes of his family
promesse f. pl. *en général consentir à* *désir* m. pl. *famille* f.

Were we sleeping then? Did you not belie your character?
dormir *démentir* *caractère* m.

The children were running about the garden. We (used to discourse
courir *dans* *discourir*

on interesting subjects. My sister (used to come) every
intéressant 2 *sujet* m. 1 *venir* *tous*

morning to see me. Did you not go out when you pleased?
les matins *sortir* *vouliez*

Did not the master punish you severely?
sévèrement

PRETERIT.

I softened my father by my submission. I foresaw that terrible
fléchir *soumission* f. *pressentir* — 2

catastrophe. Thou didst not (come again) as thou hadst pro-
— f. 1. *revenir* *comme* *le* ind-2 *pro-*

mised. He did not succeed through thoughtlessness. Did not his
mis *réussir* *par* *étourderie* f.

daughter (set out again) immediately? Did not Alexander sully
repartir *sur-le-champ* *ternir*

his glory by his pride? Did we (go out) of the city before him?
sortir *ville* f. *avant* *lui*

We never betrayed that important secret. Did not you agree to
trahir — 2 — m. 1 *consentir de*

(leave it to me?) They served their country with courage.
vous en rapporter à moi *pays*

FUTURE.

Shall I not obtain this of you? What will become of thee, if I
obtenir *cela de* *que* *devenir* * *tu*

forsake thee? Will he not embellish his country seat?
abandonner *embellir* *maison de campagne* f.

He will not sleep quietly. Shall we consent to that ridiculous
tranquillement 2

bargain? With time and patience, you (will
marché m. 1 *avec de* art. m. pr. art. f. *venir*

accomplish) your object. We shall not sully the splendour of
à bout de *dessein* m. *ternir* *éclat* m.

our life by an unworthy action. Will those men enrich their
indigne 2 — 1 *enrichir*

country by their industry? Will not our friends offer us their
pays *industrie* *offrir*

assistance? (Take off) your coat and you will run faster.
secours *ôtez* *courir*

CONDITIONAL.

PRESENT.

I should punish	*feel*	*open*	*hold*	*run*
je pu-*nirais*	sen-*tirais*	ou-*vrirais*	t-*iendrais*	cour-*ais*

PAST.

I should have punished	*felt*	*opened*	*held*	*run*
j'aurais pu-*ni*	sen-*ti*	ou-*vert*	te-*nu*	cou-*ru*

IMPERATIVE.

punish (thou)	*feel*	*open*	*hold*	*run*
pu-*nis*	sen-*s*	ou-*vre*	t-*iens*	cour*s*
qu'il pu-*nisse*	sen-*te*	ou-*vre*	t-*ienne*	cou-*re*
pu-*nissons*	sen-*tons*	ou-*vrons*	te-*nons*	cou-*rons*
pu-*nissez*	sen-*tez*	ou-*vrez*	te-*nez*	cou-*rez*
qu'ils pu-*nissent*	sen-*tent*	ou-*vrent*	t-*iennent*	cou-*rent*

CONDITIONAL.

I would open the door and the window. I should still cherish
porte f. *fenêtre* f. *chérir*

life. Would'st not thou interfere in that affair? Would
art. *intervenir* f.

my brother (set off again) without taking leave of us? You would
repartir *sans* *prendre congé*

not succeed in injuring him in the public opinion. You would
parvenir à *nuire* *lui* — 2 — f. 1.

never soften that hard hearted man. Could they foresee their
attendrir *cœur de rocher* *pressentir*

misfortune? Would men always (grow old) without growing
malheur art. *vieillir* *sans* *devenir* inf.-1

wiser, if they reflected on the shortness of life. I would
réfléchir ind.-2 *sur* *brièveté* f. art.

visit France and Italy if (I had the means.)
parcourir art. — art. = *mes moyens le permettaient.*

IMPERATIVE.

Shudder with horror and terror. Do not open the door
Frémir *de* = *de effroi* m. *ouvrir*

to any one in my absence. Let him not suffer such insults.
personne *souffrir pariel* *insulte* f.

SUBJUNCTIVE.

PRESENT.

that I may punish	*feel*	*open*	*hold*	*run*
que je pu-*nisse*	sen-*te*	ou-*vre*	t-*ienne*	cou-*re*
que tu pu-*nisses*	sen-*tes*	ou-*vres*	t-*iennes*	cou-*res*
qu'il pu-*nisse*	sen-*te*	ou-*vre*	t-*ienne*	cou-*re*
que nous pu-*nissions*	sen-*tions*	ou-*vrions*	te-*nions*	cou-*rions*
que vous pu-*nissiez*	sen-*tiez*	ou-*vriez*	te-*niez*	cou-*riez*
qu'ils pu-*nissent*	sen-*tent*	ou-*vrent*	t-*iennent*	cou-*rent*

PRETERIT.

that I may have punished	*felt*	*opened*	*held*	*ran*
que j'aie pun-*i*	sen-*ti*	ouv-*ert*	te-*nu*	cou-*ru*

IMPERFECT.

that I might punish	*feel*	*open*	*hold*	*run*
que je pu-*nisse*	sen-*tisse*	ouv-*risse*	t-*insse*	cou-*russe*
que tu pu-*nisses*	sen-*tisses*	ouv-*risses*	t-*insses*	cou-*russes*
qu'il pu-*nît*	sen-*tît*	ouv-*rît*	t-*înt*	cou-*rût*
que nous pu-*nissions*	sen-*tissions*	ouv-*rissions*	t-*inssions*	cou-*russions*
que vous pu-*nissiez*	sen-*tissiez*	ouv-*rissiez*	t-*inssiez*	cou-*russiez*
qu'ils pu-*nissent*	sen-*tissent*	ouv-*rissent*	t-*inssent*	cou-*russent*

Do not go out in the rain. Let us not run so fast. Let us
sortir à *courir*

feed the poor. Let us gain glory by our perseverance. Let
nourrir m pl. *obtenir* art. = f. —

us not divulge our secrets to every body. Do not maintain so
découvrir — *tout le monde.* *soutenir*

absurd an opinion.
— *de* 2 — f. 1.

SUBJUNCTIVE.

PRESENT.

That I may never stain my reputation. (That I may be before-hand)
flétrir f. *prévenir*

with such dangerous enemies. I will not have thee (go out) this
de art. *si* = 2 1 *veux* *que tu* *sortir*

PLUPERFECT.

I might have punished	*felt*	*opened*	*held*	*run*
que j'aie puni	senti	ouvert	tenu	cou-ru

morning. That he may not obtain his ends. That we may become
matin m. *parvenir à* *fin* f. pl. *devenir*

just, honest, and virtuous. That you may punish the guilty. (We
honnête *vertueux* *coupable* pl. *nous*

all pray) that you may return covered with laurels. That
prions tous pour *revenir* *couvert de* *laurier* m. pl.

they may establish wise and just laws. That they may agree
établir *de* 2 3 art. 1 *convenir*

about the conditions. You must run faster, if you wish to
de ——— *il faut que vous* *voulez le*

overtake him. I sincerely wish he may long enjoy his good fortune
attraper *désirer* *long-temps jouir de* *bonheur* m.

IMPERFECT.

That I might stun the whole neighbourhood. That I might not
étourdir 2 *tout* 1 *voisinage* m.

(bring about) my designs. That he might not bear his disgrace
venir à bout de *projet* m. pl. *soutenir* ——— f.

with firmness. That we might disobey the laws. That we might
fermeté *désobéir à*

belong to that great king. That you might renounce your erro
appartenir *revenir de* =

and prejudices. That they might weaken the force of their
pr. pron. *préjugé* *affaiblir* t.

reasons. That they might hold the most absurd ideas.
raisonnement *tenir à* 2 art. 1

118. THIRD CONJUGATION.

IN -*OIR*.

PARADIGM.

This conjugation contains only seven verbs, which are

perc-*evoir*	*to receive*	déc-*evoir*	*to deceive*
aperc-*evoir*	*to perceive*	d-*evoir*	*to owe*
conc-*evoir*	*to conceive*	red-*evoir*	*to owe again*

and *recevoir*, which serves as a paradigm. *Percevoir* is a law term, and *apercevoir* is often *reflected.*

In all tenses in which *c* comes before *o* or *u*, it takes the cedilla, in order that it may retain its soft sound.

INFINITIVE.

SIMPLE TENSES.		COMPOUND TENSES	
PRESENT.		PAST.	
re-*cevoir*	*to receive*	avoir re-*çu*	*to have received*

PARTICIPLES.

PRESENT.		PAST.	
re-*cevant*	*receiving*	ayant re-*çu*	*having received*
PAST.			
re-*çu*	*received*		

INDICATIVE.

SIMPLE TENSES.

PRESENT.

I receive	*we receive*
je re-ç*ois*	nous re-c*evons*
tu re-ç*ois*	vous re-c*evez*
il re-ç*oit*	ils re-ç*oivent*

IMPERFECT.

I did receive	*we did receive*
je rec-*evais*	nous rec-*evions*

PRETERIT DEFINITE.

I received	*we received*
je re-ç*us*	nous reç-*ûmes*
tu re-ç*us*	vous reç-*ûtes*
il re-ç*ut*	ils reç-*urent*

COMPOUND TENSES.

PRETERIT INDEFINITE.

j'ai	re-ç*u*	*I have received*
tu as	etc.	*thou*, etc.

PLUPERFECT.

j'avais reç-*u*	*I had received*

PRETERIT ANTERIOR.

j'eus	reç-*u*	*I had received*
tu eus	etc.	*thou* etc.

INDICATIVE.

PRESENT.

I see the summit of the Alps covered with perpetual
apercevoir *sommet* *Alpes* f.pl. *de* *éternel* 2

snow. What gratitude dost thou not owe to her who (has
neige f. pl. 1 *reconnaissance* f. *devoir* *celle* 1

discharged) (the duty of a mother) (to thee) (in thy infancy ?)
remplir 3 5 *près de* 4 2

Does not your pupil understand that rule which is so simple ? We
écolier *concevoir* *règle* f. * *

do not owe a large sum. Do you not perceive the snare ? Ought
devoir *gros somme* f. *piége* m. *devoir* 5

firm and courageous men to yield to circumstances ?
des 1 3 = 4 2 * *céder* art. *circonstance*

IMPERFECT.

I received a letter from her daily. Did he see the castle
tous les jours *apercevoir* *château*

from such a distance ? We did not receive our income
si * *loin* *percevoir* *revenu* m. pl.

regularly. Did you not receive great attentions ? Did those
régulièrement *de* *honnêteté* f. pl. *

tyrants conceive all the blackness of their crimes ?
tyran *concevoir* *noirceur* f.

SIMPLE TENSES.		COMPOUND TENSES	
FUTURE ABSOLUTE.		FUTURE ANTERIOR.	
I shall receive	*we shall receive*	j'aurai re-çu	*I shall have received*
je re-*cevrai*	nous rec-*evrons*		

CONDITIONAL.

PRESENT.		PAST.	
I should receive	*we should receive*	j'aurais re-çu	*I should have received*
je re-*cevrais*	nous rec-*evrions*	tu, etc.	

IMPERATIVE.

		re-*cevons*	*let us receive*
re-*çois*	*receive thou*	re-*cevez*	*receive ye*
qu'il re-*çoive*	*let him receive*	qu'ils re-*çoivent*	*let them receive*

PRETERIT DEFINITE.

I perceived him walking by moon-light. He saw him
le qui se promenait à art. *clair de la lune* m.

in the middle of the river struggling for his life. Did we not
au milieu *se débattant contre la mort*

immediately perceive the snare? You did not receive his letters in
lettres à

time. Did the ministers conceive the depth of his plan?
temps ——*tre* *profondeur* f. —m.

FUTURE.

Shall I receive any letters to-day? We shall soon see
de art. *aujourd'hui* *apercevoir*

the spire of the village. Go and see him; I am sure he will
clocher m. —— m. *allez* * *le voir* *que*

receive you well. Will they never understand so simple a thing?
concevoir ——2 *chose* 1

CONDITIONAL.

I would receive them more politely. Should a wise man thus
devoir 2 1 *ainsi* 2

(give himself up) to despair? You would easily perceive so
s'abandonner 1 art. *désespoir* m.

gross a trick. Would not my sisters receive their friend with
grossier 2 *ruse* f. 1. f.

tenderness?
tendresse f.

SUBJUNCTIVE.

SIMPLE TENSES.		COMPOUND TENSES.	
PRESENT.		**PRETERIT.**	
that I may receive	*that we may receive*	que j'aie reç-*u*	*that I may have received*
que je reç-*oive*	que nous rec-*evions*	que tu, etc.	
que tu reç-*oives*	que vous rec-*eviez*	qu'il, etc.	
qu'il reç-*oive*	qu'ils reç-*oivent*		
IMPERFECT.		**PLUPERFECT.**	
that I might receive	*that we might rec.*	que j'eusse re-ç*u*	*that I might have received.*
que je reç-*usse*	que nous reç-*ussions*	que tu, etc.	
que je reç-*usses*	que vous reç-*ussiez*		
qu'il reç-*ût*	qu'ils reç-*ussent*		

IMPERATIVE.

PRESENT.

Conceive the horror of his situation. Do not receive that mark
marque f.
of confidence with indifference. Let us entertain horror of
confiance —— *concevoir* * *de* art. *pour*
vice. Receive his advice with respect and gratitude. Receive
art. m. *avis* —— ——
no more of his letters.
lettre f. pl.

SUBJUNCTIVE.

PRESENT.

That I may receive consolations. It is not credible that he
de art. *croyable*
should not conceive a thought so well explained. I understand that
pensée f. *développé* *je comprends*
you may not perceive the danger of books which are contrary to
—— art. * * *contre* *
good morals. See that they do not collect unjust
art. *mœurs* f. pl. *voyez à ce qu'ils* *percevoir de injuste* 2
taxes.
art. —— f. pl. 1.

FOURTH CONJUGATION.

IN *-RE.*

119. This conjugation has five branches.

The first ends in	*-andre*	as	répandre	*to spill*
	-endre	..	vendre	*to sell*
	-ondre	..	répondre	*to answer*
	-erdre	..	perdre	*to lose*
	-ordre	..	mordre	*to bite*
the second ends in	*-aire*	..	plaire	*to please*
		..	taire	*to keep secret*
the third ends in	*-aître*	..	repaître	*to feed*
	-aître	..	connaître	*to know*
the fourth ends in	*-uire*	..	instruire	*to instruct*
the fifth ends in	*-aindre*	..	contraindre	*to constrain*
	-eindre	..	peindre	*to paint*
	-oindre	..	joindre	*to join*

IMPERFECT.

I did not believe that he perceived the secret designs of the
je ne croyais pas *caché* 2 *dessein* 1

enemy's general. We were obliged to receive every body with
2 * 1 *il fallait que vous*

civility. It was likely that you might not perceive the
honnêteté *il était probable*

depth of this book. That they might not perceive the
profondeur f.

masts of the ship.
mât m. p.. *vaisseau* m.

120. PARADIGMS OF THE FOURTH CONJUGATION.

INFINITIVE.

PRESENT.

Branch 1.	Branch 2.	Branch 3.	Branch 4.	Branch 5.
to render	*to please*	*to appear*	*to reduce*	*to join*
rend-*re*	pl-*aire*	pa-*raître*	rédui-*re*	join-*dre*

PAST. *(To have).*

rendered	*pleased*	*appeared*	*reduced*	*joined*
avoir ren-d*u*	—pl-*u*	—pa-r*u*	—ré-dui*t*	—join*t*

PARTICIPLE PRESENT.

rendering	*pleasing*	*appearing*	*reducing*	*joining*
ren-d*ant*	plai-*sant*	pa-*raissant*	rédui-*sant*	joi-*gnant*

PARTICIPLE PAST.

rendered	*pleased*	*appeared*	*reduced*	*joined*
ren-d*u*	pl*u*	pa-r*u*	rédui*t*	join*t*

COMP. PAST PARTICIPLE.

Avoir rendu Ayant rendu	plu	pa-ru	réduit	joint

INDICATIVE

PRESENT.

I render	*please*	*appear*	*reduce*	*join*
je rend*s*	pl-*ais*	pa-*rais*	rédui*s*	join*s*
tu rend*s*	pl-*ais*	pa-*rais*	rédui*s*	join*s*
il rend	pl-*ait*	pa-*raît*	rédui*t*	join*t*
nous ren-d*ons*	pl*ai-sons*	pa-*raissons*	rédui-*sons*	joi-*gnons*
vous ren-d*es*	pl*ai-ses*	pa-*raisses*	rédui-*ses*	joi-*gnes*
ils ren-d*ent*	pl*ai-sent*	pa-*raissent*	rédui-*sent*	joi-*gnent*

PRETERIT INDEFINITE. *(I have).*

rendered	*pleased*	*appeared*	*reduced*	*joined*
j'ai ren-*du*	—pl*u*	—pa-r*u*	—rédui*t*	—join*t*

17*

IMPERFECT.

Branch 1.	Branch 2.	Branch 3.	Branch 4.	Branch 5.
I did render	*please*	*appear*	*reduce*	*join*
je ren-*dais*	pl*ai-sais*	pa-*raissais*	rédui-*sais*	joi-*gnais*

PLUPERFECT.

I had rendered	*pleased*	*appeared*	*reduced*	*joined*
j'avais ren-d*u*	—pl*u*	—par*u*	—rédui*t*	—join*t*

INDICATIVE.

PRESENT.

I know his fiery and impetuous temper. I expect his
connaître *bouillant* 2 = 3 *caractère* m. 1 *attendre*

return with impatience. Does he fear death? Does not
retour *craindre* art. f.

virtue please every body? We do not compel you to adopt this
à *contraindre* *de adopter*

opinion. We suppress for the present several interesting circum-
—— f. *taire* —— m. *intéressante* 2

stances. Do you not confound these notions (with one another?)
f. 1 *confondre* *l'une avec l'autre*

You captivate your hearers by your modest exterior. Do your
séduire *auditeurs* m. pl. 2 = m. 1

sons acknowledge their errors? Do not those workmen waste their
reconnaître = *ouvrier* *perdre*

time about trifles?
à *bagatelle* pl.

IMPERFECT.

I did not displease by my conduct. I pitied those sad victims
déplaire *plaindre* *triste victime* f. pl.

of the revolution. Did not this dog bite? She pleased every
——— f. *chien* *mordre* *plaire à* *tout*

body. He never seemed satisfied. Did he not beat every body
le monde *paraître* *content* *battre*

at draughts? We did not hear well because we were too far.
aux dames *entendre* *éloigné*

She was painting. His presence diffused joy wherever he
peindre *répandre* *par tout où*

appeared. They led us into error.
se montrait *induire* *en*

PRETERIT.

Branch 1.		Branch 2.	Branch 3.	Branch 4.	Branch 5.
I rendered		*pleased*	*appeared*	*reduced*	*joined*
je	ren-*dis*	pl*us*	pa-*rus*	rédui-*sis*	joi-*gnis*
tu	ren-*dis*	pl*us*	pa-*rus*	rédui-*sis*	joi-*gnis*
il	ren-*dit*	pl*ut*	pa-*rut*	rédui-*sit*	joi-*gnit*
nous	ren-*dîmes*	pl*ûmes*	pa-*rûmes*	rédui-*sîmes*	joi-*gnîmes*
vous	ren-*dîtes*	pl*ûtes*	pa-*rûtes*	rédui-*sîtes*	joi-*gnîtes*
ils	ren-*dirent*	pl*urent*	pa-*rurent*	rédui-*sirent*	joi-*gnirent*

PRETERIT ANTERIOR.

I had rendered	*pleased*	*appeared*	*reduced*	*joined*
j'eus ren-d*u*	pl*u*	pa-r*u*	rédui-*t*	join*t*

FUTURE ABSOLUTE.

I shall render	*please*	*appear*	*reduce*	*join*
je rend-*rai*	pl*ai-rai*	pa-ra*î-trai*	rédui-*rai*	join-*drai*

FUTURE ANTERIOR. (*I shall have*)

rendered	*pleased*	*appeared*	*reduced*	*joined*
j'aurai ren-*du*	pl*u*	pa-r*u*	rédui-*t*	join*t*

PRETERIT.

I sold every thing I had before my departure. She compelled
vendre *tout ce que* ind. 2. *contraindre*

him to speak the truth. They started before us, but we joined
de dire *partir* *rejoindre*

them at Paris where they (waited for) us. After giving him a
attendre ind. 2. *donner* inf. 2

good dinner, we took him back to his cottage in our own car-
reconduire * *chaumière* f.

riage. They put out all the candles which alarmed us a little.
éteindre *lumières* f. *ce qui étonner* ind. 3

My dog ran after him and bit him in the leg.
courir ind. 3. *mordre* *à*

FUTURE.

Shall I hear him when he calls? I shall not conceal
entendre *appeler*, ind. 7 *taire* 2

my mind from you. Will not the general compel the offi-
façon de penser 3 * 1 *contraindre* *offi-*

CONDITIONAL.

PRESENT.

Branch 1.	Branch 2.	Branch 3.	Branch 4.	Branch 5.
I should render	*please*	*appear*	*reduce*	*join*
je ren-d*rais*	pl-*ai-rais*	pa-*raî-trais*	ré-dui-*rais*	join-*drais*

PAST. *(I should have).*

rendered	*pleased*	*appeared*	*reduced*	*joined*
j'aurais ren-d*u*	—pl*u*	—pa-r*u*	—ré-dui*t*	—joi-*nt*

IMPERATIVE.

render (thou)	*please*	*appear*	*reduce*	*join*
ren-d*s*	pl*ais*	pa-r*ais*	rédui*s*	join*s*
qu'il ren-*de*	pl*aise*	pa-r*aisse*	rédui*se*	joi-*gne*
ren-d*ons*	pl*ai-sons*	pa-r*aissons*	rédui-*sons*	joi-*gnons*
ren-d*ez*	pl*ai-sez*	pa-r*aissez*	rédui-*sez*	joi-*gnez*
qu'ils ren-d*ent*	pl*ai-sent*	pa-r*aissent*	rédui-*sent*	joi-*gnent*

---

cers to join their respective corps? Will not a thought,
cier à rejoindre = f.

true, grand, and well expressed, please? (We shall make our
exprimé, plaire paraî-

appearance) on this great stage next month. Shall
tre sur théâtre m. art. *prochain* 2 *mois* m. 1

we describe all the horror of this terrible night? Will you
dépeindre —— 2 *nuit* f. 1

not re-model a work so full of errors? Will you know your
refondre plein erreur f. *reconnaître*

things again? They will assiduously correspond with their
effet m. pl. * *assidûment correspondre*

friends.

CONDITIONAL.

PRESENT.

Should I, by these means, gain the desired end? I
moyen m. s. *atteindre à désiré* 2 *but* m. 1

would (carry on) the undertaking with success. Would his mother
conduire entreprise f.

wait with (so much) patience? Could sincerity displease a
attendre tant de art. = f. *déplaire à*

SUBJUNCTIVE.

PRESENT. (*That I may*).

Branch 1.	Branch 2.	Branch 3.	Branch 4.	Branch 5.
render	*please*	*appear*	*reduce*	*join*
que je ren-*de*	pl*aise*	pa-*raisse*	rédui-*se*	joi-*gne*
tu ren-*des*	pl*aises*	pa-*raisses*	rédui-*ses*	joi-*gnes*
il ren-*de*	pl*aise*	pa-*raisse*	rédui-*se*	joi-*gne*
nous ren-*dions*	pl*aisions*	pa-*raissions*	rédui-*sions*	joi-*gnions*
vous ren-*diez*	pl*aisiez*	pa-*raissiez*	rédui-*siez*	joi-*gniez*
ils ren-*dent*	pl*aisent*	pa-*raissent*	rédui-*sent*	joi-*gnent*

---

man (of sense)? Should we sell our liberty? Should we
sensé *vendre*

build our house upon that plan? Would you oblige
construire — m. *astreindre de* art.

young people to live as you do? Would you drive your child
gens pl. *vivre comme* * *réduire*

to despair? They should fear public censure. Would
art. *désespoir* m. *craindre* 2 art. f. 1

my protectors introduce an unknown person into the world?
= *introduire* *inconnu* m. *

IMPERATIVE.

Depict in thy idyl all the charms of a rural life. Do
peindre *idylle* *douceur* f. *champêtre* 2 1

not wait for me, for it is uncertain whether I shall
attendre * *douteux* *que* *re-*

return or not. Know the powers of thy mind before thou
venir subj-1 *force* f. *avant de* *

write. Let us unite prudence with courage. Let us not
écrire *joindre* art. f. *à* art. m.

descend to useless particulars. Do not appear either too
descendre *dans des* 2 —*larité* 1 *paraître* *ni*

cheerful or too grave. Ye sovereigns make the people happy
gai *ni* *sérieux* * *souverain* pl. *rendre*

Sweet illusions, vain phantoms, vanish. (Keep to yourself
doux — f. — *fantôme* m. *disparaître* *taire*

such truths as may offend.
certain f. pl. *qui peuvent offenser*

PRETERIT. *(That I may have).*

rendered	*pleased*	*appeared*	*reduced*	*joined*
que j'aie ren-d*u*	—pl*u*	—pa-r*u*	—rédui*t*	—joi-*nt*

IMPERFECT. *(That I might).*

render	*please*	*appear*	*reduce*	*join*
que je ren-d*isse*	pl*usse*	pa-r*usse*	rédui-*sisse*	joi-*gnisse*
tu ren-d*isses*	pl*usses*	pa-r*usses*	rédui-*sisses*	joi-*gnisses*
il ren-d*ît*	pl*ût*	pa-r*ût*	rédui-*sît*	joi-*gnît*
nous ren-d*issions*	pl*ussions*	pa-r*ussions*	rédui-*sissions*	joi-*gnissions*
vous ren-d*issiez*	pl*ussiez*	pa-r*ussiez*	rédui-*sissiez*	joi-*gnissiez*
ils ren-d*issent*	pl*ussent*	pa-r*ussent*	rédui-*sissent*	joi-*gnissent*

SUBJUNCTIVE.

PRESENT.

That I may fear that host of enemies. That I should please
craindre *nuée* f. *à*

every body, is impossible. That he may not reply to such
ce *répondre* *un si* 2

absurd criticism. That he may lead his pupil step by step
—— f. *critique* f. 1 *conduire* *élève* *pas* *à*

to a perfect knowledge of the art of speaking and writing. That
connaissance f. inf. 1 pr. inf-1

we may confound the arts with the sciences. That you may have
confondre *tendre à*

the same end (in view). That they may not depend on any body.
but m. * * *dépendre* *de personne*

That they may not increase our sufferings.
accroître *peines*

IMPERFECT.

He did not allow us to answer him. They were obliged
Il ne voulait pas que *répondre* *lui* *Il fallait* *que*

to appear in full uniform at dinner. He stayed a fort-
grande —forme m. *attendre* ind-3 * *quinze*

night in Paris, (in order) that we might rejoin him. That we
jours à *afin* *rejoindre*

PLUPERFECT. (*that I might have*).

rendered	*pleased*	*appeared*	*reduced*	*joined*
que j'eusse ren-d*u*	pl*u*	par-*u*	rédui*t*	join*t*

---

might take him to court. That you might hear their
conduire art. *cour* f. *entendre*
justification. That you might know your real friends. That they
vrai
might (wait for) the opinion of sensible persons.
attendre art. *sensé* 2 f. pl. 1

---

121. *Pronominal or reflected verbs* are, as it has already been said, conjugated with two pronouns, one the subject and the other the object. In their compound tenses the participle past agrees in gender and number with the subject.*

EXAMPLES.

je me blesse	*I hurt myself*
nous nous trompons	*we deceive ourselves*
elle s'est tuée	*she has killed herself*

Almost all active verbs may be made reflected, since a person may hurt and deceive himself in the same manner that he hurts or deceives others. This point is common to both languages, but there are two things in which they differ with regard to reflected verbs. First, the compound tenses are conjugated with *to have*, in English, and with *être* in French: *I have hurt myself, je me suis blessé.* Secondly, there are a good many verbs which are used in the reflected form in French which are *neuter* in English; such as *je m'arrête, je me dépêche,*

* There is one exception which will be found noticed in the chapter of the *Participle Past*

I stop, I make haste. As these latter are very frequently used in conversation, wc subjoin a list of them.

122. LIST OF COMMON REFLECTED VERBS.

s'abstenir	*to abstain*
s'abonner	*to subscribe*
s'apercevoir	*to perceive*
s'asseoir	*to sit down*
se coucher	*to lie down*
se dépêcher	*to make haste*
se défaire	*to get rid*
se désespérer	*to despair*
se dispenser	*to dispense with*
s'entretenir	*to converse*
s'endormir	*to fall asleep*
s'en aller	*to go away*
s'efforcer	*to endeavour*
s'empêcher	*to forbear*
s'emporter	*to grow warm*
s'enfuir	*to run away*
s'enquérir	*to enquire*
s'étonner	*to feel surprised*
s'éveiller	*to wake*
s'évanouir	*to faint*
s'enquérir	*to enquire*
se fâcher	*to be angry*
se fier	*to trust*
se garder	*to beware*
s'habiller	*to dress*
s'habituer	*to get used*
se hâter	*to hasten*
s'imaginer	*to fancy*
s'intéresser	*to feel an interest*
se lever	*to get up*
se méfier	*to distrust*
se moquer	*to laugh at*; *not to care for*
se nommer	*to be named*
s'occuper	*to be busy about*
se promener	*to walk*
se plaindre	*to complain*
se plaire	*to take pleasure*
se porter	*to be (ill or well)*
se rappeler	*to remember*
se réjouir	*to rejoice*
se rendre	*to go, to repair to*
se repentir	*to repent*
se ressouvenir	*to remember*
se rire	*to laugh at*; *not to care for*
se retourner	*to turn round*
se reposer	*to rest*
se réveiller	*to wake*
se savoir gré	*to be glad*
se servir	*to make use of*
se taire	*to be silent*
se tromper	*to mistake or be mistaken*
se trouver	*to be*
se vanter	*to boast*

123. PARADIGM OF A REFLECTED VERB.

INFINITIVE.

SIMPLE TENSES.	COMPOUND TENSES.
PRESENT.	PAST.
se repentir — *to repent*	*s'*être repenti *or* repenti*e* — *to have repented*
PRESENT.	
repentant — *repenting*	

PARTICIPLES.

PAST.	PAST.
repenti, *m.*; repenti*e*, *f.*; repenti*s*, *m.*; repenti*es*, *f.* — *repented*	*s'*étant repenti, *or* repenti*e* — *having repented*

INDICATIVE.

SIMPLE TENSES.			COMPOUND TENSES.			
PRESENT.			PRETERIT INDEFINITE.			
I repent.			*I have repented.*			
je	*me*	repens	je	*me*	*suis*	repenti *or* repenti*e*
tu	*te*	repens	tu	*t'*	*es*	
il, *or* elle	*se*	repent	il, *or* elle	*s'*	*est*	
nous	*nous*	repentons	nous	*nous*	*sommes*	repenti*s* *or* repenti*es*
vous	*vous*	repentez	vous	*vous*	*êtes*	
ils, *or* elles	*se*	repentent	ils, *or* elles	*se*	*sont*	
IMPERFECT.			PLUPERFECT.			
I did repent.			*I had repented.*			
je	*me*	repentais	je	*m'*	*étais*	repenti *or* repenti*e*
tu	*te*	repentais	tu	*t'*	*étais*	
il, *or* elle	*se*	repentait	il, *or* elle	*s'*	*était*	
nous	*nous*	repentions	nous	*nous*	*étions*	repenti*s* *or* repenti*es*
vous	*vous*	repentiez	vous	*vous*	*étiez*	
ils, *or* elles	*se*	repentaient	ils, *or* elles	*s'*	*étaient*	

124. INTERROGATIVE AND NEGATIVE FORMS.

je ne me repens pas	*I do not repent*
te repens-tu ?	*dost thou repent ?*
ne nous repentons-nous pas ?	*do we not repent ?*
je ne me suis pas repenti	*I have not repented*
ne se sont-ils pas repentis ?	*have they repented ?*
ne se sont-elles pas repenties ?	*have they not repented ?*
ma sœur se repent	*my sister repents*
ma sœur ne se repent-elle pas ?	*does not my sister repent ?*
vos frères se sont-ils repentis ?	*have your brothers repented ?*

INDICATIVE.

PRESENT.

I often walk by moonlight. Dost thou not
souvent se promener† *à* art. *clair de la lune* m. *se*

deceive thyself ? He (is never happy) but (when he is doing)
tromper *ne se plaire* *que* *à faire*

wrong. I complain of his bad conduct. (Do we
de art. *mal* m. *se plaindre* *mauvais* *conduite* f.

not take too much care of ourselves) ? How do you do ? They
s'écouter *trop* *se porter* *se*

intend to travel in the spring.
proposer *de voyager* *à* *printemps* m.

PRETERIT INDEFINITE.

I (have been) tolerably well for some time. Didst thou not
se porter *assez* *bien* *depuis*

lose thyself in the wood ? (It is said) that he killed himself
s'égarer *on dit* *se* *tuer*

(out of) despair. Have we flattered ourselves without foundation ?
de *se flatter* *fondement*

Ladies, have you walked (this morning) ? Did those ladies re-
Mesdames *promener* *matin* m. *dame* *se*

† It need hardly be remarked that reflected verbs do not belong to one conjugation alone, but to all. The learner must, therefore, be careful to ascertain to which of them those which come under his consideration belong. *Se promener* is of the first, *se plaindre* is of the fourth and fifth branch; and *se plaire* is fourth conjugation, second branch.

SIMPLE TENSES.			COMPOUND TENSES.			
PRETERIT DEFINITE.			PRETERIT ANTERIOR.			
I repented.			*I had repented.*			
je	*me*	repentis	je	*me*	*fus*	repenti, *or* repentie
tu	*te*	repentis	tu	*te*	*fus*	
il *or* elle	*se*	repentit	il *or* elle	*se*	*fut*	
nous	*nous*	repentîmes	nous	*nous*	*fûmes*	repentis *or* repenties
vous	*vous*	repentîtes	vous	*vous*	*fûtes*	
ils *or* elles	*se*	repentirent	ils *or* elles	*se*	*furent*	

cognise themselves in this portrait? You have mistaken the
reconnaître *à* — m. *se tromper* *de*

house We have made as much haste as we could. Has he stopped
se dépêcher autant que possible *s'arrêter*

(on the) road? I have fallen asleep.
en *s'endormir*

IMPERFECT.

I troubled myself about the affairs of others. You were always
se tourmenter *pour* *autrui.* *se*

complaining of being too warm, and now you are too cold. Were
plaindre *d'avoir trop chaud* *avoir trop froid*

you not comfortable in his house? My mother did not like the
se trouver bien *se plaire à*

country, because we went to bed so early. He was a very suspicious
se coucher de si bonne heure * *très soupçonneux*

man, who never trusted any body. Did you fancy that he would
* *il ne se fier à personne* *s'imaginer*

return early? Did you not laugh at us?
revenir cond-1 *de si bonne heure* *se moquer de*

PLUPERFECT.

I had trusted myself to (very uncertain) guides. Didst thou not
se livrer *peu sûr* 2 *des* m. pl. 1 *se*

confide too inconsiderately in this man? Had that officer rushed
confier *légèrement* *à* —*cier se précipiter*

rashly into this danger? We had condemned ourselves. Had
témérairement dans — m. *se condamner nous-mêmes*

FUTURE ABSOLUTE.			FUTURE ANTERIOR.			
I shall repent.			*I shall have repented.*			
je	*me*	repentirai	je	*me*	*serai*	repenti *or* repentie
tu	*te*	repentiras	tu	*te*	*seras*	
il *or* elle	*se*	repentira	il *or* elle	*se*	*sera*	
nous	*nous*	repentirons	nous	*nous*	*serons*	repentis *or* repenties
vous	*vous*	repentirez	vous	*vous*	*serez*	
ils *or* elles	*se*	repentiront	ils *or* elles	*se*	*seront*	

---

you not been engaged with trifles? Had those travellers
s'occuper de bagatelle f. pl. *voyageurs se*

(gone out) of the right way?
détourner droit chemin m.

PRETERIT DEFINITE.

I repented too late of having taken such a step. Were you
tard inf-2 *fait* 2 1 *démarche* f.

not well amused yesterday evening? He suffered
s'amuser hier au ne se trouver pas bien

for his imprudence. We met in the street, but we did not
de ——— f. *se rencontrer rue*

speak. Did not those rash children go too near the
se parler téméraire 2 1 *s'approcher trop de*

river? They rejoiced when they heard of his great success.
ind-3 *se réjouir apprendre* * *succès* m. pl.

PRETERIT ANTERIOR.

(As soon as) I had discovered that they sought to deceive
Dès que s'apercevoir on chercher ind-2 *à tromper*

me, I was on my guard. What didst thou, when thou
se tenir ind-3 *garde* f. pl. *fis* ind-3 *quand*

didst see thyself thus forsaken? When she recollected all the
se trouver ainsi abandonné se souvenir de

circumstances, she was quite ashamed. When we had rejoiced
f. ind-3 *toute honteux se réjouir*

sufficiently, we parted. When you had amused yourself suffi-
assez se séparer ind-3 *s'amuser*

ciently at his expence, did you not leave him alone?
à dépens m. pl. *laisser* ind-3 *tranquille*

When they had walked enough, they (sat down) at the foot of a
se promener *s'assirent à*
tree.

FUTURE ABSOLUTE.

I will yield, (if they convince me). Wilt thou remember the
se rendre si on me convainc *se souvenir de*
engagement that thou makest? What will not he reproach himself
prendre *se reprocher à lui-même*
for)? We shall not forget ourselves (so far as) to (be wanting)
* *s'oublier* *jusque* *manquer*
in respect towards him. Will you employ the means I (point
de *lui* *se servir de* *que* *indi-*
out) to you? Will not these flowers fade?
quer f. *se flétrir*

FUTURE ANTERIOR.

Shall I have betrayed myself? Wilt thou not have degraded
se trahir *moi-même* *s'avilir*
thyself in his eyes? He will have (been proud) of this trifling ad-
à *s'enorgueillir* *faible*
vantage. We shall have fatigued ourselves (to no purpose). In
avantage m. *se fatiguer* *inutilement* *à*
the end, you will have been undeceived. Will your children have
se désabuser
(loved each other) too much?
s'entr'aimer

CONDITIONAL.

SIMPLE TENSES.			COMPOUND TENSES.			
PRESENT.			PAST.			
I should repent.			*I should have repented*			
je	*me*	repentirais	je	*me*	*serais*	repenti
tu	*te*	repentirais	tu	*te*	*serais*	*or*
il *or* elle	*se*	repentirait	il *or* elle	*se*	*serait*	repentie
nous	*nous*	repentirions	nous	*nous*	*serions*	repentis
vous	*vous*	repentiriez	vous	*vous*	*seriez*	*or*
ils *or* elles	*se*	repentiraient	ils *or* elles	*se*	*seraient*	repenties

CONDITIONAL.

PRESENT.

Should I suffer myself to (be drawn) into the
se laisser • *entraîner*

party of the rebels? Wouldst thou be (so easily)
parti m. • *de si peu de chose* 2

frightened? Would not the nation submit to so just a
s'effrayer 1 — f *se soumettre* 3 4 1

law? We should not like to see the triumph of guilt.
2 *se plaire* *à voir* *triomphe* art. *crime* m.

Would you dishonour yourselves by such an action? Would those
se déshonorer 2 1

lords avail themselves of their birth and fortune,
seigneur *se prévaloir* *de* *naissance* f. pron. *richesses*

(in order to) act against our feelings.
pour *faire violence à* *sentiment.*

PAST.

Would I not then have devoted myself entirely to the
se dévouer alors *entièrement*

service of my country? (Had it not been for) thy carelessness,
pays m. *sans* *insouciance* f.

thou wouldst certainly have grown rich. Would this pleasing
certainement rule 111th *s'enrichir* *doux*

hope have vanished so soon? Should we have degraded our-
espoir m. *s'évanouir* *se dégrader*

IMPERATIVE.

AFFIRMATIVE.		NEGATIVE.		
Repent (thou).		*Do not repent.*		
	repens-toi		*ne te* repens	pas
qu'il *or* qu'elle	*se* repente	qu'il *or* qu'elle	*ne se* repente	pas
	repentons-*nous*		*ne nous* repentons	pas
	repentez-*vous*		*ne vous* repentez	pas
qu'ils *or* qu'elles	*se* repentent	qu'ils *or* qu'elles	*ne se* repentent	pas

---

selves to such a degree? You would have reduced yourselves to
* 2 1 *point* m. *se réduire*

absolute want. They would have been drowned, if (they
art. *plus grand besoin* *se noyer* *on*

had not had assistance).
ne les avait secourus

IMPERATIVE.

O man, remember that thou art mortal. Do not flatter
se souvenir *se promettre*

thyself (that thou wilt succeed easily). Let us take an exact
un succès facile *se rendre* — 2

account of our actions. Let us not deceive ourselves. Rest
compte 1 *se flatter* *se reposer*

yourself in the shade of this tree. Do not expose yourself so
à *ombre* *s'exposer*

rashly.
témérairement.

SUBJUNCTIVE.

PRESENT.

I must rise to-morrow at an earlier hour. I wish that
Il faut que se lever *de * meilleur heure* f. *souhaiter*

thou mayest be better. I wish him to conduct himself
se porter mieux *Je désire qu'il ** *se conduire*

SUBJUNCTIVE.

SIMPLE TENSES.			COMPOUND TENSES.			
PRESENT.			**PRETERIT.**			
That I may repent.			*That I may have repented.*			
que			que			
je	*me*	repente	je	*me*	*sois*	repenti
tu	*te*	repentes	tu	*te*	*sois*	*or*
il or *elle*	*se*	repente	il *or* elle	*se*	*soit*	repentie
nous	*nous*	repentions	nous	*nous*	*soyons*	repentis
vous	*vous*	repentiez	vous	*vous*	*soyez*	or
ils *or* elles	*se*	repentent	ils *or* elles	*se*	*soient*	repenties
IMPERFECT.			**PLUPERFECT.**			
That I might repent.			*That I might have repented.*			
que			que			
je	*me*	repentisse	je	*me*	*fusse*	repenti
tu	*te*	repentisses	tu	*te*	*fusses*	*or*
il *or* elle	*se*	repentît	il *or* elle	*se*	*fût*	repentie
nous	*nous*	repentissions	nous	*nous*	*fussions*	repentis
vous	*vous*	repentissiez	vous	*vous*	*fussiez*	*or*
ils *or* elles	*se*	repentissent	ils *or* elles	*se*	*fussent*	repenties

---

better. Is it not essential that we should contain ourselves? They
—tiel *se contenir* *On*

wish that you should early accustom yourselves to industry.
désirer *s'accoutumer de bonne heure* art. *travail* m.

It is time that they should rest from the fatigue of business.
se délasser —f. art. *affaires*, f

PRETERIT.

Can I have been deceived so grossly? It is
Se peut-il que *se tromper* *grossièrement!*

astonishing that thou hast determined to stay. It is not said
étonnant *se décider à* *rester* *On* * *dit*

that he interfered in this business. It will never be believed that
se mêler de *on* *croira*

we have conducted ourselves so ill. It is not suspected that you
se comporter *mal. On* * *soupçonner*

have disguised yourselves so ingeniously. (It is not reported) that
se déguiser *adroitement* *On ne dit pas*

they have behaved ill.
se conduire

IMPERFECT.

They required that I should go to bed at ten o'clock.
On exigeait *se coucher* *à* *heures.*

They wish that thou shouldst walk oftener. Did they
On voudrait *se promener* *On*

not wish that he should practise fencing? Was it ne-
voulait *s'exercer à faire des armes*

cessary that we should have recourse to this method? Did they
= *se servir* *de* *moyen*, m. *on*

wish that you should complain of their want of attention? Did
voulait *se plaindre* *manque* ———

they not wish them to make more haste?
on *désirer* ind-2 *que* *ils* *se hâter davantage*

PLUPERFECT.

Could they wish me to revenge myself? I should have
Aurait-on voulu que *se venger* *avoir* cond-1

wished that thou hadst shewn thyself more accommodating.
désirer *se montrer* *moins* *difficile*

I should have wished that he had been less negligent. Would you
avoir cond-1 *voulu* *se négliger moins* *Auriez-vous*

have wished us to have ruined ourselves in public opinion, (in order
voulu que *se perdre* 1 *pour*

to) satisfy your resentment? I might perhaps have wished that
satisfaire *ressentiment* *J'aurais pu désirer peut-être*

you had applied yourselves more to your studies. We could
s'appliquer *davantage* *Nous aurions*

have wished that they had extricated themselves more skilfully
pu désirer *se tirer* *adroitement*

from the difficulties (in which) they (had involved themselves).
embarras *où* *s'étaient mis.*

125. CONJUGATION OF PASSIVE VERBS.

A passive verb shows that the action is directed to ourselves, that we *suffer* it; whereas the *active verb* expresses that *we act*, or perform the action, and direct it towards another object, thus: *I love*, is active, *I am loved* is passive. The Greek and the Latin languages have a peculiar form of verbs, called *passive verbs* or *passive voice*, totally distinct from the *active verb* or *active voice*. The French language as well as the English and other modern languages have no such form, and express the passive voice by means of the *participle past* of the active voice with the auxiliary *être*, to be, thus: *je suis aimé*, I am loved. The participle, in that case, being as an adjective, is made to agree in gender and number with the subject of the verb.

EXAMPLES.

je suis aimé *or* aimée	*I am loved*
tu étais estimé *or* estimée	*thou wast esteemed*
ce roi fut chéri de son peuple	*that king was beloved by his people*
elle fut toujours chérie	*she was always beloved*
mon père fut respecté	*my father was respected*
ma mère fut révérée	*my mother was revered*
nous serons loués *or* louées	*we will be praised*
vous en serez blâmés *or* blâmées	*you will be blamed for it*
ils seraient craints et redoutés	*they would be feared and dreaded*
elles seraient mieux instruites	*they would be better informed*
afin que mes fils soient connus	*that my sons may be known*
je voudrais que les portes fussent ouvertes	*I should wish the doors were opened*

OBSERVE.—In future, the tenses of the verbs will be promiscuously intermixed; but directions will be given as to those which it is proper to use; that is, marks like these will be found under the verb, *ind*-1, *ind*-2, *ind*-3, etc. The learner will do well, therefore, to consult the *explanations of the abbreviations* given at the beginning of the grammar, that he may be familiar with those marks.

EXERCISES.

My brother was wounded. They were detested. Has she not
ind-3 *blesser* *ils* ind-2 *détester*

been rewarded? The robbers were apprehended in the park. Has
récompenser ind-4 *saisir*

not your sister been well received? The boys shall all be punished.
recevoir *écolier* *punir*

Is the garden door opened? When were these fruits gathered?
porte du jardin f. *ouvrir* ind-4 — m. *cueillir*

The actress has been crowned.
actrice *couronner*

126. OF NEUTER VERBS.

Neuter verbs are of two sorts. 1. Those which express a state, a quality, as: *je languis,* I languish; *il excelle,* he excels. 2. Those which express an action, which cannot pass over to another object, as: *je dîne,* I dine; *je marche,* I walk; since we cannot say: *je dîne un homme,* I dine a man; *je marche mon frère,* I walk my brother. Neuter verbs are also sometimes on that account called *intransitive.*

Some neuter verbs admit a substantive after them, as complement, that is to say, as giving full sense to the sentence: *je pense à mon père,* I think of my father; *je dépends de mon oncle,* I am dependant on my uncle; *je tremble de peur,* I tremble with fear; but that substantive is always governed by a preposition.

127. Neuter verbs are not all conjugated with the same auxiliary in their compound tenses; some have *avoir,* others have *être.*

AVOIR.

J'ai parlé,	*I have spoken.*
Nous avons ri,	*We have laughed.*
Ils ont mangé,	*They have eaten.*

ÊTRE.

Je suis parti,	*I am gone.*
Ils sont venus,	*They are* or *have come.*
Nous sommes tombés,	*We have fallen.*

128. It is important to observe that neuter verbs do not require the same preposition in both languages: Thus, *je pense à mon père,* may not be translated by I think *to* my father, but *of* my father. We must also add that a verb, which is neuter in French, is sometimes active in Eng-

lish, as: *j'obéis à mon père,* I obey my father, and vice versâ. This is one of the most material points of difference in the construction of the two languages. It is not here the place to treat it at full length, because it properly belongs to the Syntax, where it will be found; meanwhile, it is recommended that the learner should not lose sight of it, and attend to the preposition which, in the course of the exercises, will carefully be affixed to the infinitives of neuter verbs.

EXERCISE.

We will return at five o'clock. Do you speak to that man?
revenir *parler*

We resist obstacles. I have not accepted of his offers.
résister à art.—— *accepter* ind-4 *

Think of my father. They live on vegetables. We will
penser à *vivre* ind-1 *de* *légumes*

agree about the price. All at once twenty men entered
convenir *de* *entrer* *dans* ind-5

the room. She sleeps. Do not walk so fast. You will fall
dormir *marcher* *tomber* ind-7

They run. We shall arrive in the morning.
courir ind-1 *arriver* *

129. OF IMPERSONAL VERBS.

Impersonal verbs are those which have only the third person singular, such as: *il pleut,* it rains; *il neige,* it snows. We subjoin a list of the most common.

pleuvoir	il pleut	*it rains*
neiger	il neige	*it snows.*
grêler	il grêle	*it hails*
tonner	il tonne	*it thunders*
éclairer	il éclaire	*it lightens*
geler	il gèle	*it freezes*
dégeler	il dégèle	*it thaws*
bruiner	il bruine	*it drizzles*
importer	il importe	*it matters*
faire chaud	il fait chaud	*it is warm*
faire froid	il fait froid	*it is cold*
faire glissant	il fait glissant	*to be slipping*
faire crotté	il fait crotté	*to be dirty*
falloir	il faut	*it is necessary, must*
y avoir	il y a	*there is*

These verbs are also called *unipersonal,* from their having only the third person singular. *Falloir, y avoir,* being very commonly used in French, they are conjugated at full length separately.

The genius of the French language admits of using some active and neuter verbs impersonally, such as *dire, il se dit des choses singulières,* singular things are reported; *arriver, il arrive des choses singulières,* singular things happen. This peculiarity will be found noticed in the Syntax.

EXERCISE.

Does it rain this morning? Did it hail last
pleuvoir *matin* m. *grêler* ind-4 art. *dernier*

night? It does not snow. I thought it had thundered Does it
f. 1 *neiger* *Je croyais que* *tonner* ind-6

not lighten? Do you think it freezes? It is ten o'clock.
éclairer *croyez que* *geler* subj-1 *heure* pl.

It will freeze long. It (is fit) to act so. It (was of great im
long-temps *convenir de* *importer beau-*

portance) to succeed. It appears that he has not attended to
coup ind-2 *de réussir* *sembler* *s'occuper de* ind-4

that business. It is very slippery in the streets. Is it cold?
faire glissant *rue* f. *faire* *froid*

It will be very warm to-day. It was very cold all night. Open
bien ind-4 art. *nuit* f. *ouvrir*

the window, for it is too warm in this room. Will it not be too
appartement m.

cold? (I put on) thick boots, for I thought it was very dirty
mettre ind-4 *croire* ind-2 ind-2

in the streets.

130. CONJUGATION

OF THE

IMPERSONAL VERB, *FALLOIR, IL FAUT,* IT MUST, IT IS NECESSARY.

INFINITIVE.

SIMPLE TENSES.		COMPOUND TENSES.	
PRESENT	falloir	PAST	avoir fallu
PARTIC. PRES.	*none*	PAST	fallu, ayant fallu

INDICATIVE.

PRESENT	il faut	PRETERIT IND.	il a fallu
IMPERFECT	il fallait	PLUPERFECT	il avait fallu
PRETERIT DEF.	il fallut	PRETERIT ANT.	il eut fallu
FUTURE ABSOL.	il faudra	FUTURE ANT.	il aura fallu

CONDITIONAL.

PRESENT	il faudrait	PAST	il aurait fallu

SUBJUNCTIVE.

PRESENT	qu'il faille	PRETERIT	qu'il ait fallu
IMPERFECT	qu'il fallût	PLUPERFECT	qu'il eût fallu

131. COMPARISON BETWEEN MUST AND FALLOIR.

The English verb *must,* not being impersonal, may take any noun, or pronoun, for its subject; *I must, we must, my sister must;* FALLOIR, on the contrary, being impersonal, can only have the third person singular. The latter has besides too distinct meanings; it implies *necessity* or *duty,* and *want* or *deficiency.* In both acceptations, the construction is so peculiar in French, and differs so materially from the English, that it is deemed necessary to illustrate it by examples.

132. FALLOIR, in the sense of *duty, necessity.*

il faut que je *parte*	*I must go*
il faut que ma sœur *vienne*	*my sister must come*
faut-il que cet homme *entre?*	*must that man come in?*
il faudra que vous *écriviez*	*you will be obliged to write*
ne fallait-il pas qu'il lui *répondît?*	*was it not necessary that he should answer?*
n'aurait-il pas fallu que mon père le *payât?*	*must not my father have paid him?*
il faut *partir*	*we must set off*
faudra-t-il le *payer?*	*must he be paid?*

Observe that when *falloir* implies *personal or individual obligation,* it requires the *subjunctive mood* but if it implies *suggestion, general advice,* it requires the *infinitive.*

133. FALLOIR, in the sense of *want, deficiency, must have.*

il faut un habit neuf *à* mon père	*my father wants a new great coat*
il *me* faut vingt livres	*I must have twenty pounds*
ne *lui* faudra-t-il pas du papier et de l'encre?	*shall he not want paper and ink?*
il faut peu de choses *aux* enfants pour les amuser	*children require few things to be amused*
c'est là ce qu'il *lui* faut	*that is what he wants*

Observe also that when *falloir* implies *want, necessity* of having, it requires the person who wants the thing to be in the dative case.

EXERCISE.

You *must* speak to him about that affair. It *was necessary* for
sub-1 *de* f. ind-2 *que* *

him to consent to that bargain. We *were obliged* to (set out)
il * sub-2 *marché* m. ind-3 *partir* sub-2

immediately. Children *should* learn every day something by
sur-le-champ art. cond-1 sub-2

heart. *Shall* I suffer patiently such *an* insult? He *must* have
ind-7 sub-1 1 2 cond-2 *être*

been a blockhead not to understand such easy rules.
sub-2 *sot* 2 *pour* 1 *comprendre* inf-1 *des si* 2 3 *règle* f. 1

(How much) does your brother *want?* He does what is *requisite.*
combien *fait* *falloir*

Do that as it *(should be).* What *must* he *have* for his trouble?
faites *falloir* ind-1 *que* 2 *lui* 1 * *peine* f.

You are the man I *want.* Do not give me any more bread,
que * *de*

I have already more than I want. I *need* not ask you whether
en *ne m'en* * inf-1 *si*

you will come. I do not think that *it is necessary* to be a con-
vouloir ind-7 *crois* sub-1 * *sor-*

jurer to guess his motives. I could not suspect that I
cier pour deviner *motif* *pouvais* *soupçonner*

ought to ask pardon for a fault I have not committed.
sub-2 * inf-1 —— *de* *faute* f. *que* *commise*

134. CONJUGATION

OF THE

IMPERSONAL VERB, *Y AVOIR*, THERE IS.

INFINITIVE.

PRESENT	y avoir	*there to be*
PAST	y avoir eu	*there to have been*
PARTIC. PRES.	y ayant	*there being*
PARTIC. PAST	y ayant eu	*there having been*

INDICATIVE.

PRESENT	il y a	*there is* or *there are*
PRET. INDEF.	il y a eu	*there has been* or *there have been*
IMPERFECT.	il y avait	*there was* or *there were*
PLUPERFECT.	il y avait eu	*there had been*
PRETERIT DEF.	il y eut	*there was* or *there were*
PRETERIT ANT.	il y eut eu	*there had been*
FUTURE ABSOL.	il y aura	*there will be*
FUTURE ANTER.	il y aura eu	*there will have been*

CONDITIONAL.

PRESENT	il y aurait	*there would be*
PAST	il y aurait eu	*there would have been*

SUBJUNCTIVE.

PRESENT	qu'il y ait	*that there may be*
PRETERIT	qu'il y ait eu	*that there may have been*
IMPERFECT	qu'il y eût	*that there might be*
PLUPERFECT	qu'il y eût eu	*that there might have been*

This verb in English is used in the plural, when followed by a substantive plural; in French it remains always in the singular.

EXERCISE.

There must *be* a great difference of age between those two
il doit ——— f.

persons. *There being* (so many) vicious people in this world,
tant de = 2 *gens* m. pl. 1

is it astonishing that *there are* so many persons who become the
étonnant sub-1 *devenir*

victims of the corruption of the age? *It is* a thousand to
perversité f. *siècle* m. * *mille à parier contre*

one that he will not succeed. *There would be* more happiness if
réussir ind-7 *de bonheur*

every one) knew how to moderate his desires. I did not think
chacun savait * * *modérer désir croire* ind-2

that *there could be* (any thing) to blame in his conduct. *There*
subj-2 *rien à reprendre conduite* f.

would not *be* so many duels, did people reflect that one of the
—— *si l'on réfléchir* ind-2 f.

first obligations of a Christian is to forgive injuries. Could
——— f. *de chrétien de pardonner* art. *pourrait-il*

there be a king more happy than this who has always been the
celui-ci

father of his subjects?
sujets

135. OF THE IRREGULAR VERBS.

IRREGULAR VERBS OF THE FIRST CONJUGATION.

The only irregular verbs of the first conjugation are ALLER and ENVOYER.

136. INF. PRES. ALLER, *to go*.
INF. PAST. Avoir été, être allé, e, *to have gone*.
PART. PRES. Allant, *going*.
PART. PAST. Été, allé, allée, *gone*.
COMP. PAST. Étant allé, ayant été, *having gone*.

INDICATIVE.

PRESENT.

je vais	nous allons
tu vas	vous allez
il va	ils vont

IMPERF. j'allais, etc.*
PRET. j'allai, etc. *or* je fus, etc.
FUTURE j'irai, etc.
CONDIT. j'irais, etc.

IMPERATIVE.

va, qu'il aille, allons, allez, qu'ils aillent.

SUBJUNCTIVE.

PRES. que j'aille, que tu ailles, qu'il aille, que nous allions, que vous alliez, qu'ils aillent.

IMP. que j'allasse, que tu allasses, qu'il allât, que nous allassions, que vous allassiez, qu'ils allassent.

137. S'EN ALLER, *to go away*; will be given at full length because its conjugation is rather difficult on account of its two pronouns.

* In future the first person only of tenses regularly conjugated will be given.

INFINITIVE.

	SIMPLE TENSES.		COMPOUND TENSES.		
PRESENT	s'	en aller	s'	en être	allé, allés
PARTIC. PRES.	s'	en allant	s'	en étant	allée, allées
PARTIC. PAST.		en allé			

INDICATIVE.

PRES.	je	m'	en vais*	je	m'	en suis	allé or allée
	tu	t'	en vas	tu	t'	en es	
	il or elle	s'	en va	il or elle	s'	en est	
	nous	nous	en allons	nous	nous	en sommes	allés or allées
	vous	vous	en allez	vous	vous	en êtes	
	ils or elles	s'	en vont	ils or elles	s'	en sont	
IMP.	je	m'	en allais	je	m'	en étais	allé, &c.
PRET.	je	m'	en allai	je	m'	en fus	allé, &c.
FUT.	je	m'	en irai	je	m'	en serai	allé, &c.
COND.	je	m'	en irais	je	m'	en serais	allé, &c.

* *Or* je (m'en) vas.

IMPERATIVE.

AFFIRMATIVE.				NEGATIVE.			
	va	t'	en		ne t'	en va	
qu'il		s'	en aille	qu'il	ne s'	en aille	
	allons	nous	en		ne nous	en allons	pas
	allez	vous	en		ne vous	en allez	
qu'ils		s'	en aillent	qu'ils	ne s'	en aillent	

SUBJUNCTIVE.

	SIMPLE TENSES.			COMPOUND TENSES.			
PRES. que	je	m'	en aille	je	m'	en sois	allé or allée
	tu	t'	en ailles	tu	t'	en sois	
	il or elle	s'	en aille	il or elle	s'	en soit	
	nous	nous	en allions	nous	nous	en soyons	allés or allées
	vous	vous	en alliez	vous	vous	en soyez	
	ils or elles	s'	en aillent	ils or elles	s'	en soient	
P.	que je	m'	en allasse	je	m'	en fusse	allé, &c.

REMARKS.

Je fus, j'ai été, j'avais été, j'aurais été, are not synonymous of *j'allai, je suis allé, j'étais allé, je serais allé.* The former serve to express the *fact of having gone,* the latter, the *fact of being gone.*

The imperative *va* takes an *s* when followed by *y,* or by *en* as: *vas-y, vas en savoir des nouvelles,* go thither, go and make enquiries about it; however it takes no *s* when the *y* is followed by a verb, as: *va y donner ordre,* go and see about it.

Puer, to stink; is defective; it has no preterit of the indicative, nor the imperfect of the subjunctive.

Tisser, to weave; is only irregular in the participle past, which makes *tissu* instead of *tissé.*

Envoyer and *renvoyer,* make in their future absolute and conditional present, *j'enverrai, j'enverrais,* and *je renverrai, je renverrais.*

EXERCISE.

Are you going into the country this evening? I *am going* to
ind-7 *à* *campagne* f. *soir* m.

pay some visits. *Go* there with thy brother. *Go* and *do* that
faire * *faire*

errand. *Go* there and put every thing in order. Let him *go*
commission f. * *mettre* *en*

to church on holidays. I shall *go* to London. When
art. *église,* f. * art. *jour* pl. *de fête.*

do they go to Italy? My sisters *are going away* next week. We
en Italie ind-1

shall *go away* early. Do not *go away* yet. Make haste for
de bonne heure *dépêchez-vous*

they *are going away.* I shall *send* early flowers
de art. *printanier* 2 f. pl. 1

to those ladies. I would *go* to Rome, if I could. We would
dame f. pl. *pouvais*

(*send back*) our horses. Why do they *go away* so soon? My
pourquoi

brother and sister *went* yesterday to Windsor. I shall not *go*
pron. ind-4

(any more) a hunting.
plus *à* * art. *chasse* f.

wiser, if they reflected on the shortness of life. I would
réfléchir ind.- 2 *sur* *brièveté* f. art.

visit France and Italy if (I had the means.)
parcourir art. — art.= *mes moyens le permettaient.*

IMPERATIVE.

Shudder with horror and terror. Do not open the door
Frémir *de* = *de effroi* m. *ouvrir*

to any one in my absence. Let him not suffer such insults.
personne *souffrir* *pareil* *insulte* f.

138. IRREGULAR VERBS OF THE SECOND CONJUGATION.

BRANCH I. *PUNIR.*

Bénir, to bless; has two participles, *bénit, bénite,* consecrated, (by prayers or religious ceremonies); *pain bénit,* consecrated bread; *eau bénite,* holy water; *béni, bénie,* blessed, favored of God. *Peuple béni,* a blessed, happy, Godly nation.

Fleurir, in the common acceptation of *to blossom, to come to bloom,* is regular; but, in the sense of *to flourish,* it makes, *florissant, florissait.*

In *haïr,* to hate; the letters *-aï* form throughout two syllables, except in the three persons singular of the present of the indicative, *je hais, tu hais, il hait,* and in the second person singular of the imperative *hais,* which are pronounced as one syllable, as if written, *je hès, tu hès, il hèt.*

Gésir, to lie, is a defective verb, and has only retained *gisant, gît, nous gisons, ils gisent, il gisait,* and particularly *ci-gît,* here lies.

EXERCISE.

May the name of that good king be *blessed* from generation to
nom m. *en*

generation. These trees *blossomed* twice every year. The
ind-2 *deux fois tout* art. *an* pl.

arts and sciences *flourished* at Athens in the time of Pericles.
— art. —— ind-2 *à Athènes*

Horace and Virgil *flourished* under the reign of Augustus. We
Virgile ind-2 *sous* *règne* *Auguste.*

discovered from the top of the mountain a vast plain full of
découvrir *haut* *plaine* f. *rempli de*

flowery meadows. The empire of the Babylonians was
fleurissant 2 *pré* m. pl. 1 —— ——*nien* ind-3

long a *flourishing* one. We did not *hate* the man, but his
long-temps * *

vices. Does she really *hate* that vain pomp and all the display of
pompe f. *appareil*

grandeur?
art. ————

139. BRANCH II, ON *SENTIR*.

BOUILLIR, *to boil.*

Par. pres. bouillant—*Past.* bouilli
IND. *pres.* bous, bous, bout, bouillons, bouillez, bouillent
Imperf. bouillais—*Pret.* bouillis
Future. bouillirai—*Cond.* bouillirais
IMP. bous, qu'il bouille, bouillons, bouillez, qu'ils bouillent.
SUB. *pres.* bouille—*Imp.* bouillisse

Rebouillir, to boil again, and *ébouillir*, to boil away, are conjugated like *bouillir*; this latter is only used in compound tenses, and the infinitive, as: *cette sauce est trop ébouillie*, this sauce has boiled away too much.

FAILLIR, *to fail.*

Part. pres. faillant*—*Past.* failli
IND. *pres.* faux,* faux,* faut,* faillons,* faillez,* faillent*
Imperf. faillais*—*Pret.* faillis, etc.—*Fut.* faudrai*
COND. faudrais*—SUBJ. *imperf.* que je faillisse

DEFAILLIR, *to faint*, has now only the plural of the

IND. *pres.* nous défaillons, ils défaillent—*Imperf.* défaillais.
Pret. défaillis—*Pret. indef.* j'ai défailli, and INF. *pres.* défaillir.

N.B. The tenses marked with an asterisk are obsolete.

EXERCISE.

Take that water off the fire, it *boils* too fast. Do not
retirer f. *de dessus* m. f. *fort*

let the soup *(boil away)* (so much). That sauce has *(boiled*
laisser 1 *pot* 3 *tant* 2 —— f. *est* f.

away) (too much). *Boil* that meat again; it has not *boiled*
trop *faites rebouillir* *viande* f. * f. 2

long enough.
* *assez* 1

FUIR, *to fly, to run away.*

Part. pres. fuyant—*Past.* fui.
IND. *pres.* fuis, fuis, fuit, fuyons, fuyez, fuient.
Imperf. fuyais—*Pret.* fuis—*Fut.* fuirai—COND. fuirais.
IMP. fuis, fuie, fuyons, fuyez, fuient.
SUBJ. *pres.* fuie, fuies, fuie, fuyions, fuyiez, fuient.
Imperf. fuisse, *or rather*, prisse la fuite.

MOURIR, *to die.*

Part. pres. mourant—*Past.* mort.
IND. *pres.* meurs, meurs, meurt, mourons, mourez, meurent.
Imp. mourais—*Pret.* mourus—*Fut.* mourrai—COND. mourrais.
IMP. meurs, meure, mourons, mourez, meurent.
SUBJ. *pres.* meure, meures, meure, mourions, mouriez, meurent.
Imperf. mourusse—*Comp. tenses.* je suis mort, j'étais mort, etc.

REM.—*S'enfuir*, to run away, is conjugated after *fuir*. *Mourir* takes the auxiliary *être;* and when reflected, *se mourir* signifies to be dying, or emphatically and figuratively to be dying with. It is seldom used except in the present and imperfect of the indicative.

EXERCISE.

He *(was near)* losing his life in that encounter. He *(was*
faillir *perdre* * art. *rencontre* f. *faillir*

falling into the snare which was laid for him. His
ind-4 *donner* *piége* m. *qu'on* *avait tendu* * *lui* *

strength *fails* him. Give us something to eat
art. *force* f. pl. *défaillir* *lui.* *donnez-nous* * *manger* 2

directly; we *are fainting* with fatigue and hunger. I cannot get at
vite 1 *se mourir* *de* —— pr. *faim.* *ne puis rencontrer*

him, he shuns me. Would he not *avoid* flatterers, if he
fuir *fuir* art. *flatteur* m. pl.

knew all their falsehood. He *died* of a (very painful) disease.
ind-2 *fausseté* f. *de* *cruel* 2 *maladie* f. 1

She *died* of grief (for the loss of) her son. He is *dying.*
ind-4 *chagrin* m. *d'avoir perdu* *se mourir*

She *was dying* with grief, when the fear of death at l...
se mourir *de* *crainte* f. art. *en...*

wrested her secret from her.
arracher ind-3 — m. * *lui.*

Quérir, to fetch; is used, in familiar conversation, after *venir, envoyer, aller,* as: *envoyez quérir,* send for; *allez quérir,* go and fetch.

ACQUÉRIR, *to acquire.*

Part. pres. acquérant—*Past.* acquis.
IND. *pres.* acquiers, acquiers, acquiert, acquérons, acquérez, acquièrent.
Imper. acquérais—*Pret.* acquis—*Fut.* acquerrai—COND. acquerrais.
IMP. acquiers, acquière, acquérons, acquérez, acquièrent.
SUBJ. *pres.* acquièr-e, -es, -e, acquér-ions, -iez, acquièrent.
Imperf. acquisse.

S'enquérir, to enquire; and *requérir,* to request; are conjugated as *acquérir.*

Conquérir, to conquer, is seldom used but in the IND. *pret.* je conquis, etc., and in the SUBJ. *imperf.* que je conquisse. Its chief use is in the *compound tenses.*

Ouïr, to hear; is only used in the INF. *pres.* ouïr *Part. past.* ouï. IND. *pret.* j'ouïs, tu ouïs, etc. and SUBJ. *imperf.* que j'ouïsse, tu ouïsses, etc. Its prinpal use is in the *compound tenses,* as: *je l'ai* or *je l'avais ouï dire,* I have *or* I had heard it.

VÊTIR, *to clothe.*

Part. pres. vêtant*—*Past.* vêtu.
IND. *pres.* vêts,* vêts,* vêt,* vêtons, vêtez, vêtent.
Imperf. vêtais—*Pret.* vêtis—*Fut.* vêtirai—COND. vêtirais.
IMP. vêts,* vête,* vêtons, vêtez, vêtent.
SUB. *pres.* vête—*Imperf.* vêtisse.

N.B.—*Vêtir* is seldom used in the forms marked with an asterisk, and is most frequently used as reflected, *se vêtir*, to dress one's self.

Revêtir, to clothe, to invest, is used through all the tenses; *dévêtir*, to divest, is principally used as a reflected verb. and in some forms only.

Send for the physician and follow exactly his advice. *Go* and
médecin *suivez* *

fetch my cane. Every day he *acquired* celebrity by
canne f. *tout* art. *jour* m. pl. ind-3 *de* art. = f.

works calculated to fix the attention of an enlightened
de art. *ouvrage* m. pl. *fait* *pour* 2

public. Would you have me *acquire* riches at the expense
1 *voudriez-vous que* subj-2 *de* art. *dépens* m. pl.

of my honesty? He had *acquired* by his merit great influence
probité f. m. *une* —— f.

over the opinions of his contemporaries. I *have enquired about*
sing. *contemporain* *s'enquérir* ind-4 *de*

that man (every where), and I have not (been able) (to hear
homme-là *partout* *pu* *en avoir*

any thing of him). Who has *requested* it of you?
de nouvelles *Qui est-ce qui* 3 4 *en* 2 * 1

Sesostris, king of Egypt *conquered* a great part of Asia. The
ind-3 art.

formidable empire which Alexander *conquered* did not last
2 1 ——*dre* ind-6 *durer*

longer than his life. I *have heard* that he *will* not *return*.
plus long-temps f. *ouïr dire* ind-4 *revenir*

He *dressed himself* in haste and (went out) immediately.
se vêtir ind-3 *à* art. *hâte* f. *sortir* ind-3 *sur-le-champ*.

I wish she *would dress* the children with more
voudrais que *vêtir* subj-2 *de*

care. If his fortune permitted him, he *would clothe* all the
permettait 2 *le lui* 1

poor of his parish. Two servants *clothed* him in his ducal
paroisse f. *domestique* *revêtir* *de* 2

mantle. It begins to be very warm; one might
manteau m. 1 *commencer à faire chaud; pourrait*
(*throw off some clothing*).
se dévêtir.

140. BRANCH III. *OUVRIR.*

CUEILLIR, *to gather.*

Part. pres.	cueillant	*Past.*	cueilli	IND. *pres.*	cueille
Imperf.	cueillais	*Pret.*	cueillis	*Fut.*	cueillerai*
COND.	cueillerais*	IMPER.	cueille	SUBJ. *pres.*	cueille
Imperf.	cueillisse				

The irregularity of *cueillir*, in the future and the conditional, is remarkable; these two tenses are formed from the old infinitive *cueiller*. Thus, *accueillir*, to welcome; and *recueillir*, to collect.

Saillir, to project, has only *saillant*, *sailli*; and the following forms: *il saille*, *il saillait*, *il saillera*, *il saillerait*, *qu'il saille*, *qu'il saillît*. But *saillir*, to gush out; is regularly conjugated like *finir*; *saillissant*, *je saillis*, etc., *ils saillissent*, etc. Its principal use is in the third persons.

ASSAILLIR, *to assault.*

Part. pres.	assaillant	*Past.*	assailli	IND. *pres.*	assaille
Imperf.	assaillais	*Pret.*	assaillis	*Fut.*	assaillirai
COND.	assaillirais	IMPER.	assaille	SUB. *pres.*	assaille
Imperf.	assaillisse				

Tressaillir, to start, conjugated like *assaillir*, make in the fut. je *tressaillerai*, or *tressaillirai*, etc.

EXERCISE.

I *will gather* with pleasure some of these flowers and of these fruits, since you wish to have some. *Do not gather*
puisque être bien aise de en

these peaches, before they are ripe. That is a country
f. pl. *avant que* *ne* subj-1 *mûr* *Ce* *pays*

where they neither reap corn, nor (gather) grapes. We
où *on* *ne* *recueillir* *ni* *blé* *ni* * *vin*

shall *collect* in ancient history important and valuable
recueillir 2 1 *de* art. —2 *précieux* 3

facts. He *received* us in the most polite manner.
fait 1 *accueillir* 3 1 *de* 2 *manière* f. 1

Poverty, misery, sickness, persecution, in a word, all
art. f. art. f. art. *maladie* f. art. *en*

the misfortunes in the world *(have fallen upon)* him. If you
malheur m. pl. *de* *accueillir* ind-4

give six inches to that cornice, it *will project* too much.
donner *pouce* m. *corniche* f. *trop*

That balcony *projected* too much ; it darkened the dining-
balcon m. ind-2 *trop* *obscurcir* ind-2 *salle à*

room. When Moses struck the rock, there *gushed*
manger f. *Quand Moïse* *frapper* ind-3 *rocher* m. *il* ind-3

out (of it) a spring of (fresh running) water. The blood *gushed*
2 *en* 1 *source* f. *vif* 2 f. 1 ind-2

from his vein with impetuosity. We *shall assault* the enemy
veine f. *assaillir* pl.

to-morrow in their entrenchments. Were we not *overtaken* by a
demain *retranchement* ind-3. *assailli*

horrible storm? At every word which they said to him
tempête f. *à* *chaque* *que* *on* *disait* 2 *lui*

concerning his son, the good (old man) leaped for joy.
de *vieillard* *tressaillir* ind-2 *de* *joie*

141. IRREGULAR VERBS OF THE THIRD CONJUGATION.

Avoir, to have, is conjugated at length, No. 101.

Ravoir, to have again; and *se ravoir*, to recover, are only used in the present of the infinitive.

Choir, to fall, has only the participle past, ***chu, chue, être chu.***

DECHOIR, *to decay.*

(*No Part. pres.*) *Part. past.* déchu.
IND. *pres.* déchois, déchois, déchoit, déchoyons, déchoyez, déchoient
(*No Imperf.*) *Pret.* déchus—*Fut.* décherrai—COND. décherrais
IMPER. déchois, déchoie, déchoyons, déchoyez, déchoient.
SUB. *pres.* déchoie, déchoies, déchoie, déchoy-ions, —iez, déchoient.
Imperf. déchusse.

Echoir, to fall to, to expire, has only now in use the IND. *pres. il échoit*, sometimes pronounced *il échet*, the pret. *il échut*, fut. *il écherra*, cond. *il écherrait*, the imperf. SUBJ. *que j'échusse*; INF. and PAST. ***échoir, échéant, échu.***

Choir, déchoir, échoir, take the auxiliary *être* and *avoir*.

Falloir, to be necessary, is an impersonal verb, the conjugation of which has been given.

EXERCISE.

I had apartments that I liked; I will endeavour to *have* them
ind-2 *un logement* *aimer* ind-2 *veux essayer de* s.

again. Beware of *falling*. How *has* he *fallen* into
prenez garde inf-1 *comment* *en*

poverty? Since the publication of his last work, he has
pauvreté *depuis* *dernier* –

much *fallen* in the esteem of the public. If he do not
déchoir

alter his conduct, he *will gradually lose* his reputation
changer de * *déchoir de jour en jour de* —— f.

and credit. He has put in the lottery, and he hopes
pr. pron. — m. *mis à loterie* f.

that a capital prize will *fall* (to his share). That bill
* art. *gros lot* m. *échoir lui lettre* f.

of exchange *has expired* on the twenty-fifth. The first term
change échoir * *le vingt-cinq terme* m.

expires at Midsummer. You have drawn on me a bill of
à la Saint-Jean tirer sur moi

exchange; when *is it payable*? I did not believe that I *must*
échoir ind-1 *croire* ind-2 *falloir* sub-2

so soon (have taken) that journey. He must
faire voyage m. ind-4 *que*

have sunk under the efforts of (so many) enemies.
succomber sub-2 *tant de*

MOUVOIR, to move.

Part. pres. mouvant—*Part. past.* mu.
IND. *pres.* meus, meus, meut, mouv-ons, —ez, meuvent.
Imperf. mouvais—*Pret.* mus—*Fut.* mouvrai—COND. mouvrais
IMPER. meus, meuve, mouvons, mouvez, meuvent.
SUBJ. *pres.* meuv-e, —es, —e, mouv-ions, —iez, meuvent.
Imperf. musse

Thus are conjugated *émouvoir*, to move, excite, stir up; *se mouvoir*, to move, stir; *s'émouvoir*, to be moved, affected.

Promouvoir, to promote in rank or office, has only the infinitive, and participle *promu*.

Démouvoir, to induce to desist, has the infinitive only.

PLEUVOIR, *to rain (impersonal)*.

Part. pres.	pleuvant	*Past.*	plu	IND. *pres.*	il pleut
Imperf.	il pleuvait	*Pret.*	il plut	*Fut.*	il pleuvra
COND.	il pleuvrait	SUB. *pres.*	qu'il pleuve	*Imperf.*	qu'il plût

EXERCISE.

The spring which *moves* the whole machine is very inge-
ressort m. 2 *tout* 1 — f.

mous, though very simple. It was passion which *moved*
= *quoique* — *Ce* ind-1 art. —— f. ind-4

him to that action. Can you doubt that the soul, though it
—f. *pouvez* f. *

is spiritual, moves the body at pleasure? That is a man
* —*tuel ne* sub-1 *à sa volonté* *ce*

whom nothing *moves*. We had scarcely lost sight of
émouvoir. ind-3 *à peine perdu vue* f. 3 2

land, when there *arose* a violent tempest.
art. *terre*, f. 1 *que il s'émouvoir* ind-3 *grand tempête* f.

We were *moved* with fear and pity. When the famous
ind-3 *émus de crainte* f. pr. *pitié* f. *quand célèbre*

d'Aguesseau was *promoted* to the dignity of chancellor, all
ind-3 = f. *chancelier tout*

France shewed the greatest joy. That bishop well
art. f. *en témoigner* ind-3 f. *évêque*

deserved, by his talents and by his virtues, that the king
mériter ind-2

should promote him to the dignity of primate. The people
sub-2 2 *le* 1 *primat* sing.

think that it *rains* frogs and insects
croit *de* art. *grenouille* f. pl. pr. art. *insecte* m. pl.

at certain seasons. It *will* not *rain* to-day, but I
en — *temps* pl. *aujourd'hui*

(am fearful) of its *raining* to-morrow.
craindre que * *ne* sub-1

POUVOIR, *to be able.*

Part. pres. pouvant—*Part. past.* pu.
IND: *pres.* puis,* peux, peut, pouv-ons, —ez, peuvent.
Imperf. pouvais—*Pret.* pus—*Fut.* pourrai—COND. pourrais.
(No imperative). SUBJ. *pres.* puisse—*Imperf.* pusse.

* Conversation and poetry admit also *je peux*, but not *peux-je?*

There is an imperative used, not to express command, but a wish that a thing be, as a sort of imprecation. *Puissé-je, puisses-tu, puisse-t-il, puissions-nous, puissiez-vous, puissent-ils*. Ex: *puissiez-vous arriver à temps*, may you arrive in time.

SAVOIR, *to know*

Part. pres. sachant—*Part. past.* su.
IND. *pres.* sais, sais, sait, savons, savez, savent—*Imperf.* savais.
Pret. sus—*Fut.* saurai—COND. saurais.
IMPER. sache, sache, sachons, sachez, sachent.
SUBJ. *pres.* sache—*Imperf.* susse.

Seoir, to be becoming, to befit; has *only* the *part. pres. seyant*; and the third persons of the *simple* tenses, *il sied, ils siéent, il séyait, il siéra, il siérait, qu'il siéc.* But *seoir*, to sit, is used only in the two participles, *séant* and *sis*. This verb is also used impersonally.

ASSEOIR, *to set.*

Part. pres. asseyant—*Part. past.* assis.
IND. *pres.* assieds, assieds, assied, assey-ons, —ez, —ent.
Imperf. asseyais—*Pret.* assis.—*Fut.* assiérai, *or* asseyerai.
COND. assiérais, *or* asseyerais.—IMP. assieds, assèye, assey-ons, —ez, —ent—SUBJ. *pres.* assèye.—*Imperf.* assisse.

N.B.—This verb is more frequently reflected, as *s'asseoir*, to sit down. Its compound *rasseoir*, to set again, to calm, or to sit down again, is conjugated in the same manner.

EXERCISE.

When he arrived at home, he (was quite exhausted).
être ind-1 *arrivé chez lui* *n'en pouvoir* ind-2 *plus*

The minister had (so many) people at his *levee*, that I
ministre ind-3 *tant* *de monde* *à* *audience*

could not speak to him. *Are you afraid* that he cannot
ind-3 2 1 *craindre*, ind-1 *pouvoir* sub-1

accomplish that affair? I *know* that he is not your friend,
venir à bout de *de* pl.

but I *know* likewise that he is a man of probity. *Let* them *know*
aussi * *bien*

that their pardon depends on their submission. I *could wish*
grâce *dépendre de* *soumission.* *désirer* cond-1

that he *knew* a little better his lessons. Let us see if this new-
sub-2 *voyons* *d'un*

fashioned dress *becomes* you, or not. Be assured that
nouveau goût 2 *robe* f. 1 2 1 *non*

colours too rich *will* not *become* you. The head-dress which that
art. f. *voyant* *coiffure* f. *que*

lady wore did not become her at all. These
porter ind-2 *seoir* ind-2 2 *lui* 1 *du tout*

colours *become* you so well, you (would do wrong) to wear any
inf-3 *avoir tort* cond-1 *de en porter de*

others. Sit that child in this arm-chair, and take care he
asseoir m. *fauteuil* m. *prenez garde que*

does not fall. I *will sit down* on the top of that hill,
ne subj-1 *s'asseoir* *sommet* m. *côteau* m.

whence I shall discover a prospect (no less) magnificent
découvrir *scène* f. *aussi* —*que*

than diversified. We (were sitting) on the banks of the
varié *s'asseoir* ind-6 *bord* m. pl.

Thames, whence we contemplated myriads of vessels,
Tamise f. *contempler* ind-2 *de* art. *millier* *vaisseau*

which bring, every year, the riches of the two hemis-
apporter art. pl.

pheres.

VOIR, *to see.*

Part. pres. voyant.—*Part. past.* vu.
IND. *pres.* vois, vois, voit, voyons, voyez, voient.
Imperf. voyais.—*Pret.* vis.—*Fut.* verrai.—COND. verrais.
IMPER. vois, voie, voyons, voyez, voient.
SUBJ. *pres.* voie, voies, voie, voyions, voyiez, voient.—*Imp.* visse.

Revoir, to see again; and *entrevoir*, to have a glimpse of, are conjugated in the same manner; but *prévoir*, to foresee; makes in the future and the conditional, *je prévoirai*, etc. *je prévoirais*, etc.

Pourvoir, to provide; makes in the *pret. je pourvus, tu pourvus*, etc. *fut. je pourvoirai*, etc. COND. *je pourvoirais* etc., and *imperf.* SUBJ. *que je pourvusse*, etc.

Surseoir, to supersede, though a compound of *seoir*, is conjugated like *voir*, except that it makes *fut. je surseoirai*, etc. COND. *je surseoirais*, etc., and *part. past. sursis*.

VALOIR, *to be worth*.

Part. pres. valant.—*Part. past.* valu.
IND. *pres.* vaux, vaux, vaut, valons, valez, valent.
Imperf. valais.—*Pret.* valus.—*Fut.* vaudrai.—COND. vaudrais.
IMPER. vaux, vaille, valons, valez, vaillent.
SUBJ. *pres.* vaille, vailles, vaille, valions, valiez, vaillent.
Imperf. valusse.

Revaloir, to pay off, and *équivaloir*, to be equivalent to, follow *valoir*; but *prévaloir*, to prevail, makes in the SUBJ. *pres. que je prévale, que tu prévales, qu'il prévale, que nous prévalions*, etc.

VOULOIR, *to be willing*.

Part. pres. voulant.—*Part. past.* voulu.
IND. *pres.* veux, veux, veut, voulons, voulez, veulent.
Imperf. voulais.—*Pret.* voulus.—*Fut.* voudrai.—COND. voudrais.
SUBJ. *pres.* veuill-e, —es, —e, voulions, vouliez, veuillent.
Imperf. voulusse.

The imperative is *veuille, veuillons, veuillez*, but the last person only is commonly used, in the sense of *be so kind* or *so good as, please to*.

EXERCISE.

Behold the admirable order of the universe. *Has* he *again seen*
2 D
his country and his frie[illegible] (Had he *had a glimpse of)* the dawn
pays *aurore*
of this fine day? To terminate their affairs, it would be neces-
pour *falloir*
sary for them to *(see one another)*. I clearly *foresaw*,
cond-1 *que* * *ils* * *s'entrevoir* subj-2 *bien* 2

(from that time), all the obstacles he would have to surmount.
dès lors — m. *que* *à* *surmonter*

Would you have had the judge *(put off)* the execution
vouloir ind-2 *que* *juge* *surseoir* subj-2

of the sentence that he had pronounced? I *shall* not *put off* the
arrêt ind-2 *rendu*

prosecution of that affair. If men *do* not *provide* (for it),
poursuite f. pl. art. 2 *y* 1

God *will provide* (for it). (But for the cooking), this fish *(would be*
2 *y* 1 *sans la sauce* *ne valoir*

good for nothing). You have not paid for this ground more than
rien * *terre* f.

it *is worth*; (are you afraid) that it *is* not *worth* six hundred
ne * *craindre* *que* subj-1

pounds? One ounce of gold *is equivalent* to fifteen
livre f. pl. *sterling!* *once* f.

ounces of silver. Doubt not that reason and truth will
douter art. art. *

prevail at last. I *can* and I *will* tell the truth. If you
ne subj-1 *à la longue* *dire* *le*

are willing, he *will be willing* too. *Let* us *resolve* to resist
le *aussi* *vouloir* * *combattre*

our passions, and we shall be sure to conquer them. *(Be so good as)*
ne vaincre 2 1 *vouloir*

to lend me your grammar.
* *prêter* 1

142. IRREGULAR VERBS OF THE FOURTH CONJUGATION.

BRANCH I. *On RENDRE.*

RESOUDRE, *to resolve.*

Part. pres. résolvant.—*Part. past.* résolu, *or* résous.
IND. *pres.* résous, résous, résout, résolv-ons, —ez, —ent.
Imperf. résolvais.—*Pret* résolus.—*Fut.* résoudrai.
COND. résoudrais.—IMPER. résous, résolve, résolv-ons, -ez, -ent.
SUBJ. *pres.* résolve.—*Imperf.* résolusse.

This verb has two participles past, *résolu,* in the sense of *to determine, to fix; résous,* without a feminine, in the sense of *to resolve into, to turn into.*

Absoudre, to absolve, is conjugated like *résoudre;* but has neither *pret.* IND. nor *imperf.* SUBJ.; its participle past is *absous,* m. *absoute,* f.

Dissoudre, to dissolve; has the same irregularities, and wants the same tenses as *absoudre.*

COUDRE, *to sew.*

Part. pres. cousant.—*Part. past.* cousu.
IND. *pres.* couds, couds, coud, cousons, cousez, cousent.
Imperf. cousais.—*Pret.* cousis.—*Fut.* coudrai.—COND. coudrais.
IMPER. couds.—SUBJ. *pres.* couse.—*Imperf.* cousisse.

Découdre, to unsew; and *recoudre,* to sew again, are conjugated in the same manner.

METTRE, *to put.*

Part. pres. mettant.—*Part. past.* mis.
IND. *pres.* mets, mets, met, mettons, mettez, mettent.
Imperf. mettais.—*Pret.* mis.—*Fut.* mettrai.—COND. mettrais.
IMPER. mets.—SUBJ. *pres.* mette.—*Imperf.* misse.

In the same manner are conjugated the derivatives:

admettre	*to admit*	permettre	*to permit*
commettre	*to commit*	promettre	*to promise*
compromettre	*to compromise*	remettre	*to replace*
se démettre	{ *to put out of joint* / *to resign* }	soumettre	*to subject*
		transmettre	*to transmit*
omettre	*to omit*	s'entremettre	*to intermeddle*

EXERCISE.

Wood when burning *resolves itself* into ashes and smoke.
art. *bois* m. *que l'on brûle* *se résoudre* *en cendre* f. pr. *fumée* f.

Have they *resolved* on peace or war? The fog has
on * art. f. art. f. *brouillard* m. *s'*

resolved *itself* into rain. Would that judge thus lightly
résoudre ind-4 *en pluie* f. *si* *légèrement*

absolve the guilty? Strong waters *dissolve* metals.
cond-1 *coupable* m. pl. art. *fort* 2 f. pl. 1 art. *on* 1

Those drugs *were dissolved* before they were put into
drogue 3 ind-4 *avant que de* *les* * *mettre*

that medicine. My sister *did sew* all day yesterday. That piece
remède m. * *hier*

is not well *sewed*, it must (*be sewed over again*). *Unpick*
falloir *la* inf-1 *découdre*

that lace, and *sew* it *again* very carefully. *Does* he
dentelle f. 2 1 *avec beaucoup de soin*

set a great value upon riches? I never *admitted* those
mettre *prix* m. *à* art. ind-4

principles. *Has* he *committed* that fault? If he (would take my
faute f. *me*

advice), he *would resign* his charge in favour of his
croyait *se démettre* cond-1 *de* f. *en* ==

son. He *put* his arm *out of joint* yesterday. I *will omit* nothing
se démettre *le bras* ind-4

that depends on me to serve you. God frequently
de ce *dépendre* ind-7 *de* *pour* *souvent* 2

permits the wicked to prosper. *Put* this book
1 *que* *méchant* m. pl. * *prospérer* sub-1 *remettre*

its place *again*. Under whatever form of government
— f. * *quelque* *gouvernement* m. *que*

you (may live), remember that your first duty is to be
vivre subj-1 *se souvenir* *devoir* m. *de*

obedient to the laws. It frequently happens that fathers *transmit*
soumis 2 *arriver* 1 art.

to their children both their vices and their virtues.
et

He *has* long *meddled* with public affairs; but his
s'entremettre ind-4 *long-temps* *de* art. 2 1

endeavours have not been crowned with success.
effort *couronner* *de* art. m.

MOUDRE, *to grind* (corn, &c.)

Part. pres. moulant.—*Part. past.* moulu.
IND. *pres.* mouds, mouds, moud, moul-ons, —ez, —ent.
Imperf. moulais.—*Pret.* moulus.—*Fut.* moudrai.—COND. moudrais.
IMPER. mouds, moule, moulons, moulez, moulent.
SUBJ. *pres.* moule.—*Imperf.* moulusse.

In the same manner are conjugated the derivatives:

moudre { *to grind* (knives, etc.) | remoudre *to grind again* (corn, etc.) | rémoudre *to grind again* (knives, etc.)

PRENDRE, *to take.*

Part. pres. prenant.—*Part. past.* pris.
IND. *pres.* prends, prends, prend, pren-ons, —ez, prennent.
Imperf. prenais.—*Pret.* pris.—*Fut.* prendrai.—COND. prendrais.
IMPER. prends, prenne, prenons, prenez, prennent.
SUBJ. *pres.* prenn-e, —es, —e, pren-ions, —iez, prennent.
Imperf. prisse.

In the same manner are conjugated:

apprendre	*to learn*	entreprendre	*to undertake*
désapprendre	*to unlearn*	se méprendre	*to mistake*
comprendre	*to understand*	reprendre	*to retake, to reply*
déprendre	*to separate*	surprendre	*surprise*

ROMPRE, *to break.*

Part. pres. rompant.—*Part. past.* rompu.
IND. *pres.* romps, romps, rompt, romp-ons, —ez, —ent.
Imperf. rompais.—*Pret.* rompis.—*Fut.* romprai.—COND. romprais.
IMPER. romps, rompe, rompons, rompez, rompent.
SUBJ. *pres.* rompe.—*Imperf.* rompisse.

In the same manner are conjugated *corrompre*, to corrupt; and *interrompre*, to interrupt.

SOURDRE, to rush out of the ground, as water, has only the infinitive, and *il* or *elle sourd.*

EXERCISE.

I *took* great pains. *Grind* those razors with care.
ind-3 *beaucoup de* soin. *rasoir* m.

Those knives *(are just) ground.* This corn is not sufficiently
couteau m. *venir d'être* *grain* m. *assez*

ground, it *should be* *ground again.* I wish that you *would*
falloir ind-1 *le* inf-1 *vouloir* cond-1

take courage. What news have you *learnt?* Philosophy
subj-2 f. pl. art.

comprehends logic, ethics, physics, and
art *logique* f. art *morale* f. art. *physique*, f. art

metaphysics. It is (with difficulty) that he *divests himself* of
métaphysique f. *Ce* *difficilement* *que* *se déprendre*

his opinions. He *has forgotten* all that he knew. I fear
désapprendre *ce que savoir* ind-2 *craindre que*

you *will undertake* a task above your strength. *Could*
ne subj-1 *tâche* f. *au-dessus de* *forces*, f.

he *have been mistaken* so grossly? I *reproved* him
se méprendre cond-2 *grossièrement* *reprendre* ind-2 2 1

continually for his faults, but (to no purpose). We *surprised*
sans cesse *de* *défaut* *inutilement* ind-3

the enemy, and cut *them* to pieces. In the middle of the
pl. *tailler* 1 2 *en* *à*

road the axletree of our carriage broke. Bad
chemin *essieu* m. *carrosse* *se rompre* ind-3 art. *mauvais*

company *corrupts* the minds of young people. Why
compagnie pl. sing. *gens* *pourquoi*

you *interrupt* your brother, when you see him busy?
quand 2 1 *occupé*

SUIVRE, *to follow.*

Part. pres. suivant—*Part. past.* suivi.
IND. *pres.* suis, suis, suit, suivons, suivez, suivent.
Imperf. suivais—*Pret* suivis—*Fut.* suivrai—COND. suivrais.
IMPER. suis, suive, suivons, suivez, suivent.
SUBJ. *pres.* suive—*Imperf.* suivisse.

Poursuivre, is conjugated in the same way.

S'ensuivre also, but it has the third persons singular and plural only.

VAINCRE, *to conquer, to vanquish.*

Part. pres. vainquant—*Part. past.* vaincu.
IND. *pres.* vaincs,* vaincs*, vainc,* vainqu-ons,* —ez, —ent.
Imperf. vainquais—*Pret.* vainquis—*Fut.* vaincrai—COND. vaincrais.
SUBJ. *pres.* vainque—*Imperf.* vainquisse.

*All the persons of this verb, marked with an asterisk, are very little used. But its derivative, *convaincre*, to convince, is generally used in all its tenses and persons.

EXERCISE.

(For a long while) we *followed* that method, which was only
long-temps 2 ind-3 1 f. ind-2 *ne*

calculated to mislead us. What *is the consequence?* See the errors
propre que à égarer 2 1 *que s'ensuivre* f.

that *have sprung* from this proposition, which appeared so
s'ensuivre ind-4 —— f. ind-2

true. We *pursued* our course when some cries, which
suivre ind-2 *chemin lorsque de* art. *cri*, m. pl *

came from the midst of the forest struck terror into our
sortis *fond* m. *forêt* f. *porter* ind-3 art. — f.

souls. The Greeks *vanquished* the Persians at Marathon, Salamis
Grec *Perse* *à* pr. *Salamine*

Platea, and Mycale. I have at last *convinced* him, by
pr. *Platée,* pr. *convaincre enfin* ind-4 2

such powerful reasons, of the greatness of his fault, that I
des *si* 2 *fort* 3 f. pl. 1 *énormité* *faute* f.

(have no doubt) but he will repair it.
ne douter nullement *que* *ne* *réparer* subj-1 2 1

BATTRE, *to beat.*

Part. pres. battant—*Part. past.* battu.
IND. *pres.* bats, bats, bat, battons, battez, battent.
Imperf. battais—*Pret.* battis—*Fut.* battrai—COND. battrais.
IMPER. bats—SUBJ. *pres.* batte—*Imperf.* battisse.

Conjugate in the same manner:

abattre	*to pull down*	combattre	*to fight*
rabattre	*to abate*	débattre	*to debate*
rebattre	*to beat again*	s'ébattre	*to be merry*

VIVRE, *to live.*

Part. pres. vivant—*Part. past.* vécu.
IND. *pres.* vis, vis, vit, vivons, vivez, vivent.—*Imperf.* vivais.
Pret. vécus—*Fut.* vivrai—COND. vivrais—IMP. vis.
SUBJ. *pres.* vive—*Imperf.* vécusse.

In the same manner are conjugated *revivre,* to revive; and *survivre,* to survive.

EXERCISE.

It is during winter that they *thrash* the corn in cold
Ce *pendant* art. *on* *battre* *froid* 2

countries. The enemy were so completely *beaten* in that
art. *pays* m. pl. 1 pl. ind-3 ——*ment*

engagement, that they were forced to abandon thirty leagues of the
rencontre f. *de* *lieue* f. *

country. The cannon *beat down* the tower. They *were fighting*
pays *canon* *abattre* ind-3 *tour* f. ind-2

with unexampled rage when a panic terror
un sans exemple 2 *acharnement* m. 1 *panique* 2 = f. 1

made them take flight, and dispersed them in an instant.
ind-3 2 *leur* 1 art. *fuite* f. 2 — m.

Beat these mattrasses *again*. Happy those who *live* in
rebattre *matelas* m. *

solitude ! Long *live* that good king ! He
art. *retraite* f. *Que* 1 *long-temps* 4 subj-1 3 2 2 2

did not long *survive* a person who was so dear to him.
survivre ind-3 *à* f. 2 1

Fathers *live again* in their children. He was in a great
art.

dejection of mind; the news which he has received has
accablement f. pl. f. pl. *ont fait*

revived him.
inf-1 2 1

BRANCH II. *Plaire.*

Braire, to bray; is used in the third persons only and in the following tenses: *il brait, ils braient, il braira, ils brairont, il brairait, ils brairaient.*

FAIRE, *to do.*

Part. pres. faisant—*Part. past.* fait.
IND. *pres.* fais, fais, fait, faisons, faites, font.
Imperf. faisais—*Pret.* fis—*Fut.* ferai—COND. ferais.
IMPER. fais, fasse, faisons, faites, fassent.
SUBJ. *pres.* fasse, fassions—*Imperf.* fisse.

Some authors, on account of the similarity of sound, write *nous fesons, fesant*, etc. but it is contrary to the opinion of the French Academy.

In the same manner are conjugated:

contrefaire	*to counterfeit*	refaire	*to do again*
défaire	*to undo*	satisfaire	*to satisfy*
redéfaire	*to undo again*	surfaire	*to exact*
forfaire*	*to trespass*	méfaire*	*to misdo*
malfaire	*to do ill*	parfaire	*to perfect*

TRAIRE, *to milk* (defective).

Part. pres. trayant—*Part. past.* trait.
IND. *pres.* trais, trais, trait, trayons, trayez, traient.
Imperf. trayais—(*No pret.*)—*Fut.* trairai—COND. trairais.
IMPER. trais, traie, trayons, trayez, traient.
SUBJ. *pres.* traye—(*No imperf.*)

* These four verbs are only used in this form, and the partic. past, *forfait, malfait, méfait* and *parfait*.

Conjugate in the same manner:

attraire	*to allure*	rentraire	*to finedraw*
abstraire	*to abstract*	retraire	*to redeem*
distraire	*to divert*	soustraire	*to subtract*
extraire	*to extract*		

All these verbs are principally used in the compound tenses.

EXERCISE.

What will you have him *do?* *Do* not *make* (so much)
Que vouloir * *que il* sub-1 *tant*

noise. *Do* they never *exact?* That woman *mimicked* all the per-
de bruit ind-2 f.

sons whom she saw. It was with difficulty he *(divested himself)*
pl. *voir* ind-3 *Ce* ind-3 *peine que se défaire* ind-3

of the falsé opinions which had been given him in his infancy.
— f. *on* ind-2 * 2 *données* 3 *lui* 1 f.

Is there no chance of *our making again* another trip to
n'est-il donc pas probable que sub-1 *le voyage de*

Paris, Rome, and Naples. He says that you have offended him,
pr. pr. *dit* 2 *offensé* 3 1

and that, if you do not *satisfy* him quickly, he will find means
promptement art. *moyen*

to *satisfy* himself. Every night, she *milked* her
sing. *de se lui-même* art. *soir* m. pl. ind-2

cows, which gave her a (great quantity) of wholesome milk.
qui ind-2 *lui abondant* 2 * *et sain* 3 *lait* m. 1.

Have you *milked* your goats? Are the cows *milked?*
chèvre f. pl. *vache* f. pl. art.

Salt is good to *entice* pigeons. You will never know the
Sel m. *pour attraire* art. m. pl. *connaître*

nature of bodies, if you *abstract* not their accessory qualities
art. = 2 = 1 l.

from those which are inherent (in them). The least thing (diverts
2 ——— *leur* 1 *moindre le*

his attention). *Will* you not *extract* that charming passage? *Have*
distraire —— m.

you *darned* your gown? Should he not *redeem* that land?
rentraire devoir cond-1

What! would you have me *screen* those guilty
Quoi! ind-1 * *que je soustraire* sub-1 *coupable* m. pl.

persons from the rigour of the laws?
* *à* *rigueur* f.

BRANCH III. *Paraître.*

NAÎTRE, *to be born.*

Part. pres. naissant—*Part. past.* né.
IND. *pres.* nais, nais, naît, naissons, naissez, naissent.
Imperf. naissais—*Pret.* naquis—*Fut.* naîtrai—COND. naîtrais
IMPER. nais—SUBJ. *pres.* naisse—*Imperf.* naquisse.

This verb takes the auxiliary *être*; but its derivative, *renaître*, to be born again; has no participl past, and, consequently, no compound tenses.

PAÎTRE, *to graze* (defective).

Part. pres. paissant—*Part. past.* pu.
IND. *pres.* pais, pais, paît, paissons, paissez, paissent.
Imperf. paissais—*(No pret.)*—*Fut.* paîtrai—COND. paîtrais.
IMPER. pais—SUBJ. *pres.* paisse—*(No imperf.)*

Repaître, to feed to bait is, like *paraître*, regular in all its tenses, making in the *pret.* IND. je repus, etc. and in the *imperf.* SUBJ. je repusse, etc.

EXERCISE.

Was not Virgil *born* at Mantua? It is from that poisoned
ind-3 *Mantoue* *Ce* *empoisonné* 2

source that *have arisen* all the cruel wars that have desolated
f. 1 *que* *naître* f. pl. 2 f. pl. 1 *désoler*

the universe. The fable says that, as soon as Hercules had
f. *dit* *aussitôt que* *Hercule h* m. ind-2

(cut off) one of the heads of the hydra, others *sprang up.*
couper *tête* f. pl. *hydre* f. *d'autres* 2 *il* *en renaître*

While their united flocks fed on the
nd 2 1 *tandis que* *réuni* 2 *troupeau*

tender and flowery grass, they sung under the shade of a
2 *fleuri* 3 *herbe* f. 1 *chanter* ind-2 *à* *ombre*

tree the sweets of rura life. Your horses have
douceur f. pl. art *champêtre* 2 f. 1

got *fed* to-day; you must have them *fed*. That is a
repaître d'aujourd'hui ; il faut leur faire donner à manger Ce

man who *thirsts* after nothing but blood and slaughter.
ne se repaître de 2 * *que* 1 pr. *carnage* m.

145. BRANCH IV. *Réduire.*

Bruire, to roar; is defective, it has only the *part. pres.* bruyant, oftener used as an adjective, as: *des flots bruyans;* and the two third persons of the *imperf.* IND. il bruyait, ils bruyaient.

Luire, to shine; and *reluire*, to glitter; make the *part. past. lui, relui*, neither the *pret.* IND. nor *imperf.* SUBJ. are in use.

Nuire, to hurt; making *part. pres.* nuisant, *past.* nui, is regular in all its tenses.

CONFIRE, *to pickle* or *preserve.*

Part. pres. confisant—*Part. past.* confit.
IND. *pres.* conf-is, —is, it, —isons, —isez, —isent.
Imperf. confisais—*Pret* confis—*Fut.* confirai.
COND. confirais—IMP. confis—SUBJ. *pres.* confise.
Imperf. confisse.

Its derivative *déconfire*, to discomfit, is rather ob solete.

Circoncire, to circumcise, and *suffire*, to suffice, make in the *part. past. circoncis* and *suffi*, the rest is as *confire.*

EXERCISE.

The thunder which *roared* from afar announced
tonnerre m. *bruire* ind-2 *dans* art. *lointain* m ind-2

a dreadful storm. They heard the roaring of the waves of
terrible 2 *orage* m. 1 *On* ind-2 * inf-1 * *flot* m. pl.

an agitated sea. That street is too *noisy* for those who love
agité 2 *mer* f. 1 *rue* f. *bruyant*

retirement and study. I (have a glimpse of) some thing
art. *retraite* f. art. *entrevoir* *quelque chose*

that *shines* through those trees. A ray of hope *shone* upon
au travers de *rayon* m. ind-4 2 *

us in the midst of the misfortunes which overwhelmed us. Every
1 *à* *milieu* *malheur* m. pl. *accabler* ind-2

thing is well rubbed in that house: every thing *shines*, even to the
frotté *y reluire jusque à*

floor. *Would* he not *have hurt* you in that affair? Jesus
plancher m. cond-2 1

Christ was *circumcised* (a week) after his birth. *Shall* you
huit jours *naissance* f.

preserve these peaches with sugar, with honey, or with
confire *à* art. *sucre* m. art. *miel* m.

brandy? *Have* you *pickled* cucumbers,
art. *eau-de-vie* f. *de* art. *concombre* m. pr-art.

purslane, and sea-fennel? If he loses his law-suit, all his
pourpier m. pr. art. *perce-pierre* f. *procès* m.

property *will* not *suffice*.
bien

DIRE, *to say*.

Part. pres. disant—*Part. past.* dit.
IND. *pres.* dis, dis, dit, disons, DITES,* disent.
Imperf. disais—*Pret.* dis—*Fut.* dirai—COND. dirais.
IMPER. dis, dise, disons, DITES,* disent.
SUBJ. *pres.* dise—*Imperf.* disse.

* *Redire*, to say again, conformably to its primitive, makes *redites*, but

contredire	*to contradict*	make	vous contredises
dédire	*to unsay*		vous dédises
interdire	*to forbid*		vous interdises
médire	*to slander*		vous médises
prédire	*to foretell*		vous prédises

Maudire is conjugated like *punir* with the exception of the participle past which is *maudit, e* *Maudissant*, *je maudis, nous maudissons; je maudissais; je maudis; je maudirai; je maudirais; que je maudisse; que je maudisse; maudis*.

ECRIRE, *to write.*

Part. pres. écrivant—*Part. past.* écrit.
IND. *pres.* écris, écris, écrit, écriv-ons, —ez, ent.
Imperf. écrivais—*Pret.* écrivis—*Fut.* écrirai—COND. écrirais
IMP. écris—SUBJ. *pres.* écrive—*Imperf.* écrivisse.

Conjugate in the same manner :

circonscrire	*to circumscribe*	proscrire	*to proscribe*
décrire	*to describe*	récrire	*to write again*
inscrire	*to inscribe*	souscrire	*to subscribe*
prescrire	*to prescribe*	transcrire	*to transcribe*

LIRE, *to read.*

Part. pres. lisant—*Part. past.* lu.
IND. *pres.* lis, lis, lit, lisons, lisez, lisent—*Imperf.* lisais.
Pret. lus—*Fut.* lirai—COND. lirais—IMPER. lis.
SUBJ. *pres.* lise—*Imperf.* lusse.

In the same manner are conjugated :

élire	*to elect*	relire	*to read over again*

RIRE, *to laugh.*

Part. pres. riant—*Past.* ri—IND. *pres.* ris, ris, rit, rions, riez, rient.
Imperf. riais—*Pret.* ris—*Fut.* rirai—COND. rirais.
IMPER. ris—SUBJ. *pres.* rie—*Imperf.* risse.

Sourire, to smile ; is conjugated as *rire*.

Frire, to fry ; besides the present of the infinitive, has only the *part. past.* frit ; INDIC. *pres.* je fris, tu fris, il frit ; *fut.* je frirai, tu, etc. ; COND. je frirais, tu, etc. ; IMPER. sing. fris. But it has all the compound tenses. The forms that are deficient are fully supplied by *faire*, prefixed to *frire*, as : *faisant frire, je faisais frire*, etc.

EXERCISE.

Always *speak* the truth, but with discretion. Never *contradict*
dire f.
(any one) in public. You thought you were serving me in
personne *en* *penser* ind-4 * * inf-1 2 1 *en*

speaking thus ; well, (let it be so); you shall not be contradicted
parler ainsi eh bien soit en dédire

What! *would* you *forbid* him all communication with his friends ?
Quoi ! * *interdire* 2 1 ——— f.

That woman *slandered* every one. You *had foretold* that event.
ind-2 *de* ind-6

Let us *curse* no one ; *let* us *remember* that our laws forbid us
ne personne se rappeler défendre

to curse even those who persecute us. *Write down* every day
de persécuter art. pl.

the reflections which you make on the books which you *read.*

Did he not *read* that interesting history with (a great deal) of
ind-2 2 1

pleasure ? God is an infinite being who is *circumscribed* neither
2 *être* m. 1 *ne ni*

by time nor place. *Shall* you not *describe* that
art. *ni* pr. art. *lieu* m. pl.

dreadful tempest ? Have those soles and whitings *fried*
horrible 2 f. 1 *faire* 1 ——— pron. *merlan* 3 inf-1 2

If you wish to form your taste, *read* the classics *over and over.*
vouloir * *lire et relire les anciens*

He was *elected* by a great majority of voices. We *have laughed*
ind-4 *à* ——— f.

heartily and have resolved to (go on). He did not answer
de bon cœur nous résolu de continuer répondre

him (any thing) : but he *smiled* at him, as a sign of appro-
ind-3 *lui rien* ind-3 2 * *lui* 1 *en* * —

bation, in the kindest manner.
— *de gracieux* 2 *air* m. 1

BOIRE, *to drink.*

Part. pres. buvant—*Past.* bu.
IND. *pres.* bois, bois, boit, buvons, buvez, boivent.
Imperf. buvais—*Pret.* bus—*Fut.* boirai—*Cond.* boirais.
IMPER. bois, boive, buvons, buvez, boivent.
SUBJ. *pres.* boiv-e, —es, e, buvions, buviez, boivent.
Imperf. busse.

In the same manner are conjugated.

	to drink again	s'emboire	*to imbibe, a technical term used in painting*

Clore, to close; has only the *part. past.* clos; *ind. pres.* je clos, tu clos, il clôt; *fut.* je clorai, tu cloras, etc.; *cond.* je clorais, tu clorais, etc.; and the IMP. sing. clos.

Déclore, to disclose, *enclore*, to enclose, are defective in the same tenses as *clore*, but *forclore*, to debar, a law term, is only used in the *inf.* and *part. past.* forclos.

Eclore, to be hatched, as birds, or to blow like a flower, has only these forms; *inf.* éclore; *part. past.* éclos; *ind. pres.* il éclôt, ils éclosent; *fut.* il éclora, ils écloront; *cond.* il éclorait, ils écloraient; and the *subj. pres.* qu'il éclose, qu'ils éclosent. But its compound tenses, which are formed with *être*, are much used.

CONCLURE, *to conclude.*

Part. pres.	concluant—*Past.* conclu.
IND. *pres.*	conclu, conclus, conclut, conclu-ons, —ez, —ent.
Imperf.	concluais—*Pret.* conclus—*Fut.* conclurai.
COND.	conclurais—IMPER. conclus—SUBJ. *pres.* conclue.
Imperf.	conclusse.

Exclure, to exclude; is conjugated like *conclure*, except that it has two participles past, *exclu, e, exclus, e.*

CROIRE, *to believe.*

Part. pres.	croyant—*Past.* cru.
IND. *pres.*	crois, crois, croit, croyons, croyez, croient.
Imperf.	croyais—*Pret.* crus—*Fut.* croirai—COND. croirais.
IMPER.	crois, croie, croyons, croyez, croient.
Imperf.	crusse.

It has no derivative but *accroire*, which is only used with *faire*, as: *faire accroire* or *en faire accroire*, to impose upon credulity; and *s'en faire accroire*, to be self-conceited.

EXERCISE.

Seated under the shade of palm-trees, they milked their
Assis *à* art. *palmier* pl. *traire* ind-2

goats and ewes, and merrily drunk that nectar,
chèvre f. pl. pron. brebis f. pl. avec joie 2 ind-2 1 m.

which (was renewed) every day. *Would* they *drink* their
se renouveler ind-2 art. pl. boire cond-1

wine iced? This window *does* not *close* well; when you
à la glace f.

have made some alterations (in it), it *will* close better. He
ind-8 2 3 réparation f. 4 y 1 mieux

had scarcely *closed* his eyes, when the noise which they made
à peine ind-6 * art. que que on ind-3

at his door, awoke him. *Have* they not *enclosed* the suburbs
à réveiller ind-3 on faubourg

within the city? *Will* you *enclose* your park with a wall,
m. pl. ville f. parc de mur m.

or a hedge? Put the eggs of those silk-worms in the
pr. haie f. mettez œuf m. pl. ver-à-soie m. pl. à

sun, that they *may hatch.* Those flowers just *blown,*
soleil m. sub-1 nouvellement

exhale the sweetest fragrance. When *did* they *conclude* this
répandre doux parfum m. ind-4

treaty? His enemies managed so well, that he was unanimously
traité m. faire ind-3 ind-3 unanimement

excluded from the company. *Do* you *think* me capable of so
compagnie f. croire ind-1

black an act? He possesses some kind of knowledge; but
noir 2 trait m. 1 avoir espèce savoir

(not so much as he thinks).
il s'en fait trop accroire.

146. BRANCH V. *Joindre.*

Poindre, to pierce, to peep, to dawn, has only besides the infinitive *il point, il poindra.*

147. GENERAL GUIDE TO THE CONJUGATION.

The following Tables, which exhibit at one view all the primitive tenses, both of the regular and irregular verbs, and most of the defective, with references to the pages, where the other tenses are to be found, will, it is presumed, prove useful to those who will consult them.

TABLE OF THE PRIMITIVE TENSES OF THE FOUR REGULAR CONJUGATIONS.

INFIN.	PARTICIPLES.		INDICATIVE.		
PRESENT.	PRESENT.	PAST.	PRESENT.	PRETERIT.	
FIRST CONJUGATION.					
Parl*er*	Parl*ant*	Parl*é*	Je parl*e*	Je parl*ai*	172
SECOND CONJUGATION.					
FIRST BRANCH. *Punir.*					
Pun*ir*	Pun*issant*	Pun*i*	Je pun*is*	Je pun*is*	183
SECOND BRANCH. *Sentir.*					
Sen*tir*	Sen*tant*	Sen*ti*	Je sen*s*	Je sen*tis*	186
Men*tir*	Men*tant*	Men*ti*	Je men*s*	Je men*tis*	
Se repen*tir*	Se repen*tant*	Repen*ti*	Je *me* repen*s*	Je *me* repen*tis*	
Par*tir*	Par*tant*	Par*ti*	Je par*s*	Je par*tis*	
Sor*tir*	Sor*tant*	Sor*ti*	Je sor*s*	Je sor*tis*	
Dor*mir*	Dor*mant*	Dor*mi*	Je dor*s*	Je dor*mis*	
Ser*vir*	Ser*vant*	Ser*vi*	Je ser*s*	Je ser*vis*	
THIRD BRANCH. *Ouvrir.*					
Ouvr*ir*	Ouvr*ant*	Ouv*ert*	J' ouvr*e*	J' ouvr*is*	188
Offr*ir*	Offr*ant*	Off*ert*	J' offr*e*	J' offr*is*	
Souffr*ir*	Souffr*ant*	Souff*ert*	Je souffr*e*	Je souffr*is*	

INFIN.	PARTICIPLES.		INDICATIVE.		
PRESENT.	PRESENT.	PAST.	PRESENT.	PRETERIT.	
FOURTH BRANCH. *Tenir.*					
Tenir	Tenant	Tenu	Je tiens	Je tins	183
Venir	Venant	Venu	Je viens	Je vins	
FIFTH BRANCH. *Courir.*					
Courir	Courant	Couru	Je cours	Je courus	184
THIRD CONJUGATION.					
Recevoir	Recevant	Reçu	Je reçois	Je reçus	190
Devoir	Devant	Dû	Je dois	Je dus	
FOURTH CONJUGATION.					
FIRST BRANCH. *Rendre.*					
Répandre	Répandant	Répandu	Je répands	Je répandis	195
Rendre	Rendant	Rendu	Je rends	Je rendis	
Fondre	Fondant	Fondu	Je fonds	Je fondis	
Pondre	Pondant	Pondu	Je ponds	Je pondis	
Répondre	Répondant	Répondu	Je réponds	Je répondis	
Tondre	Tondant	Tondu	Je tonds	Je tondis	
Perdre	Perdant	Perdu	Je perds	Je perdis	
Mordre	Mordant	Mordu	Je mords	Je mordis	
Tordre	Tordant	Tordu	Je tords	Je tordis	
SECOND BRANCH. *Plaire.*					
Plaire	Plaisant	Plu	Je plais	Je plus	195
Taire	Taisant	Tu	Je tais	Je tus	
THIRD BRANCH. *Paraître.*					
Paraître	Paraissant	Paru	Je parais	Je parus	195
Croître	Croissant	Crû	Je crois	Je crus	
Connaître	Connaissant	Connu	Je connais	Je connus	
Repaître	Repaissant	Repu	Je repais	Je repus	
FOURTH BRANCH. *Réduire.*					
Réduire	Réduisant	Réduit	Je réduis	Je réduisis	195
Instruire	Instruisant	Instruit	J' instruis	J' instruisis	
FIFTH BRANCH. *Craindre.*					
Craindre	Craignant	Craint	Je crains	Je craignis	195
Peindre	Peignant	Peint	Je peins	Je peignis	
Joindre	Joignant	Joint	Je joins	Je joignis	

146. PRIMITIVE TENSES OF THE IRREGULAR AND DEFECTIVE VERBS.

INFIN.	PARTICIPLES		INDICATIVE.		
PRESENT.	PRESENT.	PAST.	PRESENT.	PRETERIT	
FIRST CONJUGATION.					
Aller	Allant	Allé	Je vais	J' allai	223
SECOND CONJUGATION.					
FIRST BRANCH. *Punir.*					
Fleurir	Fleurissant Florissant	Fleuri	Je fleuris	Je fleuris	229
Haïr	Haïssant	Haï	Je hais	Je hais	
Gésir*	Gisant		Il gît		
SECOND BRANCH. *Sentir.*					
Bouillir	Bouillant	Bouilli	Je bous	Je bouillis	237
Ebouillir		Ebouilli			
Faillir	Faillant*	Failli	Je faux*	Je faillis	
Défaillir		Défailli	Nous défaillons	Je défaillis	
Fuir	Fuyant	Fui	Je fuis	Je fuis	
Mourir	Mourant	Mort	Je meurs	Je mourus	
Acquérir	Acquérant	Acquis	J' acquiers	J' acquis	
Conquérir	Conquérant	Conquis	Je conquiers	Je conquis	
Ouïr	Oyant*	Ouï		J' ouïs	
Vêtir	Vêtant	Vêtu	Je vêts	Je vêtis	
Revêtir	Revêtant	Revêtu	Je revêts	Je revêtis	
THIRD BRANCH. *Ouvrir.*					
Cueillir	Cueillant	Cueilli	Je cueille	Je cueillis	241
Saillir	Saillant	Sailli	Il saille	Il saillit	
Tressaillir	Tressaillant	Tressailli	Je tressaille	Je tressaillis	
THIRD CONJUGATION.					
Recevoir.					
Avoir	Ayant	Eu	J'ai	J'eus	238
Ravoir					
Choir		Chu			
Déchoir		Déchu	Je déchois	Je déchus	
Echoir	Echéant	Echu	Il échoit	J' échus	

N.B. The forms marked with an asterisk are rather obsolete.

INFIN.	PARTICIPLES.		INDICATIVE.		
PRESENT.	PRESENT.	PAST.	PRESENT.	PRETERIT.	
Falloir		Fallu	Il faut	Il fallut	218
Mouvoir	Mouvant	Mu	Je meus	Je mus	
Promouvoir		Promu		Je promus*	
Pleuvoir	Pleuvant	Plu	Il pleut	Il plut	
Pouvoir	Pouvant	Pu	Je puis	Je pus	
Savoir	Sachant	Su	Je sais	Je sus	234
Seoir*	Seyant		Il sied		à
Seoir*	Séant	Sis			
Asseoir	Asseyant	Assis	J' assieds	J' assis	238
Surseoir		Sursis	Je sursois	Je sursis	
Voir	Voyant	Vu	Je vois	Je vis	
Prévoir	Prévoyant	Prévu	Je prévois	Je prévis	
Pourvoir	Pourvoyant	Pourvu	Je pourvois	Je pourvus	
Valoir	Valant	Valu	Je vaux	Je valus	
Vouloir	Voulant	Voulu	Je veux	Je voulus	

FOURTH CONJUGATION.

FIRST BRANCH. *Rendre.*

Résoudre	Résolvant	Résous, résolu	Je résous	Je résolus	
Soudre	Solvant				
Absoudre	Absolvant	Absous	J' absous		
Dissoudre	Dissolvant	Dissous	Je dissous		
Coudre	Cousant	Cousu	Je couds	Je cousis	
Sourdre			Il sourd		240
Mettre	Mettant	Mis	Je mets	Je mis	à
Moudre	Moulant	Moulu	Je mouds	Je moulus	
Prendre	Prenant	Pris	Je prends	Je pris	246
Rompre	Rompant	Rompu	Je romps	Je rompis	
Suivre	Suivant	Suivi	Je suis	Je suivis	
S'ensuivre	S'ensuivant	Ensuivi	Il s'ensuit	Il s'ensuivit	
Vaincre	Vainquant	Vaincu	Je vaincs	Je vainquis	
Battre	Battant	Battu	Je bats	Je battis	
Etre	Etant	Eté	Je suis	Je fus	162
Vivre	Vivant	Vécu	Je vis	Je vécus	246

SECOND BRANCH. *Plaire.*

Braire			Il brait		
Faire	Faisant	Fait	Je fais	Je fis	246
Traire	Trayant	Trait	Je trais		

THIRD BRANCH. *Paraître.*

Naître	Naissant	Né	Je nais	Je naquis	
Renaître	Renaissant		Je renais	Je renaquis*	248
Paître	Paissant	Pû	Je pais		

INFIN.	PARTICIPLES		INDICATIVE.		
PRESENT.	PRESENT.	PAST.	PRESENT.	PRETERIT.	

FOURTH BRANCH. *Réduire.*

Bruire	Bruyant				
Luire	Luisant	Lui	Je luis		
Nuire	Nuisant	Nui	Je nuis	Je nuisis	
Confire	Confisant	Confit	Je confis	Je confis	
Suffire	Suffisant	Suffi	Je suffis	Je suffis	
Circoncire	Circoncisant	Circoncis	Je circoncis	Je circoncis	
Dire	Disant	Dit	Je dis	Je dis	
Médire	Médisant	Médit	Je médis	Je médis	249
Maudire	Maudissant	Maudit	Je maudis	Je maudis	à
Ecrire	Ecrivant	Ecrit	J' écris	J' écrivis	258
Lire	Lisant	Lu	Je lis	Je lus	
Rire	Riant	Ri	Je ris	Je ris	
Frire		Frit	Je fris		
Boire	Buvant	Bu	Je bois	Je bus	
Clore, clorre		Clos	Je clos		
Conclure	Concluant	Conclu	Je conclus	Je conclus	
Exclure	Excluant	Exclu *or* exclus	J' exclus	J 'exclus	
Croire	Croyant	Cru	Je crois	Je crus	

FIFTH BRANCH. *Craindre.*

Poindre			Il point		254

N. B. The derivatives, which are not in this Table, will be found, with the primitives, to which we have given references.

CHAPTER VI.

OF THE PREPOSITIONS.

149. *Pre*positions, so called, from their being *pre*fixed to the nouns, which they govern, serve to show the relation which exists between two words. Thus, in this phrase, *le fruit de l'arbre*, the fruit of the tree, *de* expresses the relation between *fruit* and *arbre*. Likewise in this, *utile à l'homme*, useful to man; *à* shows the relation between the noun *homme* and the adjective *utile*. *De* and *à* are *pre*positions, and the word to which they are *pre*fixed, is called their *regimen*.

Prepositions being invariable parts of speech, they remain the same whatever be the gender and number of the noun which they precede.

They are generally divided into classes, according to the nature of the relation they serve to express.

Some also require another preposition after them, *de* or *à*, whilst their equivalents in English do not, and *vice versa*.

These peculiarities deserve much attention and will, therefore, be noticed in order.

150. PREPOSITIONS DENOTING *PLACE*.

CHÉZ. *Il est chez son père*, he is *at the house of* his father, *or* at his *father's*. *Nous sommes chez lui*, we are in his house. *Il est chez lui*, he is at home.

Dans. *Il se promène* dans *le jardin;* he is walking *in* the garden.

Devant. *Il est toujours* devant *mes yeux;* he is always *before* my eyes.

Derrière. *Il ne regarde jamais* derrière *lui;* he never looks *behind* him.

Parmi. *Que de fous* parmi *les hommes!* how many fools *among* men!

Sous. *La taupe vit* sous *terre;* the mole lives *under* ground.

Sur. *Il a le chapeau* sur *la tête;* he has his hat *on* (his head.)

Vers. *L'aimant se tourne* vers *le nord;* the loadstone points *towards* the north.

EXERCISE.

We find less real happiness *in* an elevated condition than *in*
On *de* 2 *bonheur* 1 2 f. 1

a middling state. One is never truly at peace but *at* home.
moyen 2 1 *véritablement tranquille que soi*

He walked *before* me. There was a delightful grove *behind*
marcher ind-4 *avoir* ind-2 2 *bosquet* m. 1

his house. Among (so many) different nations, there is not one
tant de 2 . 1 *y en avoir*

that has not a religious worship. Nature displays her riches
qui sub-1 = 2 *culte* m. 1 art. *déployer*

with magnificence *under* the torrid zone. Eternal snows
torride 3 f. 1 *de* art. 3 5 f. pl. 4

(are to be seen) *on* the summit of the Alps. *Towards* the
on 1 *voir* ind-1 2 *sommet* *Alpes* f.

north, nature presents a gloomy and wild aspect.
art. *triste* 2 *sauvage* 3 *aspect* m. 1

PREPOSITIONS DENOTING *ORDER.*

Avant. *La nouvelle est arrivée* avant *le courri*
news is come *before* the courier.

APRÈS. *Il est trop vain pour marcher* après *les autres;* he is too proud to walk *after* other people.

ENTRE. *Elle a son enfant* entre *les bras;* she holds her child *in* (for *between*) her arms.

DEPUIS. Depuis *la création jusqu'à nous, from* the creation to the present time.

DÈS. Dès *son enfance; from* his infancy; dès *sa source; from* its source.

EXERCISE.

We (were up) *before* day-light, (in order to) enjoy the
se lever ind-6 art. * *pour* *jouir de*

magnificent spectacle of the rising sun. *After* such great
magnifique 2 —m. 1. *levant* 2 1 *de si*

faults, it only remained for us to repair them (as well as
faute f. pl. *ne* *rester* ind-2 2* 1 *que à réparer* 2 1 *de notre*

we could). *Between* those two mountains is a deep hollow
mieux *profond* 3 *et creux* 2

road. Many very astonishing events (have taken place)
chemin m. 1 * *de* art. 2 4 3 *il s'est passé* 1

within these ten years. *From* my earliest infancy I have had an
depuis * . art. *tendre* , *

abhorrence for falsehood.
horreur *de* art. *mensonge* m.

PREPOSITIONS DENOTING *UNION.*

AVEC. *Il faut savoir* avec *qui on se lie,* we ought to know *with* whom we associate.

DURANT. Durant *la guerre, during* the war: durant *l'été, during* the summer.

PENDANT. Pendant *l'hiver, in* winter; pendant *la paix, in* time of peace. This preposition denotes a duration more limited than *durant.*

SUIVANT. *Je me déciderai* suivant *les circonstances,* I shall determine *according to* circumstances.

SELON. *Le sage se conduit* selon *les maximes de*

la raison, a wise man acts *according to* the dictates of reason.

EXERCISE.

With wit, politeness, and a little (readiness to
de art. pr. art. *peu de prévenance*

oblige) one generally succeeds in the world. We are fit for
réussir *on* *propre à*

meditation *during* winter. *(In the course of)* that siege the com-
art. f. *pendant* *siége* m.

mandant of the city made some very successful sallies.
ind-3 *de* art. *heureux* 2 *sortie* f. pl. 1.

Besides the exterior advantages of figure and the graces of
= 2 1 art. art.

deportment, she possesses an excellent heart, a correct judgment,
maintien m. *avoir* 2 1 *sain* 2 *jugement* 1

and a kind heart. Always act *according* to the maxims
sensible 2 1 *se conduire* * f. pl.

which I have given you.
inculquer f. pl.

152. PREPOSITIONS DENOTING OPPOSITION.

CONTRE. *Je plaide* contre *lui*, I plead *against* him.

MALGRÉ. *Il l'a fait* malgré *moi*, he has done it *in spite of* me.

NONOBSTANT. Nonobstant *ce qu'on lui a dit*, *notwithstanding* what has been said to him.

EXERCISE.

We cannot long act (*contrary to*) our own disposition
savoir cond-1 *agir* *contre* * *caractère* m.

notwithstanding all the pains we take to disguise it, it shews
que *pour* 2 1 *se mon-*

itself, and betrays us on many occasions. (In vain we
trer *trahir* 2 1 *en* *bien de* art. *avoir beau*

dissemble; *in spite of* ourselves, we are known at last.
faire *on nous connaît à la longue.*

153. PREPOSITIONS DENOTING PRIVATION, SEPARATION.

SANS. *Des troupes* sans *chefs ;* troops *without* commanders.

EXCEPTÉ. Excepté *quelques malheureux, except,* some wretches.

HORS. *Tout est perdu* hors *l'honneur,* all is lost *save* honour.

HORMIS. *Tous sont entrés* hormis *mon frère,* they are all come in *except* my brother.

EXERCISE.

(Had it not been for) your care, I should have been ignorant all
sans pl. * *un*

my life. All the philosophers of antiquity, *except* a few
art. *très-petit nom-*

bre have held the world to be eternal. All laid down their
croire * * *mettre bas* *

arms, *except* two regiments, who preferred (making their way)
art. m. *se faire jour*

through the enemy. Every thing is absurd and ridiculous in
au travers de pl.

that work, *except* a chapter or two.

154. PREPOSITIONS DENOTING THE END

ENVERS. *Il est charitable* envers *les pauvres,* he is charitable *to* the poor.

TOUCHANT. *Il a écrit* touchant *cette affaire,* he has written *respecting* that business.

POUR. *Il travaille* pour *le bien public,* he works *for* the public good

EXERCISE.

I have written to you *concerning* that business, in which I take
à laquelle
the most lively interest; and as I know your benevolence to-
vif 2 1 *connaître* *bienveillance* f.
wards the unfortunate, I (make not the least doubt) that you
ne douter nullement
(will carefully attend) (to it) (not so much) *for* the satisfac-
ne donner tous vos soins sub-1 2 *y* 1 *moins*
tion of obliging me, as *for* the pleasure of justifying innocence,
inf-1 2 1 *justifier* inf-1 art.
and confounding calumny.
pr. *confondre* art. f.

155. PREPOSITIONS DENOTING *CAUSE, MEANS*.

PAR, *Il l'a fléchi* par *ses prières,* he has softened him *by* his prayers.

MOYENNANT. *Il réussira* moyennant *vos avis,* he will succeed *by* means of your counsels.

ATTENDU. *Il ne peut partir,* attendu *les vents contraires,* he cannot sail *on account of* contrary winds.

EXERCISE.

Is there any man that has never been softened *by* tears
y avoir aucun sub-1 *fléchir* art.
or disarmed *by* submission? *Through* the precautions which
ni désarmer art. *que*
we took we avoided the rocks of that dangerous coast. *Owing*
ind-3 ind-3 *écueil* m. pl. 2 *côte* f. 1
to the bad state of my father's health, I shall not travel this
2 1 *voyager*
year.
année f.

156. The prepositions *à*, *de*, *en* are so commonly used in French, that they deserve particular attention.

A is generally used to express several relations, as *destination, tendency, place, time, situation*, etc. being often a substitute for various other prepositions: *Ex.*—destination -*to: aller* à *Londres*, to go to London.—Tendency -*to, toward: courir* à *sa perte*, to hasten *to* one's ruin.—Aim -*to, for: aspirer* à *la gloire*, to aspire *to* glory.—Residence -*at, in: être* à *Rome*, to be *at* Rome.—Time -*at:* à *midi, at* twelve o'clock.—Concern -*on:* à *ce sujet, on* this subject.—Manner -*with: supplier* à *mains jointes*, to intreat earnestly.—Means -*with: peindre* à *l'huile*, to paint *in*, or *with* oil; *des bas* à *trois fils*, three thread-stockings, that is, *with* three threads.—Situation -*at, with: être* à *son aise*, to be *at* ease.—Purpose -*for: une table* à *manger*, a dining table.—Suitableness -*for, to: homme* à *réussir*, a man likely to succeed:—desert, *crime* à *ne pas pardonner*, a crime not *to* be forgiven, etc.

EXERCISE.

Fathers! give good counsels, and still better examples
de *encore* 3 pr. *meilleur* 1 m. 2

to your children. A good minister only aims *at* the glory of
ne aspirer que à

serving his country well. When we were *in* the country we de-
inf-1 2 *pays* 3 1 ind-2 *à* *campagne* f. *con-*

voted the morning *to* study, we walked *at* noon,
sacrer ind-2 *matinée* f. art. *se promener* ind-2 *midi*

and *at* three or four o'clock, we went *a* hunting, or fishing.
heure ind-2 *à la chasse* f. pr. *à la pêche* f.

Michael Angelo has painted (a great deal) *in* fresco. It is a
Michel - Ange *beaucoup* art. *fresque* f. *ce*

bed *with* ivory posts, and mahogany feet. That man, *with* his
lit m *ivoire* *colonne* f. pr. *acajou* *pied* art.

gloomy looks and surly behaviour, seems
sombre 2 *regard* m. 1 art. *brusque* 2 *maintien* m. 1 pr a t. *ne semble*

fit only *to* serve as a scarecrow.
ropre *que* *de* * *épouvantail*.

De is generally used to express *separation*, *extraction*, *possession*, *appurtenance*, *cause*, *shift*, *result*, etc. and supplies the place of several prepositions, as—*from*: *je viens* de *France*, I come *from* France; *d'un bout* à *l'autre*, *from* one end to the other.—*Of*: *le palais* du *roi*, the palace *of* the king; *les facultés* de *l'âme*, the faculties *of* the soul; *un homme* d'*esprit*, a man *of* talent. In a partitive sense—*of*: *moitié* de, *quart* de, etc. the half of, the fourth of, etc.: it is used for PAR—*by*: *il est aimé* de *tout le monde*, he is beloved *by* every body; for—*through*, or *by*, etc.: *mourir* de *faim*, de *soif*, to die *of* hunger, *of* thirst: *on*, *upon*, *with*: *vivre* de *fruits*, to live *upon* fruit.—*On account of*, or *for*: *sauter* de *joie*, to leap *for* joy.

EXERCISE.

I come *from* London, where I have spent a week very agreeably.
où *passé huit jours*

From one end of the horizon to the other, the sky was covered
bout m. m. *ciel* m. ind-2

with thick black clouds. The marble *of* Paros is not
épais 2 *et* *noir* 3 *nuage* m. pl. 1.

finer than that which we get *from* Carrara. Montaigne, Mad. de
72 *qui* *nous vient* *Carrare.*

Sévigné, and la Fontaine, were writers *of* truly original ge-
ind-2 *de* art. *écrivain* *un* 2 3 1

nius. One half *of* the terrestrial globe is covered *with* water,
moitié f. *terrestre* 2 *globe* m. 1

and above a (third part) *of* the rest is uninhabited, either through
plus de *tiers* m. *inhabité* *ou* *par*

extreme heat, or through excessive cold. In that happy
un 2 *chaleur* f. 1 *un* = 2 *froid* m. 1

retreat, we lived *on* the milk *of* our flocks, and the delicious
asile m. ind-2 *brebis* pr. 2

fruits *of* our orchards.
1 *verger* m. pl.

En serves to mark the relations of time, place, situation, etc. and is variously expressed, as, *c'était* en *hiver*, it was *during* winter; *être* en Angleterre, to be *in* England; *aller* en *Italie*, to go *into* Italy; *elle est* en *bonne santé*, she is *in* good health; *il vaut mieux être* en *paix*, *qu'*en *guerre*, it is better to be *at* peace than *at* war; *il l'a fait* en *haine de lui*, he did it out of hatred to him, etc.

EXERCISE.

He had for a (long while) lived *in* France; the troubles
3 * *depuis* 1 * *long-temps* 2 *vivre* ind-2

which agitated that fine kingdom obliged him to retire *to*
ind-4 *royaume* m. ind-4 *de se retirer*

Switzerland, whence he soon after went *to* Italy. We were
Suisse *d'où* 3 1 2 *se rendre* ind-4 ind-2

at peace, and enjoyed all its blessings, when ambition
pron. *goûter* ind-2 *en* art. *charme* m. art.

kindled again the flames of war, and forced us *to* put our
rallumer ind-3 *feu* s. art. ind-3 *de mettre*

frontiers *in* a state of defence. The savage is almost continually
frontière f. pl. * * *presque toujours*

at war; he cannot remain *at* rest. He has acted, *on* this
pouvoir *en repos* *dans*

occasion, like a great man.
—— f. *en* *

CHAPTER VII.

OF THE ADVERB.

157. The *adverb* is a word which is generally placed after the verb to express *where*, *when*, and *how* the action is or was done. *Vous chantez bien*, you sing well; *il partira demain*, he will set out to-morrow, etc.

It is often also joined to an adjective, coupled with *être; il est vraiment digne d'amitié*, he is truly deserving of friendship.

Remark. There are adjectives which are sometimes used as adverbs, as, *il chante juste*, he sings right; *elle chante faux*, she sings out of tune; *ils ne voient pas clair*, they do not see clear; *cette fleur sent bon*, this flower has a pleasant smell, etc. The adjectives, *juste*, *faux*, *clair* and *bon*, here supply the place of adverbs.

Adverbs are of different kinds.

The most numerous are those which express manner, and are formed from adjectives, in the following manner.

158. When the adjective ends, in the masculine, with a vowel, the adverb is formed by adding *ment*: as, *modeste-ment*, modestly; *poli-ment*, politely; *ingénu-ment*, ingenuously, etc.

Exceptions. *Impuni* makes *impunément* and *traître*, *traîtreusement*.

The following six take *é* close before *-ment*, instead of the *e* mute which is in the adjective.

aveuglément	*blindly*	conformément	*conformably*
commodément	*commodiously*	énormément	*enormously*
incommodément	*incommodiously*	opiniatrément	*obstinately*

159. When the adjective ends with a consonant, in the masculine, the adverb is formed from the feminine termination, by adding *ment*; as, *grand*. *grandement*, greatly; *franc*, *franchement*, frankly; *naïf*, *naïvement*, artlessly, etc

Observe that the adverbs,

follement	*foolishly*	bellement	*softly*
mollement	*effeminately*	nouvellement	*newly*

Are to be considered as coming from the adjectives *fol*, *mol*, *bel*, *nouvel*, and accordingly belong to the foregoing rule.

Exceptions. *Gentil*, makes *gentiment*, prettily. The following eight adverbs,

communément	*commonly*	importunément	*importunately*
confusément	*confusedly*	obscurément	*obscurely*
diffusément	*diffusedly*	précisément	*precisely*
expressément	*expressly*	profondément	*deeply*

take before *ment* the *é* close instead of the *e* mute, which is in the feminine of the adjectives from which they are derived.

Rem. The six following adverbs are not derived from adjectives.

comment	*how*	profusément	*lavishly*
incessamment	*presently*	nuitamment	*by night*
notamment	*especially*	sciemment	*knowingly*

Adjectives ending in *ant*, *ent*, form their adverbs by changing them into *-mment*, as *consta-nt*, *consta-mment*, constantly; *éloque-nt*, *éloque-mment*. Except *lent* and *présent*, the only two of this class which follow the 159th rule, and make *lentement*, *présentement*.

160. Most adverbs denoting manner, and a few others, have the three degrees of comparison, as, *profondément*, *aussi*, *plus*, or *moins profondément*, *fort*, *bien*, or *très-profondément*, and *le plus profondément*.

The following degrees of comparison are irregular.

Positive.		Comparative.		Superlative.	
bien	*well*	mieux	*better*	le mieux	*the best*
mal	*badly*	pis	*worse*	le pis	*the worst*
peu	*little*	moins	*less*	le moins	*the least*

EXERCISE.

Bourdaloue and Masillon have both spoken very *eloquently*
l'un et l'autre

on evangelical truths; but the former has *principally* (pro-
évangélique 2 art. 1 *se pro-*

posed to himself) to convince the mind; the latter has *generally*
poser ind-4 *de convaincre*

had in view to touch the heart. Several of la Bruyère's cha-
en vue de art. 2 1

racters are as *finely* drawn as they are *delicately* expressed. Buf-
finement tracé * *

fon is one of the best writers of the last century: he thinks *deeply*,
2 *siècle* m. 1.

describes *forcibly*, and expresses himself (with dignity). Cor-
fortement, *noblement*

neille and Racine are the two best French tragic poets; the pieces
3 *tragique* 2 1 f.

of the former are *strongly* but *incorrectly* written; those of the lat-
2 3 1

ter are more *regularly* beautiful, more *purely* expressed, and more
beau

delicately conceived.
pensé

161. There are likewise various other sorts of adverbs:

Of	Affirmation,	as *certes*, certainly; *oui*, yes.
	Consent,	.. *soit*, be it so; *volontiers*, willingly.
	Doubt,	.. *peut-être que*, perhaps.
	Denial,	.. *non*, *ne*, *ne-pas*, *ne-point*, no, not.
	Order, or Rank.	.. *premièrement*, first: *secondement*. 2dly, etc. *D'abord*, at first; *ensuite*, *apres*, afterwards. *Avant*, *auparavant*, before.

EXERCISE.

Certainly, either I am mistaken, or the business passed (in
ou se tromper *se passer* ind-4

that manner). Do you think that he listens *willingly* to this pro-
ainsi *penser* *écouter* *

posal? Have you ever read in Racine the famous scene of Phœdra's
f. *Phèdre* 2

delirium? *Yes*, I have read it, and I own it is one of the
art. *délire* m. 1 *lue la* *avouer que ce*

finest of the French theatre. *Perhaps* you will discover, on a se-
2 m. 1 *dans*

cond perusal of la Fontaine's fables, beauties which you
lecture f. 2 art. 1 *de* art. f. pl. *que*

have not perceived at first. Will you have some? *No.* Will
aperçues d'abord 2 1 * *en* 1 3

you *not* have some? The man who (is willing) to do good is
4 1 5 * *en* 2 *vouloir* * * art. *bien* m.

not stopped by any obstacle. I will pay him what I owe, but
arrêté aucun *lui ce que lui*

not all (at once).
non pas à la fois

162. Of—place, or distance.

Où, where; *ici*, here; *là*, there.

Deçà, on this side; *delà*, on that side; *partout*, every where.

Près, *proche*, near, nigh; *loin*, far, etc.

EXERCISE.

We ought *first* to avoid doing evil; *afterwards* we ought
falloir ind-1 * *de* inf-1 art. *

to do good. Read books of instruction *first*, and *afterwards*
* art. 1 art. 3 4 2

you may proceed to those of entertainment. If you will (go
* *passer* ind-7 72 *agrément* *vouloir s'en*

away), settle *first* what is to be done. The painter had
aller régler auparavant ce que falloir * * inf-1

(brought together) in the same picture, several different objects:
rassembler un * *tableau* 2 1

here, a troop of Bacchantes; *there*, a troop of young people; *here*,
Bacchante *gens*

a sacrifice; *there*, a disputation of philosophers. Sesostris carried
dispute *pousser* ind-4

his conquests *farther* than Alexander did *afterwards*. Call
conquête *ne* ind-4 *depuis passer*

upon your cousin; he lives *near here*. I cannot see that, if I
chez *loger* 2 *ici* 1 *savoir* cond-1

am not *near* it. When he knew *where* he was, he
ind-1 *auprès* * *quand* *savoir* cond-1 ind-2

began to fear the consequence of his imprudence. Contem-
commencer ind-3 *à* *suite*

plate *(at a distance)* lofty mountains, if you wish to behold
de loin art. *haut* f. *vouloir* * *découvrir*

prospects ever varied and ever new.
de art. *site* m.

263. Some express the present, as, *maintenant*, now; *à présent*, at present; *actuellement*, this moment, etc.

— the past, as, *hier*, yesterday; *avant-hier*, the day before yesterday; *autrefois*, formerly, etc.

— the future, as, *demain*, to-morrow; *après-demain*, the day after to-morrow, etc.

— indeterminate time, as, *souvent*, often; *d'ordinaire*, generally; *quelquefois*, sometimes; *matin*, early; *tôt*, soon; *tard*, late, etc.

EXERCISE.

I have finished the work you prescribed me; what do you
achever *que* *ordonner* ind-6 *que*

wish me to do *now? Formerly*, education was neglected,
vouloir que je * subj-1 —— f. ind-2

it is *now* (very much) attended to; it is (to be hoped) that
on * 4 *beaucoup* 3 *s'occuper* 2 *en* 1 *falloir* *espérer*

new views will be adopted *soon*. They grieved (at it)
on de 3 4 *adopter* ind-7 1 2 *on* *s'affliger* ind-3 *en* 1

yesterday; now, they laugh (at it); *to-morrow*, it will no
aujourd'hui *rire* 2 *en* 1 *on* 2 * *ne*

longer (be thought) of. It is one of those accidents which
plus *penser* ind-7 2 *y* 1 *c'est*

it is *sometimes* impossible to avoid. The (evening air) incommoded
de *serein* m. ind-4

me (very much); I shall not *(in future)* walk so *late*. Rude
beaucoup *désormais se promener* *mal-*

and coarse criticism *generally* (does greater injury)
honnête 2 *grossier* 3 *un* f. 1 *nuire plus*

to the person who indulges himself in it, than to him who is
se permettre 2 * *la* 1 *celle* 2

the object (of it).
? *en* 1

164. Some express quantity; as, *peu*, little; *assez*, enough; *trop*, too much; *beaucoup*, much, very much; *tant*, so much, etc. See rule 105.

165. Others express comparison; as, *plus*, more; *moins*, less; *aussi*, so; *autant*, as much, etc.

EXERCISE.

There are many people who have pretensions; but very *few*
y avoir *beaucoup de* * * *à*

who have such as are well founded. To embellish a subject
en sub-1 * * * * *de fondé*, f. pl. * 2 3

too much, frequently betrays a want of judgment and taste. One
1 *souvent* *être* *faute*

very often experiences disgust in the midst of the most riotous
trouver art. *ennui* *à* *bruyant* 2

pleasures. She is a giddy and thoughtless woman, who speaks
1 *ce* *léger* 2 *inconséquent* 3 , 1

much and reflects *little*. She has so *much* kindness in her, that it
réfléchir *de* *bonté* * *

is impossible not to love her. These stuffs are beautiful; *conse-*
de ne pas *étoffe* f. *aussi*

quently are dear. This book has merit; but there are
elles coûter *cher* *du* *y en avoir*

others *as* good. If he has done that, I can do (*as much*). She
* *de* *en* *autant*

is six years *younger* than her brother. Nobody is *more* inte-
avoir *de moins* *ne*

rested than you are (in the success) of the affair. You do
* *à ce que* 1 *réussir* subj-1 3 * 2

not offer *enough* for this garden; give something *more*. *The more*
offrir *de* *de* 1

ignorant we are, *the less* we (believe ourselves so).
4 *on* 2 3 * *croire l'être*

CHAPTER VIII.

OF CONJUNCTIONS.

166. The conjunction is a word which serves to connect words or sentences, as, *Il pleure et rit en même temps*, he cries and laughs at the same time; the word *et* unites the first sentence, *il pleure*, with the second, *il rit*. Likewise in *Pierre et Paul rient*, Peter and Paul laugh; the word *et* unites these two sentences into one, *Pierre rit* and *Paul rit*.

167. There are different kinds of conjunctions, which serve to different purposes.

1st. To unite two sentences or words under the same affirmation, or under the same negation: *et* is used for the affirmation, and *ni*, neither, nor, for the negation.

2ndly. To denote an alternative, or distinction, *ou*, either, or; *soit que*, whether, or; *tantôt*, sometimes, etc.

3rdly. To restrict an idea; *sinon*, but, except; *quoique*, *encore que*, though, although; *à moins que*, unless, till.

EXERCISE.

Gold *and* silver are metals less useful than iron. To
art. art. *de* art. art. *

listen with joy to a slanderer, *and* to applaud him, is to cherish
* *médisant* * *lui c'est* * *réchauffer*

the serpent who stings, that he may sting more effectually. I
piquer afin que *plus sûrement*

like *neither* flatterers *nor* the wicked Those who have never
ne *flatteur* pl.

suffered, know nothing; they know *neither* good *nor*
savoir *ne connaître* art. *bien* pl.

evil. You may choose *either* a happy mediocrity, *or* a
art *mal* pl. *avoir à choisir* *de* ——— f. *de*

sphere more elevated, but exposed to many dangers. He is an
—— f. *bien de* art. —— m. *ce*

inconsistent man; he is *sometimes* of one opinion, and *sometimes*
inconséquent 2 1 *tantôt* *avis*

of another. I have (nothing more) to say to you, *only that* I
ne *autre chose* *à* *sinon que*

will have it so. I shall not yet pass to the perusal of the
vouloir 2 * *le* 1 * *encore* *lecture* f.

authors of the second class, *unless* you advise me to it.
ordre m. *ne conseiller* sub-1 *

4thly. To express conviction, *mais*, but; *cependant*, yet nevertheless; *néanmoins*, for all that, however; *pourtant*, however, though; *toutefois*, *bien que*, although.

5thly. To express a condition; *si*, if; *sinon que*, except that: *pourvu que*, save that; *à condition que*, on condition that.

To express consent; *à la vérité*, indeed; *à la bonne heure*, very well.

7thly. To explain: *savoir*, *c'est-à-dire*, viz. that is to say; *comme*, as.

EXERCISE.

The serpent bites; it is only a bite; *but* from this bite the
ce *ne* *que* *morsure*

venom communicates itself to the whole body; the slanderer
venin 2 1 3

speaks; it is but a word; *but* this word resounds every-
ce *ne que* *parole* f. *retentir* *par-*

where. (That is) certainly a superb picture; *nevertheless*, there
tout *voilà* *tableau*

is some incorrectness in the design Although Homer, according
incorrection pl. *dessin*

to Horace, slumbers (at times), he is *nevertheless* the
sommeiller sub-1 *quelquefois il n'en est pas moins*

first of all poets. You will succeed, *provided* you act with
art. *réussir pourvu que agir* sub-1

vigour. We have within us two faculties seldom united, *viz.*
en —— f.

imagination and judgment.
art. art.

8thly. To express relation, or parity; *comme*, as; *ainsi*, thus, so; *de même*, as, just as; *ainsi que*, as; *autant que*, as much as; *si que*, as, etc.

9thly. To express augmentation, *d'ailleurs*, besides, furthermore.

For diminution, *au moins, du moins, pour le moins*, at least.

10thly. To express the cause, or the reason of a thing; *car*, for; *comme*, as; *parce que*, because; *puisque*, since; *pour que*, that, in order that, etc.

EXERCISE.

The most beautiful flowers last but a moment; *thus*, human
ne durer que 3

life passes away. The (greatest part) of mankind have, *like*
art. 2 1 * *plupart* f. art. *homme* pl.

plants, hidden qualities, which chance discovers
art. *caché* 2 *de* art. *propriété* f. 1 art. *hasard faire découvrir*

Mad. de Sévigné's letters are models of elegance, simpli-
2 art. f. 1 *de* art. pr.

city, and taste; *besides*, they are replete with interesting anecdotes.
pr. *plein de* 2 f. 1

Nothing is more entertaining than history; *besides*, nothing is
* *de amusant* art. *

more instructive. Circumstances make us known to others,
de art. *occasion* pl. *faire connaître*

and still *more* to ourselves. I shall always advise you to take
encore *conseiller de*

the ancients as your guide, *at least*, leave but seldom
pour * *ne s'écarter que rarement de*

the way which they have traced for you. We must, *at least*,
route f. *que* *tracée* * * *falloir*

know the general principles of a language, before (we take
2 1 *langue* f. *de* *se*

upon ourselves) to teach it. Certain people hate grandeur,
mêler de * *enseigner* f. *gens* art.

because it lowers and humiliates them, and makes them
les rabaisser *que elle* 2 *leur* 1

feel the privation of the advantages which they love.
bien pl.

11thly. To draw a conclusion or inference; *or*, now; *donc*, then; *par conséquent*, consequently; *c'est pourquoi*, therefore.

12thly. To express a circumstance; *quand*, *lorsque*, when; *pendant que*, *tandis que*, etc. whilst, while; *tant que*, as long as; *depuis que*, ever since; *avant que*, before; *dès que*, *aussitôt que*, *d'abord que*, as soon as; *enfin*, in fine, finally, to conclude, etc.

13thly. To express a transition; *car*, for; *en effet*, indeed, in effect; *au reste*, besides, otherwise; *à propos*, now I think of it; *après tout*, after all.

EXERCISE.

We ought to love what is amiable; *now*, virtue is amia-
* *falloir* ind-1 * *ce qui* art.

ble, *therefore* we ought to love virtue. We ought to practise
* * art. * *falloir* *

what the gospel commands us; *now*, it commands us, not only
ce que *évangile* m. 2 1 *non*

to forgive our enemies, but also to love them. Despréaux was
de pardonner à *encore de*

extremely particular in not coming late, *when* he was
de la plus grande exactitude à inf-1 *trop* ind-2

invited to dinner; he said that all the faults of those who (keep
à ind-2 *défaut* *se*

others waiting) present themselves to those who wait for them.
faire attendre *attendre* *

The pride which possesses us, visible as it is, escapes our eyes,
posséder *tout* *que* *à*

while it manifests itself to the eyes of the public, and displeases
choquer

every one. *After* we had examined that singular effect, we
art. *esprit* pl. ind-5 2 1

(inquired into) its causes. We had *hardly* done, when he came
rechercher ind-3 *en* art. ind-2 *finir* *que* *entrer*

in. None but an Englishman can (be a judge of) Shak-
* *il n'y a que* *qui* subj-1 *juger de*

speare: *for*, what foreigner is sufficiently versed in the English

language to discover the sublime beauties of that author?
langue f. *pour* 2 1

168. The conjunction *que* is always placed between two ideas, and serves to connect them, so as to form of the two one proposition, as *je crois que vous vous trompez*, I think you are deceived. The conjugation *that* is almost always understood in English, whereas *que* is not only always expressed in French, but repeated before each member of the proposition. *Je crois que vous vous trompez et que vous ne réussirez pas*, I think you are mistaken, and that you will not succeed.

The frequent use of *que*, under several forms, and the government of conjunctions in general, form an important chapter of the Syntax, No. 388, which must be read attentively.

EXERCISE.

(As long as I live), this image will be before my eyes;
tout ma vie —— f. *peint*

and if ever the gods permit me to reign, I shall not forget, after
faire *

so terrible an example, *that* a king (is not worthy) to govern,
3 1 2 *n'est digne de* *commander*

(nor) happy in his power (*but* in proportion as) he subjects
et n'est *puissance* f. *qu'autant que* *soumettre*

it to reason. I am very glad to see that you do not love
art. *de* •

flattery, and *that* one (runs no risk) in speaking to you with
art. *ne hasarder rien à* inf-1 •

sincerity.
——— f.

CHAPTER IX.

OF INTERJECTIONS.

169. Interjections are words which serve to express the sudden emotion of the soul. The only point to be attended to is not to place them between words which custom has made inseparable. There are interjections for every feeling, or passion, viz. :

Of		
	pain	ahi, aïe! ouf! ah!
	grief	hélas! mon Dieu, etc.
	fear	ha! hé!
	joy	ah! bon, bon! o!
	aversion	fi! fi donc! oh, oh!
	disgust	pouah, pouah!
	indignation	foin de
	imprecation	peste de, la peste de
	disbelief	chansons, tarare
	surprise	ouais
	astonishment	oh! bon Dieu! miséricorde! peste!
	warning	gare! hem! holà, ho!
	checking	tout beau! holà.
	encouraging	alerte! allons! ça, courage
	applauding	bravo, vivat!
	encoring	bis, bis
	calling	hola! ho! hem!
	derision	oh! eh! zest! oh! oh! oh
	silence	chut! paix! st.

PART II.

SYNTAX,

OR

GRAMMATICAL CONSTRUCTION

OF

WORDS IN FRENCH.

CHAPTER I.

§ I.

OF THE SUBSTANTIVE OR NOUN.

The substantive has already been considered as to its individual nature, that is to say, its gender and number; its functions in a sentence are now to be considered.

The noun is either the subject of the verb, or the governing word; or it is governed by the verb, or what is called the regimen.

170. EXPLANATION OF THE TERMS REGIMEN DIRECT, REGIMEN INDIRECT, OR CASES.

In *le père aime ses enfants*, the father loves his children; *le père* is the subject, or governing word, or nominative case; and *enfants* is the governed word, or regimen, or accusative case. *Ses enfants* is also called a direct case, because there is no preposition intervening between it and the verb *aime*.

In *les enfants obéissent au père*, the children obey to the father; *les enfants* is the subject, and *au père* is the governed noun or regimen; and the regimen is called indirect because it has a preposition (*à*) before it. It is also called the dative case.

In *le père envoie un présent à ses enfants*, the father sends a present to his children: *les enfants reçoivent une lettre de leur père*, the children receive a letter from their father, *le père, les enfants*, are subjects, *un présent, une lettre* are objects, or accusative, or direct cases, *à ses enfants, de leur père* are indirect cases because governed by a preposition, the former being what is called the dative, and the latter, the ablative case.

In the construction of a sentence two things are to be considered: 1st. ORDER, or arrangement. 2nd. GOVERNMENT, or cases.

OF ORDER.

171. Order is invariable, 1st. the subject, whether the verb be affirmative or interrogative.

le père aime	le père aime-t-il?
le père n'aime pas	le père n'aime-t-il pas?

2ndly. The verb; 3rdly, the direct case or object; 4thly, the indirect case, or dative, or genitive or ablative.

It need hardly be told that if there is not a direct case, the indirect comes next to the verb, *les enfants obéissent au père.*

A deviation from this order or arrangement is called an INVERSION. See *Inversion*, p. 497.

EXERCISE.

My mother received two letters this morning, which (have
recevoir ind-4 *faire*

given) her * much pain. *Did* not the soldiers resist the
ind-4 2 *lui* 1 *bien de la peine* *résister à* ind-4

commands of their officers? Send this game to Mr. L. Have
ordre *Envoyer*

you not thought of your sisters? My uncle (has just) bought a
penser à *venir de* 437†

beautiful house in Paris. Has the (nurse maid) given (any thing to
bonne *à manger*

eat) to these poor children? Will not James send these
* *envoyer* ind-7

books to his cousin when he has read them?
avoir ind-7

GOVERNMENT OR CASES.

172. By government, is meant the case in which a noun is to be put after the verb, that is, whether it will be direct or accusative, indirect or dative, genitive or ablative, or, to speak more plainly, whether that noun will be preceded by *à* or *de*.

* Personal pronouns *me, te, nous, vous, lui, leur*, in the dative case, are placed before the verb, as is explained in the article *Pronoun Personal* 61. What is said here, must, in fact, be understood solely of *nouns substantives.*

† See Examples on Difficulties, Chapter XIX, to which this figure refers. The learner must bear in mind that the figures which he will occasionally meet with in the Exercises refer to the general series of rules.

173. DIFFERENCE BETWEEN THE TWO LANGUAGES AS TO THE GOVERNMENT OF VERBS.

To those who are acquainted with the Latin language, this will present little or no difficulty, accustomed as they are to the proper distinction of cases; but to those who are not, and to young ladies principally, the distinction is not so obviously clear. As in learning the French language, much of the task consists in turning English into French; and also, as, when endeavouring to speak, people first think in English, and then translate, a very natural propensity leads them to translate literally, thereby expressing themselves in a way little in accordance with the peculiar construction of the French language. We cannot devise a more efficacious method to guard them from such erroneous proceeding, than by showing the different cases used in the one or the other language, after the corresponding verb.

EXAMPLES.

penser *à* une chose	*to think* of *a thing*
obéir *à* la loi	*to obey the law*
dépendre *de* son père	*to be dependent* on *one's father*
mourir *de* peur	*to die* with *fear*
répondre *à* une question	*to answer a question*
jouir *de* sa fortune	*to enjoy one's fortune*
se réjouir *d'*une chose	*to rejoice* at *a thing*
plaire *à* ses amis	*to please one's friends*
se ressouvenir *d'*un accident	*to remember an accident*
jouer *du* violon	*to play* on *the violin*
écouter un avis	*to listen* to *an advice.*

The list of the instances in which the two languages differ, in respect to the case of the governed words, might easily be extended to several pages, but the few examples here given, must be sufficient to awake the attention and carefulness of the learner, and to make him sensible of the necessity of mastering this point.

A few more remarks may tend to impress still deeper in his mind the necessity of attending to it.

174. NECESSITY OF ATTENDING TO THE GOVERNMENT, WITH REGARD TO THE RELATIVE PRONOUNS.

Sometimes, and even frequently, verbs govern a relative pronoun representing some noun antecedently expressed, and such pronoun must be put in the proper case, according to the preposition which would be placed before the noun. For instance, to translate "such is the law *which* you have not obeyed," *telle est la loi* QUE *vous n'avez pas obéi,* would be wrong, it must be à LAQUELLE, because we have seen that *obéir* requires the dative, or the preposition *à*. Again, to say *je vous donne de bons avis* AUXQUELS *vous n'écoutez pas,* would be literal and wrong, because, as we have seen also, *écouter* is active in French, that is, requires no preposition.

EXERCISE.

I repent my idleness. Do you want this pen? I was
se repentir de *Avoir* *besoin de* *penser*

thinking of my poor brother. He did not discharge his duty
à ind-2 *s'acquitter de* ind-4 *devoir* m.

to my satisfaction. I advise you to go and change your shoes.
——— *conseiller* 2 1 *d'aller* * *changer de* *

Have we not mistaken the road? We are very grateful for your
se tromper de ind-4 * *être reconnaissant de*

kindness. You have gone too near the river. Are you not afraid
s'approcher de ind-4 * *craindre*

of that cruel man? We did not expect such an answer. If you
* 2 1 *attendre à* ind-2 2 1 3

some to-night we will agree about terms. I am not fond of
ce soir *convenir* *de* *nos conditions* *aimer* *

music. I do not know why, but your brother left the
art. *savoir* *sortir de* ind-3

room very abruptly. Do not mind his threats.*
faire *attention à*

176. KING'S PALACE, ETC. ETC.

This form of the genitive case, or of the case marking possession, is rendered in French in an inverted manner, as if it were *the palace of the king, le palais du roi.*

176. OF COMPOUND WORDS.

SILK-STOCKINGS. DINING-ROOM, ETC. ETC.

These are a sort of compound word of which the order is likewise inverted in French. *Bas de soie, salle à manger.*

Here again also, two different prepositions are used, (*à, de*) the choice of which depends upon the nature of the expression.

De is used when *made of, composed of, coming from, of the, belonging to,* can be understood.

EXAMPLES.

Silk stockings, i. e. *stockings made of silk.*	Bas de soie.
Burgundy wine, i. e. *wine coming from Burgundy.*	Vin de Bourgogne.
Chambermaid, i. e. *maid of the chamber.*	Femme de chambre.
Back door, i. e. *the door of the back of the house.*	Porte de derrière.
Garden seat, i. e. *seat belonging to the garden.*	Banc du jardin.

* The same difficulty occurs with regard to the preposition used before the infinitive in French. See *infinitive,* 394, 397.

A is used when *for the purpose of, by means of, with,* may be understood.

EXAMPLES.

moulin à vent	*wind-mill* i. e. *mill going by wind*
moulin à papier	*paper-mill* i. e. *mill for the purpose of making paper*
fille aux yeux bleus	*blue eyed girl* i. e. *girl with blue eyes*

EXERCISE.

My father's house. The mayor's authority. Shall you go to
père maison maire = *aller*
Mrs. B's party? He has bought a gold box. Go out at the
soirée f. *acheté or boîte* f. *sortir par*
front door. What is that long eared animal? Send
devant porte Qu'est-ce que c'est que longues oreilles ———
me the letter box. Where is the oil bottle? Give me a wine glass,
huile verre
and a tea spoon. Did you observe that man with the
thé cuiller f. *remarquer* ind-4 *le*
long cloak? My sister has given me a penknife with an ivory
2 1 *canif* * *ivoire*
handle. They have lately discovered a copper mine on his estate.
manche m. *on venir de découvrir cuivre* —— *terre* f.
Where is the milk jug? Is this the hay market?
lait pot foin marché

CHAPTER II.

177. OF THE INDEFINITE ARTICLE, *A, AN*.

1. The article *a, an,* used in English before national and professional names, in explanatory sentences, is not rendered in French.*

EXAMPLES.

I am a Frenchman	*je suis Français*
he is a grocer	*il est épicier*
his father was a barrister	*son père était avocat*
the Duke of York, a prince of the royal blood	*le Duc d'York, prince du sang royal*
we went to Caen, a large town of Normandy	*nous allâmes à Caen, ville considérable de Normandie*

2. But it is expressed after *c'est,* and also when an adjective is joined to the noun, or when it is followed by a relative pronoun or some other restrictive circumstance.

EXAMPLES.

he is an officer	*c'est un officier*
I am a Frenchman of an illustrious family	*je suis un Français d'une illustre famille*
I am an unfortunate prince	*je suis un prince infortuné*

3. The article indefinite is also omitted in French after, *quel, quelle,* in admirative sentences, and before titles of books.

*See personal pronouns, No. 237.

EXAMPLES.

quelle beauté!	*what a beauty.*
histoire de France	*a history of France*
il dépense beaucoup d'argent, chose qui déplaît à son père	*he spends much money, a thing which displeases his father*
l'excellent homme que votre frère!	*what an excellent man your brother is!*
la belle ville que Londres!	*what a fine city London is!*

EXERCISE.

I am *a* Frenchman and *a* merchant; after having (been at) the
négociant inf-1 *parcouru*

most famous (trading towns) in the Levant, my commercial con-
= *échelle* f. pl. *de* —— m. *les affaires de mon*

cerns have brought me here. I am *an* unhappy Frenchman
commerce *conduire*

who, a striking example of the vicissitudes of fortune,
* *mémorable* 2 1 ———— art.

seek an asylum where I may end my days in peace. He was a
chercher *asile* m. *puisse finir* *ce*

man of uncommon probity and of tried virtue; (as a)
un *rare* 2 — f. 1 *un éprouvé* 2 1 *pour*

reward for the services he had rendered to the church
le récompenser *de* *que* ind-2 m. pl. *église*

and state, the king has made him *a* bishop. Neoptolemus
pr. art. *évêque* *Néoptolème*

had hardly told me that he was *a* Greek, when I (cried out)
eut *à peine* *dit* *que* *s'écrier* ind-3

O! enchanting words, after so many years of silence and
doux *parole* f. pl. *de*

unceasing pain, O my son, what misfortune, what storm,
sans consolation 2 pr. 1 *malheur* m. *tempête* f.

or rather, what propitious wind has brought you hither to end
plutôt *favorable* 2 1 *conduire* ind-4 *pour*

my woes? He replied, I am of the island of Scyros, I
mal m. pl. *répondre* ind-3 *île*

am returning thither; (I am said) (to be) *the* son of Achilles.
retourner ind-1 *y* *on dit* *que* ind-1

What a noise you make! What a mistake! *A* letter to Lord L.

We read the account of his death, an event full of interest. He
récit

has not yet returned, a most unaccountable thing. He is modest
être *revenir* *fort* *extraordinaire* 2 *chose* 1

a rare quality among poets. He is a very rich man.
2 — f. 1 *chez les* *ce*

178. The English make use of *a* or *an*, before nouns of measure, weight, and purchase, as: *wheat is sold for a crown* a *bushel; butter sells for sixpence* a *pound*; *wine sold yesterday for forty crowns* a *hogshead, it is more than a groat* a *bottle.* The French make use of the article *le, la*, as: *le blé se vend un écu* le *boisseau*; *le beurre se vend six sous* la *livre*; *le vin se vendit hier quarante écus* le *muid, c'est plus de quatre sous* la *bouteille.*

179. When speaking of *time, a* or *an* is expressed in French by the preposition *par*, as: *so much* a *week, tant* par *semaine.* A head, is also rendered *par tête*, but *a piece* is rendered by *la pièce*; a man, *par homme* or *chacun.*

EXERCISE.

Corn sells for eight shillings a bushel, veal and
art. *blé* m. *se vendre* * *boisseau* art. *veau*

mutton cost ten pence a pound. This lace is sold at half a
art. *mouton* *coûter* *livre* f. *se vendre* * 2 1

guinea an ell. The best French wines are sold at ten shillings
3 *de France* 2 1 *se vendre* *

per bottle. I see him twice a year. How much do you give
voir 2 1 *deux fois* *combien* *donner* 2

him a day? She comes twice a week. We had an excellent
lui 1 *faire* ind-4

dinner at five shillings a head. What beautiful peaches, how much
pêche f.

do they cost a piece?

OF THE ARTICLE DEFINITE.

180. The definite article is used in French, (*but omitted in English*) before substantives spoken of i

a general sense; that is before *names of species*, *virtues*, *passions*, *sciences*, *metals*, etc., etc., taken in the abstract.

EXAMPLES.

l'homme se repaît trop souvent de chimères	*man too often feeds on vain fancies*
l'or est un métal précieux	*gold is a precious metal*
évitons la paresse	*let us avoid idleness*

Before nouns specified by an adjective or some particular and individual circumstance.

EXAMPLES.

les hommes à imagination sont toujours malheureux	*men of imagination are ever unhappy*
l'homme dont vous parlez est instruit	*the man of whom you speak is well informed*
voici la maison de mon père	*this is my father's house*

181. It is also used before adjectives used substantively.

EXAMPLES.

le riche ne donne pas toujours	*rich men do not always give*
j'aime le vert	*I am fond of green*

After *tout* when it means *every, the whole.*

EXAMPLES.

tout le monde le voit	*every body sees it*
toute la ville était en l'air	*the whole town was in a bustle*

EXERCISE.

1. The moment *elegance*, the most visible image of fine *taste*, appears, it is universally admired; *men* differ respecting the other constituent parts of * *beauty*, but they all unite without hesitation in acknowledging the power of *elegance*.

2. *Men of superior genius* 2, while 1 they * see 3 the rest of mankind painfully * struggling to comprehend obvious 2 truths 1, penetrate themselves * through * the most remote 2 consequences 1, like lightning through a track that cannot be measured.

3. *The man who lives* under an habitual 2 sense 1 of the divine 2

presence I, preserves a perpetual cheerfulness of temper, and enjoys, every moment, the satisfaction of thinking himself * in company with the dearest and best of friends.

4. Come and show me your sister's *room* for I cannot find it.
5. Yellow does not suit you at all.
6. When he returned, he found the whole school in an uproar.

(1.) The moment, *du moment que;* fine, *délicat;* appears, *se montrer;* is, *elle est;* respecting, *sur;* constituent, *(which constitute);* hesitation, *hésiter*, in, *pour.*

(2.) While, *tandis que;* struggling, *se tourmenter;* obvious, *qui s'offrent d'elle-mêmes;* penetrate, *ils pénètrent en un instant;* lightning, *foudre*, f.; through, *traverse;* track, *espace;* that, *qu'on;* be measured, *mesurer.*

(3.) Under, *dans;* sense, *conviction;* preserves, *conserver;* perpetual, *constant;* cheerfulness, *gaîté;* temper, *caractère;* enjoys, *jouir de;* of thinking, *se croire;* in, *dans*, art.; with, *de.*

(4.) Come and show, *venir montrer;* I cannot, *je ne saurais.*

(5.) Yellow, *jaune;* to suit, *convenir;* at all, *du tout.*

(6.) To return, *revenir*, ind-3; to find, *trouver*, ind-3; in an uproar, *dans la confusion.*

182. The article is put before proper names of countries, provinces, islands, regions, rivers, winds, and mountains*.

EXAMPLES

la France a *les Pyrénées* et *la Méditerranée au sud, la Suisse* et *la Savoie à l'est, les Pays-Bas au nord*, et *l'océan à l'ouest*	*France is bounded on the south by the Pyrenees and the Mediterranean, on the east by Switzerland and Savoy, on the north by the Netherlands, and on the west by the ocean*
le Japon, la Chine, le Mexique, la Martinique, le Mogol, l'Inde	*Japan, China, Mexico, Martinique, Mogul, India*
la Tamise, le Rhône, l'aquilon, les Alpes, le Cantal	*the Thames, the Rhône, the north wind, the Alps, the Cantal*

* In speaking of *monts*, we say: *le Parnasse*, or *le Mont Parnasse; le Vésuve*, or *le Mont Vésuve; l'Etna*, or *le Mont Etna; les Pyrénées*, or *les Monts Pyrénées.* But in speaking of *Montagnes*, we say: *les Alpes*, or *les Montagnes des Alpes, la Castellane*, or *la Montagne de la Castellane.*

In speaking of some *rivières*, we say: *la rivière de Seine, la rivière de Saône, la rivière de Rile*, of others we say simply *la Loire, la Tamise, la Durance*, etc.

In speaking of *fleuves*, we say: *le fleuve du Rhône, le fleuve du Tage*, but of others simply *le Volga, le Danube*, etc.

Of *Mers*, we say also: *la Mer Méditerranée, la Mer Noire, la Mer Blanche, la Mer Rouge*, etc.

These are peculiarities which have nothing to do with grammar, but which chiefly depend upon use and custom

EXERCISE.

1. *Europe* is bounded on the north by the Frozen Ocean; on the south by the Mediterranean Sea, which separates it from *Africa*; on the east by the continent of *Asia*; on the west by the Atlantic Ocean. It contains the following 2 states 1: on the north, *Norway, Sweden, Denmark* and *Russia*; in the middle, *Poland, Prussia, Germany, the United Provinces, the Netherlands, France, Switzerland, Bohemia, Hungary, the British Isles*: on the south, *Spain, Portugal, Italy, Turkey in Europe.*

2. The principal rivers in Europe are: the *Wolga*, the *Don* or *Tanaïs*, and the *Boristhenes* or *Nieper*, in Muscovy; the *Danube*, the *Rhine*, and the *Elbe*, in Germany; the *Vistula* or *Wezel*, in Poland; the *Loire*, the *Seine*, the *Rhone*, and the *Garonne*, in France; the *Ebro*, the *Tagus*, and the *Douro*, in Spain; the *Po*, in Italy; the *Thames*, and the *Severn*, in England; and the *Shannon*, in Ireland.

3. The principal mountains in Europe are the *Daarne Fields*, between Norway and Sweden; *Mount Krapel*, between Poland and Hungary; the *Pyrenean Mountains*, between France and Spain; the *Alps*, which divide France and Germany from Italy.

4. The bleak *north wind* never blows here, and the heat of summer is tempered by the cooling 2 *zephyrs* 1, which come to refresh the air towards the middle of the day.

(1.) Bounded, *borné*; on, *à*; frozen ocean, *mer glaciale*, f.; south, *sud*, or *midi*; Mediterranean sea, *Méditerranée*, f.; east, *est* or *orient*; west, *ouest* or *occident*; Norway, etc. *See* p. 74; British Isles, *îles Britanniques*, Turkey in, *Turquie de.*

(2.) Muscovy, *Moscovie*; Vistula, *Vistule*, f.; *Loire*, f., *Seine*, f.; *Rhone*, m.; *Garonne*, f.; Ebro, *Ebre*; Tagus, *Tage*, m.; Thames, *Tamise*, f.; Severn, *Saverne*, f.

(3.) Pyrenean Mountains, *Pyrénées.*

(4.) Bleak, *rigoureux*; north wind, *aquilon*; heat, *ardeur*; cooling, *rafraîchissant*; come, *venir*; to refresh, *adoucir.*

183. EXCEPTIONS. The article is omitted before the names of countries.

1. When these are governed by the preposition *en*, as: *il est en France*, he is in France; *il est en Espagne*, he is in Spain.

2. When those names are governed by some preceding noun, and have the meaning of an adjective, as: *roi de France*, king of France; *vins de France*, French wines; *noblesse d'Angleterre*, the English nobility.

3. When speaking of those countries as of places we come from, as: *je viens de France*, I come from

France; *j'arrive d'Italie*, I am just arrived from Italy. However, when speaking of the four parts of the world, custom requires the use of the article, as: *je viens de l'Amérique, j'arrive de l'Asie.*

4. The article is also omitted, before proper names of places and of persons; *Naples, Venise, César*, etc.*

EXERCISE.

1. *Naples* may be called a paradise, from its beauty and fertility. From this country 2 some suppose 1 Virgil took the model of the Elysian 2 Fields 1.

2. I have been a * prisoner *in Egypt*, as a * Phœnician; under that name I have long suffered, and under that name I have been set at liberty.

3. *He* has received French and Spanish wines, Italian silks, Provence oil, and English wool.

4. We set sail *from Holland*, to go to the Cape of Good Hope.

5. I was but just arrived *from Russia*, when I had the misfortune to lose my father.

6. I had set off *from America*, when my brother arrived there.

(1.) From, *à cause de;* from this country, *que c'est là, où;* some suppose, *quelques personnes penser que.*
(2.) Prisoner, *captif;* under that name *c'est sous ce nom que*, (both alike).
(4.) Set sail, *partir;* to go, *se rendre.*
(5.) I was but just, *ne faire que de.*
(6.) Set off, *partir;* there, *y.*

184. The definite article is not rendered in translating the following English sentences or others like them.

EXAMPLES

book the *tenth*, *chapter* the *fifth*	livre dix, chapitre cinq
Louis the *XIVth.*	Louis Quatorze
George the *Fourth*	George Quatre
he married Mary, the *daughter of Louis Philippe*	il épousa Marie, fille de Louis Philippe

* There are some proper names of authors, painters, and actors before which the article is used; *Le Tasse, le Dante, le Corrège, la Catalani, le Titien, la Chammeslé, l'Arioste, le Poussin, le Dominiquin, le Carache, l'Albane.* There are also some names of French towns which take the definite article. *La Flèche, la Rochelle, la Ferté, le Hâvre, le Perch*

the more you have, the less you give — plus vous avez, moins vous donnez
the richer you are, the less generous you are — plus vous êtes riche, moins vous êtes généreux
the more knowledge a man has, the more modest he is — plus un homme a de connaissance, plus il est modeste

The definite article is never used after *en*, but always after *dans*.

EXAMPLES.

il n'est pas en France — *he is not in France*
ce n'est pas dans la France, que vous le trouverez — *it is not in France, that you will find him*

185. The definite article is not used before the word which qualifies the substantives *espèce, genre, sorte, multitude, foule, amas, quantité*, etc.

EXAMPLES.

sorte de fruit — *a sort of fruit*
genre d'ouvrage — *a kind of work*
monceau d'argent — *a heap of money*
bande de voleurs — *a troop of robbers*
pile de livres — *a pile of books*
meute de chiens, etc. — *a pack of dogs*

186. The article is not used before substantives preceded by the pronominal adjectives *mon, ton, son, notre, votre, leur, ce, nul, aucun, chaque, tout* (used for *chaque*), *certain, plusieurs, tel*, or *cent, mille*.

EXAMPLES.

nos mœurs mettent le prix à nos richesses — *our manners fix the value of our riches*
toute nation a ses lois — *every nation has its laws*
cent ignorans, doivent-ils l'emporter sur un homme instruit? — *are a hundred blockheads to be preferred to one learned man?*

EXERCISE.

1. The roads are bordered with *laurels, pomegranates, jessamines,* and *other trees*, which * are * ever green, and ever in bloom.

The mountains are covered with *flocks*, which yield a fine wool, in great request among all the known 2 nations 1 (of the world. *)

2. The fleets of Solomon, under the guidance of the Phœnicians, made frequent voyages to the land of Ophir and Tharsis, (of the kingdom of Sophala, in Ethiopia), whence they returned at the end of three years, laden with *gold*, *silver*, *ivory*, *precious* 2 *stones* 1, and other kinds of *merchandise*.

3. *Costly furniture* 2 is not allowed there 1, nor *magnificent attire*, nor *sumptuous feasts*, nor *gilded palaces*.

4. We contemplated with pleasure the extensive fields covered with yellow ears of corn, the * *rich gifts* of bounteous Ceres.

5. He was *in a kind of ecstacy*, when he perceived us.

6. In the most corrupt age, he lived and died *a wise man**.

7. Are you surprised that the worthiest 2 men, 1 are *but men*, and betray remains of the weakness of humanity, amid the innumerable 2 snares 1 and difficulties which * are * inseparable from royalty ?

8. *He excited our pity*, when we saw him after his disgrace.

9. Hear, then, *O nations* full of valour! and you, *O chiefs*, so wise and so united! hear what I have * to * offer to you.

10. Out of this cavern issued, from time to time, a black 2 thick 3 smoke 1, which made *a sort of night* at mid-day.

11. *Those imitative* 2 *sounds* 1 are infused in all languages, and form, as it were, their * real basis.

12. *Every man* has his foibles, his moments of ill * humour, even his irregularities.

13. *Each plant* has virtues peculiar to itself, the knowledge 2 of which 1 could not but be infinitely useful.

14. *In all his instructions*, he is careful to bear in mind that grammar, logic, and rhetoric, are three sisters, that ought never to be disjoined.

(1.) Roads, *chemin*; with, *de*; pomegranates, *grenadier*; in bloom, *fleu-* : yield, *fournir*; wool, *laine*, pl.; in great request, *recherché*; among, *de*.

(2.) Made, *faire*, ind-2; end, *bout*; laden, *chargé*.

(3.) Is not allowed there, *on n'y souffre ni*: furniture, *meuble*; costly, *précieux*; attire, *ornement*; feasts, *repas*.

(4.) Extensive, *vaste*; fields, *campagne*; ears, *épi*; bounteous, *fécond*.

(5.) In a kind of, *comme en*.

(6.) Age, *siècle*.

(7.) That, *de ce que*; worthy, *estimable*; but, *encore*; betray, *montrer* remains, *reste*; snares, *piége*; difficulties, *embarras*.

(8.) He excited our pity, *il nous fit pitié*.

(9.) Hear, *écouter*.

(10.) Out of, *de*; issued, *sortir*, ind-2; thick, *et épais*; smoke, *fumée*, f. mid-day, *milieu du jour*.

(11.) Infused, *fondu*; to, *dans*; and form as it were, *et ils en sont comme* real, *fondamentale*.

(13.) Peculiar, *qui sont propres*; to it, *lui*; could, cond-1; not but, *ne que*.

(14.) He is careful to bear in mind, *ne point perdre de vue*: ought, *on devoir* ind-1; to be disjoined, *séparer*.

187. Proper names of deities, men, animals, towns, and particular places, do not take the article.

EXAMPLES.

Dieu a créé le ciel et la terre,	*God created heaven and earth*
Jupiter était le premier des dieux	*Jupiter was the first of the gods*
Bucéphale était le cheval d'Alexandre	*Bucephalus was Alexander's horse*
Rome est une ville d'une grande beauté	*Rome is a city of great beauty*

EXCEPTIONS. Proper names, however, take the article, when used in a restrictive sense.

EXAMPLES.

le Dieu des Chrétiens	the *God of Christians*
le Dieu de paix	the *God of peace*
le Jupiter d'Homère	*Homer's Jupiter*
le Bucéphale d'Alexandre	*Alexander's Bucephalus.*
*l'*ancienne Rome	*ancient Rome*
la Rome moderne	*modern Rome*

EXERCISE.

1. *Jupiter,* son of *Saturn* and *Cibele* or *Ops,* after having expelled his father from the throne, divided the paternal * inheritance with his two brothers, *Neptune* and *Pluto.*

2. On a dispute, at a feast of the gods, between *Juno, Pallas* and *Venus,* for the pre-eminence of beauty, *Jupiter* not being able to bring them to an agreement, referred the decision to *Paris,* a shepherd of mount Ida, with directions that a golden apple should be given to the fairest. *Paris* assigned to *Venus* 2 the golden * prize 1.

3. *God* said: let there * be 2 light 1, and there * was 2 light 1.

4. *The Apollo del Belvidere* and *the Venus di Medicis,* are valuable 2 remains 1 of antiquity.

5. *May* and *September* are the two finest months of the year in the south of France.

6. *The God of Abraham, Isaac,* and *Jacob,* was the only true God.

(1.) Expelled, *chasser;* divided, *en partager;* inheritance, *héritage,* m.
(2.) On, *dans;* at a feast, *qu'il y eut à un festin;* being able, *pouvoir;* to bring to an agreement, *accorder;* referred, *renvoyer;* directions, *ordre;* that a golden, etc. to give a golden apple to; assigned, *adjuger.*
(4.) Del Belvidere, *du Belvéder;* valuable, *précieux.*
(6.) Only, *seul.*

OF THE PARTITIVE ARTICLE *du*.

188. In the exercises on the verb, *avoir*, No. 102, 103, 104, 105, we have already had occasion to notice that *du, de la, des*, are used before a noun, not mentioned as if speaking of the totality of the species, but only as a part of it, and when, in English, the word *some* may be understood.

EXAMPLES.

du pain et *de l'eau* me feraient plaisir	*some bread and water would please me*
je vis hier *des savants* qui ne pensent pas comme vous	*I yesterday saw some learned men, who do not think as you do*

And also that *de* alone, without the article, is used when an adjective, an adverb of quantity or a negation precedes the noun thus spoken of in a partial sense; no regard being paid then to its gender or number.

EXAMPLES.

voilà *de beaux tableaux*	*there are beautiful pictures*
j'achetai hier *beaucoup de livres*	*I bought yesterday many books*
que de livres, j'achetai hier!	*how many books I bought yesterday!*
il n'y eût jamais *plus de lumières*	*there never was more learning*
il y a *moins d'habitants* à Paris qu'à Londres	*there are fewer inhabitants in Paris than in London*
je ne manque pas *d'amis**	*I do not want for friends*

EXCEPTION. *Bien* is the only adverb of quantity which is followed by the article.

EXAMPLES.

il a bien de l'esprit	*he has a great deal of wit*
elle a bien de la grâce	*she is very graceful*

190. OBSERVE. These expressions: *des petits-maîtres, des sages-femmes, des petits-pâtés*, etc. are

* See rule 109, *bis*.

not exceptions to the rule which requires *de* before an adjective, because, in cases of this kind, the substantives are so united with the adjectives, as to form but one and the same word. We must likewise say: *le propre* des *belles actions*, *les sentimens* des *anciens philosophes*, etc.; because, in expressions of this kind, the substantives are taken in a general sense.

191. It has been seen that, generally speaking, an article or some other sign precedes the noun in French, so as to point out whether we speak of a thing as to its general kind or merely as to a portion of it. There are however, many phrases in which no article or sign is required before the noun; we subjoin those which are most commonly used.

avoir faim
—— soif
—— dessein
—— honte
—— coutume
—— pitié
—— compassion
—— froid
—— chaud
—— patience
—— envie
—— besoin
donner envie
—— occasion
—— leçon
—— permission
—— parole
entendre raison
—— raillerie
—— malice

faire profession
—— tort
—— plaisir
—— peur
—— provision
—— défense
gagner pays
—— chemin
mettre fin
—— ordre
parler français
—— anglais
—— allemand
porter envie
—— bonheur
—— malheur
prendre parti
—— plaisir
—— leçon
—— patience
—— jour

EXERCISE.

1. We could not cast our eyes on either shore, without seeing *opulent* cities, *country houses* agreeably situated, *lands* every year 2 covered 1 with a golden 2 harvest 1, *meadows*, abounding in flocks

and herds, *husbandmen* bending under the weight of the fruits, and *shepherds* who made 1 the echoes 5 around them 6 repeat 2 the sweet sounds 3 of their pipes and flutes 4.

2. Provence and Languedoc produce *oranges, lemons, figs, olives, almonds, chesnuts, peaches, apricots,* and *grapes* of an uncommon sweetness.

3. The man who has never seen this pure light, is as * blind as one who was born blind: he dies without having seen any thing; at most, he perceives but *glimmering and false lights, vain shadows* and *phantoms* that have nothing real.

4. Among the Romans, those who were convicted of having used *illicit* or *unworthy means* to obtain an office, were excluded from it for ever.

5. Those who govern are like the celestial 2 bodies 1, which have *great splendour* and *no rest.*

6. *What beauty, sweetness, modesty,* and at the same time *what nobleness* and *greatness* of mind!

7. Themistocles, in order to ruin Aristides, made use of *many* artifices, which would have covered him with infamy in the eyes of posterity, had 1 not 4 the eminent services 2 which he rendered his country 3 blotted out 5 that stain.

8. The consequences *of great passions* are blindness of mind and depravity of heart.

9. *Noblemen* should never forget that their high birth imposes great duties on * them.

(1.) Could, *pouvoir*, ind-2; our, *les;* either, *les deux;* seeing, *apercevoir;* every year, *tous les ans;* covered with, *qui se couvrir de*, ind-2; abounding in, *remplis de;* flocks and herds, *troupeau;* bending, *qui étaient accablés;* weight, *poids;* shepherds, *bergers;* pipes, *chalumeau;* the echoes, *aux échos;* around them, *d'alentour.*

(3.) Who is born blind, *aveugle-né;* without having, *n'avoir jamais*, inf-3; any thing, *rien;* at most, *tout au plus;* perceives, *apercevoir;* glimmering, *sombre;* lights, *lueur;* real, *de réel.*

(4.) Used, *employer;* illicit, or unworthy means, *moyen illicite, ou voie indigne.* pl.; were, ind-2; from it, *en.*

(5.) Great, *beaucoup de;* splendour, *éclat;* no rest, (that have no rest) *repos.*

(6.) What, *que de.*

(7.) Ruin, *perdre;* made use of many, *employer bien;* artifices, *manœuvres;* covered, cond-3; with, *de;* infamy, *opprobre;* in, *à;* had, *si;* rendered, ind-3 *à;* blotted out, *effacer*, cond-3; stain, *tache.*

(8.) Of mind, art. *esprit;* of heart, *de*, art. *cœur.*

(9.) Noblemen *gentilhomme;* should, *devoir*, ind-1;

CHAPTER III.

OF THE ADJECTIVE.

192. CONCORD OF THE ADJECTIVE WITH THE NOUN.

It has already been said that the nature of the adjective in French is to agree in gender and number with the noun to which it is joined, thus: *un grand jardin, une grande maison, de bons livres, de bonnes plumes,* and the manner of forming the plural and the feminine of adjectives has also been explained. (No. 42.*)

An adjective referring to two or more nouns which are of the same gender, *all subject of the same verb,* must be in the plural and assume their gender.

XAMPLES.

la clémence et la majesté peintes sur son front sont, etc.	*the clemency and majesty imprinted on his countenance are, etc.*
le travail et le courage joints ensemble font surmonter des obstacles	*labour and courage together united make us surmount obstacles*

If the substantives are of different genders, the adjective must be in the masculine.

EXAMPLES.

votre frère et votre sœur sont peu instruits	*your brother and sister are not well informed*
la beauté et le vice réunis dans un même individu ne sauraient attacher, etc.	*beauty and vice united in the same individual cannot attach, etc.*

* See the peculiarities of *feu, nu, demi, bon, court, fort, bas,* No 43 *bis.*

When in speaking of *things*, (not of persons), an adjective belongs to two or more nouns which are *the object of or governed by a verb*, it is *customary* to make that adjective agree with the last noun, next to which it is placed.

EXAMPLES.

il avait la bouche et les yeux ouverts	*his mouth and eyes were open*
il avait les yeux et la bouche ouverte	*his eyes and mouth were open*

We say *customary*, because it is more *grammatical* to attach an idea of numbers to the adjective, when it expresses a quality or state common to several objects and to say,

EXAMPLES.

il avait les yeux et la bouche ouverts	*his eyes and mouth were open*
c'est un homme d'une valeur, d'une vertu et d'une fidélité éprouvées*	*he is a man of tried valour, virtue and fidelity*

EXERCISE.

His impetuosity and courage, long restrained, soon surmounted
= —— *enchaîné* 2 *vaincre* ind-3 1

all obstacles. The king and the shepherd are equal after death.

This comedian acts with delightful taste and grace. He found
acteur *jouer* *charmant* 3 1 — 2 ind-3

the rivers and ponds frozen over. His whole life (was nothing
2 *étang* m. 1 *glacé* 3 *n'être que*

* There are certain locutions on the correctness of which grammarians are not agreed: this is not the place for discussing such questions, but we will give both modes of expression, placing in the second column those which are thought preferable,

Les cotes personnelle, mobiliaire, et foncière.	*La cote* personnelle, la mobiliaire et la somptuaire.
Un cours *de langues* Française, Italienne, et Espagnole.	Un cours *de langue française*, Italienne, et Espagnole.
Les langues Française et Espagnole.	*La langue* Française et l'Espagnole.

but) constant labour and occupation. It was lost time and trouble.
ind-3 3 1 2 *c'était* 3 1 *peine* 2

Honours and riches are ever envied. Music and drawing are very entertaining. I teach the French and English tongues. Have you
amusant *enseigner* *langue* f.

read the Greek and Roman histories?
= f.

ADJECTIVES OF DIMENSION.

193. In speaking of the dimensions of an object, the French make use of a very different form from the English, thus:

EXAMPLES.

1. A tower two hundred feet high	*une tour de deux cents pieds de hauteur* or *de haut*
2. This tower *is* two hundred feet high	*cette tour* a *deux cents pieds de hauteur*

In the first example, *de* is used before the noun of numbers and before the adjective, to which the substantive of dimension may elegantly be substituted.

In the second, *to be* is rendered by *avoir*, and, consequently, the substantive of dimension *hauteur* can alone be used, since an adjective cannot be coupled with *avoir*.

EXERCISE.

This box, which is six feet *long*, is very convenient. You
coffre, m. *commode*

will be stopped in your march by a river three hundred feet *broad*.
arrêté f.

This observatory is twelve hundred feet *high*. It is a terrace
= *ce* *terrace* f.

a hundred and eighty feet *broad*, and twelve hundred feet
large *deux* *cents* *

long. The walls of our garden are twenty feet *high* and three
mur m. pl.

broad. It is one of the finest stones that was ever seen: it is
75 *on ait jamais vues*

twenty feet *long* and six *thick.* This ditch is nine feet six
longueur *épaisseur* *fossé* m.

inches deep and six feet *broad.*
pouce m. pl. *profondeur* f. *largeur*

194. Adjectives, used substantively, require the definite article.

EXAMPLE.

les fous inventent les modes, et *les sages* s'y conforment	*fools invent fashions, and wise men conform to them*

EXERCISE.

1. Were the *learned* of antiquity to come to life again, they would be much astonished at the extent of our knowledge.

The *ignorant* have, in a * large stock of presumption, what the want in real knowledge, and that is the reason they are admired by *fools.*

(1.) Were the, *si les;* to come again, *revenir,* ind-2; life, *monde;* at, *de:* knowledge, *connaissance,* pl.
(2.) Large stock, *forte dose;* they want, *il leur manque;* knowledge, *science;* the reason, *ce qui fait que;* they are, etc. the fools admire them.

When a noun is accompanied by two adjectives, expressing different qualities incompatible in the same object, the article must be repeated before each adjective.

EXAMPLES.

les vieux et les *nouveaux* soldats sont remplis d'ardeur	*the old and the newly raised soldiers are full of ardour*
il faut fréquenter *la bonne* compagnie et fuir *la mauvaise*	*we ought to frequent good and shun bad company*

REMARK. But if those qualities be not incompatible, the article is not repeated, as: *le sage et pieux Fénélon;* if merely expressing different ideas, it is perhaps better to repeat it, as: *le sensible et l'ingénieux Fénélon.*

EXERCISE.

1. The *antient* 1 and *modern* 3 writers 2 are not agreed upon that point.

2. The wise man preserves the same tranquillity of mind in *good* or *bad* fortune.

3. The man who is jealous of his reputation frequents *good* and shuns *bad* company.

4. *Grand* and *vigorous* thoughts were always the offspring of genius.

(1.) Writers, *auteur*; are agreed, *s'accorder*.
(4.) Vigorous, *fort*; offspring, *fruit*.

195. The article is used before the adjective which is joined to a proper name, either to express its quality, or to distinguish the person spoken of from those who might bear the same name.

EXAMPLES.

le sublime Bossuet	*the sublime Bossuet*
Louis le gros	*Louis the fat*
le vertueux Fénélon	*the virtuous Fenelon*
Louis le Juste	*Louis the Just*
le tendre Racine	*the tender Racine*
Louis le Grand	*Louis the Great*

Remark. If the adjective, which is joined to a proper name, precede that name, it expresses a quality which may be common to many; but if it follow, it expresses a distinguishing quality. Thus: *le savant Varron*, and *Varron le savant*, do not convey the same meaning: in the first example, *Varron* merely obtains the quality of *savant*; in the second, *Varron* is distinguished for his learning from all of the same name.

EXERCISE.

1. The *great Corneille* astonishes by beauties of the first order, and by faults of the worst taste. If the *tender Racine* does not often rise so high, at least, he is always equal, and possesses the art of always interesting the heart.

(1.) By, *par des*; order, *ordre*; is always equal, *se soutenir*; possesses, *avoir*.

2. The more we read the fables of the *good* and *artless La Fontaine*, the more we are convinced they are a book for all ages, and the manual of the man of taste.

3. It was only under the reign of *Louis the Just* (XIII.) that good taste began to show itself in France : but it was under that of *Louis the Great* that it was carried to perfection.

(2.) The more we, *plus on ;* artless, *simple ;* are convinced, *on se convaincre ;* they are, *que c'est ;* a, *le ;* for, *de ;* manual, *manuel.*
(3.) Only, *ne que ;* carried, *porter à.*

196. When a superlative relative precedes a substantive, the article is used once only; if it follow, it must be repeated before the noun and the adjective.

EXAMPLES.

les plus habiles gens font quelquefois *les plus grandes* fautes *or les* gens *les plus habiles* font quelquefois *les* fautes *les plus grandes*
*the ablest men sometimes commit the grossest blunders**

EXERCISE

1. It has been said of the Telemachus of the virtuous Fenelon, that it is *the most useful* 2 present 1 the muses have made to mankind ; for, could the happiness of man be produced by a poem, it would be by that.

2. *The smoothest* 2 *waters* 1 often conceal *the most dangerous* 2 *gulfs* 1.

(1.) It has been said, *on a dit ;* present, *don que ;* have made, subj-3 ; could, (if the, etc. could, ind-2) ; be produced by, *naître de ;* would be, *naître*, cond. .
(2.) Smoothest, *tranquille ;* gulf, *gouffre*, m.

* Observe. Cette planète est *la* plus éloignée du soleil. Lorsque cette planète est *le* plus éloignée du soleil.
There is a difference here with regard to the declinability of the article which must be understood.
If there is a comparison implied the article is declined. Thus, in the first sentence, we speak of the planets which are distant from the sun, and allude to that which is most so ; but in the second, our thought bears on one planet alone, independant of all others ; *le plus* is merely an adverb to the verb *être éloignée*, and consequently is undeclined as all adverbs are.
These remarks apply also to *le moins, la moins, les moins.*

REMARKS ON SOME PARTICULAR MODES OF EXPRESSING COMPARISONS.

197. The manner of expressing comparisons of equality and of superiority and inferiority will be explained, (No. 211). But there are some phrases which it is the place to notice here.

Equally with is used for as *well as* and is thus rendered.

EXAMPLES.

He blamed it equally with me	*il le blâma aussi bien que moi*
He was blamed equally with me	*il fut blâmé aussi bien que moi*

NOTHING *so pleasant*, *good*, *difficult*, etc., is thus rendered.

EXAMPLES.

Nothing so easy as to do it	*rien de si facile que de le faire*
Nothing so pleasant as to meet with friends	*rien de si agréable que de rencontrer des amis*

QUOI, *what* ; *quelque chose*, something ; *rien*, nothing ; before adjectives require *de*.

EXAMPLES.

Quoi de plus agréable que d'être au coin d'un bon feu ?	what is there more pleasant than to sit by a good fire ?
Il n'y a rien de doux dans sa physionomie	there is nothing sweet in her countenance
J'ai remarqué quelque chose d'extraordinaire	I noticed something extraordinary

THE PLACE OF ADJECTIVES.

198. Pronominal and numerical adjectives precede their substantive, as do generally the following six

teen; *beau, bon, brave, cher, chétif, grand, gros, jeune, mauvais, méchant, meilleur, moindre, petit, saint vieux*, and *vrai*, when taken in their literal sense.

EXAMPLES.

mon père	my father
quel homme	what man
vieille femme	old woman
dix guinées	ten guineas
plusieurs officiers	several officers
grand homme	great man
six arbres	six trees
chétive mine	mean look

EXCEPTION. The pronoun *quelconque*.

EXAMPLE.

d'une manière quelconque in whatever manner

EXERCISE.

1. There have been ages, when a *great man* was a sort of prodigy produced by a mistake of nature.

2. In almost all nations, the *great geniuses* that have adorned them were contemporaries.

3. *Young people*, says Horace, are open to the enticements of vice, lavish, presumptuous, and equally impetuous and light in their passions; *old people*, on the contrary, are covetous, dilatory, timid, ever alarmed about the future, always complaining, hard to please, panegyrists of times past, censors of the present, and great givers of advice.

4. *What man* was ever satisfied with his condition, and dissatisfied with his abilities?

5. *Thirty chambers*, which have a communication one with another, and each of them an iron door, with six huge bolts, are the places where he shuts himself up.

(1.) Ages, *des siècles*; when, *où*; produced, *enfanter*.
(2.) In, *chez*; nations, *peuple*; adorned, *illustrer*, ind-4.
(3.) Old people, *vieilles gens*; open, *souple*; lavish, *prodigue*; impetuous, *vif*; (all those adjectives are m. pl.); covetous, *avare*; dilatory, *temporiseur*; about, *sur*; complaining, *plaintif*; hard, *difficile*; please, *contenter*: times, sing.
(4.) Dissatisfied, *mécontent*; abilities, *esprits*.
(5.) Have a communication, *communiquer*; each of them, *dont chacun avoir*; huge, *gros*; bolts, *verrou*; places, *lieu*, sing.; shuts himself, *se renfermer*.

199. Adjectives of number, joined to proper names, pronouns, and substantives, are placed after the noun.

EXAMPLES.

George Trois	George III
chapitre dix	chapter 10
page trente	page the 30th

200. The adjectives mentioned 198, when connected by a conjunction with another adjective, which is to be placed after the substantive, are themselves placed after the noun.

EXAMPLE.

c'est une femme grande et bien faite	she is a tall well-made woman

201. In English, two, or even several adjectives may qualify a substantive, without a conjunction; but in French *et* is always placed before the last adjective, *c'est un homme aimable et poli,* he is an amiable, well-behaved man.

202. OBSERVE. All adjectives are put after the noun, *un homme riche, jeune et aimable,* except one of them is one of those which precede it, *c'est un grand homme sec,* he is a tall thin man.

They are placed after the noun, adjectives formed —from the participle present of verbs—*ouvrage divertissant,* entertaining work;—from the participle past; all those expressing form, physical qualities, etc. *figure arrondie,* round figure; *table ovale,* oval table;—colour, *maison blanche,* white house;—taste, *herbe amère,* bitter herb;—sound, *orgue harmonieux,* harmonious organ;—action, *procureur actif,* active attorney;—effect, *coutume abusive,* custom founded in abuse;—arrangement, *ordre grammatical,* grammatical order;—species, *qualité occulte*, occult quality; —nation, *générosité Anglaise*, English generosity;— those ending in *-esque, -il, -ule, ic, ique, -in:*

style burlesque	burlesque style
jargon puéril	childish jargon
femme crédule	credulous woman
bien public	public welfare
ris sardonique	sardonic grin
voix enfantine	childish voice

but in this, custom is the best guide.

EXERCISE.

1. An *affected* simplicity is a *refined* imposture.
2. The *smiling* images of Theocritus, Virgil, and Gessner, excite in the soul a gentle feeling.
3. In that *antique* palace are to be seen neither *wreathed* columns, nor *gilded* wainscots, nor *valuable* basso-relievoes, nor ceilings curiously *painted*, nor *grotesque* figures of animals which never had existence but in the imagination of a child or a madman.
4. If *human* life is exposed to many troubles, it is also susceptible of many pleasures.
5. A *ridiculous* man is seldom so by halves.
6. *Spanish* manners have, at first sight, something harsh and uncivilized.
7. *French* urbanity has become a proverb among *foreign* nations.

(1.) Refined, *délicat*.
(2.) Smiling, *riant;* excite, *porter;* soft, *doux;* feeling, *sensibilité*, f.
(3.) Are to be seen, *on ne voit;* wreathed, *torse;* wainscots, *lambris;* basso-relievoes, *bas-relief;* cielings, *plafond;* curiously, *artistement;* had existence, *exister*.
(4.) Many, *bien des;* troubles, *peine*.
(5.) So, *le;* by halves, *à demi*.
(6.) Spanish, *Espagnol;* manners, *mœurs;* at first sight, *au premier abord;* uncivilized, *sauvage*.
(7.) Become, *passer en;* among, *chez*.

203. Although it may seem that adjectives expressing moral qualities are placed indifferently before, or after the substantive, yet taste and a correct ear will assign them their proper situation.

Nevertheless if spoken in a broken, loose style, it

may be indifferent to say *femme aimable*, or *aimable femme*; *talents sublimes*, or *sublimes talents*, etc.; but in the dignified style, the place of the adjective may, in a variety of instances, affect the beauty of a sentence.*

EXERCISE.

1. An *amiable* woman gives to every thing she says an *inexpressible* grace; the more we hear, the more we wish to hear her.
2. The *majestic* eloquence of Bossuet is like a river, which carries away every thing in its rapid course.
3. The *sublime* compositions of Rubens have made 1 an English traveller 3 say 2, that this *famous* painter was born in Flanders, through a mistake of nature.

(1.) Give to, *répandre sur*; we, *on*.
(2.) River, *fleuve*; carries away, *entraîner*; its rapid course, *la rapidité de son cours*.
(3.) Say, *dire à*; famous, *célèbre*; through, *par*; mistake *méprise*.

GOVERNMENT OF ADJECTIVES.

204. Adjectives are frequently followed by another substantive than that which they qualify, thus: *un homme digne de récompense, un homme enclin au bien*, they are also sometimes followed by an infinitive, *capable d'aimer*, *prompt à bien faire*, etc. In such cases a preposition is used according to the case or regimen which the adjective requires. This is called the government of adjectives.

205. Adjectives which govern the preposition DE.

digne	comblé	fou
indigne	taxé	avide
capable	chargé	ennuyé
incapable	plein	libre
aisé	accusé	qualifié.
ravi	fatigué	vide
joyeux	las	dépendant
content	contrit	chéri
mécontent	enragé	

* Such adjectives are more expressive when placed before the noun; but taste and harmony must be consulted. None but those well versed in the French Language can *feel* the proper place of the adjective; we recommend to the *learner* always to place it after the noun; which is quite correct, if not ele-

206. Adjectives which govern the preposition *à*.

adroit
bon
beau
laid
agréable
ingénieux
contraire
opposé
conforme
semblable
pareil
porté
enclin
adonné
sujet
propre
inexorable
désagréable
agile
alerte
habile
ardent
âpre
lent
nuisible
prompt
prêt
utile
inutile
sensible
aisé
facile
cher

207. Adjectives which require ENVER. *Complaisant, généreux, affable, indulgent, prévenant, cruel, bon,* and any other expressing kindness or unkindness of feeling towards individuals.

EXERCISE.

Are you pleased with your horse? Do not be so greedy
content *avide*
after riches. I am not unworthy of his friendship. They say
indigne *on dit que*
he is very dissatisfied with his son. We were tired with
mécontent ind-2 *fatigué*
running after him. Are we (not at liberty) to go? My
courir *libre* *partir*
brother is not fit for that place. Send me some gloves
propre *gant*, m.
like those which my sister has. If you are ready to go,
pareil
I will order the carriage. Too much exercise may be
commander ind-7 *pouvoir être*
injurious to the health. You will not find that easy to do
nuisible *cela facile*
Let us be kind (to one another). He was so kind to
les uns envers les autres *bon*
his sisters.

208. **Observe.** A noun may be governed by two adjectives, provided they do not require two different prepositions. Thus you may say: *cet homme est utile et cher à sa famille*, that man is useful and dear to his family; but you may not say, *il est utile et chéri à sa famille*, because *chéri*, beloved, requires the genitive, or preposition *de* before a noun. Such sentences must be turned thus, *il est utile à sa famille et en est chéri*, he is useful to his family and beloved of them.

ÊTRE WITH ADJECTIVES.

209. *Je suis bien aise, fâché, contrarié*, etc., or any other phrase expressing gladness or regret at a thing, requires the subjunctive mood, or the infinitive with DE, as:

je suis enchanté que *vous* soyez de retour	I *am delighted that* you *have returned*
je suis enchanté d'être de retour à temps	I *am delighted that* I *have returned in time*

In the first example, there are two different subjects *je, vous;* the verb is on that account put in the subjunctive mood.

In the second example, there is but one and the same subject, the second verb is in the infinitive.

EXERCISE.

She will be delighted to see you. How sorry I am you
enchanté 2 1 *que* 2 1

were not at home last night. Call upon him, he will be
subj-2 *chez vous hier au soir.* *aller* 1 *voir* 3 2

glad to see you. I cannot tell you how vexed I am
bien aise *je ne saurais* *contrarié* 2 1

at my servant being so slow, and at your not receiving
être subj-3 *ne recevoir pas* subj-3

my note. We are all very sorry you cannot come, for
billet m. *bien fâché* *pouvoir* subj-1

we shall have a delightful evening.
passer 2 *soirée* f. 1

210. Il est, impersonal, joined to an adjective requires *de* before the infinitive. *C'est* requires *à*.

EXAMPLES.

il est beau de mourir pour sa patrie	it is noble to die for one's country
c'est horrible à voir	it is horrid to see.

EXERCISE.

It was amusing to see them. How pleasant it is to
il ind-2 *que* *agréable* 2 *il* 1

enjoy good health! This is most painful to hear.
jouir de *ce* *on ne peut plus pénible*

It was very disagreeable (for me) to witness all their
il 2 ind-2 3 *me* 1 *être présent à*

quarrels. It may be pleasant to look at, but is it very
cela *voir* *

useful?

ADJECTIVES IN THE COMPARATIVE DEGREE.

211. The verb which follows an adjective in the comparative requires *ne* before it.

EXAMPLE:

vous êtes plus heureux que vous n'étiez	you are happier than you were.

But if the first member of the sentence is negative or interrogative the *ne* is suppressed.

EXAMPLES.

vous n'êtes pas plus heureux que vous l'étiez	you are not happier than you were
peut-on être plus heureux que vous l'êtes?	can any one be happier than you are?

The *ne* is also suppressed after *quand, dans le temps*, or any adverb.

EXAMPLE.

vous êtes plus heureux que quand vous étiez en France	you are happier than when you were in France

Tout autre, autrement, mieux, moins bien, plus mal, also require the *ne*, before the verb.

EXAMPLE.

il est tout autre qu'il n'était	he is quite different from what he was

EXERCISE.

He is much richer than you think (*penser*). You sing better than you did (*faire* ind-2). He has been better received than he thought (*croire* ind-2). Sciences are now more cultivated than they were (*être* ind-2). Since the invention of gun (2) powder (1) battles are less bloody than they were. That war was (*être* ind-3) not less successful (*heureuse*) than it was (*être* ind-2) just. (Can any one) (*peut-on*) be more amiable than she is? Is he not much richer than he was? The poor (pl.) are not so sick, (*moins malade*) (for want of) (*faute de*) food, as (*que*) the rich (pl.) are for taking (*en prendre*) too much.

ADJECTIVES IN THE SUPERLATIVE DEGREE.

212. An adjective in the superlative degree requires that the verb which follows it should be in the subjunctive mood, or that the noun should be in the genitive case, that is. have the preposition *de* before it.

EXAMPLES.

donnez-moi la meilleure plume que vous ayez	give me the best pen you have
la plus belle fleur du jardin	the prettiest flower in the garden

The absolute *le seul, l'unique, le premier, le dernier, aucun,* must be considered as superlatives, and included in this rule.

EXERCISE.

You see the largest tree there is in the park. Is he
grand arbre qu'il y ait

not the richest man in the town? I gave you the only one
riche * *donner* ind-4

I had. They say he is the cleverest boy in the school
avoir subj-2 *on dit que c'est* *habile*

She is certainly the prettiest girl I ever saw. I am not the
c'est *personne* *voir* subj-3

only one, I believe, who accepted his invitation. There
à ce que je crois *accepter* subj-3 *il y*

were present some of the most celebrated men in Europe,
avait là quelques-uns

but (no one could get a peep at them), so great was the
il était impossible d'en approcher *tant* 1 4 3

crowd.
2

213. By, after a comparative, is rendered by DE.

EXAMPLE.

il est plus grand d'un pouce	he is taller by one inch

ADJECTIVES OF NUMBER.

214. *Unième* is used only after *vingt, trente, quarante, cinquante, soixante, quatre-vingt, cent* and *mille*. *C'est la vingt-et-unième fois,* it is the twenty first time.

Cent, in the plural takes an *s*, except when followed by another noun of number, as:

ils étaient deux cents	there were two hundred
trois cents hommes	three hundred men
ils étaient deux cent dix	there were two hundred and ten

Vingt in *quatre-vingt*, and *six-vingt*, also takes an *s*, when followed by a substantive, as:

quatre-vingts hommes	eighty men
six vingts abricots	six score apricots

But it takes no *s*, when followed by another term expressing number, *quatre-vingt-un arbres*, *quatre-vingt-dix hommes*.

The ordinal numbers, collective and distributive, always take the sign of the plural: *les premières douzaines*, the first dozens; *les quatre cinquièmes*, the four fifths.

For dates the French write *mil*, as: *mil sept cent-quatre-vingt-dix-neuf*, one thousand seven hundred and ninety-nine, etc.

REMARK. *Cent* and *mille* are used indefinitely, as

il lui fit cent *caresses*	he shewed him *a hundred* marks of kindness
faites-lui mille *amitiés*	present him *a thousand* compliments

EXERCISE.

1. It was the *thirty-first* year after so glorious a peace, when the war broke out again with a fury of which history offers few examples.

2. There were only *three hundred*, and in spite of their inferiority in numbers*, they attacked the enemy, beat and dispersed them.

3. He has sold his country house for* *two thousand five hundred and fifty* pounds.

4. Choose out of your nursery ground *eighty* fruit trees and *ninety* dwarf-trees, divide them into dozens, and put in the two first dozens of each sort, those whose fruits are most esteemed.

5. When Louis the Fourteenth made his entry into Strasbourg, the Swiss deputies having come to pay their respects to him, Le Tellier, archbishop of Rheims, who saw among them the bishop of Basle, said to one near him: that bishop is apparently some poor beggar.—How, replied the other, he has a *hundred thousand* livres a year.—Oh! oh! said the archbishop, he is then a respectable man, and shewed him a thousand civilities.

(1.) Year, *année*; when, *que*; broke out again, *se rallumer*, ind-3.
(2.) Only, *ne que*; in spite of, *malgré*.
(3.) Pounds, *livre sterling*.
(4.) Out of, *dans*; nursery-ground, *pépinière*; fruit-trees, *pied d'arbre fruitier*; dwarf-trees, *arbre nain*.
(5.) Swiss, (of the Swiss); pay, *présenter*; respect, *hommage*, pl.; one near him, *son voisin*: that bishop, etc. *c'est un misérable apparemment que cet évêque*; a year, *de rente*; shewed, *faire*, ind-3; civilities, *caresses*.

The French say, *le onze, du onze, au onze, sur les onze heures, sur les une heure,* pronouncing the words *onze* and *une*, as if they were written with an *h* aspirated.

215. The cardinal numbers are used for the ordinal.

1. In reckoning time, that is, the *hour* of the day, the *day* of the month, the *year* of an era, as: *il est trois heures*, it is three o'clock; *le vingt de Mars*, the twentieth of March; *l'an mil sept cent dix*, etc.,

216. 2. In speaking of the order of succession of sovereigns, as: *Louis seize, George trois,* except the first two of the series, as: *Henri premier, George second. Quint* for *cinq* is only said of the *Empereur Charles-quint*, and the *Pape Sixte-quint*.

EXERCISE.

1. They made in the parish and in the neighbouring places a collection which produces a *hundred and twenty-one* guineas.

2. William, surnamed the Conqueror, king of England and duke of Normandy, was one of the greatest generals of the *eleventh* century: he was born at Falaise, and was the natural son of Robert, duke of Normandy, and of Arlotte, a furrier's daughter.

3. Make haste; it will soon be *ten* o'clock. We shall have a great difficulty to arrive in time.

4. The winter was so severe in *one thousand seven hundred and nine*, that there was but one olive tree that resisted it*, in a plain where there had been more than ten thousand.

5. It was the *twenty-first* of January, one thousand seven hundred and ninety-three, that the unhappy Louis *the sixteenth* was led to the scaffold.

(1.) They, *on*; neighbouring places, *voisinage*, sing.; collection, *quête*.
(2.) William, *Guillaume*; furrier, *fourreur*.
(3.) Make haste, *se dépêcher*; will be, ind-1; great difficulty, *bien de la peine*
(4.) Severe, *rude*; but, *ne que*; had been, *y en avoir*, ind-2.

CHAPTER IV.

PRONOUNS.

§ I.

PERSONAL PRONOUNS.

DISTINCTION BETWEEN THE SUBJECT AND THE OBJECT.

217. Personal pronouns, like the substantives which they represent, whether persons or things, are either the *subject* or *object* of a verb.

As object or regimen, they are also *direct* or *indirect*. See 170, 173.

SUBJECT.

Common to persons and things *je, tu, il, elle, nous, vous, ils, elles*.

Also *moi, toi, lui, eux*.

OBJECT DIRECT.

Common to persons and things, *me, te, le, la, nous, vous, les*, m. f.

Also *moi, toi*.

OBJECT INDIRECT. (DATIVE.)

Of persons, *me, te, lui*, m. f. *nous, vous, leur*, m. f.
Also, *moi, toi*.

Also *à moi, à toi, à lui, à elle, à nous, à vous, à eux à elles.*

Of things, *y* of both genders and numbers.

OBJECT INDIRECT, (*genitive or ablative.*)

Of persons, *de moi, de toi, de lui, d'elle, de nous, de vous, d'eux, d'elles*; sometimes *en.*

Of things, *en* of both genders and numbers.

PRONOUNS GOVERNED BY PREPOSITIONS.

Moi, toi, lui, elle, nous, vous, eux, elles.

PRONOUN SUBJECT.

218. The place of the subject is before the verb, if affirmative, after it, if interrogative.

EXAMPLES.

je parle	*I speak*
il raconta son histoire	*he related his history*
est-il heureux?	*is he happy?*

219. Sometimes there are two or more subjects to the verb, such as *you, he, and I are agreed to go*; in such cases, *moi, toi, lui, eux,* are used instead of *je, tu, il, ils,* and it is polite to place the first person last.

EXAMPLES.

vous et moi, nous irons — *you and I we shall go.*

EXERCISE.

My sister and I we were walking by the last rays of the
se promener ind-2 *à* *rayons* m. pl.

setting sun, and we were saying, what a soft splendour does it
couchant 2 1 *dire* ind-2 *doux éclat* m. * 2

still spread over all nature! In the long winter even-
pas 3 5 *ne répand* 1 art. *de* 2 *soi*

ings, my father, my brothers, and I used (to spend) two
réc f. pl. 1 *nous passer* ind-2

hours in the library, and to read there, (in order to)
bibliothèque f. *nous lire,* ind-2 *y* *pour*

(unbend our minds) from the serious studies of the day, those
se délasser = 2 1

amiable poets who interest most the heart, by the charms of a
2 1 *le plus*

lively imagination, and make us love truth, by disguising it
riant 2 1 2 1 art. *en déguiser*

under the mask of an ingenious fiction You and your friend
trait m. pl. = 2 f. 1

shall accompany me to the museum, where we shall study nature
—pagner 2 1 *musée* m. *où*

in her three kingdoms.
règne m. pl.

220. *Moi, toi, lui, eux* are also used instead of *je, tu, il, ils.*

1st. After *que* in comparisons.

EXAMPLE.

vous êtes plus grand que moi	*you are taller than I.*

2nd. After *c'est,* and in answer to a question.

EXAMPLES.

ce n'est pas moi qui l'ai fait	*it is not I who did it*
que vous reste-t-il ? Moi	*whom have you left ? Me.*

3rd. Before a relative pronoun or an infinitive, speaking emphatically and by apposition.

EXAMPLES.

moi, dont il déchire la réputation	*I, whose reputation he destroys*
toi, qui fais le brave	*thou who lookest so valiant*
moi, trahir le meilleur de mes amis !	*I, betray my best friend ?*
voudriez-vous me perdre, moi votre allié ?	*would you ruin me, who am your ally ?*
eux m'ont relevé, et lui m'a pansé	*they picked me up, and he dressed my wounds*

OBSERVE. In English, it is allowed to place the adverb between the subject and the verb, *I certainly did not think he would come.* The adverb must always come last in French, *Je ne pensais certainement pas qu'il viendrait.*

EXERCISE.

You write (a great deal better) than I do. If you are not so rich
beaucoup mieux *

as he is, I think you are as happy. Who calls? I do
oue * tout aussi heureux *

Is it you or he who said so? It is not I. I! stoop to the
l'avez dit m'abaisser devant

man who dipped his hands in the blood of his king! Your
tremper ind-4

brothers and mine undertake it. They find the money and he
s'en charger fournir

will manage the work. It is I who have prevailed upon him to un-
conduire 2 engagé 3 * le 1 à

dertake that journey. Can you act so towards him, he who ever
2

was your best friend?
ind-3 1

THINGS MASCULINE OR FEMININE.

221. It is almost useless to repeat that inanimate things in French are either masculine or feminine, and consequently that the pronouns *il, elle, ils, elles,* are used accordingly in speaking of such.

Thus speaking of a rose, *rose* f. we say

EXAMPLES.

elle est belle, *it is beautiful*
ne sent-elle pas bon? *does it not smell nice?*

Of a book, *livre,* m.

EXAMPLES.

il est bien écrit *it is well written*
vous a-t-il amusé? *has it amused you?*

EXERCISE.

(Look at) that magnificent building; *it* unites grace to
Regarder —*fique* *bâtiment* m *réunir* art. *grâce* f. art.

beauty, and elegance to simplicity. Ignorance is jealous,
= f. art. — f. art. = f. — f.

presumptuous, and vain: *it* sees difficulties in nothing, (is
présomptueux — *ne* *de* = f. pl. *à* *rien* *ne*

nothing, and stops at nothing. Let us gather
ne *s'arrêter* *à* *cueillir*

these roses; what a sweet fragrance *they* exhale Never judge
quel * *parfum* *—ler.*

from appearances; *they* are often deceitful: the wise man ex-
sur art. f. *

amines them, and does not decide upon *them,* till he has
* *se décider d'après* f. *que lorsque*

had time to fix his judgment.
art. m. *de* *fixer*

AUSSI, ENCORE, PEUT-ETRE, ETC. FOLLOWED BY THE INTERROGATIVE FORM.

222. Although placing the personal pronoun *subject,* after the verb, is the sign of a question, there are some cases in which custom requires or admits, that the pronoun should be so placed, though no interrogation is meant.

1st. After *aussi,* and on that account, and for this reason, *peut-être,* may be, perchance; *encore,* and yet, besides, with all that; *toujours,* still; *en vain,* in vain, *du moins, au moins,* at least.

2nd. In narrations, as in English, said I, *dis-je*; replied I, *répondis-je.*

3rd. In the imperative mood of *pouvoir, devoir.*

EXAMPLES.

puissé-je le voir !	*oh that I may see him*
dussé-je mourir	*were I to die*

F PRONOUNS BEING DIRECT AND INDIRECT REGIMEN.

223. It has been shown (No. 170), in speaking of the government of the substantive, that the use of the proper preposition, before the noun, or the using no preposition at all, entirely depends upon the knowledge of the regimen of the verb; and it has also been shown, by comparison, that the two languages are far from agreeing in that respect, because the French equivalent of an active English verb, may be

neuter, and vice versâ; *obéir*, for instance, requires *à*, *obeir à la loi*, whereas in English *to obey* is active, *to obey the law.* Now, if instead of a noun, a pronoun is used, as the object of a verb, it must necessarily be put in the same case as the noun itself would; pains must therefore be taken to ascertain whether the governing verb requires a direct or an indirect case. *I resist him*, for example, must not be rendered by *je* LE *résiste*, but by *je* LUI *résiste*, because *to resist a man*, is, in French, *résister à un homme. I want them*, cannot be *je les ai besoin*, but *j'ai besoin d'eux*, because *to want a person*, is *avoir besoin d'une personne.* Again, the English make no difference between the *direct* and *indirect* case; *him*, *her*, *them*, serve for both; not so in French, *him* is rendered by *le* or *lui*, not indifferently, but according to circumstance. Thus we say, *I see him*, *je le vois*, and *I send him a book*, *je lui envoie un livre*, because *him* being the case direct or accusative of *I see;* so is *le* of *je vois;* but *him* is the indirect case or dative of *I send*, and book the direct case, consequently *lui* must be used in French, to show that difference.

Having endeavoured to point out the different manner of using personal pronouns in French and in English, we will now give rules as to the place they are to occupy in French, as direct and indirect cases of the verb.

In order to give every assistance to the learner, the proper preposition will be placed after the infinitive, in the exercises.

224. The pronouns *me*, *te*, *se*, *lui*, *leur*, *le*, *la*, *les* *nous*, *vous*, *y* and *en*, are generally placed before verbs

EXAMPLES.

Il me dit	*He tells me*	Je lui parle	*I speak to him*
Je le vois	*I see him*	J'y songerai	*I will think of it*
Je les écoute	*I listen to them*	J'en suis ravi	*I am delighted at it*

EXERCISE.

(As soon as) he had explained to *us* the maxims of Socrates,
Dès que *yaer* ind-5 * *Socrate*

he said: you see that it is not without reason he (is looked
ind-3 *ce* *qu'on le* *regarde*

upon) as truly wise. He was continually saying *to me*, yet a little
un vrai ind-2

patience, and you will disarm even envy itself. You have
de *désarmer* * art. *être*,

no doubt (some ground) for reproaching *him* with faults; is
sans doute *fondé* *à reprocher* inf-1 *des fautes;*

there (any man) on earth that is exempt *(from them)*? To
quelqu'un art. *qui* subj-1 *en* *pour*

please *her*, you must never flatter *her*. To abandon *one's self* to
lui *falloir* *flatter*

metaphysical abstractions, is to plunge into an unfathomable
*des métaphysique*2 —1 *ce* * *se jeter* *sans fond* 2

abyss.
abîme m. 1

225. The pronouns *moi*, *toi*, *soi*, *nous*, *vous*, *lui*, *eux*, *elle*, and *elles*, are placed after verbs, when they are preceded by a preposition.

EXAMPLES.

cela dépend de moi	*that depends on me*
je pense à toi	*I think of thee*
on s'occupe trop de soi	*we think too much about ourselves*
que dites-vous d'eux?	*what do you say of them?*

EXERCISE.

My father loved me so tenderly, that he thought of none but
ind-2 *ne penser* ind-2 *à* * *que*

me, (was wholly taken up) with *me*, and saw none but *me* in the
ne s'occuper ind-2 *que* *de* *voir* ind-2 * *que* *dans*

universe. If you wish to obtain that favour, you must speak *to him*
de * *falloir*

himself. It depended on *you* to excel your rivals, but you
ind-2 *de* *de l'emporter sur*

would not. Philip, father of Alexander, being advised
le vouloir ind-4 *Philippe* 2 *comme on conseil-*

to expel from his dominions a man, who (had been speaking
lait à de chasser *état* m. pl. *parler* ind-6

ill of *him*; I shall take care not to do that, said he, he would go and
se garder bien * * * *en* ind-3 *aller* *

slander *me* every where.
médire de

225*. In imperative phrases, when affirmative, *moi*, *toi*, *nous*, *vous*, *lui*, *leur*, *le*, *la*, *les*, *y*, and *en*, are placed after the verb; but, when negative, *me*, *te*, *se*, *nous*, *vous*, *lui*, *leur*, *le*, *la*, *les*, *y*, and *en*. are placed before it.

EXAMPLES.

dites-*moi*	*tell me*	ne *me* dites pas	*do not tell me*
donnez-*m'en* la moitié	*give me half of it*	ne *m'en* donnez point	*do not give me any*
songez-*y* sérieusement	*think of it seriously*	n'y songez pas	*do not think of it*

REMARK. If the pronouns *me*, *te*, *moi*, *toi*, intervene betwixt an imperative and an infinitive, *me*, *te*, are used when the imperative is without a regimen direct.

EXAMPLES.

venez me parler, *come and speak to me*
va te faire coiffer *go and get thy hair dressed*

But *moi*, *toi*, are used if the imperative have a regimen direct.

EXAMPLES.

laissez-moi faire *let me do it*
fais-toi coiffer *get thy hair dressed*

226. If *moi*, *toi*, when placed after the imperative, be followed by the pronoun, *en*, they are changed into *me*, *te*.

EXAMPLES.

donnez-m'en *give me some* | retourne-t en *go back*

227. When there are two imperatives joined together by the conjunctions *et*, *ou*, it is more elegant to repeat the pronoun before the second verb.

EXAMPLES.

polissez-*le* sans cesse et *le* repolissez — *polish and re-polish it continually*
gardez *les*, ou *les* renvoyez — *keep them or send them back*

EXERCISE.

Listen to *me*, do not condemn *me*, without a hearing. *Com-*
écouter * * *m'entendre* *se*

plain, thou hast just cause of complaint; however, do not *com-*
plaindre *un* *sujet* *plainte*

plain too bitterly of the injustice of mankind. Give *some*. Do
amèrement art. *homme* pl.

not give *any*. Think (*of it*). Do not think *of it*. Repeat *to them*
y

continually, that, without honesty, one can never succeed in the

world. Do not repeat *to them* continually the same things. Ac-

knowledge *him* as your master, and obey *him*. Tread upon
reconnaître *pour* *lui* *marcher*

that spider and kill it.
araignée f. *écraser*

228. When several pronouns accompany a verb, *me*, *te*, *se*, *nous*, *vous*, must precede the others: *le*, *la*, *les*, come before *lui*, *leur*; *y* comes before *en*, and *en* is always the last.

EXAMPLES.

Prêtez-moi ce livre; je vous *le* rendrai demain; si vous *me* *le* refusez, je saurai *m'en* passer — *lend me that book; I will return it to you to-morrow; if you refuse me, I can make shift without it*

aurez-vous la force de *le leur* dire?	*will you have resolution enough to tell it them?*
il n'a pas voulu *vous y* mener	*he would not take you there*
je *vous y en* porterai	*I will bring you some there*

EXCEPTION. In an imperative sentence, when affirmative, *le*, *la*, *les*, are always placed first, as, *donnez-le-moi*, give it me, *offrez-la-lui*, offer it to him; *conduisez-les-y*, conduct them thither: and *moi* is placed after *y*, as *menez-y-moi*, carry me thither: but *nous* must precede *y*, as, *menez-nous-y* carry us thither.

EXERCISE.

You wish to make a present to your sister. (There is) a beau-
vouloir * *Voilà*

tiful fan, you should present *her* with it. (How many
éventail m. *devoir* cond-1 *offrir lui* * *que de*

people are there without merit and without occupation, (who would
gens * * *ne tenir*

be mere nothings) in society, did not gaming introduce
à rien cond-1 art. *si* art. *jeu* m. *introduire* ind-2

them (into it). I shall speak *to them (about it)* and give *you* a
y *en* *je rendre* ind-7

faithful account *of it*. It is certain that old Géronte has re-
exact 2 *compte* m. 1 art.

fused his daughter to Valere; but because he does not give *her to*

him, it does not follow. that he will give *her to you*.
s'en suivre

229. REMARK. The word *même* is sometimes added to the pronouns *moi*, *toi*, *soi*, *nous*, *vous*, *eux*, *lui*, *elle*, *elles*, to assist in specifying more particularly the person, or thing spoken of.

EXAMPLES.

ils se sont perdus eux-mêmes	*they have ruined themselves*
le monde estime bien des choses qui, en elles-mêmes, sont fort méprisables	*the world prizes many things which, in themselves, are worthless*

DIRECTIONS ON THE USE OF THE PROPER PERSONAL PRONOUNS.

230. The direct regimen *me, te, le, la, nous, vous, les*, m. f. are used when the verb is active, i.e. when it requires no preposition before the noun which it governs, such as *donner un livre.*

EXAMPLES.

je le donne	*I give it*
vous le donnerez	*you will give it*
ne le donnez pas	*do not give it*

Aimer une personne.

EXAMPLES.

nous l'aimons	*we love him*
aimez-la	*love her*
il ne les aime pas	*he does not like them*
aimez-moi	*love me*

INDIRECT, (*dative.*)

231. The indirect *me, te, lui*, m. f. *nous, vous, leur*, m. f. are used when the preposition *à* must be placed before the noun they represent.

Thus, *donner une chose à une personne.*

EXAMPLES.

nous lui donnerons un gâteau	*we will give her a cake*
lui avez-vous envoyé la lettre?	*have you sent him the letter?*
ne me donnez pas de vin	*do not give me any wine*

À moi, à toi, à lui, à elle, à nous, à vous, à eux a elles, also express the dative; but in four cases only.

1st. After *penser, aller, courir, venir, boire en avoir.*

EXAMPLES.

nous penserons à lui	*we will think of him*
ils coururent à elle	*they ran to her*
en avez-vous à moi?	*are you angry with me?*

2nd. After reflected verbs,

adressez-vous à lui	*apply to him*

3rd. After *c'est*.

EXAMPLES.

c'est à moi à y aller	*it is my turn to go*
est-ce à vous à parler ainsi?	*is it for you to speak to me in this manner?*

4. When there are two datives

EXAMPLES.

je l'enverrai à vous et à elle	*I will send it to you and her*
il parlait à mon frère et à moi	*he was speaking to my brother and me*

232. *Y* is used in speaking of things in all cases, and is of both genders and numbers.* Thus, of a *lettre* f. we say:

mettez-y l'adresse	*put the direction to it*
j'y ajouterai un mot	*I will add a word to it*

Of a project, *projet* m.

EXAMPLES.

vous n'y réfléchissez pas assez	*you do not sufficiently think upon*
pensez-y un peu plus	*consider it a little more*

Of threats, *menaces*, f. pl.

EXAMPLE.

je n'y fais aucune attention	*I do not mind them*

* There are one or two exceptions mentioned in the following pages.

EXERCISE.

1. He has been speaking *to them* with such energy, as has astonished *them.*

2. Women ought to be very circumspect; for a mere appearance is sometimes more prejudicial *to them* than a real fault.

3. He comes up to me with a smiling air, and pressing my hand, says: My friend, I expect you to-morrow at my house.

4. He said *to me*: Wilt thou ever torment thyself for advantages, the enjoyment 2 of which 1 could not render *thee* more happy? Cast thy eyes round thee: see how every thing smiles on *thee*, and seems to invite *thee* to prefer a retired and tranquil life to the tumultuous pleasures of a vain 2 world 1.

5. The ambitious man * agitates, torments, and wastes *himself* to obtain the places or the honours to which he aspires; and when he has obtained *them*, he is still dissatisfied.

6. I have known *him* since his childhood, and I always loved *him* on account of the goodness of his temper.

7. That woman is always engaged in doing good works: you see *her* constantly consoling the unhappy, relieving the poor, reconciling enemies, and promoting the happiness of every one around *her*.

8. The more you live with men, the more you will be convinced that it is necessary to know *them* well before you* form a connection with them.

9. Enjoy the pleasures of the world, I consent *to it;* but never give yourself up *to them.*

(1.) Such energy as, *une force qui.*
(2.) *Mere*, simple; to be more prejudicial, *faire plus de tort.*
(3.) Comes up with, *aborder de;* pressing, *serrer;* my hand, *la main;* says, *il me dit;* at my house, *chez moi.*
(4.) Incessantly. *sans cesse;* advantages, *des biens;* could, *savoir*, cond-1; cast, *porter;* thy. *art;* smiles, *sourire à.*
(5). Destroys, *consumer;* to, *pour.*
(6.) Have known, *connaître*, ind-1; loved, ind 4; on account, *cause;* the goodness of his, *(his good);* temper, *caractère*, m.
(7.) In, *à;* works, *œuvres*, f. pl.; constantly, *sans cesse;* consoling, etc. inf-1 relieving, *assister;* promoting, *faire;* every one around her, *tout ce qui l'environne.*
(8). Live, ind-7; be convinced, *se convaincre*, ind-7; before, *avant de;* form a connection, *vous lier.*
(9.) Enjoy, *jouir de;* give yourself up, *se livrer.*

233. The regimen indirect *de moi, de toi, de lui, d'elle, de nous, de vous, d'eux, d'elles,* (the genitive and ablative cases) are used when the preposition *de* comes before the noun they represent. Thus,

Parler d'une personne, d'un homme.

EXAMPLE.

nous ne parlons pas de lui	*we do not speak of him*

Dépendre de son père.

EXAMPLES.

je dépends de lui	*I am dependant on him*
ils n'ont pas le droit de me parler ainsi, puisque je ne dépends pas d'eux.	*they have no right to speak to me in this manner, I am not their dependant.*

234. *En* is used in speaking of things, and is of both genders and numbers; as *s'abstenir de vin.*

EXAMPLES.

le vin m'est contraire, je m'en abstiendrai	*wine is bad for me I will abstain from it*
vous devriez vous en abstenir	*you should abstain from it*

EXERCISE

1. He was suddenly taken ill of the cholera and died of it
2. He is so absurd that every one laughs at him.
3. What reason has he to complain of me, what harm have I done him?
4. His fortune is very large, it is true, but he does not know how* to enjoy it.
5. Those are things which make a deep impression on the mind, I will remember them as long as I live.
6. Your things are exactly as they were when you left, no one has used them.
7. If you meet my brother, have the goodness to tell him that I shall want him at 5 o'clock precisely.
8. She must not be uneasy; we will think about her, but she must have patience.

(1.) *Avoir une attaque soudaine de,* ind-4; *mourir de,* ind-4.
(2.) To laugh, *se moquer de.*
(3.) *Se plaindre de;* harm, *mal.*
(4.) It is true, *j'en conviens;* to enjoy, *jouir de.*
(5.) Those are things, *ce sont de ces choses;* to remember, *se souvenir de;* to live, *vivre,* ind-7.
(6.) Things, *affaires;* as they were, *dans l'état où elles étaient;* to leave, *partir,* ind 4; to use, *se servir de,* ind-4.
(7.) To tell, *de dire;* to want, *avoir besoin de.*
(8.) To be uneasy, *s'inquiéter;* to think about, *s'occuper de;* to have patience, *patienter.*

PARTICULAR USE OF *y* AND *en*.

235. These two pronouns are very frequently used in French, in cases when they have no equivalent in English, or at least when it is always understood; they may be then considered as relative personal pronouns.

EN.

En stands for *some of them, some of it, any of them, any,* and refers to a noun antecedently named.

EXAMPLES.

si vous n'avez pas de manteau, je vous *en* prêterai un	*if you have no cloak, I will lend you one*
avez-vous un canif? oui, j'*en* ai un	*have you got a pen-knife? yes, I have*
ces oranges sont fort bonnes, envoyez-m'*en* deux douzaines	*these oranges are very good, send me two dozen*
à propos de fleurs, j'*en* ai de bien belles à vous montrer	*talking of flowers, I have beautiful ones to show you*

Y.

236. *Y* has generally been called an adverb because it may commonly be rendered by *there, here.* always understood; but it is frequently used for *in it, into it,* when it relates to *things* as well as to *places.*

EXAMPLES.

cette affaire est fort obscure, je n'y conçois rien	*this is a very obscure affair, I can make nothing of it*
cela ne m'intéresse nullement, je n'y suis pour rien	*this does not at all concern me, I have nothing to do with it*
si vous allez au spectacle, je serai bien aise d'y aller avec vous	*if you go to the play I shall be glad to go with you*

Y is used in speaking of persons with the verb *se fier*, and with *penser* in reference to a dead person.

EXAMPLES.

c'est un honnête homme, vous pouvez vous y fier	*he is an honest man, you may trust to him*
il est mort, on n'y pense plus	*he is dead, no one thinks of him any more*

EXERCISE.

1. Do you want a pen? here is a very good one.
2. He was in the garden then, but I do not think he is now.
3. Since you like game, I will send you a basket.
4. As to their father, although he has not been dead six months, they think no more of him.
5. I never could play chess; I cannot imagine, what pleasure you find in it.

(1.) To want, *falloir à*; here is, *voici*.
(2.) *Etre*, ind-2; he is, *être*, subj-1.
(3.) Game, *gibier*, m.
(4.) Although, etc., *quoiqu'il y ait six mois qu'il est mort*.
(5.) Could, *pouvoir*, ind-4; I cannot, *je ne saurais*.

USE OF *ce* INSTEAD OF *il, elle, ils, elles*, IN DESCRIPTIVE AND EXPLANATORY SENTENCES.

237. When we speak in reference to an object already named, *il, elle, ils, elles* are used according to its gender and number; but when we define objects, when we express what they are, *ce* must be used, as well of persons as of things, thus:

qu'est-ce que c'est que ce grand bâtiment, est-ce une église?	*what is that large building, is it a church?*
non, c'est la maison commune	*no, it is the town-hall*
savez-vous qui est ce monsieur?	*do you know who that gentleman is?*
oui, c'est un Allemand	*yes, he is a German*
chacun admire Cicéron et Démosthènes; ce sont les plus grands orateurs de l'antiquité	*every one admires Cicero and Demosthenes, they are the greatest orators of antiquity*

EXERCISE.

1. White negroes are degenerated blacks, but they are not a distinct species of men.
2. I will not trouble myself about them, they are ungrateful children.
3. What flowers are those? they are tulips just come from Holland; they cost me ten guineas each.
4. I do not know him, but they tell me he is a clever architect.
5. Have you noticed this box? it is a snuff-box which belonged to my grand-father.
6. She is certainly the prettiest girl in the room.

(1.) Distinct, *particulière.*
(2.) To trouble one's self about, *s'occuper de.*
(3.) What, etc., *comment nommez-vous ces fleurs-là?* just, *fraîchement.*
(4.) They tell me, *on me dit que.*
(5.) Noticed, *remarqué;* to belong, *appartenir,* Ind-2.
(6.) Certainly, *bien certainement.*

CASES WHERE THE PRONOUNS *lui*, *eux*, *elle*, *elles*, MAY APPLY TO THINGS.

238. The personal pronouns *lui*, *elle*, *eux*, *elles*, after some prepositions, apply to persons only. Thus in speaking of a woman, we must say: *je m'approchai d'elle, je m'assis près d'elle;* but in speaking of a table: *je m'en approchai, je m'assis auprès.*

However with the prepositions *avec*, *après*, *à*, *de*, *pour*, *en*, etc., *lui*, *elle*, *eux*, *elles*, may be applied to things. Thus it is correct to say of a river,

EXAMPLE.

cette rivière est si rapide quand elle déborde, qu'elle entraîne avec elle tout ce qu'elle rencontre; elle ne laisse après elle que du sable et des cailloux	*that river is so rapid when it overflows, that it carries away every thing it meets with in its course; it leaves nothing behind but sand and pebbles*

Of an enemy's company.

EXAMPLE.

nous marchâmes à elle	*we marched up to them*

Of things, reasons, truth, virtues and vices personified, etc. as:

ces choses sont bonnes d'elles-mêmes	*these things are good in themselves*
j'aime la vérité au point que je sacrifierais tout pour elle	*I love truth to that degree, that I would sacrifice every thing for it*
ces raisons sont solides en elles-mêmes	*those reasons are solid in themselves*

239. After the verb *être*, they are applied only to persons, and likewise when they are followed by the relatives *qui* and *que*, as: *c'est à elle, c'est d'elles que je parle, c'est elle-même qui vient.*

The same may be said of the pronoun *eux*, which is also generally applied to persons only, yet custom allows us to say,

ce chien et ces oiseaux font tout mon plaisir, je n'aime qu'eux; eux seuls sont mon amusement, je ne songe qu'à eux	*this dog and these birds are all my pleasure, I love nothing but them; they alone are my diversion, I think of nothing else*

240. *Lui* and *leur* are generally applied to persons, but are sometimes used in speaking of animals, plants, and even inanimate objects, with *donner*, *rendre*, *être redevable*, *devoir*, etc., as:

ces chevaux sont rendus, faites-leur donner un peu de vin	*those horses are exhausted, give them a little wine*
ces orangers vont périr, si on ne leur donne de l'eau	*these orange-trees will die unless they have a little water*
ces murs sont mal faits, on ne leur a pas donné assez de talus	*those walls are badly built, they have not sufficient inclination*

EXERCISE.

1. Virtue is the first of blessings; it is *from it* alone we are to expect happiness.

2. The labyrinth had been built upon the lake Meris, and they had given *it* a prospect proportioned to its grandeur.

3. Mountains are frequented on account of the air one breathes on them: how many people are indebted *to them* for the recovery of their health?

4. War brings in its train numberless evils.

5. It is a delicate 2 affair 1 which must not be too deeply investigated, it must be lightly passed over.

6. I have had my house repaired, and have given *it* an appearance quite * new.

7. Those trees are too much loaded: strip *them* of part of their fruit.

8. This book cost me a great deal, but I am indebted *to it* for my knowledge.

9. Self-love is captious; we, however, take *it* for our * guide; *to it* are all our actions directed, and *from it* we take counsel.

10. These arguments, although very solid *in themselves*, yet made no impression upon him, so strong a tie is habit.

11. These reasons convinced me, and *by them* I formed my decision.

12. I leave you the care of that bird; do not forget to give *it* water.

(1.) Blessings, *bien;* are, *devoir.*
(2.) Had been built, *on bâtir,* ind-6; prospect, *vue.*
(3.) On account, *à cause;* breathes, *respirer;* on them, *y;* are indebted for, *devoir;* recovery, *rétablissement.*
(4.) Brings, *entraîner;* in its train, *avec elle;* numberless, *bien des.*
(5.) Affair, *matière;* must, ind-1; be deeply investigated, *approfondir,* inf-1; be passed, *glisser;* over, *dessus.*
(6.) Have had, *faire,* ind-4; appearance, *air.*
(7.) Strip, *ôter à;* of part, *une partie.*
(8.) A great deal, *cher;* knowledge, *instruction.*
(9.) We, *(it is* it *that we);* to it, *(it is* to it *that we direct all, etc.);* direct, *rapporter;* from it, *(and it is* from it *that, etc.)*
(10.) No, *ne aucun;* so strong, etc. *(so much habit is a, etc.)* habit, *habitude.*
(11.) And from, *(and it is from them that);* by, *d'après;* formed my decision, *se décider.*

DIFFICULTY RESPECTING THE SUPPLYING PRONOUN *le* EXPLAINED.

241. Le is used in French to supply the place of an antecedent phrase, of a substantive or an adjective. In such case, its equivalent in English is *so* or *it*, which is almost always understood.

EXAMPLES.

je suis père, et vous *le* serez aussi un jour	*I am a father, and some day or other, you will be (one) also*
ils ne sont pas aussi riches que nous *le* sommes	*they are not so rich as we are (it, i. e. rich)*
je le ferai, si je *le* puis	*I will do it, if I can (do it)*

Le, thus used, is declined in some cases, and not in others.

When *le* supplies the place of a substantive, it then assumes the gender and number of that substantive, as: *Madame, êtes-vous la mère de cet enfant?—Oui, je la suis;* Madam, are you the mother of that child?—Yes, I am. *Mesdames, êtes-vous les parentes dont Monsieur m'a parlé?—Oui, nous les sommes.*

EXERCISE.

1. The laws of nature and decency oblige us equally to defend the honour and interest of our parents, when we can do *it* without injustice.
2. We ought not to condemn, after their death, those that have not been *condemned* during their life.
3. Is that your idea?—Can you doubt that it is?
4. Are you Mrs. Such-a-one?—Yes, I am.
5. Are those your servants?—Yes, they are.
6. Ladies, are you glad to have seen the new piece?—Yes, we are.
7. I, a * slave! I, born to command! alas! it is but too true that I am *so*.
8. She was jealous of her authority, and she must be *so*.
9. Was there ever a girl more unhappy, and treated with more ridicule than I am?
10. You have found me amiable: why have I ceased to appear so to you?

(1.) Decency, *bienséance*.
(2.) We ought, *falloir;* condemned, *le*.
(3.) Idea, *pensée;* that it is, *ce être*, subj-1.
(4.) Mrs. *madame;* such-a-one, *un tel*.
(5.) Those, *ce là;* they, *ce*.
(6.) Ladies, *mesdames*.
(7.) Slave, *esclave;* but, *ne que*.
(8.) Must, *devoir*, ind-2.
(9.) With more ridicule, *plus ridiculement*.

11. Have we ever been so quiet as we are?
12. Madam, are you married?—Yes, I am.
13. Madam, are you the bride?—Yes, I am.

242. When *le* supplies an antecedent, adjective or a verb, it is undeclined.

EXAMPLES.

je le ferai si je le puis (le faire) *I will do it if I can*
Madame, êtes-vous enrhumée?—Oui, je le suis.
Mesdames, êtes-vous contentes de ce discours?—Oui, nous le sommes.
Fut-il jamais une femme plus malheureuse que je le suis?

REMARK. The *le* is also undeclined, when substantives are used adjectively, as:

Madame, êtes-vous mère?—Oui, je le suis.
Mesdames, êtes-vous parentes?—Oui, nous le sommes.
Elle est fille, et le sera toute sa vie.

But it is declined if the adjectives be used substantively, as:

Madame, êtes-vous la malade?—Oui, je la suis.

Therefore this question: *êtes-vous fille de M. le duc?* is to be answered, *oui, je le suis;* but this, *êtes-vous la fille de M. le duc?* it is to be by *Oui, je la suis.*

REPETITION OF THE PERSONAL PRONOUNS.

243. Pronouns in the first and second persons, when the subject, must be repeated before every verb, if each of them is in different tenses. It is always even preferable to repeat them, when the verbs are in the same tense.

EXAMPLES.

je soutiens et je soutiendrai toujours	*I maintain, and (I) will always maintain*
vous dites, et vous avez toujours dit	*you say, and (you) have always said*
accablé de douleur, je m'écriai, et je dis	*overwhelmed with sorrow, I exclaimed and (I) said*
nous nous promenions sur le haut du rocher, et nous voyions sous nos pieds, etc.	*we were walking upon the summit of the rock, and we saw under our feet, etc.*

In all cases, these pronouns must be repeated, though the tenses of the verbs be the same, if the first is followed by a regimen, or accusative.

EXAMPLE.

vous aimerez le seigneur votre Dieu, et vous observerez sa loi	*you shall love the Lord your God, and (you shall) observe his law*

244. The pronouns of the third person, when the subject, are hardly ever repeated before verbs, except those verbs be in different tenses.

EXAMPLES.

la bonne grâce ne gâte rien; elle ajoute à la beauté, relève la modestie, et y donne du lustre	*a graceful manner spoils nothing; it adds to beauty, heightens modesty, and gives it lustre*
il n'a jamais rien valu, et ne vaudra jamais rien	*he never was good for any thing, and never will be*
il est arrivé ce matin, et il repartira ce soir	*he is arrived this morning, and (he) will set off again this evening*

EXERCISE.

1. My dear child, *I* love you, and *I* shall never cease to love you: but it is that very love that I have for you which obliges me to correct you for your faults, and to punish you when you deserve it.

2. *I* heard and admired these words, which comforted me a little, but my mind was not sufficiently free to make him a reply.

3. *Thou* art young, and *thou* aimest, no doubt, at the glory of surpassing thy comrades.

4. God has said : *you* shall love your enemies, bless those that curse you, do good to those that persecute you, and pray for those who slander you. What a difference between these morals and those of philosophers !

(1.) Correct for, *reprendre de.*
(2.) Heard, *écouter*, ind-2; words, *discours*, sing.; my mind, etc. *(I had not the mind, etc.)*; sufficiently free, *assez libre*; to make a reply, *répondre à.*
(3.) Aimest at, *aspirer à*; surpassing, *l'emporter sur*, etc.
(4.) Slander, *calomnier*; between, *de*; morals, *morale, f.*; and that, *à celle.*

However, perspicuity requires the repetition of the pronoun, when the second verb is preceded by a long incidental phrase, as : *il fond sur son ennemi, et, après l'avoir saisi d'une main victorieuse, il le renverse, comme le cruel aquilon abat les tendres moissons qui dorent la campagne.*

EXERCISE.

1. *He* took the strongest cities, conquered the most considerabl provinces, and overturned the most powerful empires.

2. *He* takes a hatchet, completely cuts down the mast which was already broken, throws it into the sea, jumps upon it amidst the furious billows, calls me by my name, and encourages me to follow him.

3. *He* marshals the soldiers, marches at their head, advances in good order towards the enemy, attacks and routs them, and after having entirely routed them, (he) cuts them to pieces.

(1.) *Overturned*, renverser.
(2.) Completely cuts down, *achever* - *couper*; jumps upon it, *s'élancer dessus*; billows, *onde.*
(3.) Marshals, *ranger en bataille*; routs, *renverser*; entirely routed, *achever de mettre en désordre*; cuts, *tailler.*

245. A personal pronoun, when the *subject*, must be repeated before verbs, when passing from an affirmation to a negation, and *vice versâ*, or when the verbs are joined by a conjunction, except *et* and *ni.*

EXAMPLES.

Il veut, et il ne veut pas — *he will and he will not*

il donne d'excellents principes, parce qu'il sait que les progrès ultérieurs en dépendent	*he lays down excellent principles, because he knows that upon them depends all further progress*
il donne et reçoit	*he gives and receives*
il ne donne ni ne reçoit	*he neither gives nor receives*

Pronouns, when the regimen or the object are repeated before every verb.

EXAMPLES.

l'idée de ses malheurs le poursuit, le tourmente et l'accable	*the idea of his misfortunes pursues (him), torments (him), and overwhelms him*
il nous ennuie et nous obsède sans cesse	*he wearies (us) and besets us unceasingly*

EXCEPTION. They are not repeated before such compound verbs as express the repetition of the same action, and when the verbs are in the same tense, as:

Je vous le dis et redis, il le fait et refait sans cesse.

EXERCISE.

1. It is inconceivable how whimsical she is; from one moment to another *she* will and *she* will not.

2. The Jews are forbidden to work on the sabbath; *they* are as it * were * locked in slumber; *they* light no fire, and carry no water.

3. For nearly a week *she* has neither eaten nor drunk.

4. The soldier was not repressed by authority, but stopped from satiety and shame.

(1.) *(She is of a whimsical cast inconceivable)* whimsical cast, *bizarrerie* f.
(2.) *(It is forbidden to)*, forbidden, *défendre*; sabbath, *jour du sabbat*; locked, *enchaîné*; slumber, *repos*; light, *allumer*.
(3.) For, *depuis*; nearly, *près de*, a week, *huit jours*; has eaten....drunk, Ind-1.
(4.) Repressed, *réprimer*; stopped, *s'arrêter*, Ind-3; from, *par*.

RELATION OF THE PRONOUN OF THE THIRD PERSON TO A NOUN EXPRESSED BEFORE.

246. The pronouns of the third person, *il*, *ils*, *elle*, *elles*, *le*, *la*, *les*, must always relate to a noun, whether subject or regimen, taken only in a definite

sense, antecedently expressed; but they must not be applied to a subject and regimen, at the same time.

EXAMPLES.

la rose est la reine des fleurs, aussi est-*elle* l'emblême de la beauté	*the rose is the queen of flowers; therefore it is the emblem of beauty*
j'aime l'ananas; il est exquis	*I like the pine-apple; it is delicious*

EXERCISE.

1. It is taste that selects the expressions, that combines, arranges, and varies *them*, so as to produce the greatest effect.

2. Horace answered his stupid critics not so much to instruct *them*, than to shew their ignorance, and let *them* see that they did not even know what poetry was.

3. Man embellishes nature itself; he cultivates, extends, and polishes it.

4. The Messiah is expected by the Hebrews; *he* comes and calls the Gentiles, as had been announced by the prophecies; the people that acknowledge *him* as come, is incorporated with the people that expected *him*, without a single moment of interruption.

(1.) So as to, *de manière à ce qu'elles*, subj-1.
(2.) Stupid, *sot;* not so much, *moins;* to, *pour;* show, *(to them)*, their, etc.; let see, *faire entendre;* was, *c'était que.*
(4.) Gentiles, *Gentil;* (the prophecies had announced it); acknowledges, *reconnaître;* with, *à;* without, *sans qu'il y ait;* single, *seul.*

But the two following sentences would be equivocal:

Racine a imité *Euripide*, en tout ce qu'*il* a de plus beau dans sa Phèdre	*Racine has imitated Euripides in all that he has most beautiful in his Phedra*
le légat publia une sentence d'interdit; *il* dura trois mois	*the legate published a sentence of interdiction; it lasted three months*

because, in the first of these two sentences, *il* may relate, either to *Racine*, or to *Euripides;* and, from the construction of the second sentence, *il*, relating to *interdit*, appears also to relate to *légat*. Again, it is not altogether correct to say:

nulle paix pour l'impie; il *la* cherche, *elle* fuit	no peace *for the wicked: he seek it, it flies*

Because, from the construction, the pronouns *la* and *elle* seem to relate to *nulle paix,* whereas their real antecedent is the substantive *paix*, but without the negative *nulle.*

EXERCISE.

1. Poetry embraces all sorts of subjects; *it* takes in every thing that is most brilliant in history; *it* enters the fields of philosophy; *it* soars to the skies; *it* plunges into the abyss; *it* penetrates to the dead; *it* makes the universe its domain; and if this world be not sufficient, *it* creates new ones, which *it* embellishes with enchanting abodes, which *it* peoples with a thousand various inhabitants.

2. Egypt aimed at greatness; and wished to * strike the eye at a distance, always pleasing *it* by the justness of proportion.

3. Egypt, satisfied with its own territory, where every thing was in abundance, thought not of conquests; *it* extended itself in another manner, by sending colonies to every part of the globe. and with *them* politeness and laws.

(1.) Subjects, *matière;* takes in, *se charger de;* that is, *y avoir de; (in)* the fields, soars to, *s'élancer dans;* plunges, *s'enfoncer;* to, *chez; (its domain of the universe);* be sufficient, *suffire;* ones, *monde;* enchanting, *enchanté;* abodes, *demeure;* various, *divers.*

(2.) Greatness, *grand;* wished, *vouloir;* eye, pl.; at a distance, *dans l'éloignement; (in)* pleasing, *contenter.*

(3.) Was in abundance, *abonder;* thought of, *songer à;* in, *de;* by, *en;* to, *par:* part of the globe, *terre.*

ON THE PRONOUN *soi.*

247. *Soi* is generally accompanied by a preposition, and is used in phrases, where there is an indeterminate pronoun either expressed, or understood: *on doit rarement parler de soi ; il est essentiel de prendre garde à soi.* In this case, it is the regimen indirect; but it may be employed without a preposition.

1. With the verb *être*, as: *en cherchant à tromper les autres, c'est souvent* soi *qu'on trompe* or *on est souvent trompé soi-même,* in attempting to deceive others, we frequently deceive ourselves. In this situation it is the subject.

2. After *ne que*, or by opposition, as:

n'aimer que soi, c'est n'être bon à rien	*to love only ourselves, is being good for very little*
penser ainsi, c'est s'aveugler soi-même	*to think in this manner, is to blind one's-self*

It is, in these examples, the regimen; but when *de soi* and *en soi* are used in a definite sense, in speaking of things, they mean *de sa nature* and *dans sa nature.*

EXERCISE.

1. To excuse in *one's-self* the follies which one cannot excuse in others, is to prefer being a fool *ones-self* to seeing others so.
2. To be too much dissatisfied with *ourselves* is a weakness; but to be too much satisfied *(with ourselves)* is *(a)* folly.
3. We ought to despise no one: how often have we needed the assistance of one more insignificant than *ourselves?*
4. If we did not attend so much to *ourselves,* there would be less selfishness in the world.
5. Vice is odious in *itself.*
6. The loadstone attracts iron (to *itself.*)

(1.) Follies, *sottises;* others, *autrui;* prefer, *aimer mieux;* fool, *sot;* to seeing, *que de voir;* so, *tel.*
(3.) We ought, *falloir,* ind-1; how often, *combien de fois;* we, *on;* needed the assistance, *n'avoir pas besoin;* insignificant, *petit.*
(4.) We, *on;* attend to, *s'occuper de;* selfishness, *égoïsme.*
(6.) Loadstone, *aimant.*

POSSESSIVE PRONOUNS.

248. Possessive pronouns, conjunctive as: *mon, ma, mes;* relative, as: *le mien, la mienne, les miens, les miennes,* agree in gender and number with the noun to which they are joined or are related.

Its, their, (his, her,) which, in English, are used in reference to things, are rendered by *son, sa, ses,* according as the case requires; thus, in speaking of England, we say:

son parlement est le *sanctuaire de* la plus sage politique	*her parliament is the seat of the wisest policy*

son roi n'*a de* pouvoir que pour faire le bien	*her king possesses power only to do good*
elle envoie *ses* flottes dans toutes les mers	*she sends her fleet in all the seas*

249. But, sometimes by the construction of the phrase, ITS may be turned by *of it;* then, it is not rendered by a possessive pronoun, but by the personal pronoun *en*, which, is it not been explained, is placed before the verb, Thus, speaking again of England, we say:

tout enfin contribue à m'*en* faire aimer *le* séjour; j'*en* admire surtout *l*'exacte police, en même temps que *les* lois m'*en* paraissent extrêmement sages	*in short every thing conspires to make me love its sojourn; I particularly admire the strictness of her police, at the same time that her laws appear to me extremely wise*
regardez cet arbre, n'*en* admirez-vous pas la fraîcheur?	*look at that tree, do you not admire its freshness?*

EXERCISE.

1. A new custom was a phenomenon in Egypt; for which reason, there never was a people that preserved so long *its* customs, *its* laws, and even *its* ceremonies.

2. Solomon abandons himself to the love of women: *his* understanding declines, *his* heart fails and *his* piety degenerates into idolatry.

3. That superb temple was upon the summit of a hill: *its* columns were of Parian marble, and *its* gates of gold.

4. Laocoon is one of the finest statues in France: not only the whole, but all *its* features, even the least, are admirable.

5. The Thames is a magnificent river: *its* channel is so wide and so deep, below London Bridge, that several thousands of vessels lie at their ease in it.

6. This fine country is justly admired by foreigners: *its* climate is delightful, *its* soil fruitful, *its* laws wise, and *its* government just and moderate.

7. The trees of that orchard have sun enough, yet *its* fruits are but indifferent.

8. The Seine has *its* source in Burgundy, *its* mouth is at Havre-de-Grace.

9. The pyramids of Egypt astonish, both by the enormity of *their* bulk, and the justness of *their* proportions.

10. Egypt alone could erect monuments for posterity: *its* obelisks are to this day, as well for *their* beauty as for *their* height, the principal ornaments of Rome

11. History and geography throw mutual light on each other: a * perfect knowledge *of them* ought to enter into the plan of good education.

(1.) Phenomenon, *prodige;* for which reason, *aussi;* a, *de;* preserved, subj.-s.
(2.) Understanding, *esprit;* declines, *baisser;* fails, *s'affaiblir.*
(3.) Summit, *haut;* hill, *colline;* Parian, *de Paros.*
(4.) In, *qu'il y ait en;* the whole, *l'ensemble;* even, *jusqu'à.*
(5.) Magnificent, *superbe;* channel, *lit;* below, *au-dessous de;* lie at, *être à*, their, *art.;* in it, *y.*
(6.) Justly, *avec raison;* soil, *sol;* *the verb* être *must be repeated.*
(7.) Have sun enough, *être bien exposé;* but indifferent, *assez mauvais.*
(8.) Mouth, *embouchure;* Havre, *le Hâvre.*
(9.) Both, *également et;* bulk, *masse;* and, *et par.*
(10.) Egypt alone could, *il n'appartenait qu'à l'Egypte de;* erect, *élever;* to this day, *encore aujourd'hui;* as well for, *autant par;* height, *hauteur.*
(11.) Throw mutual light, etc. *s'éclairer l'une par l'autre;* of them, (their).

250. *Mine, thine, his, hers, ours, yours, theirs,* which, in English, are used with *to be,* in the sense of *to belong,* are expressed, in French, by *à moi, à toi, à lui, à elle, à nous, à vous, à eux, à elles.*

EXAMPLES.

ce cheval est-il *à vous?*	*is this horse yours?*
on dirait à l'entendre que le monde est *à lui*	*he talks as if the world were his*

251. The forms *my father's, your uncle's,* etc., etc. are also rendered *à mon père, à votre oncle.*

EXAMPLE.

la maison que nous habitons est (ou appartient) à Monsieur B.	*the house we inhabit is Mr. B's*

EXERCISE.

The carriage is not theirs, it is their uncle's. If this house was mine I would sell it, for I do not like its situation. You have no right to give what is not yours. This pretty dog is my sister's, I have promised to take care of it in her absence.

No right, *le droit de.* In, *pendant.*

252. *Les miens, les tiens, les siens, les nôtres, les vôtres,* are used to express one's family, relations, clients, etc.

EXAMPLES.

il est allé en Amérique avec tous les siens	*he has gone to America with his family*
toi et les tiens vous avez toujours mal parlé de moi	*you and your whole race have always spoken ill of me*

253. *A friend of yours, a horse of mine*, and such phrases, are turned in this manner in French, *un de vos amis, un de mes chevaux.**

EXAMPLE.

c'est un de ses tours	*this is a trick of his*

254. In speaking to a person of his own relations, politeness requires that we put: ***monsieur***, ***madame***, ***mademoiselle***, ***messieurs***, ***mesdames***, ***mesdemoiselles***, before the possessive pronoun.

EXAMPLES.

j'ai rencontré Monsieur votre père	*I met your father*
Messieurs vos frères sont-ils arrivés ?	*are your brothers come ?*

255. Custom requires the use of the possessive pronoun before the names of relations, in addressing them.

EXAMPLES.

ma sœur, venez ici que je vous parle	*sister, come here, I want to speak to you*
mon oncle, quand partez-vous ?	*uncle, when do you go ?*

EXCEP. *Papa, maman.*

* ***This is no business of yours***, must be rendered by ***ce n'est pas là votre affaire***, or ***cette affaire là ne vous regarde pas***. This is applicable to any sentence which may not be turned, like the above, by *this is one of his tricks*; *that brother of yours* must, therefore, be turned by *your brother*.

256. Possessive pronouns are repeated before every noun of the same sentence.

EXAMPLES.

mon père et ma mère* sont venus.	*my father and mother have come.*
donnez-moi mon habit et mon chapeau.	*give me my coat and hat.*

257. When two adjectives qualify the same noun, the pronoun possessive is repeated, if they express opposite or incompatible qualities; it is not repeated, in the contrary case.

EXAMPLES.

je lui ai montré mes beaux et mes vilains habits.	*I showed him both my fine and ugly dresses.*
je lui ai montré mes beaux et magnifiques habits.	*I showed him my beautiful and magnificent dresses.*

EXERCISE.

1. I fear neither you nor yours.
2. He left France with all his family at the time of the revolution.
3. A friend of mine told me this morning that Parliament is to be dissolved.
4. That son of yours will give you a great deal of trouble.
5. Is your mother returned from the country?
6. Allow me to congratulate you on your brother's appointment.
7. Cousin, I am glad to see you; when did you return?
8. I believe that his father and mother are dead.

(1.) *Ne craindre ni.*
(2.) To leave, *abandonner.*
(3.) *Dire*, ind-4; is to be, etc., *que l'on va dissoudre le.*
(4.) Trouble, *embarras.*
(6.) Appointment, *nomination.*
(7.) When did you, etc., *depuis quand êtes-vous de retour?*

* Custom admits *mes père et mère*, my father and mother, instead of *mon père et ma mère;* it admits also, *ses père et mère. vos père et mère.*

PARTS OF THE BODY, PHYSICAL AND INTELLECTUAL FACULTIES.

258. There is peculiarity of construction, with regard to these, which requires particular attention and notice. The French in speaking of them do not generally, make use of the possessive pronoun, but of the definite article.

EXAMPLES.

j'ai mal à la tête*,	*I have a pain in my head.*
j'ai reçu un coup de feu au bras droit,	*I received a shot in my right arm.*
il a perdu l'esprit,	*he has lost his senses.*
mieux vaut perdre la vie que l'honneur,	*better lose one's life than one's honour.*
la tête me fait mal,	*my head aches.*

259. When speaking of any thing done to any part of the body, or of the understanding, such as *to wash one's hands, to improve one's mind*, a pronoun, in the dative case, is placed in conjunction with the verb, in order to show *whose hands, whose understanding* are thus affected; *me laver les mains, lui former l'esprit*, to wash my hands, to form his mind.

If the thing is done *to ourselves*, and *by ourselves*, the verb is reflected.

EXAMPLES.

je me lave les mains,	*I wash my hands*, or *I wash the hands to myself.*
tu te coupes le doigt,	*you cut your finger.*
il se fait la barbe,	*he shaves his beard.*
nous nous rinçons la bouche,	*we wash our mouths.*
nous nous sommes lavé les mains,	*we have washed our hands.*
vous vous formez l'esprit,	*you improve your mind.*
ils s'enrichissent la mémoire,	*they enrich their memory.*

* The reason of this custom is that there cannot be any ambiguity as to whose head is aching, and, consequently, that the definite article is sufficient.

260. If the thing is done *to another*, the indirect regimen, *me, te, lui, nous, vous, leur,* are used with the verb, according to the rules 224, 225, and 225*.

EXAMPLES.

vous me blessez la main,	*you hurt my hand,* or *you hurt the hand to me.*
tenez-moi la tête,	*hold my head.*
vous lui avez cassé le bras,	*you have broken his arm.*
ils nous ont fendu la tête,	*they split our head.*
vous ai-je marché sur le pied ?	*did I tread on your foot?*
on leur a arraché les yeux,	*they tore their eyes out.*

EXERCISE.

1. Our carriage passed over his body, and broke two ribs.
2. Writing so long makes* my hand ache.
3. She was so shocked by the sudden death of her husband, that she lost her mind.
4. Come, give me your hand, let us be friends.
5. Do not cut your nails with my penknife, you will spoil it.
6. Where did he lose his leg?
7. You have not washed your face.
8. Who has cut your hair?
9. Have you not cut your finger?
10. Last year, I sprained my foot, by leaping over a ditch.
11. The wound is so bad that they say they will be obliged to amputate his leg.
12. She took my hand, and put a pretty ring on my little finger.

(1.) To pass over, *passer sur.*
(2.) *A force d'écrire;* to ache, *faire mal.*
(3.) Shocked, *affecté;* to lose, *en perdre,* ind-3.
(5.) Nails, *ongles.*
(6.) To lose, *perdre,* ind-4.
(8.) Hair, *les cheveux.*
(10.) To sprain, *se donner une entorse à.*
(11.) They will be obliged, *il faudra.*
(12.) Put, *mettre,* ind-3; on, *à.*

261. If however the part of the body spoken of be the subject of the verb, it is then necessary to use the possessive pronoun, otherwise there would be ambiguity.

EXAMPLES.

je vois que ma jambe enfle, *I see my leg is swelling.*
son esprit succomba, *his mind failed.*

In some other cases, it is also necessary to use the possessive pronoun for the sake of clearness.

EXAMPLES.

il lui donna *sa* main à baiser, *he gave him his hand to kiss.*
elle a donné hardiment *son* bras au chirurgien, *she courageously presented her arm to the surgeon.*

EXERCISE.

1. In this interview, they made each other presents; she gave him *her* portrait, and he gave her his finest diamond.
2. A young surgeon preparing to bleed the great Condé, this prince said to him smiling, do not you tremble to bleed me? I, my lord, no, certainly; it is not I, it is you who ought to tremble. The prince, charmed with the reply, immediately gave him *his* arm.

(1.) Interview, *entrevue;* made each other, *se faire mutuellement.*
(2.) Preparing, *se disposer;* bleed, *saigner;* smiling, *d'un air riant;* it is not I, (it is not to me); it is you, (it is to you); who ought to, *de;* reply, *repartie.* f.

262. Although verbs which are conjugated with two pronouns of the same person generally remove every kind of amphibology, yet custom authorizes some familiar expressions, although the possessive pronoun seems to be redundant, as:

il se tient ferme sur *ses* pieds, *he stands firm upon his feet.*
je l'ai vu, *de mes propres yeux*, *I have seen it with my own eyes.*

When speaking of an habitual complaint, the possessive pronoun is also properly used, as:

Sa *migraine l'a repris,* *his head-ache is returned.*

EXERCISE.

1. Whatever he may do, he always finds himself safe.
2. Can you still doubt the truth of what I tell you? Would you

ask a stronger proof than that I give you, it is that I heard it, yes, heard it with *my* own ears.

3. *My* gout does not allow me a moment's repose.

4. It is in vain that I exhort you to work and study; *your* idleness, that cruel disease under which you labour, renders useless all the exhortations of friendship.

(1.) Finds himself, *se retrouver*; safe, *sur ses jambes*.
(2.) Can, cond-1; doubt, *douter de*; ask, *exiger*.
(3.) Allow *laisser*.
(4.) It is in vain that I, *je avoir beau*; you labour, *qui vous travaille*.

DEMONSTRATIVE PRONOUNS.

For their concord with the noun, see Nos. 70, 71, 72.

263. ETRE, used in conjunction with *ce*, must be in the singular, although relating to the first and second person plural.

EXAMPLES:

c'est moi qui l'ai dit,	*it is I who said so*
ce sera vous qui en jouirez,	*you will be the person to enjoy it.*
est-ce nous qui vous avons trompé?	*is it we who deceived you?*
ce n'est pas lui que j'ai envoyé chercher,	*he is not the person I sent for.*

264. With regard to the third person plural, the verb ÊTRE is sometimes plural, sometimes singular; this difference does not arise from any rule or principle, but merely from custom, and, as it cannot be explained, an example of each case is given for reference.

C'EST with *eux*, *elles*.

EXAMPLES.

ce sont eux,	est-ce eux?
ce sont elles,	est-ce elles?
ce furent eux,	est-ce que ce furent-eux?
ce seront eux,	sera-ce eux ou elles?
que ce soient eux,	seraient-ce eux ou elles?
que ce fussent eux.	

265. C'EST with nouns substantives.

EXAMPLES.

ce sont les français qui,	sont-ce les français qui.
c'étaient les gardes qui,	étaient-ce les gardes?
ce seront les anglais qui,	est-ce que ce seront les anglais?
ce furent les allemands qui,	est-ce que ce furent les allemands?

ce sont ses élèves, qui lui ont fait ce présent,	*his pupils have made him this present.*
on dit que ce seront les grenadiers, qui feront le service du château,	*they say the grenadiers are to be on duty at the castle.*
sont-ce les honneurs que vous cherchez?	*is it honours that you seek?*

266. CE is used before *être*, instead of the pronouns *il*, *elle*, *ils*, *elles*, in reference to a noun, singular or plural, antecedently named, at the beginning of the sentence which declares the nature or the actions of such a noun. Thus, having mentioned the Phenicians, we say:

ce furent eux qui inventèrent l'écriture,	*they were the inventors of writing.*
lisez Homère et Virgile: *ce sont les* plus grands *poètes* de l'antiquité.	*read Homer and Virgil: they are the best poets of antiquity.*
la douceur, l'affabilité et une certaine urbanité, distinguent l'homme qui vit dans le grand monde; *ce sont là les marques* auxquelles on le reconnaît,	*gentleness, affability, and a certain urbanity, distinguish the man that frequents polite company; these are marks by which he may be known.*
avez-vous lu Platon? *c'est un* des plus beaux génies de l'antiquité,	*have you read Plato? he is one of the greatest geniuses of antiquity.*

But, when the verb *être* is followed by an adjective, or by a substantive taken adjectively, *il* or *elle*, must be used.

EXAMPLES.

lisez Démosthènes et Cicéron ; *ils sont très-éloquents,*	*read Demosthenes and Cicero ; they are very eloquent.*
j'ai vu l'hôpital de Greenwich ; *il est magnifique et digne* d'une grande nation,	*I have seen Greenwich Hospital; it is superb, and worthy of a great nation.*
compteriez-vous sur Valère ? ignorez-vous qu'*il est homme à* ne jamais revenir de ses premières idées ?	*would you rely upon Valère ? do you not know that he is a man who will never abandon his first opinions ?*

267. A distinction is made in English, as to the singular or the plural, in sentences like these, *this is my horse, these are my children ; ce* is again used in French before both numbers.

EXAMPLES.

c'est-là mon cheval,	ce sont mes enfants.

or

voici *or* voilà mon cheval,	voici mes enfants.

EXERCISE.

1. It is *we* who have drawn that misfortune upon * us, through our thoughtlessness and imprudence.

2. *It was* the Egyptians that first observed the course of the stars, regulated the year, and invented arithmetic.

3. Peruse attentively Plato and Cicero : *they are* the two *philosophers* of antiquity who have given us the most sound and luminous ideas upon morality.

4. If you are intended for the pulpit, read over and over again Bourdaloue and Massillon : *they are* both very *eloquent ;* but the aim of the former is to convince, and that of the latter to persuade.

5. Are not these the gloves you *bought* yesterday? This is not my house. These are not my books ; mine are in another room.

(1.) Have drawn, *s'attirer ;* thoughtlessness, *légèreté.*
(2.) First, *les premiers ;* stars, *astre.*
(3.) Peruse, *lire ;* sound, *sain :* morality, *morale.*
(4.) Are intended for, *se destiner à ;* pulpit, *chaire ;* read over and over again, *lire et relire sans cesse ;* aim, *but*
(5.) To buy, *acheter,* ind-4.

268. Ce is much used in conjunction with *qui, dont, à quoi, que*, in the sense of *what, that which, that thing which.* It is used in speaking of things only, and the adjective which relates to it, is of the masculine gender singular.

EXAMPLE.

ce qui flatte est plus dangereux que *ce qui offense*,	*what flatters is more dangerous than what offends.*

Ce, joined to the relative pronouns, *qui, que, dont*, and *quoi*, has, in some instances, a construction peculiar to itself. Both *ce* and the relative pronoun that follows it, form, with the verb which they precede, the subject of another phrase, of which the verb is always *être*. Now, *être* may be followed by another verb, an adjective, or a noun.

When *être* is followed by another verb, the demonstrative *ce* must be repeated, as:

ce que j'aime le plus, *c'est* d'être seul.	*what I like most is to be alone.*

When followed by an adjective, the demonstrative *ce* is not repeated, as:

ce dont vous venez de me parler *est* horrible,	*what you have been mentioning to me is horrid.*

When *être* is followed by a substantive, the demonstrative may either be repeated, or not, at pleasure, except in the case of a plural, or of a personal pronoun. Thus:

ce que je dis, *est* la vérité, *or*, *c'est* la vérité	*what I say is truth*
ce qui m'indigne, *ce sont* les in-	*what provokes me, are the injuries*

justices, qu'on ne cesse de faire	*which are continually committed*
ce qui m'arrache au sentiment qui m'accable, *c'est vous*	*what alleviates the grief that oppresses me, is you*

EXERCISE.

1. *What* is astonishing *is* not always *what is* pleasing.
2. *What* the miser thinks least *of*, is to enjoy his riches.
3. *What* pleases us in the writings of the ancients, *is* to see that they have taken nature as a model, and that they have painted her with noble simplicity.
4. *What* that good king has done for the happiness of his people, deserves to be handed down to the remotest posterity.
5. *What* constitutes poetry *is not* the exact number and regular cadence of syllables: but *it is* the sentiment which animates every thing, the lively fictions, bold figures, and the beauty and variety of the imagery: *it is* the enthusiasm, fire, impetuosity, force, a something in the words and thoughts which nature alone can impart.
6. *What* we justly admire in Shakspeare *are* those characters always natural and always well* sustained.
7. *What* keeps me attached to life, *is you*, my son, whose tender age has still need of my care and advice.

(1.) To be astonishing, *étonner*; to be pleasing, *plaire*.
(2.) What, (that to which); miser, *avare*.
(3.) As a, *pour*.
(4.) Deserves, *être digne*; to be handed down, *être transmis*; remotest, *la plus reculée*.
(5.) Constitutes, *faire*; exact, *fixe*; lively, *vif*; imagery, *image*, pl; a something, *un je ne sais quoi*; words, *parole*; impart, *donner*.
(6.) We, *on*; justly, *avec justice*; natural, *dans la nature*; sustained, *soutenu*.
(7) Keeps attached, *attacher*; care, advice, pl.

269. *Celui, celle, ceux, celles* are frequently used in conjunction with the relatives *qui, dont, auquel, à laquelle*, and *que* in the sense of *he who, she who, they who*, or *whom, whichever, whoever*, and *that which*, etc.

EXAMPLES.

celui qui ne pense qu'à lui seul, dispense les autres d'y penser	*he who thinks of nobody but himself, excuses others from thinking of him*

votre nouvelle est plus sûre que celle qu'on débitait hier,	*your intelligence is more authentic than that which was circulated yesterday.*
celui qui arrivera le premier l'aura,	*whichever comes first shall have it.*
ce n'est pas là celui dont nous parlions,	*this is not the one we were speaking of. It was not this we were speaking of.*

In these two cases it is applied both to persons and things.

270. *Celui, celle, etc.* are also followed by a genitive case.

EXAMPLE.

cette maison ne m'appartient pas, c'est celle de mon oncle,	*this house does not belong to me, it is my uncle's.*

271. WHICH, standing for *that which, a thing which*, and having a sentence for its antecedent, is rendered by *ce qui* in French.

EXAMPLES.

il a plu toute la nuit, ce qui nous a empêchés de sortir ce matin	*it rained all night, which prevented our going out this morning*

272. *This day week, this day month, this day twelve months*, are rendered thus: *d'aujourd'hui en huit, dans huit jours, dans un mois, au bout d'un an.*

273. *Celui* is sometimes omitted, and this turn gives strength and elegance to the expression, as:

qui veut trop se faire craindre, se fait rarement aimer	*he who wishes to make himself too much feared, seldom makes himself beloved*

274. *Ceci* and *cela* apply only to things, and when they have not been named, and are mentioned in an indeterminate manner.

ne touchez pas à cela	*do not touch that*

However, in the familiar style, custom authorizes us to say, in speaking of one person individually, or of many collectively; cela *est heureux! cela croupit dans la fange; cela est gueux et fier, etc.*

EXERCISES.

1. *Whichever of you* shall be found to excel the others both in mind and body, shall be acknowledged king of the island.

2. These are admirable pictures: *these* are after the manner of Rubens, and *those* after the manner of Van-Huisum.

3. Why are the statues of the most celebrated modern sculptors, notwithstanding the perfection to which the arts have been carried, so much inferior *to those* of the ancients?

4. *He* whose soul, glowing, as it were, with divine fire, shall represent to himself the whole of nature, and shall breathe into objects that spirit of life which animates them, those affecting traits which delight and ravish us, will be a man of real genius.

5. *He that* judges of others by himself, is liable to many mistakes.

6. *He that* is easily offended, discovers his weak side, and affords his enemies an opportunity of taking advantage of it.

7. *He who* loves none but himself, deserves not to be loved by others.

8. I have shown my flowers to you, but you have not seen my sister's yet.

9. I cannot lend you my horse to-day, but you may ride my brother's, he is not going out.

10. Come this day week, and I will pay you.

(1) Be found to excel the other, *on juger vainqueur*; both in, *et pour* (repeated.)
(2.) These are, *voilà de*; picture, *tableau*; are after, *être dans*; manner, *genre*.
(3.) Are, (to be placed before *so much inferior)*; have been carried, (active voice), with, *on*; inferior, *au-dessous*.
(4.) Glowing with, *enflammé de*; as it were, *pour ainsi dire*; the whole of, *tout*; shall breathe into, *répandre sur*; affecting, *touchant*; delight, *séduire*; real, *vrai*.
(5.) By, *d'après*; liable, *exposé*; mistake, *méprise*.
(6.) Is offended, *s'offenser*; weak side, *faible*; affords, *fournir à*; of taking advantage, *profiter*.

275. It signifying *that, that thing,* is also expressed by *cela.*

vous rentrez tard, et *cela* lui déplait,	*you keep late hours, and it displeases him.*

RELATIVE PRONOUNS.

276. *Qui*, when it is the subject, relates equally to persons and things, of both numbers and genders.

EXAMPLES.

l'homme *qui* joue perd son temps,	*the man who games loses his time.*
le livre, qui plaît le plus, n'est, pas toujours le plus utile,	*the book which pleases most is not always the most useful.*

But when *qui* is the regimen, that is, the object or accusative of a verb, or when it is governed by a preposition, such as *de*, *à*, *sans*, *par*, etc. it can only be used of persons, or of things personified.

EXAMPLES.

quand on est délicat et sage dans ses goûts, on ne s'attache pas, sans savoir *qui* l'on aime,	*he who is wise and discriminate in his choice, does not form an attachment, without knowing whom he loves.*
l'homme à qui appartient ce beau jardin est très-riche,	*the man to whom this fine garden belongs, is very rich.*
de qui parlez-vous?	*of whom do you speak?*
à qui en enverrez-vous?	*to whom will you send some?*
ne voulez-vous pas me dire avec qui vous étiez?	*will you not tell me whom you were with?*
qui inviterons-nous?	*whom shall we invite?*

277. *Qui* for *whom*, is particularly used in interrogative sentences. In any other, as in the second of these examples, *auquel* may properly be substituted for it.

278. *What*, as the object or direct regimen of an interrogative verb, is rendered by *que*.

EXAMPLES.

que faites-vous?	*what are you doing?*
que dit-il?	*what is he saying?*

279. When the regimen indirect is expressed by the preposition *de*, then *dont* should be preferred to *de qui*. It is better to say: *la femme* dont *vous parlez*, than *de qui*; however, when the verb expresses transmission from one individual to another, *de qui* must be used, as,

celui de qui je tiens cette nouvelle,	*the person from whom I had that intelligence.*

280. Relative pronouns must not be separated from their antecedent, when that antecedent is a noun.

EXAMPLE.

un jeune homme qui est docile aux conseils qu'on lui donne, et *qui* aime à en recevoir, aura infailliblement du mérite,	*a young man who is obedient to the advice that is given him, and who loves to receive some, will infallibly acquire merit.*

REMARK. In some phrases, *qui* may be separated from the substantive by several words, when these words serve to qualify the substantive, and are so connected with it, as to give the idea of one thing only, as

Il a fallu, avant toute chose, vous faire lire dans l'écriture sainte, *l'histoire du peuple de Dieu, qui* fait le fondement de la religion.

This sentence is very correct, because as *du peuple* determines the kind of history, and *de Dieu* the kind of people, the mind necessarily goes back to the substantive *histoire*, to which the incidental phrase, *du peuple de Dieu*, refers.

EXERCISE.

1. I will show you a watch which did not cost me half so much as yours, and which is a great deal better.

2. If you buy any furniture, buy that which will be durable, in preference to that which is elegant only.

3. Could I ever expect that a man for whom I made such sacrifices, and to whom I devoted so much of my time, would thus abandon me in the moment of need?

4. I cannot name the man whom I have this report from, but I can tell you he is trustworthy.

5. Whom is this letter for?

6. Pray, what have you done with the pencil case which was upon the table this morning? I cannot find it any where.

7. That man is truly happy who can be content with his lot.

(1.) Cost, *coûter*, ind-4; half so much as, *la moitié de la*; to be better, *valoir mieux*.
(2.) Any furniture, *des meubles*, m.; in, *de*; only, *ne-que*.
(3.) *Pouvoir*, ind-2; to expect, *s'attendre que*; to make, *faire*, ind-4; such, *tant de*; to devote, *consacrer*, ind-4; so much of, *une si grande partie de*; would abandon, *abandonner*, subj-3; in the, *au*.
(4.) Cannot, *savoir*, cond-1; man, *personne*, f.; trust-worthy, *digne de confiance*.
(6.) Pray, *dites-donc*; with, *de*; to be, *être*, ind-2; any where, *nulle part*.
(7.) To be content with, *se contenter de*.

280.* *Qui*, may likewise be separated from its antecedent, by the verb, when the antecedent is a pronoun used as the regimen direct, or object of the verb.

EXAMPLES.

Il *la* trouva *qui* pleurait à chaudes larmes,	*he found her crying bitterly.*
je *le* vois *qui* joue,	*I see him playing* *.

281. A whole sentence may also be the antecedent of the relative pronoun *qui*.

EXAMPLE.

ceux-là ne sont pas les plus malheureux, *qui* se plaignent le plus,	*those are not the most unhappy, who complain the most.*

But it is more according to grammar to say, *ceux qui se plaignent le plus ne sont pas les plus malheu-*

* See manner of rendering the English participle present, No. 398, 399.

reux. Observe also that the first manner of construing would be incorrect without the addition of the particle *là.*

EXERCISE.

1. A young man *who* loves vanity of dress, like a woman, is unworthy of wisdom and glory; glory is only due to a heart *that* knows how* to* suffer pain and trample upon pleasure.

2. Thyself, O my son, my dear son, thou* thyself *that* now enjoyest a youth so cheerful and so full of pleasure, remember that this delightful age is but a flower *which* will be 1 withered 3 almost as soon 2 as blown.

3. Men pass away like flowers, *which* open in* the morning, and at night are withered and trampled under foot.

4. You must have a man *that* loves nothing but truth and you, *that* will speak the truth in spite of you, *that* will force all your entrenchments; and that indispensable being is the very man whom you have sent into exile.

5. We perceived him waiting for us, quietly sitting under the shade of a tree.

(1.) Vanity of dress, *à se parer vainement;* trample upon, *fouler aux pieds.*
(2.) Cheerful, *vif;* full of, *féconde en;* remember, *se souvenir;* delightful, *bel;* withered, *sécher;* blown, *éclore.*
(3.) Open, *s'épanouir;* and (which); at night, *le soir;* withered, *flétrir;* under, *à;* foot, art. pl. *pied,* m.
(4.) You must have, *il vous falloir;* nothing but, *ne que;* will speak, will force, subj-1; entrenchments, *retranchement;* indispensable being, *être si utile;* very man, *homme même;* sent into exile, *exiler.*
(5.) Waiting for, (who waited), *attendre,* ind-2. under, *à.*

282. The relative *qui* must always have reference to a noun taken in a determinate sense.

EXAMPLES.

L'homme est un animal raisonnable, qui, etc. *Il me reçut avec* une politesse, qui, etc.

But we cannot say, *l'homme est* animal raisonnable, qui, etc. *Il me reçut avec* politesse, qui, etc.

283. When the antecedent of *qui* is the subject of

a verb in the negative or the interrogative form, the following verb must be in the subjunctive mood.

EXAMPLES.

il n'a point *de livre, qui* ne soit de son choix,	*he has not a* book *that is not of his own selecting.*
y a-t-il *ville dans le royaume qui* soit plus favorisée ?	*is there* a city *in the kingdom that is more favoured ?*

284. *Que* relates both to persons and things. It is always the regimen direct, and always follows its antecedent.

EXAMPLES.

l'homme que je vois,	*the man whom I see.*
les pêches que je mange,	*the peaches which I eat.*

The antecedent of *que* may also be a noun, qualified or determined by several words, which separate it from the relative; as

Qu'est-ce qu'une armée ?—*Un corps* animé d'une infinité de passions différentes, *qu*'un homme habile fait mouvoir pour la d fense de la patrie.

EXERCISE.

1. He received us with such *goodness, civility,* and *grace*, as charmed us, and made us forget all we had suffered.

2. There is no *city* in the world *where* there are more riches and a greater population.

3. Is there a *man* who can say, I shall live till to-morrow ?

4. He has not a *friend* but would make for him every kind of sacrifice.

5. He is surrounded by *enemies, who* are continually watching him, and would be very glad to detect him in a * fault.

6. In his retreat, he lives like a *philosopher who* knows mankind and mistrusts them.

7. The pine-apple is *a sort of fruit* which, in Europe, ripens only in hot-houses

8. That man is *a sort of pedant, who* takes words for ideas, and facts confusedly heaped up for knowledge.

(1.) Civility, *politesse;* such, *une;* as, *qui.*
(2.) There are, *y avoir,* subj-1.
(3.) Man, (who); *cun,* subj 1. to live, *vivre.*
(4.) But, *qui ne;* would make, subj-2.
(6.) Like a, *en;* philosopher, *sage;* mistrusts, *se défier de.*
(7.) Pine apple, *ananas;* hot-houses, *serre chaude.*
(8.) Heaped up, *entasser;* knowledge, *savoir.*

285. Observe that the relatives *whom, which, that,* being the object or accusative, are almost always understood in English, but *que* is always expressed in French.

EXAMPLES.

les hommes que nous avons vus,	*the men we saw.*
le vin que nous avons bu,	*the wine we drank.*

286. There are some cases in which it is customary to use *que* for *à qui,* or *dont,* as: *C'est à vous* que *je parle; de la façon* que *j'ai dit la chose. That* is used in the same way, in English; it is to you *that* I speak; in the way *that* I did the thing. See 295.

287. *Lequel* and *dont* relate both to persons and things. But *lequel, duquel,* ought never to be used either as a subject or object, except in cases when a distinction is to be made between objects of the same nature, and to avoid ambiguity; for whenever the sense is clear, *qui* or *que* must be used, thus:

la Tamise *dont* le lit, and not, *de laquelle.*
le prince *dont* la protection, and not, duquel.

288. Sometimes, *duquel, de laquelle,** (common to persons and things,) and *de qui,* are separated from

* It is generally allowed, in English, to place the preposition governing *which* last; *The thing you think of,* for *the thing of which you think;* that must not be the case in French, the preposition must be first, *la chose à laquelle vous pensez.*

their antecedent by another noun substantive governed by a preposition.

EXAMPLES.

la Tamise dans le lit de laquelle mille poissons se jouent,	*the Thames, in the bed of which myriads of fish are playing.*
le prince à la protection duquel je dois ma place,	*the prince to whose protection I owe my place.*

EXERCISE.

1. The *God whom* the Hebrews and Christians have always served, has nothing in common with the deities full of imperfection and even of vice worshipped by the rest of the world.

2. The Epic Poem is not the panegyric of a *hero who* is proposed as a * pattern, but the recital of great and illustrious *actions, which* are exhibited for imitation.

3. The *good which* we hope for * presents itself to us, and disappears like an empty *dream, which* vanishes when we awake: to teach us, that the very *things which* we think we hold fast in our hands, may slip away in an instant.

4. Plato says, that, in writing, we ought to hide ourselves, to disappear, to make the world forget us, that we may present nothing but the *truths* we wish to impress.

5. She is a woman on whose character nothing can be said.

6. The sheep, to the spoils of which men are indebted for their garments.

7. Religion, whose maxims we despise, is, however, our greatest comfort in adversity.

8. The grand principle *on which* the whole turns is, that all * the world is but one republic, *of which* God is the common father, and in *which* every nation forms, as it were, one great family.

9. Homer, *whose* genius is grand and sublime like nature, is the greatest poet, and perhaps the most profound moralist of antiquity.

10. The celebrated Zenobia, *whose* noble firmness 2 you have admired 1, preferred dying with the title of queen, rather * than accept the advantageous 2 offers 1 which Aurelian made her.

11. The Alps, on the summit *of which* the astonished eye discovers perpetual snow and ice, present, at sun-set, the most striking and most magnificent spectacle.

12. A king, *to whose* care we owe a good law, has done more for his own glory, than if he had conquered the universe.

(1.) (That the rest of the world worshipped.)
(2.) Is proposed, *on propose*; as, *pour*; pattern, *modèle*; is exhibited, *on donner*; imitation, *exemple*.

(3.) Good, *bien*; disappears, *s'envoler*; empty, *vain*; vanishes, etc. *le reveil fait évanouir*; we * hold fast, *tenir le mieux*; in our hands *; slip away, *nous échapper*.
(2.) We, *on*; to make the world forget, *se faire oublier*; that we may present but, *pour ne produire que*; wish, *vouloir*; impress, *persuader*.
(5.) She is, *c'est*; character, *compte*; nothing can be said, *on ne saurait rien dire*.
(6.) Spoils, *dépouille, f.*; to be indebted, *devoir*.
(7.) However, *pourtant*.
(8.) Turns, *rouler*; every, *chaque*; as it were, *comme*.
(9.) Preferred, *aimer mieux*; than, *que de*.
(10.) Perpetual, *éternel*; snow, ice, pl.; sun-set, *soleil couchant*; striking, *imposant*.
(11.) Care, *solicitude*.

289. *Lequel*, *laquelle*, are used in conjunction with prepositions, in speaking of things, but *qui* is preferable, in speaking of persons.

EXAMPLE.

la place à laquelle il aspire,	*the situation he aims at.*
les rois à qui on doit obéir,	*the kings to whom one must obey.*

EXERCISE.

1. The ambitious man * sees nothing but pleasure in the possession of the places *to which he* aspires with so much eagerness, instead of seeing the trouble that is inseparable from them.
2. Kings, *whom* religion makes it our duty to obey, are, upon earth, the true representation of the providence of God.

(1.) (To) whom; makes it our duty to, *faire un devoir de*; representation, *image*.

290. *Quoi* is said of things, and when speaking in a vague or indefinite manner; that is, when the object is not specifically named. It is generally preceded by a preposition, and rendered by *what* in English.

EXAMPLES.

c'est de quoi je m'occupe sans cesse,	*this is what I am always thinking about.*
à quoi pensez-vous?	*what are you thinking of?*
avec quoi fait-on l'encre?	*what is ink made of?*

Quoi is sometimes used relatively to a thing named and of which the gender is known; but *lequel, laquelle* would be more correct.

EXAMPLES.

la chose à quoi on pense,	*the thing of which they are thinking.*
voilà les conditions sans quoi la chose ne peut se faire,	*these are the terms without which the thing cannot be done.*

WHOSE.

291. *Whose is, whose are*, are generally rendered by *à qui est, à qui sont*, or *à qui appartient, à qui appartiennent*, etc. etc.

EXAMPLES.

whose house is this? I cannot tell you whose it is,	à qui est cette maison? je ne saurais vous dire à qui elle appartient.
whose gloves are these?	à qui appartiennent ces gants?
God, whose we are,	Dieu à qui nous sommes.
God, whose creatures we are,	Dieu dont nous sommes les créatures.
that man, on whose account I came, disappointed me,	cet homme pour le compte duquel, à cause de qui, pour l'affaire duquel je suis venu, m'a trompé.

292. *Which* is used antecedently, as a sort of demonstrative pronoun, in *which case* it is rendered as follows:

I had some business, on which account (on account of which) I came to town,	j'avais quelques affaires pour lesquelles, à cause desquelles, ou de quoi, je suis venu à Londres.
he might come to-night, in which case we had better not go out,	il pourrait se faire qu'il vînt ce soir, dans ce cas -là nous ferons bien de ne pas sortir.
I had determined to go to Paris, for which purpose I saved all the money I could,	j'avais résolu d'aller à Paris; à ce dessein, je faisais toutes les épargnes possibles.

EXERCISE.

1. Do you know whose beautiful carriage this is?
2. This dog was found this morning in the stable, and no one knows whose it is.
3. That man, whose slave you have been, despises you, and will cast you off when you are no longer useful to his purpose.
4. His poor daughter, on whose account he had undertaken a journey to Italy, died at Genoa, almost immediately on landing.
5. He wished to get up early, in which intention he had desired his servant to call him up at four o'clock.

(1.) *Savoir.*
(2.) To find, *trouver*; pass. voice, ind-2.; no one, *personne.*
(3.) To cast off, *abandonner*; you are, *être*, ind-7; no longer, *ne plus.*
(2.) A journey to, *le voyage de*; to die, *mourir*, ind-3; on landing, *après avoir débarqué.*
(5) To wish, *avoir le désir de*, ind-2; to desire, *dire à*, ind-6; to call up, *de réveiller.*

293. *Où, d'où, par où,* relate only to things. They are never used, but when the nouns, to which they refer, express some kind of motion, or rest, at least metaphorically; they stand for *auquel, duquel,* thus:

voilà le but, *où* (auquel) il tend,	*that is the end he aims at.*
c'est une chose *d'où* (de laquelle) dépend le bonheur public,	*it is a thing upon which the public happiness depends.*
les lieux par *où* (lesquels) il a passé,	*the places through which he has passed.*
par *où* commencerons-nous (par quelle chose?)	*what shall we begin with?*
par *où* a-t-il passé? (par quel endroit, quel chemin)	*which way has he passed?*
par *où* êtes-vous venu?	*which way have you come?*
d'où venez-vous? (de quel endroit, de quelle place)	*whence are you coming? what place are you coming from?*

EXERCISE.

1. *What* a young man, who begins the world, ought principally to attend *to*, is not to give it a high opinion of his understanding, but to gain numerous friends by the qualities of his heart.
2. A youth passed in idleness, effeminacy, and pleasure, lays up for * us nothing but sorrow and disgust in old age: this, however, is *what* we little think of when we are young.

3. There is nothing *by which* we are more affected than the loss of fortune, although, being frail and perishable by its nature, it cannot contribute to our happiness.

4. A grove *in which* I defy the ardours of the dog-days, a retired valley *where* I can meditate in peace, a high hill, *whence* my eye extends over immense plains, are the places *where* I spend the happiest moments of my life.

5. No one could tell which way he had come into the room.

6. This is what we are to begin with.

(1.) To what, *ce à quoi;* begins, *entrer dans;* to attend, *s'attacher;* it, *y;* opinion, *idée;* understanding, *esprit;* to gain, *se faire;* numerous, *beaucoup de.*

(2.) Idleness, *inutilité;* effeminacy, *mollesse;* pleasure, *volupté;* lays up, *prénarer;* of, *à;* we, *on.*

(3.) By, *à;* we, *on;* affected, *sensible;* frail, *frêle;* by, *de;* cannot, subj. 1. our, (the).

(4.) Grove, *bosquet;* defy, *braver;* dog-days, *canicule;* spend, *passer.*

(5). Had come, *était entré.*

(6.) We are, *il faut.*

IV.

ABSOLUTE PRONOUNS.

294. *Qui* is used in interrogations, with reference to persons, in a vague and indeterminate way.

EXAMPLES.

Qui sera assez hardi pour l'attaquer?	*who will be bold enough to attack him?*

It is likewise used in the feminine, and in the plural, as,

Qui est cette *personne*-là?	*who is that person?*
Qui sont ces femmes-là?	*who are those women?*

Que and *quoi* relate to things only, as,

Que pouvait la valeur en ce combat funeste?	*what could valour do in that fatal combat?*
A *quoi* pensez-vous?	*what are you thinking of?*

295. *Que* is sometimes used for *à quoi*, *de quoi*, as,

Que sert la science sans la vertu? (à quoi sert)	*what avails learning without virtue?*
Que sert à l'avare d'avoir des trésors? (de quoi sert)	*what use is it to the miser to possess treasures?*

Quoi, *de quoi*, *à quoi*, may be used in reference to a sentence antecedent, as a sort of pronoun *neuter*, the thing to which it refers being neither *masculine* nor *feminine*.

la vie passe comme un songe: c'est cependant *à quoi* on ne pense guères.

296. *Que* and *quoi* require the preposition *de* before the adjective or substantive that follows them, having then the force of an adverb of quantity, as;

Que dit-on de nouveau? quoi de plus agréable!
Que d'inconséquences dans sa conduite!

Quel relates both to persons and things, as:

Quel homme peut se promettre un bonheur constant?
Quelle grâce! quelle beauté! mais quelle modestie!

EXERCISE.

1. *Who* could ever persuade himself, did not daily experience convince us of it, that, out of a hundred persons, there are ninety who sacrifice, to the enjoyment of the present, all the best founded hopes of the future?

2. *Who* would not love virtue for its own sake, could he see it in all its beauty?

3. He who does not know how * to apply himself in his youth, does not know *what* to do when arrived at maturity.

4. He was a wise legislator, who, having given to his countrymen laws calculated to make them good and happy, made them swear not to violate any of those laws during his absence: after *which*, he

went away, exiled himself from his country, and died poor in a foreign land.

5. *What* people of antiquity ever had better laws than the Egyptians? *What* other nation ever undertook to erect monuments calculated to triumph over both time and barbarism?

6. *What is more instructing and entertaining* than to read celebrated authors in their own language? *What beauty*, *what delicacy* and *grace*, which cannot be thrown into a translation, are discovered in them!

7. When Ménage had published his book on the Origin of the French Language, Christina, queen of Sweden, said: "Ménage is the most troublesome 3 man 1 in the world 2: he cannot let one word 2 go 1 without its passport: he must know *whence* it comes, *where* it has passed *through*, and *whither* it is going."

(1.) Did, *si*; out of, *sur*; future, *avenir*.
(2.) Its own sake, *elle-même*; could he, *si on pouvoir*; ind-2
(3.) (To) what; to do, *s'occuper*; when arrived, etc., *dans l'âge mûr*.
(4.) He, *ce*; calculated, *propre*; not to, (that they would not;) went away, *partir*.
(5.) Calculated to, *fait pour*; both, *également*; over, *de*.
(6.) Language, *langue*; delicacy, *finesse*; which cannot, *qu'on ne peut*; be thrown, *faire passer*; translation, *traduction*; are, etc. *n'y découvre-t-on pas*.
(7). When, *après que*; Christina, *Christine*; troublesome, *incommode*; the, *de*, art.; cannot, *ne saurait*; go, *passer*; must, *vouloir*.

V.

PRONOUNS INDEFINITE.

297. These pronouns have been divided into four classes in the grammar. (No. 85). The following remarks are arranged in the same order.

FIRST CLASS.

Of those which are never joined to a noun substantive.

ON

298. Examples have already been given, (No. 86) of the use of ON, in French, with an explanation of its reasonably supposed etymology. As it is a

word which frequently occurs, and in a manner totally different from the English idiom, it has been thought necessary to devote another chapter to it, in which its use will be more fully explained.

The general meaning of *on* is: one, people, men, we.

EXAMPLES

on secourt plus volontiers les malheureux quand on l'a été soi-même,	*we succour the unfortunate more readily when we have been so ourselves.*
on ne doit pas attribuer à la religion les défauts de ses ministres,	*man ought not to charge religion with the faults of her ministers.*
on relit tout Racine, on choisit dans Voltaire,	*people read the whole of Racine again, they chuse in Voltaire.*
on fait du bruit dans la rue,	*people are making a noise in the street.*
on n'est pas toujours heureux,	*people are not always fortunate.*
on dit qu'il va se marier,	*people say, they say, he is going to be married.*

Observe, that the adjective referring to *on* is in the masculine gender, when that pronoun is taken in a vague and indeterminate sense; but when it applies to any person in particular, as in the case stated No. 298, then the adjective agrees with the person understood. Thus, a woman would say: *on n'est pas toujours jeune et jolie*, we cannot be young and pretty for ever.

Observe also that we must not say *qu'on, et on, aussi on*, but *que l'on, et l'on, aussi l'on*. Ex: *je crois que l'on frappe.* The *l'* thus prefixed is for euphony's sake. But if the word following begins with an *l*, then we say: *je crois qu'on l'appelle*, because *je crois que l'on l'appelle* would equally be disagreeable.

298. On, according to the above examples, has a vague and indefinite meaning; it is indeed the subject of the verb, but not specified, not applied to any one person in particular.

There are, however, two cases in which *on* is very

significantly used in French, in a definite sense, and as applicable to one individual alone.

1. A master speaking to his servants, a father to his child, a tutor to his pupil, says *on*, instead of *vous* or *tu*, either to put greater distance between the persons, or to assume a more serious tone, or also a sort of mock gravity.

EXAMPLES.

a-t-on passé chez le Colonel Sainville ?	*did you call at the house of Colonel Sainville ?*
eh bien, a-t-on été bien sage en mon absence ?	*well, have you been good in my absence ?*
finira-t-on ce bruit-là bientôt ?	*will you put an end to that noise ?*

2. A person, speaking of himself, says *on*, as the English sometimes say *we ;* or applies it to another, also in the same manner as the English use *we* for *you*.

EXAMPLES.

on n'est pas des esclaves pour essuyer de si mauvais traitements,	*we are not slaves (I am not a slave) to bear such ill usages.*
on vous l'a dit mille fois,	*I have told you so a thousand times.*
depuis quand est-on de retour ?	*how long have we (you) been back?*

299. On is also much used in French as the subject of an active verb, when the passive voice is used in English. (*See* 95.)

EXAMPLES.

on me trompe,	*I am deceived.*
on m'a dit ce matin que le roi va en Irlande,	*I have been told this morning that the king is going to Ireland.*

This form is adopted in almost every case, except when the verb expresses *love, esteem, hatred, feeling*

EXAMPLE.

they are much loved,	*ils sont très-aimés.*

EXERCISE.

1. If we knew how to limit our wishes, we would spare ourselves many troubles and we should be happier.
2. At the last judgment we shall not be asked what we have read, but what we have done.

3. I will not have him be teased.
4. People do not come into the world musicians.
5. When men regulate their wants on nature, they save themselves many cares and difficulties.
6. They praise him, they threaten him, they caress him; but whatever they do, they cannot conquer him.
7. They say the town has been taken.
8. My father has been robbed.

(1.) To limit, *borner;* to spare, *s'épargner;* troubles. *maux.*
(2.) To ask, *demander.*
(3.) To will, *vouloir que;* to teaze, *tourmenter.*
(4.) To come into the world, *naître.*
(5.) To save one s self, *s'épargner;* difficulties, *travaux.*
(6.) Whatever they do, *quoique l'on fasse;* cannot, *savoir,* cond-1.

300. *Quelqu'un* is relative, and agrees in gender with the noun to which it refers.

EXAMPLES.

nous attendons des hommes, il en viendra quelqu'un,	*we expect men, some of them will come.*
plusieurs femmes m'ont promis de venir, il en viendra quelqu'une.	*several ladies have promised me to come, some one of them will come.*
quelques-uns assurent,	*some people affirm.*
entre les nouvelles qu'il a débitées, il y en a quelques-unes de vraies,	*among the reports he has circulated, there are some which are true.*

Quelqu'un taken absolutely and substantively, is of the masculine gender.

EXAMPLES.

j'attends ici quelqu'un,	*I wait here for somebody.*
quelqu'un en doute-t-il?	*does any one doubt it?*

Quiconque, whoever, signifies *quelque personne que ce soit, qui que ce soit,* any person whatever; the verb which it governs is in the singular and the adjective, which refers to it, is masculine.

EXAMPLE.

ce discours s'adresse à quiconque est coupable,	*this speech is addressed to whoever is guilty.*

Quiconque is also used for *celui qui, celle qui, celui de nous, de vous, celle de nous, de vous.*

EXAMPLE.

quiconque (de vous) fera du bruit, je l'en punirai,	*whoever makes a noise, I shall punish him.*

301. *Chacun,* each, every one, is used either distributively or collectively.

Distributively, it means *chaque personne, chaque chose,* each person or thing. It is then of both genders.

EXAMPLES.

chacun de nous vit à sa mode,	*each of us lives as he pleases.*
donnez à chacune sa part,*	*give to each his share.*

Collectively, it signifies *toute personne,* every person.

EXAMPLE.

chacun a ses défauts,	*every body has his faults.*

EXERCISE.

Can *any one* (be still ignorant) that it is from the
pourrait-il 2 1 *ignorer encore* *ce* *dès*

earliest infancy we ought to form the mind, the heart and
tendre enfance f. *que l'on doit* * *former*

the taste? Will not *some one* of these ladies be of the party?
f. *partie* f.

* There is apparently some difficulty in determining whether the possessive pronoun after *chacun* is to be plural or singular; some examples will illustrate and explain the case.

il a donné à chacun sa part,	each man can have but *one* share.
toute la compagnie se retira chacun chez soi,	each to his own house.
ils apportaient des offrandes chacun suivant sa dévotion,	according to the devotion of each.

Ils ont apporté chacun leur offrande. *Chacun,* is here taken collectively, and may be considered as an adverb having the sense of *all, generally.*

Some people like to read (every thing new). (These are
aimer à *toutes les nouveautés.* *voilà de*

beautiful pictures; I would wish to buy *some*. *Whoev*
superbe *tableau* m. *vouloir en* * *acheter*

has studied the principles of an art, knows that it (is only) (by
——*pes* —— m. *savoir* *ce n'est que* *à*

length of time) and by deep reflections, that he can succeed in
la longue *de profond réflexion* f. *réussir* *à*

making it, his own. All the ladies at the ball were
se 1 *rendre* 3 *le* 2 * *propre* 4 *bal* m. ind-2

very finely dressed, and *each* differently.
* *superbement* *paré* *avait une parure différente.*

Every one should, for (the sake of) his own happiness, listen
devrait, *pour* * *propre* m. *n'écouter*

only to the voice of reason and of truth. What is the price
que * *voix* f. art. *raison* f. art. *vérité* f. *prix* m.

of *each* of these medals?
f. *médaille* f.

Autrui, others, only applies to persons, is never joined to an adjective, has no plural, and is always preceded by a preposition.

EXAMPLE.

la charité se réjouit du bonheur d'autrui, — *charity rejoices in the happiness of others.*

302. *Personne*, as an indeterminate pronoun, and signifying *no one*, *nobody*, is always masculine. It requires *ne* before the verb.

EXAMPLES.

personne n'est venu?	*no one has come?*
n'est-il venu personne?	*has nobody come?*
nous ne voyons personne,	*we see nobody.*

When it is used substantively it is feminine.

EXAMPLES.

c'est une personne active,	*he is an active person.*
ces personnes sont-elles riches?	*are those people rich?*

In interrogative phrases, not negative, or in those expressing doubt, *personne* signifies *quelqu'un* any body.

EXAMPLES.

personne oserait-il nier?	*would any body dare deny?*
je doute que personne soit assez hardi,	*I doubt whether any body be bold enough.*

When *personne* is placed in the second member of a comparison, it also means *any body.*

EXAMPLE.

cette place lui convient mieux qu'à personne,	*that place suits him better than any body.*

303. *Rien,* nothing; which is masculine and singular, generally requires the negation, before the verb; in which case it signifies *nulle chose,* nothing.

EXAMPLE.

il ne s'attache à rien de solide,	*he applies himself to nothing solid.*

When used without a negation, it means *quelque chose,* something.

EXAMPLE.

Je doute que rien soit plus propre à faire impression que, etc.	*I doubt whether any thing be more suited to make an impression, than, etc.*

Rien is sometimes used absolutely, in answer to a question; *que vous a coûté cela? rien,* how much did you pay for it? nothing.

Rien always requires the preposition *de* before the adjective, or participle that follows it, when the verb and the negative are understood. Thus, we say, *rien de beau que le vrai*, nothing is noble but truth; as if it were, *il n'y a rien de beau que le vrai.*

304. NI L'UN NI L'AUTRE, require *ne* before the verb.

EXAMPLES.

ni l'un ni l'autre n'ont fait leur devoir,	*they have not either of them their duty.*
ni l'un ni l'autre ne l'aura,	*neither of them shall have it.*
ils ne sont morts ni l'un ni l'autre,	*they are not dead either of them.*
ni l'un ni l'autre n'est mort,	*neither of them is dead.*

305. TOUT means every thing, *all.*

EXAMPLES.

il rit de tout,	*he laughs at every thing.*
il ne lui a pas tout dit, parce que tout n'est pas bon à dire,	*he did not tell him all, because every thing is not to be told.*

Tout is adverb and adjective, see No. 44.

EXERCISE.

To most men, the misfortunes of *others* are but
Pour la plupart de art. *mal* m. *ne que*

a dream. Do not to *others* what you would not wish to be
songe m. *ne vouloir pas que* cond-1 *on*

done to you. *No one* knows whether he deserves love or
faire sub-3 *savoir si être digne*

hatred. An egotist loves *nobody*, not even his own children;
égoïste pas même propre

in the whole universe he sees no one but himself. He is more
dans * *univers ne voit* * *que lui seul*

than *(any body)* worthy of the confidence with which the king
digne confiance f.

honours him. I doubt whether *any one* ever painted
honorer de que ait jamais peint

nature, in its amiable simplicity, better than the feeling Gessner.
—— f. = f. *sensible* ——

Has any body called on me this morning? *Nobody*. There
venir ind-4 *chez* *matin* m. *y avoir*

was *nothing* (but what was great) in the designs and
ind-2 *que de grand* *dans* *dessein* m. pl. art.

works of the Egyptians. I doubt whether there is
ouvrage m. pl. ——*tiens* *que* * subj-1 2

any thing better calculated to exalt the soul than the contemplation
1 *plus* *propre* —— f.

of the wonders of nature.
merveille f. art. —— f.

SECOND CLASS.

OF THOSE WHICH ARE ALWAYS JOINED TO A SUBSTANTIVE.

306. *Quelque*, some, signifies, *un*, *une entre plusieurs*, one out of several; it is of both genders, and takes the number of the substantive, before which it is placed.

EXAMPLE.

adressez-vous à quelque autre personne, *apply to somebody else.*

Quelque, *quel que*, may be considered as adjectives on account of their being declinable, see No. 44.

307. *Chaque*, each every; which is of both genders, has no plural.

EXAMPLE.

chaque pays a ses coutumes *each country has its customs.*

308. *Aucun*, followed by *quelconque* or *que ce soit*, agrees in gender with the noun to which it is joined; it is always used with a negative phrase.

EXAMPLE.

Il ne veut se soumettre à aucune autorité quelconque,	*he will submit to no authority whatever.*

309. *Quelconque*, is sometimes used as synonimous with *que ce soit*, *quel qu'il soit*, and with an affirmative phrase; it takes the sign of the plural.

EXAMPLE.

deux points quelconques étant donnés,	*any two points being given*

310. *Certain*, certain, some; in this sense is used alike of persons and things, with which it agrees in gender; but it is always placed before the substantive.

EXAMPLE.

j'ai ouï dire à certain homme, ou, à une certaine femme,	*I have heard some man*, or *woman say.*

311. *Un, une*, a *or* an; when used indeterminately for *quelque, certain*, some person, or some thing, takes the gender of the substantive with which it is joined.

EXAMPLES.

j'ai vu un homme qui courait,	*I saw a man who was running.*
je me suis promené dans une grande et belle prairie,	*I walked in a large and beautiful meadow.*

EXERCISE.

Some enlightened people among the Egyptians preserve
éclairé 2 *esprit* m. pl. 1 *parmi* ——*tiens conserver*

the idea of *a* first being, whose attributes they
ind-2 *idée* *être* art. ——*but* m. pl. 3 1

represented under various symbols; this (is proved)
représenter ind-2 2 *différent symbole* m. *c'est ce que prouve*

by the following inscription upon *a* temple, "I am all that
o * *cette* * ——f. *de* ——m. *ce qui*

has been, is and shall be; no mortal ever removed the veil that
3 *mortel* 2 1 *lever* ind-4 *voile* m.

covers me." *Every* nation has (in its turn) shone on the
f. *à son tour* 2 *brillé* 1

stage of the world. There is no reason *whatever* that can
théâtre *raison* f.

bring him to it. *Some* figure appear monstrous and
déterminer le 1 *y* 2 ——f. —*trueux*

deformed, considered separately, or too near; but, if they are
difforme f. pl. *séparément* *de* *près* *on* *les*

put in their proper light and place, the true point of view
met * *jour* *à leur* —— —m. *vue* f.

restores them to *beauty* and grace. Yesterday I saw
leur rendre * art. = f. art. — f. 2 *voir*

a lady remarkably beautiful.
ind-4 1 *d'une rare* 2 *beauté* 1.

THIRD CLASS.

OF THOSE WHICH ARE SOMETIMES JOINED TO A SUBSTANTIVE, AND SOMETIMES NOT.

312. *Nul* and *pas un*, no, not any, not one; are used either relatively to, or with a substantive, with which they agree in gender, and require *ne* before the verb which they govern.

EXAMPLES.

nul de tous ceux qui y ont été, n'en est revenu,	*not one of those who went there has returned.*
pas un ne croit cette nouvelle,	*not one believes that intelligence.*
je n'en ai nulle connaissance,	*I have no knowledge of it.*
il n'y a pas une seule personne qui le croie,	*there is not a single person that believes it.*

313. *Aucun* signifies *nul*, no, not any, when accompanied by a negation, and may be followed by the preposition *de*.

EXAMPLE.

vous n'avez aucun moyen de réussir dans cette affaire,	*you have no means of succeeding in that affair*

This pronoun is seldom used in the plural, except before substantives, which, in some particular sense, are better employed in that number.

EXAMPLE.

il n'a fait aucunes dispositions,	*he has made no preparations.*

Rem. *Aucun* may be used without the negation in interrogative sentences, or in those which express doubt, or exclusion.

EXAMPLES.

aucun homme fut-il jamais plus heureux ?	*was ever any man more successful?*
on doute qu'aucune de ces affaires réussisse,	*they doubt whether any of those affairs will succeed.*
le plus beau morceau d'éloquence qu'il y ait dans aucune langue, etc.	*the finest piece of eloquence that exists in any language, etc.*

EXERCISE.

No one likes (to see himself) as he is. *No* expression, *no*
à se voir *tel que* — f.

truth of design and colouring, *no* strokes of genius in that great
f. *dessein* *de coloris* *trait*

work. He is as learned as *any one*. *Not one* of these en-
ouvrage m. *savant*

gravings announces any great skill. *None* of his works will
gravure f. pl. *annoncer* *un* *talent* m.

descend to posterity. He is so ignorant, and at the same
passer art. = f. —— *en* * *même*

time so obstinate, that he will not (be convinced) by *any*
temps *obstiné* * *se rendre* ind-1 *à*

reasoning. Did *any* man ever attain to such a
raisonnement m. *jamais* 2 *parvenir* ind-4 1 *à*

pitch of glory! I doubt whether there be in any science a
comble m. = *que* *y avoir* subj-1 —— f.

more evident principle.
plus *lumineux* 2 ——*pe* m. 1

314. *Autre*, other, expresses a difference between two objects, or between one and several, as: *quelle autre chose souhaitez-vous de moi?* what else do you wish of me?

Rem. *Autre* is sometimes used relatively of persons, but in an indeterminate manner, as: *j'aime mieux que vous l'appreniez de tout autre que de moi*, I had rather you learn it of any other person than me.

315. *L'un l'autre*, is of both genders and numbers, *l'un l'autre, les uns les autres, les unes les autres*, each other, one another.

EXAMPLE.

il faut se secourir l'un l'autre,	*we ought to assist one another.*

Of one another, to one another, of each other, to each other, are rendered by, *l'un de l'autre, l'un à l'autre*, the preposition being placed before *l'autre**.

When used separately, they denote a difference.

EXAMPLE.

les passions s'entendent les unes avec les autres; si l'on se laisse aller aux unes, on attire bientôt les autres,	*our passions correspond with one another; if we abandon ourselves to the ones, the others will soon follow.*

Rem. In the latter case *l'un* is used for the person, or thing first mentioned, and *l'autre*, for the person, or thing last spoken of.

* This is according to common rules of grammatical construction; *l'un* being the subject and *l'autre* the object. *Ils médisent l'un de l'autre*, that is, *l'un médit de l'autre*.

316. *L'un et l'autre*, both; these two words mark union; *l'une et l'autre sont bonnes*, both are good.*

EXERCISE.

Ask another. Would any other have been so
Demander à | *avoir* cond-2 | *assez*

self-conceited as to think that his private opinion could
d'amour-propre * *pour penser que* *particulier* 2 — f. 1 *pouvoir*

counterbalance the public sentiment? Reason and faith
sub-3 *balancer* 2 *opinion* f. 1 *Raison* f. *foi* f.

equally demonstrate that we were created for another life.
2 *démontrer* 1 *créer* ind-4 f.

They speak ill of one another. The happiness of the people con-
parler mal de m

stitutes that of the prince; their true interests are connected with
faire — m. *intérêt* m. *lié à*

each other. Presumption and pride easily insinuate them-
pl. pl. art. *présomption* f. art. *orgueil* 2 *se glis-*

selves into the heart; if we allow one admission, it is
ser 1 m. *l'on y donne à* 2 f. 3 *entrée* 1

much to (be feared) that we shall soon (abandon ourselves) to the
bien *craindre* *on* * *bientôt* 2 *ne se livre* 1

other. Both relate the same story, though neither believes
rapporter *fait* m. *ne penser*

it to be true.
que * *soit*

317. *Le même, la même, les mêmes*, the same, the very same are used relatively to, or with a noun, and agree in gender and number with it.

* *L'un et l'autre, ni l'un ni l'autre.* In the new edition of the *Dictionnaire de l'Académie*, the following examples are given.

l'un et l'autre y a manqué,	each of them has failed.
l'un et l'autre sont venus,	both have come.
ni l'un ni l'autre ne viendront,	they will not come either of them.
ni l'un ni l'autre ne viendra,	neither of them will come.

It seems that the verb is in the plural when *l'un et l'autre, ni l'un ni l'autre*, may be transferred after the verb, as an adverb, *ils sont venus l'un et l'autre*, but when there is no distinction, but union in the action.—See *Peculiarities* No 226

EXAMPLES.

ce sont les mêmes raisons,	*they are the same reasons.*
ce poème est le même que celui dont je vous ai parlé.	*this poem is the same that I was mentioning to you.*

318. *Tel, telle,* although properly adjectives, may also be used relatively in speaking of persons.

EXAMPLE.

tel fait des libéralités, qui ne paie pas ses dettes,	*such is liberal in giving, who does not pay his debts.*

319. *Plusieurs,* which is always, as an adjective, joined to a noun plural, may also be used absolutely in reference to persons. The verb which it governs must be in the third person plural.

EXAMPLE.

plusieurs ont cru le monde éternel.	*some* or *several have thought the world to be eternal.*

EXERCISE.

Does he always maintain the *same* principles? Yes, they are
soutenir —*pe* *oui* *ce*

absolutely the *same.* That general is the *same* who commanded
—*ment* pl. — —*der* ind-2

last year. *Such* a conduct is inexplicable.
art. *dernier* 2 *année* f. 1 2 1 *conduite* f. —

There are no *such* customs in this country. I never
de *coutumes* f. *pays* m. *ai*

heard (any thing) *like it.* Such a *man* sows who
entendu dire *rien* *de* * *tel* * *semer*

often reaps nothing. I this morning received *several*
recueillir 1 3 *matin* 4 *recevoir* ind-4 2

letters. Of those manuscripts, there are *several* much
lettre f. p. *Parmi* —*crits* *y en avoir* *qu'on beau-*

esteemed. *Many* by endeavouring to injure others,
coup 2 *estimé* 1 *en* *s'efforcer* *de nuire à* art.

injure themselves more than they think.
se nuire à *ne penser*

FOURTH CLASS.

320. OF THOSE WHICH ARE FOLLOWED BY THE CONJUNCTION *que*, AND WHICH REQUIRE THE SUBJUNCTIVE MOOD.

They are *qui que ce soit*, *quoi que ce soit*, *quoi que*, *quelque*, *quel que*.

Qui que, whoever, is only said of persons, and signifies *quelque personne que*, whatever person; it requires the verb following to be in the subjunctive.

EXAMPLES.

qui que ce soit qui ait fait cela, c'est un habile homme,	*whoever has done that, is a man of talents.*
qui que je sois,	*whoever I may be.*
qui que ç'ait été,	*whoever it may have been.*
qui que c'eût été,	*whoever it might have been.*
qui que ce puisse être,	*whoever it may be.*
je n'ai vu qui que ce soit,	*I saw nobody; I did not see anybody whatever.*
quoi que ce soit qu'il fasse, *ou* qu'il dise, on se défie de lui,	*whatever he does or says, he is distrusted.*
quoi que vous disiez, je le ferai,	*whatever you may say, I will do it.*
sans application, on ne peut réussir en quoi que ce soit,	*without application, it is impossible to succeed in any thing whatever.*

EXERCISE.

Whoever has told you so, he is mistaken. Passenger, *whoever* thou be, contemplate with religious veneration,
ce soit qui — *le* — *se tromper* ind. 4 — *Passant* — *contempler* — *un* — =2 — *respect* m. 1

this monument erected by gratitude; it is the tomb of a just and benevolent man. How can he hope to be
— m. — *élevé* — art. *reconnaissance* f. — *ce* — *tombeau* m. — 2 — *bienfaisant* 3 — 1 — *Comment* — *espérer de*

beloved who has regard for *no one?* *Whatever* he may do or say, he (will find it) very difficult to destroy
lui — *ne* — *d'égards* — *qu'il* — *aura* — *bien de la peine* — *détruire*

prejudices so deeply rooted. A vain, presumptuous,
des préjugé m. *si profondément enraciné* — *présomptueux*

and inconsistent mind will never succeed in *any thing whatever.*
sans consistance *réussir*

Whatever a frivolous world may think of you, never swerve
frivole 2 *monde* 1 *puisse* *à* *se détourner*

from the path of virtue.
chemin m. art. f.

CHAPTER V.

OF THE VERB.

321. CONCORD BETWEEN THE VERB AND THE SUBJECT.

The subject is that of which something is affirmed, and may always be known by the answer to this question, *qui est-ce qui?* who, or what is it? as: *Pierre vit*, Peter lives; *l'oiseau vole*, the bird flies; if it be asked, *qui est-ce qui vit?* who is it that lives? *qui est-ce qui vole?* what is it that flies? The answers *Pierre* and *l'oiseau*, shew that *Pierre* and *l'oiseau* are the subjects of the verbs *vit* and *vole.*

There are three subjects or persons, *je, tu, il, elle, I, thou, he, she,* singular; *nous, vous, ils, elles,* plural.

The verb must be of the same number and person as its subject.

EXAMPLES.

je ris	*I laugh*	nous parlons	*we speak*
tu joues	*thou playest*	vous plaisantez	*you jest*
il aime	*he loves*	ils sont fous	*they are mad*

la vertu est aimable, *virtue is amiable*

Ris is in the singular number, and the first person, because *je*, its subject, is in the singular, and the first person. *Joues* is in the singular, and the second person, as *tu* is in the singular, and the second person, etc.

EXERCISE.

The most free of men is he who can be free even in
libre art. *celui* *même*

slavery. Are we not often blind to our defects?
art. *esclavage* m. * *s'aveugler* ind-1 *sur* *défaut*

All men (are inclined) to laziness, but the savages of hot
art. *tendre* ind-1 art. *sauvage* *chaud* 2

countries are the laziest of all men. Do you think of imposing
art. *pays* 1 * *en imposer*

long on the credulity of the public! Thou canst not deny
long-temps *à* =f. —m. *pouvoir* *nier*

that he is a great man.
ne subj-1

When a verb is governed by two or more nouns, in the singular, it must be in the plural.

EXAMPLE.

Mon père et ma mère m'aiment tendrement, *my father and mother love me tenderly.*

EXERCISE.

His uprightness and honesty, make him courted by
droiture f. pron. *honnêteté* *faire* *rechercher* *de*

every body. Strength of body and of mind meet
art. f. art. *celle* art. *se rencontrer*

not always together. A good heart and a noble soul are
ensemble. m. *beau* f. *de* art.

precious gifts of nature.
= 2. *don* m pl. 1 art. —f.

322. When a verb relates to subjects of different persons, it agrees with the first, rather than with the

other two, and with the second rather than the third. The person addressed is named *first*, and the person addressing *last*. On this occasion, the pronoun plural *nous*, is generally placed before the verb, as its principal subject, if one of the several subjects, is in the first person, and the pronoun plural *vous*, if there is no first person.

EXAMPLES.

vous, votre frère et moi, nous lisons ensemble la brochure nouvelle,	*you, your brother, and I, read together the new pamphlet.*
vous et votre ami, vous viendrez avec moi,	*you and your friend will come with me.*

XERCISE.

You, your friend, and I, have each a different opinion. In
chacun 2 f. 1

our childhood, you and I (were pleased) with playing toge-
enfance f. *se plaire* ind-2 *à* inf-1

ther. Neither I, nor (any one else) have been able to un-
ni *ni* *d'autres* *ne* *pouvoir* ind-4 * *com-*

derstand (any thing) in that sentence, (Take good care), you
prendre 2 *rien* 1 *à* *phrase* f. *se garder bien*

and your brother, not to (give way) to the impetuosity of your
* *de s'abandonner* =

disposition.
caractère m.

323. When a verb has the relative pronoun *qui* for its subject, it is put in the same number and person as the noun, or pronoun, which is the antecedent of that relative.

EXAMPLES.

est-ce moi qui ai dit cette nouvelle ?	*is it I who told this news ?*
est-ce nous qui l'avons voulu ?	*is it we who desired it ?*
ceux qui aiment sincèrement la vertu sont heureux,	*those who sincerely love virtue are happy.*

EXERCISE.

He that complains most of mankind, is not always he
celui *se plaindre* *le plus* art. *homme* pl.

that (has most reason) to complain (of them). You that wish
être le plus fondé *en* *vouloir*

to enrich your mind with thoughts vigorously conceived and
* *enrichir* *esprit* *de* f. pl. *fortement* *conçu* f. pl.

nobly expressed, read the works of Homer and Plato.
noblement *exprimé* *ouvrage*

324. There are some cases in which a verb, although governed by several nouns in the singular, is not put in the third person plural. A few examples of such cases are here given, with remarks on the cause and nature of their deviation from the rule given, No. 322.

EXAMPLES.

le roi, *aussi bien que* son ministre, *veut* le bien public,	*the king*, as well *as his ministry*, wishes *for the public good.*
son honnêteté, *autant que* son esprit, le *fait* rechercher,	*his honesty*, as much as *his wit*, makes *him courted.*
l'envie, *comme* l'ambition, *est une* passion aveugle,	*envy*, like *ambition*, is *a blind passion.*
la séduction, *ou* la terreur, l'*a* entraîné dans le parti des rebelles	*either persuasion*, or *terror*, has *drawn him into the party of the rebels.*

Observe. *First*, that: *aussi bien que son ministre*, *autant que son esprit*, *comme l'ambition*, are, as it were, adverbial phrases, which might be placed at the end of the sentence, *le roi veut le bien public, aussi bien que son ministre*, etc. and consequently that, although there are apparently two subjects, there is really but one.

Secondly, we do not affirm that *la séduction* in conjunction with *la terreur* has acted, but that either the one or the other has done so. There is consequently no unity in the action, no collective effort.

325. A verb may be in the singular, when preceded by nouns substantives in the plural.

EXAMPLES.

biens, dignités, honneurs, *tout disparaît* à la mort,	*riches, dignities, honours, every* thing vanishes *at death.*
jeux, conversations, spectacles, *rien* ne la *distrait*,	*games, conversations, shows,* nothing diverts *her.*
perfidies, noirceurs, incendies, massacres, ce n'*est* là qu'une faible image, etc.	*perfidies, enormities, conflagrations, massacres,* all this is *but a feeble representation, etc.*
non seulement toutes ses richesses et tous ses honneurs, *mais toute sa vertu s'évanouit*,	*not only all his riches and honours,* but all his virtue vanishes.

In the three first examples, all the things enumerated *biens, dignités, honneurs, jeux, conversations, spectacles,* are summed up in the words *tout, rien, ce n'est-là,* which, being singular, must necessarily have the verb they govern in the same number

EXERCISE.

1. Fear *or* inability prevented them from moving.
2. The fear of death, *or* rather, the love of life, began to revive in his bosom.
3. Alcibiades, *as well as* Plato, was among the disciples of Socrates.
4. Lycurgus, *like* Solon, was a wise legislator.
5. Euripides, *as much as* Sophocles, contributed to the glory of the Athenians.
6. Riches, dignities, honours, glory, pleasure, every thing loses its charms from the moment we possess it, because none of those things can fill the heart of man.

(1.) Inability, *impuissance;* moving, *remuer.*
(2.) Began to revive, *se réveiller;* in, *au fond de;* bosom, *cœur.*
(3.) Among, *au nombre de.*
(6.) We, *on;* none, *rien;* those things, *tout cela.*

326. PECULIARITIES.

La gloire et la prospérité des méchants est courte.

might have been *sont courtes;* but as each subject may form a separate proposition, *la gloire des méchants est courte, la prospérité des méchants est courte,* Fénélon has put the verb in the singular as being applicable to each subject.

Racine has said :

> Quelle était en secret ma honte et mes chagrins.

Quels étaient would have been more regular, but in point of elegance, and as a latinism, the verb has been made to agree with the first noun.

> Ni l'un ni l'autre ne sera l'ambassadeur.
> Ni la force ni la douceur n'y peuvent rien.

One alone can be the *ambassadeur*, and consequently the verb can only be applicable to one of them.

Force and *douceur* are both unavailing, consequently the verb is in the plural.

327. NOUNS OF MULTITUDE AND NOUNS COLLECTIVE PARTITIVE.

1. The words *armée*, army ; *peuple*, people ; *nation*, nation ; *parlement*, parliament ; *flotte*, fleet ; *assemblée*, assembly ; or any other nouns of multitude have the verb which they govern in the singular, especially when preceded by the definite article.

EXAMPLES.

l'assemblée a été tumultueuse,	*the assembly has been tumultuous.*
le peuple veut la paix,	*the people wish for peace.*
la nation aime son roi elle le protégera,	*the nation love their king they will protect him.*
un peuple de héros va naître,	*a nation of heroes will spring up.*

2. Nouns collective partitive as *la plupart*, most part ; *quantité*, quantity ; *multitude*, multitude ; *nombre*, number ; *beaucoup*, much ; *peu*, few ; etc., etc.,

have the verb in the plural, if they are qualified by a noun in the plural, otherwise the verb is in the singular.

EXAMPLES.

la plupart du monde le croit,	*most people believe it.*
la plupart des hommes le pensent.	*most men think so.*
une troupe de jeunes gens couraient après lui,	*a crowd of young people ran after him.*

Whatever be the noun which follows *la moitié, le tiers, le quart*, the verb must be in the singular.

328. The words *infinité* and *la plupart*, used by themselves, require the verb to be in the plural, as: *une infinité pensent, la plupart sont d'avis*, whenever *de personnes*, or *des hommes*, etc. are understood.

EXERCISE.

1. *Many persons* experience that human life is, every where, a state in which much is to be endured, and little to be enjoyed.

2. *Many poets* think that poetry is the art of uniting pleasure with truth, by calling imagination to the help of reason.

3. *Few persons* consider that time, like money, may be lost by unreasonable avarice.

4. *So many years* of familiarity were as* chains of iron which linked me to those men who beset me every moment

5. *How many wise* men* have thought that, to seclude one's self from the world, was to pull out the teeth of devouring animals, to take away from the wicked the use of his poniard, from calumny its poisons, and from envy its serpents!

6. *A company of young Phœnicians* of uncommon beauty, clad in fine linen, whiter than snow, danced a * long while the dances of their own * country, then those of Egypt, and lastly, those of Greece.

7. *A troop of nymphs*, crowned with flowers, whose lovely tresses flowed over the shoulders and played in the wind, swam in multitudes behind her car.

8. At the time of the invasion of Spain by the Moors, an *innumerable multitude of people* retired into the Asturias, and there proclaimed Pelagius king.

9. *A third part of the enemy* was left dead on the field of battle; the rest surrendered at discretion.

10. *The innumerable crowd of carriages* which are to be seen in London during the winter, astonishes foreigners.

(.) Much is, *etc.* (*one has a great deal of pains, and little of real enjoyments.*)
(3.) To be lost, *se perdre;* unreasonable, *hors de propos.*
(4.) Familiarity, *habitude;* linked, *lier;* beset, *obséder.*
(5.) How many, *que de;* to seclude one's self, *se retirer;* pull out of, *arracher à;* to take away from, *ôter à.*
(6.) Company, *troupe;* clad in, *et vêtu de;* linen, *lin.*
(7.) Lovely, *beau;* tresses, *cheveu;* flowed, *pendre;* to play, *flotter;* with, *au gré de;* swam, *nager;* shoals, *foule;* car, *char.*
(8.) Moors, *Maure;* retired, *se retirer;* Asturias, *Asturies;* Pelagius, *Pélage.*
(9.) A third part, *un tiers;* enemy, pl.; surrendered, *se rendre.*
(10.) Crowd, *quantité;* which are, (*active voice on*).

PLACE OF THE SUBJECT WITH REGARD TO THE VERB.

329. The subject of the verb when a noun must always precede the verb, and cannot be separated from it, except by a negation, or personal pronoun in the dative or the accusative case.

EXAMPLES.

le roi est revenu,	*the king has returned.*
le roi ne reviendra pas,	*the king will not return.*
le roi lui a parlé,	*the king has spoken to him.*
le roi le lui a donné,	*the king has given it to him.*
le roi reviendra-t-il?	*will the king return?*
le roi le lui a-t-il donné?	*has the king given it to him?*
le roi ne le lui a-t-il pas donné?	*has not the king given it to him?*

330. When the subject is a pronoun, it precedes the verb, in the affirmative form, and follows it in the negative.

EXAMPLES.

je parle,	*I speak.*
parle-t-il?*	*does he speak?*
ne lui a-t-il pas parlé?	*has he not spoken to him?*

EXERCISE.

1. *Youth* is full of presumption; *it* expects every thing from itself: although frail, *it* thinks itself all-sufficient, and that *it* has nothing to fear.

* The use of the hyphen has been explained, No.

2. *Commerce* is like certain springs; if *you* attempt to * divert their course, *you* dry them up.

3. *It* is enough that falsehood is falsehood, to be unworthy of a man who speaks in the * presence of God, and who is to sacrifice every thing to truth.

4. The *ambition* and *avarice* of man are the sources of his unhappiness.

5. *They* punish, in Crete, three vices, which have remained unpunished in all other nations: ingratitude, dissimulation, and avarice.

6. Like the Numidian lion, goaded by cruel hunger, and rushing upon a flock of feeble sheep, *he* tears, *he* slays, *he* wallows in blood.

(1.) Full of presumption, *présomptueux;* expects, *se promettre;* itself all-sufficient, *pouvoir tout;* that it has, *avoir.*
(2.) Springs, *source;* attempt, *vouloir;* dry up, *faire tarir.*
(3.) It is enough, *suffire;* falsehood, *mensonge;* is, *subj.* in, *en;* is to sacrifice, *doit.*
(5.) Punished, *ind-2;* have remained, *être;* in, *chez.*
(6.) Like the, *semblable à un;* Numidian, *de Numidie;* goaded by, etc. *(that cruel hunger goads) dévorer;* rushing, *(which rushes upon), entrer dans;* tears, *déchirer;* slays, *égorger;* wallows, *nager.*

331. When an interrogation begins with *que, où, combien, à quoi,* the noun subject may be placed after the verb, and *il, elle, ils, elles* are suppressed.

EXAMPLES.

Que dit votre ami? à quoi s'occupe votre frère? où demeure votre cousin? combien coûte cet habit?

332. Verbs of the first conjugation require the acute accent before *je,* in interrogations, *parlé-je, aimé-je.*

Cours-je, dors-je, sens-je, would be harsh; such questions are to be turned thus: *est-ce que je cours? est-ce que je dors?*

EXERCISE.

1 *Have you* forgotten all that Providence has done for you? how *have you* escaped the shafts of your enemies? how *have you* been preserved from the dangers which surrounded you on all sides? *could you be* so blind as not to acknowledge and adore the all-powerful hand that has miraculously saved you?

2. What *will posterity say* of you, if, instead of devoting to the happiness of mankind the great talents which you have received from nature, you make use of them only to deceive and corrupt them.

3. Do not *the misfortunes* which we experience often contribute to our * prosperity ?

4. Why are *the works of nature* so perfect ? Because each work is a whole, and because she labours upon an eternal plan, from which she never deviates. Why, on the contrary, are *the productions* of man so imperfect ? It is because the human mind being unable to create any thing, and incapable of embracing the universe at a single glance, can * produce only after having been enriched by experience and meditation.

(1.) Escaped, *échapper à;* shafts, *trait;* preserved, *garantir;* on all sides, *de toutes parts;* so as, *assez pour;* saved, *conserver.*
(2.) Devoting, *consacrer;* mankind, *homme, pl.* deceive, *égarer.*
(3.) Experience, *éprouver;* contribute to, *tourner en.*
(4.) Because, *c'est que;* and because, *et que;* being unable, *ne pouvoir;* incapable, *(not being able)* at, *de;* glance, *vue;* enriched, *fécondé.*

Replied I, said I, says he, used in narrations, are literally translated in French.

EXAMPLES.

je meurs innocent, a dit Louis XVI	*I die innocent, said Louis XVI.*
je le veux bien, dit-il,	*I am very willing, said he.*

The subject of impersonal verbs is placed after the verb.

EXAMPLES.

il est arrivé de grands malheurs,	*great misfortunes have happened.*
il vint à ma voix un bon vieillard,	*at my call, there came an old man.*

333. When the adverb and adjective *ainsi, tel,* begin the sentence, the subject is placed after the verb.

EXAMPLES.

tel était l'acharnement du soldat, que, etc.	*such was the fury of the soldier that, etc.*
ainsi finit cette sanglante tragédie,	*thus ended that bloody tragedy.*

EXERCISE.

1. True glory, *said he*, is founded on humanity; whoever prefers his own glory to the feelings of humanity, is a monster of pride, and not a man.

2. There have happened, for these * ten years, *so many events* exceeding all probability, that posterity will find it very difficult to credit them.

3. *Such was that incorruptible Phocion*, who answered the deputies of Alexander, who were telling him that this powerful monarch loved him as the only honest man; well, then 2, let him allow me 1 to be and to appear so.

4. *Thus* ended, by the humiliation of Athens, *that dreadful war* of twenty-seven years, to * which ambition gave rise, which hatred made atrocious, and which was as fatal to the Greeks, as their ancient confederation had proved advantageous to them.

(1.) Is founded, *ne se trouver pas hors de;* feelings, *sentiment.*
(2.) There have happened for, *il se passer depuis;* exceeding, *hors de;* probability, *vraisemblance;* will find very difficult, *avoir bien de la peine;* to credit, *ajouter foi à.*
(3.) Loved, *chérir;* honest man, *homme de bien;* well, *ho!* to be so, *d'être tel;* appear so, *le paraître.*
(4.) Ended, *se terminer;* gave rise, *faire naître;* made, *rendre;* had proved, *être.*

After *aussi, peut-être, aussi bien*, the verb assumes the interrogative form. *Il est riche, aussi est-il recherché*, he is rich, and therefore sought after.

334. The noun or pronoun subject comes also after the imperative of *pouvoir*, *devoir*, and *faire*.

EXAMPLES.

puissent tous les peuples se convaincre de cette vérité,	*may all nations be convinced of this truth.*
dussé-je y périr, j'irai,	*though I perish there, I will go.*
fasse le ciel que....	*heaven grant that....*

There are some other cases in which the subject may be placed after the verb, but only as a matter of taste and elegance. Such transpositions must be left to the experienced writer.

EXERCISE.

1. The gods grant that you may never experience such misfortunes!

2. May you, oh wise old man, enjoy the happiness you deserve.

3. Though I were to perish in this enterprise, I will not give it up.

(1.) Grant, *faire;* experience, *éprouver de.*
(2.) To enjoy, *jouir de;* happiness, *le bonheur que.*
(3.) To give up, *renoncer à.*

335. The distinction between the active, passive, and neuter verbs has already been explained, No. 94, 95, the regimen direct and indirect have also been explained, No. 170.

The noun, which is the object or accusative case of a verb active, as also the indirect cases, are all placed after the verb.

EXAMPLES.

une mère chérit ses enfants,	*a mother cherishes her children.*
un père donne tous ses soins à sa famille,	*a father gives all his attention to his family.*
je reçois une lettre de mon frère,	*I receive a letter from my brother.*

N.B. The place of personal pronouns has also been fully explained, No. 223 and following.

EXERCISE.

He has discovered to all other nations his ambitious
montrer art. * *peuple* m. pl. =2

design of enslaving them, and has left
dessein m. 1 *mettre dans l'esclavage* inf-1 *ne laisser*

us no means of defending our liberty, but by endeavouring
aucun moyen inf-1 *que en tâcher* inf-3

to overturn his new kingdom. Homer represents Nestor as
de renverser *royaume* m.

the man who restrained the ungovernable wrath of Achilles,
celui *modérer* ind-2 *bouillant* *courroux* m.

the pride of Agamemnon, the haughtiness of Ajax, and the
fierté f.

impetuous courage of Diomed. He dared not (lift up)
=2 —m. 1 *Diomède* *oser* ind-2 *lift up*

his eyes, lest they should meet those of his
* art. *de peur de* * * *rencontrer* inf-1

friend, whose very silence condemned him. He caresses
art. *même* 2 m. 1 ind-2

them, because he *loves* them.

336. When an interrogative sentence begins with *quel, de quel,* the object comes before the verb.

EXAMPLES.

quel objet voyez-vous ?	*what object do you see?*
quelle science vous appliquez-vous ?	*to what science do you apply yourself?*
de quelle affaire s'occupe votre frère ?	*what is your brother about?*

337. Though the natural order of the ideas seems to require that the regimen direct be placed before the indirect, the perspicuity of the sentence does not allow it in all cases.

When a verb has two regimens, the shorter is generally placed first; but if they be of equal length, the regimen direct will precede the indirect.

EXAMPLES.

les hypocrites s'étudient — à parer *le vice*—des dehors de la vertu.	*hypocrites make it their study to deck vice with the appearance of virtue.*
les hypocrites s'étudient à parer—*des dehors de la vertu*—les vices les plus honteux et les plus décriés.	*hypocrites make it their study to deck with the appearance of virtue the most shameful and the most odious vices.*
ambition sacrifie—*le présent*—à l'avenir, mais la volupté sacrifie—*l'avenir*—au présent.	*ambition sacrifices the present to the future, but pleasure sacrifices the future to the present.*

EXERCISE.

1. Illustrious examples teach us, that God has hurled *from their thrones* princes who contemned his laws: he reduced *to the condition of a beast* the haughty Nebuchadnezzar, *who wanted to usurp divine honours.*

2. Wretched is * the man who feeds *his mind with chimeras.*

3. Our interest should prompt us to prefer *virtue* to vice, *wisdom* to pleasure, *and modesty* to vanity.

(1.) Illustrious, *fameux*; teach, *apprendre*; hurled, *renverser*; haughty, *superbe*; *Nabuchodonosor*; wanted, *vouloir.*
(2.) Feeds, *repaître.*
(3.) Should, *devoir,* ind-1; prompt, *porter*; pleasure, *volupté.*

338. A noun may be governed at the same time by two verbs, provided those verbs do not require different regimens.

EXAMPLES.

on doit aimer et respecter *les rois,*	*we ought to love and respect kings.*
ce général attaqua et prit *la ville.*	*that general attacked and took the city.*

But we must not say:

cet officier attaqua et se rendit maître de la ville,	*that officer attacked and made himself master of the city.*

But turn the sentence thus:

cet officier attaqua *la ville* et *s'en* rendit maître,	*that officer attacked the city and made himself master of it.*

because *attaquer* is active, and *se rendre* requires *de.*

EXERCISE.

1. Luxury is like a torrent, which *carries away,* and *overthrows* every thing it meets.

2. Nothing can * resist the operation of time; it, at length, *undermines, alters,* or *destroys* every thing.

3. Among the Spartans, public education had two objects: the first, to harden their bodies by fatigue; the second, to *excite* and *nourish*, in their minds, the love of their country, and an enthusiasm for what is great.

(1.) Carries away, *entraîner*; overthrows, *renverser*; every thing, *tout ce que*.
(2.) Operation, *action*; at length, *à la longue*; undermines, *miner*.
(3.) Among the Spartans, *à Sparte*: to, *de*; harden, *endurcir*; by, *à*; their *must be rendered by the article*; for what is great, *des grandes choses*.

339. PASSIVE VERBS.

Passive verbs require the prepositions *de* or *par*, generally *de* with those verbs which express a moral action, and *par* with those which express a physical one.

EXAMPLES.

un jeune homme vertueux est estimé de tout le monde,	*a virtuous young man is esteemed of all.*
la poudre à canon fut inventée par Berthold Schwartz,	*gun powder was invented by B. Schwartz.*

In this sentence *votre ouvrage a été loué d'une manière fort délicate par un grand académicien*, *par* is used to avoid the repetition of *de*.

Puristes pretend we ought not to say *le monde a été crée par Dieu*, but *de Dieu*. This opinion has for its object to avoid an equivocation, with the oath or, rather, interjection, *pardieu!* this is being over nice, as the words *par Dieu*, in the above sentence, convey no idea of irreverence, but on the contrary of admiration to God.

EXERCISE.

The city of Troy was taken, plundered, and destroyed by the
Troie *pris* f. *saccager* *détruit*
confederate Greeks, 1184 years before the Christian æra: this
confédéré 2 1 *ans avant* 2 *ère* f. 1

event has been celebrated by the two great poets of Greece
art.

and Italy. You will only be beloved, esteemed and
pr. art. ne

courted by men, (in proportion as) you join the
rechercher de que autant que joindre ind-7

qualities of the heart to those of the mind. God pu-
= f. pl. pr. 3 pu-

nished the Jews every time that,
nir (passive voice ind-3 2) peuple Juif 1 toutes les fois

deaf to the voice of the prophets, they fell into
sourd prophète sing. tomber ind-3 dans

idolatry and impiety
art. = art. =

340. NEUTER VERBS.

The nature of these verbs has been explained at full length, No. 96, 126. Their chief difficulty consists in the preposition which they require before the noun coming after them; pains must be taken to ascertain it, especially as it almost always differs from that which is used in English.

341. Some neuter verbs are used absolutely, as: *je dors*, I sleep; *je marche*, I walk.

342. Some govern the preposition, *à*, such as: *plaire*, *obéir*, *résister*, *applaudir*, *croire*, *penser*, etc. etc.*

EXAMPLES.

vous plaisez à cette dame,	*you please that lady.*
avez-vous pensé à mon affaire?	*have you thought of my affair?*

343. Others govern the preposition *de*, such as: *jouir*, *se moquer*, *se servir*, *se tromper*, *se repentir*. *mourir*, *dépendre*, *avoir besoin*, etc., etc.*

* The government of verbs is the greatest difficulty the English learner has to encounter in his study of the French language, as the correct construction of the

EXAMPLES.

il jouit d'une bonne santé,	*he enjoys good health.*
la fortune dont il jouit,	*the fortune which he enjoys.*

OBSERVE. That many neuter verbs have the reflected form, thus: ***s'arrêter***, to stop; ***se plaire à***, to take pleasure in.

EXERCISE.

This sentiment has pleased the king and all the nation.
à *à*

In his retirement, he enjoys the faculties of his
dans *retraite* f. *jouir de* *tout* =f. pl.

soul. To slander (any one) is to assassinate him in cold blood.
* *médire de quelqu'un c'est* * *de* 2 *sang* 1

The honest man seldom (permits himself) to jest
rarement 2 *se permettre* 1 *de* * art. *plaisanterie*

because he knows the most innocent jests may
f. pl. *parce que* *savoir que* f. pl. * *pouvoir*

sometimes hurt the reputation. It is only in retirement
quelquefois nuire à f. *ce* *ne que* art.

that one truly enjoys one's self. His work has
on *véritablement* 2 *jouir* 1 *de soi.* *ouvrage* m.

pleased every one, because it unites to real utility
à art. *monde* *joindre* *un* 2 =f. 1

the charms of style, and the beauties of sentiment.
agrément m. pl. art. m. sing. art. pl

whole sentence depends upon it. Suppose, for instance, you had to translate, *you have resisted orders on the execution of which our success depended.* If you have previously ascertained that *résister* governs the *dative* and *dépendre* the *genitive*, then you will say correctly, *vous avez résisté* à *des ordres* de *l'exécution desquels notre succès dépendait.* Neglect to ascertain this point, and you will translate literally thus: *vous avez résisté* les *ordres* sur *l'exécution desquels dépendait notre succès.*

The Dictionnaire des Verbes or Dictionary of French Verbs, showing their regimen, 1 vol. 12mo will it is hoped, be found a great assistance to those who wish to write correctly.

The Familiar and Conversational exercises, containing a selection of about 150 pages of English sentences, chosen on account of their peculiarity of construction and frequent recurrence in every day's conversation, will also afford good and useful practice on this subject.

344. *Neuter verbs*, do not all take the same auxi liary ; some have *avoir*, others have *être*.

XAMPLES.

ils sont partis,	*They have gone.*
les soldats ont couru,	*the soldiers have run.*

Some in one sense, take the auxiliary *être*, and in another, *avoir*.

EXAMPLES.

1. ils ont échappé. 2. ils sont échappés.

The first implies the *actual fact* of some people having escaped, the second implies the *state or position* of people having escaped.

These are points which require much attention, and we subjoin three lists of examples which the learner will do well to commit to memory.

345. The neuter verbs which take the verb *être* are, *aller*, *arriver*, *choir*, *convenir*, *déborder* (to overflow) *décéder*, *devenir*, *échoir*, *éclore*, *intervenir*, *mourir*, *naître*, *partir*, *parvenir*, *provenir*, *repartir* (to set off again), *résulter*, *retourner*, *revenir*, *survenir*, *tomber* and *venir*.

EXAMPLES.

les enfants *sont* allés au jardin,	*the children are gone to the garden.*
elle *était* arrivée avant moi,	*she had arrived before me.*
nous *sommes* convenus de nos torts,	*we have confessed our wrongs.*
la rivière *est* débordée,	*the river has overflown.*
ces grands hommes *sont* tous décédés,	*those great men are all dead.*
les vrais littérateurs *sont* devenus rares,	*true learned men have become scarce.*

* These lists are taken from Mr. Sievrac's edition.

votre billet *sera* échu avant votre retour,	*your bill will fall due before you return.*
ces œufs sont *éclos,*	*those eggs are hatched.*
il *est* intervenu dans cette affaire,	*he has interfered in that affair.*
on dit que son père et sa mère *sont* morts,	*they say that his mother and father are dead.*
nos malheurs *sont* nés de nos dissentions,	*our misfortunes have sprung from our dissentions.*
ma sœur *était* partie avant lui,	*my sister had set off before him.*
elle *est* enfin parvenue à son but,	*she has at last obtained her end.*
les enfants qui *sont* provenus de ce mariage,	*the children that are issued from that marriage.*
ils *sont* repartis pour la campagne,	*they are gone into the country again.*
il en *est* résulté un grand inconvénient,	*a great inconvenience has been the result of it.*
nous *étions* retournés au château,	*we had all gone back to the castle.*
elles *seraient* revenues avec nous,	*they would have come back with us.*
cette agréable nouvelle *est* survenue ce matin,	*this agreeable news came this morning.*
il a voulu courir et il *est* tombé,	*he would run, and he fell.*
pourquoi *sont*-ils venus ici ?	*why did they come hither ?*

346. Neuter verbs, which take the verb *avoir*, are *comparaître, contrevenir, convenir, courir, échouer, paraître, subvenir.*

EXAMPLES.

les témoins *ont* comparu ce matin,	*the witnesses have appeared this morning.*
ils *ont* contrevenu aux principaux articles du traité,	*they have infringed the chief articles of the treaty.*
cette maison et cet ameublement m'*auraient* bien convenu,	*that house and furniture would have suited me much.*
les soldats *ont* couru vers leur général,	*the soldiers have run towards their general.*
un vaisseau américain *a* échoué devant le port,	*an American vessel has run aground near the port.*
nous *avons* paru quand on nous a appelés,	*we appeared, when we were called for.*
mon bon père *a* subvenu à tous mes besoins,	*my good father has provided for all my exigencies.*

347. Neuter verbs which take either of the auxi

tiaries according to the idea expressed, *accoucher, accourir, accroître, apparaître, cesser, changer, commencer, croître, déchoir, demeurer, descendre, diminuer, disparaître, échapper, embellir, entrer, expirer, grandir, rajeunir, monter, passer, périr, rester, sonner* and *vieillir*.

EXAMPLES.

With AVOIR *(fact)*.	*With* ÊTRE *(state)*.
j'ai accouru sur-le-champ à son secours, *I immediately ran to his assistance.*	la garde *est* accourue sur-le-champ, *the guard ran up in all haste.*
il *a* accru sa fortune en bien peu de temps, *he has increased his fortune in a short time.*	son orgueil *est* accru avec ses richesses, *his pride has increased with his riches.*
il dit qu'un spectre lui *a* apparu pendant la nuit, *he says that a ghost has appeared to him during the night.*	Dieu *est* apparu à Moïse, *God has appeared to Moses.*
la fièvre *a* cessé pendant une heure, *the fever has ceased for an hour.*	la fièvre *est* cessée depuis une heure, *the fever has ceased an hour ago.*
les circonstances *ont* changé la face des affaires, *circumstances have altered the face of affairs.*	cette femme *est* changée à faire peur, *that woman is so altered as to frighten one.*
le bal *a* commencé vers minuit, *the ball began towards midnight.*	le bal *était* commencé lorsque nous entrâmes, *the ball had began when we came in.*
cet enfant *a* crû pendant sa maladie, *that child has grown during his illness.*	cette plante *est* crûe prodigieusement, *that plant is prodigiously grown.*
depuis ce moment il *a* déchu de jour en jour, *he has been on the decay ever since.*	il *est* bien déchu de son credit, *he has lost much of his credit.*

j'ai demeuré vingt ans à Paris,
I have lived twenty years in Paris.

il *est* demeuré à Paris pour y étudier la médecine,
he has remained in Paris to study physic.

ils *ont* descendu la montagne beaucoup plus vite qu'ils ne l'*avaient* montée,
they have descended the hill much quicker than they had ascended it.

ils *sont* descendus,
they have come down.

le prix du blé n'*a* pas diminué depuis six mois,
the price of wheat has not fallen for these six months.

il *est* enfin diminué de moitié,
it has at last fallen by half.

elle *a* disparu subitement,
she has disappeared all on a sudden.

elle *est* disparue depuis quinze jours,
it is now a fortnight since she has disappeared.

ils *ont* échappé au danger,
they have escaped the danger.

ils *sont* échappés depuis hier,
they have made their escape since yesterday.

elle *a* fort embelli pendant son voyage,
she is grown handsome on her journey.

on croirait qu'elle *est* embellie,
one would think that she is grown handsomer.

j'*ai* entré en ce lieu,
I have entered that place.

vous *êtes* entré, restez-y,
you are in, stay.

Jésus-Christ *a* expiré sur la croix,
Jesus-Christ expired on the cross.

la trève *est* expirée,
the truce has expired.

ce jeune homme *a* grandi depuis peu de temps,
that young man has grown very lately.

assurément vous *êtes* bien grandi,
indeed you are much grown.

vous *avez* rajeuni dans votre voyage,
you are grown younger in your journey.

vous *êtes* rajeuni à mes yeux de dix ans,
you are grown younger in my eyes by ten years.

il *a* monté quatre fois à sa chambre pendant la journée,
he went up into his room four times in the course of the day.

il *est* monté dans sa chambre et il y *est* resté,
he is gone up into his room and has remained there.

la procession *a* passé sous mes fenêtres, *the procession has passed under my window.*	la procession *est* passée, *the procession has gone by.*
ces malheureux *ont* tous péri dans le combat, *those unfortunate men have all perished in the battle.*	que *sont* devenus ces malheureux qu'on avait entassés dans vos prisons? ils *sont* péris, *what has become of those unfortunate men who had been heaped in your dungeons? they are dead.*
combien de temps *avez*-vous resté en Angleterre? *what stay did you make in England?*	cent combattants *sont* restés sur la place, *one hundred combattants have remained on the field of battle.*
la pendule *a* sonné cinq heures, *the clock has struck five.*	trois heures *étaient* sonnées, lorsqu'on s'est mis à table, *it had struck three, when we sat down at meat.*
j'*ai* bien vieilli depuis deux ans, *I am grown much older within these two years.*	avouez que nous *sommes* bien vieillis, *confess that we are grown very old.*

OF THE VERB BEING REGIMEN.

348. When two verbs come together the second may be, 1st. in the infinitive; 2dly, in the indicative mood; 3dly, in the subjunctive.

OF THE VERB IN THE INFINITIVE AFTER ANOTHER.

349. The second verb is in the infinitive, when we speak of one person only, *i.e.* when the subject of both verbs is the same

EXAMPLES.

je veux sortir,	*I wish to go out.*
nous espérons voir le roi,	*we hope to see the king.*

The subject of *vouloir* and *sortir* is the same; *I*

wish *I* may go out; so of *espérer*, *we* hope *we* shall see the king.

350. But here again is a difficulty for the learner; the infinitive following is sometimes governed by the preposition *à*, sometimes by *de*, sometimes by *pour*, and sometimes there is no preposition at all.

EXAMPLES.

j'aime *à* lire,	*I like* to *read.*
je crains *de* tomber,	*I fear* to *fall.*
je travaille pour vivre,	*I work to get my living.*
je dois partir,	*I am to go.*

This difference depends on the preceding verb of which the government must be ascertained.

351. *Aimer mieux*, *valoir mieux*, *aller*, *espérer*, *falloir*, *devoir*, *pouvoir*, *savoir*, *vouloir*, etc., require no preposition before the following infinitive.

EXAMPLES

j'aimerais mieux mourir,	*I had rather die.*
vous devriez sortir,	*you ought to go out.*

352. *Achever*, *finir*, *affecter*, *se dépêcher*, *se hâter*, *craindre*, *appréhender*, *désirer*, etc., require the preposition *de*.

EXAMPLES.

il affecte de l'aimer,	*he affects to like it.*
elle craignait de tomber,	*she feared to fall.*

353. *Aimer*, *apprendre*, *consentir*, *se plaire*, *s'apprêter*, etc. require *à*.

EXAMPLES

j'aime à danser,	*I like dancing.*
consentez-vous à l'épouser?	*do you consent to marry her?*

The preposition *pour* is used when *in order to*, is either expressed or understood in English.

EXAMPLE.

il va à la campagne pour chasser, *he is going in the country to shoot.*

354. Verbs generally require, before the infinitive, the same preposition which they require before the noun.

EXAMPLES.

je vous blâme de votre refus,	*I blame you for your refusal.*
je vous blâme de refuser,	*I blame you for refusing.*

355. Sometimes a verb governs two different prepositions, because it has two different acceptations.

S'efforcer de, to endeavour, is taken in the moral sense; *s'efforcer à*, in the physical.

EXAMPLES.

il s'efforce de plaire,	*he tries to please.*
il s'efforce à parler,	*he exerts himself to speak.*

These peculiarities of the language cannot be taught by rule; they belong to individual words which must be consulted. See *Dictionnaire des Verbes.*

EXERCISE.

1. Do you prefer living * in the country?
2. Come, when you have done writing.
3. Are you afraid of falling?
4. He cannot walk.
5. Does he not like travelling?
6. She takes delight in teasing.
7. Has he not consented to pay you?

8. They are gone to London to see if they can find a house for the season.
9. My sisters learn drawing.
10. I was getting ready to go out when he came.
11. They hope to arrive in time.
12. Make haste to get up and to dress.

(1.) Préférer, vivre; *in*, à.
(2.) Finir, *ind*-8.
(3.) Craindre.
(4.) Pouvoir.
(5.) Aimer voyager.
(6.) Se plaire, tourmenter.
(7.) Consentir.
(8.) Aller, voir, pouvoir.
(9.) Apprendre, dessiner.
(10.) S'apprêter, sortir, venir, *ind*-4.
(11.) Espérer; *in time*, à temps.
(12.) Se dépêcher, se lever, s'habiller.

OF THE VERB IN THE INDICATIVE AND THE SUBJUNCTIVE MOOD.

356. When the subjects of the two verbs are different, the second verb must be in the indicative mood or in the subjunctive.

EXAMPLES.

je crois que vous avez raison,	*I think you are right.*
je doute que vous ayez raison,	*I doubt your being right.*

Here are two persons or subjects; the one *thinking* or *doubting*, and the other *being or not being in the right.*

357. The indicative mood is used after all verbs expressing an act of the mind, and when speaking *in an affirmative and positive manner*; among such may be enumerated *croire*, *imaginer*, *concevoir*, *réfléchir*, *considérer*, *observer*, *remarquer*, *compter*, *espérer*, *démontrer*, etc., etc.

EXAMPLES.

je crois *qu*'il est venu,	*I believe he has arrived.*
espérons *que* la chose ira bien,	*let us hope the thing will succeed.*

OBSERVE. That the conjunction *que* is never omitted in French.

358. If the same verbs are used interrogatively

or negatively, they require the subjunctive mood after them.

EXAMPLES.

je ne crois pas qu'il soit venu	*I do not think he is come*
espérez-vous que la chose aille bien ?	*do you expect the thing will go on well?*

359. There are some verbs expressive of *fear*, *doubt*, *apprehension*, *desire*, which always have the subjunctive mood after them, whether in the affirmative or the negative form.*

EXAMPLES.

je doute qu'il vienne	*I doubt his coming*
je crains que cela ne soit	*I fear its being so*

EXERCISE.

1. She thinks you have not sufficiently attended to her interest :
2. Do you imagine it is an easy thing to convince him ?
3. They say he is going abroad.
4. Do you imagine I have done it on purpose ?
5. I wish you may succeed, but I doubt it.
6. We fear he will come in our absence, and he will be vexed not to find us at home.

(1.) Croire ; *to have attended*, s'être occupé de ; *interest*, intérêts.
(2.) S'imaginer, chose facile, convaincre.
(3.) *Abroad*, à l'étranger.
(4.) *To do on purpose*, faire exprès.
(5.) Désirer, réussir, douter de.
(6.) Craindre, venir ; *vexed*, contrarié de.

* This is more fully explained at the article, subj. mood, No. 391.

OF THE NATURE AND USE OF MOODS AND TENSES.

OF THE INDICATIVE

360. *The indicative* is the mood which declares affirmatively or negatively. It has eight tenses which are:

the present	je parle
the imperfect	je parlais
the preterit definite	je parlai
the preterit indefinite	j'ai parlé
the preterit anterior	j'eus parlé
the pluperfect	j'avais parlé
the future simple	je parlerai
the future anterior	j'aurai parlé

361. The *present* marks that a thing is *now* passing, that is. either existing or doing.

EXAMPLES.

j'aime,	*I love, do love, am loved.*
ils jouent,	*they play, do play, are playing.*

361. The present may be used in speaking of a thing that is going to be done, or take place, as being more expressive than the future.

EXAMPLE

je suis de retour dans un moment,	*I shall be back in an instant*

It is also used, in a narrative, instead of the preterite, in order to give more force and vivacity to the description, and to make the thing, as it were, present.

EXAMPLE.

le cheval blessé, se démène et secoue son maître; Cyrus tombe.	*the horse being wounded, struggled, shook off his rider; Cyrus fell.*

EXERCISE.

1. *He* is in his chamber, where he *is relaxing* his mind from the fatigue of business, by some instructive and agreeable reading.
2. Truth, eternal by its nature, *is* immutable as God himself.
3. I never *let* a day *pass* without devoting an hour or two to reading the ancients.
4. It is this week that the new piece *comes* out.
5. The armies were in sight: nothing was heard on all sides but dreadful cries: the engagement began. Immediately a cloud of arrows *darkens* the air and *covers* the combatants; nothing *is* heard but doleful cries of the dying, or the clattering of the arms of those who *fall* in the conflict; the earth *groans* beneath a heap of dead bodies, and rivers of blood *stream* every where; there *is* nothing in this confused mass of men enraged against one another but slaughter, despair, revenge, and brutal fury.

(1.) Is unbending, *délasse*; reading, *lecture.*
(2.) By, *de*; immutable, *immuable.*
(3.) Let, devoting, *consacrer*; reading, *la lecture de.*
(4.) Come out, *on donner.*
(5.) Sight, *présence*; nothing was, etc., *on ne que*, ind-2; the engagement began, *on en venir aux mains*, ind-3; cloud, *nuée*; arrows, *trait*; darkens, *obscurcir*; nothing is, etc., *on ne plus que*; doleful, *plaintif*; clattering, *bruit*; conflict, *mêlée*; groans, *gémir*; beneath, *sous*; heap, *monceau*; rivers, *ruisseau*; stream, *couler*; there is nothing in, etc. *ce ne être dans*; mass, *amas*; enraged, *acharné*; but, *que*; slaughter, *massacre.*

362. The *imperfect, je parlais,* I was speaking, I did speak, I used to speak, I spoke; expresses a thing being done at the moment another takes place.

EXAMPLE.

j'entrais au moment où vous êtes entré,	*I came in at the moment you entered.*

The imperfect expresses also repetition, habit, description of things habitual and stationary.

EXAMPLES.

je recevais de ses nouvelles toutes les semaines,	*I heard from him every week.*
quand j'étais à Paris, j'allais souvent aux Champs Elysées,	*when I was in Paris I often went to the Champs Elysées.*
voilà la place où elle aimait à s'asseoir,	*this is the place where she liked to sit down.*
son père était fier,	*his father was very proud.*
le livre était sur la table ; quelqu'un l'aura pris,	*the book was laying upon the table, somebody must have taken it.*

EXERCISE.

1. When I *was* at Paris, I *went* every morning to take a walk in the *Champs Elysées*, or the *Bois de Boulogne:* afterwards I *came* home, where I employed myself till dinner, either in reading or writing ; and, in the evening, I generally *went* for amusement to the French Theatre or the Opera.

2. When I *was* in the prime of life, like the light butterfly, I *fluttered* from object to object, without being able to settle to any thing : eager for pleasure, I *seized* every thing that *had* its appearance · alas ! how far *was* I then from foreseeing that I should deplore with so much bitterness the loss of that precious time.

3. For a short time after Abraham, the knowledge of the true God still *appeared* in Palestine and Egypt. Melchisedec, king of Salem, *was* the priest of the Most High 2 God 1. Abimelech, king of Gerar, and his successor of the same name, *feared* God, *swore* by his name, and *reverenced* his power. But in Moses' time, the nations *adored* even beasts and reptiles. Every thing *was* God but God himself.

(1.) Take a walk, *se promener ;* in, *à ;* came home, *rentrer chez soi ;* was busy, *s'occuper ;* reading, *(by the verb) ;* for amusement, *me délasser ;* French Theatre, *Comédie Française.*

(2.) Prime of life, *fleur de l'âge ;* butterfly, *papillon ;* fluttered, *voler ;* being able, *pouvoir ;* settle, *me fixer ;* eager for, *avide de ;* had its appearance, *m'en presentait l'image ;* how, *que ;* with so much bitterness, *(so bitterly.)*

(3.) Swore, *jurer ;* reverenced, *admirer ;* the nations, *on ;* even, *jusqu'à ;* but, *excepté*

363. *The preterit definite, je parlai*, is used in speaking of things done during a period, *a year, a month or a week*, entirely elapsed, and when the precise moment is specified or understood in which the action took place.

EXAMPLES

je lui écrivis à mon arrivée à Bath,	*I wrote to him on my arrival at Bath.*
nous nous rencontrâmes l'année dernière aux eaux,	*we met last year at a watering place.*

This preterit has been called the ***historical tense,*** on account of its serving to express things which have happened at a period distant from the present.

EXERCISE.

Amenophis *conceived* the design of making his son a conqueror. He *set about* it, after the manner of the Egyptians, that is, with great ideas. All the children who were born on * the same day as Sesostris, *were brought* to court by order of the king: he *had* them educated as his own children, and with the same care as Sesostris. When he *was* grown up, he made him serve his apprenticeship in a war against the Arabs: this young prince *learned* there to bear hunger and thirst, and *subdued* that nation, till then invincible. He afterwards *attacked* Lybia, and *conquered* it. After these successes, he *formed* the project of subduing the whole world. In consequence of this *, he entered Ethiopia, which he *made* tributary. He *continued* his victories in Asia. Jerusalem *was* the first to feel the force of his arms: the rash Rehoboam *could* not resist him, and Sesostris *carried* away the riches of Solomon. He *penetrated* into the Indies, farther than Hercules and Bacchus, and farther than Alexander did afterward. The Scythians *obeyed* him as far as the Tanais; Armenia and Cappadocia *were* subject to him. In a word, he *extended* his empire from the Ganges to the Danube.

Making, *faire de;* set about it, *s'y prendre:* after, *à;* ideas, *pensée;* brought, *amener;* had educated, *faire élever;* grown up, *grand;* made serve, *fit faire.* apprenticeship, *apprentissage;* in, *par;* entered, *entrer dans;* made, *rendre;* as far as, *jusqu'à;* Cappadocia, *Cappadoce.*

364. *The preterit indefinite, j'ai parlé,* is the tense which is the most used in French; it expresses things done, or which have happened in the course of the day, recently, within the week, the month or the year in which

EXAMPLE.

j'ai rencontré votre frère ce matin,	*I met your brother this morning.*

The preterite indefinite is used also to express assertion of a thing having been done, without any reference to time.

EXAMPLES.

j'ai voyagé en Italie,	*I travelled in Italy.*
j'en ai parlé à votre oncle,	*I have mentioned it to your uncle.*
n'avez-vous remarqué aucune faute?	*have you noticed no mistakes?*

It is also used figuratively instead of the future.

EXAMPLES.

avez-vous bientôt fini?	*shall you have done soon*
oui, j'ai fini dans un moment,	*yes, I shall have done in a minute.*

EXERCISE.

1. Enflamed with the desire of knowing mankind, I *have travelled*, not only among the most polished nations, but even among the most barbarous. I *have observed* them in the different degrees of civilization, from the state of simple nature to the most perfect state of society, and wherever I went, the result *was* the same: that is to say, I *have* every where *seen* beings occupied in drying up the different sources of happiness that nature had placed within their reach.

2. I *have travelled* this year in Italy, where I *had* an * opportunity of seeing several master-pieces of antiquity, and where I *made* a valuable collection of scarce medals. I there *admired* the perfection to which they *have brought* architecture, painting, and music; but what *pleased* me most there, was the beauty of the climate of Naples.

(1.) With, *de;* mankind, *homme, pl.* to, *chez;* polished nations, *peuple policé;* barbarous, *nation sauvage;* from, *depuis;* simple, *pur;* to, *jusqu'à;* wherever I went, *dans tous les pays;* the result was the same, *(I had the same result);* in drying up, *à tarir;* within their reach, *à leur portée.*

(2.) Opportunity, *occasion;* master-pieces, *chef-d'œuvre;* scarce, *rare;* pleased me most, *faire le plus de plaisir;* was, ind-1.

365. *The two preterit anterior, j'eus parlé, j'ai eu parlé,* are commonly used after an adverb of time, such as *dès que, aussitôt que, quand.*

EXAMPLES.

dès que j'eus dîné je sortis,	*as soon as I had dined I went out.*
dès que j'ai eu dîné je suis sorti,	*I did go out as soon as I had done dinner.*

There is the same difference between these two tenses as between the preterit definite and the preterit indefinite. The first, *j'eus parlé,* is principally used in reference to time long past; the second, *j'ai eu parlé,* is said of things recently occured. The latter expresses also assertion of facts, as *j'ai parlé* does.

EXAMPLE.

aujourd'hui j'ai eu déjeùne en dix minutes,	*i was not more than ten minutes about my breakfast to day.*

366. *The pluoerfect, j'avais parlé,* expresses the completion of an action, at the moment another took place.

EXAMPLE.

j'avais soupé quand il entra,	*I had done supper when he entered.*

It is generally preceded of *dès que, quand, lorsque, aussitôt que,* and, like the imperfect, serves to express habitual things, repetition, and to describe.

EXAMPLES.

j'allais à la chasse dès que j'avais déjeûné,	*I went out shooting as soon as I had done breakfast.*

EXERCISE.

1. As soon as I *had examined* this phenomenon, I tried to find out its causes.

2. As soon as we *had crossed* the river, we found ourselves in a wood where there was not a single foot-path traced.

3. As soon as the great Sesostris *had satisfied* his ambition by the conquest of so many empires, he returned into Egypt, where he devoted the whole of the day to administering strict justice to his people, and, in the evening, he recreated himself by holding conferences with the learned, or by conversing with the most upright people of his kingdom.

4. I *had* only *received*, like most of the grandees, an education in which I *had imbibed* nothing but sentiments of pride and insensibility; that is, they *had done* every thing in their power, to stifle in me the happy and benevolent dispositions which I *had received* from nature.

(1.) As soon as, *dès que*; tried to find out, *en rechercher*.
(2.) Crossed, *traverser*; found ourselves, *se trouver engagé*; foot-path, *sentier de*.
(3.) The whole of the day, *jour entier*; administering, *rendre*, inf-1; strict, *exact*; recreated, *délasser*; by holding conferences, *à s'entretenir*; upright, *honnête*; people, *gens*.
(4.) Grandee, *grand*; imbibed, *puiser*; they, *on*; in their power, *ce qu'on pouvoir*, ind-6; stifle, *étouffer*; benevolent, *bienfaisant*.

367. The *future absolute, je parlerai*, is that tense which expresses that an action or event will take place at a time which does not yet exist.

EXAMPLE.

j'irai demain à la campagne,	*I shall go to-morrow into the country.*

The *future anterior* is the tense which expresses that, at a time when a thing will take place, another thing will have already taken place.

EXAMPLE.

quand j'aurai fini, je sortirai,	*when I have done, I shall go out.*

368. It is customary in English, to put the *present tense* after *when*, it is not so in French, the

future tense must always be used, if speaking of things to come.

EXAMPLES.

I will show it to you when I have done,	je vous le montrerai, quand je l'aurai fini.
when he comes, do let me know,	quand il viendra, faites-le-moi savoir.

369. The future is also used after *si*, when it means *whether*, that is, when a doubt is expressed.

EXAMPLE.

je ne sais si mon père viendra,	*I do not know whether my father will come.*

When *si* means *if*, the future must not be used.

EXAMPLE.

nous irons à la campagne demain, s'il fait beau temps,	*we shall go into the country to-morrow if it is fine*

The future is used in French in rendering sentences like this, do as you please, *faites comme il vous plaira* or *comme vous voudrez.*

EXERCISE.

1. Remember that youth is but a flower, which *will wither* almost as soon as it * opens. Thou *wilt see thyself* gradually changed. Smiling graces, sweet pleasures, strength, health, and joy, *will vanish* like a pleasing dream; nothing but the sad remembrance will be left thee.

2. I *shall* next year *take* a journey into Greece, and I am preparing myself for it by reading the travels of the young Anacharsis.

3. When you *have read* the celebrated discourse of Bossuet on Universal History, and *studied* in it the causes of the rise and fall of states, you *will be* less astonished at the revolutions, more or less sudden, that modern empires have experienced, which appeared to you in the most flourishing state.

(1.) Will wither, *(will be almost as soon withered as. 47), sécher;* opens, *éclose*: gradually, *insensiblement*; lively, *riant*; pleasing, *beau*; nothing will be left, *il n'en rester*.

(2.) Take, *faire*; for it, *y*; reading, *lecture de*; (*the travels*, celui.)

(3.) Have read, ind-8; and, *que vous*, ind-8; in it, *y*; rise, *grandeur*; fall, *chute*; sudden, *subite*; (*that have experienced the modern empires, which, etc.*) appeared, ind-2.

ILLUSTRATIVE EXAMPLES OF *JE PARLAIS, JE PARLAI, J'AI PARLÉ.*

370. The choice of the proper tense, between *je parlais, j'ai parlé, je parlai* is so difficult for the learner, it requires such perfect understanding of the peculiar acceptation of each of them, that the following passages selected and analysed for their illustration, may prove useful in addition to the foregoing rules.

We read in Marmontel—

Célicour, à l'âge de quinze ans, *avait été* dans le monde ce qu'on appelle un petit prodige,	*Célicour, at the age of fifteen*, had been *in the world what is called a little prodigy*.

The author uses the pluperfect, because he describes what was at a period of time anterior to all those which he is going to mention.

Again,

Il *faisait* des vers les plus galants du monde; il n'y *avait* pas dans le voisinage une jolie femme qu'il n'eût célébrée: *c'était* dommage de laisser tant de talents enfouis dans une petite ville; Paris *devait* en être le théâtre,	*he* composed *the most agreeable love-sonnets imaginable: there* was *not a pretty woman in the neighbourhood that he had not celebrated*: *it* was *a pity to let so many talents be buried in a little town; Paris* was *the stage on which they ought to be exhibited.*

Here the author makes use of the imperfect, because he speaks of the habitual occupation of Célicour.

EXAMPLE.

et l'*on fit* si bien, que son père se *résolut* de l'y envoyer,	*and they* contrived *matters so, that his father* determined *to send him there.*

Now, the author passes to the preterit definite, because he is no longer speaking of what was habitual or repeated, but of an action which once occurred, and long ago.

EXAMPLE.

ce père *était* un honnête homme, qui *aimait* l'esprit sans en avoir, et qui *admirait*, sans savoir pourquoi, tout ce qui *venait* de la capitale. Il *avait* même des relations littéraires, et du nombre de ses correspondants *était* un connaisseur nommé M. de Fintac,	*this father* was *a good sort of man, who* was *fond of wit, without having any, and* admired, *without knowing why, every thing that* came *from the metropolis. Nay, he* even *had some literary connexions, and among his correspondents* was *a connoisseur of the name of Fintac.*

Here again, the author resumes the form of the imperfect, as he is now speaking of the habitual state of Célicour's father, in his little town.

EXAMPLE.

ce *fut* principalement à lui que Célicour *fut* recommandé	*it* was *particularly to him that Célicour* was *recommended*

The form of the preterit definite is now resumed, because this is said of action passed at a time long elapsed.

And in Molière's Fourberies de Scapin, we read

comme nous sommes grands amis, il me *fit* aussitôt confidence de son amour, et me *mena* voir cette fille que je	*as we are great friends, he immediately imparted the secret of his love to me, and took me to see that girl whom I certainly*

trouvai belle, à la vérité, mais non pas tant qu'il *voulait* que je la trouvasse, | *thought pretty, but not so much as he wished me to do.*

Here *fit*, *mena*, *trouvai* are all referring to actions past long ago, and they serve also to state facts but not to describe permanent things. *Voulait*, on the contrary, is in the imperfect, because it expresses the constant and continued desire of Leandre that his mistress should be thought pretty.

Again Scapin says:

c'est ce que *je lui ai dit*. *J'ai rejeté* bien loin de pareilles propositions, et je lui *ai bien fait* entendre que vous *n'étiez* point une dupe, pour vous demander des cinq ou six cents pistoles. Enfin, après plusieurs discours voici où *s'est réduit* le résultat de notre conférence, | *that is what I said to him; I would not hear of such proposals, and I gave him to understand that you were not a dupe to ask you five or six hundred pistols. Finally, after several speeches, this is what has been the result of our interview.*

Here the preterit indefinite, *j'ai parlé* is used, because Scapin relates what he has done since he saw Argante, consequently in the course of the day in which he is speaking. There is no description of a continued state of things, except in *étiez*, which refers to the general character of Argante.

OF THE CONDITIONAL.

371. The *conditional* is the mood which affirms a thing would be on some conditions; it has two tenses, the *present* and the *past*.

The *present of the conditional (je parlerais)* is that tense which expresses that a thing would take place on certain conditions.

EXAMPLE.

Je ferais votre affaire avant peu, | *I would settle your business be-*

si elle dependait uniquement de moi, — *fore long, if it only depends upon me.*

The *past of the conditional (j'aurais parlé)* is that tense which expresses that a thing would have taken place at a time which no longer exists, dependant on certain conditions.

EXAMPLE.

j'aurais, *ou* j'eusse* fait votre affaire, si vous m'en aviez, *ou* m'en eussiez parlé, — *I would have settled your business if you had mentioned it to me.*

372. The conditional is used to express a wish, as,

que je serais, *or*, que j'aurais été content si j'avais réussi ! — *how glad I should be, or should have been had I succeeded !*

AND after *si*, whether, expressing a doubt, as,

demandez-lui s'il serait venu avec nous, supposé qu'il n'eût pas eu affaire ? — *ask him whether he would have come with us, had he not been engaged ?*

373. It is used also before, or after the imperfect, or pluperfect of the indicative, when they are preceded by *si*, as,

nous nous épargnerions bien des peines, si nous savions modérer nos désirs, — *we should spare ourselves much pain, did we know how to moderate our desires.*

vous auriez été plus heureux, si vous aviez suivi mes conseils, — *you would have been more happy, if you had followed my advice.*

374. After *quand, quand même;* in the sense of *though even, were I to.*

EXAMPLE.

quand l'avare posséderait tout l'or du monde, il ne serait pas encore content, — *were the miser to possess all the gold in the world, he would not be satisfied.*

* Some writers, and Voltaire especially, often make use of this form, *j'eusse parlé*, for *j'aurais parlé*. It is here given as an example, but it will be well to follow the first.

And in questions like the following, in the sense of *is it possible that, could I? could you? really?*

EXAMPLES.

croiriez-vous votre fils ingrat?	*could you think your son ungrateful?*
l'auriez-vous soupçonné d'un tel vice?	*could you have suspected him of such a vice?*

which means, ***croyez-vous, pouvez-vous croire.*** etc ***auriez-vous pu,*** etc.

Voltaire makes a happy use of this form, in his Mérope.

EXAMPLES

serais-tu vraiment son fils?	*can it really be that you should be his son?*
tu n'aurais employé qu'une juste défense,	*really, you had only recourse to self-defence.*

EXERCISE.

1. If it *were* even possible for men always to act conformably to equity, as it is the multitude that must judge their conduct, the wicked would always blame and contradict them from malignity, and the good sometimes from mistake.

2. What false steps I *should have made* but for you, at my entrance into the world!

3. But for your counsels, I *should have failed* in this undertaking.

4. How satisfied I *should have been,* if you had sooner informed me of your happiness!

5. If we gave to infancy none but just and clear notions, *there would be* a much less considerable number of false wits in the world.

6. *Had* Alexander *conquered* the whole world, his ambition *would not have been* satisfied: he *would* still *have found* himself straitened in it.

7. *Could you believe* him vain enough to aspire to that high degree of honour?

8. *Could you* ever *have thought* him capable of deserting the good cause, to go and side with rebels?

9 *Would you renounce* being useful to the present generation because envy fastens on you?

(1.) If even, *quand même;* were, cond-1; for men, (that men); to act, subj-2; judge, *juger de;* would blame, ind-7; contradict, *croiser*, ind-7.
(2.) What, *que de;* steps, *démarche;* but for, *sans*.
(3.) But for, *sans;* failed, *échouer*.
(4.) How, *que*.
(5.) We, *on;* a much less considerable number, *bien moins*.
(6.) (When Alexander would have conquered); straitened, *trop à l'étroit*.
(8.) Deserting; *abandonner;* to go and side with, *pour se ranger sous les drapeaux de*.
(9.) Renounce, *renoncer à;* fastens, *s'attacher;* on you, *à vos pas*.

375. Foreigners are very apt to use the conditional after *si*, when meaning *supposé que*. They say,

vous auriez vu le roi, *si* vous *seriez* venu,	*you would have seen the king if you had come.*

This mistake cannot be made if attention is paid to the actual meaning of SI, which signifies both *if* and *whether;* when it is taken in the acceptation of *whether* the conditional is used, not otherwise.

EXAMPLES.

je ne savais si nous irions ou non,	*I did not know whether we should go or no.*
si nous allions à la campagne, je vous en préviendrais,	*if we went into the country, I would tell you of it.*

OF THE IMPERATIVE.

376. The *imperative* is that mood which commands, exhorts, entreats, forbids or reproves.

In many verbs a compound of the imperative may be used to express an injunction to have a thing done previously to another, as, *ayez dîné avant que je revienne*, have dined before I return.

EXERCISE.

Be not fond of praise; but seek virtue, which
sing. *passionné pour* art. *louange* f. art.

procures it. Let us remember that unless virtue guide
attirer *se souvenir* *à moins que* art. *ne*

us, our choice must be wrong. Let us not be deceived by
devoir ind-1 mauvais se laisser prendre à

the first appearances of things; but let us take time, to
art. se donner art. de

fix our judgment. Arbiters of the destinies of men, do good
arbitre — née art. art. bien

if you wish to be happy; do good, if you wish that your memory
vouloir *

should be honoured; do good, if you wish that heaven should
subj-1 art. sub.

open to you its eternal gates.
1 2 porte f. 1.

OF THE SUBJUNCTIVE MOOD.

377. Remarks have already been made (No. 113) on the use of the subjunctive mood in French, and some examples have been given, by way of comparison, to show that the two languages by no means agree on this point. Many verbs in English, are put in the *future*, the *conditional* and the *present tense* which, in French, must be in the *subjunctive* mood. Thus,

je ne crois pas *qu'il soit* si âgé,	*I don't think* he is so old.
je ne crois pas qu'il *vienne*,	*I don't think* he will come.
je craignais qu'il ne *vînt*,	*I feared* he would come.
elle est la plus jolie que je *connaisse*,	*she is the prettiest* I know.

Observe that the *present* and *future* are the same in the subjunctive mood, the context alone shows of which of the two we speak.

EXAMPLES.

je ne crois pas qu'il vienne,	*I do not think he is coming.*
je ne crois pas qu'il vienne,	*I do not think he will come.*

The use of the present or of the past tenses of the

subjunctive is determined by the preceding verb, as will be seen No. 388.

378. The subjunctive mood is used in French after the following conjunctions.

à moins que*	*unless*
afin que	*in order that*
à Dieu ne plaise que	*God forbid that*
au cas que	*in case*
avant que	*before*
bien que	*although*
bien loin que	*far from*
ce n'est pas que	*it is not that*
de crainte que*	*for fear that, lest*
de manière que	*so that, in a manner that*
de peur que*	*for fear that*
Dieu veuille que	*God grant that*
encore que	*although*
excepté que	*except*
jusqu'à ce que	*until*
loin que	*far from*
malgré que	*although, spite of*
moyennant que	*on consideration that*
non pas que	*not that*
plût à Dieu que	*would to God that*
posé le cas que	*suppose*
pour que	*in order that, that*
pour peu que	*ever so little*
pourvu que	*provided that*
que	*(in the place of another conjunction)*
quelque	*whatever, however*
quoique	*although*
sans que	*without*
si ce n'est que	*except that*
si non que	*but that*
soit que	*whether, or*
supposé que	*suppose*
tant s'en faut que	*far from it that*

EXAMPLES.

entrez sans qu'il vous voie,	*get in without his seeing you.*
à dieu ne plaise qu'il en soit ainsi,	*God forbid it should be so*

* *Ne* is frequently put before the verb which follows *avant que*; yet I believe it ought to be only whenever *avant que* may be rendered by *lest*, and when there is an apprehension that a thing should happen before another.

Those conjunctions which are marked * require *ne* before the verb, though not having a negative sense

EXAMPLE.

allez doucement de peur qu'il ne vous entende,	*go gently lest he should hear you.*

EXERCISE.

Get up early to-morrow morning, that we may start in good time Shall the day pass away without my seeing you? God forbid that I should wrong a man who has ever showed me so much kindness. Make haste, lest he should set off without you. I shall wait until you have done.

379. It has been observed, (No. 357) that the conjunction *que*, used before the indicative mood, coming after a verb, expressing an act of the mind in the affirmative form, is never to be omitted in French. This shows that that conjunction does not *in itself* govern the subjunctive mood, as is erroneously thought by most learners; but there are, however, several cases in which *que* requires that mood after it. They are when *que* is used instead, or in the sense, of the following conjunctions: *à moins que, avant que, sans que, jusqu'à ce que, quoique, soit que,* which are themselves always followed by the subjunctive.

EXAMPLES.

j'attendrai *que* la pluie soit passée *(jusqu'à ce que)*	*I shall wait until the rain be over.*
je ne sortirai pas *que* vous ne m'ayez payé *(avant que)*	*I shall not leave the house before you pay me.*

EXERCISE.

1. Give me your letter *that* I may send it to the post-office.
2. He says he will not marry *until* he has a profession.
3. He cannot play, but he hurts himself.
4. We shall not go into the country, *unless* he consents to come with us.

(1.) *Que* for *afin que;* to send, *envoyer.*
(2.) To marry, *se marier, que* for *avant que ne;* profession, *état* m.
(3.) Cannot, *il ne saurait, que* for *sans que -ne.*
(4.) *Que* for *à moins que -ne;* to consent, *consentir à;* to come, *y aller.*

380. When the conjunction *si* governs two verbs the second must be in the subjunctive mood.

EXAMPLE.

si votre frère vient demain, et qu'il fasse beau temps, nous le mènerons à la chasse,	*if your brother comes to-morrow, and the weather is fine, we will take him hunting*

EXERCISE.

1. If men were wise and followed the lights of reason, they would save themselves many troubles.
2. If you go to Paris, and will take me with you, I shall be most happy.

(1.) *Etre,* ind-2, *suivre;* to save, *s'épargner.*
(2). To take, *mener;* to be happy, *en être enchanté.*

381. An adjective in the superlative degree, requires that the verb following be in the subjunctive.

EXAMPLE.

donnez-moi la meilleure plume que vous ayez,	*give me the best pen you have.*

Obs. Among such adjectives must be included *le premier, le dernier, le seul, l'unique, personne.*
See No. 212.

382. The relative pronouns *que, qui,* following a negative phrase, govern the subjunctive mood.

EXAMPLES.

il n'y avait là personne que je connusse,	*there was there no one that I knew.*

ne pourriez-vous m'indiquer un homme qui voulût se charger de cette affaire?	*could not you recommend some man to me, who would undertake that business?*

283. *Qui, que,* require also the subjunctive when following a sentence expressing ***a wish*** or ***a doubt***: *où*, for in which, has the same power.

EXAMPLES.

indiquez-moi un endroit où l'on puisse trouver cela,	*ell me of a place where that can be found.*
choisissez une femme qui soit prudente,	*choose a woman who is prudent.*

EXERCISE.

1. The largest stage there is for virtue, is conscience.
2. The motions of the planets are the most regular that we know.
3. There is no one who, in such case, would neglect so important a matter.
4. It may be said that the dog is the only animal whose faithfulness be proof.
5. This is the largest elephant that ever was seen.
6. Show me a man who calls himself perfectly happy.

(..) Stage, *théâtre*, m. there is, *y avoir*.
(2.) Motions, *mouvement*, m.
(3.) To neglect, *négliger;* matter, *intérêt*, m.
(4.) *On peut dire*, to be proof, *soit à l'épreuve*.
(5.) *Turn*, that one has ever seen.
(6.) To call one's self, *se dire*.

384. There are also a great many verbs which govern the subjunctive mood; they generally express *wish, determination, permission,* such as *désirer, souhaiter, prier, prétendre, vouloir, entendre, aimer mieux que, souffrir, s'étonner, ordonner,* etc.

EXAMPLES.

permettez que je vous dise ce qui est arrivé,	*allow me to tell you what has happened.*
je veux qu'il le fasse à l'instant,	*I will have him do it this moment*

Nier, *douter*, require the subjunctive, and, when used interrogatively or negatively, *ne* must precede the verb.

EXAMPLES

je nie que cela soit,	*I deny its being so*
je ne nie pas que cela ne soit,	*I do not deny but that it may be so.*
doutez-vous qu'il ne le fasse ?	*do you question his doing it ?*

Craindre, *appréhender*, *avoir peur*, *empêcher*, *trembler*, have also *ne* before the subjunctive, except when they are in the negative form.

EXAMPLES.

j'ai peur que cela ne vous fasse de la peine,	*I fear that will give you pain.*
je n'ai pas peur que cela vous fasse de la peine,	*I do not fear that it will give you pain.*

EXERCISE.

1. Do you doubt his coming? No, I do not doubt but he will come after so pressing an invitation.
2. I am afraid he will see me.
3. Do not let that child ride this horse, I am afraid he will throw him down.
4. The rain prevented us from going out.
5. Can you prevent his doing what he pleases ?
6. We all pray that he be soon relieved from his sufferings.
7. I do not like people to talk when I am reading.
8. Shall I read the letter aloud?

(1.) *Douter que;* to come, *venir.*
(2.) To be afraid, *craindre.*
(3.) To let, *permettre que;* to ride, *monter;* to throw down, *jeter à bas.*
(4.) To prevent, *empêcher que;* to go out, *sortir.*
(5.) What he pleases, *ce que bon lui semble.*
(6.) Relieved, *délivré;* sufferings, *peines.*
(7.) People, *on.*
(8.) Shall I, *voulez-vous que.*

385. *Etre ravi, bien aise*, etc. etc. have been noticed, No. 209, as governing also the subjunctive.

REMARKS ON THE ENGLISH SIGNS OR AUXILIARIES *DO, DID, WILL, WOULD, SHOULD, CAN, COULD, MAY, MIGHT.**

386. *Do, did, will, would, should, can, could, may,* and *might*, are sometimes to be considered as being simply signs of tenses; in other cases, they are real verbs.

There can be no difficulty about *do* and *did;* these are mere expletives, denoting interrogation, negation or merely emphasis, when they are joined to a verb.

EXAMPLES.

j'aime,	*I do love*
j'aimais, *or* j'aimai,	*I did love.*
aimé-je?	*do I love?*
aimais-je, *or* aimai-je?	*did I love?*
je n'aime pas,	*I do not love.*
je n'aimais *pas*, *or*, je n'aimai pas,	*I did not love.*

In all these cases, they are not expressed in French.

But when they are followed by a noun, or a pronoun, in short, by any thing else, except the verb with which they are connected, then they are real verbs, and mean, *faire*.

EXAMPLES.

faites-moi ce plaisir,	*do me that favour.*
il le fit,	*he did it.*
il fit plus qu'on n'eût pu espérer.	*he did more than could have been expected.*

* See the manner of rendering *might, should, ought* No. 19, of Models or Phrases on Difficulties, at the end

Should is only a sign of the conditional, when it expresses a thing which may happen upon some condition, and, in fact, it is used for *would.*

EXAMPLE.

j'aimerais la vie champêtre, si mes affaires me permettaient de suivre mon goût,	*I should like a country life, if my affairs would permit me to indulge my inclination.*

But when it implies duty or obligation, it is a distinct verb, and must be expressed by *devoir*, as,

nous ne devrions jamais nous écarter du sentier de la vertu,	*we should never swerve from the path of virtue.*

Can, could, may, and *might*, are not so difficult as they appear at first sight; because, in almost every instance, there is no impropriety in rendering them by the verb *pouvoir*. In general, the first two imply a power, a possibility, a capability, etc. and the others a permission, probability, etc.

EXAMPLES.

je puis le faire,	*I can do it.*
il pourrait le faire,	*he could do it.*
elle pourrait venir,	*she might come.*
elle aurait pu venir,	*she might have come.*
puis-je vous parler?	*may I speak to you?*

Can is rendered by *savoir*, when it is used for *to know how.*

EXAMPLE.

elle sait chanter,	*she can sing.*

Do, did, shall, will, etc. in English, are sometimes used elliptically in answer to an interrogation, or in an affirmation. In such cases the full sense is always given in French, that is, the verb, which is understood in English, is repeated.

See No. 20 of models of phrases, at the end.

EXAMPLE.

ferez-vous votre thème aujourd'hui?—Oui, je le ferai,	*shall you do your exercise to-day? yes, I shall.*

CONCORD BETWEEN THE TENSES OF THE INDICATIVE

387. When the first verb is in the imperfect, the preterit, or the pluperfect, the second verb is put in the imperfect, if we speak of the present time.

EXAMPLE.

je croyais, j'ai cru, j'avais cru que vous étudiez les mathématiques,	*I thought, I have thought, I had thought that you were studying the mathematics.*

And in the pluperfect, if we speak of past time.

EXAMPLE.

il m'assura qu'il n'avait jamais tant ri,	*he assured me that he had never laughed so much.*

And in the present of the conditional, if we speak of a future time.

EXAMPLE.

on m'a dit que votre frère viendrait à Londres l'hiver prochain,	*I was told your brother would come to town next winter.*

when it relates to things of common occurrence, or states a fact of general application.

EXAMPLE.

je vous disais, je vous ai dit, je vous avais dit, que la santé fait la félicité du corps, et le savoir celle de l'âme,	*I told you, I have told you, I had told you, that health constitutes the happiness of the body, and knowledge that of the soul.*

In phrases where the imperfect is preceded by *que*, it denotes, sometimes a thing past, sometimes a thing present. It denotes a thing past, when the verb which is joined to it by the conjunction *que*, is in the present or the future.

EXAMPLE.

vous savez, *ou* vous saurez *que* le peuple Romain *était* aussi avide qu'ambitieux	*you know* or *you must know that the Romans were a people as covetous as they were ambitious.*

But it denotes a thing present, when the verb, which precedes it, is in the imperfect, the preterit, or the pluperfect.

EXAMPLES.

on disait, on a dit, on avait dit que Phocion *était* le plus grand et le plus honnête homme de son temps,	*it was said, it has been said, it had been said, that Phocion was the greatest and most upright man of his age.*
dès qu'on eut appris à Athènes qu' Alcibiade *était* à Lacédémone, on se repentit de la précipitation avec laquelle on l'avait condamné,	*as soon as it was known at Athens that Alcibiades was at Lacedemon, the Athenians repented the precipitation with which they had condemned him.*

Nevertheless, the imperfect denotes the past, in this last instance, when it signifies an action which was past before that, which is expressed by the first verb.

EXAMPLE.

en lisant l'histoire des temps héroïques, vous devez avoir remarqué que ces hommes, dont on a fait des demi-dieux, *étaient* des chefs féroces et barbares, dignes à peine du nom d'homme,	*in reading the history of heroic times, you must have remarked that those men who have been made demi-gods, were ferocious and barbarous chiefs, scarcely deserving the name of men.*

EXERCISE.

1. I *thought* you *were not ignorant* that, to teach others the principles of an art or science, one needs to have experience and skill.

2. I *have been told* that your dearest occupation *was* to form your taste, your heart and your understanding.

3. Darius, in his flight, being * reduced to the necessity of drinking water muddy and infected by dead bodies, *affirmed* that he never *had drunk* with so much pleasure.

4. Care *has been taken* to inculcate in me, from infancy, that *I should succeed* in the world, only in proportion as I should unite with the desire of pleasing, a great deal of gentleness and civility.

5. Ovid *has said*, that study *softens* the manners, and *corrects* every thing that is found in us rude and barbarous.

6. You *know* that those pretended heroes, of whom Pagan antiquity has made gods, *were* only barbarous and ferocious kings, who overran the earth, not so much to conquer as to ravage it, and who left every where traces of their fury and of their vices.

7. It *has been said of* Pericles, that his eloquence was like a thunderbolt, which nothing could resist.

8. As soon as Aristides *had said*, that the proposal of Themistocles *was* unjust, the whole people *exclaimed*, that they must not think of it any longer.

9. Had you read the history of the early ages, *you would know* that Egypt *was* the most enlightened country in the universe, and that whence knowledge *spread* into Greece and the neighbouring countries.

(1.) Were ignorant, *ignorer;* teach, *instruire dans;* needs, *avoir besoin;* skill, *habileté*.

(2.) I have, etc. (by the active voice) on.

(3.) Flight, *déroute;* muddy, *bourbeux;* affirmed, *assurer.*

(4.) Care has, etc. (active voice) *on avoir;* in me, *me;* in proportion, *autant* civility, *honnêteté.*

(5.) Corrects, *effacer;* is found, *se trouver de.*

(6.) Overran, *parcourir;* not so much, *moins.*
(7.) It, *on;* thunderbolt, *foudre,* m.; (to) which.
(8.) Exclaimed, *s'écrier;* they must, *falloir.* ind-2; of it, *y;* any longer, *plus.*
(9.) Ages, *temps;* whence, *celui d'où;* neighbouring, *circonvoisin;* countries *lieux.*

CONCORD BETWEEN THE TENSES OF THE SUBJUNCTIVE AND THOSE OF THE INDICATIVE

388. When the verb of the principal proposition is in the present, or future, that of the subordinate proposition is put in the present of the subjunctive, to express a thing present, or future; but in the preterit, to express a thing past, we say,

il faut que celui qui parle *se mette* à la portée de celui qui l'écoute,	*he that speaks should accommodate himself to the understanding of him that listens.*
il voudra que votre frère *soit* de la partie,	*he will wish your brother to be one of the party.*

But we must say,

pour s'être élevé à ce point de grandeur, il faut que Rome *ait eu* une suite non interrompue de grands hommes,	*to have risen to that pitch of grandeur, Rome must have had an uninterrupted succession of great men.*

Exception. Though the first verb be in the present, or future, yet the second may be put in the imperfect, or pluperfect of the subjunctive, when some conditional expression is introduced into the sentence.

EXAMPLES.

il n'est point d'homme, quelque mérite qu'il ait, qui me *fût* très-mortifié, s'il savait tout ce qu'on pense de lui,	*there is no man, whatever merit he may have, that would not feel very much mortified were he to know all that is thought of him.*
où trouvera t'on l'homme qui	*where will you find the man who*

ne *fît* la même faute, s'il était exposé aux memes tentations?	*would not have committed the same error, had he been exposed to the same temptations?*
Je doute que votre frère *eût réussi* sans votre assistance,	*I doubt whether your brother would have succeeded, had it not been for your assistance*

EXERCISE.

1. He who wishes to teach an art, must *know it* thoroughly, he must *give* none but clear, precise and well-digested notions of it: he must *instil* them, one by one, into the minds of his pupils, and, above all, he must not overburthen their memory with useless, or unimportant rules.

2. He *must yield* to the force of truth, when they *shall have suffered* it to appear in its real light.

3. There is no work, however perfect people may suppose it, that would not be liable to criticism, if it were examined with severity and in every point of view.

4. I doubt whether his piece would have had the approbation of *connaisseurs*, if he had not determined to make in it the changes you judged necessary.

(1.) It must (that he who, etc. know it); he must (not repeated), *que;* instil, *faire entrer;* by, *à;* overburthen, *surcharger;* unimportant, *insignifiant.*

(2.) (It must, ind-7, that he); yield, *se rendre;* suffered, *permettre;* it to appear, (that it appear); real light, *vrai jour.*

(3.) Would be liable, *prêter,* subj-2; with severity, *à la rigueur;* in, *sous;* point of view, *face.*

(4.) Approbation, *suffrage;* had determined, *se décider;* in it, *y;* judged, ind-4.

When the first verb is in the imperfect, the preterit, the pluperfect or the conditional, the second is put in the imperfect of the subjunctive, if we mean to express a thing present, or future; but it is put in the pluperfect, if we wish to express a thing that is past.

Je voulais, j'ai voulu, j'eus voulu, je voudrais, or *j'eusse voulu qu'il* finisse *cette affaire.*

Je ne savais pas, je n'ai pas su, etc. *que* vous eussiez étudié *les mathématiques.*

REMARK. With the preterit indefinite, the second verb is put in the present, if it expresses a thing of common occurrence.

EXAMPLES.

Dieu a entouré les yeux de tuniques fort minces, transparentes au dehors, afin qu'on puisse *voir à travers*,	*God has surrounded the eyes with very thin tunics, transparent on the outside, that we may see through them.*

And in the preterit, if we mean to express a thing past, as,

il a fallu qu'*il ait sollicité* ses juges,	*he must have been obliged to solicit his judges.*

EXERCISE.

1. Mr. de Turenne never *would* buy any thing on credit, of tradesmen, for fear, said he, they *should lose* a great part of their demand, if he happened to be killed. All the workmen who were employed about his house, had orders to bring in their bills, before he set out for the campaign, and they were regularly paid.

2. It *would be better*, for a man who truly loves himself, *to lose* his life, than to forfeit his honour by some base and shameful action.

3. Lycurgus, in one of his laws, *had forbidden* the lighting of those who came from a feast in the evening, that the fear of not being able to reach their houses might *prevent* them from getting intoxicated.

4. People *used* the bark of trees, or skins, to write upon,* before paper was known.

5. Go and* ask that old man: for whom are you planting? he will answer you: for the immortal gods, who *have ordered* both that I *should profit* by the labour of those that have preceded me, and that those who should come after me, *should profit* by mine.

(1.) Would, *vouloir*, ind-2; buy on credit, *prendre à crédit*; of, *chez*; happened, *venir*; were employed, *travailler*; about, *pour*; bills, *mémoire*; he, *on*; set out for, *se mettre en.*

(2.) To lose, (that he *would lose)*; forfeit, *ternir.*

(3.) In, *par*; the lighting of, *que on éclairer*, subj-2; that, *afin que*; reach their houses, *se rendre chez eux*, getting intoxicated, *s'enivrer.*

(4.) People, *on*; bark, *écor*[illegible] skins, *peau*; known, *en usage.*

(5.) Have ordered, *voulo*[illegible]; by, *de.*

The subjunctive is elegantly used in elliptical

phrases, where the principal proposition is omitted, as,

qu'il vive *(je souhaite qu'il,)*	*may he live!*
qu'il se soit oublié jusqu'à ce point! *(je suis surpris qu'il)*	*that he should so forget himself.*
qui m'aime, me suive! *(je veux que celui qui)*	*whoever loves me, let him follow me.*
heureux l'homme qui peut, ne fût-ce que dans sa vieillesse, jouir de toute la force de sa raison! *(quand ce ne serait que),*	*happy the man that can, were it only in his old age, enjoy the whole strength of his reason.*

CONCORD BETWEEN THE TENSES OF THE DIFFERENT MOODS.

389. Remark. Our intention is not to give the concord of all the tenses, but simply to mention some of the principal.

THE INDICATIVE.

After the imperfect may come three tenses.

EXAMPLES.

Je lisais { *quand vous écriviez.*
quand vous avez écrit.
quand vous écrivîtes.

The preterit anterior requires the preterit definite, as, *quand j'eus fini, vous entrâtes.*

After the pluperfect may come, the preterit definite, the preterit indefinite, the preterit anterior, and the imperfect.

EXAMPLES.

J'avais lu { *quand vous entrâtes*
quand vous êtes entré
quand vous fûtes entré
quand vous entriez

After the preterit anterior indefinite, comes the preterit indefinite, as, *quand j'ai eu díné, vous êtes entré.*

In conjunction with *si* for *supposé que*, the future absolute requires the present, and the future anterior, the preterit indefinite.

EXAMPLE.

Vous partirez, si je veux
Il sera parti, si vous l'avez voul

CONCORD BETWEEN THE CONDITIONAL AND THE IMPERFECT AND THE CONDITIONAL.

The conditional, first and second, are used in conjunction with the imperfect, and the pluperfect governed by *si*.

EXAMPLE.

Vous partiriez, si je le voulais.
Vous seriez parti { *si je l'avais voulu* / *si je l'eusse voulu* }

The present of the conditional and the two past tenses of the conditional may be used in conjunction with each other.

EXAMPLES.

Quand l'avare posséderait tout l'or du monde, il ne serait pas encore content.
Quand Alexandre aurait conquis tout l'univers, il n'aurait pas été content.
Vous fussiez parti, si je l'eusse voulu.

CONCORD BETWEEN THE PRESENT AND THE FUTURE AND THE OTHER TENSES OF THE INDICATIVE MOOD.

391. These two tenses may be joined to all the tenses of the indicative and conditional.

EXAMPLES.

On dit / *On dira* } *que* {
vous partez aujourd'hui.
vous partirez demain
vous serez parti, quand, etc.
vous partiez hier.
vous partîtes hier.
vous êtes parti ce matin
vous fûtes parti hier, quand, etc.
vous étiez parti hier, quand, etc.
vous partiriez aujourd'hui, si, etc.
vous seriez parti hier, si, etc.
vous fussiez parti plutôt, si, etc.

REMARK. The same concord exists when the sentence is negative; except that for the present absolute of the indicative, the present of the subjunctive is substituted. Instead of, *on ne dit pas que vous partez aujourd'hui,* the genius of the French language requires that we should say, *on ne dit pas que vous partiez aujourd'hui.*

The imperfect, the preterit definite, the preterit indefinite, and the pluperfect, are followed either by the imperfect, or the pluperfect.

EXAMPLES.

On disait / *On dit hier* / *On a dit* / *On avait dit* } *que* {
vous partiez aujourd'hui.
vous étiez parti.

The future anterior requires the preterit indefinite, as, *on aura dit que vous avez menti.*

The conditional present may be followed by the present, the imperfect, the preterit indefinite, the pluperfect, the future of the indicative, as well as by the three conditionals.

EXAMPLES.

On croirait {
qu'il se trompe
qu'il se trompât
qu'il s'est trompé
qu'il s'était trompé
qu'il se trompera
qu'il se tromperait, si, etc.
qu'il se serait trompé, si, etc.
qu'il se fût trompé, si, etc.

The first conditional past may be followed by the imperfect, the pluperfect, as well as by the two other conditionals.

EXAMPLES.

On aurait cru {
qu'il tombait
qu'il était tombé
qu'il serait tombé
qu'il fût tombé.

The second conditional past may be joined to the same tenses.

PRINCIPAL CONCORD WITH THE TENSES OF THE SUBJUNCTIVE.

392. To the present, the future absolute, and the future anterior of the indicative is generally joined the present of the subjunctive.

EXAMPLES.

il veut
il voudra } *que vous partiez*
il aura voulu

To the imperfect, the preterit definite, the preterit indefinite, the pluperfect, and the preterit anterior may be joined the imperfect of the subjunctive.

EXAMPLES.

je voulais *je voulus* *j'ai voulu* *j'avais voulu* *j'eus voulu*	*que vous partissiez.*

To the future anterior the preterit of the subjunctive, as: *il aura voulu qu'il soit parti.*

The conditional present is accompanied either by the imperfect, or by the pluperfect of the subjunctive.

EXAMPLES.

je voudrais que	*vous partissiez* *vous fussiez parti.*
j'aurais voulu *j'eusse voulu*	*que vous fussiez parti.*

OF THE INFINITIVE.

393. The *infinitive* is that mood which conveys the abstract idea of an action unconnected with time or persons; thus, *aimer*, *parler*. The use of the infinitive after another verb, the prepositions *de*, *à*, *pour*, placed before it according as the case requires, etc. have been noticed No. 350, which see.

394. The participle present is used in English in many cases which require the infinitive in French. The principal, and most common, are when the English participle is governed by a preposition. See Exception, 400.

EXAMPLES.

I blame you for *having refused,*	je vous blâme *d'*avoir refusé.
he has gone without speaking to me,	il est parti sans me parler.
she takes delight in *teazing,*	elle se plaît *à* tourmenter.
I like dancing,	j'aime *à* danser.

Observe that the same, or the corresponding, prepositions are not always used, because, as it cannot too often be repeated, the two languages differ essentially in this point.

EXERCISE.

We only shut our eyes to truth, because we fear to
ne * art. art. *que parce que* *de*

see ourselves as we are. We were yet far from the castle,
2 *nous* 1 *tel que* ind-2 *encore*

when one of our friends came to join us. I did not think I was
ind-3 * ind-2 * *devoir*

to set out so soon. He promises every day that he will
* art. pl. *de* * *

amend, but I do not rely upon his promises. They talk
se corriger *compter* *promesse* f. pl. *on*

of a secret expedition; he hopes to be (in it). He relies upon
2 — f. 1 * *en*

seeing you very soon to terminate amicably his affair
inf. 1 *au premier jour* *pour* *à l'amiable*

with you. You expected to take a journey this year; but
s'attendre ind-2 *faire* *voyage* m.

your father has changed his mind. He threatens to punish us se-
de * *avis* *de* *sé-*

verely, if we (fall again) into the same error.
vèrement *retomber* *faute*

OF THE PARTICIPLE.

395. The *participle* is a part of the verb which

partakes of the properties both of a verb and an adjective; of a verb, as it signifies action and state, of an adjective, as it expresses the quality of a person, or thing.

There are two participles, the *participle present*, and the *participle past*.

OF THE PARTICIPLE PRESENT.

The *participle present* always terminates in *ant*: as, *aimant*, *finissant*, *recevant*, *rendant*.

396. The participle present is undeclined, that is takes neither gender nor number, when it expresses an action, and may be turned by the present or the imperfect of the indicative mood, *une montagne*, or *des montagnes dominant* (i.e. *qui dominent ou dominaient*) *sur des plaines immenses*, a mountain or mountains commanding immense plains; *un homme, des hommes, une femme, des femmes lisant, parlant, marchant*, (*qui lisent, qui parlaient, qui marchent)* a man, men, a woman, women reading, speaking, walking. But when, like an adjective, it expresses simply a quality, it takes both the gender and number of its substantive; as, *un homme obligeant*, an obliging man; *une femme obligeante*, an obliging woman; *des tableaux parlants*, speaking portraits; *la religion dominante*, the established religion; *à la nuit tombante*, at night falling. It is known to partake of the nature of the adjective when it is put before the noun in English.

What grammarians call *gerund*, is nothing but the participle present, to which the word *en* is prefixed; *on se forme l'esprit en lisant de bons livres*, we form our minds by reading good books.

EXERCISE.

That mountain being very high, and thus commanding a vast
élevé *ainsi* *dominer sur* *grand*

extent of country, was very well calculated for our observations.
étendue *pays* ind-2 * *propre* *à*

This woman is of a good disposition, obliging every one, when-
caractère m. *tout le monde* *quand*

ever she (has it in her power). They go cringing before the great,
le pouvoir * *ramper* *devant* pl.

that they may be insolent to their equals. The state of pure
afin de * * inf-1 pl. *avec* *égal*

nature is the savage living in the desert, but living in his family,
famille f.

knowing his children, loving them, (making use) of speech, and
connaître *user* art. *parole*

(making himself understood). An agreeable languor impercep-
se faire entendre 2 *langueur* f. 1. *insensi-*

tibly (laying hold) of my senses, suspended the activity of my
blement *s'emparer* *sens* *suspendre* ind-3

soul, and I fell (asleep). Time is a real blunderer, placing,
s'endormir ind-3 art. *vrai* *brouillon* *mettre*

replacing, ordering, disordering, impressing, erasing, approaching,
remettre, *ranger* *déranger* *imprimer* *effacer* *approcher*

removing, and making all things good and bad; and almost always
éloigner *rendre* f. pl. *quasi*

(impossible to be known again).
méconnaissable

397. The participle present is frequently used in English as a substantive, which is not the case in French.

EXAMPLE.

his ruling *passion is hunting,* sa passion *dominante* est *la chasse*

When preceded by a preposition, it is rendered in French by the infinitive. (No. 394)

EXAMPLES.

prevent him from doing mischief,	empêchez-le de faire le mal.
there is a pleasure in silencing great talkers,	il y a plaisir à fermer la bouche aux grands parleurs.

398. The participle present frequently takes the place of the *indicative* in English; it must not then be rendered literally, but in the following manner.

EXAMPLE.

I met them riding post,	*je les ai rencontrés qui couraient la poste.*

399. Sometimes also it is used substantively with a possessive pronoun; then, it must be rendered in French by the indicative or the subjunctive, according as the case requires.

EXAMPLES.

the fear of his coming (lest he should come) harassed us,	la crainte qu'il ne vînt nous tourmentait.
I doubt his being faithful,	je doute qu'il soit fidèle, etc.
what do you think of his writing to me?	que pensez-vous de cela? il m'a écrit. Savez-vous qu'il m'a écrit? qu'en pensez-vous?

400. In No. 394, it has been said that the infinitive is used after prepositions in French, and not the participle present. The only exception to this rule is *en*.

EXAMPLES.

nous en parlerons en marchant,	*we will talk about it as we walk.*
on apprend en enseignant,	*we learn by teaching others.*

401. The participle present always forming a phrase incidental and subordinate to another, must necessarily relate to the subject of the principal phrase, when it is not preceded by another noun, as in this sentence:—

je ne puis vous accompagner à	*I cannot accompany you into the*

la campagne, ayant des affaires qui exigent ici ma présence, — *country, having some business that requires my presence here.*

The participle present *ayant* relates to the subject *je*, since the subordinate proposition, formed by *ayant*, could have no kind of relation to the principal proposition, if it could not be resolved into this, *parce que j'ai des affaires qui, etc.* But, in this sentence :

combien voyons-nous de gens, qui, connaissant le prix du temps, le perdent mal-à-propos ! — *how many people do we see, who, knowing the value of time, waste it improperly !*

Connaissant relates to the substantive *gens*, because this is the word which it modifies, and because the relative *qui*, placed between that substantive, as the regimen, and the participle present, obviates every kind of ambiguity.

Remarks. Two participles ought never to be used together without being united by a conjunction, as, etc,

EXAMPLE.

c'est un homme aimant et craignant Dieu, — *he is a man loving and fearing God.*

2. The relative *en* ought never to be put either before a participle present, or before a gerund. We cannot say,

Je vous ai remis mon fils entre les mains, en *voulant faire quelque chose de bon,*

because the sense would be ambiguous : for, the meaning is not :

As I wish to do something good, or, *as I wish to do well, I have put my son into your hands.*

But,

I have put my son into your hands, as I wish to make something of him.

We should say: *Voulant* en *faire*, etc.

Likewise this sentence would be improper:

Le prince tempère la rigueur du pouvoir, en en *partageant les fonctions.*

On account of the repetition of the word *en*, used in two different senses, viz., as a preposition and a relative. Another turn must be then adopted, as,

C'est en *partageant les fonctions du pouvoir, qu'un prince* en *tempère la rigueur.*

OF THE PARTICIPLE PAST.

The participle past has various terminations; as, *aimé*, *fini*, *reçu*, *ouvert*, *dissous*, etc.

402. The participle past is sometimes declined, sometimes not, thus,

Avez-vous mangé *toutes les fraises que vous avez* cueillies *ce matin?*

Avez-vous mangé, vous avez cueillies are two verbs in the same tense, and person, yet one participle *mangé*, is undeclined, the other, *cueillies*, is feminine plural. This difference, apparently contradictory, is grounded upon a principle which must be explained.

OF THE PARTICIPLE WITH ETRE.

403. The participle past, when accompanied by the auxiliary verb *être*, agrees with its subject in gender and number.

EXAMPLES.

mon frère est tombé,	*my brother is fallen.*
mes frères sont tombés,	*my brothers are fallen.*

ma sœur est tombée, *my sister is fallen.*
mes sœurs sont tombées, *my sisters are fallen.*
la nuit sera bientôt passée, *the night will soon be over.*
les spectacles sont fréquentés, *the theatres are frequented.*
cette fleur est fort recherchée, *this flower is much sought after.*
ils sont fort estimés, *they are very much esteemed.*

There is an exception which is explained at No. 410, *participle past of Reflective Verbs.*

EXERCISE.

Fire-arms were not known to the ancients. Ishmael, the
art. *arme à feu* f. pl. ind-4 *connu de* *Ismaël*

son of Abraham, is known among the Arabs, as (the man) from
— *parmi* *Arabe* *celui*

whom they sprung, and circumcision has remained (among
être sorti art. f. *être demeuré* *leur*

them) as the mark of their origin. Heaven is that permanent
f. art. — 2

city, (into which) the just are to be received after this life.
cité f. 1 *où* pl. *devoir* * *après*

In Abraham's time, the threatenings of the true God were
de 2 art. 1 *menace* f. pl. ind-2

dreaded by Pharaoh, king of Egypt; but, in the time of Moses, all
redouté de Pharaon *Moïse* art.

nations were corrupted, and the world, which God has made to
f. *perverti* *pour*

manifest his power, was become a temple of idols. That dread-
pouvoir m. *devenu* *ter-*

ful crisis which threatened the state with instant destruc-
rible 2 *crise* f. 1 ind. *de* *prochain* 2 f. 1

tion, was happily soon over. She is come to bring us all
ind-3 *heureusement* *passé* *

kinds of refreshments. The sciences have always been pro-
sorte f. sing. *rafraîchissement* f. *pro-*

tected by enlightened governments.
tégé art. *éclairé* 2 1

PARTICIPLE PAST WITH AVOIR.

404. A participle past with *avoir*, may be the compound tense of a *neuter verb*, or of an *active verb*.

405. The participle past of a neuter verb is invariable.

EXAMPLE.

elle a *dormi*,	*she has slept.*
nous avons *ri*,	*we have laughed.*
ils ont *pensé*,	*they have thought.*

406. The participle past of an active verb is declined in one case, and not in the other.

Avez-vous mangé *les fraises que vous avez* cueillies?

1. The participles never agree with the subject or nominative of the verb, but with the accusative.

EXAMPLES.

mon frère a écrit,	*my brother has written.*
mes frères ont écrit,	*my brothers have written.*
ma sœur a écrit,	*my sister has written.*
les Amazones ont acquis de la célébrité,	*the Amazons have acquired celebrity.*
j'ai contraint les soldats à marcher,	*I have forced the soldiers to march.*

2. It does not, nevertheless, agree with the accusative when it precedes it. See 407.

EXAMPLES.

les soldats ont attaqué la ville,	*the soldiers have attacked the town.*
mes filles ont dessiné ces fleurs,	*my daughters have painted these flowers.*

EXERCISE.

The Romans successively triumphed over the most warlike
Romain successivement 2 ind-4 1 *de* *belliqueux* 2

nations. Lampridius relates that Adrian erected to Jesus
1 *raconter* *Adrien* *élever* ind-6

Christ some temples, which (were still to be seen) in his
de art. *on* *encore* 2 *voir* ind-2 1 *de*

time. Happy those princes who have never (made use) of their
* art. *user*

power but to do good! We have spent the whole day
pouvoir *que pour* art. *bien* *journée* f.

in tormenting ourselves. One has seldom seen a great stock
à inf-1 2 *nous* 1 *rarement* *fonds* m.

of good sense in a man of imagination. The errors of Descartes
sens — = —

proved very useful to Newton.
* *beaucoup* *servir* ind-4 —

407. The participle past of an active verb agrees with the object or accusative when it follows it; that is, it agrees with the noun substantive, which is the antecedent of *que, me, te, se, le, la, nous, vous, les.*

EXAMPLES.

les livres que j'ai lus	*the books which I have read.*
la lettre que j'ai écrite,	*the letter which I have written.*

lus agrees with *que* of which the antecedent is *livres*, m. pl.

Écrite agrees with *que* of which the antecedent is *lettre* f. s.

Nous avons cueilli *des fraises et nous* les *avons* mangées.

Cueilli is undeclined, becauses it precedes the object *fraises* : *mangées* is feminine plural, because it follows *les* antecedent *fraises*.

A woman says,

vous m'avez trompée, *you have deceived me.*

Trompée agrees with *me*, of which the antecedent *femme* is understood.

In admirative and interrogative sentences, the participle agrees with the noun following *que de*, *combien*, *quel*.

EXAMPLES.

que de soins elle a eus!	*what attentions she has met with!*
quelle affaire avez-vous entre-	*what affair have you undertaken?*

EXERCISE.

All the letters which I have *received* confirm that important
f. pl. *confirmer* 2

news. The agitated life which I have *led* till now,
s. 1 *agité* 2 f. 1 *mener jusqu'à présent*

makes me sigh for retirement. The sciences which
soupirer après art. *retraite* f. f. pl.

you have *studied*, will prove infinitely useful (to you). The
être

persons whom you have *instructed* appear to me possessed of
f. pl. *plein*

reason and taste. Nothing can equal the ardour of the troops
pr. *égaler* f. pl.

which I have *seen* (setting off). What measures have I not
inf-1 *démarches* f. pl.

taken! What fortunes has not this revolution *ruined!* What
faire f. pl. *renverser que*

tears has she not *shed;* what sighs has she not *heaved!*
de f. pl. *verser* m. pl. *pousser*

I have *thought* her agitated by the furies. This day is one of
croire =

those which they have *consecrated* to tears. The language in
m. pl. *consacrer* art. *langue* f. *

which Cicero and Virgil have *written*, will live in their works
Cicéron *par ouvrage*

I could have wished to avoid entering into those details, but I
* *vouloir* * *éviter d'entrer* — m.

thought them necessary. The tribunes demanded of Clodius
croire ind-4 *tribun* m. pl. ind-3 *à*

the execution of the promises which the consul Valerius had
f

given them.
faire les

408. The participle past takes neither gender nor number, either when the participle and the auxiliary verb to which it is joined are used impersonally, or when that participle is followed by the verb, which governs the noun, or pronoun preceding it.

EXAMPLES.

es chaleurs excessives qu'il a fait cet été, ont beaucoup nui à la récolte,	*the excessive heats, which we have had this summer, have done great injury to the corn.*
quelle fâcheuse aventure vous est-il arrivé ?	*what unpleasant adventure have you met with?*
la maison que j'ai fait bâtir,	*the house which I have ordered to be built.*
imitez les vertus que vous avez entendu louer,	*imitate the virtues which you have heard praised.*
les mathématiques que vous n'avez pas voulu que j'étudiasse,	*the mathematics which you would not permit me to study.*

To make a right application of the second part of this rule, we ought to examine whether we can put the regimen immediately after the participle. As we cannot say; *J'ai fait la maison, vous avez entendu les vertus, vous n'avez pas voulu les mathématiques*, it follows that the regimen belongs to the second verb. Sometimes, however, the regimen may relate either to the participle, or to the following verb, according to the meaning of the speaker. Thus, *je l'ai* vu *peindre*, means, I saw her picture drawn; but *je l'ai* vue *peindre*, signifies, I saw her painting.

Sometimes it happens likewise, that, in sentences which seem to resemble each other, the regimen in one belongs to the participle, and in the other to the verb which follows it. For instance, this question, *avez-vous entendu chanter la nouvelle actrice?* Have you heard the new actress sing? Should be thus answered, *aui, je l'ai* entendue *chanter*, yes, I have. (I have heard her when she sang) but this question, ***avez-vous entendu chanter la nouvelle ariette?*** have you heard the new air sung? must be answered, ***oui, je l'ai*** entendu ***chanter***, yes, I have. (I have heard it to be sung).

409. The participle past does not agree with the antecedent of ***en.***

EXAMPLE.

sachant que nous aimions le gibier, il nous en a envoyé un panier,	***knowing that we were fond of game, he sent us a basket full.***

EXERCISE.

The great changes which (have *taken* place) in ad-
changement *y avoir* ind-4 art.

ministration, have astonished many people. The heavy
bien des personnes *grand*

rains which we have *had* in the spring, have been
pluie f. pl. * *il* *faire* ind-4

the cause of many diseases. The scarcity which there *was*
maladie f. pl. *disette* f. ind-4

last winter, has afforded the opportunity of doing
art. *dernier* 2 1 *donner* *occasion* inf-1

much good. What news has *reached* you? How many
bien *est-il venu* *que* *de*

imprudent steps were *taken* on that occasion! How
faux *démarche* f. pl. *il s'est faire* *en*

many large ships have been *built* in England within these fifty
gros *il se construire* ind-4 *depuis* *

years! The figures which you have *learned* to draw *are* of
— *apprendre* *dessiner*

great beauty. We ought never to swerve from the
un * *falloir* ind-1 * *s'éloigner*

good path which we have *begun* to follow. The measures
route f. *on* *mesure* f. pl.

which you *advised* me to adopt, have not succeeded.
conseiller ind 4 *de prendre* *réussir*

The rule, which I have *begun* to explain, seems to me very
règle f. *expliquer* *sembler*

easy to (be understood). You see that I have not been mistaken
saisir *se tromper* ind-4

respecting the affairs which I had *foreseen* you would have
prévoir que

in hand. I asked for some pencils, and he has sent
* * *demander* ind-4 * *envoyer*

me some very good ones.
en

PARTICIPLE PAST WITH REFLECTED VERBS.

410. It has been said, No. 121, that all active verbs may be used reflectedly.

The participle past of such verbs agrees with the subject or nominative.

EXAMPLES.

elle s'est blessée,	*she has hurt himself.*
nous nous sommes ennuyés,	*we have got tired.*

Here *blessée, ennuyés,* agree with *se, nous,* of which *elle, nous,* are the antecedents; *se, nous* being also besides the accusative of *blesser, ennuyer.*

But here,

il s'est cassé la jambe,	*he has broken his leg.*
Lucrèce s'est donné la mort,	*Lucrecia destroyed herself.*

Cassé, donné are undeclined, because they precede *jambe, mort,* which are the objects or accusatives of the verbs *casser, donner.* *Se,* is also in both examples an indirect case or dative. But, speaking of the *broken leg* we say,

je ne sais comment il se l'est cassée,	*I don't know how he broke it.*

Because *cassée* follows *la,* of which *jambe* is the antecedent.

EXERCISE.

Our troops have fought with great courage. They have not
se battre
sufficiently made haste. Did not your sisters stop (on the)
se *dépêcher* *s'arrêter* *en*
road. I have *put* my shoulder *out of joint.* Show me the hand
se démettre l'épaule
which you have cut. The Amazons have made themselves
se couper *se rendre*
famous by their courage. What strange fancies she has got
chimères *se mettre*
into her head! I don't think you have cleaned your teeth
la *se nettoyer*
this morning? Indeed I have cleaned them before I went out.
avant de *sortir*

CHAPTER VI.

GENERAL REMARKS ON THE USE AND MEANING OF SOME OF THE FRENCH PREPOSITIONS.

411. The office of prepositions is to connect two nouns substantives, and show the relation which they bear to one another.

412. Those who know Latin are apt to mistake the meaning of *à* and *de;* the former never means *from,* but *to;* it is the sign of the dative case; *de* means *of, from, with,* and is the sign of what is called the genitive and ablative cases, that is, it expresses, *possessions, source, accompaniment, instrumentality.*

EXAMPLES.

approchez-vous du feu,	*come near the fire.*
éloignez-vous du feu,	*go from the fire.*
il le fait de bon cœur,	*he does it with readiness.*
écrivez à Jean,	*write to John*

En and *dans* have nearly the same meaning; but they differ in this, that the former is used in a more vague, the latter in a more determinate sense.

EXAMPLE.

J'étais en Angleterre, dans la province de Middlesex.

À, *en*, are rendered by *to* or *in* before names of countries and places, but they must not be used indifferently. *A* is used before proper names of places, *en* before names of *countries*, *provinces*.

EXAMPLES.

il est allé en France,	*he is gone to France.*
elle est allée à Rome,	*she is gone to Rome.*
ils demeurent en Normandie,	*they live in Normandy.*
elles résident à Rouen,	*they live in or at Rouen.*

From what has just been said, it follows then that *en*, on account of its indeterminate nature, ought not to be followed by the article, except in a small number of phrases sanctioned by usage.

EXAMPLES.

En la présence de Dieu; en la grand' chambre du parlement; en l'absence d'un tel; en l'année mil huit cent dix-sept, etc.

with respect to the expressions,

En l'honneur, en l'âge, it is better to say, *à l'honneur, à l'âge.*

413. *Avant* is a preposition in this phrase:

avant le jour,	*before day-light.*

But it is an adverb in this:

n'allez pas si avant,	*do not go so forward.*

Autour and *alentour*, must not be confounded; *autour* is a preposition, and *alentour* an adverb.

39**

EXAMPLES.

tous les grands étaient autour du trône,	*all the grandees stood round the throne.*
le roi était sur son trône, et les grands étaient alentour,	*the king was upon the throne, and the grandees stood round.*

Avant and *auparavant* are not used indifferently. *Avant* is followed by a regimen.

EXAMPLES.

avant Pâques,	*before Easter.*
avant ce temps,	*before that time.*

Auparavant is followed by no regimen

EXAMPLE.

si vous partez, venez me voir auparavant,	*if you set off, come and see me first.*

Prêt à and *près de*, are not the same expressions. *Prêt* is an adjective :

je suis prêt à faire ce que vous voudrez,	*I am ready to do what you please*

But *près* is a preposition :

mon ouvrage est près d'être fini,	*my work is nearly finished.*

Au travers and *à travers* differ in this : the first is followed by the preposition *de*, the second is not.

EXAMPLE.

il se fit jour au travers des ennemis, il se fit jour à travers les ennemis,	*he fought his way through the enemy.*

Avant denotes priority of time and order.

EXAMPLE.

Il est arrivé avant *moi*, l'article se met avant le *nom*

Devant is used for *en présence. vis-à-vis.*

EXAMPLE.

Il a paru devant *le juge ; il loge* devant *l'église.*

Devant is likewise a preposition marking order, and is the opposite of *après.*

EXAMPLES.

il a le pas *devant* moi,	*he has precedence of me.*
si vous êtes pressé, courez *devant*,	*If you are in a hurry, run* before.

Envers and *vers*, towards, are also different as to their meaning, the former is put before names of persons, with a moral sense, the other expresses motion, and is put before names of places and persons.

EXAMPLES.

comportez-vous bien envers lui,	*behave well towards him, with regard to him.*
ils marchaient vers la ville,	*they were marching towards the city.*
elle s'avança vers moi,	*she advanced towards me.*

THE USE OF THE ARTICLE WITH PREPOSITIONS.

414. Some prepositions require the article before their regimen; others do not; and others again, sometimes admit, sometimes reject it.

The following prepositions generally require the article before the noun, which they govern.

avant,	depuis,	envers,	nonobstant,	selon,
après,	devant,	excepté,	parmi,	suivant,
chez,	derrière,	hors,	pendant,	touchant,
dans,	durant,	hormis,	pour,	ver

avant l'aurore,	chez le prince,	envers les pauvres,
après la promenade,	dans la maison,	devant l'église, etc.

There are, however, exceptions.

EXAMPLES.

avant terme,	avant dîner,	pour lit une paillasse,
avant midi,	après midi,	depuis minuit, etc.

A noun governed by the preposition *en*, is not, in general, preceded by the article.

EXAMPLE.

En ville, en campagne, en extase, en songe, en pièces, etc.

L'armée est entrée en campagne, means the army has taken the field; but *M. N. est allé à la campagne*, means, Mr. N. is gone into the country.

These eleven prepositions, *à*, *de*, *avec*, *contre*, *entre*, *malgré*, *outre*, *par*, *pour*, *sur*, *sans*, sometimes admit, sometimes reject the article before their regimen.

If the article is used in these phrases:

Jouer *sur le* velours.
St. Paul veut de la subordination *entre la* femme et *le* mari.
Sans les passions, où serait le mérite?

It is suppressed in,

Etre *sur pied*; un peu de façons ne gâte rien *entre mari* et femme.
Vivre *sans passions*, c'est vivre *sans plaisirs* et *sans peines*.

This difference arises of course from the noun being taken in a general and definite sense, or in a partial and restricted signification.

REPETITION OF THE PREPOSITIONS.

415. The prepositions *de*, *à*, and *en*, must be repeated before all nouns which they govern.

EXAMPLES.

voyons qui l'emportera *de* vous, *de* lui, ou *de* moi,	*let us see which of us will excel, you, he, or I.*
elle a *de* l'honnêteté, *de* la douceur, *des* grâces, et *de* l'esprit.	*she has politeness, sweetness, grace, and abilities.*
la loi, que Dieu a gravée au fond de mon cœur, m'instruit de tout ce que je dois à l'auteur de mon être, *au* prochain, à moi-même,	*the law which God has deeply engraven on my heart instructs me in every thing I owe* to *the author of my being,* to *my neighbour, and* to *myself.*
en Asie, *en* Europe, *en* Afrique, et jusqu'*en* Amérique, on trouve le même préjugé,	in *Asia,* in *Europe,* in *Africa, and even* in *America, we find the same prejudice.*

The other prepositions, especially those consisting of two syllables, are generally repeated—before nouns, which have meanings totally different; but seldom before nouns, that are nearly synonimous.

EXAMPLES.

rien n'est moins *selon* Dieu et *selon* le monde,	*nothing is less according to God and according to the world.*
cette action est contre l'honneur et contre toute espèce de principes,	*that action is contrary to honour and to every kind of principle.*

But we ought to say,

il perd sa jeunesse *dans* la mollesse et la volupté,	*he wastes his youth in effeminacy and pleasure.*
notre loi ne condamne personne *sans* l'avoir entendu et examiné,	*our laws condemned nobody without having heard and examined him.*

OF THE GOVERNMENT OF PREPOSITIONS.

4.7. Some prepositions govern nouns without the help of another preposition.

EXAMPLES.

devant la maison,	*before the house.*
hormis son frère,	*except his brother.*
sans son épée,	*without his sword, etc.*

Others require the help of the preposition *de.*

EXAMPLES.

près de la maison,	*near the house.*
à l'insu de son frère,	*unknown to his brother.*
au-dessus du pont,	*above the bridge, etc.*

These four, *jusque, par rapport, quant* and *sauf* are followed by the preposition *à*

EXAMPLES.

jusqu'au mois prochain,	*till the next month.*
quant à moi,	*as for me, etc.*

Practice alone can teach these different regimens.

A noun may be governed by two prepositions, provided they do not require different regimens; thus we may say with propriety,

celui qui écrit selon les circonstances, *pour* et *contre* un parti, est un homme bien méprisable,	*he who writes according to circumstances, both for and against a party, is a very contemptible man.*

But it would be wrong to say,

Celui qui écrit *en faveur* et *contre* un parti, etc.

because *en faveur* requires the preposition *de.*

Prepositions which, with their regimen, express a circumstance, are generally placed as nearly as possible to the word to which that circumstance relates.

EXAMPLES.

on voit des personnes qui, *avec beaucoup d'esprit*, commettent de très-grandes fautes,	*we see persons who, with a great deal of wit, commit very great faults.*
j'ai envoyé *à la poste* les lettres que vous avez écrites,	*I have sent to the post-office the letters which you have written*
croyez-vous pouvoir ramener *par la douceur* ces esprits égarés ?	*do you think you can reclaim by gentleness, those mistaken people ?*

If we attempt to alter the place of these prepositions, we shall find that the sentences will become ambiguous.

CHAPTER VII.

OF THE ADVERBS.

PLACE OF ADVERBS.

418. In the simple tenses, the adverb is generally placed after the verb; and, in the compound tenses, between the auxiliary and the participle.

EXAMPLES.

l'homme le plus éclairé est *ordinairement* celui qui pense *le plus modestement* de lui-même,	*the man who is most learned is generally he who thinks most modestly of himself.*
avez-vous *jamais* vu un pédant plus absurde et plus vain ?	have you ever seen a pedant more *absurd and more vain ?*

Compound adverbs, or adverbial phrases are placed after the verb, and even after the participle past in a compound tense.

EXAMPLES.

c'est à la mode,	*that is fashionable.*
il eût fallu se lever plus matin,	*it would have been necessary to rise earlier.*
nous nous sommes levés à la hâte,	*we got up hastily.*

EXCEPTIONS. 1.—Adverbs of order, rank, and those which express a determinate time, are placed either before, or after the verb.

EXAMPLES.

nous devons *premièrement* faire notre devoir; *secondement* chercher les plaisirs permis,	*we ought, first, to do our duty, secondly, enjoy lawful pleasures.*
aujourd'hui, il fait beau; il pleuvra peut-être *demain*,	*to-day, it is fine; it will rain perhaps to-morrow.*

2. These adverbs, *comment*, *où*, *d'où*, *par où*, *combien*, *pourquoi*, *quand*, used with, or without interrogation, are always placed before the verb which they modify.

EXAMPLES.

comment vous portez-vous?	*how do you do?*
où allez-vous?	*whither are you going?*
il ne sait comment s'y prendre,	*he does not know how to set about it.*

The adverbs *très*, *fort*, *infiniment*, etc. are always placed before the adjective which they modify.

EXAMPLE.

c'est une femme *fort* belle, *très*-sensible, et *infiniment* sage,	*she is a woman very beautiful, of great sensibility, and infinitely prudent.*

Adverbs of quantity and comparison, and the adverbs of time, *souvent*, *toujours*, *jamais*, are placed before the other adverbs.

EXAMPLES.

si poliment, fort poliment,	*so politely, very politely.*
très-heureusement,	*very happily.*
le plus adroitement,	*the most skilfully.*
ils ne seront jamais étroitement unis,	*they never will be intimately united.*
ils sont toujours ensemble,	*they are always together.*
c'est souvent à l'improviste qu'il arrive,	*he often comes unexpectedly.*

Souvent may, however, be preceded by an adverb of quantity, or comparison, as, *si souvent, assez souvent, fort souvent, plus souvent, moins souvent trop souvent.*

When adverbs of quantity and comparison meet together in a sentence, the following is the order, which custom has established.

si peu,	bien peu,	beaucoup* trop,	tant mieux,
trop peu,	bien plus,	beaucoup plus,	tant pis, etc.
très-peu,	bien davantage,	beaucoup moins,	

Bien before another adverb means *very much, quite.*

EXAMPLES.

bien assez,	*quite enough.*
bien tard,	*very late.*
bien moins,	*much less.*

When after the adverb it signifies *well.*

EXAMPLES.

assez bien,	*pretty well.*
fort bien,	*very well.*

OF THE NEGATIVE *ne*.

419. It is customary to use two negatives in French, *ne* comes before the verb; *pas* or *point*

* *Beaucoup* is not, as the English *much*, susceptible of being modified by any adverb preceding, thus, *très-beaucoup, trop heureux*, etc. would be barbarisms.

comes after it. The French Academy have discussed the four following questions.

1. Which is the place of the negatives?

2. When is *pas* to be used in preference to *point* and *vice versa?*

3. When may both be omitted?

4. When *ought* both to be omitted?

As this subject is of very material importance, we shall treat it upon the plan of the Academy, and agreeably to their views.

FIRST QUESTION. Where is the place of the negatives?

Ne is always prefixed to the verb; but the place of *pas* and *point* is variable.

When the verb is in the infinitive, these are placed indifferently before, or after it; for we say,

Pour ne point voir, *or*, pour ne voir pas.

In the other moods, except the imperative, the tenses are either simple, or compound. In the simple tenses, *pas* or *point* is placed after the verb.

EXAMPLES.

Il ne parle pas; ne parle-t-il pas?

In the compound tenses, it is placed between the auxiliary and the participle.

EXAMPLES.

Il n'a pas parlé; n'a-t-il pas parlé?

In the imperative, it is placed after the verb.

EXAMPLES.

badinez pas. Ne vous en allez pas.

SECOND QUESTION. When is *pas* to be used in preference to *point*, and *vice versa?*

Point is a stronger negative than *pas*. besides, it denotes something permanent: *il ne lit point*, means he *never* reads.

Pas denotes something accidental: *il ne lit pas*, means, he does not read *now*, or he is not reading.

Point de denotes an absolute negation. To say:

Il n'a point d'esprit, is to say, he has no wit at all.

Pas de, allows some sort of restriction. To say:

Il n'a pas d'esprit, is to say, he has nothing of what can be called wit.

Hence the Academy concludes, that *pas* is more proper.

1. Before *plus, moins, si, autant*, and other words denoting comparison.

EXAMPLE.

Milton n'est pas moins sublime qu'Homère,	*Milton is not less sublime than Homer.*

2. Before nouns of number.

EXAMPLE.

il n'y a pas dix ans,	*it is not ten years ago.*

Point is elegantly used,

1. At the end of a sentence.

EXAMPLE.

on s'amusait à ses dépens, et il ne s'en apercevait point,	*they were amusing themselves at his expense, and he did not perceive it.*

2. In elliptical sentences.

EXAMPLE

je croyais avoir à faire à un honnête homme; mais point,	*I thought I had to deal with an honest man: but no.*

3. In answer to interrogative sentences.

EXAMPLE.

irez-vous ce soir au parc?— point,	*shall you go this evening to the park?—no.*

The Academy also observes, that when *pas* or *point* is introduced into interrogative sentences, it is with meanings somewhat different. We make use of *point,* when we have any doubt on our minds.

EXAMPLE.

n'avez-vous point été là?	*have you not been there?*

But we use *pas,* when we are persuaded.

EXAMPLE.

n'avez-vous pas été là?	*but you have been there, have not you?*

THIRD QUESTION. When may both *pas* and *point* be omitted?

They may be suppressed,

1. After the words *cesser, oser,* and *pouvoir;* but this omission is only for the sake of elegance.

EXAMPLES.

je ne cesse de m'en occuper,	*I incessantly think about it.*
je n'ose vous en parler,	*I dare not speak to you about it.*
je ne puis y penser sans frémir,	*I cannot think of it without shuddering.*

We likewise say, but only in familiar conversation,

ne bougez,	*do not stir.*

2. In expressions of this kind,

y a-t-il un homme dont elle ne médise?	*is there a man that she does not slander?*
avez-vous un ami qui ne soit des miens?	*have you a friend but is not likewise mine?*

FOURTH QUESTION. When ought both *pas* and *point* to be omitted?

They are omitted,

420. When the extent which we mean to give to the negative is sufficiently expressed either by the words which restrict it, by words which exclude all restriction, or when the verb is joined to an adverb, or pronoun having a negative sense, as, *jamais*, *plus*, *aucun*, *personne*, *rien*, *nul*, *nullement*; and also to the words *bien*, *goutte*, *mot*, which in some cases, have been through *custom* considered as negatives.

To exemplify the first part of this remark, we say,

EXAMPLES.

je ne sors guère,	*I go out but seldom.*
je ne sortirai de trois jours,	*I shall not go out for three days.*

To exemplify the second, we say,

EXAMPLES.

je n'y vais jamais,	*I never go there.*
je n'y pense plus,	*I think no more of it*
nul ne sait s'il est digne d'amour, ou de haine,	*nobody knows whether he be deserving of love, or hatred.*
n'employez aucun de ces stratagèmes,	*use none of these stratagems*
il ne plaît à personne,	*he pleases nobody.*
rien n'est plus charmant,	*nothing is more charming.*
je n'y pense nullement,	*I do not think of it at all.*

To exemplify the third, we say,

EXAMPLES.

il n'y voit goutte,	*he cannot see at all.*
je n'en ai cueilli brin,	*I did not gather a sprig.*
il ne dit mot,	*he speaks not a word.*

But if to *mot* we join an adjective of number, *pas* must be added, as

EXAMPLES.

il ne dit pas un mot qui n'intéresse,	*he speaks not a word but what is interesting.*
dans ce discours, il n'y a pas trois mots à reprendre,	*in that speech, there are not three words that are exceptionable.*

421. The substantive which follows a negative phrase is governed by the preposition *de*.

EXAMPLES.

il n'a jamais d'argent,	*he never has any money.*
n'avez-vous pas de cheval ?	*have you got no horse?*
il ne fait pas de démarche inutile,	*he does not take any useless step.*

If, after such sentences as we have just mentioned, either the conjunction *que*, or the relative pronouns *qui* or *dont*, should introduce a negative sentence, then in this last, *pas* and *point* are omitted.

EXAMPLES

je ne fais jamais d'excès que je n'en sois incommodé,	*I never commit any excess, without being ill after it.*
je ne vois personne qui ne vous loue,	*I see nobody but what commends you.*

422. When two negatives are joined by *ni*, *pas* is omitted.

EXAMPLE.

je ne l'aime ni ne l'estime,	*I neither love nor esteem him.*

When the conjunction *ni* is repeated, *pas* is also left out.

EXAMPLES.

n. l'or ni la grandeur ne nous rendent heureux,	*neither gold nor greatness can make us happy.*
il n'est ni prudent ni sage,	*he is neither prudent nor wise.*
il n'a ni dettes ni procès,	*he has neither debts nor lawsuits.*

Pas is used, when *ni* is not repeated, and when it serves only to unite two members of a negative sentence.

EXAMPLE.

je n'aime pas ce vain étalage d'érudition prodiguée sans choix et sans goût, ni ce luxe de mots qui ne disent rien,	*I do not like that vain display of erudition lavished without choice and withont taste, nor that pomp of words which have no meaning.*

Pas is omitted when the question used for *pourquoi* begins with *que* and after *à moins que*, *si*, instead of *pourquoi*, and with *à moins que*, or *si*, used instead of it.

EXAMPLES.

que n'êtes-vous aussi posé que votre frère ?	*why are you not as sedate as your brother?*
je ne sortirai pas à moins que vous ne veniez me prendre,	*I shall not go out, unless you come to fetch me.*
je n'irai pas chez lui, s'il ne m'y engage,	*I shall not go to his house, if he do not invite me.*

With *ne—que* used instead of *seulement*, and in the sense of *only*, *but*, *pas* is not used.

EXAMPLE.

une jeunesse qui se livre à ses passions, ne transmet à la vieillesse qu'un corps usé,	*youth, which abandons itself to its passions, transmits to old age nothing but a worn-out body.*

Ne, before, and *que*, after the verb in the sense of *nothing but* does not require *pas*.

EXAMPLE.

il ne fait que rire,	*he does nothing but laugh.*

Pas is again omitted when that conjunction may be changed into *sinon*, or *si ce n'est.*

EXAMPLES.

il ne tient qu'à vous de réussir,	*the success wholly depends upon* you.
trop de maîtres à la fois ne servent qu'à embrouiller l'esprit,	*too many masters at once only serve to perplex the mind.*

With a verb in the preterit, preceded by the conjunction *depuis que*, or by the verb *il y a*, denoting a certain duration of time, *pas* and *point* are omitted.

EXAMPLES.

comment vous êtes-vous porté depuis que je ne vous ai vu ?	*how have you been since I saw you?*
il y a trois mois que je ne vous ai vu,	*I have not seen you for these three months.*

But they are not omitted, when the verb is in the present.

EXAMPLES.

comment vit-il depuis que nous ne le voyons point ?	*how does he live now we do not see him?*
il y a six mois que nous ne le voyons point,	*we have not seen him these six months.*

It has been seen, No. 211, that *ne* is used in comparative sentences, but as it has not then a negative sense, *pas point* are of course omitted.

EXAMPLES.

on méprise ceux qui parlent autrement qu'ils ne pensent,	*we despise those who speak differently from what they think.*
il écrit mieux qu'il ne parle,	*he writes better than he speaks.*

c'est pire qu'on ne le disait,	*it is worse than was said.*
c'est autre chose que je ne croyais,	*it is different from what I thought.*
peu s'en faut qu'on ne m'ait trompé,	*I have been very near being deceived.*

Ne is also used before the subjunctive mood after certain verbs noticed No. 384, in which case *pas point*, are also omitted.

EXAMPLES.

je ne doute pas qu'il ne vienne,	*I doubt not that he will come.*
ne désespérez pas que ce moyen ne vous réussisse,	*do not despair of the success of these means.*
je ne nie pas, *ou*, je ne disconviens pas que cela ne soit,	*I do not deny but that it may be so.*
j'empêcherai bien que vous ne soyez du nombre,	*I shall prevent your being of the number.*
prenez garde qu'on ne vous séduise,	*take care that they do not corrupt you.*
prenez garde que vous ne m'entendiez pas,	*mind, you do not understand what I mean.*
il craint que son frère ne l'abandonne,	*he is afraid his brother should forsake him.*
je crains que mon ami ne meure,	*I fear my friend will die.*

The Academy says, that after *nier*, *douter*, *disconvenir*, *ne* may be omitted.

EXAMPLES.

Je ne nie pas, *ou*, je ne disconviens pas que cela soit.

When we say, *de crainte qu'il ne perde son proces*, we express a fear lest he should lose his law-suit.

When we say, *de crainte qu'il ne soit pas puni*, we express an apprehension, lest he should escape punishment.

Remark. In these phrases,

je crains que mon ami ne meure,	*I am afraid my friend will die.*
vous empêchez qu'on ne chante,	*you prevent them from singing.*

Ne has the meaning of the *ne* of the Latin language, which equally governs the subjunctive mood

423. The conditional of ***savoir*** is frequently used negatively, instead of ***pouvoir*** in which case ***pas point*** are omitted.

EXAMPLE

je ne saurais en venir à bout	*I cannot accomplish it*

When ***ne savoir*** means ***être incertain***, it is best to omit ***pas*** and ***point***.

EXAMPLES

je ne sais où le prendre,	*I do not know where to find him.*
il ne sait ce qu'il dit,	*he does not know what he says.*

But ***pas*** and ***point*** must be used when ***savoir*** is taken in its true meaning, to know.

EXAMPLE.

je ne sais pas le Français,	*I do not know French.*

We also say, without ***pas*** or ***point***,

ne vous déplaise, ne vous en déplaise,	*by your leave, under favour*, or, *let it not displease you.*

Plus and *davantage* must not be used indifferently. *Plus* is followed by the preposition ***de***, or the conjunction ***que***.

EXAMPLES.

il a plus de brillant que de solide,	*he has more brilliancy than solidity.*
il se fie plus à ses lumières qu'à celles des autres,	*he relies more upon his own knowledge than upon that of others.*

Davantage is used alone and at the end of sentences.

EXAMPLE.

la science est estimable, mais la vertu l'est davantage,	*learning is estimable, but virtue is still more so.*

Although *davantage* cannot be followed by the preposition *de*, it may be preceded by the pronoun *en*.

EXAMPLE.

je n'en dirai pas davantage,	*I shall not say any more about it.*

It is incorrect to use *davantage* for *le plus*. We must say,

de toutes les fleurs d'un parterre, l'anémone est celle qui me plaît le plus,	*of all the flowers of a parterre, the anemone is that which pleases me most.*

---

424. *Si*, *aussi*, *tant*, and *autant*, are always followed by the conjunction *que*, expressed or understood.

Si and *aussi* are joined to adjectives, adverbs, and participles; *tant* and *autant* to substantives and verbs.

EXAMPLES.

l'Angleterre n'est pas si grande que la France,	*England is not so large as France.*
il est aussi estimé qu'aimé,	*he is as much esteemed as he is beloved*
elle a autant de beauté que de vertu,	*she has as much beauty as virtue.*

REMARK. *Autant* may, however, be substituted for *aussi*, in comparisons of equality.

EXAMPLE.

il est modeste autant que sage,	*he is as modest as wise*

It has been said, No. 47, that, in comparisons, *aussi* is used with the affirmative, and *si* with the negative; *si*, may, however, be used in an affirmative sentence, in the sense of *tellement*.

EXAMPLE.

Il est devenu si gros, qu'il a de la peine à marcher,	*he is become so bulky that he can hardly walk.*

Jamais takes sometimes the preposition *à*, and *toujours* the preposition *pour*.

EXAMPLES

soyez à jamais heureux,	*be for ever happy.*
c'est pour toujours,	*it is for ever.*

CHAPTER VIII.

OF THE CONJUNCTIONS.

425. Que is a conjunction so much used in French that, although it has been already noticed in every part of this grammar with which it might have reference, it may not be unnecessary to present here a series of examples of the various ways in which it is used.

EXAMPLES.

QUE	expressing *comparison*	*l'Asie est plus grande* que *l'Europe.*	Asia is larger *than* Europe.
	for *rien* que	*on ne parle* que *de la nouvelle victoire.*	they talk of *nothing but* the new victory.
	for *je souhaite* que	qu'*il vive pour, je souhaite* qu'*il vive.*	may he live, for, *I wish that* he may live.
	for *à moins* que *avant* que *sans* que	*cela* ne *finira pas* qu'*il* ne *vienne.*	there will be no end to it, *unless* he come.

QUE for	*dès* que / *aussitôt* que / *si*, or *quand*	qu'*il fasse le moindre excès, il est malade.*	*if* he commits the least excess, he is ill.
—	*soit* que	qu'*il perde, ou* qu'*il gagne son procès, c'est un homme ruiné.*	*whether* he gains, or loses his law-suit, he is a ruined man.
—	*jusqu'à ce* que	*attendez* qu'*il vienne.*	wait *till* he comes.
—	*pourquoi?*	que *ne se corrige-t-il?*	*why* does he not reform?
—	*comme*	*méchant* qu'*il est.*	wicked *as* he is.
—	combien	que *Dieu est grand!*	*how* great is the Almighty!
		que *je hais les méchants!*	*how much* I hate the wicked!

Another very frequent use of this conjunction is to save the repetition of *comme, parce que, puisque, quand, quoique, si,* etc. when, to phrases beginning with these words, others are added under the same regimen, by means of the conjunction *et.*

EXAMPLE.

si l'on aimait son pays, et qu'on en désirât sincèrement la gloire, on se conduirait de manière, etc.	*if we loved our country, and sincerely wished its glory, we should act so as, etc.*

426. *Particular construction* with *que* before a noun or an infinitive.

EXAMPLE.

c'est un homme singulier que votre frère,	*your brother is a strange man.*

For *votre frère est un homme singulier.*

EXAMPLE.

c'était quelque chose que d'avoir commencé,	*having begun was already something.*

For *avoir commencé était déjà quelque chose.*

EXERCISE.

We have every thing to fear from his wisdom, even more
encore
than from his power. What men term greatness, glory,
ce que art. *appeler*
power, profound policy, is in the eyes of God *only*
profond politique, f. *à*
misery, weakness, and vanity. *May* they understand, at last,
comprendre
that without internal peace there is no
avec soi-même 2 art 1 *point*
happiness. *May* she be as happy as she deserves to be.
de *de le*
Never write *before* you have thoroughly examined
sous toutes ses faces 2 1
the subject which you propose to treat. *Let* him but hear
se proposer de traiter
the least noise, his terrified imagination presents to him nothing
bruit *effrayé* 2 f. 1 *
but monsters. Do not sift this question, *till*
ne que de art. *approfondir*
I can (be your guide). Do not go out *till* your brother
ne subj-1 *vous mette sur la voie*
comes in. *Why* does he not (take advantage) of his youth,
ne rentrer * *profiter*
(in order to) acquire the knowledge he wants? This
pour *connaissance* pl. *dont avoir besoin?*
town is a very pretty place. My uncle was a terrible man when
he was in a passion.

Full *as* he was of his prejudices, he would not own
Rempli ind-2 *préjugé* *convenir* ind-3
(any thing). Full of self-love (*as* he is), except nothing
de rien *pétri* 1 3 2 *de*
good (from him). *How* beautiful is that cultivated nature.
en 1 6 5 2 4

How, by the care of man, it is brilliantly and richly adorned!
par *pompeusement orné*

Had profound philosophers presided at the formation of
si ind-6 *de* *à*

languages, and had they carefully examined the elements of
art. *langue* subj-4 *avec soin* — m.

speech, not only in their relations (to one another), but also
art. *discours non* *entr'eux* *encore*

in themselves, it is not (to be doubted) that languages
en m. *douteux* art. *ne*

would present principles more simple, and at the same time,
offrir subj-2 *de* art.

more luminous.

GOVERNMENT OF CONJUNCTIONS.

427. The conjunctions which unite sentences to one another, are followed either by the *infinitive*, the *indicative*, or the *subjunctive*.

Those that are followed by an infinitive, are,

1. Such as are distinguished from prepositions, only by being followed by a verb.

EXAMPLE.

il faut se reposer après avoir travaillé,	*one ought to rest after having laboured.*

2. Those which have the preposition *de* after them.

EXAMPLE.

il travaille afin de vous surpasser,	*he works that he may surpass you.*

EXERCISE.

They were going to spend a few days in town,
ne * ind-2 * *passer* * *quelques* *à* art.

only *that* they might return with more pleasure to
que pour * * *se retrouver* inf-1

their charming solitude. Many persons work only (in order to
ne que *afin de*
acquire consideration and riches, but the honest and
de art. pr. art. 2 *et*
humane man spends (so much) time in study, only
sensible 3 1 *ne employer* *tant de* *à* art. *que*
to be useful to his fellow-creatures. I reveal to you the
pour *semblables.* *dévoiler*
plot which your enemies have concerted in secret in
trame f. *ourdir* art. *ténèbres* f. pl.
order to warn you against their artifices.
prémunir

428. Conjunctions that govern the indicative,

bien attendu que,	autant que,	puisque,	peut-être que,
à condition que,	non plus que,	lorsque,	comme,
à la charge que,	outre que,	pendant que,	comme si,
de même que,	parce que,	tandis que,	quand,
ainsi que,	attendu que,	durant que,	pourquoi,
aussi bien que,	vu que,	tant que,	comment, etc.

They are followed by the indicative, because the principal sentence, which they unite with that which is incidental, expresses the affirmation in a direct, positive and independent manner.

The use of the six following conjunctions,

si non que,	de sorte que,	tellement que,
si ce n'est que,	en sorte que,	de manière que,

varies according to the meaning expressed by the principal sentence.

EXAMPLE OF THE INDICATIVE.	EXAMPLE OF THE SUBJUNCTIVE.
je ne lui ai répondu autre chose, *si non que* j'avais exécuté ses ordres,	je ne veux autre chose, *si non que* vous travailliez avec plus d'ardeur.
I made him no other answer, but that *I had executed his orders*.	*I desire nothing else*, but that *you would study with greater ardour*

The indicative is required, in the first sentence, by the verb *j'ai répondu* expressing a positive affirmation, and the subjunctive in the second, because *je veux* expresses a command, or desire.

EXERCISE.

When you have a more extensive knowledge of geometry,
ind-7 2 1 art. f.

and algebra, I shall give you a few lessons in astro-
pr. art. *algèbre* f. * *quelque* *de*

nomy, and optics. Form your mind, heart, and taste
pr. *optique* pron. pron.

while you are still young. Do not keep truth a prisoner,
encore *retenir* art. * *captive*

though you should (draw upon you) a cloud of enemies.
quand *devoir* cond-1 *s'attirer* *nuée* f.

I will give you this fine picture *upon condition* that you
tableau m. *à*

keep it as a testimony of my friendship.
conserver ind-7 *témoignage* m.

429. The conjunctions which govern the subjunctive are,

soit que,
sans que,
pour que,
quoique,
jusqu'à ce que,
encore que,
à moins que,
pourvu que,
supposé que,
au cas que,
avant que,
non pas que,
afin que,
de peur que,
de crainte que, etc.

They require the subjunctive, because they always imply doubt, desire, ignorance. See No. 378.

EXERCISE.

You know too well the value of time, *to* make
connaître *prix* m. art. *pour que être* 2

it necessary to tell you to (make a good use of) it. Study only
il 1 *de* *de* *bien employer*

great models, *lest* those which are but middling
art. *de peur que* * *médiocre ne*

should spoil your taste, *before* it be entirely formed. I
gâter subj-1

(make not the least doubt) that your method will succeed,
ne douter nullement f. *ne* subj-1

provided it be well known. Several phenomena of nature are
f. art.

easy (to be explained), *supposing* the principle of universal
(by the active) art. 2

gravitation to be true.
f. 1 *

PROMISCUOUS EXERCISES ON THE NINE PARTS OF SPEECH.

The Good Mother.

What a fine morning! said the amiable Charlotte to her
matinée f. ind-3

brother George. Come let us go into the garden and enjoy
sing. * inf-1

the magnificent sight of rich and abundant nature.
de 2 *spectacle* m. 1 *une* 2 *fertile* 3 1

We will gather the freshest and sweetest flowers. We
y *cueillir* *frais* 2 art. adv. *odorant* 3 f. pl. 1

will make a nosegay, which we will offer to mamma. You
bouquet m. *maman* sing

know she is fond of flowers. This attention will give her
savoir que *aimer* *faire lui*

pleasure. Ah! brother, it will obtain us a smile, a caress,
mon f. *valoir* *sourire* m. f.

perhaps even a kiss. Ah! sister, replied George, your
baiser m. *ma* *répondre* ind-3 sing.

proposal delights me, let us run, let us hasten, that we may
projet *enchanter* *courir* *voler* *afin de* * *

offer her, (when she gets up), this tribute of our gratitude and
lui *à son lever* *hommage* —

our love. Full of this idea, Charlotte and George hastened
pr. *plein* *se hâter* ind-3

into the garden. Charlotte gathered violets jes-
de se rendre ind-3 *de* art. pr. art.

samine, and young rose-buds which (had but just begun)
pr. *de* 2 *bouton* m.1 *ne commencer que* ind-2

to open their purple cups, while George prepared
entr'ouvrir *de pourpre* 2 *calice* 1 ind-2

green sprigs of myrtle and thyme, intended to
de art. *verdoyant* 2 *jet* m. 1 *myrte* pr. *thym* *destiné*

hold up the flowers. Never had these amiable children
soutenir 1 ind-2 3 2

exerted themselves with (so much) zeal and ardour. Satis-
travailler *tant de* *zèle* pr. art.

faction and pleasure were painted in all their features, sparkled
f. art. m. ind-2 *peint* *trait* m. *pétiller*

in their eyes, and added still to their beauty.

While they (were engaged) (in this manner), their mother,
s'occuper ind-2

who had seen them in the garden, came to join them. (As
ind-3 * *joindre*

soon as) they perceived her, they flew to her, and said : (Ah
dès que ind-3 ind-3 *elle* *lui*

mamma, how glad we are to see you! how (impatient we
que aise 3 1 2 *de* *il tardait à notre*

were) for this pleasure. In the pleasing expectation (of
impatience *d'avoir* *ce* *doux* *attente* f. *

it) we (were preparing) this nosegay for you. What satisfaction
ind-2 f.

should we have had in presenting it to you! Look at these
ne *pas* *à* *offrir* *voir* *

rose-buds, these violets, this jessamine, this myrtle, and this

thyme. Well, we intended them for you. These flowers,
Eh bien *destiner* ind-2 *

coming from u would have been dear to you. In wearing
cher *En* *porter* inf-2

them, you would have said: My children (were thinking) of me
s'occuper ind-2

while I slept. I am always as present to their minds as
dormir ind-2 sing.

to their hearts. They love me, and it is by giving me every

day new proofs of their affection, that they acknowledge
art. pl. *de* *preuve* f. *reconnaître*

the care I have taken of them in their childhood,
soin m. pl. *que*

all the marks of tenderness I am unceasingly giving them.
que *ne cesser de* inf-1 *leur.*

My dear children, replied the mother, embracing them,
répondre ind-3 *en embrasser*

how happy you make all my days! your gratitude, your
quel charme *répandre sur* *

tenderness, your attention to me, make me forget my former
pl. *pour* *oublier* *ancien*

misfortunes, and open my heart again to the sweet impressions
malheur m. *rouvrir* * f.

of pleasure. May Heaven continue to bless my
art. *Pouvoir* subj-1 art. *continuer de*

labour! May it be your guide and your support in the career
soin *Pouvoir* = *soutien* *carrière* f.

which (will soon be opened) to you! may it complete
aller ind-1 *s'ouvrir* *devant* *mettre le comble à*

its kindness by preserving you from the dangers to which
bienfait pl. *en* *garantir* inf-2 *de*

you cannot fail to be soon exposed! Alas! I
* *ne pas tarder* ind-7 *

shudder (at them) beforehand, my dear children; the moment
frémir *en* *d'avance*

is come when you must enter the world. Your persons,
où *devoir* *dans* *figure* sing

your birth, and your fortune call you there, and insure you
naissance *appeler* *y* *assurer*

a distinguished rank (in it), I cannot always be your guide.
2 m. 1 *y* ind-7

Young and inexperienced, you will find yourselves surrounded
sans expérience *aller* ind-1 inf-1 *entouré*

by every kind of temptation. (Every thing), even
sorte f. *séduction* *tout* *jusque à* art. m.

vice, presents itself there under an agreeable form, and
offrir *y* *sous* * *de* art. 2 pl. 1

almost always in the shape of pleasure, which has (so many)
sous *image* art. *tant de*

attractions for youth. They will try to mislead you, to
attrait f. art. *jeunesse* f. *On* *chercher* *égarer*

corrupt you; they (will make use of) artifice, raillery, and
employer art. art. =

even the mask of virtue. If you abandon yourselves
jusque à *masque* m. art. *se laisser aller*

to first impressions, you are lost. The poison of example will
art.

insinuate itself into your hearts, will corrupt the innocence and
se glisser *altérer*

purity (of them) and will substitute violent passions for
en *de* art. *déchirant* 2 f. pl. 1 *à*

the sweet affections which have hitherto made your happiness.
doux *faire*

Do not imagine, my dear children. that, in placing before your
croire *en mettre sous*

eyes a picture of the dangers of the world, my intention
le tableau m.

is to prohibit you every kind of pleasure. God for-
subj-1 *de* *interdire* * *espèce* f. *à* *ne plaire*

bid Pleasure is necessary to man; without it, our
subj-1 art. art. *lui*

existence would be dreadful; (and therefore) Providence, al-
affreux *aussi* art. f.

ways attentive to our wants, has multiplied the sources of
besoin *a-t-elle*

it, both in and out of ourselves. But, in tasting the pleasures
* *en nous* *en goûter*

of the world, never (abandon yourselves) (to them). Take care
se livrer *y* *Avoir*

they do not govern you; know how to quit them the mo-
dominer subj. 1 *savoir* * * *ne*

ment they have acquired (too much) empire over you. It is
que *prendre* ind-7 *trop de* *Ce*

the only way to enjoy with delight that exquisite plea-
moyen de *volupté de délicieux* 2

sure which we can only find in ourselves, and which has its
1 *en*

source in an upright and pure conscience. Ah! why cannot I
dans droit 2 3 f. 1 *que*

give all my experience? why cannot you like me read the
dans

depths of the heart? With what astonishment would you often
abîme sing. pl.

see vexation, agitation, and trouble, disguised under the
art. —m. art. art. —m. *déguisé sous*

appearance of joy and tranquillity; hatred and envy
apparence pl. art. pr. art. *calme* art. f. art. f.

concealed under the air of confidence and friendship;
caché art. *confiance* f. pr. art.

indifference and selfishness, affecting the most lively interest;
art. *égoïsme* *vif*

the most dreadful and perfidious plots contrived
2 art. adv. 3 *trame* f. pl. 1 *ourdi*

deliberately in the dark; in a word, the most odious
de sang froid et ténèbres f. pl. *en* 2

vices endeavouring to show themselves under the features
art. 1 *s'efforcer de* *traits*

of (their opposite) virtues! In the world there is but
qui leur être opposé 2 art. 1 *ne que*

one (moving principle); that is self-interest. To that
seul mobile m. *ce* art. *personnel* 2 1 *C'est à lui que*

every action refers, every thing tends to that as to its
art. pl. *se rapporter* *lui*

end. I know very well, my dear children, that your hearts
fin f. *savoir*

will not be infected by this vice. The sentiments of universal
de 2

benevolence with which I (have always) inspired you and
bienveillance 1 * *ne point cesser* ind-4 *de* inf-1

of which I have seen you give (so many) proofs, (remove
tant de preuve rassurer 1

already every fear) (I might have) upon that subject: but will
d'avance 3 *me* 2 *sur point* m.

you not yield to other vices not less dangerous? Cruel idea!
de non f.

terrible uncertainty? If this misfortune were to happen.
affreux f. * * *arriver* ind-2

ah! my dear children, instead of being the joy and conso-
art. f.

lation of my life, you would be the torment, the shame and the
honte f.

disgrace (of it). You would poison my days, and you
opprobre *en* *empoisonner*

would plunge a dagger into the very bosom which gave
porter art. *mort* f. *même* 2 *sein* m. 1 ind-3

you life. But whither is my tenderness for you carrying me?
art. *où* * *emporter*

No, my children, no, I have nothing to fear; you love me (too
Non

much) to wish to grieve me so cruelly; and I shall have
trop *pour* *vouloir* *

the pleasure, (as long as) I live, of seeing you walk in the ways
tant que ind-7 *sentier*

of honour and virtue.
art. pr. art.

CHAPTER IX.

OF GRAMMATICAL CONSTRUCTION.

430. Grammatical construction is the order which the genius of a language has assigned, in speech, to the different sorts of words into which it is distinguished. Construction is sometimes mistaken for syntax; but there is this difference: the latter consists in the rules which we are to observe, in order to express the relations of words one to another, whereas grammatical construction consists in the

various arrangements which are allowed while we observe the rules of syntax. Now this arrangement is irrevocably fixed, not only as phrases may be interrogative, imperative, or expositive, but also as each of these kinds may be affirmative, or negative.

In sentences simply interrogative, the subject is either a noun, or pronoun.

If the subject be a noun, the following is the order to be observed: first, the noun, then the verb, then the corresponding personal pronoun, the adverb, if any, and the regimen in the simple tenses: in the compound tenses, the pronoun and the adverb are placed between the auxiliary and the participle.

EXAMPLE.

les lumières sont-elles un bien pour les peuples? ont-elles jamais contribué à leur bonheur?	*are sciences an advantage to nations? Have they ever contributed to their happiness?*

If the subject be a pronoun, the verb begins the series, and the other words follow in the order already pointed out.

EXAMPLES.

vous plairez-vous toujours à médire?	*will you always take pleasure in slandering?*
aurez-vous bientôt fini?	*shall you have soon done?*

N.B.—[When the verb is reflected, the pronoun forming the regimen begins the series, this pronoun always preserves its place before the verb, except in sentences simply imperative.]

In interrogative sentences, with a negation, the same order is observed; but *ne* is placed before the verb, and *pas* or *point*, after the verb in the simple tenses, and between the auxiliary and the participle in the compound tenses

EXAMPLES.

votre frère ne viendra-t-il pas demain ?	*will not your brother come to-morrow ?*
n'aurez-vous pas bientôt fini ?	*shall you not have soon done ?*

REMARK. There are in French several other ways of interrogating.

1. With an absolute pronoun.

EXAMPLE.

qui vous a dit cela ? *or* qui est-ce qui vous a dit cela ?	*who told you that ?*

2. With the demonstrative pronoun *ce*.

EXAMPLES

est-ce vous ?	*is it you ?*	est-ce qu'il pleut ?	*does it rain ?*

3. With an interrogative verb.

EXAMPLES.

pourquoi ne vient-il pas ?	*why does he not come ?*
comment vous trouvez-vous ?	*how do you find yourself ?*

Hence we see that the absolute pronouns and the interrogative adverbs always begin the sentence: but the demonstrative pronoun *ce* always follows the verb.

In sentences, simply imperative, the verb is always placed first, in the first and second persons; but in the third, it comes after the conjunction *que* and the noun or pronoun.

EXAMPLES.

allons-là,	*let us go there.*
venez-ici,	*come here.*
qu'ils y aillent,	*let them go there.*
que Pierre aille à Londres,	*let Peter go to London.*

With negation, *ne* and *pas* are placed as in interrogative sentences.

For the place of the pronouns, See No. 218.

Sentences are expositive, when we speak without either interrogating, or commanding. The following is the order of the words in those which are affirmative: the subject, the verb, the adverb, the participle, and the regimen.

EXAMPLES.

un bon prince mérite l'amour de ses sujets et l'estime de tous les peuples,	*a good prince deserves the love of his subjects, and the esteem of all nations.*
César eût inutilement passé le Rubicon, s'il y eût eu de son temps des Fabius,	*Cæsar would have crossed the Rubicon to no purpose, had there been Fabii in his time.*

The negative sentences differ from this construction, only as *ne* is always before the verb, and *pas*, or *point*, either after the verb, or between the auxiliary and the participle.

EXAMPLES.

un homme riche ne fait pas toujours le bien qu'il pourrait,	*a rich man does not always do all the good he might.*
Cicéron n'eût pas peut-être été un si grand orateur, si le désir de s'élever aux premières dignités n'eût enflammé son âme,	*Cicero would not perhaps have been so great an orator, had not the desires of rising to the first dignities inflamed his soul.*

Sentences are either simple, or compound. They are simple, when they contain only one subject and one attribute.

EXAMPLES.

vous lisez,	*you read.*
vous êtes jeune,	*you are young.*

They are compound, when they reunite several

subjects with one attribute, or several attributes with one subject, or several attributes with several subjects, or several subjects with several attributes.

This sentence, *Pierre et Paul sont heureux*, is compound by having two subjects; this, *cette femme est jolie, spirituelle et sensible*, is compound by having more than one attribute; and this, *Pierre et Paul sont spirituels et savants*, is composed at once of several subjects and several attributes.

A sentence may be compound in various other ways; by the subject, by the verb, or by the attribute.

By the subject, when this is restricted by an incidental proposition.

EXAMPLE.

Dieu, qui est bon.

By the verb, when it is modified by some circumstance of time, order, etc.

EXAMPLE.

Dieu, qui est bon, n'abandonne jamais.

By the attribute, when this attribute is modified by a regimen which is itself restricted.

EXAMPLE.

Dieu, qui est bon, n'abandonne jamais les hommes, qui metten sincèrement leur confiance en lui.

These simple, or compound sentences may be joined to others by a conjunction.

EXAMPLES.

quand on aime l'étude, le temps passe sans qu'on s'en aperçoive,	*when we love study, time flies without our perceiving it.*

The two partial phrases here form but one.

When a sentence is composed of two partial phrases, joined by a conjunction, harmony and perspicuity generally require the shortest to go first.

EXAMPLES.

quand les passions nous quittent, nous nous flattons en vain, que c'est nous qui les quittons,	*when our passions leave us, we in vain flatter ourselves that it is we that leave them.*
on n'est point à plaindre, quand, au défaut de plaisirs réels, on trouve le moyen de s'occuper de chimères,	*he is not to be pitied, who for want of real pleasures, finds means to amuse himself with chimeras.*

Periods result from the union of several partial phrases, the whole of which make a complete sense. Periods, to be clear, require the shortest phrases to be placed first. The following example of this is taken from Fléchier.

N'attendez pas, Messieurs,

1. Que j'ouvre une scène tragique ;
2. Que je représente ce grand homme étendu sur ses propres trophées ;
3. Que je découvre ce corps pâle et sanglant, auprès duquel fume encore la foudre qui l'a frappé ;
4. Que je fasse crier son sang comme celui d'Abel, et que j'expose à vos yeux les images de la religion et de la patrie éplorée.

This admirable period is composed of four members, which go on gradually increasing. It is a rule not to give more than four members to a period, and to avoid multiplying incidental sentences.

Obscurity in style is generally owing to those small phrases which divert the attention from the principal sentences, and make us lose sight of them.

The construction which we have mentioned is called direct, or regular, because the words are placed in those sentences according to the order which has been pointed out. But this order may be altered in certain cases, and then the construction is called indirect, or irregular. Now, it may be irregular, by *inversion*, by *ellipsis*, by *pleonasm*, or by *syllepsis*; these are what are called the four figures of words.

INVERSION.

431. *Inversion* is the transposition of a word into a place, different from that which, by usage, is properly assigned to it. This ought never to be done except when it introduces more perspicuity, energy, or harmony into the language; for it is a defect in construction, whenever the connexion subsisting between words is not easily perceived.

There are two kinds of inversion: the one, by its boldness seems to be confined to poetry: the other is frequently employed even in prose.

We shall speak here of the latter kind only.

The following inversions are authorized by custom.

The subject by which a verb is governed may with propriety be placed after it.

EXAMPLE.

tout ce que lui promet l'amitié des Romains,	*all that the friendship of the Romans promises him.*

REMARK. This inversion is a rule of the art of speaking and writing, whenever the subject is modified by an incidental sentence, long enough to make us lose sight of the connexion between the verb governed and the subject governing.

The noun governed by the prepositions *de* and *à* may likewise be very properly placed before the verb

EXAMPLES.

d'une voix entrecoupée de sanglots, ils s'écrièrent,	*in a voice interrupted by sobs, they exclaimed.*
à tant d'injures, qu'a-t-elle répondu?	*to so much abuse, what answer did she give?*

The verb is likewise elegantly preceded by the prepositions *après*, *dans*, *par*, *sous*, *contre*, etc. and the nouns which they govern, as well as by the conjunctions *si*, *quand*, *parce que*, *puisque*, *quoique*, *lorsque*, etc.

EXAMPLES.

par la loi du corps, je tiens à ce monde qui passe,	*by the law of the body, I am connected with this passing world.*
puisqu'il le veut, qu'il le fasse,	*since he wishes it, let him do it.*

OF THE ELLIPSIS.

432. *Ellipsis* is the omission of a word, or even several words, which are necessary to make the construction full and complete. An ellipsis is bad, if the mind does not easily and rapidly supply the words omitted.

EXAMPLE

J'accepterais les offres de Darius, si j'étais Alexandre :— et moi aussi, si j'étais Parménion,	*I would accept the offers of Darius, if I were Alexander :— and so would I, if I were Parmenio.*

Here the mind easily supplies the words *je les accepterais* in the second member.

The ellipsis is very common in answers to interrogative sentences.

EXAMPLE.

quand viendrez-vous?—demain, *when will you come?—to-morrow.*

that is, *je viendrai demain.*

In order to know whether an ellipsis be good, the words that are understood must be supplied. It is correct, whenever the construction completely expresses the sense denoted by the words which are supplied; otherwise it is not exact.

OF THE PLEONASM.

433. *Pleonasm*, in general, is a superfluity of words: in order to constitute this figure good, it must be sanctioned by custom, which never permits its use, except it give greater energy to language, or express, in a clearer manner, the internal feeling with which we are affected.

EXAMPLES.

Et que m'a fait *à moi* cette Troïe où je cours!
Je *me* meurs. S'il ne veut pas vous le dire, je vous le dirai, *moi.*
Je l'ai vu *de mes propres yeux.*
Je l'ai entendu *de mes propres oreilles.*

—*A moi*, in the first sentence;—*me*, in the second; —*moi*, in the third;—*de mes propres yeux*, in the fourth; and—*de mes propres oreilles*, in the fifth, are employed merely for the sake of energy, or to manifest an internal feeling; but this manner of speaking is sanctioned by custom.

REMARK. Expletives must not be mistaken for pleonasms.

EXAMPLE.

c'est une affaire, où il y va du salut de l'état,	*it is an affair in which the safety of the state is concerned.*

Which is better than *c'est une affaire, où il va*, etc. that is, than omitting *y*, which is in reality useless on account of *où*: this is a mode of expression from which it is not allowed to deviate.

OF THE SYLLEPSIS.

434. The syllepsis is a figure by which a word relates more to our meaning, than to the literal expressions, as in these phrases:

Il est onze heures; l'an mil sept cent quatre-vingt-dix-neuf.

When using them, the mind, merely intent upon precise meaning, pays no attention to either the number, or the gender of *heure* and *an*.

There is likewise a syllepsis in these sentences:

Je crains qu'il ne vienne.
J'empêcherai qu'il ne vous nuise.
J'ai peur qu'il ne m'oublie, etc.

Full of a wish that the event may not take place, we are willing to do all we can, that nothing should present an obstacle to that wish. This is the cause of the introduction of the negative, which, although unnecessary to complete the sense, yet must be preserved for the sake of the idiom.

There is again a very elegant syllepsis in sentences like the following from Racine:

Entre le *peuple* et vous, vous prendrez Dieu pour juge;
Vous souvenant, mon fils, que caché sous ce lin,
Comme *eux* vous fûtes pauvre, et, comme *eux*, orphelin.

The poet forgets that he has been using the word *peuple:* nothing remains in his mind but *des pauvres* and *des orphelins*, and it is with that idea of which he is full that he makes the pronoun *eux* agree. For the same reason, Bossuet and Mézengui have said,

Quand le *peuple Hébreu* entra dans la terre promise, tout y célébrait *leurs* ancêtres.—BOSSUET.

Moïse eut recours au Seigneur, et lui dit: que ferai-je à *ce peuple?* bientôt *ils* me lapideront.—MÉZENGUI.

Leurs and *ils* stand for *les Hébreux.*

CHAPTER X.

OF GRAMMATICAL DISCORDANCES, AMPHIBOLOGIES, AND GALLICISMS.

435. We have chiefly to take notice of two incorrect modes of construction, which are contrary to the principles laid down in the preceding chapters—grammatical discordances, and—amphibologies.

OF DISCORDANCES.

In general, there is a discordance in language, when the words, which compose the various members of a sentence, or period, do not agree with each other, either because their construction is contrary to analogy, or because they bring together dissimilar ideas, between which the mind perceives an opposition, or can see no manner of affinity.

The following examples will serve to illustrate this:

Notre réputation ne dépend pas des louanges qu'on nous donne, mais des actions louables que nous faisons.

This sentence is not correct, because the first member being negative, and the second affirmative, cannot come under the government of the same verb. It ought to be:

notre réputation dépend, non des louanges qu'on nous donne, mais des actions, etc.	*our reputation depends, not upon the praises which are bestowed on us, but upon the praiseworthy actions which we perform.*

But the most common discordances are those which arise from the wrong use of tenses, as in this sentence:

Il regarde votre malheur comme une punition du peu de complaisance que *vous avez eue* pour lui, dans le temps qu'il vous *pria*, etc.

Because the two preterits, definite and indefinite, cannot well agree together; it should be:

Que vous eûtes pour lui dans le temps qu'il vous pria

There is discordance in this sentence:

On en ressentit autant de joie que d'une victoire complète dans un autre temps.

Because the verb cannot be understood after the *que* which introduces the second member of the comparison, when that verb is to be a different tense; it should be:

On en ressentit autant de joie qu'on en aurait ressenti, etc.

This line of Racine,

Le flot, qui l'apporta, recule épouvanté.

is also incorrect, because the form of the present cannot associate with that of the preterit definite; it should have been: *qui l'a apporté*

OF AMPHIBOLOGIES.

436. Amphibology, in language, is when a sentence is so constructed as to be susceptible of two different interpretations: this must be carefully avoided. As we speak only to be understood, perspicuity is the first and most essential quality of language; we should always recollect that *what is not clearly expressed in any language, is no language at all.*

Amphibology are occasioned, 1. By the misuse of —moods, and—tenses. 2. Of—personal pronouns, *il, le, la,* etc. 3. Of—possessive pronouns, *son, sa, ses,* etc. 4. By giving a wrong place to nouns.

EXAMPLE

Of an Amphibology of the first Kind.

Qu'ai-je fait, *pour venir* accabler en ces lieux
Un héros, sur qui seul j'ai pu tourner les yeux?—RACINE.

Pour venir forms an amphibology, because we do not know whether it relates to the person who speaks, or to the person spoken to: it should have been: *pour que vous veniez*

EXAMPLE

Of an Amphibology of the second Kind.

César voulut premièrement surpasser Pompée ; les grandes richesses de Crassus *lui* firent croire, qu'*il* pourrait partager la gloire de ces deux grands hommes.

This sentence is faulty in its construction, because the pronouns *il* and *lui* seem to relate to *César*, although the sense obliges us to refer them to *Crassus*.

EXAMPLE

Of an Amphibology of the third Kind.

Valère alla chez Léandre ; il y trouva *son* fils.

The pronoun *son* is ambiguous, because we do not know which it relates, to *Valère*, or to *Léandre*.

EXAMPLE

Of an Amphibology of the fourth Kind.

J'ai envoyé les lettres, que j'ai écrites, à la poste.

A la poste, thus placed, is equivocal, because we do not know whether it is meant that the letters have been *written at* the post-office, or *sent to* the post-office.

OF GALLICISMS.

In the "Grammaire Philosophique et Littéraire," four sorts of gallicisms have been pointed out. Notice will be taken here of those only which have reference to construction.

The gallicisms of construction are, in general, irregularities and deviations from the customary rules of syntax: there are some, however, which are mere ellipses, and those which can only be attributed to the caprice of custom.

General Principle. Every gallicism of construction, which renders the meaning of the sentence obscure, ought to be condemned. Those only ought to be allowed which do not impair perspicuity, by introducing irregularity of construction, and which are, at the same time, sanctioned by long practice.

According to this principle, this elliptic gallicism is now rejected:

Et qu'ainsi ne soit, *meaning* ce que je vous dis est si vrai que,

because it renders the sentence obscure. For instance:

J'étais dans ce jardin, *et qu'ainsi ne soit*, voilà une fleur que j'y ai cueillie, *that is*, et pour preuve de cela, voilà une fleur, etc.

Molière and La Fontaine seem to have been the last great writers that have used this expression.

One of the most common gallicisms is that in which the impersonal verb *il y a*, is used for *il est*, *il existe*. These expressions:

Il y avait une fois un roi ;—il y a cent à parier contre un,

are gallicisms. There are two in the following sentence:

il n'y a pas jusqu'aux enfants, *even children will meddle with it* qui ne s'en mêlent,

The verb *falloir* forms a sort of gallicism with the pronoun *en*, when it is conjugated like pronominal verbs with the double pronouns *il se*.

EXAMPLE.

Il s'en faut, il s'en fallait, etc.

It then means *to be wanting*, and when preceded by an adverb of quantity, the first pronoun is omitted.

EXAMPLE.

Peu s'en faut, tant s'en faut.

These several manners of using the verb *falloir* will be found in the following sentences:

EXAMPLES.

il s'en faut bien qu'il soit aussi habile qu'il croit l'être,	*he is far from being so clever as he thinks.*
peu s'en est fallu qu'il n'ait succombé dans cette entreprise,	*he was very near falling in that undertaking.*
il ne s'en est presque rien fallu qu'il n'ait été tué,	*he was as near as possible being killed.*
vous dites qu'il s'en faut vingt livres que la somme entière n'y soit, mais vous vous trompez, il ne peut pas s'en falloir tant,	*you say it wants twenty pounds to complete the sum, but you are mistaken, it cannot want so much.*
son rhume est entièrement guéri, ou peu s'en faut,	*his cold is entirely cured, or very near.*
que s'en est-il fallu que ces deux amis ne se soient brouillés ?	*how near were these two friends quarrelling ?*
je ne suis pas content de votre application à l'étude, tant s'en faut,	*I am not satisfied with your application to study, far from it.*
tant s'en faut que cette comédie me plaise, elle me semble au contraire détestable,	*so far from this play pleasing me, I think it insufferable.*
il s'en fallait beaucoup que je vous approuvasse dans cette circonstance,	*I was far from approving your conduct on that occasion.*

The sentences:

il n'est rien moins que généreux,	*he is far from being generous.*
vous avez beau dire,	*you may say what you please, but, etc.*

à ce qu'il me semble,	*by what I can see, as the matter appears to me, etc.*
nous voilà à nous lamenter,	*we began to lament, here we are lamenting, crying, etc.*
qu'est-ce que de nous !	*what wretched beings we are, etc., etc.*

are also gallicisms.

The use which is made of the preposition *en*, in many sentences, is likewise another source of gallicisms; some of this kind will be found in the following expressions:

à qui en avez-vous ?	*whom are you angry with ?*
où en veut-il venir ?	*what does he aim it? what would he be at?*
il lui en veut,	*he owes him a grudge.*

The preposition *en* changes, also, sometimes, the signification of verbs, and then gives rise to gallicisms.

The conjunction *que* produces as great a number of gallicisms.

EXAMPLES.

c'est une terrible passion que le jeu,	*gaming is a terrible passion.*
c'est donc en vain que je travaille,	*it is in vain then that I work.*
ce n'est pas trop que cela,	*that is not too much.*
il n'est que d'avoir du courage,	*there is nothing like having courage.*

See No. 426.

Many others will be found in the use which is made of the prepositions *à*, *de*, *dans*, *après*, etc. but enough has been said on this subject.

Gallicisms are of very great use in the simple style: therefore La Fontaine and Mme. de Sévigné abound in them. The common style has not so many, and the solemn oratorical but few, and these even of a peculiar nature. Only two examples of this kind, both taken from the tragedy of Iphigenia, by Racine, will be here inserted.

> Avez-vous pu penser qu'au sang d'Agamemnon
> Achille préférât une fille sans nom,
> *Qui*, de tout son destin, ce qu'elle a pu comprendre,
> C'est qu'elle sort d'un sang etc.

And,

> *Je ne sais qui m'arrête* et retient mon courroux,
> *Que* par un prompt avis de tout ce qui se passe
> *Je ne coure* des dieux divulguer la menace.

In the first sentence, *qui* is the subject though without relating to any verb; and in the second, *je ne sais qui m'arrête que je ne coure*, is contrary to the rules of common construction. "But," says Vaugelas, "these extraordinary phrases, far from being faulty, possess the more beauty, as they belong to a particular kind of language."

FREE EXERCISES.

I.

MADAME DE MAINTENON TO HER BROTHER.

We can only be 1 unhappy by our own fault; this shall always be my text, and my reply to your lamentations. Recollect 2, my dear brother, the voyage to America, the misfortunes of our father, of our infancy and our youth 3; and you will bless Providence instead of murmuring against fortune Ten years ago, we were both very far (below our present situation 4;) and our hopes were so feeble 5, that we limited our wishes to an (income of three thousand livres 6.) At present we have four times that sum 7, and our desires are not yet satisfied! we enjoy the happy mediocrity which you have so often extolled 8; let us be content. If possessions 9 come to us, let us receive them from the hand of God, but let not our views be 10 too extravagant 11. We have (every thing necessary 12) and comfortable 13; all the rest is covetousness 14; all these desires of greatness spring from 15 a restless heart. Your debts are all paid, and you may live elegantly 16, without contracting more 17. What have you to desire? must 18 schemes 19 of wealth and ambition occasion 20 the loss of your repose and your health? read the life of St. Louis; you will see how unequal 21 the greatness of this world is to the desires of the human heart; God only can satisfy them 22. I repeat it, you are only unhappy by your own fault. Your uneasiness 23 destroys your health, which you ought to preserve, if it were 24 only because I love you. Watch 25 your temper 26: if you can render it less splenetic 27 and less gloomy, (you will have gained a great

1. On ne être—que. 2. Songer à. 3. The misfortunes of our infancy and those of our, etc. 4. Du point où nous sommes aujourd'hui. 5. Si peu de chose. 6. Trois mille livres de rente. 7. *That sum*, en. . .plus. 8 *Have so often extolled*, vanter si fort, ind-2. 9. *Possessions*, biens. 10 Let us not have views. 11. Trop vaste. 12. Le nécessaire. 13. Le commode. 14. *Covetousness*, cupidité. 15. *Spring from*, partir du vide de. 16. Délicieusement. 17. *Contracting more*, en faire de nouvelles. 18. *Must*, faut-il que. 19. Projet. 20. *Occasion*, coûter, subj-1. 21, *Unequal*, au-dessous de. 22. *Satisfy them*, le rassasier. 23. *Uneasiness*, inquiétude pl. 24. *If it were*, quand ce être, cond-1. 25 Travailler sur. 26. Humeur. 27. Bi-

advantage 28.) This is not the work of reflection only; exercise, amusement, and a regular life, (are necessary for the purpose 29.) You cannot think well (whilst your health is affected 30;) when the body is debilitated 31, the mind is without vigour. Adieu! write to me more frequently, and in a style less gloomy.

II.

THE CONVERT.

AN EASTERN TALE.

Divine mercy 1 had brought a vicious man into a society of sages, whose morals were holy and pure. He was affected by their virtues; it was not long 2 before 3 he imitated them and lost his old habits: he became just, sober, patient, laborious and benevolent. His deeds nobody could deny, but they were attributed 4 to odious motives. They praised his good actions, without loving his person: they would always judge him by what he had been, not by what he had become. This injustice filled him with grief; he shed tears in the bosom of an ancient sage, more just and more humane than the others. "O my son," said the old man to him, "thou art better than thy reputation; be thankful to God for it. "Happy the man who can say: my enemies and my rivals censure "in me vices of which I am not guilty. What matters 5 it, if thou "art good, that men persecute thee as wicked? Hast thou not, to "comfort thee, the two best witnesses of thy actions, God and thy "conscience?"

SAINT-LAMBERT.

Mr. de Montausier has written a letter to Monseigneur upon the king of Philipsbourg, which very much pleases me. "Monseigneur, I do not compliment you on the capture of Philipsbourg; you had a good army, bombs, cannon, and Vauban: neither shall I compliment you upon your valour; for that is an hereditary virtue in your family. But I rejoice that you are liberal, generous, humane, and that you know how to recompense the services of those who behave well: it is for this that I congratulate you."

SÉVIGNÉ.

lieux. 28. Ce être un grand point de gagné. 29. Il y faut de. 30. Tant que vous se porter mal 31. *Debilitated*, dans l'abattement.

1. Miséricorde. 2. Ne pas tarder. 3. A inf. 4. On donner des motifs. 5. Importer.

III.

THE GOOD MINISTER.

AN EASTERN TALE.

The great Aaron Raschild began to suspect that his vizier Giafar was not deserving of the confidence which he had reposed in him. The women of Aaron, the inhabitants of Bagdad, the courtiers, the dervises, censured the vizier with bitterness. The calif loved Giafar; he would not condemn him upon the clamours of the city and the court: he visited his empire; every where he saw the land well cultivated, the country smiling, the cottages opulent, the useful arts honoured, and youth full of gaiety. He visited his fortified cities and sea-ports: he saw numerous ships, which threatened the coasts of Africa and of Asia; he saw warriors disciplined and content; these warriors, the seamen and the peasantry, exclaimed: "O God, pour thy blessings upon the faithful, by giving them a calif like Aaron, and a vizier like Giafar." The calif, affected by these exclamations, enters a mosque, falls upon his knees, and cries out: "Great God, I return thee thanks: thou hast given me a "vizier of whom my courtiers speak ill, and my people speak well."

SAINT-LAMBERT.

Providence leads us with so much goodness through the different periods of our life, that we (are not sensible of our progress 1.) This loss takes place gently 2, it is imperceptible, it is the shadow of the sun-dial whose motion we do not see. If, at twenty years of age, we could see 3 in a mirror the face we shall have at three-score, we (should be shocked at the contrast 4,) and terrified at our own figure; but it is day by day that we advance: we are to-day as we were yesterday, and shall be to-morrow as we are to day; so we go forward without perceiving it, and this is a miracle of that Providence which I adore.

SÉVIGNÉ.

IV.

THE MAGNIFICENT PROSPECT.

This beautiful house was on the declivity of a hill, from whence you beheld the sea, sometimes clear and smooth as glass, sometimes

1. Ne le sentir quasi pas 2. Va doucement. 3. On nous faire voir.
4. Tomber à la renverse.

idly 1 irritated against the rocks on which it broke, bellowing 2 and swelling its waves like mountains. On another side was seen a river, in which were islands bordered with blooming limes, and lofty poplars, which raised their proud heads to the very clouds. The several channels, which formed those islands, seemed sporting 3 in the plain. Some rolled their limpid waters with rapidity: some had a peaceful and still course; others, by long windings, ran back again, to reascend as it were, to their source, and seemed not to have power to leave these enchanting borders. At a distance were seen hills and mountains, which were lost in the clouds, and formed by their fantastic figure, as delightful a horizon (as the eye could wish to behold. 4.) The neighbouring mountains were covered with verdant (vine branches, 5) hanging in festoons; the grapes brighter than purple, could not conceal themselves under the leaves, and the vine was overloaded with its fruit. The fig, the olive, the pomegranate, and all other trees, overspread the plain, and made it one large garden. FENELON.

Long hopes wear out 7 joy, as long maladies wear out pain.

All philosophic systems are only good when one (has no use for them 8.) SÉVIGNÉ.

V.

A GENERAL VIEW OF NATURE.

With what magnificence does nature shine 1 upon earth! . pure light, extending from east to west, gilds successively the two hemispheres of this globe; an element, transparent and light, surrounds it; a gentle fecundating heat animates, gives being 2 to the seeds of life: salubrious running streams contribute to their preservation and growth; eminences diversified over the level land, arrest the vapours of the air, make these springs inexhaustible and always new; immense cavities made to receive them divide the continents. The extent of the sea is as great as that of the earth; it not a cold, barren element; it is a new empire, as rich, as populous as the first. The finger of God has marked their boundaries.

The earth, rising above the level of the sea, is secure 3 from its

1. Follement. 2. En gémir. 3. Se jouer. 4. A souhait pour le plaisir de. 5. Pampre, m. 6. Vigne, f. 7. User. 8. N'en avoir que faire.
1. Ne briller pas. 2. Faire éclore. 3. A l'abri de.

eruptions: its surface, enamelled with flowers, adorned with ever-springing verdure, peopled with thousands and thousands of species of different animals, is a place of rest, a delightful abode, where man, placed in order to second nature, presides over all beings. The only one among them all, capable of knowing and worthy of admiring. God has made him spectator of the universe, and a witness of his wonders. The divine spark with which he is animated enables him to participate in the divine mysteries: it is by this light that he thinks and reflects; by it he sees and reads in the book of the universe, as in a copy of the Deity.

Nature is the exterior throne of the divine Majesty: the man who contemplates, who studies it, rises by degrees to the interior throne of Omnipotence. Made to adore the Creator, the vassal of heaven, sovereign of the earth, he ennobles, peoples, enriches it; he establishes among living beings order, subordination, harmony; he embellishes nature herself; he cultivates, extends, and polishes it; lops off the thistle and the briar, and multiplies the grape and the rose.

BUFFON.

VI.

ANOTHER GENERAL VIEW OF NATURE.

Trees, shrubs, and plants are the ornaments and clothing 1 of the earth. Nothing is so melancholy 2 as the prospect of a country naked and bare 3, exhibiting to the eye nothing but stones, mud, and sand. But, vivified by nature, and clad 4 in its nuptial robe, amidst the course of streams and the singing of birds, the earth presents to man, in the harmony of the three kingdoms, a spectacle full of life, of interest and charms, the only spectacle in the world of which his eyes and heart are never weary 5.

The more a (contemplative man's soul is fraught with sensibility 6), the more he yields to the extacies which this harmony produces in him. A soft and deep melancholy then takes possession of his senses, and, in an intoxication of delight, he loses himself in the immensity of that beautiful system, with which he feels himself identified. Then, every particular object escapes him, he sees and feels nothing but in the whole. Some circumstance must contract his ideas and circumscribe his imagination, before 7 he can observe by parcels that universe which he was endeavouring to embrace.

J. J. ROUSSEAU.

1. Vêtement. 2. Triste. 3. P 'é. 4. Revêtu. 5. Se lasser.
6. Contemplateur, avoir l'âme sensible. 7. Pour qu'il.

VII.

CULTIVATED NATURE.

How beautiful is cultivated nature! And, by the labours of man, how brilliant it is, and how pompously adorned! He himself is its chief ornament, its noblest part; by multiplying himself, he multiplies the most precious germ; she also seems to multiply with him; by his art, he (brings forth to view 1) all that she concealed 2 in her bosom. How many unknown treasures! What new riches! Flowers, fruits, seeds brought to perfection, multiplied to infinity; the useful species of animals transported, propagated, increased without number; the noxious species reduced, confined, banished: gold, and iron more necessary than gold, extracted from the bowels of the earth; torrents confined 3, rivers directed, contracted 4; the sea itself subjected, explored 5, crossed, from one hemisphere to the other; the earth accessible in every part, and every where rendered equally cheerful and fruitful: in the vallies, delightful meadows; in the plains, rich pastures, and still richer harvests; hills covered with vines and fruits; their summits crowned with useful trees and young forests; deserts changed into cities inhabited by an immense population, which, continually circulating, spreads itself from these centres to their extremities; roads opened and frequented, communications established every where, as so many witnesses of the strength and union of society: a thousand other monuments of power and glory sufficiently demonstrate that man, possessing dominion over the earth, has changed, renewed the whole of its surface, and that, at all times, he shares the empire of it with nature.

VIII.

THE SAME SUBJECT CONTINUED.

However, man only reigns by right of conquest: he rather enjoys than possesses, and he can preserve only by means of continual labour. If this ceases every thing droops, every thing declines, every thing changes and again returns 1 under the hand of nature; she reassumes her rights, erases the work of man, covers

1. Mettre au jour. 2. Recéler. 3. Contenu. 4. Resserré. 5. Reconnu.
1. Rentrer

with dust and moss its most pompous monuments, destroys them in time, and leaves him nothing but the regret of having lost, through his fault what his ancestors had conquered by their labours. Those times, in which man loses his dominion, those barbarous 2 ages, during which every thing is seen to perish, are always preceded by war, and accompanied by scarcity and depopulation. Man, who can do nothing but by number, who is strong only by union, who can be happy only by peace, is mad enough to arm himself for his misery, and to fight for his ruin. Impelled by an insatiable thirst of having, blinded by ambition still more insatiable, he renounces all the feelings of humanity, turns all his strength against himself, seeks mutual destruction, actually 3 destroys himself; and, after these periods of blood and carnage, when the smoke of glory has vanished, he contemplates with a sad eye, the earth wasted, the arts buried, nations scattered, the people weakened, his own happiness ruined, and his real power annihilated.

BUFFON.

IX.

INVOCATION TO THE GOD OF NATURE.

Almighty God! whose presence alone supports nature, and maintains the harmony of the laws of the universe: Thou, who from the immoveable throne of the empyrean, seest the celestial spheres roll under thy feet, without shock or confusion: who, from the bosom of repose, reproduced every moment their immense movements, and alone governset, in profound peace, that infinite number of heavens and worlds; restore, restore at length tranquillity to the agitated earth! let it be silent at thy voice; let discord and war cease their proud clamours! God of goodness, author of all beings, thy paternal eye takes in 1 all the objects of the creation; but man is thy chosen being; thou hast illumined 2 his soul with a ray of thy immortal light: complete the measure of thy kindness by penetrating his heart with a ray of thy love: this divine sentiment, diffusing itself every where, will reconcile opposite natures; man will no longer dread the sight of man; his hand will no longer wield the murderous steel 3; the devouring flames of war will no longer dry up 4 the sources of population: the human species, now weakened, mutilated, mowed down in the blossom, will spring anew 5 and multiply without number; nature, overwhelmed under the weight of scourges 6, will soon re-assume, with a new life, its for-

2, De barbarie. 3. En effet.

1. Embrasser. 2. Eclairer. 3. Le fer..., ..arme sa main. 4. Tarir.
5. Germer de nouveau. 6. Fléau.

mer fruitfulness; and we, beneficent God, will second it, we will cultivate it, we will contemplate it incessantly, that we may every moment offer thee a new tribute of gratitude and admiration.

BUFFON.

X.

Happy they who are disgusted with 1 turbulent pleasures, and know how to be contented 2 with the sweets of an innocent life! Happy they who delight in being instructed 3, and who take a pleasure 4 in storing their minds with knowledge! Wherever adverse fortune may throw them, they always carry entertainment with them; and the disquiet which preys upon others, even in the midst of pleasures, is unknown to those who can employ themselves in reading. Happy they who love to read, and are not like me deprived of the ability. As these thoughts were passing in my mind, I went into a gloomy forest, where I immediately perceived an old man holding a book in his hand. The forehead of this sage was broad, bald, and a little wrinkled: a white beard hung down to his girdle; his stature was tall and majestic; his complexion still fresh and ruddy, his eyes lively and piercing, his voice sweet, his words plain and charming. I never saw so venerable an old man. He was a priest of Apollo, and officiated 5 in a marble temple, which the kings of Egypt had dedicated to that God in this forest. The book which he held in his hand was a collection of hymns in honour of the Gods. He accosted me in a friendly manner; and we discoursed together. He related things past so well, that they seemed present, and yet with such brevity that his account never tired me. He foresaw the future by his profound knowledge, which made him know men, and the designs of which they are capable. With all this wisdom he was cheerful and complaisant, and the sprightliest youth has not so many graces as this man had at so advanced an age. He accordingly loved young men when they were teachable 6, and had a taste for study and virtue.

FENELON.

XI.

THOUGHTS ON POETRY.

Wherever I went, I found that poetry was considered as the high-

1. Se dégoûter de. 2. Se contenter de. 3. S'instruire. 4. Se plaire. 5. Servir. 6. Docile.

est learning 1), and regarded with a veneration (somewhat approaching to 2) that which men would pay to angelic nature.

It yet fills me with wonder that, in almost all countries, the most ancient poets are considered as the best; whether (it be that 3) every kind of knowledge is an acquisition gradually attained, and poetry is a gift conferred at once, or that the first poetry of every nation surprised them as a novelty, and retained the credit by consent, which it received by accident at first, or whether, as the province 4 of poetry is to describe nature and passion, which are always the same, the first writers (took possession 5) of (the most striking objects for description 6), and (the most probable occurrences for fiction 7,) and left nothing to those that followed them, but transcription 8 of the same events, and new combinations 9 of the same images. Whatever be the reason, it is commonly observed, that the early writers are in possession of natrue, and their followers 10 of art: that the first excel in strength and invention, and the latter in elegance and refinement.

I was desirous to add my name to this illustrious fraternity 11. I read all the poets of Persia and Arabia, and was able to repeat by memory the volumes that are suspended in the mosque of Mecca. But I soon found that no man was ever great by imitation. My desire of excellence 12 impelled 13 me to transfer 14 my attention to nature and to life 15. Nature was to be my subject, and men to be my auditors: I could never describe what I had not seen: I could not hope (to move those with delight or terror 16) whose interests and opinions I did not understand 17.

XII.

THE SAME SUBJECT CONTINUED.

Being now resolved to be a poet, I saw every thing (with a new purpose 18;) my sphere of attention was suddenly magnified: no kind of knowledge (was to be overlooked 19.) I ranged mountains and deserts for 20 images and resemblances and (pictured upon my mind 21) every tree of the forest and flower of the valley. I observed with equal care the crags of the rock and the pinnacles of the palace. Sometimes I wandered along the mazes of the rivulet

1. Partie la plus sublime de la littérature. 2. Qui tenait de. 3. Cela vienne de ce que. 4. But. 5. S'emparer. 6. Objets qui fournissaient les plus riches descriptions. 7. Evénements qui prêtaient le plus à la fiction. 8. De copier. 9. Faire de nouvelles combinaisons. 10. Successeurs. 11. Famille. 12. Exceller. 13. Engager. 14. Reporter...sur. 15. Tableau de la vie. 16. Réveiller le plaisir ou la terreur dans ceux. 17. Ne connaître ni. 18. Sous un nouveau jour. 19. Je ne devais négliger. 20. Pour recueillir. 21. Pénétrer mon esprit du tableau de.

and sometimes watched the changes of the summer-clouds. To a poet nothing can be useless. Whatever is beautiful, and whatever is dreadful, must be familiar to his imagination: he must (be conversant 22) with all that (is awfully vast or elegantly little 23). The plants of the garden, the animals of the wood, the minerals of the earth, and the meteors of the sky, must all concur to store his mind with inexhaustible variety; for every idea is useful for the (enforcement or decoration 24) of moral or religious truth; and he who knows most, will have most power 25 of diversifying his scenes 26, and gratifying his reader with remote allusions and unexpected instruction.

All the appearances of nature (I was, therefore, careful to study,) 27, and every country which I have surveyed has contributed something to my poetical powers.

In so wide a survey, interrupted the prince, you must surely have left much unobserved. I have lived, till now, within the circuit of these mountains, and yet cannot walk abroad without the sight of something which I had never beheld before, or never heeded 28.

XIII.

THE SAME SUBJECT CONTINUED.

The business of a poet, said Imlac, is to examine, not the individual, but the species; to remark general properties and (large appearances 29:) he does not number the streaks of the tulip, or describe the different shades in the verdure of the forest. He is to exhibit, in his portraits of nature, such prominent and striking features, as 30 recal the original to every mind; and must neglect the minuter discriminations 31, which one may have remarked, and another neglected, for those characters 32 which are alike obvious 33 to vigilance 34 and carelessness 35.

But the knowledge of nature is only half 36 the task of a poet: he must be acquainted likewise with all the modes 37 of life. His character requires that he estimate 38 the happiness and misery of every condition: observe the power of all the passions, in all their combinations, and trace the changes 39 of the human mind, as they

22. Bien connaître. 23. Etonne par sa grandeur, ou charme par son élégante petitesse. 24. Fortifier, ou embellir. 25. Ressources pour. 26. Tableau. 27. Etudier avec soin toutes les, etc. 28. Remarquer. 29. Considérer les objets en grand. 30. De ces traits saillants et frappants qui, etc. etc. 31. Ces petits détails. 32. Pour s'appliquer à caractériser, etc. etc. 33. Frappe également. 34. Œil observateur. 35. Esprit insouciant. 36. The half of. 37. Tous les différents aspects. 38. Apprécier. 39. Suivre les vicissitudes.

are modified by various institutions, and accidental influences of climate or custom; from the sprightliness of infancy to the despondence of decrepitude. He must divest himself 40 of the prejudices of his age or country; he must consider right and wrong 41 in their abstracted and invariable state 42; he must disregard present laws and opinions, and rise to general and transcendant truths, which will always be the same; he must, therefore, (content himself with the slow progress of his name 43,) to contemn the applause of his own time, and commit his claims to the justice of posterity. He must write as the interpreter of nature, and the legislator of mankind, and consider himself as presiding 44 over the thoughts and manners of future generations, as a being superior to time and place.

His labour is not yet at an end: he must know many languages and many sciences; and, that his style may be worthy of his thoughts, he must, by incessant practice, familiarize himself to every delicacy of speech and grace of harmony.

S. Johnson.

XIV.

First follow nature and your judgment frame
By her just standard, which is still the same:
Unerring nature, still divinely bright,
One clear, unchanged, and universal light,
Life, force, and beauty, must to all impart; 1
At once the source, and end, and test of art. 2
Art, from that fund, each just supply provides:
Works without show, and without pomp presides:
In some fair body thus th' informing soul
With spirits feeds, with vigour fills the whole,
Each motion guides, and every nerve sustains
Itself unseen, but in th' effect remains. 3
Some, to whom heav'n in wit has been profuse,
Want as much more to turn it to its use:

40. Se dépouiller. 41. Ce qui est juste ou injuste. 42. Abstraction faite de ces divers préjugés. 43. Se résigner à voir son nom percer difficilement. 44. Influer.

1. Light, clear, immutable, and universal nature, which never errs, and shines always with a divine splendour, must impart to all she does life, force and beauty.

2. She is at once the source, etc, etc.

3. So in a fair body, unseen itself, but always sensible by its effects, the soul continually acting, feeds the whole with spirits, fills it with vigour, guides every motion of it and sustains every nerve.

For wit and judgment often are at strife,
Tho' meant each other's aid, like man and wife. 4
'Tis more to guide, than spur the muse's steed;
Restrain his fury, than provoke his speed: 5
The winged courser, like a gen'rous horse,
Shows most true mettle, when you check its course. 6

POPE

4. Some to whom heaven has given wit with profusion, want as much yet to know the use they ought to make of it; for wit and judgment, though made, like man and wife, to aid each other, are often in opposition.

5. It is more difficult to guide than spur the courser of the muses, and to restrain its ardour than provoke its impetuosity.

6. The winged courser is like a generous horse: the more we strive to stop it in its rapid course, the more it shows unconquerable vigour.

437. EXAMPLES OF PHRASES ON THE PRINCIPAL DIFFICULTIES OF THE FRENCH LANGUAGE.

N.B.—It is strongly recommended that these examples be learnt by heart. They will also be found very useful, in point of reference, whenever the learner is at a loss on some point of grammar or construction. The better to enable him to find what he wants, the different chapters have been numbered, and will be found minutely described in the Table of Contents.

1. *Sur les Collectifs Partitifs.*	On the Collective Partitives.
La plupart des fruits verts sont d'un goût austère.	*The greater part of green fruit is of a harsh taste.*
La plupart des gens ne se conduisent que par intérêt.	*Most people are guided only by interest.*
La plupart du monde se trompe.	*The greater part of mankind are in error.*
Il méprise par philosophie les honneurs, que la plupart du monde recherche.	*As a true philosopher he despises those honours which mankind in general court.*
Il devait me fournir tant d'arbres; mais j'en ai rejeté la moitié qui ne valait rien.	*He was to furnish me so many trees, but I refused half of them which were good for nothing.*
Un grand nombre de spectateurs ajoutait à la beauté du spectacle.	*A considerable number of spectators added to the splendour of the scene.*
Toute sorte de livres ne sont pas également bons.	*Every kind of books are not equally good.*
Beaucoup de personnes se sont présentées.	*Many people presented themselves.*
Bien des personnes se font des principes à leur fantaisie.	*Many persons form principles to themselves, according to their fancy.*

2. *Sur quelques Verbes qu'on ne peut conjuguer avec* Avoir *sans faire des barbarismes.*

2. On some verbs which cannot be conjugated with the verb *Avoir*, without making barbarous phrases.

Il lui est échu une succession du chef de sa femme.

An estate fell to him in right of his wife.

Il est bien déchu de son crédit.

He has lost much of his credit.

Ne sommes-nous pas convenus du prix ?

Have we not agreed about the price?

N'est-il pas intervenu dans cette affaire, comme il l'avait promis ?

Did he not interfere in that affair as he had promised?

Il est survenu à l'improviste.

He came up unawares.

La neige, qui est tombée ce matin, a adouci le temps.

The snow which fell this morning has softened the weather.

Que de neige il est tombé ce matin !

How much snow has fallen this morning!

Toutes les dents lui sont tombées.

All his teeth have fallen out.

Ce propos n'est pas tombé à terre.

That remark was not allowed to escape.

Etes-vous allé voir votre ami?

Have you been to see your friend?

Ils sont arrivés à midi et sont repartis de suite.

They arrived at noon and set out again immediately.

Ces fleurs sont à peine écloses.

These flowers are scarcely blown.

Il est né de parents vertueux, qui n'ont rien négligé pour son éducation.

He was born of virtuous parents, who bestowed on him the best education.

Mademoiselle votre sœur est-elle rentrée?

Is your sister returned?

Madame votre mère n'est-elle pas encore venue?

Is not your mother come yet?

3. *Sur les Mots de Quantité.*

On Words of Quantity

Il a beaucoup d'esprit, mais encore plus d'amour-propre.

He has a great deal of sense but still more vanity.

Il a d'assez d'argent pour ses menus plaisirs.

He has pocket-money enough for his pleasures.

Il y avait bien du monde à l'Opéra.

There were a great many people at the Opera.

Il y avait hier au Parc je ne sais combien de gens.

There were I do not know how many people in the park yesterday.

Il boit autant d'eau que de vin.	*He drinks as much water as wine.*
Il a tant d'amis qu'il ne manquera de rien.	*He has so many friends that he will want for nothing.*
Personne n'y a plus d'intérêt que lui.	*Nobody has more interest there than he.*
Il n'a pas plus d'esprit qu'il n'en faut.	*He is not overburthened with sense.*
Trop de loisir perd souvent la jeunesse.	*Too much leisure time is frequently the ruin of youth.*
J'y ai bien moins d'intérêt que vous.	*I am much less concerned in it than you.*

4. *Sur les Pronoms Personnels.*	On the Personal Pronouns.
Sors et te retire.	*Go out and retire.*
Cours vite et ne t'amuse point.	*Go quick and do not loiter.*
Il dit aujourd'hui une chose et demain il se démentira.	*He advances a thing to-day, and will contradict himself to-morrow.*
Il s'est démenti lui-même.	*He has contradicted himself.*
La jeunesse est naturellement emportée; elle a besoin de quelque entrave qui la retienne.	*Youth is naturally hasty, it needs some curb to restrain it.*
Il ne peut voir personne dans la prospérité sans lui porter envie.	*He can see the prosperity of nobody, without envying them.*
Ce que vous me dites est une énigme pour moi.	*What you tell me is a perfect riddle to me.*
C'est un homme extrême en tout; il aime et il hait avec fureur.	*He is a man that carries every thing to excess; he is alike violent in his love and in his hatred.*
Si vous n'y avez jamais été, je vous y mènerai.	*If you have never been there, I will take you.*
Je l'ai connu doux et modeste; il s'est bien gâté dans le commerce de ses nouveaux amis.	*I knew him when he was gentle and modest; he has been much corrupted by associating with his new acquaintances.*
Elle n'est pas encore revenue du saisissement, que lui a causé cette nouvelle.	*She is not yet recovered from the consternation into which that news threw her.*
Il menace de l'exterminer, lui et toute sa race.	*He threatens to exterminate him and all his family.*
Si vous n'avez que faire de ce livre-là, prêtez-le-moi.	*If you have done with this book, lend it me.*
Je lui avais envoyé un diamant, il l'a refusé, je le lui ai renvoyé.	*I had sent him a diamond, and he refused it, but I sent him it back again.*

Il apprend facilement et oublie de même.

He learns easily and forgets the same.

Je lui pardonne facilement d'avoir voulu se faire auteur ; mais je ne saurais lui pardonner toutes les puérilités dont il a farci son livre.

I can easily pardon him for having attempted to turn author; but I cannot pardon him all the absurdities with which he has stuffed his book.

Je me plains à vous de vous-même.

I complain to you of yourself.

Si vous ne voulez pas être pour lui, au moins ne soyez pas contre.

If you will not be for him, at least do not be against him.

Quand sera-ce que vous viendrez nous voir ?

When will you come to see us?

5. Sur *soi*, *lui*, *soi-même*, et *lui-même*.

On soi, lui, soi-même, *and* lui-même.

Quand on a pour soi le témoignage de sa conscience, on est bien fort.

The approbation of our conscience imparts great courage.

L'estime de toute la terre ne sert de rien à un homme qui n'a pas le témoignage de sa conscience pour lui.

The good opinion of the whole world is of no use to a man who has not the approbation of his own conscience.

Un homme fait mille fautes, parce qu'il ne fait point de réflexions sur lui.-même.

A man commits a thousand faults, because he does not reflect on future consequences.

On fait mille fautes, quand on ne fait aucune réflexion sur soi.

We commit a thousand faults, when we neglect to reflect on ourselves.

Il aime mieux dire du mal de lui-même, que de n'en point parler.

He had rather speak ill of himself than not talk of himself at all.

L'égoïste aimera mieux dire du mal de soi-même, que de n'en point parler.

The selfish man prefers speaking ill of himself rather than not be the subject of his own conversation.

On a souvent besoin d'un plus petit que soi.

We frequently want the assistance of one who is below ourselves.

Un prince a souvent besoin de beaucoup de gens plus petits que lui.

A prince frequently needs the assistance of many persons inferior to himself.

C'est un bon moyen de s'élever soi-même, que d'exalter ses pareils ; et un homme adroit s'élève ainsi lui-même.

It is an excellent method of exalting ourselves to exalt our equals, and a man of address by this means exalts himself.

6. *Sur les Pronoms Relatifs.*	On the Relative Pronouns.
Il n'y a rien de si capable d'efféminer le courage, que l'oisiveté et les délices.	*Nothing is so calculated to enervate the mind as idleness and pleasure.*
Il faut empêcher que la division, qui est dans cette famille, n'éclate.	*The dissension in that family must be prevented from becoming public.*
Il y a bien des événements que l'on suppose se passer pendant les entr'actes.	*There are many events in a piece which are supposed to happen between the acts.*
Je le trouvai qui s'habillait.	*I found him dressing*
Qui le tirera de cet embarras, le tirera d'une grande misère.	*Whoever extricates him from this difficulty, will relieve him from much distress.*
Ceux-là sont véritablement heureux, qui croient l'être.	*Those are really happy, who think themselves so.*
Il n'y a que la vertu, qui puisse rendre un homme heureux en cette vie.	*Virtue alone can render a man happy in this life.*
Il n'y a règle si générale, qui n'ait son exception.	*There is no rule so general but it admits of exceptions.*
C'est un orateur qui se possède et qui ne se trouble jamais.	*He is an orator who is master of himself, and who is never embarrassed.*
Il n'y a pas dans le cœur humain de repli, que Dieu ne connaisse.	*There is no recess of the human heart but God perceives it.*
On n'a trouvé que quelques fragments du grand ouvrage qu'il avait promis.	*Only some fragments of the great work he had promised have been found.*
La faute, que vous avez faite, est plus importante que vous ne pensez.	*The error you have committed is of more consequence than you imagine.*
Les premières démarches qu'on fait dans le monde, ont beaucoup d'influence sur le reste de la vie.	*The first steps we take on entering the world have considerable influence on the rest of our lives.*
Cette farce est une des plus risibles qu'on ait encore vues.	*That farce is one of the most truly comic that ever was seen.*
Amassez-vous des trésors que les vers et la rouille ne puissent point gâter, et que les voleurs ne puissent point dérober.	*Lay up for yourselves treasures which neither moth no rust can corrupt, and which thieves cannot steal.*
L'incertitude, où nous sommes de ce qui doit arriver, fait que nous ne saurions prendre des mesures justes.	*Our uncertainty as to what shall happen makes us incapable of properly providing against it*

Je m'étonne qu'il ne voie pas le danger où il est.

I am astonished he does not see the danger he is in.

L'homme dont vous parlez n'est plus ici.

The man whom you are speaking of, is not here now.

Celui de qui je tiens cette nouvelle ne vous est pas connu.

The person from whom I received the intelligence is not known to you.

Celui à qui ce beau château appartient ne l'habite presque jamais.

The proprietor of that beautiful seat seldom resides there.

Ce sont des événements auxquels il faut bien se soumettre.

These are events to which we must submit.

C'est ce à quoi vous ne pensez guère.

It is what you seldom think of.

7. *Sur les Pronoms Démonstratifs.* — On the Demonstrative Pronouns.

Ne point reconnaître la divinité, c'est renoncer à toutes les lumières de la raison.

Not to acknowledge the divinity, is totally to renounce the light of reason.

Mentir, c'est mépriser Dieu et craindre les hommes.

To lie is to despise God and to fear man.

Il y a des épidémies morales, et ce sont les plus dangereuses.

There are moral contagious diseases, and they are the most dangerous.

Je crois que ce que vous dites, est bien éloigné de ce que vous pensez.

What you advance is, I think, widely different from your sentiments.

Les hommes n'aiment ordinairement que ceux qui les flattent.

Men in general love only those who flatter them.

Celui qui persuade à un autre de faire un crime n'est guère moins coupable que celui qui le commet.

He who persuades another to the commission of a crime, is hardly less guilty than he who commits it.

Penser ainsi, c'est s'aveugler soi-même.

To think in this manner is to be wilfully blind.

Ce qu'on rapporte de lui est inconcevable.

The reports concerning him are hardly conceivable.

Ce qui m'afflige, c'est de voir le triomphe du crime.

What distresses me is to see guilt triumphant.

Connaissez-vous la jeune Emilie? c'est une enfant dont tout le monde dit du bien.

Do you know little Emily? she is a child of whom every body speaks well.

Imitez en tout votre amie; elle est douce, appliquée, honnête et compatissante.

Imitate your friend in every thing; she is gentle, assiduous, polite and compassionate.

8. *Sur le Verbe* avoir *employé à l'Impersonnel*	On the Verb *Avoir, to have,* employed impersonally.
Remarque.—Quand le verbe *avoir* s'emploie à l'impersonnel, c'est dans le sens d'*être*, et alors il se joint toujours avec *y*.	*When the verb* avoir *is used impersonally it signifies* être, *to be, and in this sense it is always accompanied by the adverb* y.
Il y a un an que je ne vous ai vu.	*It is a twelvemonth since I saw you.*
Y a-t-il des nouvelles?	*Is there any news?*
Non, il n'y en a pas, du moins que je sache.	*No, there is none at least that I know.*
N'y a-t-il pas cinquante-quatre milles de Londres à Brighton?	*Is not it fifty-four miles from London to Brighton?*
Il y avait déjà beaucoup de monde lorsque j'arrivai.	*There were already a great many people when I arrived.*
Il n'y avait hier presque personne au Parc.	*There was hardly any body in the Park yesterday.*
Y a-t-il eu de grands débats?	*Were there violent debates?*
N'y avait-il pas beaucoup de curieux?	*Were there not many spectators?*
Je l'avais vu il y avait à peine vingt-quatre heures.	*I had seen him scarcely four-and-twenty hours before.*
Il n'y avait pas deux jours qu'il avait dîné chez moi.	*He had dined with me not two days before.*
Y avait-il si long-temps que vous ne l'aviez vu?	*Was it so long since you had seen him?*
Il y eut hier un bal chez M. un tel.	*There was yesterday a ball at Mr. A's.*
Il n'y eut pas hier de spectacle.	*There was no play yesterday.*
Y eut-il beaucoup de confusion et de désordre?	*Was there a great deal of confusion and disorder?*
N'y eut-il pas un beau feu d'artifice?	*Were there not beautiful fireworks?*
Il y a eu aujourd'hui une foule immense à la promenade.	*There was an immense crowd to-day in the public walks.*
Il n'y a pas eu de bal, comme on l'avait annoncé.	*There has not been any ball as had been mentioned.*
Est-il vrai qu'il y a eu un duel?	*Is it true that there has been a duel?*
N'y a-t-il pas eu dans sa conduite un peu trop d'emportement?	*Was there not rather too much hastiness in his behaviour?*
Quand *il y eut eu* une explication, les esprits se calmèrent.	*After there had been an explanation, tranquillity was restored.*
N'y avait-il pas *eu* un plus grand nombre de spectateurs?	*Was not there a greater number of spectators?*

Il y aura demain un simulacre e combat naval.	*To-morrow there will be a moc sea-fight.*
Il n'y en aura aucun de vous.	*There will be none of you.*
Y aura-t-il une bonne récolte cette année ?	*Will not there be a good harvest this year ?*
N'y aura-t-il pas quelqu'un de votre famille ?	*Will not there be some of your family ?*
A coup sûr *il y aura eu* bien du désordre ?	*There must certainly have been much disorder.*
Sur cent personnes, il n'y en aura pas eu dix de satisfaites.	*Out of a hundred persons there will not have been ten satisfied.*
Y aura-t-il eu un bon soupé ?	*Will there have been a good supper ?*
N'y aura-t-il pas eu de mécontents ?	*Will there not have been some dissatisfied people ?*
Il y aurait de la malhonnêteté dans ce procédé.	*Such a step would have been uncivil.*
Il n'y aurait pas grand mal à cela.	*There would be no great harm in that.*
Y aurait-il quelqu'un assez hardi pour l'attaquer ?	*Would there be any one bold enough to attack him ?*
N'y aurait-il pas quelqu'un assez charitable pour l'avertir de ce qu'on dit de lui ?	*Would there be nobody kind enough to acquaint him with what is said of him ?*
Il y aurait eu de l'imprudence à cela.	*There would have been some imprudence in that.*
Il n'y aurait pas eu tant de mésintelligence, si l'on m'en avait cru.	*There would not have been so great a misunderstanding had I been believed.*
Il n'y aurait pas eu dix personnes.	*There would not have been ten persons.*
Y aurait-il eu de l'inconvénient.	*Would there have been any inconvenience ?*
N'y aurait-il pas eu de jaloux pour le traverser dans ses projets ?	*Would there not have been some envious persons to thwart him in his designs ?*
Je ne crois pas qu'*il y ait* un spectacle plus magnifique.	*I do not think there can be a more superb spectacle.*
Je désirerais qu'*il y eût* moins de fausseté dans le commerce de la vie.	*I wish there was less duplicity in the concerns of life.*
Je n'ai pas oui-dire qu'*il y ait eu* hier des nouvelles du continent.	*I have not heard that there was any news from the continent yesterday.*
Auriez-vous cru qu'*il y eût eu* tant de personnes compromises dans cette affaire ?	*Could you have thought so many persons would have been exposed in that affair ?*

9. *Phrases Diverses.*	Promiscuous Phrases.
Sa vie, ses actions, ses paroles, son air même et sa démarche, tout prêche, tout édifie en lui.	*His life, his actions, his very look and deportment, every thing in him instructs and edifies.*
On craignait qu'il n'arrivât quelque désordre dans l'assemblée, mais toutes choses s'y passèrent fort doucement.	*It was apprehended some disorder would take place in the assembly, but every thing went off very quietly.*
La vigne et le lierre s'entortillent autour des ormes.	*The vine and the ivy twist round the elms.*
On ne disconvient point qu'il ne soit brave, mais il est un peu trop fanfaron.	*They do not deny that he is brave, but he boasts rather too much.*
Le cadet est riche, mais l'aîné l'est encore davantage.	*The youngest is rich, but the eldest is still more so.*
Le ciel est couvert de nuages, et l'orage est prêt à fondre.	*The sky is covered with clouds, and the storm is preparing to burst.*
Après qu'il eut franchi les Alpes avec ses troupes, il entra en Italie.	*After having crossed the Alps with his troops, he entered Italy.*
La frugalité rend les corps plus sains et plus robustes.	*Temperance imparts an increase of health and strength to the body.*
Ce discours est peut-être un des plus beaux morceaux d'éloquence, qu'il y ait jamais eus.	*This speech is perhaps one of the finest pieces of eloquence that were ever delivered.*
C'est un homme qui aime la liberté; il ne se gêne pour qui que ce soit.	*He is a man fond of liberty, he will be constrained by nobody.*
Il est plus haut que moi de deux doigts.	*He is taller than I by two inches.*
Irez-vous vous exposer à la barbarie et à l'inhospitalité de ces peuples?	*Will you go and expose yourself to the barbarity and inhospitality of those nations?*
A la longue, les erreurs disparaissent, et la vérité surnage.	*In time, errors vanish and truth survives.*
Si vous le prenez avec moi sur ce ton de fierté, je serai aussi fier que vous.	*If you treat me with that haughtiness, I can be as haughty as you.*
C'est un homme rigide, qui ne pardonne rien, ni aux autres ni à lui-même.	*He is a stern man, who pardons nothing either in himself or others.*
Les uns montent, les autres descendent, ainsi va la roue de la fortune.	*Some rise, others descend; thus goes the wheel of fortune.*

Je ne vois rien de solide dans tout ce que vous me proposez.

I see nothing certain in all thy propose to me.

L'art n'a jamais rien produit de plus beau.

It is one of the finest productions of art.

Lequel est-ce des deux qui a tort?

Which of the two is in the wrong?

On aime quelquefois la trahison, mais on hait toujours les traitres.

We sometimes like treason, but we always hate the traitor.

10. *Continuation.* — Continuation.

L'éléphant se sert de sa trompe pour prendre et pour enlever tout ce qu'il veut.

The elephant makes use of his trunk to take and lift anything he pleases.

Plus j'examine cette personne, plus je crois l'avoir vue quelque part.

The more I look at that person, the more I think I have seen him somewhere.

La nuit vint, de façon que je fus contraint de me retirer.

Night came on, so that I was obliged to retire.

Il faut vivre de façon qu'on ne fasse tort à personne.

We must live in such a manner as to injure nobody.

Elle sut qu'on attaquait son mari; elle courut aussitôt tout éperdue pour le secourir.

She knew her husband was attacked, and in a state of distraction, ran to his assistance.

Je trouvai ses parents tout éplorés.

I found his relations all in tears.

Cet arbre pousse ses branches toutes droites.

The branches of that tree grow quite straight.

J'en ai encore la mémoire toute fraîche.

It is still quite fresh on my memory.

Il a voulu faire voir par cet essai qu'il pouvait réussir en quelque chose de plus grand.

He wished to show by that attempt that he could succeed in an enterprise of more consequence.

Il fut blessé au front et mourut de cette blessure.

He was wounded in the forehead, and died of his wound.

Ces chevaux prirent le mors aux dents et entraînèrent le carrosse.

Those horses ran away with the carriage.

C'est un homme qui compose sans chaleur, ni imagination: tout ce qu'il écrit est froid et plat.

He is a man that writes without the least warmth or animation: all his productions are cold and insipid.

Ce bâtiment a plus de profondeur que de largeur.

That building has more depth than it has breadth.

Cet homme est un prodige de savoir, de science, de valeur, d'esprit et de mémoire.

That man is a prodigy of knowledge, judgment, courage, sense, and memory.

Il est attaché à l'un et à l'autre, mais plus à l'un qu'à l'autre.

He is attached to both, but to one more than the other.

Ils ont bien l'air l'un de l'autre.

They very much look like one another.

Si l'on ruine cet homme-là, le contre-coup retombera sur vous.

If that man is ruined, his misfortune will recoil upon you.

Il serait mort, si on ne l'eût assisté avec soin.

He would have died if he had not been kindly assisted.

Ce poème serait parfait, si les incidents, qui le font languir, n'interrompaient la continuité de l'action.

That would be a perfect poem, if the incidents which give a heaviness to it, did not break the connexion of the subject.

11. *Continuation.*

Continuation.

Quand je le voudrais, je ne le pourrais pas.

If I were disposed, I could not do it.

Je serai toujours votre ami, quand même vous ne le voudriez pas.

I shall ever be your friend, even though you should not wish it.

Quand vous auriez réussi, que vous en serait-il revenu ?

Though you had succeeded, what were you to have derived from it?

Quand on découvrirait votre démarche, on ne pourrait la blâmer.

Should the steps you have taken be discovered they could not be blamed.

Quand vous auriez consulté quelqu'un sur votre mariage, vous n'auriez pas mieux réussi.

Had you consulted somebody about your marriage, you could not have succeeded better.

Le tonnerre et l'éclair ne sont sensibles que par la propagation du bruit et de la lumière jusqu'à l'œil et à l'oreille.

Thunder and lightning are only perceptible by the transmission of sound and light to the ear and eye.

Le langage de la prose est plus simple et moins figuré que celui des vers.

Prose language is much more simple and less figurative than poetry.

Le commencement de son discours est toujours assez sage ; mais, dans la suite, à force de vouloir s'élever, il se perd dans les nues : on ne sait plus ni ce qu'on voit, ni ce qu'on entend.

The beginning of his speech is always tolerably sensible : but afterwards, by affecting the sublime, he loses himself, and we no longer understand either what we see or hear.

C'est une faute excusable dans un autre homme, mais à un homme aussi sage que lui, elle ne se peut pardonner.

This fault would be excusable in another man, but in a man of his sense it is unpardonable.

Il ne suffit pas de paraître honnête homme, il faut l'être.

It is not enough to appear to be an honest man, we must be so.

Il nous a reçus avec bonté, et nous a écoutes avec patience. — *He received us with kindness and heard us patiently.*

Tout y est si bien peint qu'on croit voir ce qu'il décrit. — *Every thing in it is so well delineated you think you see what he describes.*

On ne pense rien de vous, qui ne vous soit glorieux. — *They think nothing of you but what is to your honour.*

Les eaux de citernes ne sont que des eaux de pluie ramassées. — *Cistern water is generally only rain water collected*

S'il n'est pas fort riche, du moins a-t-il de quoi vivre honnêtement. — *If he is not rich at least he has enough to live upon respectably.*

Quel quantième du mois avons-nous? — *What day of the month is it?*

Il lui tarde qu'il ne soit majeur; il compte les jours et les mois. — *He longs to be of age and counts the days and months.*

Des qualités excellentes, jointes à de rares talents, font le parfait mérite. — *Excellent qualities joined to distinguished talents constitute perfect merit.*

Il a une mauvaise qualité, c'est qu'il ne saurait garder un secret. — *He has one bad quality, he cannot keep a secret.*

12. *Modèles de Phrases dans lesquelles, on doit faire usage de l'Article.* — Examples of Phrases in which the Article is used.

L'homme est sujet à bien des vicissitudes. — *Man is liable to a variety of changes.*

Les hommes d'un vrai génie sont rares. — *Men of real genius are scarce*

Les hommes à imagination sont rarement heureux. — *Men of a visionary character are seldom happy.*

L'homme, dont vous parlez, est un de mes amis. — *The man you speak of is a friend of mine.*

La vie est un mélange de biens et de maux. — *Life is a compound of good and evil.*

La perfection en tout genre est le but auquel on doit tendre. — *Perfection in every thing ought to be our object.*

La beauté, les grâces et *l'esprit* sont des avantages bien précieux quand ils sont relevés par la modestie. — *Beauty, gracefulness, and wit, are valuable endowments when heightened by modesty.*

Voilà *des tableaux* d'une grande beauté. — *These are very beautiful pictures.*

Faites-vous *des principes*, dont vous ne vous écartiez jamais. — *Establish rules for yourself, and never deviate from them.*

Cet arbre porte *des fruits* excellents.	*This tree bears very excellent fruit.*
Ces raisons sont *des conjectures* bien faibles.	*These reasons are very idle conjectures.*
Servez-vous *des termes* établis par l'usage.	*Use the expressions established by custom.*
On doit éviter l'air *de l'affectation.*	*We ought to avoid the appearance of affectation.*
Le Jupiter de Phidias était d'une grande beauté.	*The Jupiter of Phidias was extremely beautiful.*
Continuation des même Phrases.	The same Phrases continued.
La mémoire est le trésor *de l'esprit*, le fruit *de l'attention* et *de la réflexion.*	*Memory is the treasure of the mind, the result of attention and reflection.*
J'achetai hier *des gravures* précieuses et rares.	*I yesterday bought some valuable and scarce engravings*
La France est le plus beau pays de l'Europe.	*France is the finest country in Europe.*
L'intérêt de l'Allemagne était opposé à celui *de la Russie.*	*The German interest was contrary to the Russian.*
La longueur *de l'Angleterre* du nord au sud est de 360 milles, et sa largeur de l'est à l'ouest est de 300.	*The length of England from north to south is 360 miles, and its breadth from east to west is* 300.
Il arrive *de la Chine, du Japon,* et *des Indes Orientales*, etc.	*He comes from China, Japan, and the East Indies.*
Il arrive *de l'Amérique, de la Barbade, de la Jamaïque*, etc.	*He comes from America, Barbadoes, Jamaica, etc.*
Il vient *de la Flandre* Française.	*He comes from French Flanders.*
Il s'est établi dans *la province* de Middlesex.	*He has settled in the county of Middlesex.*
Des petits-maîtres sont des êtres insupportables dans la société.	*Coxcombs are insufferable beings in society.*
C'est l'opinion *des nouveaux* philosophes.	*It is the opinion of the new philosophers.*
Elle a *bien de la grâce* dans tout ce qu'elle fait.	*She does every thing most gracefully.*
Cette étoffe se vend une guinée l'aune.	*This stuff sells at a guinea the ell.*
Ce vin coûte 70 livres sterlings *la pièce.*	*This wine costs seventy pounds the hogshead.*

13. *Modèles de Phrases dans lesquelles on ne doit pas faire usage de l'Article.*	Examples of phrases in which the Article is omitted.
Nos connaissances doivent être tirés *de principes* évidents.	*Our knowledge ought to be derived from evident principles.*
Cet arbre porte *d'excellents fruits.*	*This tree produces excellent fruit.*
Ces raisons sont *de faibles conjectures.*	*These reasons are idle conjectures.*
Evitez tout ce qui a un air *d'affectation.*	*Avoid whatever bears the appearance of affectation.*
Ces exemples peuvent servir *de modèles.*	*These examples may serve as models.*
Il a une grande présence *d'esprit.*	*He has great presence of mind.*
La mémoire *de raison* et *d'esprit* est plus utile que les autres sortes *de mémoire.*	*The memory of reason and sense is more useful than any other kind of memory.*
Peu *de personnes* réfléchissent sur la rapidité de la vie.	*Few people reflect on the rapidity of life.*
Que *d'événements* inconcevables se sont succédés les uns aux autres !	*How many inconceivable events have followed in succession !*
Il y a plus *d'esprit*, mais moins *de connaissance*, dans ce siècle que dans le siècle dernier.	*There's more wit but less knowledge in this age than in the last.*
On ne vit jamais autant *d'effronterie.*	*So much assurance never was met with.*
Je pris hier beaucoup *de peine* pour rien.	*I took a great deal of trouble yesterday about nothing.*
Candie est une des îles les plus agréables de la Méditerranée.	*Candia is one of the most agreeable islands in the Mediterranean.*
Il arrive *de Perse, d'Italie, d'Espagne, etc.*	*He comes from Persia, Italy, Spain, etc.*
Il est revenu *de Suisse, d'Allemagne, etc.*	*He is returned from Switzerland, Germany, etc.*
Les vins *de France* seront chers cette année ; les vignes ont coulé.	*French wines will be dear this year ; the vines have ran.*
L'empire *d'Allemagne* est composé de grands et de petits états.	*The German empire is composed of great and small states.*
Les chevaux *d'Angleterre* sont excellents.	*The English horses are excellent.*
Après mon départ *de Suisse* je me retirai à Rome	*On my leaving Switzerland, I retired to Rome.*

14. *Continuation des mêmes Phrases.*	Continuation of the same Phrases.
Vous trouverez ce passage *page* 120, *livre* premier, *chapitre* dix.	*You will find this passage in page* 120, *book the first, chapter the tenth.*
Il s'est retiré en *Angleterre.*	*He has retired to England.*
Il vit dans sa retraite *en vrai philosophe.*	*He lives in his retreat, like a real philosopher.*
Quand il réfléchit sur sa conduite, il en eut *honte.*	*When he reflected on his conduct, he was ashamed of it.*
C'est un homme qui cherche *fortune.*	*He is a man that seeks fortune, he is a fortune hunter.*
Il entend *malice* à tout.	*He puts a malicious construction on every thing.*
Ne portez *envie* à personne	*Envy nobody.*
Si vous promettez, tenez *parole.*	*If you promise, keep your word.*
Dans les affaires importantes ne vous décidez jamais sans prendre *conseil.*	*In matters of consequence never decide without advice.*
Courage, *soldats,* tenons fermes; la victoire est à nous.	*Cheer up, soldiers, let us continue firm, the day is our own.*
Cette femme n'a ni *grâce* ni beauté.	*This woman is destitute both of grace and beauty.*
Monseigneur le duc, etc. prince du sang, alla hier à la campagne.	*The duke of, etc. a prince of the blood, went yesterday into the country.*
Montrer tant de faiblesse, c'est n'être pas *homme.*	*To shew so much weakness is not acting like a man.*
Cet homme est une espèce *de misanthrope,* dont les brusqueries sont quelquefois très-plaisantes.	*This man is a kind of misanthropist, whose oddities are sometimes comical.*
L'ananas est une sorte de *fruit* très-commun aux Antilles.	*The pine-apple is a kind of fruit very common in the Antilles,*
C'est un genre de *vie* qui ne me plaît point.	*It is a kind of life that is no agreeable to me.*

15. *Continuation des mêmes Phrases.*	The same sentences continued.
Cette dame plaît à tout le monde par son honnêteté et sa douceur.	*This lady pleases every one for her good breeding and mildness.*
Tout homme a des défauts plus ou moins sensibles.	*Every man has defects more or less obvious.*
Cette conduite augmentait *chaque jour* le nombre de ses amis.	*This beahviour daily increased the number of his friends*

Tous les biens nous viennent *de Dieu.*

Every blessing comes from God.

Vénus était la déesse de la beauté, et la mère de l'amour et des grâces.

Venus was the goddess of beauty and the mother of love and the graces.

Selon les païens, *Jupiter* était le premier des dieux.

According to the Heathens, Jupiter was the first of the gods.

Apollon était frère jumeau de Diane.

Apollo was twin brother to Diana.

Rubens a été un grand peintre.

Rubens was a great painter.

Homère et *Virgile* sont les deux plus grands poètes épiques.

Homer and Virgil are the two greatest epic poets.

Londres est la plus belle ville que je connaisse.

London is the finest city that I know.

L'eau *de rivière* est douce, et l'eau *de mer* est salée.

River water is sweet, and sea water is salt.

C'est un excellent poisson *de mer.*

It is an excellent sea fish.

Voilà une superbe table *de marbre.*

There is a superb marble table.

L'eau *de Seine* est celle qu'on préfère à Paris.

The water of the Seine is preferred at Paris.

Pauvreté n'est pas *vice.*

Poverty is not a vice.

Citoyens, étrangers, grands, peuples, se sont montrés sensibles à cette perte.

Citizens, strangers, grandees, people, have shewn themselves sensible of this loss.

16. *Modèles de Phrases sur le pronom* Le.

Forms of Phrases upon the pronoun *Le.*

Est-ce-là votre *opinion?*—ne doutez point que ce ne *la* soit.

Is that your opinion?—do not question it.

Sont-ce là vos *domestiques?*—oui, ce *les* sont.

Are those your servants?—yes they are.

Mesdames, êtes-vous les *étrangères* qu'on m'a annoncées?—*oui,* nous les sommes.

Ladies, are you the strangers that have been announced to me? yes, we are.

Madame, êtes-vous *la malade* pour laquelle on m'a appelé?—oui, je *la* suis.

Madam, are you the sick person, for whom I have been called? yes, I am.

Madames, êtes-vous *la mère* de cet enfant?—ou, je *la* suis.

Madam, are you the mother of this child?—yes, I am.

Mesdame, êtes-vous *contentes* de cette musique?—oui, nous *le* sommes.

Ladies, are you pleased with this music?—yes, we are.

Elle est *malheureuse,* et je crains bien, qu'elle ne *le* soit toute sa vie.

She is unhappy, and I much fear she will continue so for life.

Madame, êtes-vous *mère ?*—oui, je *le* suis.

Madam, are you a mother?—yes, I am.

Madame, depuis quel temps êtes-vous *mariée ?*—je *le* suis depuis un an.

Madam, how long have you been married? I have been married a year.

Y a-t-il long-temps que vous êtes *arrivée ?*—je *le* suis depuis quinze jours.

Have you long been arrived?—a fortnight.

Aristote croyait que le monde était de tout éternité; mais Platon ne *le* croyait pas.

Aristotle believed the world to have been from all eternity, but Plato did not.

Quoique cette femme montre plus de fermeté que les autres, elle n'est pas pour cela *la* moins affligée.

Although this woman shows more resolution than the others, she is nevertheless not the least distressed.

Cette femme a l'art de répandre des larmes daus le temps même qu'elle est *le* moins affligée.

This woman had the art of shedding tears, ever when she is least distressed.

17. *Modèles de Phrases sur les différentes règles du participe passé.*

Forms of Phrases upon the different rules of the participle past.

La nouvelle *pièce* a-t-elle été *applaudie ?*

Did the new piece meet with applause?

Vos *parents* y seront-ils *arrivés* à temps?

Will your relations arrive there in time?

Elle s'est *donné* de belles robes.

She has given herself fine gowns.

Elles nous ont *apporté* de superbes œillets.

They have brought us beautiful pinks.

Cette ruse ne lui a pas *réussi.*

He has not succeeded in this stratagem.

La *vie* tranquille que j'ai *menée* depuis dix ans, a beaucoup contribué à me faire oublier mes malheurs.

The quiet life I have led these ten years, has greatly contributed to make me forget my misfortunes.

Les *lettres* que j'ai *reçues*, m'ont beaucoup affligée.

The letters I have received have greatly distressed me.

Que de *peines* vous vous êtes *données !*

What a deal of trouble you have given yourself!

Quelle tâche vous vous êtes *imposée !*

What a task you have imposed on yourself!

C'est une *satire* que j'ai *retrouvée* dans mes papiers.

It is a satire that I have again found within my papers.

Les *lettres* qu'a *écrites* Pline le ieune, quelque agréables qu'elles soient, se ressentent néanmoins

The letters which the younger Pliny has written, however agreeable they may be, savour never-

un peu de la décadence du goût parmi les Romains. — *theless a little of the decline of taste among the Romans.*

Je ne serais pas entré avec vous dans tous ces détails de grammaire, si je ne *les* avais *crus* nécessaires. — *I would not have entered into these grammatical details with you, had I not thought them necessary.*

*L'Egypte s'*était *rendue célèbre* par la sagesse de ses lois, long-temps avant que la Grèce sortît de la barbarie. — *Egypt had become celebrated for the wisdom of its laws, long before Greece had emerged from barbarism.*

C'est une des plus grandes *merveilles* qu'on ait *vues*. — *It is one of the greatest wonders that has ever been seen.*

L'homme de lettres, dont vous m'avez *parlé*, a un goût exquis. — *The man of letters you spoke to me of has an excellent taste.*

Vous avez très-bien *instruit* vos élèves. — *You have taught your pupils extremely well.*

Lucrèce s'est *donné* la mort. — *Lucretia killed herself.*

La sécheresse qu'il y a *eu* au printemps a fait périr tous les fruits. — *The dry weather we had in the spring has destroyed all the fruit*

Je n'ai point réussi, malgré les mesures que vous m'avez *conseillé* de prendre. — *I have not succeeded, notwithstanding the steps you advised me to take.*

Quelle aventure vous est-il *arrivé?* — *What adventures have you met with?*

Cette femme s'est *proposée* pour modèle à ses enfants. — *This woman proposed herself as a model for her children.*

Cette femme s'est *proposé* d'enseigner la géographie et l'histoire à ses enfants. — *This woman proposed to teach geography and history to her children.*

18. *Modèles de Phrases sur les principaux rapports des modes et des temps.* — Forms of Phrases upon the principal relations of moods and tenses.

Je l'attendais depuis long-temps quand il vint me joindre. — *I had waited a long time for him, when he came to me.*

Il sortit au moment même que j'entrais. — *He was going out at the time I was entering.*

Je commençais à avoir des craintes sur la réussite de votre affaire, lorsque j'ai reçu votre lettre. — *I was beginning to be apprehensive of the success of your business when I received your letter.*

Dès que j'eus fait quelques visites indispensables, je rentrai chez moi, et je ne sortis plus. — *As soon as I had paid some indispensable visits, I went home and did not go out afterwards.*

J'avais déjà tout préparé pour mon départ, lorsque des affaires — *I had already made every preparation for my departure, when* imprévues m'ont forcé à le différer de quelques jours. — *some unexpected business occurred, that obliged me to defer it for some days.*

Vous étiez déjà sorti, quand je me présentai chez vous. — *You were already gone out when I called upon you.*

J'avais déjà livré à l'impression mon ouvrage, lorsque vous me demandiez, si je le donnerais bientôt au public. — *My work had been sent to be printed, when you asked me if I should soon bring it out.*

Lorsque j'ai eu terminé mon affaire, vous avez commencé la vôtre. — *When I had terminated my business, you began yours.*

Lorsque j'eus déjeûné, je montai à cheval, et je fus à Londres. — *When I had done breakfast, I got on horseback, and went to London.*

Lorsque j'aurai lu la nouvelle pièce, je vous dirai avec franchise ce que j'en pense. — *When I have read the new play, I will candidly give you my opinion of it.*

19. *Modèles de Phrases sur l'emploi des Auxiliaires* aller, venir de, devoir, pouvoir. — Examples on the use of the Auxiliaries *aller, venir de, devoir, pouvoir.*

Je vais partir à l'instant même. — *I am off this very instant.*

Nous allons vous expliquer cela en deux mots. — *We will explain it to you in two words.*

Nous allions nous mettre à table lorsqu'il est entré. — *We were going to sit down to table when he entered.*

J'allais lui offrir mon bras, lorsque je m'aperçus de ma méprise. — *I was on the point of offering my arm to her, when I saw my mistake.*

On allait en venir aux mains, mais la nuit venant à tomber, on remit l'attaque au lendemain. — *They were on the moment of engaging, but night falling, they put off the attack until the next day.*

Je viens de les voir ensemble. — *I have this moment seen them together.*

Elle vient de se marier avec un homme fort riche. — *She has just married a very rich man.*

Leur père vient de mourir, ainsi il n'est pas probable qu'elles aillent en société. — *Their father has recently died it is not likely therefore they should go into company.*

Mon frère venait de sortir. — *My brother had just gone out.*

Nous venions de dîner. — *We had not long dined.*

Si vous avez quelque chose à leur dire, je m'en chargerai; je dois les voir aujourd'hui. — *If you have any message to send to them, I will take it, for I am to see them to-day.*

Vous ne devez pas lui répondre ainsi. — *You are not to answer him in this manner.*

Dois-je attendre? — *Am I to wait, or must I wait?*

Elle doit avoir quinze ans au moins. — *She must be fifteen at least.*

Il doit être à la maison car je ne l'ai pas vu sortir. — *He must be at home, for I did not see him go out.*

Je devais sortir, mais le mauvais temps m'en a empêché. — *I intended to go out, I was to have gone out, but the bad weather prevented me.*

Ne deviez-vous pas vous mettre en route lundi dernier. — *Were you not to have set off on Monday last.*

Ils devaient m'en prévenir. — *They ought to have told me of it.*

Cela devait être le meilleur parti. — *That must have been the best determination.*

Vous devriez lui dire la vérité. — *You should speak the truth to him.*

Devrais-je obéir à des ordres si injustes. — *Ought I to obey such unjust orders?*

Il aurait dû revenir de suite. — *He ought to have returned directly.*

Nous n'aurions pas dû dépenser follement. — *We ought not to have spent extravagantly.*

Mon frère pourrait vous reconduire. — *My brother must see you home.*

Nous pourrions lui en parler, lorsqu'il sera moins occupé. — *We might mention it to him when he is less engaged.*

Ne pourrions-nous pas passer par Bath? — *Might we not return through Bath?*

Il me semble qu'elle aurait pu mieux faire. — *It appears to me that she might have done better.*

Les troupes auraient pu débarquer sur nos côtes. — *The troops might have landed on our coasts.*

20. *Models to show how to render* will, shall, would, should, *elliptically used.*

Iriez-vous à Rome, si vous le pouviez?—oui, j'irais. — *Would you go to Rome if it were in your power? yes, I would.*

Auriez-vous consenti à ces conditions, si on vous les avait proposées? oui, sans doute. — *Would you have agreed to these terms, had they been proposed to you? yes, I would.*

Irez-vous demain à Londres, si vous le pouvez?—oui, j'irai. — *Shall you go to London tomorrow, if you can? yes, I shall.*

Il sera sûrement parti, si vous l'avez voulu. — *He will certainly have set out, if you have wished it.*

J'ai bien dormi, *mais non pas lui.*	*I have slept well,* but he has not.
N'a-t-il pas une jolie terre en Normandie? *oui, Monsieur.*	*Has he not a pretty estate in Normandy?* yes, he has.
Nous avons été au spectacle hier au soir. *Vraiment!* or *ha!*	*We went to the play last night* Did you?
Elle n'a pas de fortune. *Vraiment!*	*She has no fortune of her own* Has she not?
Mes compliments chez vous. *Je n'y manquerai pas.*	*My compliments at home.* I will.
Je dis qu'il y était; mais ma sœur dit que non.	*I say he was there, but my sister says he was not.*
Je vous dis que oui, et moi, je vous dis que non.	*I tell you it is, and I tell you it is not.*
Vous eussiez laissé échapper une occasion si favorable, si l'on ne vous eût averti à temps.	*You would have let so favourable an opportunity slip, had you not been warned in time.*

21. *Continuation des mêmes Phrases.*	The same Phrases continued.
On dit que vous partez aujourd'hui pour Paris.	*It is said that you set off to-day for Paris.*
Tout le monde soutient que vous accepterez la place qu'on vous offre.	*Every one maintains that you will accept the place that is offered to you.*
On soupçonne que vous aviez hier reçu cette agréable nouvelle quand on vous rencontra.	*It is suspected that you had received this agreeable intelligence when you were met yesterday.*
Beaucoup de vos amis croient que vous partîtes hier pour la campagne.	*Many of your friends believe that you set out yesterday for the country.*
Le bruit se répand que vous avez fait une grosse perte.	*There is a report that you have met with a considerable loss.*
J'apprends dans l'instant que vous fussiez parti il y a trois jours, si des engagements, que vous aviez contractés depuis long-temps, ne vous avaient retenu.	*I have this moment learnt that you would have set out three days since, had not engagements which you had formed long ago, detained you.*
N'est-il pas vrai que vous partiriez aujourd'hui, si vous le pouviez?	*Is it not true that you would set out to-day, if you could?*
Est-il vrai que vous seriez parti depuis long-temps pour la campagne, si votre amour pour les arts ne vous avait retenu à la	*Is it true that you would have set out for the country long since, had not your love for the arts detained you in town?*

Je ne crois pas que vous partiez, quoique tout le monde l'assure.

I do not imagine that you will set out, although every body asserts it.

Je ne croyais pas qu'il fût sitôt de retour.

I did not believe he had gone back so soon.

Il a fallu qu'il ait eu affaire à bien des personnes.

He must have had business with a great many people.

Je doute que votre ami fût venu à bout de ses projets, s'il n'avait pas été fortement protégé.

I doubt that your friend would have succeeded in his plans, had he not been strongly patronised.

Il n'est point d'homme, quelque mérite qu'il ait, qui ne fût très-mortifié, s'il savait tout ce qu'on pense de lui.

There is not a man, whatever merit he may possess, that would not be very much mortified, were he to know every thing that is thought of him.

Vous ne vous persuadiez pas que les affaires pussent si mal tourner.

You never persuaded yourself that matters could have taken so unfortunate a turn.

22. *Modèles de Phrases sur la Négative* Ne.

Forms of Phrases upon the Negative *Ne*.

Il *n*'y a *pas* beaucoup d'argent chez les gens de lettres.

There is not much money to be found among men of letters.

Il *n*'y a *point* de ressource dans une personne qui *n*'a *point* d'esprit.

There are no resources in a person deprived of sense.

C'est à tort que vous l'accusez de jouer; je vous assure qu'il *ne* joue *point*.

You accuse him wrongfully of gaming; I assure you he never does.

Entrez dans le salon; vous pourrez lui parler; il *ne* joue *pas*.

Go into the room, you may speak to him; he is not playing.

Si pour avoir du bien, il en coûte à la probité, je *n*'en veux *point*.

I do not wish to make a fortune, if it can only be done at the expense of honesty.

Rien n'est sûr avec les capricieux: vous croyez être bien en faveur, *point* du tout: l'instant de la plus belle humeur est suivi de la plus fâcheuse.

Nothing is certain with capricious people: you think yourself in favour, by no means: the moment of the best humour is followed by that of the worst.

Vous *ne cessez* de nous répéter les mêmes choses.

You are constantly repeating the same thing to us.

Je *n*'aurais *osé* vous en parler le premier.

I should not have dared to be the first to speak to you of it.

Malgré ses protections, il *n*'a pu réussir dans ses projets.

With all his interest he has not been able to succeed in his plans.

Cet ouvrage serait fort bon, *n*'était la négligence du style. — *This work would be very good, were it not for the negligence of the style.*

Y a-t-il quelqu'un dont elle *ne* médise ? — *Is there any one she does not slander?*

J'ai pris tant de goût pour une vie retirée, que je *ne* sors presque *jamais.* — *I have acquired so great a taste for retirement, that I seldom go out.*

Voilà ce qui s'est passé ; *n*'en parlez à *personne.* — *This is what has passed; do not mention it to any one.*

Mon parti est pris ; *ne* m'en parlez *plus.* — *My resolution is fixed; talk to me no more of it.*

N'employez *aucun* de ces moyens : ils sont indignes de vous. — *Do not employ any one of these measures, they are unworthy of you.*

Rien n'est plus joli. — *Nothing is more beautiful.*

Je *ne* dis *rien* que je ne pense. — *I never speak but what I think*

Je *ne* fais *jamais* d'excès que je n'en sois incommodé. — *I never commit any excess without suffering by it.*

23. *Continuation des mêmes Phrases.* — Continuation of the same Phrases.

C'est un homme pour qui je *n*'ai *ni* amour, *ni* estime. — *He is a man for whom I have neither love nor esteem.*

Il *n*'est *ni* assez prudent *ni* assez éclairé. — *He is neither sufficiently prudent nor enlightened.*

Je vous assure que je *ne* le fréquente *ni ne* le vois. — *I assure you I neither associate with him nor see him.*

Ne faire *que* parcourir les différentes branches des connaissances humaines sans s'arrêter à aucune, c'est moins chercher à s'instruire, qu'à tuer le temps. — *To go through the different branches of human knowledge only, without fixing upon any one of them, is not to seek for instruction, but to kill time.*

Que n'êtes-vous toujours aussi complaisant? — *Why are you not at all times equally obliging?*

Il ne le fera pas, *à moins que* vous *ne* l'y engagiez. — *He will not do it, unless you persuade him to it.*

Il n'ira pas, *si* vous *ne* l'en priez. — *He will not go, if you do not request it of him.*

Il nous a menacés de se venger ; nous *n*'avons fait *qu*'en rire. — *He has threatened us with vengeance; we only laughed at him.*

Trop d'insouciance *ne* peut *que* nuire. — *Too great supineness cannot but be hurtful.*

Que devenez-vous ? *il y a* trois mois *que* nous *ne* vous avons vu? — *What has become you? we have not seen you these three months.*

Comment vous êtes-vous porté *depuis que* nous *ne* vous avons vu? — *How have you been since we saw you?*

C'est bien *pire* qu'on *ne* le disait. — *It is much worse than was said.*

Peu s'en faut que je *n'* aie donné tête baissée dans le piége. — *I was near running headlong into the snare.*

Dites la vérité en toute occasion; on méprise toujours ceux qui parlent *autrement* qu'ils *ne* pensent. — *Tell the truth on all occasions: those who speak what they do not think are always despised.*

Ne désespérez pas que la vérité *ne* se fasse jour à la longue. — *Do not despair that truth will appear in time.*

Je *ne disconviens* pas que la chose *ne* soit ainsi. — *I do not deny but the thing may have been so.*

Prenez garde qu'on *ne* vous entraîne dans quelque fausse démarche. — *Take care that you are not led into some false step.*

J'*empêcherai* bien qu'on *ne* vous nuise dans cette affaire. — *I shall prevent them from doing you any harm in this business.*

Il *craint* qu'on *ne* le soupçonne d'avoir trempé dans ce complot. — *He is apprehensive that he is suspected of being concerned in this plot.*

On lui a donné d'excellents conseils, *de crainte* qu'il *ne* manquât l'occasion de faire connaître ce qu'il est en état de faire. — *They have given him excellent advice, lest he should lose the opportunity of showing what he was capable of doing.*

J'y ai long-temps travaillé; je *ne saurais* en venir à bout. — *I have been long employed about it; I cannot accomplish it.*

Vous feriez mieux de vous taire; vous *ne* savez ce que vous dites. — *You had better be silent, you do not know what you are saying.*

Vous *ne* sauriez me faire un plus grand plaisir. — *You cannot do me a greater favour.*

24. *Phrases sur quelques Délicatesses de la Langue Française.* — Phrases on some Niceties of the French Language.

Irez-vous ce soir à l'opéra?—oui, j'irai. — *Shall you go to the opera this evening?—yes, I shall.*

Iriez-vous avec plaisir à Rome? oui, j'irais. — *Would you cheerfully go to Rome?—yes, I would.*

La justice qui nous est quelquefois refusée par nos contemporains, la postérité sait nous la rendre. — *Posterity knows how to do us that justice which is sometimes refused us by our contemporaries.*

Cette grandeur qui vous étonne — *That greatness which so much*

si fort, il la doit à votre nonchalance.

astonishes you he owes to your indifference.

Il périt, ce héros, si cher à son pays.

That hero, so dear to his country perished.

Je l'avais bien prévu que ce haut degré de grandeur serait la cause de sa ruine.

I foresaw that the greatness of his elevation would be his ruin.

Citoyens, étrangers, ennemis, peuples, rois, empereurs, le plaignent et le révèrent.

Citizens, strangers, enemies, nations, kings, emperors, pity and respect him.

L'assemblée finie, chacun se retira chez soi.

The assembly being over, each returned home.

Heureux le peuple qu'un sage roi gouverne.

Happy are the people who are governed by a wise king.

Il refusa les plus grands honneurs, content de les mériter.

He refused the greatest honors, satisfied with having deserved them.

Prières, remontrances, commandements, tout est inutile.

Entreaties, remonstrances, injunctions, all are useless.

Le vent renverse tours, cabanes, palais, églises.

The wind overturns towers, cottages, palaces, churches.

Notre réputation ne dépend pas du caprice des hommes; mais elle dépend des actions louables que nous faisons.

Our reputation does not depend on the caprice of men, but on the commendable actions we perform.

Il y a beaucoup de choses qu'il n'importe point du tout de savoir.

There are many things which it is of no consequence at all to know.

La vue de l'esprit a plus d'étendue que la vue du corps.

The eye of the mind reaches much farther than the bodily eye.

Ce qui sert à la vanité, n'est que vanité.

What promotes vanity is only vanity.

Tout ce qui n'a que le monde pour fondement, se dissipe et s'évanouit avec le monde.

All that is confined to this lower world disperses and vanishes with the world.

C'est le privilége des grands hommes de vaincre l'envie; le mérite la fait naître, le mérite la fait mourir.

It is the prerogative of great men to conquer envy: merit gives it birth, and merit destroys it.

L'amour-propre est plus habile que le plus habile homme du monde.

Self-love is more ingenious than the most ingenious man in the world.

En quittant le monde, on ne quitte le plus souvent ni les erreurs, ni les folles passions du monde.

In renouncing the world we generally renounce neither the errors nor foolish passions of the world.

END.

CPSIA information can be obtained
at www.ICGtesting.com
Printed in the USA
LVHW031301210223
739960LV00006B/349

9 783375 144104